Guardians of the Flame:
THE WARRIORS

Guardians of the Flame:
THE WARRIORS

THE SLEEPING DRAGON
THE SWORD AND THE CHAIN
THE SILVER CROWN

Joel Rosenberg

Nelson Doubleday, Inc.
Garden City, New York

Published by arrangement with
New American Library
1633 Broadway
New York, New York 10019

Printed in the United States of America

CONTENTS

Guardians of the Flame:
THE WARRIORS

THE SLEEPING DRAGON

for Felicia

Acknowledgments

I want to thank the people who helped me through this: Allan Schmidt, who gave me the crazy idea in the first place and helped to make the gaming aspects work; Cara Herman, who gave much needed encouragement as I struggled through the first draft; Harry F. Leonard, who annoyed the hell out of me by quibbling endlessly over minor flaws until I saw the light and corrected them, much to the betterment of the story, if not my disposition; Robert Lee Thurston and Judith Heald, who gave me good criticism and better friendship; Doug Kaufman, who put his money where his mouth was; Barry B. Longyear, whose advice always helps when I'm wise enough to take it; Kim Tchang, who told me to relax and write the damn thing; my agent, Cherry Weiner, whose help and support went beyond the call of duty; my editor, Sheila Gilbert, who not only knew a good thing when she saw it, but knew how to make it better; and the members of Haven: Deborah Atherton Davis, Mary Kittredge, Mark J. McGarry, and Kevin O'Donnell, Jr., who gave this book the line-by-line, word-by-word examination and dissection that a first novelist so desperately needs.

And, most particularly, I'd like to thank Robert Anson Heinlein, whose work has been both example and inspiration, for Thorby, Colonel Baslim, Oscar Gordon, and so much more.

The great problems of life . . . are always related to the primordial images of the collective unconscious. . . .

The unconscious is not just evil by nature, it is also the source of the highest good: not only dark but also light, not only bestial, semihuman, and demonic, but superhuman, spiritual, and, in the classical sense of the word, "divine."

—Carl Gustave Jung

. . . for every human being there is a diversity of existences . . . the single existence is itself an illusion. . . .

—Saul Bellow

It seems to me that there might well be the equivalent, with regard to the collective unconscious, of the concept in physics of "critical mass." Are we approaching it? Quite possibly—consider the resurgence of spiritualism, in all its guises, and don't neglect the function of the fantasy role-playing games. The characters, the situations . . . all seem to touch something that is basic and fundamental.

But where would the locus of crisis be? And how can it be exploited? *The Elder Edda, The Song of the Harper, The Book of the Dead,* even *The Great Hymn to the Aten* offer only hints, suggestions, intimations.

Perhaps the best approach would be neither induction nor deduction, but, rather, empirical experimentation. Perhaps . . .

—Arthur Simpson Deighton

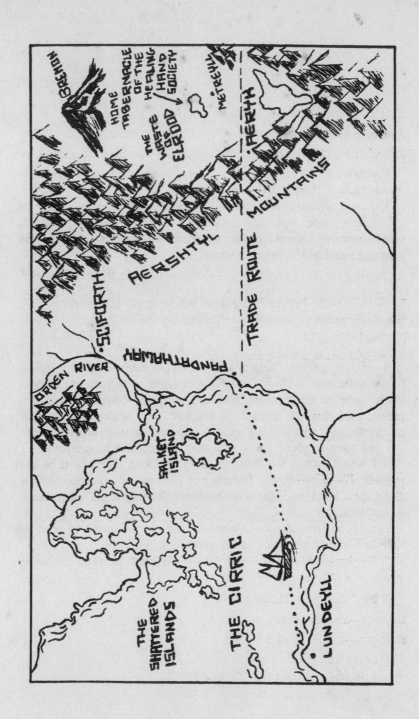

DRAMATIS PERSONAE

Karl Cullinane/Barak—dilettante and acting major/warrior

Andrea Andropolous/Lotana—English major/novice wizard

James Michael Finnegan/Ahira Bandylegs—computer sciences major/dwarf warrior

Doria Perlstein/Doria of the Healing Hand—domestic arts major/master cleric

Walter Slovotsky/Hakim Singh—agricultural sciences major/journeyman thief

Jason Parker/Einar Lightfingers—history major/master thief

Louis Riccetti/Aristobulous—civil engineering major/master wizard

Arthur Simpson Deighton, Ph.D.—Associate Professor of Philosophy, gamemaster

Wen'l of Lundescarne—peasant and freefarmer

Frann of Pandathaway—innkeeper

Lordling Alahn Lund—heir to the throne of Lundeyll

Marik, Arno—men-at-arms

Avair Ganness—captain and owner of the *Ganness' Pride*

Airvhan ip Melhrood—customs official

Challa—man-at-arms

Callutius—Junior Librarian of the Great Library of Pandathaway

Oreen—Specializing Librarian of the Great Library of Pandathaway

Ellegon—a young dragon

Tommallo—owner of the Inn of Quiet Repose

Khoralt ip Therranj—Wineseller's Delegate to the Pandathaway Guilds' Council, Games official

Ohlmin—master slaver

Blenryth—master wizard

The Dragon at the Gate

The Matriarch of the Society of the Healing Hand

PART ONE

The Student Union

CHAPTER ONE

The Players

Karl Cullinane reached out his fork and speared the last stick of asparagus from the stainless-steel serving plate in the middle of the table, not bothering to set the asparagus on his own plate before taking a bite. It was cold and mushy, almost tasteless; he swallowed quickly.

"Karl, you're a pig. A skinny one, granted, but a pig." Andrea Andropolous' smile took most of the sting out of her words, pitched low enough so that nobody else in the crowded cafeteria would have been able to hear her over the clatter of dishes and the chatter of a hundred or so students.

Karl put it down to a natural gentleness. Hell, she'd been able to make him like it—almost—when she'd turned him down. Usually, the let's-just-be-friends routine drove him into a silent, stomach-churning rage.

"I gotta rush, Andy-Andy. There's a game tonight." He took another bit, added a mouthful of lukewarm black coffee, and swallowed quickly. "If I'm late, sure as hell they'll start without me, put Barak out to pasture for the night."

"You mean that they'll put him out to *stud.*" She chuckled, revealing a mouthful of even, white teeth.

Karl liked her laugh, her smile. He had always thought that the notion of somebody brightening a room with a smile was just a fantasy. Until he had met Andy-Andy, that is. Not that he had anything against fantasy, quite the—

"It's bullshit, Karl," she said, smiling sweetly. "Just an absurd male power fantasy." She reached out and stroked his skinny forearm with a long, dark finger. Was it tanned, or not? Andy-Andy always seemed to find something better to do during afternoon tanning hours than loll in the sun like some well-oiled, roasting slug. Probably the olive tone of her skin was natural coloration. Maybe not. Of course, there was a way to tell. Trouble was, Karl had never had the chance to check her for bikini marks.

Damn. "No, it's just a game. A way to spend a little time, have a little fun."

"A little fun?" She arched an eyebrow. "You call pretending to chop up a pixie, rape a virgin or three, slice an ogre—you call that fun?" Quirking a smile, she sat back in her chair, crossing her arms almost defensively over her blue velour pullover. Which was amply filled out, but not tight. Karl liked that; Andy-Andy was more than a little pretty, but not an exhibitionist.

"First of all"—he tapped his index finger on the table, forcing himself to pay attention to the conversation—"you're missing the point. Pretending isn't the same thing as really doing it. I mean— take last week's session, for instance. Barak strangled an elf, chopped a half-orc in two—hey, now the critter's really two halves of an orc. Or should that be 'quarter-orces'? Never mind, the point is that he took three points of damage. One's a light wound, two's more serious, going up to five, which is certainly lethal. Three's the equivalent of getting sliced up pretty bad." He reached for his shirt's top button. "Care to check for scars?"

"Some other time." She tossed her head, sending shoulder-length black hair whipping around her face. "Maybe." A strand came to rest on her slightly too long, slightly bent nose. She blew it off. "Then again, maybe not."

"Teaser."

"That's only half the word, Karl. You don't have to use that bullshit with me."

"In my neighborhood, *mother* was only half a word." That might sound good, but it wasn't true: Karl was a product of middle-class suburbia. "And besides, I was . . . kind of pointedly told to watch my language around—women." If you consider having your mouth liberally washed out with Lifebuoy to be a pointed telling. Which it was, after a fashion. "But to get back to the point, it's all just a fantasy, a game. No harm; no damage. Anyway, Barak isn't that sort of character—he'll violate a *law*, but he's no rapist." That was true, but omitted a new character Doc Deighton had helped him roll up, one Lucius of Pandathaway. Lucius was not a nice person. Not at all. "The trouble with you is that you feel perfectly free to judge something you haven't tried. How many times since the start of the semester have I invited you—ten? Twenty?"

She shook her head. "I don't have to jump out a window to decide that I'm not going to like it."

"Irrelevant. If you try role-playing and you don't like it, you quit. Period. No scars—not even on your psyche. Which is part of the fun." He shrugged. "Besides, it's probably beneficial. You get to work out some aggressions without hurting anybody. Not yourself, not anybody else."

"Stop trying to sound like a psych major. You're supposed to be studying to be an actor, these days."

"I used to be a psych major—"

"—and a poli sci major. Plus American lit, engineering, philosophy, sociology—am I missing something?"

"Prelaw. And two weeks of premed, back when I was a freshman. What's your point?"

"You're a dilettante, Karl. This role-playing stuff is just another one of your temporary obsessions. Remember last year, when it was bridge? You spent a whole semester nattering about Stayman conventions and South American Texas transfers, whatever the hell they are—"

"South African Texas, not South American." He dipped two fingers into his shirt pocket and pulled out a cigarette, then lit it with his shiny new Zippo. Karl let the flame flare for a moment before snapping the cover shut. He figured that he might as well enjoy it while he could; he'd lose it soon. Karl could never seem to keep track of *things;* the Zippo was the third lighter he'd bought that semester. "I still play bridge," he said, exhaling a cloud of smoke. "It's just that this is more fun—particularly with this group. Sometimes . . ." He let his voice trail off.

"Yes?"

"Sometimes, when you get the mechanics of the game out of the way—rolling the dice, keeping track of what you're carrying—it's almost like you're there." He lifted his head and smiled. "And that's *something.* How often do you think I'm going to get the chance to, say, rescue a princess or slay a dragon?" He glanced down at his wrist. 6:48. Karl pushed himself to his feet. "Well, I've got to run, if I'm not going to be late. See you later?"

Andy-Andy's brow furrowed. "How late are you going to be? Getting back, I mean."

"Mmmm, probably be back before midnight. If you want to meet me in the lounge, I'll help you go over *Deerslayer*, if that's what you mean. It's a rotten book, though—I've got a Twain piece on it that pretty much—"

"No." She shook her head. "I'm caught up with that, but I do have a quiz in astronomy tomorrow. If you're sure we can be back by twelve, I'll come along, give it a try. If the invitation's still open." She stood, taking her bulky yellow ski jacket from the back of her chair and slipping it on.

"You know it is."

She sighed. "Yes, I do." Andy-Andy shook her head slowly. "Which is part of the problem. Never mind; let's get going, shall we?"

James Michael Finnegan was the first player to get to Room 109 in the Student Union. It was a matter partly of habit, but mainly of pride. The others, well, they'd wait for him, sure. *Only* for him, dammit.

They wouldn't wait for him because he was now the most accomplished player in the group. Davy Davidson had been the best in the group until he'd dropped out last year, and nobody would wait for Davy and his character, Erik of the Three Bezants, on the not too infrequent occasions that he'd arrive late.

James Michael shifted uncomfortably in his chair, his hands limp in his lap.

No, they wouldn't wait for him because he was a nice person to be around, with a dry sense of humor and an always friendly smile. That monomaniac flake Karl Cullinane cracked better jokes; that hick jock Walter Slovotsky always seemed to have a grin pasted on his face—and everybody *always* liked being around Doria. But if one of *them* showed up late, it was well-too-bad-it-seems-your-character-is-down-with-a-cold-tonight. Just last week, Doria had fluttered in breathless, just five minutes after they'd started, and even Riccetti had ignored her implied promises and threats; Doc Deighton had just turned a very cold eye her way and suggested that lateness was an implicitly hostile act.

He spun his chair in a tight circle and swore softly under his breath.

It wasn't all that bad, not always. The one time he'd had to wait for the Special Student Services truck (all the way muttering a spell to change the driver into a toad, a particularly small, unusually ugly toad—with one eye) and had been wheeled into the elevator late, coming out on the first floor *late*, his car-battery-powered chair zipping down the tiled hall and into Room 109 LATE—

—nobody had said anything. Except, "Hi, James," and "Nice to see you, James," and "Let's play, James."

The tolerance, the implied pity, was bad. Not playing would have been worse. Much worse.

All cripples fantasize, you see. They have to, just like normal people, although not always about the things normal people do.

And when you've spent your whole life with muscular dystrophy, you're really lucky, in a way. There's *lots* more things to dream about. Like being able to punch a computer keyboard at better than a scorching ten words per minute. Like sleeping in a top bunk. Like feeding yourself quickly, wolfing down food so you could run off somewhere. Like using a goddam bathroom without having someone else wipe you off.

Like not having to be so goddam cheerful all the time since because you're a feeb in a chair, people will let you get away with anything as long as you don't touch them.

But the game . . . ah, there it was. All at once. "I'll walk across the room, heft my axe, and chop at the ogre," you'd say, and everybody would react to it, *just as though you'd really done it.*

A miracle? Well, not quite. An addiction, *yes.*

James Michael lifted his right hand to the steering knob and wheeled himself over to the long table in the middle of the bright room, getting himself so close that his chin was directly over the edge of the battered mahogany surface. He reached into the denim bag on his lap, secured there by a long cloth loop around his neck, and pulled out a large plastic bag, bringing it up to the tabletop.

And the whole . . . wonder of it depended on this little bag, and the dice inside it. Standard six-sided dice for the attack tables. A twenty-sided die, generating a random number to compare to Ahira's intelligence, or endurance, or strength. And Ahira was *strong,* although not terribly wise, perhaps, and certainly not handy with anything except an axe or hammer.

And then there were the pyramidal four-sided dice, and the eight-sided ones to—but why bother thinking about the mechanics of it? They didn't matter; the rules were soon learned and subsumed, the way a normal person would learn to ride a bicycle by technique, and then forget the technique, to ride. . . .

James Michael closed his eyes and dreamed of riding a bicycle, seeing the ground slip by smoothly beneath him. Sort of like riding in a car, but being there, and—

"James!"

His eyes snapped open like twin shutters. Doria Perlstein stood over him, concern creasing her too round, too smooth face, her short blond hair only making her seem chubbier.

"James, are you okay?"

"I'm fine." He smiled up at her, making a special effort to keep the traitor muscles of the right side of his face under control. Doria . . . *tried,* that was it. The little dwarf in the chair revolted her and scared her, as though his disability could rub off. But she tried to hide it.

He brought his hands down into his lap, out of sight. No shame, just a reflexive kindness, although he really wanted to reach out and shake her. *I'm not contagious.* "I'm just fine. It's been a busy week; I guess I was just dozing off."

She dropped into a chair, visibly considered the possibility that it would seem to him to be too far away, took a half second to fight with her own fear of James Michael Finnegan, and compromised by wiggling herself a scant inch closer.

Someday, he thought, *I'm going to tell her that she doesn't have to sit next to me, if she's so uptight. Then again, maybe this is better for her than sitting across the table from me; it's natural for her to avoid my eyes, this way.*

She forced a smile, drumming crimson fingernails against the tabletop. "I see I'm early this time."

"I'm glad you're here. We ran into a fairly heavy-duty goblin last time; could have used a cleric."

"How bad?"

"Both Barak and Ahira took quite a bit of damage. He got three points; I got away with just two."

"Wait a minute—where was Sandy?"

"Dropped out. Which leaves you as the only cleric around. The team's topheavy with warriors."

"Ooo." She grimaced. "Sorry I was late last time." She tossed her head, brightening. "But don't worry. Soon as Doc works me back into the campaign, I'll heal both of you up."

James Michael smiled. "Make that 'heal Barak up.' Ahira's just fine."

She wrinkled her forehead. "How? I know Barak had some healing draughts in his bag—but Ahira—"

"—persuaded him to fork them over."

She toyed with the ruffles of her blouse. "What did you offer him? As though I didn't know." She raised a finger in mock accusation.

"Not bashing him with my axe."

"Sounds fair." She reached up and scratched the tip of her stubby nose. Slovotsky claimed it was artificial; James Michael had a standing bet that it was natural. Unfortunately, there was no way to find out; Doria ignored all questions on the subject. "But one of these times he's not going to stand for it, if you keep it up. Bully. He might—" She caught herself. "Never mind."

James Michael sighed. It was obvious why Cullinane didn't want to fight him, despite the way he'd been provoking the confrontation. If Ahira killed Barak, Cullinane would lose—and if Barak managed to win, James Michael would be, at least temporarily, out of the game. Cullinane wouldn't want to kick a cripple out of the game, would he? "I guess he recognized that it was more useful to the whole team to have Ahira up and healthy, what with us being underground, and all." A dwarf's natural habitat was in underground warrens, where his ability to see in the infrared gave him a clear advantage.

"That sounds like a bit too . . . sound reasoning for Barak. His IQ's not that high, is it?"

"Wisdom, Doria, wisdom. Barak is the wisest fighter around. Not a berserker, like Ahira." He formed his hands into clumsy fists, and pounded himself lightly on the chest. "Arg."

A new voice bellowed from the doorway. "You going berserk, *again?*" Walter Slovotsky swaggered into the room, smelling vaguely of Ivory, his hair damp. "Doria, James." He nodded, dropped his books to the floor, kicked his shoes off and in the general direction of a far corner, and perched himself tailor-fashion on the table. "How goes it?"

Of all the people on campus that he knew—hell, of *all* the people he knew, specifically including his parents—James Michael was most comfortable around Walter Slovotsky. Jealous, sure—but not unusually so; James didn't particularly want to Be a Football Hero. The thing was that the big man was so sure of himself, without being offensive about it. Whether he was stomping quarterbacks out on the field or spending extra time in the Ag Library, cramming for a final in Meat Science (a course that Slovotsky couldn't mention without chuckling), Slovotsky seemed certain that the universe centered on him, and that all was well with the universe.

A massive hand reached out and chucked Doria under the chin. "And where the hell were you last Friday, m'love?"

"Thursday." She shoved his hand away. "And you know damn well where I *wasn't;* you were the one yelling 'Come on time if you want to play,' weren't you?"

"No, I meant Friday. I thought you were going to come over, spend the night."

"Shh." She started to jerk a thumb toward James Michael, stopped herself. "I don't think—"

"Pre*cise*ly. You don't think." He turned to James, running blunt fingers through his damp black hair. "Jimmy me boy, would it be any surprise to you to learn that Doria and I sleep together, every now and then?"

*"Wal*ter!"

"No, not really," James Michael said. Doria's pale skin went from light pink through various shades of red before settling on a nice, hot crimson. He looked her in the eye, suppressing an urge to reach out and pat her arm. "Not that he ever said anything about it. I'm pretty good at reading people for a . . ."—an impish impulse made him pause—"computer sciences major."

Walter's broad face went somber. "Exactly. Beautiful, I don't tell on ladies. Wouldn't mention it in front of Cullinane, say—he's an explosion, looking for a place to happen. Trouble with you Jewish girls is that your desire to *do* it is in inverse proportion to your willingness to *talk* about it."

Doria's skin had gone back to its normal shade, which made her glare at Slovotsky a trifle less comical. "Another one of Slovotsky's Laws?"

"Actually"—he cocked his head to one side—"I think that I got that from one of my many roommates—Bernstein-the-rabbi, I think."

Many roommates was a fair statement of fact, James Michael thought. Not a whole lot of people liked spending their nights mainly on the couch in the lounge.

Slovotsky brightened. "But I don't mind stealing it. Make it Slovotsky's Law Number Twenty-three, right after 'Never date a woman with a brother named Nunzio.' " He bounced to his feet. "I'm going for coffee. Either of you need anything from the snack bar?"

"Shoes," James Michael supplied.

"Sorry, they don't serve them there. A burger close enough?" He patted the hip pocket of his jeans. "On me. Had a nice bet we wouldn't beat the spread against Yale."

"No, you've got to *wear* shoes."

Slovotsky looked down at his blue-sock-clad feet, then blanked his face. "James, when you're six-foot-one-and-a-fraction, weighing in at two-twenty-three, *nobody* tells you you've got to wear shoes." His eyes glazed over. "Walter not un-der-stand. Per-son half his size telling him he not come in? Walter must have mis-un-der-stood." He shrugged, a bit sadly. "You wouldn't *believe* how easily people believe that if you're big, you've gotta be dumb. And violent. Now, do you want anything?"

Doria shrugged. "Coffee sounds fine."

"James?"

"Herb tea. Red Zinger, if they've got it. With plenty of sugar." He mimicked Slovotsky's big-and-dumb voice. "Ahira need to keep strength up."

"That's the ticket." Walter paused in the doorway. "But if it takes me more than a couple of minutes, don't let them start without me. Assuming that the rest get here on time."

"I wouldn't dream of it." Doria's voice held a definite chill.

"Hey, Dr. Deighton, wait up." Jason Parker broke into a lope, letting Riccetti fall behind.

The thin, stoop-shouldered man stopped under a streetlight and turned, the harsh green casting his face into shadow. He wore a tan wool suit, amply decorated with burn marks from his ever-present bulldog briar pipe; the suit, like the pipe, the battered briefcase, and the man, had come a long way since new, the wrinkles having developed a life of their own, as though they would be resistant to even the stubbornest, most persistent dry cleaning.

"Good evening, Mr. Parker." The voice was out of place; it was a strong young tenor, the voice of a prepubescent boy, not a sixtyish philosophy professor. "And good evening to you, Mr. Riccetti," he added, as Lou Riccetti panted up to join them under the streetlight. "I trust you're ready for the test tomorrow?"

Lou Riccetti shrugged, his round face covered with a light sheen of sweat. "I hope so, Doc. I've got the *Apologia* practically memorized, and this is my second go-round with the *Republic.*"

Jason chuckled. It was a good bet that Lou would flunk again; he never seemed to be able to understand anything that didn't have a number attached. Engineering students—"Hey, no teaching tonight, Doc. You're gamemastering tonight, not using your conclusions to prove your postulates." He took an impatient step toward the Student Union building.

Deighton took a few puffs on his pipe, then followed. "You have that reversed, Mr. Parker." He blew a smoke ring; it shattered and drifted away in the light, cool breeze. "One uses one's postulates to prove one's conclusions, not the other way around."

Jason shrugged his bony shoulders and tucked his hands into the pockets of his fraying army jacket. "That's what you say. Seems to me you philosophers do both. Sort of bootstrap levitation."

"A nice phrase, that. Not true, mind you, but a nice phrase." Deighton sighed deeply. "But your major premise was correct: We are gaming tonight. Mr. Riccetti, I apologize if I seemed to be pressuring you about the test tomorrow."

"No problem, Doc." Riccetti cocked his head to one side. "Any clues about what we're going to run into after we get through the treasure room?"

"Ricky, *don't* ask." Jason tried to keep irritation out of his voice; he failed. "Either he won't tell us, in which case you're just wasting your breath, or he will—and that'd ruin the game. Let it flow, don't—"

"—force it. Okay, okay. I was just asking."

"Actually, I can tell you something without spoiling anything." Deighton smiled crookedly around his pipestem. "But if you'd prefer to wait . . ."

"Go ahead." Jason was curious. Doc never gave anything away, except at the start of a campaign, of course, where the gamemaster would have to set the scene, give out a clue or two.

"We are beginning a new campaign tonight. From scratch."

"Wait one minute." Riccetti slapped his bookbag. "I've spent one hell of a lot of time turning Aristobulus into a K-Class wizard—I don't want to have to start again back in A-Class, with just one spell. Sleep, probably."

At least Ricky was keeping his wits. Of all the spells available to an A-Class wizard, the Sleep spell—technically, Herstell's Spell of Induced Somnolence—was the most useful. Once you had an enemy sleeping, he, she, it, or they were as good as dead if you wanted them to be.

"That was not what I meant, Mr. Riccetti. We will be starting a new campaign, yes, but not with A-Class characters. They wouldn't be likely to survive. You can run Aristobulus, if you like. The balance should be about right that way, as a matter of fact."

Jason ticked players and characters off on his fingers. "Let's see . . . Cullinane and James are going to run their warriors—I'm sure about that: I talked to Karl about it earlier. And James always runs Ahira, of course."

"Jase, I don't think he always does. Didn't he—"

"Nope. You should pay attention." It was obvious why the poor little guy always wanted to be a warrior; the game was the closest he was ever going to get to being like Slovotsky. It was kind of pitiful, the way James Michael tried to pretend he wasn't jealous of Walter— or, possibly more accurately, Walter and Doria. "Let's see . . . Doria's the only one who likes being a cleric—God knows why— cleaning up after everybody else's fights. Slovotsky could play either as a wizard or a thief."

"Or a monk. I like Master Kwan."

"Too limited. Depending on the situation, we might need a thief, but a monk is a waste. He can't advance fast enough, can't carry enough—most of the time, everybody else has to carry him."

Deighton's slate-gray eyes went vague. "Actually, I think you might well need a thief. Or two. For this campaign, a balanced team would be best. I think you'll find all of the archetypical situations in this one."

"Fine," Jason said, "we'll have him run Hakim. That gives us two warriors, one cleric, one wizard—take a bow, Ricky; looks like Aristobulus is going to be on his own—and one thief."

"Plus you, Jase."

"Right. Any suggestions, Doc? I really don't care what sort of character I get. Long as I get to *do* something."

"Hmmm . . . quite possibly a thief would be best."

"Or a thief/assassin? I've got Lendwyl ready to run."

"No, I doubt that you'll need to have anyone poisoned. You might want to choose someone more dexterous than Lendwyl."

"Jase, how about running Einar Lightfingers? You haven't run him for a while."

"He is kind of fun."

They walked up the stone steps of the Student Union, Riccetti bustling ahead to hold the door. "Give it a try, Jase. Not that I'd turn my back on him, but Lightfingers is awful good at what he does, all things considered."

"You first, Doc—age before beauty. On the other hand, if he hurts his other arm, he'd be pretty much out of the picture." Jason shrugged. "But what the hell; I'll run him." As they crossed the yellowed marble floor to the stairwell, Jason stopped. "But I don't like having just one wizard. What if Ari gets killed?"

Deighton shrugged. "You could find an R-Class cleric, and have him resurrected. Or, conceivably, help Doria of the Healing Hand rise to that height."

"Fat chance—I don't think I've ever run into a cleric past N-Class. And what is she now, J?"

"K, Ricky. As a cleric, she's one step farther along than Aristobulus is as a magic usurer."

"That's magic *user.*"

Jason returned Riccetti's glare. "I meant exactly what I said. I didn't like the way you charged everybody a thousand gold—*each*—to charm the Eater."

Riccetti shrugged. "Wizard's got to make a living, just like anybody else. You'd rather I let him eat Doria?" He took the lead in the hall, their footsteps echoing hollowly on the tiles.

"No, but—"

"But nothing. Value is relative; first law of economics. At that point, Aristobulus' value was pretty huge. I think you should have been happy to pay."

Deighton stroked his chin. "I think you are asking a bit too much of Mr. Parker. Perhaps the . . . fee for your services was proper; certainly, adding gratitude to it does seem excessive."

"That the gamemaster talking, or you?"

"Just me. Just me—and here we are. If you would get the door, please?"

Riccetti swung the door open; Jason ushered him and Deighton in before following.

"Seven-thirty on the nose. Nice timing, Doc, Ricky, Jason," Walter Slovotsky said, from his usual spot on the table, where he sat like an improbably massive sprite.

"Hi, Hakim." Jason dropped his jacket in a corner, setting his books on top. He took a moment to check out the other players as he took his own seat across the table from Deighton, next to Doria. As usual, to Doria's left was James Michael, huddling in his wheelchair like a vulture waiting to pounce.

Next was Karl Cullinane. Jason shook his head; Karl was *still* trying to persuade his sparse growth of facial hair to become a beard.

Actually, he might have been able to make it, if he wouldn't give up and shave after a few weeks—but that was the trouble with Karl: He never followed through with anything.

On the other hand, he thought, *that might be a bit of a hasty judgment.* From the way Karl was perched protectively close to the woman sitting next to him, it seemed that perhaps here was something he'd follow through with. She was a bit too, well, Mediterranean for Jason's taste, but Karl seemed to go for that type.

And another mystery solved. Now we know why Karl's been ignoring Doria's come-on. His mind, such as it is, is elsewhere.

"Hakim?" Slovotsky interrupted his thoughts with a friendly bellow. "Something going on that I don't know about?" There was just a hint of threat in the question.

"Ask Doc. Ricky, toss me a cigarette."

Riccetti obediently pulled a box of Marlboros out of his faded blue workshirt and rolled one across the table.

"And a match?"

Without pausing in his hushed conversation with the woman next to him, Karl Cullinane pulled out a shiny new Zippo and slid it across the table to him.

"Thanks, Karl. You going to introduce us all to your friend, or do we have to wait until Doc issues us psi ratings?"

"Cute." Karl's face made the word a lie. "Andrea Andropolous, Jason Parker."

Jason nodded. As Andrea smiled in response, he decided to reconsider his original appraisal. Nice.

"The one with the maps, charts, and calculator"—Karl jerked a thumb toward Riccetti—"is Luigi Riccetti."

"Lou." Riccetti didn't bother to look up.

"Doesn't matter; call him Ricky, just like everybody else. You've met the rest, except for Dr. Deighton, and—"

"By the process of elimination, she should be able to infer that I'm he, no?" Deighton set his briefcase on the table and opened it, careful as always to keep the open back toward the table, the contents hidden from view. "And, as everyone is here, shall we begin?"

"Hold it, Doc," Karl objected. "We haven't rolled up a character for Andy yet."

Deighton smiled indulgently. "That was what I meant by beginning, at least in part. Do you think you can help her with that— honestly, mind you—while paying attention to my briefing?"

"What briefing? We're still stuck in the treasure room, a whole

bunch of dead critters and jewels lying around, Barak cut up pretty
bad, and—"

"Actually, I am terminating this campaign. We start a new one
tonight. From scratch." Deighton raised a palm. "All I ask is that
you give it a try. If, say, after half the evening—even just an hour,
perhaps?—the consensus is that the old one is more entertaining, we
will resume where we left off." He tapped his briefcase with a gnarled
forefinger. "But I've spent quite a bit of time on this new campaign. I
expect—I am certain that it will appeal to you." Deighton smiled,
momentarily appearing much younger than his sixty-odd years.
"Quite certain."

Slovotsky shrugged. "Let's give it a try, then. James, that okay
with you?"

"Fine."

The big man gave Jason a meaningful glance. "And now I understand what you were up to before. I'm supposed to run a thief this
time. Hakim Singh, just as a guess?"

"It would help balance the team." Jason puffed on his cigarette.
"But it's up to you."

"What do you know that I don't know?"

"Quite a—"

"Gentlemen." Deighton rapped the stem of his pipe on the table.
"In answer to your question, Mr. Slovotsky, Mr. Parker knows nothing that a few minutes of listening to me won't teach you." He raised
a bushy eyebrow. "If that's acceptable. Mr. Riccetti, if you will be
kind enough to close the door and spin the dimmer switch down to
low, we will begin." Deighton took a deep breath.

"Now."

CHAPTER TWO

The Game

The chess board is the world, the pieces are the phenomena of the universe, the rules of the game are what we call the laws of Nature. The player on the other side is hidden from us. We know that his play is always fair, just and patient. But we also know, to our cost, that he never overlooks a mistake, or makes the smallest allowance for ignorance.

—Thomas Henry Huxley

While Deighton began to speak in low, mysterious tones, Karl Cullinane borrowed five four-sided dice from James Michael, then slid a well-chewed pencil and a sheet of paper in front of Andy-Andy.

She picked up one of the dice. "Funny-looking little pyramid. But how do you get the numbers to come up on top?"

"You don't. Look at it a bit closer." Instead of being stamped in the center of the faces, the numbers, zero through three, were along the edges; when the die was thrown, the player would read the upright number, the one closest to the table. "But I want to keep half an ear on what Doc's saying, so we'll make this mechanical—I'll fill you in on the background later. Okay?"

"Fine. But bear with me if I'm slow."

He couldn't let that pass without turning to look her straight in the eye, letting a tight grin creep across his face. She didn't have the grace to blush.

"This campaign," Deighton intoned, his face lit demonically by the light of the flashlight in his opened briefcase, "is the Quest for the Gate Between Worlds. . . ."

"Now write this down on the paper: ST, S, I, W, MD, WP, E, and C."

". . . find yourselves on a hilltop, overlooking a vast walled city, and—"

"Doc?" Karl half-raised a hand, then brought it down.

"*Yes?*" Deighton snapped.

"Sorry for interrupting, but I've got to know: How do you want me to generate her character? And what level? This sounds like a pretty heavy-duty campaign; you're not sending in an A-Class character, are you?"

"Good point." Deighton nodded a quick apology. "Try . . . three rolls for each characteristic, and set Miss Andropolous up as a C-Class whatever. If her Intelligence is high enough, try for a wizard; the company is a trifle light in that department—"

"Wait a minute!" Riccetti's head snapped up. "I—"

"—*despite* the great skills and talents of Aristobulus. Now, if I may proceed . . ."

Andy-Andy tilted her head close to his. "Intelligence? If he's suggesting—"

"No, he was talking about your *character's* intelligence. But let's roll Strength, first." He gestured at the five dice. "Go ahead."

Andy-Andy shrugged, took the dice, and rolled them gently. "Three, three, one, and two zeros—how's that?"

"Not too good; strictly average, in fact. The top possible score's fifteen. Try again; twice more, in fact. I think we can better a seven."

The next roll brought a total of five, the one after, a nine. "That's not too bad, but it's not too good; your character's barely above average Strength. Speed next. It's related to Strength; we throw out all rolls that aren't within two points of your Strength score of nine."

Her first roll was five zeros. "Doesn't count," Karl said. "Three more tries."

In the three tries, she couldn't do better than eight. "So you've got average Speed. Roll for Intelligence, now."

Her best score out of three rolls was *the* best score. "A full fifteen, and that's good. Means you can be a wizard—like being a magician, except for real."

"Almost."

"Right."

Deighton droned on, ". . . to the north, you see a great body of water stretching out to the horizon. It could be an inland sea, but the wind blowing across it brings no smell of salt; you suspect that it is a lake, instead . . ."

"Roll for Wisdom."

"Wisdom? What's the difference between that and Intelligence?"

"Edith Bunker."

"*What?*" She flinched as the others glared as though in chorus. "What?" she whispered.

"I said, 'Edith Bunker'—from *All in the Family?* Not too bright, but wise as all hell. Or to take a counterexample, Richard Nixon. Get it?"

"Fine."

Three rolls gave her a ten. "That's not too bad," he said. "Manual Dexterity is next."

"As opposed to electric dexterity?" She arched an eyebrow.

"As opposed to Weapon Proficiency—wizards can be dexterous as hell, but not with weapons. It comes with the territory. Roll."

". . . beside your party is a collection of large wooden boxes. Except for weapons and personal effects, they are the only equipment you have with you . . ."

The best she could do was five. "Too bad. Guess I'm clumsy, eh?"

"And cold." He smiled. "Now, Weapon Proficiency."

Her first roll was a total of twelve. "Which is a waste of some good numbers," Karl said. "The best WP a wizard can have is five, which is what we'll give you. Now try Endurance."

". . . you have no sure recollection of how you got to this hillside, and the only possibility that suggests itself is too incredible to be taken seriously . . ."

"Hmm, a thirteen." She lifted her head. "Which means I'm hardy as hell, right?"

"Close. One more to go."

"What's the C stand for?"

"Charisma. Roll."

Her first roll was a perfect five threes. "Which figures," he mumbled.

Andy-Andy just smiled back.

". . . and now," Deighton straightened himself, "all that remains is for you to decide who you are, and what to do next."

"Not quite, Doc." Karl tapped Andy-Andy's sheet. "Still got to work out her spells, decide on a character."

"Quite right. Miss Andropolous, if you'll step over here, you and I can work that out. Mr. Cullinane tends to be a bit too . . . generous with spells, as I recall."

"Not fair." James Michael's voice held a decided edge. "I was there the time Karl rolled up Martin the Illusionist. Righteous rolls, all of them."

"As it may be." Deighton motioned Andy-Andy over to his side of the table. "And now, it is time for you to decide on your characters, weapons, and effects."

James Michael Finnegan held himself back from the arguments over who was going to do what. There was no question that he was going to be Ahira Bandylegs, a dwarf warrior of great Strength and Weapon Proficiency, average Intelligence, Wisdom, and Charisma, low Speed—because of the three-point penalty for his short dwarf's legs—but with an Endurance level that was just this side of magical. That was settled, for certain. On the other hand—

"Dammit. I *don't* want to be the cleric this time." Doria thumped her hand on the table. "Let me run a warrior, a thief, a wizard—and get to *do* something. One of you be the cleric."

Cullinane shook his head. "Who? The only one of us with a reasonably high-level cleric is Walter. And as I recall, his cleric's only about a D-Class—we'll be better off with Walter as a thief." Cullinane shrugged. "It makes sense to do it that way."

Slovotsky shifted position uncomfortably. "I do have a cleric character." He licked his thumb and riffled through the character sheets in front of him. "Gin. But it's Rudolph—"

"—the Incompetent," Jason Parker finished, his voice taking on a whining tone that made James Michael itch. "Forget it. A D-Class cleric in a killer campaign? C'mon, Dore—stick with what you're best at."

Riccetti sucked air in through his teeth. "Why don't we let her decide for herself? If she's tired of being a cleric, if she wants to do something else, let her."

"Thanks, Ricky." Doria smiled a promise at him.

Now *that* was strange. Riccetti always followed Parker's lead, but . . .

Of course. James Michael nodded. The only character of a higher class than Riccetti's Aristobulus was Doria's cleric, and Riccetti wanted to be the most advanced character in the game.

Cullinane spun around. "You want to be the cleric?"

Riccetti sneered. "And have our only wizard be a C-Class novice? Don't be silly."

James Michael sighed. If this haggling went on much longer, it would threaten to cut heavily into playing time. And that would be intolerable. "Excuse me." Five pairs of eyes fastened on him. "Ricky, it seems to me that you're being kind of . . . generous. Usually, you're the one pushing for a balanced team. At least you were, until Doria went up to K-Class."

"Yes, but . . ." Riccetti obviously couldn't think of a but.

"But nothing. The fact is that Doria of the Healing Hand is K-Class. Aristobulus is J-Class, one level lower. I'm sure, Ricky, that you'll put aside your jealousy. For the good of the group." He turned to Doria. "If you're willing to be the cleric, that is."

Suddenly, he was ashamed of himself. Not that he'd meant it that way, but Doria was taking it as a request from a cripple. And she wouldn't turn down a little feeb, would she? *Please, Doria, say no. You wouldn't give in to anyone else on this. Treat me like everyone else, for once. Please?*

She nodded. "I'll be the cleric—but I want to have a say in your characters. You choose mine, I get to veto yours if I don't like it. Agreed?"

"Agreed," James Michael sighed.

"Fine," Parker said. "Ricky and I were talking to Doc on the way in; he kind of agreed that it would be a good idea for Walter to run Hakim, if that's—"

"Yippee!" Walter leered at Doria. "This thief's going to steal your heart, he is." He riffled through his character sheets and selected one. "I like that greasy bastard. Please don't veto him, Doria-beautiful, please?" He clasped his hands below his chin and ducked his head.

"Okay, okay." Doria turned to Parker. "And I suppose you've decided on a character already?"

Parker shrugged. "Einar Lightfingers, I guess—Doc suggested that we might want to have a couple of thieves along. Particularly if we're going to have to steal this Gate thing."

Cullinane's head snapped back from his almost constant staring at the new girl, who was still talking with Doc in the corner of the room. "Steal it? Do we know that it's portable? I was helping Andy roll up her character; must've missed something."

"No." James Michael made it final. "We don't know what it is, where it is, or how it does what it does—although I'm willing to bet I know *what* it does."

"Big fat hairy deal." Walter waved it away. "Getting to it, and then doing whatever the hell we're supposed to do after we get to it—"

"—is the problem." Parker tapped a pencil against the table. "But we're getting a bit ahead of ourselves. Doria hasn't okayed me as Lightfingers, James as Ahira, or Ricky as Aristobulus—you want to veto them, Dore?"

James Michael suppressed a scowl. Cute—by lumping his and Riccetti's characters in with James Michael's Ahira, Parker was making it more than a little awkward for Doria to exercise a veto.

Doria opened her mouth, closed it again. A quick glance at James Michael, then, "No. No veto."

"Fine." Parker slid a sheet of paper in front of him and picked up his pencil. "Now, on to weapons. . . . I don't see any problem for Lightfingers: shortsword, dagger, and a few throwing darts should do it." He looked over at Riccetti. "Unless you think I can get away with armor."

"Out of character. But how about tools?"

Parker lifted his head. "Doc? Do thief's tools come under the heading of personal effects?"

"Don't worry about it. I suspect rather strongly that you'll find all that you need in the wooden boxes next to your party, on the hillside." Deighton turned back to Andrea.

"Fine." Parker glared at his back. "Just fine."

James Michael tapped Slovotsky's leg. "Do you think I could arrange to borrow Hakim's plus-three battleaxe?"

"Nope." Walter didn't bother to take the sting out of the refusal. "Hakim doesn't *lend* anybody anything. You want to talk buying?"

"With Hakim? What would the price be? Two or three times whatever I could come up with?"

Doria laughed. "He's got you. Probably four. James, you'd better stick with your usual stuff; the battleaxe, crossbow, and . . ." she wrinkled her forehead.

"Flail. I like to go well armed."

"Flail," she agreed. "If you think you can carry all . . ."

Everyone was silent for a moment. *Damn it, why can't you forget about it for one bloody second?*

Walter raised himself and stretched. "Hakim, m'friends, will be carrying a scimitar, and two braces of throwing knives."

"Be more specific, please. How many knives in a brace?" James Michael kept his words as acid as possible, but couldn't help smiling his thanks.

"Two. Always two in a brace." Walter quirked a smile at Karl. "And if you're running Barak, I assume he still turns up his nose at anything except his two-handed broadsword?"

"Yup." Cullinane sat back. "Established character trait."

"Wait a minute." Doria sounded more calculating than peeved. "I'm thinking about changing my mind and vetoing Barak."

Karl snatched his lighter from the table, stuck a cigarette in his mouth, and lit it. "Make up your mind." He *snapped* the lighter closed. "I've been running Barak all semester, but if you've got an objection, let me know. You think I've got another character that'll be better for the team?"

"No, but . . ."

"Doria's within her rights, Karl," James Michael said. *You stupid bastard. You treat her like a piece of furniture, then get offended when she insists on a bit of attention.*

"Thank you, James. But go ahead, Karl, run Barak." She smiled ingratiatingly.

James Michael tried to keep his face straight, but brought his hands up to rub at his eyes in case he failed. *All the dynamics of a kindergarten. Doria's still chasing after Cullinane. He's hooked on Andrea—badly, unless I miss my guess. And to make it worse, Parker has been shooting meaningful glances Andrea's way, and Cullinane's looking as though he wishes he had a real sword to run through Parker's guts.*

So Doria tries a quick I-don't-have-to-let-you-but-I-will to get some attention. All of which means—

Walter Slovotsky leaned over. "Looks to be an interesting evening, all things considered." He tapped his temple with a stubby finger that was almost the size of a hotdog. "Wal-ter may look dumb. Doesn't mean he is."

"Just what I was thinking. On both counts." James Michael raised his voice. "And since neither Aristobulus nor Doria carry weapons, I think we're all set. Except for picking a team leader, of course."

Parker sat smugly in his chair. Which wasn't totally unreasonable;

he'd been doing an adequate job as team leader in the Draa Dungeon campaign, the adventure that Deighton had just terminated. But that was as a warrior, not a thief.

Walter reached out and laid a massive hand on James Michael's shoulder. "You think you're up to it, Jimmy me boy?"

"What?" Parker was stunned; Cullinane, Doria, and Riccetti smiled their approval in unison, as though they had rehearsed it. Even Riccetti? Hell, Ricky followed Parker around like an obedient spaniel.

"Makes sense," Riccetti said, drumming his impatience on the table with nail-bitten fingers. "Can't have a thief as team leader; nobody'll trust him farther than I could throw Walter." For Ricky, the game came first.

"Yes, but—"

"But nothing, Jase." Cullinane was enjoying this, perhaps a little too much. "James has been gaming longest here; he hasn't been team leader in quite a while. Give him a chance." His glance over toward Andrea took most of the pleasure out of hearing that. James Michael wished there hadn't been . . . superfluous reasons.

"Doria-beautiful, speak up." Walter slipped down from the table, stretching broadly. "If you're in agreement, then let's have Doc finish getting Andrea's character ready, and play." He rubbed his hands together in mock impatience.

"It's okay with me. Besides, there'll be plenty of time to argue—and fight—once we start playing." She turned to James Michael, and actually smiled as if she meant it. "You're on, Ahira."

"Fine." James Michael folded his hands in his lap. "Okay, everybody—character sheets to Doc. Start an encumbrance list."

"With what?" Parker was still chafing.

"With just your weapons and armor, so far. Once we open the boxes, you'll add to that. Doria of the Healing Hand?"

"Yes, Ahira?"

"I'll need to know your spells—that goes for you, too, Aristobulus."

Riccetti—*no,* Aristobulus; *get into the spirit of it*—nodded. "You want me to write them down for you?"

"Ahira doesn't carry sheets of paper. Orally, of course. You first."

"Okay." Riccetti closed his eyes. If James Michael could remember his spells, so could he.

Good.

"I'm carrying . . . Herstell's Spell of—"

"Just the short names."

"Make that Sleep, Lightning, Fire, Glow Temporarily, the two-way version of Charm, Injure, Preserve, Shatter Metal, and Dispel Magic. That's nine, isn't it?"

"Yes. And that's fine. Don't waste them, now." One of the rules of the game was that a wizard's spells were immediately forgotten when used. It was sort of like firing a gun; the gun could be reloaded, but a spent cartridge was gone. And it would take valuable time out of a campaign for a wizard to relearn his spells from his spell books. Often that time couldn't be spared. "Doria?"

She had to consult her notes. "I'll memorize them, Ahira. . . . Here they are: Heal Minor Wounds—I've got that one three times—Make Edible—"

"Handy. Good choice." Situations could come up where there wouldn't be food at hand. But with that spell, the company could survive for a long time on *anything;* she could even make cafeteria food edible.

"Thanks, Ja—Ahira. . . . Ah, and Warm, Glow, Heal Disease, the Gift of Tongues, Heal Serious Wounds, and—ta-da!—Locate. That last could be handy, no?"

"Very. But be careful. You'll have to know what the Gate is, roughly where it is . . . and we'll have to be reasonably close before you use it." He turned to Cullinane, smiling. "I know what your special skills are."

Karl Cullinane cracked a smile and stroked at the stubble that he no doubt thought of as a beard. *"Arrgh."*

"Arg, indeed. Hakim."

Walter Slovotsky bounced to attention and bowed from the waist, clasping his hands in front of him. "Thy servant, O short sahib."

"Don't waste the oil on *me.* You might need it later.—We're going to need a thief on this quest, probably."

"Yes, O Source of All Wisdom, but what is thy point?" His look of total innocence was perhaps a bit overdone.

"It would be a shame to have to execute you for stealing from members of the party." James Michael mimed hefting an axe. "A great loss."

"As it would be to thy servant." Walter felt at his neck. "So this unworthy one shall keep thy counsels in mind."

"See that you do." This was getting better all the time. "And Lightfingers."

Visibly, Parker considered giving him a hard time, not playing along. James Michael was counting on Parker's basic desire to play to overcome his irritation at not getting to be team leader for once. For a moment, opposed desires balanced. Finally, Parker shrugged and answered in a harsh whisper. "And what do *you* want?"

Good. "I want you to listen very closely to me, *thief.*"

"I always listen closely. To humans, at least. Not to a filthy little dwarf."

"Barak? Do you think I should have to take this?"

"No. You want me to persuade him, Ahira?"

James Michael glanced over at Deighton, who was again standing in front of his open briefcase, his hands hidden inside. One of the things James Michael liked—a lot—about Doc Deighton's gamemastering was that Doc almost always chose to do the dice-rolling himself, freeing the players from as much of the mechanics of the game as was possible. It helped to maintain the illusion, the atmosphere. "Will that be necessary, Einar Lightfingers? Barak would lop off your remaining hand if I asked him to." And Karl Cullinane would probably enjoy kicking Jason Parker out of the game by killing off Parker's character.

Lightfingers/Parker sighed. "What do you want me to do?"

"Good. And it's not what I want you to do, it's what I want you *not* to do. Understood?" He rapped on the table. "I know your habits; we won't have any of that nonsense in this company."

Pause. "Understood."

And we're off. He gave a slight nod at Deighton.

"You have just awoken on a hillside," Deighton intoned, "a company of . . . six adventurers, seeking treasure and fame."

"Wait a minute," Aristobulus grated. "How did we get here? And I thought that there was—"

"Patience, please. Last night, you all slept in an inn, which was located in a village just south of the great walled city, D'tareth. You don't know how you got here." He stopped.

Doria picked up the hint. "Where the hell are we?"

"Yeah."

"What're we doing on this hilltop?"

"Last thing I knew, I was kicking the serving girl out of bed so I could get some sleep." That was from Slovotsky/Hakim; Ahira leaned back, closed his eyes, and smiled.

"From the top of this hill, you can see the dawn sun, rising over another walled city. It is not D'tareth; the walls of this city are of some wet-looking gray stone."

"Forget the distance—what's close up?" Ahira understood Parker's impatience, but wished that he'd contain himself. They would learn, soon enough.

"Beside you on the hillside are half a dozen large wooden boxes. They are plain, almost cubical, each side roughly the height of a dwarf."

Eyes still closed, Ahira spoke up. "Nobody touch the boxes. We don't know what's in them."

"I'll dispel any spells."

"You're not thinking, Aristobulus," Ahira shot back. "First, if it's harmless, you're wasting a spell. Second, there could be, say, a magic carpet inside. You want to turn it into a throw rug?"

"But what can we *do?*"

"Hakim." He voiced it as a command.

"Here, sahib."

"You want to give the boxes a try? Careful, now."

A deep chuckle. "So you want me to be the sacrificial meat? Very well. I walk over to the nearest of the boxes and run my fingertips lightly over its top surface."

Deighton: "You feel nothing unusual, although your . . ." As he paused, dice clattered. "Your suspicion is that there is a hidden catch."

"For some reason or other, I suspect that there is a hidden catch, Ahira. You want me to find it?"

Deighton: "From behind you, you hear a voice."

"Quick!" Ahira said. "Everybody, turn around. Barak, loose your sword—but don't draw it. Aristobulus, get ready to throw a spell—if anything funny happens, throw it."

"Which one?"

"Lightning." James Michael knew that the new voice would be Andrea's character, joining the group, but Ahira was a suspicious sort, who wouldn't know that, anyway. Best to be prepared.

"As you turn around, you see a young human woman, dressed in the gray robes of a user of magicks. Go ahead."

"I . . . I'm supposed to say . . ." Andrea was uncomfortable; James Michael resigned himself to having a hard time getting her into the spirit of things.

Hakim/Slovotsky's basso boomed, "Speak for yourself—are you possessed by a demon, wench?"

"Wench? Oh. No, I'm not possessed by a demon. I'm, uh, Lotana," she said, the accent firmly on the second syllable, "and,"

she added in a low monotone, "I'm going to get even with you for this, Karl Cullinane."

Never mind; get back into it.

"Greetings, little girl, would you like a piece of candy?"

"Barak," Ahira snapped out, "if Einar Lightfingers opens his mouth again, stick a sword through his lips."

*"De*lighted."

Bringing a new player—a new *person* into the company was always a touchy situation. Ahira didn't need Lightfingers complicating matters, not with a nov—a not terribly experienced magic user. "Lotana, we are a band of adventurers, seeking . . . something, although we don't quite know what, *yet.*"

Deighton: "You have a vague, unexplainable feeling that what you are looking for is something called the Gate Between Worlds."

"Although we all share a vague suspicion that we're looking for the Gate Between Worlds, whatever that is. Would you like to join us?"

"Sure. Uh, what were you going to do about those boxes on the hillside?"

Doria's voice was almost a whine. "Open them, silly."

"Okay, fine, I'll open them."

"No, don't—"

"As the first box was opened, you are overwhelmed by a rush of . . ."

James Michael couldn't hear the rest; a rush of sound like the roar of an impossibly loud, impossibly near jet buffeted his ears, acrid smoke invading his nostrils until he found himself on his knees in a coughing spasm, his tearing eyes jammed shut.

He bounced to his feet on the damp grass, reflexively reaching for the axe strapped to his chest, loosening the straps with two quick jerks and taking the axe in his gnarled, well-muscled hands.

Well-muscled hands?

He opened his eyes.

He was standing on the side of a grassy hill, a dwarf with an axe in his hands.

"Ohmygod."

PART TWO

Lundeyll

CHAPTER THREE

"It Isn't a Game Anymore"

*I do not know whether I was then a man dreaming I
was a butterfly, or whether I am now a butterfly dreaming
I am a man.*

—Chang-tzu

"Jason, *wake up,*" James Michael's voice rasped.

Jason Parker shrugged the hand from his shoulders, reaching for
the covers, to pull them over his head. But the covers weren't there.

"Want me to try?" The voice was Karl Cullinane's, but changed: a
deep, rich baritone.

"No, we'll do it. You go back to your little friend," Doria said.
"Maybe she's over her crying jag by now."

Jason pried an eye open, squinting painfully in the bright sunlight.
Doria knelt on the grass next to him. But it wasn't Doria, not exactly. She was older, gaunt, the rounded features of her face having
changed into the well-defined ones of a thirtyish woman. And her
eyes were strange; *nobody* had yellow irises.

But Doria did. And that seemed . . . right, familiar.

"What the hell?" Jason jerked upright, now totally awake.

Maybe.

He was sitting on damp morning grass, wearing a musky-smelling
leather jerkin and dew-damp gray woolen leggings, an ivory-hilted

shortsword in its scabbard at the right side of his waist, a sheathed dagger strapped to his chest beneath his jerkin.

He reached his right hand up to his face, to slap himself awake. This had all the makings of a *bad* bad dream.

He missed; air brushed his cheek. *Missed?* He looked down at his arm. Instead of a hand on the end of his withered, age-spotted right arm, there was nothing but a naked stump, covered with brown keloid scars.

My hand . . . The world went gray.

James Michael's voice came from behind. "Take it easy, Jason. Deep breaths. But you've got to get yourself together. You're next to the last—we still can't get Arist—Ricky to wake up."

He kept his eyes closed. A massive hand gripped the back of his neck, pulling him forward. Reflexively, he retrieved his dagger with his left hand, thrust it over his shoulder—

And found his wrist caught in a bone-crushing grip. The dagger was wrenched out of his fingers, thudding on the ground beside him.

"*Don't* try that again."

"You just go easy on him, Ahira." There was a strength, a confidence in Doria's voice that Jason had never heard before. "It's going to be harder on him than it was on you." Gentle fingers stroked his face. "We'll just have to take this one step at a time."

"Maybe you're right, but I don't like it. Aristobulus is still—"

"Shh. One step at a time."

Jason opened his eyes. Somehow it was fitting that James Michael was a dwarf, a broad-shouldered creature with a huge, broken nose and a jutting jaw. But it was still James Michael's eyes that peered at him from beneath heavy brows.

"You're Ahira."

"That's right." The dwarf smiled, running a hand down the front of his gapped chainmail vest. "We're here, on the other side."

"Other side?"

Ahira shrugged. "Somehow or other . . . never mind, for now. But if I'm Ahira, who are you?"

Doria glared at the dwarf, then clasped Jason's good hand in her two. She was wearing a long, high-necked robe, belted tightly around her waist. "Easy, now. Don't let him rush you."

Jason snatched his hand away and slapped at Doria's sleeve. It didn't even dent; it was like slapping a brick wall. "It works." In the game, Doria of the Healing Hand had a robe like that, a magical one.

She smiled reassuringly and waved her arm, the tightly woven cloth flapping. "It's just like in the game. Feels like a cotton robe from the inside, but from the outside it's like armor. Just like in the game." Her face sobered. "And all of us, we're our characters. Sort of."

"Which means that I'm Lightfingers." A small leather pouch dangled by a thong from her sash. He let his head loll forward as though he were fainting again, slipped his hand across her body while his head movement distracted her, and fingered open the pouch without disturbing the strap that attached it to her belt. He dipped two gnarled fingers in, lifted and palmed a coin, closed the pouch with a gentle tug, and tucked the coin into a pocket inside his sleeve with a practiced flip.

Elapsed time less than three seconds. It felt natural, as though he'd done it thousands of times before. *But I've never stolen anything. It's—*

"A nice try, Jason." Ahira shook his head. "But I was watching for it. Give it back."

"Watching for *what?*" Doria's brow furrowed in exasperation. Now *that* was strange; she always deferred to the little cripple.

Oh. He isn't little anymore. Or crippled. Just short. The snotty bastard must be having the time of his life.

"He just picked your purse." The dwarf chuckled. "Give it back. Now."

"I don't know what you're talking about—and who are you to be giving orders, anyway?" He braced himself on his stump and slid his feet under him. It was the practiced routine of a thief when caught: First deny, then challenge, then *run.*

Ahira grabbed his sleeve and shook the coin out. Picking it up, he handed it to Doria. "Don't worry; I'm not going to give him a hard time. This once." He turned back to Jason. "But we're in enough trouble as it is; I don't want you adding to it. Understood, Lightfingers?"

"My name is Jason." But the name felt strange in his mouth. "And I want to go home."

The dwarf helped him to his feet. Standing, Ahira's head barely came up to his chest. Ahira picked up his battleaxe from the damp grass and tapped a well-chewed thumbnail against the blade. "Two things. In answer to your question, *this* says that I'm in charge here. Back home, the group chose me as team leader. That's the way it is; that's the way it's going to be.

"And second, we are going home." Ahira opened his mouth; shut it. He shook his head. "Just take it easy for a while, get your bearings. Doria, let's go see to the wizard."

Karl Cullinane had often thought of holding Andy-Andy in his arms, but nowhere in his imaginings had she been crying. "Everything will be fine." He patted her clumsily on the back.

But these weren't his arms, this wasn't his body. Not quite. Karl was of average height, and skinny. *Was.* Now, he towered over her as he held her, careful not to squeeze her tightly; somehow, he knew that his grip could break a strong man's back.

After a while, her weeping died down. He let her go, then took a loose sleeve of her gray robe and wiped at her eyes. "Feeling better?"

"N-no. I'm *scared.* What happened?" She rubbed at her temples. "I . . . feel so strange—how do I know that I could turn invisible, or make you fall asleep, or charm—it's like there's something in my head, trying to get *out.*"

Her mouth started to move; he clapped a hand over it. "Don't. Just listen to me, but don't say anything." Her eyes grew wide; she brought up her hands, vaguely pulling at his arm. *"No.* Nod if you understand me, and I'll take my hand away."

Her head moved; he let his hand drop. "Don't do that again," she said, planting a palm against his chest, shoving.

He could have laughed, almost. But he took a step back. "Okay, but be careful what you say. You've got three spells in your head, and they're trying to get out."

"How do you know?"

He shrugged. *I don't know. But I do.* "It's . . . like I've got two minds. One is Barak; the other is me." That a wizard had to constantly rein in spells was something Barak would know. It had to be: Karl hadn't known it; it wasn't part of the game. He stooped slowly, and lifted his scabbarded sword from the grass. "Barak knows how to use this, not me." The sword was long, almost three-fifths his height. Without drawing it from its scabbard, he knew that it was single-edged like a Japanese katana, but straight, not curved; primarily a slashing weapon, it still could be used to thrust. "And why not to strap it to anything; it'd take too long to draw it." He gripped the cord-wound handle with his left hand almost at the pommel. To draw the sword, he would slip the scabbard away, add his right hand in its place on the grip, and strike. That was one of the rules: Get your sword into play, and worry about picking up the scabbard later.

It was important to keep the blade clean and dry; an image of his hands—*his* hands—cleaning the blade with a dead enemy's hair welled up, unbidden.

"But what *happened?*" She gestured at her robes, at him, at the boxes on the hillside. "We're in the place that Dr. Deighton described. Look."

He looked to the east. The early-morning sun sat over the far walls of the city below. Karl raised his hand to his forehead to shield his eyes. The walls were solid and wide; a few bowmen stood on the pathways girdling them. People, and horses drawing two-wheeled carts, swarmed in and out of the gate.

To the north, a vast expanse of dark water spread across the horizon, waves rippling in toward a rocky shore. Off in the distance a broad-beamed schooner glided slowly in toward the docks.

But there was more than Deighton had described; he hadn't mentioned the fishing village to the north, and Karl hadn't visualized it.

How did he know that it was a fishing village?

It was too complicated, too strange. He shook his head. "You're right. I don't know how, but somehow we're *here.*" He stretched his arms, letting his shoulders strain against the seams of his leather jerkin, and drew in a deep breath. It was clean air, fresh and sweet with a tang of ozone; this world had never known the stink of the internal combustion engine. "But doesn't it feel fine?"

"For you." She was nearing tears again. "But how do I get home?"

"I don't know. And I didn't mean it that way—not that I wanted to stay here forever." It was one thing to play at being a warrior, but a fuzzy memory of his sword opening someone's belly like an over-ripe fruit . . . that didn't feel right, not to Karl Cullinane. *But I'm not just Karl, not anymore. There's a lot of Barak in me, now. Then again, maybe that's not all bad.* He and Andy-Andy used to be close to the same height, although when she wore heels she'd look down at him. Now he towered over her by a foot, or more. When he stood close to her, she had to crane her neck to look up at him. She wasn't changed, though, at least on the outside, except for the loose robes that had replaced her jeans and shirt.

And the fear in her eyes. That was new. "Karl, how are we going to—"

"I don't know." He shook his head. "But someh—"

"This a private conversation, or can anyone join?" Walter Slovotsky's voice boomed from behind him.

Karl spun around. He hadn't heard the big man—*no, not big anymore; I'm half a head taller than he is.* "Don't do that."

"Don't do what?" Slovotsky smiled innocently. Except for Andy-Andy, he was the least changed of the group, at least physically. His skin had darkened a shade or two, his black hair was slightly straighter and a bit longer, and there were hints of epicanthic folds around his eyes, but that was all. Even his all-is-right-with-the-world smile was intact.

"Don't sneak up on me. I don't like it."

Slovotsky shrugged, muscles playing under the bare skin of his chest. He was dressed as Hakim would be: shirtless, a blousy pair of pants belted tightly to his waist, the cuffs tucked into the lacing of his sandals. From the left side of his waist, a wickedly curved scimitar hung in a leather scabbard; from the right, a tangle of knives and straps. Slovotsky rubbed at his temples. "I guess I should apologize, or something. It's just that moving silently seems to come naturally to me. It's sort of like a new toy, Karl. Or should I call you Barak?"

"Karl." He forced a smile. "Barak would give you a clout on the head as a reminder."

"Good point. You had better call me Walter. Hakim would slip a knife between your ribs, for—" He stopped, puzzled, raising a palm. "Sorry. That wasn't me."

"I understand." Karl unclenched his hand from the hilt of his sword. "But the question is—"

"What the *hell* are we going to do?" There was a new strength in Andy-Andy's voice. Just a little.

Karl gave her a smile. "Right." She was adjusting. A few minutes before, she would have put the emphasis on *do* instead of *hell.*

"In theory, it's simple," Slovotsky said.

"Nonsense." She waved a hand at their surroundings. "Simple?"

"Everything's simple, actually." He held up a well-manicured finger. "First, you figure out what you want."

Karl didn't like the way Slovotsky's eyes roamed up and down her as he said that, but he let it pass.

"Second, you figure out what you have to do to get it." Another finger. "And three"—he added a third, tapping all three fingers against his other hand—"you do it. That's the way life works." He jerked a thumb toward the city below. "Somehow or other, we're in the world that Doc described, no?"

"Yes, but—"

"But nothing, Karl. That has to be our operating assumption, until and unless we find out differently. Which is unlikely. I mean, I've got skills I never had, Doria's got cleric spells trying to bust their way out of her head, you're a full foot taller than you should be, James is—"

"I get the point. But what does that do for us?"

"Simple, again. The name of the campaign Doc designed is, if you'll remember, the Quest for the Gate Between Worlds. How we got here, I don't know. But if we want to get back, then obviously we've got to find this Gate thing." He pointed at the six wooden boxes, just over fifty yards away. One of the boxes stood open and empty; the other five, smooth, dark, and seamless, closed. "I'm willing to bet that there's something inside that'll give us a clue. Or more than a clue."

Hushed voices whispered behind the cluster of boxes.

"They haven't woken Riccetti yet?"

"They're trying. Jimmy—make that Ahira; he likes it better—Ahira thinks that we should have a fully conscious wizard on hand before we try to open any of the rest. And no offense, Lotana—"

"Andrea."

"Andrea, then—no offense, but the way you fell apart, I wouldn't want to count on you to sniff out any spells on them. You think you could spot a Glyph of Shrouding?"

"I don't know what you're talking about—wait." Her hands flew to her temples, her fingers digging into her scalp. "It's strange. I know things that I don't know, if you understand what I mean."

Karl laid a gentle hand on her arm. "We all do."

She grabbed his hand, squeezing it with white-knuckled fingers. "A glyph is like a magical charm, usually placed on a doorway or entrance. It can hurt anybody trying to get past it, unless it's tuned to leave them alone, or unless they break its spell," she said, her voice calm and businesslike. "Like the ones on the city." She jerked her hand toward the walled city, below. "Right?"

"What ones?" Karl and Walter said in unison.

She chuckled. "C'mon, don't play games with me—I don't need that."

Karl sighed and looked back toward the city. Just a walled city, no writing on it. "You see anything, Walter?"

"No." Slovotsky raised an eyebrow. "And that was a part of the game I always had trouble swallowing."

Karl nodded. "Me, too." He shrugged. "Well, another—"

"If you don't mind, I'd like to know what you're talking about. Please?"

"We can't see magical writing," he said. "To Walter and me, that's just a wall."

"Don't be silly, it's plain as . . ." She turned back. "Really?"

"Really. As Deighton said, unless you've got the genes for wizardry, all magical writing is totally transparent to you. What does it say?"

"I can *see* it, not read it. Besides, it isn't something that can be pronounced, but it would fry Aristobulus or me to a crisp if we got inside the city." She wrinkled her forehead. "Wait a minute. How did I—"

"Comes with the territory," Slovotsky said. "Looks like wizards aren't too popular there; probably cost the locals quite a bit to hire one to do the work." He smiled. "But it looks like there's a pony in the bottom of this shitbucket; want to check out the boxes for Glyphs?"

Karl frowned. "I thought you said Ahira wanted to wait."

"I'll check it out with him, first. But"—he clapped a hand to Andy-Andy's shoulder—"it looks like you've got what it takes."

Karl suppressed an urge to knock Slovotsky's hand away from her. "Why don't you go clear it with him, then?"

"Which was something else I wanted to talk to you about. You got any objection to him being in charge? Somebody's got to do it." Slovotsky's face was studiously blank.

Karl thought about it for a moment. In the game, he'd always enjoyed his occasional chances to be the team leader. *But this is for real. I may be good at the game, but this is for real.* "No. No objection. As long as there're no PMDs, or anything like that."

"PMD?" Andrea asked. "What's that?"

Slovotsky grinned broadly. "Stands for Polish Mine Detector." He covered his ears with both hands and mimed stomping fearfully on the ground. *"Boom.* Seriously, it's a technique for checking for traps. You send the lowest-class character on ahead. If there's no trap, there's no harm. And if there is, then you bring the player back into the game with a new character. It's kind of hard on the old character, but—"

She looked up at him. "You mean that it kills him. Or her."

"Right, but—"

"But we won't have any of that," Karl said. "Not as long as I'm around."

"I can speak for myself, Karl." She scowled at both of them. "And I'm not going to let myself be a guinea pig."

"Understood, Andrea." Slovotsky nodded and walked away.

"Karl, he seems so . . . sure of himself."

"That's Walter. Possibly Hakim, too." Which was one of the things he'd always envied about Slovotsky. Always so sure of himself, no matter what. And so comfortable around women.

Karl shook his head. Even around Andy-Andy he felt awkward, gawky. And she was a *friend.*

"What are you thinking?"

He returned her smile with interest. "Nothing much." This was ridiculous. Here he was, God knew where, more scared than he cared to admit, even to himself. And thinking about how good it had felt to hold her. "And you wouldn't believe it, anyway."

"Bets?"

"Well, what's the diagnosis?" Ahira asked.

"I think he's in shock." Kneeling over the limp form of Aristobulus, Doria looked up at him. "Shallow breathing, thready pulse." Her fingers dipped into the wizard's short gray hair. "And I think he might have hit his head on one of the boxes; there's a bit of a lump here." She bent over, examining his head more closely. "Although the skin isn't broken. Do you think there might be a blanket or two in one of these boxes? We should keep him warm."

"No."

"What do you mean, no? He could *die.*"

Ahira repressed a smile; she wouldn't have understood. But that felt good; Doria would never have contradicted James Michael Finnegan, would never, ever have argued with a little cripple.

But I'm not a cripple anymore. He bounced on the balls of his feet, reveling in how good, how natural it felt. *I'm Ahira Bandylegs, and I'm strong. Better than normal.* "No, he won't die. Try your Healing spell, the one for minor wounds. I think this should count as a minor wound."

"But, James—"

"But nothing. You're a cleric, a healer. You've been complaining about spells buzzing around your head. Here's your chance to get rid of one. You'll have to pray for it, to get it back—but we'll have plenty of time for that later."

Her face paled. "I—I don't know if—"

"I trust you, Doria of the Healing Hand. And so would Aristobulus. Do it. Now."

She nodded a reluctant agreement, and planted spread-fingered hands on the old man's chest. The polish was gone from her nails, just as the fear of him was gone from her manner. Perhaps, somewhere inside, Doria Perlstein was confused, frightened. But not the cleric.

"Easy," he whispered. "It's going to be easy. You've done this a thousand times."

Slowly, her eyes sagged shut, as her weight bore down on her arms, on Aristobulus' chest. The old man looked to be in bad shape; his skin was ashen, his breathing barely perceptible.

Strange, liquid syllables issued from her barely parted lips, starting slowly, then becoming a torrent. Ahira could hear the words distinctly, tried to memorize them.

But he couldn't. Not a phrase, not a word, not a syllable. They vanished from his mind like a snowflake melting on a palm.

The volley of sound flowed into Aristobulus, his breathing becoming deeper, a tinge of pink replacing the fishbelly pallor of his face. The fingers of an outflung arm twitched, then curled, as his eyes snapped open.

Aristobulus sucked in air with a desperate gasp, and a stream of sound issued from his mouth, obscenely guttural and harsh.

And like a striking snake, a bolt of lightning crackled from the tips of his fingers, shattering the nearest of the boxes into a thousand charred, smoking pieces.

"You idiot!" Ahira reached out, grabbed the wizard's throat, setting broad thumbs against his windpipe.

"Stop it! *Stop it!*" Doria's fists beat a rapid tattoo on his back.

Reluctantly, Ahira released Aristobulus, bouncing the old man's head against the grass.

The wizard's eyes were wide. "You told me, have the spell ready— you told me, Ahira." He rubbed at his head. "Ahira? Or are you James . . . ?" He bit his lip.

Ahira spat in disgust and stood. "Take care of him, Doria. Just get him out of my sight." He raised his voice. "Barak, Hakim, Lightfingers, Lotana—get over here. Let's see if there's anything we can salvage out of this . . . mess."

"I . . . don't understand," the wizard whined. He began to cry, to weep like a frightened child.

After more than half an hour on their hands and knees, sorting through charred pieces of bone and horn, smashed vessels of glass and clay, Ahira called a halt.

"Anybody find anything salvageable?"

Barak shook his head, rubbing a sooty finger against a smudge on his nose, which only made it worse. "No, whatever was in here is gone." He lifted a jagged scrap of horn and scraped a clean spot with a thumbnail. "What do you think this was?"

Hakim shrugged. "A Joshua's Horn?"

Lightfingers swore softly under his breath. "And unless I miss my guess, these scraps of leather and parchment were spell books. *Were.* Unless there are duplicates in one of the others, we can kiss Lot—Andrea's and Ari's relearning their spells goodbye." He pitched a shard at the wizard. "You stupid little *shit.*"

This couldn't go on. Ahira agreed with Lightfingers—emphatically—but what was done was done. The problem was what to do now. He wasn't sure that he knew.

Never mind. The leader has to seem to know what he's doing. At least. "Shut up, Lightfingers. We go on from here. Lotana?"

"Andrea," she said, with a friendly nod. Good—at least somebody was on his side. "Yes, Ahira?"

"Do you think that you can check out the rest of the boxes for magic? Without touching them, I mean."

Hakim held up a hand. "I'd better check for mechanical traps."

"Fine. You two do that. And if it seems safe, have Barak open them."

Barak nodded slowly. "You don't think there's any trap."

No, I don't. But if there is, you're probably the most expendable. Without the spell books, we can't afford to risk either of the wizards. And we've only got one cleric, and one two-handed thief. "I'm certain of it. I think that what's in the boxes is our supplies, or what's left of them. But be careful, anyway." He beckoned to Lightfingers. "Come here for a moment."

"What do you want?" the thief asked, walking over, stopping a few feet away.

Just about half a foot farther away than I could swing my axe. Which was good; at least it showed caution, if not respect. "We're going to need somebody to scout around, check out the city down there. The wizards are out, what with the glyphs Andrea sees on the walls. And I don't think Barak or I tend to be subtle enough. You think you're up to it? *Jason,* " he added, deliberately. Not a whole lot was clear to Ahira, not yet. But one thing he was certain of was that he wanted to encourage the other's Jason-part, not the Lightfingers persona.

Lightfingers stood silently for a moment, rubbing his stump against the point of his jaw. "Yes." He stopped himself in mid-nod. "You do want me to pick up more than information, of course."

"No. Just find out whatever you can. We're going to have to find this Gate thing. Whatever and wherever it is. Which means, among other things, that we'll have to find out where *we* are. And, Jason, you're too valuable to lose. Don't pick any pockets; don't try any swindles. We've got quite a few coins in our pouches; we need information a lot more than money."

"Yes?" Lightfingers tilted his head to one side. "And how much is one gold piece worth, here? It could buy half a town, if gold is scarce. But if not . . ."

"Then maybe we couldn't buy half a sandwich. If they have sandwiches here. Good point."

"It is, isn't it?" Lightfingers' hand came to rest on the hilt of his shortsword, perhaps accidentally.

But perhaps not. Ahira pretended not to notice. "You know, maybe I made a mistake. Declaring myself in charge, that is. You've always been a bit sharper than me. Maybe—"

"Don't be silly. You think Slovotsky or Cullinane and his little friend would follow me? A one-armed thief?"

The dwarf took a slow step forward and laid a hand on Lightfingers' arm. "Perhaps no. But if I am going to be in charge, I'll need your full support. Or I won't be able to do it. If you want—"

Lightfingers cut him off with a full-throated laugh. "James Michael, you little *bastard*. You're damn good at manipulating people, aren't you?" His smile was almost friendly.

Ahira shrugged. "You have to learn a lot of things when you spend your whole life in a wheelchair. Lots of things you can't do for yourself; you have to get other people to do them for you. In your case," he said, smiling, "all the technique in the world isn't going to do any good, is it?"

"Maybe, maybe not. For the time being, I'll follow your lead." He jerked a thumb at the city below. "You want me to leave now?"

Ahira hadn't thought about it. In the game, daytime was safer than night. But a thief was at his best in the dark. "Hmmm. How far away would you say that the city is?"

"Five miles, or close to it. You want another opinion?"

"No, I'm sure you're right." That sounded phony, even in his own ears. But the point, that he was going to trust Lightfingers, had gotten across; Lightfingers was smiling. "What do you think the chances are that they lock up the city at sundown?"

"If they don't, I'd be surprised. Why build a wall around a city if you don't lock up?"

"Right. So, time it so you get there just about an hour before sundown. Plan to spend the night inside. Find out whatever you can, then get back up here, first thing in the morning. Understood?"

"Fine." The thief nodded. "Which means—figure it'll take two hours to get down there—that I ought to leave, say, about three hours after noon. Sounds good?"

Noon was still a while off; the sun was at about a forty-five-degree angle. "Right. So get Hakim. We'll see if there're any blankets in those boxes. You two duck into the woods and get some sleep." It would be best for them to stay awake all night. In preindustrial cities, the night was a time of danger, when the only safe place to sleep would be behind locked, barred doors.

"*Hakim?*" Lightfingers glared down at him. "What do you mean?"

"He's going along." *I may have to trust you a bit, Jason, but I'm not going to go overboard about it.* "Two is better than one. Besides, I want you to keep an eye on him."

A snicker. "Don't play games with me. It's me that—"

"*Ahira, Lightfingers—we found something.*" Andrea jumped up from in front of a now-open box, waving a sheaf of paper. "It's a letter. From Dr. Deighton."

CHAPTER FOUR

"It Should Be Relatively Easy"

There is no one who can return from there
To describe their nature, to describe their dissolution,
That he may still our desires,
Until we reach the place where they have gone.

—*The Song of the Harper,* Stanza Five

Jason threw his arms up in disgust. "I can't read that. What the hell language is it in?" It was frustrating. The letters on the page looked familiar, but strange. Clearly, they formed words. But not for him.

Andrea's brow wrinkled. "It's easy. Listen: 'Tikrach amalo, ift recet quirto blosriet az . . .'"

Dear friends, please accept my sincere apologies . . .

She raised her head. "Can't any of you *read?*"

Barak tugged at his beard. "No." He shook his head sadly. "I can understand it, but I'm not literate. Not in Erendra."

Erendra. Eren meant man, or human; *dra* was a shortened form of *dravhen,* mouth. Man-mouth: a language for humans. But how did he know that? No, Jason didn't know that—Lightfingers did. *And that's who I am.*

Ahira shrugged. "That makes sense, actually. Aristobulus, Doria —take a look. Bet you can read it."

They could. "It's easy," Doria said. "But you can't . . . ?"

No, Hakim, Barak, Ahira, and Lightfingers couldn't.

"Damn." Lightfingers rubbed his fingertips against his stump. It did make sense, of a sort. They all had the abilities of their characters, plus their memories of the other side. But no more than that. Barak, Lightfingers, Hakim, and Ahira weren't literate in the game; warriors and thieves didn't need to be. On the other hand, clerics and wizards had to be able to read.

He licked the tip of his index finger and wrote his other name in the dust on top of an unopened box. *JASON.* He could read *that,* at least. Thank God.

"Right." Ahira looked down at the letters, just a few inches below his eyes. "We haven't lost anything, but"—he smiled—"alu n'atega nit damn ekta, pi agli." *We haven't gained too damn much, either.*

Interesting. Damn was the same word in both languages. And that suggested a possibility. . . .

He looked at the others. Barak was the most bothered by it; the big man sat on the ground, his face buried in his hands. Or was it Barak that was bothered? Quite probably, illiteracy was more distressing to Karl.

Hakim stood easily, confidently. "Well, which of you magical folks is going to give me reading lessons? Damned if I'm not going to be able to *read.*"

"That's the spirit." Ahira clapped him on the back. "But maybe we're not going to have to hang around here long enough for that to be a problem. Andrea, how about reading the letter? Out loud, for the sake of us"—he smiled—"disabled types."

Barak shook his head. "Why the hell didn't he just write it in English?"

Andrea, sitting with the letter on her lap, smiled reassuringly at him. "He did, I think. But the letter translated across, just as our bodies did. Either that, or he was trying to show off. Ari?"

The old man twined his fingers in his gray beard. "I don't know; it could work either way." He closed his eyes. "Which . . . depends on the complexity of the spell he used. And that depends on how magic works there." He opened his eyes and shrugged. "Which is something I can only guess at. Let me see the letter." He held out a hand. "I—"

"No." It was bad enough that he'd been robbed of his literacy, at least for all practical purposes. But Jason didn't want to become some sort of second-class citizen. "No, you read it. Out loud. Give all of us a chance to understand it at the same time."

Ahira nodded. "Go ahead."

She began, reading in Erendra, pausing only occasionally for breath.

Dear Friends,

Please accept my sincere apologies for not warning you about what was to happen. I am sorry for any distress you suffered, but I really had no choice: Had I warned you, you never would have believed me.

As I am sure you have gathered by now, you are in the world on which I modeled the little games we played together. Except they weren't just games.

I am not going to bore you with a long rendition of the difficulties this caused me as a child, but I have always had an ability to see into another world—this world that you are now in, since you are reading this. Quite clearly, I am not the only one who has ever had these visions, although I flatter myself by feeling that no one has ever had them so clearly. Not that it is ever terribly clear; the different time rates of our two worlds have always made events on the other side—your side—seem to happen so quickly that they are difficult to follow, even when my fleeting visions are so powerful that they overwhelm my senses.

My friends, I hunger for this world; given the chance, here, I know that I would be the most powerful wizard that this world has ever known. Were I able to transfer myself, as I did you, I would have.

But I can't. Magic works differently in the two worlds; in ours, it is an erratic force. As I write this, I have been trying to transfer material objects for twenty years, succeeding only slightly better than one percent of the time. And always, the objects change; only recently have I been able to control that change.

People, or any sentient creatures, are a different matter. There is a force in our world, called the collective unconscious, which inhibits the transfer of such. To put it simply, all of you belonged in our world, and there was nothing that I could do to transfer you as long as that obtained.

But there is ample evidence of individuals who have been liberated from the collective unconscious, and, given the proper set of conditions, have popped from one world to the other. Benjamin Bathurst and Ambrose Bierce are the two best known examples; no doubt there have been others.

As I write this, I don't know if I will be able to duplicate those conditions with any success; I do know that I can't do it for myself. A corollary of self-referential theory may, indeed, make that an impossibility for one confined to our world.

But, as you read this, you know that I have been able to duplicate those conditions for you, with the aid of much preparation and your participation in our game. I don't know who you are—as I write this, I have been trying different combinations of enchantments and individuals for a number of years, setting up caches of supplies at many different sites. The sites have been, as I'm sure you have gathered by now, always the places where our campaigns have started.

I would be very surprised if you all are not angry with me right now. But please try to understand: With what I know from my sight, I could be the greatest wizard, the most powerful user of magic that this world has ever known; instead, I find myself in the grips of academia, this world hovering in front of me like a ripe fruit.

But there is a way across. In this universe, there is a device called a Gate, a Gate Between Worlds, that can open up a pathway between our universes. I ask that you go to the Gate, and bring me through.

And in return, I promise to gratify your every wish.

To make this possible, along with the various supplies you will find in the other boxes, there is one box which I am certain you will regard as a treasure chest. Its contents are the result of years and years of research and experimentation. You will find a Horn, a lengthy book of spells, ten Cloaks of Transposition—but I don't need to go on; the contents are self-explanatory. Use and enjoy them.

These devices, together with the map of this world, will enable you to get from where you are to where the Gate is, and help you subdue the Gate's guardian so that you can bring me through with ease.

As for the rest of the supplies, they should prevent your having to buy anything locally. Please distribute the

brandy among yourselves as a treat from me, and in par-
tial apology for the discomfort I have caused you.

When you bring me through, you will receive the rest of
my apology. Those among you foolish enough to wish to
return to our dull, drab world will be given a ton of gold.
And for those of you who wish to remain with me, I prom-
ise to gratify your every wish. And I mean that literally.

Andrea lifted her head, and looked directly at Barak. "And it ends, 'with most sincere best wishes.' "

Barak rose to his full height, slipping his scabbard from his sword, and dropped the scabbard to the grass. "Can you hear me, you bastard? *This* is what you get, when I get my hands on you." He spun on Aristobulus. "Get a sword."

"What?" The old man cowered.

"Get a sword, so I can kill you fairly. That box!" He waved his sword at the shards littering the hillside. "The one with the treasures. You broke it, you—"

"Enough, Barak." Ahira moved in front of him, his battleaxe held easily in his massive hands. "We're in enough trouble as it is. I'm not going to have you—or anyone else—killed. Is that understood?"

Barak snickered. The dwarf was threatening him? Ahira might be a lot stronger, but his sword had the reach. "Me killed? Don't be more stupid than—"

"Karl!" Andy-Andy moved between the two. "Stop it."

Karl? Who is— "Oh." He took a deep breath. He was Karl Cullinane, and Karl Cullinane did not carve up a helpless old man like a side of beef.

He stooped slowly and picked up his discarded scabbard, slipping the sword easily home.

Aristobulus got to his feet. "I understand your anger. I was most . . . disoriented upon awakening." He turned to the others. "And I do apologize, to the entire company." He sucked in air through his teeth. "But it is worst for Andrea and myself. The box I inadvertently destroyed contained the spell book. Unless we can find duplicates, I am limited to the spells in my head. Just those, and when they are gone, no more." The wizard took a step back and raised his hands. "It would be a shame to waste one—Fire, say—in defending myself."

Barak smiled and took a step forward. "Try it. I bet I get my hands around your throat bef—" The prick of a knifeblade at the back of his neck stopped him.

"Easy, Karl." Walter was calm as always. "No fights. You heard Ahira."

If he moved forward quickly enough, while kicking back hard enough, he could—*no*, Barak thought, *not a good risk.* "Then how about—"

Ahira held up a palm. "I'll deal with Aristobulus." He turned to the wizard. "Put your arms down."

"I—"

"Put them *down!*" The dwarf planted himself in front of the old man, dropped his axe to the ground, and folded his arms over his massive chest. "We had better settle this now. Are you willing to take orders like everyone else, or do you want to strike out on your own?"

Aristobulus sneered. "That's an empty threat. You don't dare abandon me." He waved a hand at Andy-Andy. "And leave her as your only wizard?"

Ahira turned his back on him. "Then get going. Hakim, put the knife away. Barak, you agree that I'm in charge?"

He rubbed at the spot where the knifepoint had been, surprised to find no blood on his finger. "For now." Was the dwarf really going to get rid of Aristobulus? With the loss of the treasure box, that would make things more than difficult. But he was right. They were in enough trouble; there just wasn't room for internal dissension. "As long as you think you can get us home, Ahira."

The dwarf nodded. "I don't just think it, I swear it." He turned back to the wizard and did a double take, as though he were surprised to see Aristobulus still there. "I thought I told you to get going."

"Now wait a minute. You—"

"No. You're either one of us, or you're not. You decided not. So leave."

"But . . . how can I—how do you expect me to—"

"Frankly, I expect you to die. A wizard, without spell books, alone? You don't have a chance. You needed us more than we needed you." Ahira planted a hand against Aristobulus' chest and pushed him sprawling. He turned to Karl. "If he's not gone in two minutes, you get a chance to see whether you can work that sword faster than he can work his mouth." The dwarf closed one eye in a broad wink.

Good for you. I just hope that this works. "Understood." He took a step toward the fallen wizard.

"Wait!" The fear in Aristobulus' voice matched the ashen pallor of his face. "I agree. You're in charge."

Karl didn't look at Ahira as he advanced on the wizard. "You want to give him another chance?"

"Yes." The dwarf walked away. "Help him up."

Karl smiled at Ahira's back. *I'm not sure I like you. But I'm sure as hell not going to cross you.* He looked from Doria to Lightfingers to Walter, then let his eyes rest on Andy-Andy's. They had all gotten the point, too.

But you'd better make it work. You'd damn well better.

Ahira had been off by himself for a while, sitting on a fallen tree and staring at an anthill, when Doria walked over.

"James? Mind if I join you?"

"Sit." He kicked a heel against the rough bark, feeling it crunch satisfactorily. He quelled a muted resentment at her presence; it had been good to be by himself, not have to juggle six, twelve personalities. No, *fourteen*—including both of his own.

She smoothed her robes around her legs and seated herself gracefully on the grass in front of him, peering at him out of unblinking, yellow-irised eyes.

He looked away. A strange reversal this was. Usually, she was the one who avoided his eyes. "What is it?"

"We have a problem."

"Really?" He arched a brow. "Just one? That would be nice. Very nice. Which one are you referring to? Right now, I'm busy chewing my nails over Hakim and Lightfingers. I can think of half a score of things that could go wrong down there, and not much we could do about any of them. How long have they been gone, anyway?"

"A couple of hours. But I meant that we have a new problem." She rubbed at her eyes. "I can't get my spell back."

"What?" A cleric wasn't like a wizard, dependent on rememorizing spells from books. For a cleric, getting a used spell back was just a matter of praying for it. At least, it was supposed to be.

"I tried. Honest, I tried. But it just didn't work."

He didn't bother to keep the anger, the frustration out of his voice. "You tried what?"

"Praying. To the Healing Hand. But nothing *happened.*" She scratched at the back of her hand, leaving long red weals. "I can feel the other spells in my head. All of them—but I can't get the one I used back." A stray blond strand came to rest over one eye; she pushed it away. "Maybe . . ."

"Maybe *what?*" This was frightening; the one thing he had been able to count on was their magic working.

"Maybe if I believed . . ."

He grabbed her shoulders and shook her. "You mean to tell me that with all that's happened to us, *you don't believe in magic?*"

"Stop it. *Stop it.*" He let her shrug his hands away. "It's not that. It's just that the notion of a god of the Healing Hand, a . . ."

"Benign deity?"

". . . doing good, healing people—it just seems so absurd." She fastened slim fingers in her hair. "After all that's happened to us— after all that's happened to *me*—I just can't accept that. Not really."

"You're not just talking about here." This was a side of Doria he had never really seen. But beyond the friendly facade, the polished nails and slightly awkward manner, he had, sometimes, sensed a deep sadness.

"No, not just here." She worked her mouth, but no words came. Doria buried her face in her hands.

"You don't have to talk about it if you don't want to," he said, then cursed himself for putting it that way. Confession was a powerful cleanser of the psyche; he should have asked her to talk about it, made her talk about it. "But tell me, anyway." That sounded lame. Damn.

"I can't."

He reached out, gently pulling her hands from her face. "Don't worry about it." Ahira forced a smile. "I'm sure that everything will work out. And if you want to talk about it later, I'll be here. Wherever here is." He stood and helped her to her feet. "I saw some cans in one of the boxes. How about you read them for me? If one of them's salmon, we'll split it."

Her smile was almost natural. "But did you see a can opener?"

He hefted his axe. "Yup."

CHAPTER FIVE

Lundeyll

The day is for honest men, the night for thieves.

—Euripides

Lightfingers sidestepped a rut on the dusty road. "How do you want to play it?"

Hakim smiled. "The first thing we do," he said, "is find ourselves a tavern, and get ourselves a drink." He cocked his head to one side. "Unless, of course, we can find ourselves a willing tavern girl."

They were half a mile from the city, the walls looming dark and massive ahead of them. Lightfingers found it strange, actually, that there was still spring in Hakim's walk; the hike down the hill and along the road hadn't made an impact on the younger man.

Lightfingers raised his hand. "Hold it a moment; got to catch my breath." He forced a chuckle. "Besides, since when have you been willing to share? 'We'?" Not that anything interested him after that walk, except a place to sit down, and something to drink. Preferably something cool.

Hakim clapped him on the back. "That's the spirit. Jason, m'friend, we may be down here on business, but I didn't hear the dwarf say we couldn't have fun, too. How much do you have on you?"

He shrugged. "I don't know exactly. One platinum piece, five gold, eight silver, six copper—something like that."

"Pretty good for not knowing exactly, Jason."

"Call me Lightfingers." He rubbed at his stump. Jason Parker was a young man with a full complement of limbs. *Was* . . .

"Lightfingers, then. Look, Doc apparently went to one hell of a lot of trouble to get us here and get us supplied. I doubt that he would've outfitted us with money that wasn't good—at least at bullion rates."

"Whatever they are."

"Right."

A creaking from ahead sped them around the bend. A stocky peasant, dragging a creaking handcart, smiled a greeting through gapped teeth. He stopped to run the blunt fingers of one hand through his greasy blond hair while he balanced the cart with his other.

"Greetings, friends," he said in Erendra, his vowels overlong to Lightfingers' ears. "Bound for Lundeyll?"

Lightfinger walked over and brushed an imaginary speck of dirt from the peasant's shoulder. His jerkin was similar to Lightfingers', but cut more broadly. "Yes, we are. —There. That looks better, friend. And how is the trading today?"

The peasant patted his pouch, then waved a hand at the muslin sacks on his cart. "Good." He lowered the cart, letting it balance on the two struts that depended from the handles. "In fact"—he rummaged around in the cart, producing a bulging winesack—"good enough that Wen'l of Lundescarne would share a drink with two strangers. For luck." He uncorked the bag and drank deeply, two trickles of purple running from the corners of his mouth and into his beard. "If you would honor me?"

"Delighted." Hakim elbowed Lightfingers aside, accepted the winesack, and tilted it back. "Good. Very good." He wiped his mouth on the back of an arm, handing the sack to Lightfingers.

Lightfingers drank. Hakim was right; the wine was good. The dark, lukewarm liquid washed the dust from his mouth, replacing it with a tingling, a rippling effervescence that burbled down his throat, setting up warm vibrations in his middle. Lightfingers propped the bottom of the winesack on his stump and considered taking another swallow. No, it wouldn't do to seem too greedy. Better to *be* greedy.

He handed the wine back to Wen'l. "I thank you."

The peasant frowned; an unsummoned memory welled up: A drink for luck was a ritual that had to be accompanied by an introduction.

"Einar . . . One-handed thanks you."

Wen'l smiled, his forehead wrinkling as he turned to Hakim.

"And Hakim Singh thanks you, as well."

Wen'l's puzzled smile didn't change. "I can see that friend Einar is of Osgrad, but you are from . . . ?"

"Secaucus."

Wen'l nodded knowledgeably. "Ahh. And that land is to the . . ." He snapped his fingers, as though the direction were on the tip of his tongue.

"West," Hakim supplied. "Far to the west."

The peasant's eyes widened. "Beyond the Bitter Sea?"

"Far beyond."

"Beyond fabled D'tareth, even?"

Hakim shot Lightfingers a quick glance. D'tareth had been the jumping-off point of the last game. The last one before this one—no, this wasn't a game. "Yes, beyond even D'tareth."

Wen'l nodded wisely. "Oh, yes, I have heard of Seecacuse—it just escaped me for a moment." He shrugged, dismissing the subject. "Do you need a place to stay in Lundeyll?" At Lightfingers' nod, the peasant brightened. "Good. If I may, let me suggest the tavern of Frann of Pandathaway, on the Street of Two Dogs. It is just beyond the public well. Tell Frann that you are friends of Wen'l, and I am sure he will give you a special rate, a good one." Wen'l turned to put the winesack back in his cart.

"Permit me." Lightfingers stepped up and stumbled slightly to distract the peasant while he opened and emptied Wen'l's pouch, then flicked his haul into his sleeve before taking the sack. He tucked the winesack under a blanket in the cart. "To keep it out of the sun, and cool." Lightfingers raised his good hand to his forehead. "And a good day to you, friend Wen'l."

The peasant nodded, picked up the handles of his cart, and started down the road. "And a good evening to you, friends—you should hurry, if you wish to reach Lundeyll before sundown."

"We will." Lightfingers tugged at Hakim's arm. "Let's *hurry,* friend Hakim." In a few moments, Wen'l and his cart were out of sight. Lightfingers emptied his sleeve pocket into his hand. "Look at these."

"Where did you—you stupid son of a—"

"*Look at them.*"

Hakim held the scattering of coins in cupped hands. They were just like the ones they had in their own pouches: roughly circular, covered with a rippling pattern on one side like a stylized representation of waves; the other side decorated with a poorly stamped bust of a bearded man. He couldn't read the writing—*damn, I should have had Doria read it to me before we left.*

"See?" Lightfingers said. "That solves the money problem—this is local coin. But look at the amount. Wen'l said he did well, but there's a full dozen coppers to one silver coin. Which means that we're rich."

Hakim's face darkened. "No, that means that you're disobeying orders. Ahira said no stealing."

He shrugged. "Put them in your pouch." Hakim hesitated. "Unless you want to run after the peasant and tell him you're sorry we robbed him. Look, didn't the dwarf say that we were supposed to gather information?"

"Well, yes."

"And isn't the fact that we have legitimate money important information? Well, isn't it?"

"Yes, but—"

Lightfingers spat on the ground. "Don't be more of a fool than you have to be. He tried to steal from us—'stay at Frann's Inn'—he's probably getting a kickback from the innkeeper, who'd know to charge us extra."

As Hakim tucked the coins in his pouch, Lightfingers kept a smile from his face. The bigger thief—hah!—wasn't thinking. Why would Lightfingers have him hold his haul? No reason—unless Lightfingers intended to add to his take, add enough to it that would make a paltry dozen coppers and one silver coin seem too small to bother with.

If only I'd known how well off we were, I wouldn't have bothered to come along. Just lift all the money in their pouches, and run. Which is what I'll do when we get back—won't let that opportunity escape me again.

"Ja—Einar?" Concern creased the big man's face. "Are you all right?"

"Never mind. Just thinking about something." He waved a hand at the guard squatting at the latticework gate ahead of them. "Let's get him on his feet, and get some directions." He raised his voice and switched to Erendra. "You—how do we get to the Street of Two Dogs?" Lightfingers smiled at Hakim. "After all, we don't *have* to tell him that Wen'l sent us, eh?"

Frann of Pandathaway mopped at his gleaming pate and seated himself across the table from them. "I thank you," he said, tossing back a quart-sized mug of the sour beer that already had Lightfingers' head buzzing. "And would you care to ply me with more beer before you start to extract information from me? Not that it will do any good." He gestured at the scraggly occupants of the low-ceilinged room. "There's little enough wealth here. Not enough to interest a pair of thieves." Frann raised a bushy eyebrow. That appeared to be the only hair on the beefy man's body; his mottled forearms and huge hands were as naked and hairless as his head.

The tavern was dark and dank, the gloom hardly alleviated by a dozen oil lamps sputtering out clouds of smoke where they hung from the overhead beams. The low, roughhewn tables were littered with pools of spilled beer and gobbets of meat.

Lightfingers sipped his beer. Hardly a well-kept place, this was. But even at this early hour, Frann's tavern was crowded, several scores of men gathered around the tables, shouting at the three harried barmaids to bring them more beer.

Hakim smiled broadly. "And what makes you accuse us of being thieves? As we told you, we are men-at-arms." He dropped a hand to the hilt of his scimitar. "If you have any doubts, I'd be happy to demonstrate. Quite happy."

As Lightfingers set his mug down and reached his hand into his jerkin to loosen his dagger in its sheath, Frann chuckled deeply, raising both palms in mock surrender. "As you say." Shaking his head, he pinched a passing barmaid, the bedraggled girl rewarding him with a squeal and a scowl. "More beer, or I'll feed you to the hogs." He turned back to Lightfingers and Hakim. "As long as you don't annoy my customers, it's of no interest to me whether you're soldiers, or thieves . . . or whores in disguise, for that matter."

Hakim returned his smile. "A rather good disguise."

"Indeed." Frann accepted the fresh tankard and took a healthy swig before setting it down and folding his hands on the table in front of him. "And now, my two well-disguised trollops, what is it that you want to know?"

Lightfingers considered it for a moment. This interrogation of the innkeeper was a waste of time, but it couldn't be helped. He had to stay in Hakim's good graces until they got back to the hill. And, for now, that meant getting information out of Frann.

If the innkeeper knew anything. "Let us suppose something," Lightfingers said, idly running a fingertip through a puddle of beer

on the tabletop. "Let us suppose that my friend and I were thieves?"
He stared sternly at Frann. "Untrue as that is, of course."

Frann pursed his mouth. "Why not? And?"

"And let us suppose that we two thieves were newly arrived from
the west—from the far west—looking for something worth stealing,
say."

"Then you would probably pay well for information, I suppose."

Lightfingers produced a silver coin, spun it on the table in front of
him. "Possibly so." As Frann reached for it, he slapped his hand
over the coin. "Possibly we would pay for such information, *after* we
had received it." Lightfingers left the coin on the table as he sipped
his beer. "Remember, we are supposing that my friend and I are
thieves, not fools."

"Well put." The innkeeper rested his many chins on his fists.
"Then I would say this: Take passage from Lundeyll. We are poor
here." Frann shook his head sadly. "It's all I can do to make ends
meet, keep the lord's men from booting me out into the street. Now,
if I were a younger man, I'd go back to Pandathaway." He scowled,
then sighed. "There is much worth having, there. I remember once,
back home, a dwarf paid for a night's lodging with a diamond. It was
the size of my thumbnail." He stared at his dirty, split thumbnail. "I
swear, it was."

Lightfingers didn't ask why Frann had left Pandathaway. In the
second place, the innkeeper probably wouldn't tell him. Possibly he
had been chased out, exiled, or left just a few moments ahead of the
authorities.

But in the first place, Lightfingers really didn't care. "And how
would you suggest we get to Pandathaway?"

Frann shrugged. "The usual way. Book passage at Lundeport."
He smiled. "I know a captain who might give you a good rate for
deck passage."

"Like you gave us here? I don't see the need."

Hakim elbowed him in the side. All this talk of stealing was not
what the big man was interested in. "Perhaps there would be something else, some other—"

"Quiet." Lightfingers shook his head. "I find what our host is
saying to be most interesting."

Frann smiled knowledgeably. "What are you really looking for?"

"Actually," Hakim said, quashing Lightfingers' objection with a
glare, "we've heard of something called the Gate Between Worlds."

"Then you're not thieves. You *are* fools." Frann spread his hands.

"Even if it exists, then it would seem a waste of—" He interrupted himself with a shrug. "But it's none of my concern." He turned to Lightfingers, palm up. "But I would be happy to tell you . . ." He accepted the coin, beckoned to a barmaid, and tucked it into her cleavage. ". . . what everybody else knows, that it's said to be east of Pandathaway, somewhere past Aeryk." The innkeeper set his palms on the table and levered himself to his feet. "And I will add this for free: If you have any talent, you would be wise to stay in Pandathaway. Steal from the dwarves, from the elven. The risk is great, but so are the rewards—if you're good enough." He turned away, muttering, "The size of my thumbnail, it was. . . ."

Lightfingers drained his tankard and shook his head. "A genius, that's what you are. A genius."

"What did I do?"

"You told him the truth, stupid. Look, as long as we didn't seem too eager, I could have kept him talking, probably all night. A silverpiece is worth a lot here—haven't you been listening? Hell, we could buy this place, serving girls and all, for what we've got in our pouches."

Hakim shrugged his bare shoulders. The big man was completely unaffected. By Lightfingers' scorn, by the hike down, by the chill drafts blowing through the tavern, by the quarts of beer he had consumed. "As you pointed out, money isn't a problem for us." His expression grew grave. "And no more stealing, by the way. Understood? There's nothing worth taking here, and we don't need any trouble with the locals. How'd you like to try climbing those walls?"

Lightfingers rubbed his stump against the edge of the table. "Wouldn't be hard; they've got a walkway around the top, and staircases leading up to it—the walls are intended to keep people *out,* not in. It would be tough to get over them from the outside. And I could have done that barehanded, before I lost my—"

"Jason." Hakim's face creased with concern. "What the hell are you thinking of? You sound as if you think . . ."

"That I'm Einar Lightfingers?" He sneered. "Who do I look like? And who do I have one hand like?" He slammed his stump down on the table. "For all I know, this *Jason Parker* was only a dream. Here is real." He waved his stump under Hakim's nose. *"This* is real."

He pushed himself to his feet, wobbling. The beer, that was the trouble. He'd had enough to get angry on, but not enough to relax on. Yes, that was it—time for some more, to smooth things out.

The room canted off to the left; he snatched his tankard from the table and veered right, toward a stoppered keg in the corner.

He was halfway there when the huge oak door swung open and three men stepped into the tavern. Two were soldiers, tall and muscular in chain armor, swords belted to their waists, each leaning a short stabbing spear against the wall.

The third man, though, made Lightfingers' palm itch. Man? Maybe boy was more accurate: he looked to be about sixteen, blond, with sunken dark eyes in a narrow face. His soft purple cape, the many-jeweled ring on the thumb of his ungloved right hand, the bulging pouch at his waist—all of it screamed *Wealth*.

Frann bustled over as the background chatter died, the new stillness almost painful. "Lord Lund! I am honored!"

With a crooked smile, the boy removed his other glove and slapped it lightly across the innkeeper's face, his men-at-arms smiling at his side. *"Not* Lord. Not yet. Just Lordling, until my blessed father dies. . . ." He cocked his head to one side and laid a hand on the larger soldier's arm. "Marik, I believe that this fat beerseller has just insulted my father."

"M-my apologies, Lordling," Frann sputtered, his fingers knotting at his waist. "I meant no insult to your noble father, may he live forever."

"Oh? Then you think me incompetent to rule Lundeyll?"

"No, not at all . . . I . . . I mean, what may I bring you?" The innkeeper clumsily dodged the paradox. Clearly, the lordling would choose to take offense at whatever Frann said. He gestured four men away from a nearby table, and wiped at its top, then his own face. "Beer? Wine?" He held a chair for the boy.

Lund stood silent for a moment, then shrugged. "Let's let it pass, for once." He sat. "And you, innkeeper, will bring us nothing." He jerked a finger at the least bedraggled of the serving girls. "Wine. Your best. Which, I suspect, is none too good. Oh—and clean glasses, if you please?"

The barmaid scurried off toward the back.

Lightfingers kept his face blank as he filled his tankard, then returned to his table. He sipped his beer slowly as the level of noise in the room began to pick up, returning to only a fraction of its previous level. Everybody in the room was patently terrified of the slumming lordling. Which was an advantage, of sorts. It might make it—

"Don't even think about it!" Hakim hissed.

Lightfingers smiled, taking a deep draught of the sour beer. The

taste actually got better after a while. "Easy, my friend. I wouldn't."
*Unless the opportunity presents itself. Then I wouldn't bother going
back to the hill with you. I'd just book myself a passage to Pandathaway, and spend my time picking up diamonds the size of an innkeeper's thumbnail.* "Wouldn't think of it."

"Good." Hakim sat back. "I think it would be a good idea if we
get out of here quietly, make our way back to our room. It's a bit
stuffy there, but I don't like—"

"*You.*" The smaller of the two soldiers stood in front of them,
glaring down at Lightfingers. "Didn't you see me beckon to you?"

"No, I—"

"Very well." The soldier tugged at his forelock in a sarcastic genu-
flection. "Lordling Lund requests the great honor of your company
at his table. He likes to drink with the common people. If you will
come this way?"

Lightfingers called up an expression of terror. *Speaking of opportunity* . . . "M-my pleasure, s-sir." He stood slowly and walked shakily over to where the boy sat, a cruel smile flickering across his thin
lips.

"Be seated." He nodded at a chair. "And you are . . . ?"

"Einar. Einar One-Hand, Lordling." Lightfingers was too obviously the name of a thief.

A clay winebottle and four glasses arrived, the barmaid setting
them in front of the boy, then scurrying away, her smile unchanging,
as though it had been painted on.

"Allow me," the boy said, pulling the cork, then pouring wine in
two of the mottled glasses. "My . . . friends don't like to drink
while they are working." He raised a glass to his lips and took a sip.
Lund frowned. "Too tannic." He lowered his glass and smiled. "I
hope you won't be offended by their abstinence?"

"Oh no, Lordling. I follow the same custom."

Lund picked up his glass again and drank deeply, the overflow of
the purple liquid running down his chin and onto his tunic. That was
good; either the boy was normally a slob, or he was more than a little
drunk. "Please drink, Einar One-Hand. After all, you are paying for
the wine, are you not?" The two soldiers looked at each other, smiling knowingly. Obviously, this was not Lund's first stop on a night of
slumming, drinking with the common folk, forcing them to pay for
his wine.

"Of course. I am honored." Lightfingers drained his own glass,
then let his hand fall into his lap. *It should be easy, actually. The*

purse dangled from the near side of Lund's belt, hanging next to Lightfingers as though it were a ripe fruit, begging to be picked. He reached out his hand—

"Would you be kind enough to pour me another glass?" Lund rapped his wineglass against the table. "It shee—seems that I am a bit uncoordinated this evening."

Lightfingers kept his scowl off his face. "Delighted, Lordling." He poured, then set the bottle down. A bit of distraction seemed called for; he brought his stump up to the table as he let his hand drop to his side.

The boy recoiled. "I . . . I understand your name now. How did you lose it?"

Easy, now . . . Lightfingers dipped two fingers into the mouth of the boy's pouch and pried them apart gently, slowly. *Easy* . . . "An accident. It was crushed in a mill." Inside the pouch was a jumble of coins; he grasped one between his fingers and eased it out.

It was platinum, thick and heavy.

Lightfingers fingerflipped it into his sleeve pouch, then took another, careful to be slow enough, smooth enough to prevent it from clinking against the others.

"Long ago?"

"Many years, Lordling. Many years." He took another, then another, slipping them carefully into his sleeve pocket. *That's enough for now. No sense in being too greedy, Jason.*

Jason? I'm Jason? Then what—

His hand slipped.

Its full weight came to rest on the pouch.

And tugged firmly on the boy's belt.

Lund's eyes shot downward. "My pouch!" He snatched at Lightfingers' wrist, his glass clattering on the table.

Rough hands grasped Lightfingers' shoulders; a sharp blow to the back of his neck sent the world spinning.

"Marik—grab his friend, too," Lund rasped.

He opened his eyes. Hakim was in the doorway, his scimitar in his hand, off-balance as though he had decided to run, then changed his mind. He snatched a knife from his belt, sent it spinning toward the soldier holding Lightfingers.

The knife clanked against chainmail, then clattered harmlessly, uselessly to the floor.

"Don't be a fool, *run.*" He put all his strength into a scream. *"Now!"*

The big man hesitated. The smaller soldier picked up the knife and flung it at him.

With a meaty *thunk*, it sank into Hakim's shoulder. Dripping blood, he staggered through the doorway and into the night.

"Get him, Marik." The soldier, sword in hand, ran after him.

The other wrestled Lightfingers to his feet.

Lordling Lund stood easily in front of him, hefting a spear. "We will deal with your friend. I promise." He twirled it, the foot-long steel head catching and shattering the light of an overhead lamp. "But you won't see that, will you?" He touched the spearpoint to Lightfingers' tunic.

His arms were held behind him; no way to reach his dagger. Not that that would do a lot of good. "Lordling, let me *explain*. Please." *What can I say? But I've got to say* something, *talk my way out. It* can't *end like this.*

The boy hesitated, then nodded. "Of course."

"You misunderstood me. I—" An explosion of pain burned through his belly.

He screamed.

Bloody vomit choked his throat, spewed out of his mouth and down the front of his tunic.

He looked down. Half of the spearhead was sunk into his midsection.

Lund pulled the spear out and considered its bloody head. "A gut wound. I always liked gut wounds."

He was a long time dying. He only stopped screaming toward the end.

CHAPTER SIX

Second Blood

. . . a soldier,
Full of strange oaths, and bearded like the pard,
Jealous in honor, sudden and quick in quarrel,
Seeking the bubble reputation,
Even in the cannon's mouth.

—William Shakespeare

Barak came awake at a touch, flinging away the blankets, reaching for his sword—

"Easy." Ahira's voice was a harsh whisper. "It's only me."

He set the sword back on the grass and tightened his cotton loincloth around his hips. That had been enough to sleep in, on a warm night.

He looked around. Within the circle of wooden boxes, everyone else was asleep, sprawled out under their blankets like a collection of corpses—except for Andy-Andy, who was huddled under hers in a fetal position, shivering in her sleep. Barak shrugged. It was her own fault: Not only had she turned down his suggestion that they share each other's warmth, but she had stubbornly ignored his reminder to make certain she kept at least two-thirds of her covering underneath her. The ground stole a body's warmth more readily than even the chilliest air.

Rubbing his eyes, he glared up at the dwarf, not able to make out his expression in the dim starlight. "My turn to go on watch? Already?"

"No." Ahira beckoned him to his feet. "Look down the hill, down toward the city."

Barak drew air into his lungs and stared off into the distance. Nothing. A few lights twinkling in the city, stars shimmering over the sea, but that was all.

Wonderful. Our leader is jumping at shadows. "So?"

"You don't see anything on the road?"

Below them, the road was a black ribbon on a black background. "Don't be silly. You do?"

"I . . . I thought I saw a shape, like somebody fallen—there it is. Can't you see it? It's glowing like a—"

"Glowing?" He stared. Nothing. *Oh.* "I don't see in the infrared, remember?"

"Sorry—*wait.*" The dwarf pointed. "But you can see that, can't you?"

Barak followed the other's gesture. Farther down the road, lanterns twinkled like fireflies. Three—no, four of them. They were too far off, too dim for Barak to make out the shapes holding them, but . . . "I do see the lanterns. But why are they out—"

"Ohmygod. The shape on the road—it's *Hakim.*" The dwarf spun around. "Everybody, up. *Now.*"

Barak stooped to pick up his scabbarded sword. Best to keep it in its dark sheath, lest the bright steel reflect light, announcing his presence. He cast a longing look at his leather armor, heaped next to his blankets on the grass. "I'd better take it."

"Like hell you will. No time."

"No, I didn't mean the armor. I meant I'll get him, bring him back. Your legs are too short to run fast." *Four of them, eh? He would have to take out two quickly, before they became aware of his presence. And even two-on-one would be a chancy shot.* "Get your crossbow, follow me."

Ahira's face was still unreadable. He hesitated. Then: "Go."

Barak sprinted away. Behind him, Ahira called to the others. "Get up, damn you all."

Barak reached Hakim when the soldiers were still a few hundred yards away, the flicker of their lanterns announcing their coming. "Walter!" He reached out a hand and felt at the thief's neck. Good; there was a pulse. He slipped his hand down, his fingers coming away sticky. There was a knife in the thief's shoulder, dripping blood.

He rubbed his hand on his thigh. Where the hell was Lightfingers? No time to worry about that now. He could try to move Hakim off the road, but that might be too dangerous. There could be other wounds; moving him might kill him.

He smiled. Besides, there was some business to take care of first. Slipping silently into the bushes beside the road, he loosened his sword in its sheath. *Well, Karl, now we find out if you have it.*

Karl? No—*Barak.* Karl Cullinane hadn't raised a hand in anger since the third grade. Karl wouldn't squash a spider; he'd lift it on a piece of paper and fling it out of a window instead.

Karl was a peasant, Barak a warrior. So it had to be Barak, not Karl.

And to a warrior, everything is a challenge, or a reward. But he had to decide what the challenge was. Merely chasing them away wouldn't do; perhaps they could dig up reinforcements. He had to take out four soldiers—*no euphemisms, kill them*—and he had to do it without getting hurt himself. Doria had none too many healing spells left; Walter might need all of them.

"Arno, I think I see him," the closest of the soldiers said in curiously accented Erendra, then broke into a trot. Chainmail and a shortsword, plus his lantern—Barak could save him for later. But the lantern, dangling from a pole—that had to go quickly, before anyone spotted him crouching in the bushes.

Barak felt around the ground. His fingers located a jagged rock, half the size of his fist. He hefted it experimentally, and threw.

The lantern shattered, drenching the soldier in flames. He dropped his sword and screamed, his skin *crackling.*

The screams were like a signal to the other three; they dropped their lantern poles, the nearest two drawing their swords, the other, probably the leader, bringing up his crossbow. Its tip weaved, uncertainly.

The wind brought a stench of burning flesh to Barak's nostrils. He slipped his sword from its scabbard, keeping the blade low, next to the ground.

"Where?"

"I don't see—"

"It's the thief—he's shamming." The leader's crossbow leveled itself at Hakim's crumpled form.

Barak gripped his sword and charged out of the bushes, directly at the leader, a growl forcing itself from his throat.

The crossbow wavered as Barak closed, breaking stride to kick one of the swordsmen sprawling, ducking under the other's wild swing. *Too bad. You want to live too much.* The leader's drill was obvious: Kill one enemy, ignore the other one charging you.

He smacked the flat of his sword against the side of the crossbow, sending it spinning away in the dark, the bolt discharging harmlessly to his left.

The leader's eyes grew wide; he reached for his sword as Barak's backswing caught him at the base of the neck, the swordtip cleaving his throat effortlessly, dark blood fountaining.

The heavyset man clapped both hands to his throat, trying to hold the wound closed, his cry of pain only a gurgle as a dark torrent poured out through his fingers.

Barak spun around, leaving him at his back. No time to finish him off, not yet. When it's one-on-many, you can't worry about killing a disabled enemy when there are still unhurt ones around.

The one he had kicked away was gone, vanished in the dark, his sword lying still on the ground. *Where is he? Never mind—worry about him when you've killed the other.*

The small dark man in front of him smiled, crouching, his sword in his right hand, a long, curved dagger in his left. "Many thanks for the promotion, friend," he said in Erendra, stepping lightly forward, his sword weaving like an eager cobra. "I never liked Arno anyway."

No time for chatter; there was still one man unaccounted for. Barak slashed, the blade of his sword parallel to the ground.

The soldier slid to one side, easily deflecting Barak's sword with the flat of his dagger. Before Barak could bring his sword back into line to parry, the slim rapier had nicked at his biceps. It stung, terribly.

"Not used to two-swords, eh?" He lunged, in full extension.

And gasped down at his right wrist, almost severed by Barak's blade. The sword dropped to the dirt.

Barak smiled down at the crumpling figure. "Then again, maybe I a—"

An arm closed on his throat, dragging him back, off-balance. At the edge of his vision, a gleaming dagger rose, and started to fall.

Time seemed to slow. *You stupid idiot. You know better than to chat while a fight's going on.* He released his grip on the sword, bringing his hands up to block the downward thrust, knowing that he'd never make it in time.

It just wasn't possible; the knife only had to travel a few inches to reach his throat, but his hands would have to seize the wrist, stop the downward movement—

Both hands met at the soldier's flaccid arm, as the other arm loosened at his throat. He grabbed, twisted, brought an elbow back into his enemy's midsection, and spun around.

"No need," Ahira's voice rasped from behind.

Barak looked at the soldier. A crossbow bolt transfixed the man's head from temple to temple, its dark iron head bent, crumpled.

The dead soldier stared up at him, eyes wide in reproach.

Twang! Barak turned to see Ahira standing over Walter, drawing the string of his crossbow back, slipping in another bolt and sending it whistling into the leader. "Never worry about conserving bolts. Better to make sure that they stay dead." The dwarf sent another bolt into the smoldering body of the first soldier, the one whose lamp Barak had shattered, then looked up, a crooked grin on his broad face. "Not bad, Barak. Not too bad at all." He frowned. "Except for that *stupid* bit of bravado. But never mind; just do it better next time. Right now, we've got to get these bodies hidden, have Doria heal Hakim—and you, come to think of it; don't want your arm getting infected—then get ourselves packed up and out of here. There's probably going to be hell to pay—hey, what's wrong?"

Karl Cullinane was on his hands and knees in the dusty road, the stench of burning flesh in his nostrils, vomiting like a fiend.

Squinting in the dawn light, Ahira tugged at the cords lashing his two rucksacks together, then shook his head. It would tend to keep him off balance, having two packs on his back, but that couldn't be helped. Somebody had to carry the extra—either that, or leave behind supplies that might be needed.

"Hakim?"

The thief stopped fiddling with his pack and lifted his head. "What is it?"

Ahira held out a hand. "Toss me one of your knives. If I have to, I want to be able to cut these loose."

"Fine." Hakim flipped a knife point-first into the ground at Ahira's feet, then turned back to his work.

Ahira opened his mouth, then closed it. Ever since Doria had healed Hakim, he had been distant, quiet, not himself. Not at all.

Best to leave him alone, at least for a while. What had happened in Lundeyll must have been bad—climbing down a sheer wall with a knife in his shoulder, running flat-out for five miles with soldiers after him, wanting his blood. . . .

He'll get over it. He's always been strong.

Doria gave her rucksack a final pat, then raised an eyebrow in an unvoiced question. There would be a bit of time until the others were ready to leave; Ahira had assigned loads based on physical strength, and the only one with less to carry than Doria was Aristobulus. Less to carry; less time to pack.

He gave her a nod and the warmest smile he could come up with. "Go ahead." Even if she was almost out of healing spells, maybe she could do some good.

As Doria crouched beside Hakim, Ahira beckoned the others to him.

"You almost ready?" Ahira kept his voice low. No need to distract Doria or Hakim.

Andrea nodded. She was keeping her distance from Barak. That was strange, considering the way she'd behaved the previous morning. Then she had clung to him like a leech. "Just a couple more minutes."

Barak frowned, rubbing fingertips against the bloodstained tear on the arm of his jerkin. The blood had dried, and Doria had healed the wound, so it couldn't be hurting him.

Then again, not all wounds are to the body.

Barak shrugged. "I'll be done shortly. I can take more, if necessary. No need to have the rest put out a lot of effort carrying what I can haul easily." He flexed his shoulders, threatening to split the seams of his jerkin.

Ahira smiled. Barak was getting damn cocky, after the way he'd almost gotten himself killed. Then again, that was better than his Karl-self exercising his guts about a few local soldiers who had been trying to kill Hakim and him when they died. "You too, Ari? Good. Just as soon as Doria's done talking to Hakim, we head down to Lundeport, and see if we can book passage to Pandathaway." He stooped to pick up Hakim's knife and stuck it diagonally under his belt, the cutting edge up, then bent carefully at the waist to make certain it was secure, and that it wouldn't cut him. A quick check on the straps binding his battleaxe to his chest showed that they were tight, too, although it would take only two quick tugs to undo the loops and free the axe.

"Pandathaway?" Andrea's forehead wrinkled. "God, that sounds familiar." She turned to Barak. "Doesn't it, Karl?"

He shook his head. "No. First I've heard of it. Maybe you over-heard something, when Hakim was telling Ahira what happened down there." He glared down at the dwarf. "Not that he's seen fit to share it with the rest of us."

The warrior had all the sensitivity of a stone. "He didn't want to have a bunch of people around," Ahira said, not bothering to keep the scorn out of his voice. "How would you feel if you'd been cut up like he was?"

"Listen—"

"*Karl.*" Andrea took a careful step closer to him. "Didn't you tell me once, quite a while back, about another character of yours? Something of Pan-something . . . ?"

Barak nodded, quizzically, stroking at his beard just the way Karl Cullinane used to stroke at the stubble on his face. "Sure. Lucius of Pandathaway—*Pandathaway.*" His face lit up; he dropped his sword, grabbed her by the arms, whirling her around. "Pandathaway! Of *course.* I know where we are, we—"

"Put me *down!*" As he did, she rubbed at her shoulders, arms crossed defensively across her chest. "You practically pulled my arms off, you clumsy—"

"Quiet." Ahira turned to the big man, who was still grinning like an idiot. "Two things: First, what do you mean, you know where we are? Second: Why the *hell* didn't you mention it before?"

"It was a . . . character Deighton and I rolled up, once. I never got a chance to use him, but he filled me in on the background— where he came from, like that." He rubbed his fists against his tem-ples. "I . . . I don't know why I didn't think of it before. It's like there's too much inside my head, too much to manage."

"I understand." Ahira had been wrong to give him trouble for not remembering. Things in James Michael Finnegan's life seemed like something distant; it took a bit of effort to *be* James Michael, some-times, to think like him.

But that didn't cure his impatience. "Would you please tell us what you know about Pandathaway? It could be—"

"*Damn* important." Barak nodded, still smiling. "And it's all good. Pandathaway's a port city, on the Cirric—"

"The Cirric?"

"It's a huge freshwater sea, sort of like one of the Great Lakes, only big—" He caught himself, pointed an eager finger at the vast expanse of water spreading out over the horizon. "That's the Cirric!"

"Almost certainly. You were talking about Pandathaway?"

"You're going to like it. Nice place. No government—well, not much of one. The city's run by a council of guilds. Lot of them are merchants, so they like to keep the city open and safe, to keep the customers coming. Doc said that you can buy most anything there. There's a saying: Tola ergat et Pandathaway ta." *Everything comes to Pandathaway,* in Erendra. Barak shook his head, puzzled. "But he didn't say it in Erendra, he said it in—"

"It translated." Aristobulus nodded wisely. "As we did. It makes sense, if you think about it."

"Not to me," Barak said, shrugging. "But I was saying—you can get anything there: jewels, silks, spices, slaves, horses—Lucius owns a Pandathaway-bred mare; keeps a quarter horse's pace for a full two miles—anything." He beamed. "And I haven't even given you the best."

Ahira returned his smile. The swordsman's enthusiasm was positively contagious. "Do I have three guesses?"

"No. You wouldn't guess right, anyway. In the city—right smack in the *middle* of the city—is the Great Library of Pandathaway. Doc said, and I quote, 'The Great Library of Pandathaway is to the Great Library of Alexandria as a broadsword is to a paring knife.' "

Andrea chuckled. "You mean that it's big and awkward, no good for paring an apple?"

"Get off my—"

"Shut up." Ahira couldn't help joining in the laughter. "What he's trying to say is that there might be a map there, to show us where the Gate is."

"Might? If it's known, it's there. It seemed kind of strange, then, how he kept going on about it. I thought Doc was patting himself on the back."

Aristobulus had been listening quietly, his lined face somber, his head cocked to one side. "And there might be something else there. Something we need, badly." His gesture included both Andrea and himself. "Spell books. Give me sufficient time, and I'll make two copies of—"

Ahira shook his head. "I hope we have time for that. But we might not. Consider—"

"I will consider *nothing.* Do you have any idea what it is like for a wizard to be without spell books? It's like being a, a . . ."

"Being a cripple?" Ahira kept his voice low, as his hands balled themselves into fists at his side. "I . . . have some idea of what that feels like." He forced himself to open his hands. "Believe that. But tell me: How long does it take to write a spell? Just one spell, a simple one."

Aristobulus shrugged, indifferent. "Given the right materials and enough quiet . . . ten days, perhaps. But I don't see—"

"Precisely. You *don't* see. And if you don't have everything you need on hand? How long would it take?"

"That depends, of course. For the Lightning spell, the ink must contain soot from a lightning-struck tree—preferably oak, of course. And then the pen has to be made. . . ." The wizard spread his hands. "But it doesn't *matter.* I *have* to have spell books. So does she."

Ahira shook his head. Didn't the old fool see that anything— *everything*—had to take a back seat to getting to the Gate? This world was dangerous. It had already cost the life of one of them. They had to get home.

And me? Am I going to exchange security for the ability to be a full person? Here, I'm not a cripple. "Just listen—"

Barak stepped between them. "Let's leave this alone for the time being. We should have enough time to argue about it on our trip, no?" He frowned.

Ahira nodded, accepting the implied criticism. Barak was right, of course: The leader had no business getting involved in an argument, not when there were things to be done. Maybe Barak should take over—no, he hadn't acted very intelligently during the fight. An excess of bravado was bad enough in a team member.

And besides, I took on the obligation. It's mine, not his. "Correct, Barak. My fault. —You haven't packed your armor, have you?"

"Huh? What does that have to do with anything? I haven't, but I don't see what—"

"Take off your clothes—I need your jerkin, but you can keep your leggings. You can put your armor on over your bare hide."

"What?"

Ahira smiled. "I said, take your clothes off." Not a good time to bring it up, but he didn't want Barak musing on the leader's short-comings. Best to keep him off-guard. He sobered. "I don't intend to make a habit of explaining myself, but . . . what do you think the chances are that they're looking for Hakim, down there? A big man, dressed only in pants, no shirt? That can't be too common around here, not from what we've seen and heard of the locals. So we make sure he isn't dressed only in pants, go for more standard clothing. You're the only one bigger than he is, so you get to provide the clothes." Ahira extended a palm. "It'll be a bit scratchy for you—the inside of boiled leather isn't too smooth—but that's the way it goes." He tapped a thumb against his axe. "Come to think of it, give me your leggings, too. You can switch pants with him; they won't look so loose on you."

"Now? Here?"

"Now."

Aristobulus snickered; Andrea giggled.

Glaring at all three of them, Barak began unlacing the front of his jerkin, then shook his head. He chuckled. "You little *bastard.*"

"Right." Ahira returned his smile. "But hurry up; I want another chance to talk to Hakim before we get going. The sooner I get finished with that, the less time you have to wander around in your bare skin."

Ahira seated himself in front of Doria and Hakim, dropping the pile of clothing to the grass. He jerked his head at Doria. "Go put your pack on. We're leaving in a few minutes."

She nodded and walked away, shaking her head when she got behind Hakim. Clearly, she hadn't gotten anywhere with him; he was sitting against one of the now-empty boxes, running stiff fingers over the thin pink scar that was all that remained of his wound, staring blankly off into space.

"I want you to put those clothes on, before we leave. You can give your trousers to Barak. And you'd better stash your scimitar in your pack—I'll give you my crossbow, so you don't feel naked."

"Fine." He made no move to pick up the jerkin and leggings; he just sat there, rubbing the small scar as though he were trying to rub it away.

"And you'll be glad to know that Barak knows quite a lot about Pandathaway. Sounds like a nice place." Ahira crabbed himself sideways, into Hakim's line of sight. "No lords."

"That's nice."

The best thing to do would be to try—gently, gently—to get him to talk it out. But there just wasn't time. The area around Lundeyll was probably not a healthy place for any of them. The graves of the dead soldiers were shallow, and nearby; it was only a matter of time until the bodies were discovered. And that would be one hell of a problem.

Quite possibly a fatal one. They could all end up like Jason Parker. *But why don't I feel anything for Jason? Granted, I never liked him —but I should feel something for him, now that he's dead.*

Ahira shook his head. Introspection could come later; for now, he had to get Hakim up and moving. *One more try the nice way.* "I thought I could count on you. You disappointed me."

The thief's head snapped up. *"What?* How the hell was I supposed to know that he was going to pick Lund's pouch, get himself killed? You told him not to take chances, *I* told him not to . . ."

Good. Anger was better than shocked numbness. "That's not what I meant. We've got to get going. But you're just sitting there, feeling sorry for yourself—I expected better of you."

Hakim spat. "What do you know about it? You ever have to run a few miles with a knife in you, a bunch of people behind you, wanting your goddam blood?"

"No." Ahira shrugged, then started to rise. "I had better go give Doria a talking-to. Looks to me like she did a pretty poor job of healing you, if it still hurts you like this."

"Wait." Hakim held up a palm; Ahira lowered himself back to the grass. "It's not that. The time I played in the . . . game against Cornell—the time I played a half with a torn triceps . . ."

"I remember." He nodded. "That must have hurt almost as much as this did."

"It hurt *more.* But that was different. We won, that time."

"We won this time."

"But *I* didn't." Hakim slammed a fist against the ground. "I was supposed to get back intact—with Jason, with information."

"One out of three isn't bad, considering the situation."

"You don't understand, do you? I've never *failed* at anything before. I'm big, I'm strong, and I'm smart. I've always just assumed that was enough. This time, it wasn't." His eyes bored into Ahira's, as though daring him to deny it. "If you and Karl had been just a few seconds slower, I'd be dead. Like Jason." He shuddered. *"God,* James, you should have heard him screaming. I could have been next. I was lucky."

And you're terrified that you won't be lucky next time. I don't blame you for that.

Once, he had envied Walter Slovotsky. His attitude, his perfect faith and complete confidence that he was firmly at the center of the universe, and that all was well with him and his universe—that didn't seem so enviable. Not now. A self-image cast in stone could shatter. "Of course I never failed at anything." That was easy, as long as you didn't run into a situation you couldn't handle; that was fine, until you had to stagger down a road, armed men chasing you, knowing that if you fall, you die.

But when that self-image shatters, where do you go from there?

He clapped a hand to the thief's shoulder. "I don't know about next time. No promises." He shrugged. "But I'll be there, if you need me." He rose to his feet. "And for right now, I need *you* to get back on top of things. We had better get down to Lundeport and book passage the hell out of here. There could be trouble, if anyone recognizes you. On top of that, Barak is giving speeches when he should be fighting, Aristobulus is objecting to anything and everything, Doria can't get her spells back—and I'm waiting for Andrea to give me a problem; so far, she's the only one who hasn't." He held out a hand. "So I need your help."

Hakim sat motionless, then nodded weakly. "I'll do my best. I . . . I can't promise that that'll be good enough." He accepted the hand, and let the dwarf pull him to his feet.

"Welcome to the real world." Ahira found himself smiling. Almost. "Now, get the hell out of your clothes and into Karl's." He raised his voice. *"Everybody—*we're moving out."

Aristobulus, standing sweatily in his robes, bent to lower his rucksack to the sunheated wood of the pier. There was no need to keep it on his back while Ahira and Hakim negotiated with Avair Ganness, captain of the *Ganness' Pride*—it looked to be a long bargaining session, and Aristobulus' muscles were already complaining from the strain.

He rubbed a fist against the small of his back and closed his eyes, trying to ignore the constant babble from merchants arguing over the price of grain, the squawking of the gulls overhead, the foul stench of rotting fish.

Eyes closed, he could see his own power wrapped about him, a strong crimson aura that warmed him—and pleasantly, despite the heat of the day. He raised his hand in front of his face, working his fingers, enjoying the way the redness outlined his unseen hand, even as it moved.

It was magic, of course. Which meant that it was good. And which meant that it was power—something Lou Riccetti had always wanted, but never known.

Off to his side, another source blazed—but less intensely, much less so. Andrea simply wasn't in his league. Was that just because her character had been of a lower class than his? Or was it that she just hadn't *wanted* this as badly as he had?

He shrugged. It really didn't matter. The only thing that did matter was that he had been reprieved by Deighton. Life had condemned Lou Riccetti to be an inconsequential little man; at best, a second-rate civil engineer in an age when damn close to nothing important was being built. No more great suspension bridges to span mighty rivers, few if any dams; the future of American engineering was in electronics—diddling with little circuit diagrams, not *building* things, not making magic.

And if you couldn't make magic with stone and steel, all that was left was to dream about real magic. All that *had* been left. . . .

He let his remaining spells cycle through his brain, making sure each one was ready and complete. Not that that was necessary; an incomplete spell wouldn't make his mind pulse, wouldn't push at him night and day to release it, as though it were some sort of huge sneeze, backed up in his nostrils. He could live with that, easily, in exchange for the power.

He could even live with the knowledge of his best friend's death. His *only* friend's death. Probably he should be mourning Jason; perhaps Lou Riccetti would be going over all his contacts with Jason, dredging up pleasure and pain from their friendship, regretting that Jason was gone.

But he couldn't do it. Not with his power wrapping him, keeping him warm. The death of one powerless human just didn't seem significant. Now, the loss of the spell books, *that* hurt.

Which makes me a small person, perhaps?

If that was so, then so be it. He—

"Are you falling asleep?" Andrea asked, nudging him. "Standing up?"

He opened his eyes regretfully, the warm glow of his power overwhelmed by the bright sunlight. "No."

"Well, Ahira says to keep an eye out for anybody who looks official—since the soldiers chasing Hakim didn't come back, the locals may be looking for him. And I don't think that would be very healthy for the rest of us."

"Very well." Although Aristobulus didn't see why *he* had to be the lookout—probably there was something interesting going on at the boat. Keeping an eye on the shoreside crowd, he moved closer to where Hakim was haggling with the captain.

Avair Ganness tapped bare toes on the wood, his heavy calluses clicking like dice. "Well then, make up your mind. It hardly matters to me. I can make a profit of five, perhaps six gold by carrying good Lundess wine, instead of you." He spoke Erendra in a pleasant rhythm, his r's rolling melodiously. Huge shoulders shrugged inside his sweat-stained sailcloth tunic, belted at the waist with a length of rope. The tunic stopped abruptly at midthigh; below, his thick legs projected like treestumps.

Hakim smiled, raising an eyebrow. "There would be advantages to carrying us, instead."

Ganness nodded. "That is so." He sighed. "I do have this problem —happens to many a man my age. It would cost me much to have it cured in Pandathaway. Perhaps even more than your passages will cost me, all things considered. But only perhaps."

Problem? He looked healthy enough.

"That wasn't what I meant." Hakim gestured at the crewmen swarming around the sloop, checking lines, stowing cargo, pausing occasionally to leer at Doria and Andrea. "I have been watching the way they check their bows, their arrows. There are few spots on deck that don't have a weapon within reach. You are concerned about pirates, no?"

"Not concerned. Properly cautious. I've sailed the Cirric for . . . forty years, man and boy. Only run into pirates seven, eight times." He grinned, a gap-toothed smile that was not at all friendly. "And I have managed to give a good account of myself, those few times." He tossed his head, his waist-length pigtail curling around his torso like a snake. "So I have no need of wizards or warriors to protect me. But"—he extended his arm toward Doria, frowning as Hakim moved between them—"I do require a cleric's help." His face went blank. "But that can wait until we dock in Pandathaway. I won't need . . . I won't have any use for it until then. I don't bugger my seamen." He smiled at Doria.

Well, that explained what his "problem" was—a case of impotence, eh? And just perhaps Avair Ganness was a bit more eager to have her cure it than he appeared to be—otherwise, he might well have set his price for passage at enough money to overcompensate the loss of cargo space.

Aristobulus nodded to himself. Yes, that made sense—but best to whisper it quietly to Ahira or Hakim, rather than confront Ganness. The trouble with most people was that they weren't rational; the captain might refuse to carry them, just out of stubbornness.

He took a few steps closer, and called to the dwarf.

"What is it?" Ahira snapped. "We're talking, here—and I thought you were told to—" He cut himself off, his eyes going wide, as he looked past Aristobulus' shoulder.

The wizard turned. A troop of ten—no, twelve soldiers were working their way toward the pier, stopping and questioning passersby as they came. He moved toward the end of the pier, trying to carry his rucksack casually.

"We had best conclude this quickly, no?" he said, careful to speak in English rather than Erendra.

Ahira turned to the thief. "Hakim?"

Hakim shrugged in the loose tunic. "I don't think they'll recognize me, not unless—cancel that. The one with the long-bow is Marik—he'll know me, if he sees me. Maybe."

"Then turn *around.*"

Ganness frowned. "What tongue was that?"

Barak took a step toward him, smiling faintly. "I don't think that is any of your concern, is it?" He switched to English. "Better agree to *something,* folks—other than her Heal Disease spell, the only decent one she's got left is for Minor Wounds. And she's only got one of those left. If we get in a fight . . ."

Doria spoke up. "I don't remember anyone asking me if I wanted to cure him, and then . . . prove that I have."

Aristobulus sneaked a glance over his shoulder. The soldiers were still working their way toward the end of the pier, where the *Ganness' Pride* was tied up. But unless the one that knew Hakim recognized him at a distance, they still had a few minutes; the soldiers were a few hundred yards away on the crowded pier.

Barak shrugged. "I don't see what your problem is. After all, you've always been willing to make it with practically any—"

Her hand struck Barak's face with a loud *whack!* It probably wasn't the force of the blow that staggered him, it was the surprise.

Aristobulus sighed. It was starting to look like he'd have to waste a spell or two. *The stupid, overmuscled, underbrained—*

"That is *it,*" Ahira snapped, then switched back to Erendra as he turned to Ganness. "We have been trying to reach an accommodation with you, captain, but clearly you're unwilling to talk business," And in English: "I'm a lot of things, but I'm not a pimp. Hakim, keep your head turned away; everybody, up packs and move quietly down the pier. And I do mean quietly." He fiddled with the straps holding his battleaxe to his chest. "We just might be able to get out of this without—"

Doria raised a palm as she shot a look back at the approaching soldiers. "Wait. I . . . I agree to your terms, Avair Ganness," she said in Erendra to the captain. "Free passage for all, in return for . . . in return for . . ."

"Agreed," Ganness smiled gently, then spoke to the others. "Your cabins are forward, belowdecks. A bit cramped, perhaps, but I do keep a clean ship. And my cook is of the best; I bought him in Pandathaway." Ganness vaulted over the railing, landing lightly on the deck. "And you, Lady, I will see in my cabin, as soon as we clear the harbor"—he ran blunt fingers across his stubbled cheeks—"and I shave myself. I'll be gentle, I swear." He smiled. "You might even enjoy it."

Her knuckles whitened as she clutched the railing. "This is a *business* affair, Ganness. And I'm only agreeing for reasons—"

"—that are nobody else's concern," Ahira interrupted. "Captain, you were about to show us our cabins?"

"That's him!" A rough voice shouted, from down the pier. The twelve soldiers broke into a trot. Aristobulus sucked air into his lungs. "I'll slow them down—yes?"

Ahira nodded, unstrapping his axe. "Everybody else—get on board. Captain, you're about to be in the same trouble we are, if you don't get this ship moving quickly." Idly, he tore through the leather strap that slung his crossbow across his shoulders and tossed the bow and his quiver to Hakim. "Use it."

Ganness stood motionless for a long moment, then shrugged. "It seems I have little choice. All hands! Cast off!"

Aristobulus turned, raising his arms. *Now, let the power flow. . . .* It would have to be the flame spell; nothing else would slow down the charging soldiers.

So I'll give you fire. He let the spell click to the forefront of his mind, his chest tightening, straining as though he had drawn in twice as much air as his lungs could handle. The red glow brightened, a hot envelope enshrouding him, tingling his skin, so intense it blanketed his vision.

And the urgency grew; the spell had been pushing constantly at the back of his mind—but pushing gently. Now it roared, demanding use, painfully growing in his skull until he thought his head would explode from the pressure and heat.

Aristobulus released it, the rush of sound so loud he couldn't begin to hear or understand the words issuing from his own mouth.

The charging soldiers were a scant hundred feet away; halfway between the two men at the head of the group, the pier exploded into fire. The wood glowed with white heat for a moment before it could start to flame.

The wall of fire grew, tongues of flame licking easily two hundred feet into the sky, roaring, crackling.

Aristobulus dropped his hands. It was done.

"You stupid—" Ahira grabbed the collar of his robes; the pier dropped away under his feet as the dwarf threw him over the rail. He landed on his shoulder on the deck of the *Ganness' Pride*, sliding until he banged into a mast.

Pain lanced through him; he staggered to his feet.

And then he understood: He had cast the spell too far away; the lead soldiers had been able to get past the wall of fire before it blocked the way for the rest.

Ahira waited for them, his battleaxe held easily in his hands.

"Cast off, damn you all!" Ganness shouted at his crew, following his own orders as he raced to the front of the boat to slash through the bow line. *"Get those sails up—a hard hand on the tiller, there."*

The first soldier glanced at the boat as seamen pushed it from the pier, then moved toward the dwarf, only his outline visible against the wall of fire.

Aristobulus had known that the dwarf was strong, but he had never realized just *how* strong; Ahira ducked under the swing of the soldier's sword, planted the stock of his axe against the man's chest, and *pushed.*

The soldier tumbled back, head over heels, a full fifty feet into the leading edge of the fire. He jerked to his feet, gibbering and flaming, and twitched himself over the side of the pier, splashing into the water.

Ahira turned to the other soldier.

A crossbow bolt *spanged!* into the pier at Ahira's feet. Aristobulus turned to see Hakim, swearing, pull back the bowstring, then reach for another bolt.

The dwarf moved smoothly toward the remaining soldier, feinted with the blade of his axe, caught the soldier's swordthrust on the haft of his axe, and swung, once.

Once was more than enough. The soldier, chainlink armor and all, dropped to the pier, his torso twitching itself a few feet away from his legs before it stopped. Ahira had sliced the man neatly in half.

Raising his bloody axe over his head, Ahira threw it at Aristobulus. It thunked into the deck beside him, only a yard from his sandaled feet. The dwarf took a running start and jumped across the ten feet separating the boat and the pier.

"Not too bad, though," he smiled. *"Captain,* let's get out of here."

Ganness swore under his breath as he bounded across the deck to the tiller.

PART THREE

Pandathaway

CHAPTER SEVEN

In the Midst of the Sea

The entire land sets out to work,
All beasts browse on their herbs,
Trees, herbs are sprouting,
Birds fly from their nests . . .
Ships fare north, fare south as well,
Roads lie open when you rise;
The fish in the river dart before you,
Your rays are in the midst of the sea.

—*The Great Hymn to the Aten,* Stanza Three

Barak stood by himself at the bow, leaning on the rail. Starlight shimmered on the flat black water ahead; an occasional wash of cool spray tingled his face.

He unhitched a small waterskin from the railing, taking a small swig of the leathery water to wash out his mouth. Which didn't do much good; his tongue still tasted like vomit. At least he was adjusting, thank whatever. The first two days aboard the *Ganness' Pride* had been a continual bout with nausea—of all of them, why the *hell* did he have to be the only seasick one?

It was getting better, a little. His feet had picked up the rhythm of the pitching deck and his gut had unknotted; while he had no urge to let anything but water past his lips, he could keep from throwing up, as long as he kept his eyes on the horizon. Sleep was impossible, except for a few brief snatches—a nap was an almost certain invitation to another battle with the dry heaves.

He rubbed at the back of his neck. It could be worse; he could be dead. At least he was alone for a while, or as close to that as possible; the bow of the boat was long and slender. He could ignore the scurrying of feet on the deck, and just watch starlight.

Footsteps sounded behind him. Sandaled feet, walking overheavily.

"Come to push me overboard, Walter?"

The thief chuckled. "As I understand it, that might have been a favor, yesterday, or the day before—to more people than you. On the other hand, I owe you my life. You think that letting your stupidity pass is a fair trade, Karl?"

There was just a touch of emphasis on the name; he let it pass. "At least you're talking to me. The only other words I've heard from any of you during the two days we've been on this garbage scow were to the effect of 'Don't throw up on me.' " He found himself shivering, so he picked up the blanket from between his feet, gathering it around his shoulders. Another night sleeping on deck—or not sleeping . . . well, that was better than putting up with the stony silence of his so-called friends.

Walter took a position at his side, joining in his staring campaign at the Cirric. He was back in his normal clothing—or lack of it—but the chill air coming across the water didn't seem to affect him. "You're getting off easy, Karl. You did a dumb thing—two, actually, if Ahira wasn't exaggerating about your trying to strike up a conversation during the fight."

"He wasn't. And I did know better. It was just that—"

"It was just that you were acting like Karl Cullinane, when you should have been busy *being* Barak. If that makes any sense to you." Walter shrugged. "Which I hope it does. I think that's what killed . . . Jason."

He raised an eyebrow. "You're sure he's dead?"

"Yeah. I heard his screams as I was running away." Walter shuddered. "Which makes me hope to God he's dead. We'll be lucky if he's the only one of us to die before we reach the Gate."

"If we reach the Gate."

"Right." Walter produced a piece of jerky, tore it in half. "Chew on it slowly, eh?" He stuck the other half in his own mouth.

"Thanks." It wasn't bad, actually. As tough as a piece of old leather, but the flavor was rich and strangely sweet, reminiscent of hickory. Hardly salty at all—he suppressed *that* thought; just the notion of salt made him gag. "But you didn't ask the right question."

"I didn't ask any question—but what do you think the right one is?"

"Try this: *Should* we try to find the Gate?" He felt Walter's gaze, turned to see the smaller man staring quizzically. "Or hasn't that occurred to you?"

A shrug. "It has—particularly an hour or so back—but never mind that. Tell me: How do your teeth feel?"

Barak started at the non sequitur. "Huh?"

"Your teeth, your teeth. You know, the things you chew with? How do they feel?"

"Well, fine, but—oh." He nodded.

"Right. The only dentistry they've got here is clerical spells. And that gets to be expensive; magic isn't that common. I spent a bit of time pumping some of the sailors; there's one—*one*—cleric in Lundeport, and he sounds to be about B-Class, from their description. Pandathaway's going to be different, so I hear, but clerics and wizards will hardly be growing on trees even there." He sighed. "So if you decide to stay, you can say goodbye to medicine and dentistry, among other things. Bet your teeth rot right out of your head within a few years."

" 'Among other things'? Like football, for example?" He chuckled. "You that eager to stomp more quarterbacks?"

"Yes, football, too. As well as reasonably safe homes and streets— you can forget that, if you stay here. And you can give up on any profession other than cutting people up. And you can probably count on not making it to old age." He cocked his head. "You may be a heavy-duty swordsman, m'friend, but you're going to run up against somebody better—or luckier—if you stay in the profession."

Barak sighed. Walter was right, of course; he was just being contrary, still burning because the others were shunning him for talking that way to Doria. Not that she—

Don't get off the track. Remember the smell of that soldier's burning flesh? He wrinkled his nose. "I didn't exactly have much of a profession, back there. Andy-Andy was right; I've always been a dilettante." He stopped talking to chew on the jerky, keeping it slow, ignoring his stomach's protestations. "She isn't speaking to me, either. I think she blames me for getting her into this."

"You could be right." Walter took a final nibble and tossed his stub of jerky forward. "And I don't think Doria's exactly thrilled with you. She doesn't understand."

He snorted. "And you do?"

"I think so. I'm not sure your stupidity is your fault. Though it damn well is your responsibility." Walter shook his head slowly. "When you talk about a woman's sexual habits, Karl, it's not exactly nice to make her sound like a . . . public utility. You wouldn't have done that, say, a week ago, back on the other side. Hope you get over it soon."

"What the hell are you talking about?" He didn't bother to keep the irritation out of his voice. Maybe being ignored was better than being nagged at. Nagged at by a thief who didn't have the slightest notion what it was like to be a warrior. The stupid . . .

"Remind me to gamble with you some time. I wish I could have read Doc's letter as easily as I can read your face." He scuffed a sandal against the deck. "Trouble with you, Karl, is that you spend too much time thinking like a warrior. 'To a warrior, everything is either a challenge, or a reward'—right?"

"That's right."

"Including, say, a woman?"

"Now, wait—"

"You wait. Hear me out. If a woman is supposed to be one or the other, it would stand to reason that one who sleeps around a lot isn't much of a challenge, no? And if anybody can have her—that isn't true for any woman I know, but let it pass—then she isn't much of a reward, either. Eh? I didn't hear you."

"Why don't you just leave me alone?" If he didn't, Barak could break him like a twig. Idly, he glanced down at the other's waist. Walter wasn't even wearing his knives.

Which reminds me—he turned to make sure his sword was still lashed to the forward mast. It hung there reassuringly.

Walter went on as though he hadn't interrupted. "I'm not talking about Doria, now. She's got some problems. Which are none of your business—although you might have known about them if you'd *talked* to her, that time, instead of grabbing your pants and—"

"Shut up." The time Karl made it with Doria wasn't exactly one of his favorite memories. "Sounds like somebody talks too much. As well as—"

"You keep your mouth closed when you don't know what you're talking about. Okay?" Walter glared up at him. "Now, as I was saying, consider this: Maybe, just maybe, there's nothing wrong with

a woman—or a man, for that matter—having sex with somebody she likes, for her own damn reasons, not yours. And not because it's a reward, but just because she wants to."

"So?" He rubbed at his eyes. It was . . . confusing. To his Karl-self, that sounded reasonable, even obvious. But to Barak, it was absurd. Worse—immoral, and—

"So if you try thinking of Doria as a person, instead of a . . . community facility, maybe you won't make such an ass of yourself again." Walter smiled. "Or not over that, anyway."

"Thanks a lot." He put all the sarcasm he could muster into his voice. "But I don't remember asking you to come over and tell me what a jerk I am. Why the hell are you bothering me?"

The thief considered it for a moment. "Two reasons. I'll reserve one, for the time being, but the other . . . is kind of complicated. Part of it is that I owe you. I kept slipping in and out of consciousness, the other night, but I do remember you stopping one of those bastards who was after my blood." Walter toyed with the spot on his shoulder where the knife had been. Even the scar was gone now. "But mainly it's that it seems to me you've got one hell of a lot of potential. You use it right, and you can be one fine human being, Karl Cullinane."

Barak smiled. "And if I don't?"

"Depends on the situation." Walter's smile was icy. "I care about Doria. Maybe I couldn't take you in a fair fight, but you hurt her like that again, you *damn* well better make sure you never turn your back to me. Ever. Understood, my friend?" There was no trace of sarcasm in that last.

Barak shook his head. He didn't understand Walter; he never had. Football hero Walter Slovotsky could have had practically any woman on campus—and frequently did. But why Doria?

"Why Doria?" Walter echoed his thoughts. "I tell you, we've *got* to get up a poker game, once we get back." He chuckled, then sobered. "Because I know more about her than you do—remind me to tell you about it, the next time I'm into breaking confidences."

"How about right now?"

"Well . . ." Walter shrugged. "As long as you understand you have to keep your big mouth—"

"There you are. Walter, I—oh." Andy-Andy's voice cut off as if someone had thrown a switch. Possibly her eyes hadn't adjusted from the lighted cabins below, spotting Hakim's light skin and white trousers before she had been able to see Barak, wrapped in a dark blanket, concealed in shadow.

Walter waved her away. "I'll be back down in a minute."

"Then you told him—you *didn't.*"

"He didn't tell me what?" Barak turned.

She was barefoot, wearing only a loosely belted silken robe, probably borrowed from Ganness. Her long hair was mussed, as though she had been sleeping. Or *not* sleeping. "What were you going to tell me, Walter?"

The thief answered calmly, "I've got nothing to tell you, Karl." He backed off a step. "Just take it easy."

"I said, *what is it you were going to tell me?*"

She glared at him. "You don't own me, Karl. I can—"

"*Shut your mouth.*" Walter jerked a thumb at Barak. "You don't have to rub his nose in it. Now get back belowdecks, *please.*"

Barak moved away from the railing, his weight transferred to the balls of his feet. Plenty of room . . . "Yes, please do," he said, never taking his eyes from the thief. *Watch his navel—the center of gravity is always there. He can't fake you out if you don't let him.* "So, you were going to reserve telling me you'd slept with her, eh? This whole thing wasn't about Doria, was it? You were just taking out a bit of insurance."

"I thought you might take it wrong." Walter balanced himself lightly on his feet, his eyes flicking from side to side. He moved away slowly, the soles of his sandals *whisking* on the deck.

"Bad choice. Much better to keep bare feet on deck. This way, you're liable to slip, fall overboard." He circled around, the traces of nausea vanishing. The only weapons nearby were the stacked crossbows, the boltbins, and Barak's sword, all lashed to the forward mast. And they were at Barak's back—if Walter didn't want to take him on barehanded, he'd have to go through him in order to lay his hands on a weapon.

"I doubt it, Karl." Walter held out both palms. "Just take it easy, and we'll talk about—"

"Don't stall. She's gone. And if I hear anybody behind me, I'll break your neck before I send you on your way. You don't have much of a chance at best. Want to try for none?"

"No. I don't want to fight at all." Walter shifted to a fighting stance, his body angled slightly away from Barak, his hands held chest-high. "Because I'm under a handicap. I don't want to hurt you—"

"That's too bad." Barak smiled, mirroring Walter's position, keeping his hands open, relaxed, ready to form fists, or parry a kick with an openhanded block. "Take your best shot." *He's liable to try a feint toward the head, then actually go for the body. Or vice versa. But it's going to be something tricky.*

Walter smiled. "Fine. Then, think about this. If you—"

"I meant to try to hit me, little man. Not talk."

"Doesn't the condemned man get a last speech? If you kill me now, it's because you think I've violated your property rights. And that would mean that Andrea's your property, Karl. You go around owning people, do you?"

Barak moved in, kicked out sideways. Walter blocked it with a forearm, but the force of the kick sent him crashing up against the rail.

He sprang off the rail at Barak. The thief extended a hand, reaching for Barak's throat—

Barak clubbed it aside with a heavy fist, then brought both fists down on Walter's rising knee. A backhanded slap sent the thief skittering toward the bow, half stunned.

It would be easy, now. All he'd have to do is flip Walter up and over. He took a step forward—

You go around owning people, do you?

Why not? said Barak.   *Of course not,* said Karl.
What's wrong with that?   *You don't own people.*
     It's wrong.

—grabbed the thief's upper arms, lifted him—

He slept with my woman. I   *If she's ever going to be my*
have *to kill him. Honor*   *woman, it's going to be in the*
demands it.   *same sense as* my friend, *not*
     my dog.

—and set him on his feet. Karl Cullinane glared down at him. "You manipulating *bastard.*"

"Karl?" Walter shook his head to clear it. "I'm sorry—"

"Don't press your luck. I'm not going to kill you, but don't expect me to—"

Footsteps thundered on the deck behind him. He turned; Andy-Andy, Aristobulus, Doria, and Ahira stopped a few feet away, sleepy-eyed seamen crowding the deck behind them.

Ahira hefted his axe. *"What the hell is going on here?"*

Walter rubbed at the side of his neck. "Can't a couple of people have a quiet discussion without drawing a crowd?"

Karl sighed, letting his adrenaline high fade into a deep weariness. Ignoring raised eyebrows and half-voiced questions, he shouldered his way through the crowd, toward the forward hatch. "Wake me when we get to Pandathaway. I've got some sleep to catch up on."

Walter nodded, unfastening Karl's sword from the mast. He tossed it to him. "Don't lose it."

"Thanks." He started down the ladder.

Andy-Andy grabbed at his arm. "Karl, wait. I . . . I want to talk to you, explain—"

He pried her fingers from his sleeve. "There's nothing I want to hear from you." *I am Karl Cullinane. Karl, not Barak. I'll learn from my Barak-self, but I won't be* him.

Ever.

But damned *if I'm going to be the same Karl Cullinane you've been leading on as long as I've known you.* "I don't want you to talk to me, except when it's in the line of duty. Is that clear?" He didn't wait for an answer before turning to Doria. "I owe you an apology, Dore. And I pay my debts—do you want it long and flowery, or is the intention good enough?"

Doria nodded gently, her face studiously blank, but her eyes smiling. "Long and flowery, I think. Since I have a choice."

A tightness in his chest grew, as though steel bands were being clamped on his heart. He forced a chuckle. "Later, then. You deserve to have it when I'm completely awake." He pursed his lips. "But for now—you've always played fair with me. I had no business passing judgment on you. I promise it won't ever happen again." He exhaled deeply. "And now, goodnight."

Doria cocked her head to one side, her expression becoming infinitely tender. "Are you sure you want to sleep alone? Just sleep."

If I accept the invitation, it'd hurt Andy just as much as she hurt— "I think I'd better be by myself." *No, it wouldn't.*

Besides, playing people off against each other isn't the sort of thing that Karl Cullinane is going to do.

He gripped the pommel of his sword tightly, so tightly that his white knuckles stood out in broad relief.

But I would *have. Last week, last month—even yesterday. What is happening to me?*

He shrugged, and walked slowly to the nearest cabin, ignoring the rush of sound on deck.

I guess I must be growing up.

It must be that. He sat on a bunk and buried his face in his hands. *Nothing else could hurt this much.*

CHAPTER EIGHT

"Welcome to Pandathaway . . ."

That is no country for old men. The young
In one another's arms, birds in the trees
—Those dying generations—at their song,
The salmon-falls, the mackerel-crowded seas,
Fish, flesh, or fowl, commend all summer long
Whatever is begotten, born, and dies.
Caught in that sensual music all neglect
Monuments of unaging intellect.

—William Butler Yeats

Ahira frowned up at Doria as she clung to the rigging a couple of yards above his head, the wind whipping her hair, rippling her robes.

"You should see this, Ahira. Pandathaway is . . . beautiful."

He shrugged. "I'll wait until we see it close up. Probably has warts, just like everything else." Besides, while his night vision was much better than any human's, a dwarf's eyes were not built for looking across a sun-spattered sea.

She stiffened. "There's a ship—it's coming toward us, fast—"

"Shi-ip," the lookout at the top of the forward mast called out. "Just a hair off starboard, captain."

Avair Ganness chuckled. "Nothing to fear, Lady. It's just the guideboat." He raised his voice. "Drop all sails. Helmsman, bring us about. Secure all weapons—we've made it again." He glared at the dwarf. "Although I'd want more than a few bows and swords before I'd sail into Lundeport again." He considered it for a moment. "Perhaps you'd care to reimburse me for that?"

Ahira let his hands rest on his battleaxe's hilt.

Ganness shrugged. "Then again, perhaps not. Do you always leave such friends behind you as you did in Lund's territory?"

Ahira scowled at him. "Shouldn't you be doing something nautical?"

Ganness laughed, reaching out a hand, then thought better of it, letting his arm drop by his side. "It would waste my time and effort. That's what the guideboat is for, to bring us in."

"You can't do it?" Doria asked, lowering herself carefully to the slowly rolling deck.

"I wouldn't want to try. Can you see—no, you'd have to know what to look for." With an easy familiarity, he put an arm around her shoulder, a blunt finger pointing shoreward. "See that . . . darkening in the water . . . right . . ." his finger wavered, then stiffened—*"there."*

"Yes?"

"It's a sparling, metal-tipped, it is—lead, I think—sunk solidly into the bottom, canted outward. There's thousands of them in the harbor; they'd gut the *Pride* and sink us, were I foolish enough to try to dock without a guideboat." He leaned against the forward mast, idly twirling the end of his pigtail around his fingers. "Can you imagine what a prize Pandathaway would be for pirates? Not that it'd be easy to take, but the Guilds' Council doesn't like to take chances. Particularly the wizards—they want Pandathaway to be absolutely safe for them. Anyone trying to sail into the harbor without a guideboat is asking to die." A crooked grin flickered across his dark face. "Besides, it's another way for the Council to make a few extra gold. Not that they need it."

Ahira looked up. "What are you talking about?"

Ganness chuckled. "Oh—this is your first time in Pandathaway. You'll see." He walked over to the railing as the guideboat braked smoothly, then swung around so that its high, broad stern was a scant few yards from the port side of the *Ganness' Pride.*

Hakim coughed discreetly behind him. Ahira turned.

"How the hell is that thing moving?" The thief's brow wrinkled as he looked at the smaller, stubby craft. "I don't see any oarports—and if there's a mast and sail, they're both invisible."

As crewmen slid a gangplank from the guideboat to the *Pride,*

Ahira moved to the rail. Under the water, dark shapes crowded around the guideboat's tubby hull. He blinked twice, then squinted, trying to make out their forms; could they be—

"Silkies," Hakim breathed. "They've got silkies chained to the hull."

Joining them at the rail, Andrea frowned. "Silkies?"

Ahira nodded. "Silkies—sort of were-seals. Except in seal form, they're big—about the size of sea lions. In our world, they're mythical; probably the myth came about the same way dugongs were thought of as mermaids." Or maybe not. And maybe mermaids weren't as mythical as he'd always thought. Slippage between the universe wasn't limited to humans; and it could happen in both directions.

Both ends of the plank were made fast, as the guideboat's crew gathered on deck: fifty or so humans in heavy, center-ridged breastplates, their bows strung and arrows nocked, although the bowstrings weren't drawn, and the arrows weren't quite pointed at the *Ganness' Pride.* From the stern of the guideboat, a tall, slender man in a silvery tunic stepped lightly across the gangplank, not bothering to touch its low rails as he made his way quickly to the rail of the *Pride,* then dropped lightly to the deck. He was followed by two hulking swordsmen, who made their way across more carefully, walking in a half-stoop, hands clinging to the gangplank's railing.

Ganness walked up to the slim man and bowed deeply.

Andrea shook her head. "I wouldn't want to just bounce across, not while wearing that much metal. If he'd missed, he would have sunk like a stone."

Barak—no, he said to call him Karl—*Karl* snorted. "He's an elf. See the ears? There's as much chance of his missing a jump as there is of you—"

Ahira cut him off. "Enough." He turned to Hakim. "How do they manage to keep the silkies chained? Seems to me all they'd have to do is revert to human, and slip out of the collar, no?"

Hakim nodded knowledgeably, as though to say, *Anything to keep those two from going at each other, eh?* "I can think of a couple of ways. For one thing, say the transformation takes a few minutes— any of those archers could put enough bolts into it, when it's in human form, to be a fine example to the others."

"A couple of ways, you said?"

He nodded. "Yeah. Maybe some of the silkies have wives, husbands, or children. Don't think I'm going to like these people a whole lot."

Particularly if they find out what your specialty really is.

Karl's fingers whitened on the hilt of his sword, as a slick black shape broke the surface and gasped a lungful of air. Then it dove sharply, its chain whipping behind it.

Ahira tried to seem casual as he put a hand on Karl's arm. "What's bothering you?"

"This." He pointed his chin at the guideboat. "I've half a mind—"

"Exactly." *At best.* "We don't buck local customs." Ahira forced a chuckle. "What were you thinking of, diving overboard, sword in hand? This your week to play Abe Lincoln?"

Karl cracked a weak smile. "More like a human pincushion."

"Right." He jerked a thumb at Ganness and the elf, who were quietly examining a series of parchment sheets, almost certainly cargo manifests. "I read this as a customs inspection. You?"

A nod. "And it looks like he's done."

The elf favored Ganness with a brief smile, clapped him condescendingly on the shoulder, and walked aft toward where Ahira and the others stood near their rucksacks.

"Greetings," he said airily in Erendra, then tossed his head, the tips of his ears momentarily peeking out of his neck-length blond hair. He was strangely thin, as though he were a normal man— except for the ears—who had been stretched, or distorted in a funhouse mirror. "I am Airvhan ip Melhrood, the delegate of the Guilds' Council of glorious Pandathaway." His words came quickly, as though this were a set speech, down to the adjective. "I will need your names and occupations, so that I may assess your entry tariffs. You may, of course, decline to state your business here, in which case the maximum tariff will be levied." He sneered at Karl. "You needn't bother; you're a warrior, no?"

Karl took a step forward. "You have something against warriors?"

The elf's two guards moved quickly; they took up positions behind Airvhan, hands on their swordhilts. Over on the guideboat, fifty bows swung into line.

"Stand easy, Karl," Ahira snapped.

Karl stepped back. The elf chuckled, shaking his head, then leaned against the railing, supporting himself on spread-fingered hands. He nodded lightly; the guards and bowmen relaxed. "Personally, or professionally?" Airvhan responded to Karl's question as though there had been no interruption. "Not that it matters; it is the policy of the

Council to allow free entry to warriors, provided they agree to participate in the Games." He shrugged. "Not that we need to enforce that; you professional killers seem eager enough to win large purses at little risk." Raising a slim eyebrow, he smiled. "I take it you claim to be a swordsman. A true *master* of the blade, no doubt."

Ahira never saw Karl move. One moment, the big man was just standing there, his scabbarded sword in his hand.

And the next, the tip of his blade had *snicked* out a chip of wood from the railing, from between the middle and ring fingers of the elf's left hand.

As the guards went for their own weapons, Karl slapped their hands with the flat of his sword, then returned it to its scabbard, all in one smooth motion. He leaned it against the mast, then folded his arms across his chest.

"So I claim." He stroked at his beard. "Hakim, here, is even better. He taught me everything I know. He would have gotten both fingers, instead of missing, as I did. Try him?"

Airvhan glared at his two guards, as they stood sheepishly, swords half drawn. He held up a shaky hand. "No need. No need at all, friend . . . ?"

"Karl. And yes, I know of the Games. Hakim, Ahira, and I will be happy to attend."

The elf nodded, fidgeting. Ahira suppressed a chuckle, as Airvhan moved away from the rail; it seemed that the elf was eager to finish.

But it didn't take much to suppress laughter; Ahira followed the elf's gaze sideways, to the deck of the guideboat. Had Karl been just a touch slower, they might all well have found themselves filled with arrows.

Airvhan spoke quickly. "And I take it that the others of you are two wizards and a cleric? That-will-be-a-total-of-three-gold-pieces-and-seven-silver-if-you-please." Clearly, the elf had no desire to spend any more time than necessary standing next to a human crazy enough to risk becoming a pincushion in order to make a point.

But Karl's action hadn't been wise. Not at all. A bit of discipline was in order. "Pay the nice elf, Karl."

"You sure, Ahira?"

"Certain." The dwarf kept his face serious. "I'm sure that *friend* Airvhan is eager to get back to his boat." And antagonizing a customs official further didn't make any sense. "And I, for one, have no desire to spend any more time in the hot sun. I take it we will find good taverns near the docks?"

Airvhan nodded quickly. "Quite good. *All* the inns in Pandathaway are superb, friend Ahira. Much wine. Good wine." Cautiously, he held out a palm, keeping it near his body.

Karl lumbered over to him, smiled at the guards . . . and paid.

Karl and the rest followed Ahira into a sidestreet off the docks. The street opened into a cobblestone courtyard, surrounded by two-story buildings, white marble houses curved to accommodate the courtyard, and the fountain in its center.

The stones were hard under Karl's sandals, and his legs had grown used to the rolling of the *Pride;* he was glad when Ahira called a halt.

Karl dropped his rucksack and leaned his sword against the fountain's rim, taking a moment to smile at the two dolphin sculptures spouting water into the breeze. He smiled as he wiped the spray from his face; the dolphins seemed to smile back as they stood, frozen in midleap. "I like that."

The dwarf scowled. "Business first. Then, if there's time, you can rubberneck all you want."

Doria spoke up. "That's unfair, Ahira. We've got time." She smiled at Karl. "Plenty of time."

Walter took a knife from the sheaths at his hip and flipped it end over end, catching it absently as its hilt thunked into his palm. "Matter of fact, I think *friend* Karl is owed a thank-you." His mouth quirked into a smile; he took two more, juggling all three knives in a steady, effortless flickering of steel. "Without that diversion, I wouldn't have been able to pass as a warrior. A juggler, maybe," he said, picking the knives one by one out of the air and replacing them in their sheaths, "but not a swordsman." He patted at his scimitar. "I can't use this damn thing worth shit." He stood. "But you're right. Let's find ourselves a place to stay, then go exploring."

"Exploring?" Aristobulus hissed. "What we have to do is find the Great Library, and—"

"How about getting something to eat?"

Karl quashed his own resentment at the way the dwarf had snapped at him. "Everybody, *shut up.* Ahira's in charge, and he's talking."

Ahira rewarded him with a puzzled nod. "Fine. But first of all, what is this about games? I don't remember you telling me anything about it. Them."

"Whatever." But the dwarf was right. He hadn't said anything about the Games. Karl scratched at his ribs. But why think about all that now?—what he really needed was a bath and some sleep, on safe, dry, unmoving land.

No, don't let yourself get lazy now. He hadn't remembered, not until the elf had mentioned the Games. It was the same problem he'd been having, ever since they landed on this side. Memories of things he'd known back home were irregular, elusive. When he could remember something, it was reliable; but it was much easier to think like Barak, be the swordsman—

No. "Sorry . . . I didn't remember."

"Wonderful." Andy-Andy glared at him. "And what else don't you remember?"

He forced himself to ignore her and spoke to Ahira. "If it's as Deighton said, then the Council likes to encourage the best warriors to stay around, to stay in Pandathaway. Some are hired for the local . . . police force; helps to keep the city a nice place to be. As for the rest, well, having the best around keeps up Pandathaway's reputation as *the* place to buy or hire anything, anybody.

"For wizards or clerics, there's no problem: There's always good-paying work. Besides, there's a bunch of churches and magical guilds, who pretty much run the city—so guild members get a stipend from the Council when they're out of work. It's easy to do that —*hey!* I forgot all about the prices." Information, images crowded his mind. Deighton had shown him a listing. A night's stay in a relatively low-cost tavern would run more than two pieces of gold. A good bottle of wine would cost ten, twelve silvers. And it was a full—"It'll cost us at least a gold piece—each—just to get into the Library. And that won't include . . ." He curled his fists in frustration. What wouldn't it include? It was just on the edge of his mind.

But he couldn't think of it. That was—

"Easy, Karl." Andy-Andy held his arm, then visibly remembered she wasn't speaking to him. She turned away.

"Relax." Walter smiled at him. "You were telling us how they manage to keep mercenaries around."

"Right. Since there isn't much work here, they put on Games. If you're good enough, you can support yourself in the once-a-tenday ones, if only just barely. But in the Seasonals, you can make a killing." He smiled. "So to speak. You can't get much more than bruised; the contact events use blunt, wooden weapons."

"Wonderful." Ahira spat on the cobblestones. "Do you think we have to waste our time on these Games, or can we just hit the Library, buy what we need, and get out?"

"I don't know." Karl shrugged. "What's our total worth?"

Ahira turned to Aristobulus. "Give me your best guess."

The wizard's eyes went vague. "Assuming standard rates of exchange . . . maybe two thousand gold." He shook his head slowly. "And from what Hakim—"

"Walter."

"—said about Lundeyll, that would have been almost enough to have bought the whole town, back there."

"So what?" Ahira turned to Walter. "We're here now. How far away do you guess the Gate is?"

"Mmmm, it's got to be some distance; Frann only knew that it was east of Pandathaway, and he's from here. I don't know; maybe we have enough, if we don't spend too much money on room and board while we're here."

Karl snorted. "Two thousand? That isn't a lot; Lucius paid five hundred just for one horse. We need six."

"Five and a pony," Ahira snapped. "Fine. Here's what we have to do." He extended a blunt finger. "One, find a place to stay, at least for the night. Two"—another finger—"get to the Great Library, find out where the Gate is, figure out how we'll need to equip ourselves in order to get there."

"Which wouldn't be a problem," Karl said thoughtfully, looking at Aristobulus, "if somebody hadn't blown up the box with all the goodies."

"Shut up. Three, we need to know what the situation is here, find out how to raise the money we'll need. Which also means we'll need to know when the next Games are—is."

"Whatever." Karl nodded. "We might be able to do well enough in the tendays, if we're good enough." He fondled the hilt of his sword. *I bet I am.*

"Don't." Walter didn't look at him.

"Don't *what?*"

"Don't be sure you're good enough."

"Damn you, just because I got a bit sloppy, that first time—"

"It isn't that. Think it out." The thief's expression proclaimed that Karl wasn't going to like it. "We're all G-Class or so, right?"

"Right, but if that corresponds to the way things work—"

"As it seems to, then you think we're pretty much up there, right?"

Karl thought as hard as he could, *If you don't stop reading my mind, I'm going to break some bones,* making sure that his face showed what he was thinking.

"Well," Walter went on, "we aren't pretty much up there if they've got the best warriors in this world in Pandathaway, are we? We might be big fishes in—"

Karl smiled and held up a hand. It had been a long time since he'd been able to outthink Walter. *"You* think it out. Look, what would a really high-level fighter do? Go around looking for work? Hell, no. They gather followers, claim some land—either dragging in peasants to farm it, or using locals. There's not going to be a whole lot of folks as good as we are—as good as *I* am—who are still wandering around, trying to build a name. Maybe we'll have to deal with a local champion or two, but not more than that. Right?"

"Not bad, Karl. Not bad at all."

Ahira rapped his axehilt on the fountain's rim. "Enough. I came up with three things we have to do; anybody else have a fourth?"

"No."

"Uh-uh."

"I don't."

"I want to see about finding myself a tavern girl. It's been . . ." Walter trailed off at Karl's glare. "Sorry."

"As I was saying," Ahira went on, "there are three things to do. Since this is a safe city, we'll split up into three groups. I'll take the Library, but I want one of you literate types with me. Andrea?"

"Wait," Aristobulus snapped. "I need to—"

"Fine. You, instead, since she hasn't used a spell, yet."

Andrea smiled. "I've only got three; I haven't wanted to waste them. But if you need somebody put to sleep, or charmed, or want me to disappear . . ."

Right now, Karl thought, *there isn't much I'd like better.* "That last could be useful, if we need a bit of extra money, no?"

"True." Ahira raised an eyebrow. "Your charm spell—think you can get us a decent rate for lodging with it?"

"Maybe. You want me to see to the rooms?"

"Fine. You take the thief with you."

I won't be jealous. I won't. I'm just going to—

Walter shook his head. "I'd rather go look around; I'll keep an eye on Karl and Doria—Andrea should be able to handle the innkeeper by herself, no?"

"Okay. Why don't you get going, meet the rest of us back here, say, at sundown?"

She nodded and left, her sandals slapping against the cobblestones.

Ahira turned to Karl. "You three are to stay out of trouble, understood? I just want you to find out when the Games are, get an idea of the prices of things like horses and supplies, then meet us back here. No fights, *and make damn sure that there's no stealing.* We won't have another Jason. Yes?"

Good. While Walter was his best friend, Ahira was too smart to leave the responsibility of seeing that he didn't steal with him. "I'll watch him."

"And he'll watch you to make sure you don't pull another stunt like the one you did with the elf." He picked up his two rucksacks and beckoned to Aristobulus. "See the rest of you at sundown—in case somebody misses it, everybody else stays put." The dwarf beckoned to Aristobulus, and both of them walked away.

Walter waited until they had vanished into an alleyway beyond the fountain before turning to Karl. "Beer?" He smiled. "Just one or two."

Of all the irresponsible—

No. No more kneejerk reactions. "I guess one beer wouldn't hurt any." Karl shrugged. "And I could use a drink, at that. Doria?"

She looked up at him sadly. "You never asked me out for a drink before, Karl." Her hand stole toward Walter's. "I couldn't turn you down, even if I wanted to." She gripped Walter's much larger hand, with shaking, white-knuckled fingers.

Great. Maybe I'd better have that talk with Walter, and soon. This is getting too damn complicated.

The three armored guardsmen at the top of the broad stone steps nodded in unison at Aristobulus, then glared suspiciously down at Ahira.

The dwarf forced himself to keep his hands at his sides, although his palms itched to feel the smoothness of his axe's handle. Probably this was just the guards' professional demeanor, but perhaps there was more to it: Dwarves were not renowned as scholars, and Ahira's presence might have excited their professional suspicions. If he didn't keep cool, that could lead to a fight.

And three-on-one would not be something Ahira would look forward to, not even after going berserk. Besides, it wouldn't be just *three*-on-one; these guards were wearing the same center-ridged breastplates that Airvhan's guards had worn; patently, they were part of the Pandathaway police force, or whatever passed for such.

They had seen similarly equipped men on their way toward the Library—there would be, easily, half a dozen within shouting distance.

The largest of the three, a pale-skinned man with a heavy brow and a small sharp nose, gestured with his spear. "What are you doing here?"

Aristobulus raised an eyebrow; the guard lowered his spear, and touched his free hand to his forehead. "Your pardon—I was addressing the dwarf, sir."

At the wizard's sideways glance, Ahira nodded slightly. Best to keep the guards thinking that Aristobulus was in charge, since they were treating him respectfully.

"The dwarf," Aristobulus said, "would like to use the Library, as would I. Is his coin not good?" The wizard smiled thinly.

A chuckle. "It had better be. Sir. The last one trying to get counterfeit coin past the Librarians found himself full of arrows." He turned to the guard at his left. "Challa, take the dwarf's packs and weapons—everything except his pouch." Through yellow teeth, he grinned at Ahira. "That, you are going to need." The guard bowed slightly at Aristobulus. "If you and your . . . companion will come this way?"

"What do you want with my pack and—"

"We can't have you taking anything out of the Library, now can we?"

Ahira lowered his two rucksacks to the broad stone steps, then handed his crossbow, flail, and battleaxe to Challa, holding back a grin as the man staggered under the load. "You will make certain that nothing of mine . . . walks away?"

"You must be new to Pandathaway," Challa panted through gritted teeth, as he led the two of them through the entrance, past the open oak doors. The doors were massive, towering easily ten times Ahira's height, inlaid with gold and silver tracings. "We're under oath to the Library. An accusation, even, would put us out on the streets—at least until it was decided on." He set Ahira's gear down on top of a pile of other goods: swords and bows, sealed boxes and mesh bags. "But don't get any notions, *dwarf.* A suspension would give us *plenty* of time to find whoever accused us, and take our pay out of his small hide. Do you get my meaning?"

The entrance foyer of the Great Library of Pandathaway was a large, bare room, illuminated only by spears of golden light from tiny, fist-sized windows high above, only a few feet below the juncture of the stone walls and the ceiling. Below the windows, a wooden walkway ran the length of the front wall. No—*not* windows; those were arrowports. Whoever had designed the Library had provided for its defense.

Their sandals scuffed against the floor as Challa led them toward the rear of the room, with its two exits.

One was a small archway, leading into a lamplit corridor. Ahira started toward it, stopped by Aristobulus' tug on his sleeve.

"That is my entrance," the wizard whispered. "Glyphs over the doorway—they say, roughly: 'If you can read this, pass in safety.' I'll see to my needs, then locate you."

Without waiting for an answer, Aristobulus stepped briskly toward the archway and walked through. As he did, a bare glimmer of red outlined his body, then faded as the wizard walked quickly out of sight, not looking back.

I'll have to discuss this sort of thing with him later, Ahira thought, idly toying with images of bashing Aristobulus' head against a wall. Until they reached the other side, they were all in danger. Walking away without consulting him was not going to be repeated. By anyone.

Challa brushed Ahira toward the other exit, where a bored, white-bearded human sat behind a door made of thick steel bars, reading a leather-bound book. With a deep sigh, he closed the book and raised his head. "What is it?"

Challa jerked himself to a semblance of attention. "The dwarf is here to use the Library, sir. At least, that's what his friend said."

"A dwarf? And what friend?"

"A wizard, sir."

"You're certain about that?" The old man raised a skeptical eyebrow. "With the likes of this?"

"Certain, Librarian. He walked right through Wizard's Arch. There isn't any other possibility, is there?"

A shrug. "Well, if there is, it's no concern of ours. Wizards Guildmasters built it; it's their responsibility." He extended a palm through the bars. "That will be two gold."

Ahira reached into his pouch and drew out a single gold coin. "I thought that it was one?"

"Two." The Librarian pointed at a plaque set into the wall next to the door. "Can't you read?"

"No." Ahira shrugged, drawing out another coin.

"Then what are you doing here? Never mind, it's no concern of mine. Just an old man's curiosity. We don't get many dwarves here."

And at these prices, you're not going to get many more. Ahira dropped the coins into a withered palm.

The Librarian sighed, slipping the coins into the slot of a stone box, its lid secured by a steel strap and heavy padlock. "Enter-and-be-welcome," he said. "And guard, you can hurry back to your post. If you would care to keep your position." The door creaked open; the Librarian hurried Ahira inside with a quick gesture. "Come along, now. I don't have all day."

Ahira stepped through. The room was small, but tightly packed with bookshelves and scrollracks, labeled and unlabeled tomes exuding the pleasant reek of old paper and aged parchment. Beyond the farthest stack, an open doorway gave him a glimpse of a marble-floored corridor.

The Librarian seated himself on his highbacked chair and folded his hands on his lap. "Well, now, why are you here? You can't read, and—"

"That is none of your business." An explanation was out of the question; Ahira wasn't sure how they treated the supposedly insane here, but he was damn sure that he didn't want to find out firsthand.

"Very well." The old man sighed. "But your insolence is going to cost you. Another gold, please."

Ahira took a half-step forward. "I could break you with—"

Wheeet! The man gave out a piercing, pursed-lips whistle, rewarded instantly by the thumping of feet in the corridor. Within seconds, Ahira found himself at the focus of an arc of five crossbowmen, weapons cocked and aimed at his head.

"And that will be enough of *that,*" the Librarian said. "I am Callutius, Junior Librarian. You will address me either by my title, or simply as 'sir'—and always, *always* with respect. Is that understood?"

"Yes. Sir."

Callutius gave him a sour smile. "One gold for insolence plus another for the information is two, please."

"Information?"

Callutius didn't seem to hear him.

"—sir?"

"My name and title, fool." He held out his palm and accepted Ahira's gold, dropping one coin into the box, the other into a fold of the yellow sash at his waist. Callutius steepled his hands in front of his chin. "And now, what can the Great Library of Pandathaway do to serve you?"

Ahira scowled. "I'm afraid to say. How much will the answer to that question cost me, Librarian?"

"Junior Librarian—which is why I'm on greeting duty." He turned in his chair to face the bowmen. "You may go now; I think our customer is learning proper deportment."

As the bowmen shuffled off, he turned back to the dwarf. "How much it costs depends on what you wish to know. I assume that you'll need an apprentice to read for you? That will be three gold, for his services until the close of the Library today." He raised a warning finger. "And don't think to pump him for location information; there are severe penalties for that." Callutius smiled. "And as to how much the location of whatever it is that you wish to know will cost you, that is negotiable with me. Quite a lot, probably—nobody except a wizard comes to the Library unless he needs to know something very badly." He snickered. "Of course, you could just look around with the apprentice, and try to find out whatever it is that you need to know."

Ahira nodded. "That sounds good to me."

"Don't be silly!" Callutius was shocked. "There are four hundred fifty-three rooms in the Library, with an average of five thousand three hundred twelve books or scrolls in each. Conceivably, you could cover one room each day—it could easily take you better than a year to find out what you want. At two gold each day." The Librarian leaned back and closed his eyes. "I'll wait until you've made your decision."

Ahira thought it over. He could just wait there for Aristobulus, but that might be a while—and spending time around Callutius was not a pleasant prospect. Or he could hire an apprentice—no. A compromise was in order. "I won't need an apprentice, but I do want to find directions to the Gate Between Worlds. A map, if there is such a thing."

Callutius chuckled. "A treasure hunter, eh? You choose an expensive form of suicide—sixty goldpieces for directions."

"One."

"Fifty."

"One."

"Forty-five."

"One."

"Really? Is that all you're willing to pay?" Callutius shrugged. "Well, it's none of my concern. Look around; you've already paid for that." He raised a finger in admonition. "But if you damage one *page,* its replacement will be the skin of your back, suitably tanned and cured." Callutius closed his eyes again.

"Ten gold. And that's all."

"Done!" Callutius' smile was genuinely friendly as he took the proffered coins in his cupped palms, tucking all of them into his sash. "And a well-struck bargain, little one."

"Meaning that I gave in too easily?"

"Not at all." The Librarian's grin made his words a lie. He whistled again, this time a complex four-tone theme that was picked up down the corridor, then echoed off into the distance. Callutius picked up his book, then gestured at the doorway leading deeper into the Library. "Go on—an apprentice will meet you, to guide you," he said, ushering Ahira along. "And it has been a true pleasure aiding you in your search for knowledge." He patted at his sash.

"An enriching experience?"

"Quite. I take it this is your first time in Pandathaway?"

"Yes."

"Welcome to Pandathaway, then. And if you hurt anything, I'll see your head on a pole."

CHAPTER NINE

Maps and Dragons

Wilt thou send up avenues of ill?
Pay every debt, as though God wrote the bill.

—Ralph Waldo Emerson

Karl enjoyed himself as the three of them wandered through the open-air markets of Pandathaway. The markets were a rainbow of sights, sounds, and smells: dwarf blacksmiths hawking mailshirts and steelplate greaves; jewelers selling rubies and sapphires in settings both plain and ornate; foodsellers displaying spits of garlic-laden meat and glass bowls of tangy fruitices; bakers calling all to sample golden, fist-sized loaves of bread, dripping butter and fresh from stone ovens.

The prices were high for most things, although a beerseller let them drink three huge tankards for a copper; it occurred to Karl that bread and circuses might have translated into beer and games, here.

At an armorer's canopied stall, they stopped to haggle with a dwarf blacksmith over the price for charming a blade—Walter had suggested that Andrea's and Aristobulus' spells might earn some extra money if needed.

"Well," Karl finally said, quickly bored with the bargaining that the smith seemed to enjoy, "if it's only worth one gold for two swords to you, it's probably not worth bothering our friends. But we might take you up on it later."

The dwarf spat, muttering in some tongue that Karl couldn't follow. "No promises that my offer will stay open. Many wizards in Pandathaway."

Walter looked at him, raising an eyebrow. His unvoiced question: Maybe it would be worth it to nail down the deal now?

"*Out* of my way," Doria snapped, shoving her way between Karl and Walter. "You two have the bargaining sense of—never mind." She slammed her palm down on the weathered counter. "*Look, you,*" she said in Erendra, "we don't have the patience for that sort of nonsense. Understood?"

The dwarf spread his hands. "I don't know—"

"*None of that.* A charmed sword has to be worth, easily, a hundred, hundred-fifty gold if it has any kind of edge—that would be about twice standard—and you're trying to get these two poor fools to agree to half a gold, *each?* Don't bother keeping *that* offer open; we don't need it."

The dwarf chuckled deeply. "Well, it was worth trying for a fast bargain. They look new. You're a Hand cleric, aren't you?"

"Yes."

"It figures. No offense intended, but I don't care for your sect. I'm just an honest armorer and smith, trying to turn a bit of profit, and—"

Karl took a step forward. "And cheat us just a little?"

"Well," the dwarf shrugged, "maybe take a bit of advantage. From the way you three keep spinning your heads around, I figured you might be new to Pandathaway." He eyed Karl's sword. "You any good with that thing?"

Karl slipped his right hand to his swordhilt. "I manage."

The dwarf held up both palms. "Be easy, friend. I'm not threatening. It's just that I have a few spare coins, just now. Since you're new here, the oddsmakers probably will undervalue you; I might be persuaded to put a bet down."

Doria nodded. "*And* give us a good price on a spell or two."

The dwarf dismissed that with an airy wave. "I don't see the need—"

Doria reached out and grabbed him by the collar, pushing her face close to his. "You're familiar with healing spells?"

The dwarf could have pushed her away with ease. Instead, eyeing Karl and Walter, he nodded slightly.

"And," she continued, "have you ever seen one work in reverse?" She ran a fingertip lightly across the dwarf's throat.

He shook his head.

"Then," she said as she released him, "if you don't want to, maybe you'll stop trying to take advantage of my friends, no?"

The dwarf looked curiously at Karl and Walter. "Where did you get this one? I thought that Hand clerics were nonviolent."

And I didn't know Doria was capable of this sort of thing. Karl eyed her curiously. "She's a new kind."

"I'll go along with that—I'll make you a deal. Put *her* in the Games, and we'll all bet on her and get rich as elves. The stupid swordsmen will never know what hit them, eh?" The dwarf laughed, a deep-throated roar that came across as sincere, not just a bargaining technique. "But seriously, if you'll cover half my losses if you don't place, I'll give you say, twenty gold for glowing a sword, thirty for charming one. Agreed?"

"*No,*" Doria said. "You'll give us those prices anyway—and your wagers are your own profit or loss. Agreed?"

The dwarf's mouth quirked into a frown. "Can't get away with anything around you, eh?" He picked up his hammer and turned back to his forge, pumping his elbows with a muscular arm. "Go on, now—find somebody else to persecute. If you win, come back and I'll do well by you." As they started to walk away, he called out, "*And don't bring her with you next time.*"

Karl chuckled. "It seems you gained some skills during the transfer that we didn't know about, Doria."

"Not quite." She smiled up at him. "I spent a summer in Tel Aviv, back at the end of high school. That little dwarf has nothing on the Arab merchants in the Jaffa flea market—you've got to take the first offer as an insult, threaten a bit of violence . . . *then,* you can get down to business. Otherwise, you can end up spending the rent money on a pair of sandals—or take the whole afternoon just picking up lunch." She glared at both him and Walter, but there was a bit of pride mixed in. "It seems as though the two of you are going to need a keeper—or at least a teacher. Watch." She paused in front of a fruit vendor's stall and picked out three ripe, red apples from the slanted bin, examining the back sides of the fruits—"you've got to check for worm holes"—before pulling a copper coin from her pouch, holding it out to the vendor in offer of payment.

The vendor, a frowzy, overweight woman, brushed away the two dirty children clinging to her tattered skirts, nodded, and walked over to take the coin.

As they walked on, she handed Karl the reddest of the apples,

Walter another, and took a bite out of the last. "Good. See," she said around a mouthful, "if you look like you know what you're doing, you'll save a bit of money, and a lot of time."

Karl crunched a bite out of his apple. It had been too long since his last meal, aboard the *Pride;* the cool, sweet fruit tasted almost *too* good. "We've still got to find out when the next Games are." He eyed the afternoon sun. "And then get back to the fountain—I make it about three hours till sundown."

Walter took a last bite out of his apple and threw the shreds of stem and core away. "I could use another beer."

"No." That was a rule he'd learned back when he was a freshman: always set your limits *before* you have your first drink. "Let's walk this way."

Ahira found the Librarian in charge of the Room of Gold and Gray to be an unlikely occupant of the post: The man was tall and well muscled, his shoulders straining at the seams of his gold-trimmed gray woolen tunic as he bustled over to the door to greet the dwarf and dismiss Ahira's escort.

"Welcome, welcome to the Room of Gold and Gray," he boomed. His voice was a deep baritone, his handclasp firm and friendly. "I am Oreen; I am the Specializing Librarian in charge of"—he interrupted himself to chuckle—"all that you now survey. And you are . . . ?"

"Ahira." *And I am also confused.* This Librarian's manner was diametrically opposite to Callutius'.

"Ahira," the Librarian repeated, drawing up two three-legged stools, seating himself on the shorter one and gesturing Ahira to the other. "This will let us have our eyes on the same level, or close to it. Please, make yourself comfortable. You are both my first patron of the day, and my first dwarvish patron ever—let us enjoy the moment, shall we?"

"Do I get charged extra for the friendly treatment?"

Oreen's brow furrowed under a shock of brown hair. "Friendly?— oh. Callutius is on greeting duty today, isn't he? I haven't seen the old bastard for months. Does he still look as though he'd just discovered half a maggot in his meat?"

Ahira chuckled. "Quite."

Oreen shrugged. "Well, it's his own fault. He never specialized, you see—instead of trying to learn one room, he went in for indexing, trying to learn *what* is kept *where.*" Oreen punctuated the words by thumping himself on the knee. "He wants to be Chief Librarian someday. Which he may be, though I doubt it. And, in any case, he is certain to be unhappy in the interim." Oreen gestured at the shelves and racks lining the small, bright room. "As for me, I know every page of every book, every section of every scroll here. Vellum maps and hand-copied books; printed scrolls and explorers' notes—I know them all." Oreen folded his thick arms across his chest. "Which makes me the master of all I see, and a happy man. Now, what is it that we're looking for today?"

"I'm trying to find a map that will show me where the Gate Between Worlds is, if you've ever heard—"

"There's no such map." Oreen held up a hand. "But please, let me show you . . ." He stood, sucking air through his teeth, and walked over to a scrollrack, flipping aside several scrolls before selecting one. "Hmmm . . . I think that this will give you the best overview of the situation." Oreen beckoned Ahira over to a wide table and rolled the scroll open, carefully pinning his selected panel open with four springy clamps. "My own design, these clamps—they keep the scroll firmly open, without hurting it at all.—You see, here we are: Pandathaway." The Librarian held his finger over the designated spot, not touching the yellowed parchment. "I could show you the floor plans of most of the structures here. Do you follow me, so far?"

"Yes, but—"

"Be patient for a moment, friend Ahira, be patient. We now move north and east . . ." His finger traced a path through a scattering of upside-down V's. ". . . where we reach the Aershtyl Mountains, and Aeryk, there. This is the trade route into the mountains; we have much contact with the Aerir. So, I could show you maps of the landholding around Aeryk—contour maps, if you're familiar with them; much of the land is on its side." His finger went farther north. "Now, here's a problem: the Waste of Elrood. Do you know of it?"

"No." Oreen's friendliness tempted Ahira to be more complete—but it was better to be safe. "I'm new to this area."

"Oh?" Oreen's lifted eyebrow invited him to go on.

"I believe you were saying something about a Waste?"

Oreen nodded. "It was almost a thousand years ago—I don't have the date on the tip of my tongue, but I could get it for you if you want me to—it was a thousand years ago, that two powerful wizards dueled on the plain of Elrood. It was a lush farmland, back then. They destroyed everything around them, for a great distance. Now, it's devastated. Nothing grows." He shook himself. "But . . . you pass through just the edge of the Waste, and—"

"Wait." Ahira indicated a patch of green in the large brown circle that marked the Waste. "What's this? I thought you said that it was all destroyed. That's farmland or forest, isn't it?"

"*Very* good." Oreen's smile held no trace of condescension. "That's the forest surrounding the home tabernacle of the Society of the Healing Hand—oh, you know the Society?"

"Slightly," Ahira admitted. "I have a friend who is a member." *In a manner of speaking, that is.*

Oreen stood back, impressed. "Really. They're powerful healers. Their Grand Matriarch is said to be able to raise the dead, although I couldn't swear to the truth of that. I've never heard of a Hand cleric's talking about it, though." He snorted. "On the other hand, the damn Spidersect clerics claim *they* can do anything, and they lie. But, as I was saying, the Matriarch is *most* powerful; she fully protected the tabernacle and its grounds from the battle."

Ahira frowned. "I thought you said it was a long time ago— hundreds of years, no?"

Oreen's face wrinkled. "Where are you from, friend Ahira?"

"What do you mean?" There was a challenge in Oreen's voice that made Ahira's hands itch for the handle of his battleaxe.

The Librarian sighed, and shook his head. "My apologies; it's not my place to pry. But it must be a strange land, where powerful clerics can't maintain their own life functions."

The James Michael part of him welled up with an image of old Father Mendoza, his parish priest, who had collapsed with a heart attack while celebrating Mass, and died a few hours later. It *was* strange, come to think of it: Why couldn't the gods—God take care of his own?

He shook his head. That was beside the point; the problem was how to deal with Oreen. Possibly the best thing to do would be to lay his situation before the Librarian, and ask his advice. But how could he put it? *I used to be a cripple on another world, until a would-be wizard sent me here, to clear the way for him?*

No. That wouldn't do. Just because magic worked here didn't mean that there was nothing that the locals wouldn't consider insane.

And how do they treat the insane here? Beat them, to drive the demons out? And might that even work here?

It might, at that. But the cure could easily be worse than the disease. "You were showing me the route, I believe."

Oreen looked at him for a long moment before shrugging. "Very well. As I was saying, I can't show you detailed maps of the Waste, simply because nobody has ever made one. At least, not to my knowledge—anyone going through there would be more interested in getting out than they would be in mapmaking." He smiled. "And to every rule, an exception: I could show you a map of the road from Metreyll to the tabernacle of the Healing Hand." His finger hovered over a line from a lake to the green spot that marked the forest preserve of the Society. "But that would take you out of your way. Far out of your way, if you're going to Bremon."

"Bremon?"

"Bremon." Oreen tapped at a lone inverted V, near the Waste. "That's where the Gate Between Worlds is supposed to be. I have a description—no map, just some notes—of an entrance into the mountain. A hundred years back, someone gave up on finding the Gate when he was just outside of the mountain. So, I can show you where *that* is. But I can't show you a map of the inside of the mountain, simply because—"

"Nobody who has ever gone in has ever come out again, to tell the tale."

"Of course." Oreen was puzzled. "What do you think I've been getting at?"

An easterly wind brought a stink to Karl's nostrils, as the three of them walked along a quiet cobblestone street. It was a stench of dung, and sweat, and fear. He was about to pick up the pace, to urge the others along, when Walter plucked at Karl's sleeve.

"I think there's a slave market over that way—I can just barely hear an auction. You two want to go look?" The thief shrugged. "I know we can't spend any serious money right now, but it might be worth our while to find out how much some bearers cost. Could be cheaper—" He was interrupted by the crack of a distant whip, immediately followed by a scream of pain. Walter winced. ". . . than buying horses and such."

Karl shook his head. "We won't own people. It's wrong."

Doria frowned at Walter. "How could you even *think* of such a thing? That's—"

"Thinking it through. Which you two aren't. Look, what would we do with a bunch of slaves, after we reach the Gate? We'll let them go, no? In effect, it'd be more like a temporary indenture than real chattel slavery; they'd trade a bit of service for their freedom."

"No." Karl clutched his sword more tightly. "That's out. Just forget about it. One of the few virtues our world has is—"

"Don't be silly. In our world, it's been the norm for most of history. Even in our time, chattel slavery isn't unknown. It's still legal in half a dozen places I can think of—Saudi Arabia, f'rinstance. You—"

"I won't stand for it." *You don't own people. It's wrong.*

Doria interposed herself between the two of them. "Just let it be. We're supposed to be seeing the sights, no?"

"Fine."

The street sloped gradually downward as it narrowed, the one- and two-story stone houses that lined it becoming progressively more ill-kept. Through latticed windows, Karl could see an occasional head, peering out at him, ducking aside when he returned the occupant's gaze. Idly, he let his free hand rest on the hilt of his sword, loosening it in its scabbard. Probably that was an unnecessary precaution, but that was the trouble with precautions: You couldn't know which one was necessary until it was too late.

Ahead of them, where the now narrow street opened into some sort of plaza, there was a distant roaring, as though of a fire.

Fire? Karl sniffed the air. No good; the wind was at his back. "You two hear that?"

Doria and Walter nodded, stepping up their pace to keep abreast of him. "Sounds like a fire," Doria said. "A fire? This whole place is built out of stone. There can't be a fire."

"Bets?"

They reached the end of the street. What had seemed to be a plaza was more of a large, railed balcony, overlooking a vast pit, easily two thousand feet across, a hundred feet deep at its center.

And in the center of the pit, chained by the neck to a massive boulder, was an only slightly less massive dragon.

It was a huge brown beast, easily twice Karl's height at its front shoulder, only slightly shorter at the hips. Two leathery wings sprouted from behind its shoulders, curling and uncurling constantly as the dragon flamed patches of brown muck into ash and steam, its tail flicking nervously from side to side.

The head was a horror. It was shaped much like an alligator's head, but it was massive, teeth easily the size of daggers, wicked red eyes that bore into Karl's, sending him reeling away from the pit's edge.

A gout of flame issued from its mouth, roaring as it touched the stream of sludge that poured out of one of the pipes feeding into the pit.

Go away, sounded in his head, accompanied by waves of nausea.

Karl fell to his knees, gagging, his tearing eyes jammed shut.

"Karl?" Walter knelt beside him. "What happened to you?"

"Karl—are you all right?" Doria's face went ashen as she crouched in front of him.

Another burst of flame sent up a cloud of steam from a sludge pipe.

Karl forced his eyes open. No, there was nobody else there—all of the buildings that circled the pit presented it with only blank walls.

After all, no one would want to look out on a sewer, would he?

This time, the voice was unaccompanied by nausea; Karl staggered to his feet, wiping his mouth on the back of his hand. "You're talking, in my head."

Very clever, swordsman. The dragon's directionless voice dripped with sarcasm. *And you are talking with your mouth. And the mixed-up little healer and the smug thief beside you are standing mute. Have you any more subtle observations to make? If not, please taunt me in my captivity, and then be on your way.* The dragon's forepaw idly clawed at the coils of chain around its neck—no, it wasn't chain, exactly; more like cable. And in spots where the filth that covered it had flaked away, specks of gold showed through.

That is so I can't flame myself free, fool. Were I so foolish as to try, I would only burn myself. It had tried that, more than once. The gold plating on the steel cable conducted the heat away. To the dragon's neck.

Karl's hands flew to his burning neck, circled by a ring of fire.

But the fire wasn't there; the pain faded instantly, until it was only a memory, as distant as a half-forgotten pain from a childhood fall.

How do you like the feeling, human? Your kind—

"No, not me."

"Karl, would you—"

"Shut up." *You're not hearing my voice, are you?*

Why would I be interested in your voice?

I . . . don't know. But . . . how can your own flame burn you? And why are you angry at—

A magical creature the dragon is, but not immune to flame, to heat, to burning. I control my own flame, of course, but the . . .

indirect effects, no. And I hate you because . . . wait. Who are you?*

"My name is Karl Cullinane. This is Doria and Walter." *And I don't know why you're angry at me. I never did anything to you.*

I am Ellegon. The disposer of wastes.

I . . . don't understand.

Wait until the wind changes, Karl Cullinane. This pit is where the sewers of Pandathaway empty, so as not to foul their precious harbor. I must flame the wastes into ash, or sit here buried in human filth. They captured me, when I was only half a century out of the egg, and chained me here, dumping their excrement on me for these three centuries.

You're more than three hundred years old?

The dragon had been chained in sewage for three centuries; it let Karl feel what that was like.

For just a moment.

As he lay retching on the stones, Walter pulled at his shoulders. "C'mon, we've got to get him out of here. It's killing him."

Yes, I'm only a child. Do you think it's right, to treat a child like this? Do you?

Nausea.

Karl shrugged their hands away, closing his eyes, trying to close his mind. *Please. Don't do that again.*

You wouldn't have done it? No, I see that you wouldn't, not even to a dragon.

The nausea ceased. "Take it easy, you two. Everything's okay." *No, I wouldn't do it to a dragon.*

Karl would *kill* a dragon, if it endangered him. If he could. But this was wrong. Karl had felt just a trace of Ellegon's suffering, and that was more than enough. Unless the dragon wasn't as sensitive to—

Do you want to feel it again?

No. This was wrong, but it didn't look as though there was anything that Karl could do about it: The dragon looked hungry, and the cable was thick.

I am hungry, and I haven't asked you to cut the cable. Not that I need to eat; dragons are magical, don't you know. We like to eat—the satisfaction of crunching a cow, eating it in two bites, sent the last traces of nausea away—*but we don't have to.*

I didn't know. I didn't know anything about dragons.

A mental shrug. *Are you stupid, or merely ignorant?*

Just ignorant, I hope.

Hmmm. I have a proposition for you. If I do two things for you, would you do one thing for me?

That depends. You can't—

I can't reach your mind from much farther away, yes. You could run away, and I wouldn't be able to talk to you, or do thi—

DON'T. I don't want you to make me vomit again. But you were offering me a proposition? I . . . I'm not sure I trust you enough to go down there, and try to free you.

Flame roared. *Fool. I wasn't asking for that. Not from a filthy human. But if you could see your way to bringing me something to eat? A sheep, maybe? I'll do something for you, I'll start by telling you something you need to know, if you are going to find the Gate Between Worlds, Karl Cullinane.*

How—how do you know?

Blistering scorn. *I read minds, remember?* Ellegon roared.

Sorry.—And yes, if I can afford a sheep, if you do something for me that makes it worthwhile, I'll bring you one. Or something else to eat, if I can't manage to buy a sheep.

Agreed. First: You will find the Gate deep under the mountain Bremon, just north and west of the Waste of Elrood. And—

I thank you, but maybe Ahira—

*—I know. Your companion may already have found that out. I wasn't finished. I was going to tell you something else, something that he could *not* have found out. Something that I know, simply because I am a dragon, and know where all of my kind are.*

"Karl, what is—"

"Shut *up*. I'm talking to the dragon."

"You're talking to a dragon?"

Yes, he's talking to a dragon.

Walter and Doria both jumped, as Ellegon included them.

But it's easier to talk to only one.

You were telling me that there's a dragon there, at the Gate. That was bad. But maybe, if they were lucky, the dragon wouldn't be as large as Ellegon.

No, He won't. He will be much larger. He has lain there long enough for the mountain Bremon to grow up around him, as He sleeps there, guarding the Gate.

"Wonderful." He turned to the others. "Ellegon just told me that there's a dragon at the Gate, guarding it."

"Karl," Doria shrilled, "would you tell me what is going *on?*"

Tell them to go away. Their minds are even narrower and more cramped than yours. Although the woman's holds more. Strange. And the other's is built differently, as though it's not quite the same kind. I . . . don't understand.

"Ask him," Walter said, "what the other dragon's name is. Maybe Ari can put together a name-spell, and—"

Fool.

"I heard that." Walter glared.

And fool you are. He was the first dragon, created before all the rest of us.

"So?"

So, in the old days, when there was but one thing of His kind in all the world, why would He have need of a name? Just so, billions of years later, some stupid human could cast a spell using it? No. He is The Dragon, oldest of us all, and has no need of a name.

So what can we do to protect ourselves against him?

Don't wake Him. He is older than the mountain, and you could break the mountain more easily than you could dent the smallest of His scales. Karl Cullinane?

Yes?

I have done one thing for you, no? Will you bring me my sheep now, or must I do the other?

You make that sound like a threat. And I don't like threats, Ellegon.

Very well. Ellegon sighed mentally. *Then, I will let you understand.*

Understand wha—

The universe fell apart.

He was fifteen, and a nice Jewish girl. Or, at least, she was supposed to be. But there were things she wasn't supposed to be, and things she wasn't supposed to do. Like grope in the dark with Jonathan Dolan, and slip out of—

Enough? Or do you really want to understand Doria?

You're letting me into her memories? Why?

So you'll understand.

No, wai—

And she couldn't tell Daddy, of course. He called her his one-and-only, and Mommy thought she was still a virgin. That was one of the rules: You don't talk about it. But it wasn't only that she was late, there was this burning—and that damn Jonny Dolan was telling everybody that *she'd* given *him* the clap. And that couldn't be true. It couldn't. He was the first, and the only one, so far.

And it hadn't even been any fun. Just a sticky mess. He lied. They all lied. It wasn't any fun at all.

You still don't see it.

But I can't tell anybody. Besides, it's probably not *that.* Maybe, if I just forget about it, it'll go away?

I think, perhaps, just a bit more.

"She's a sick little girl, Mr. Perlstein, but with a bit of luck we'll have the fever down in a few hours." She lay panting beneath the plastic, no longer able to paw at the tubes in her nose and arms— they'd fastened her hands down.

"But it can't be gonorrhea. Not my little—"

"You know, Mr. Perlstein, you make me sick."

"Doctor, I—"

"If she'd been able to tell anybody—if she'd felt able to tell anybody . . . if there'd been *one goddam person* for her to talk to, maybe she wouldn't be lying there now. We could have treated it easily, if we had gotten to it. Before."

"Before?"

"Before it grew into one hell of a raging pelvic infection that'll leave her sterile, if it doesn't kill her."

"Sterile? My little—"

"Sterile. Unable to conceive. Ever. If we're lucky. Nurse." A cold hand felt at her forehead. "I want a temp and BP every five minutes. If her temp doesn't start to drop within the hour . . ."

And the last portion of the payment.

And I guess it doesn't matter anymore and besides in a lot of ways I'm perfect because nobody ever has to worry about getting Doria Perlstein pregnant ever which means that every cloud has a silver lining because now I can have any boy I want to but they all treat me like I was a cigarette they pass around but I guess that doesn't matter because that's what I deserve isn't it because becausebecausebe-causebe—

Enough.

"Karl, are you okay?"

"I don't care what he said, Walter, we've got to get him out of here."

"No—*wait.* I think he's coming around."

Karl pried an eye open. Doria and Walter bent over him, concern creasing their faces. "It's okay," he said, not surprised to hear his voice coming out as a harsh croak. "Help me up."

"What did he do to you?" Doria asked. "He hurt you again. That—"

"Shh." *Understanding, eh?*

Understanding. It's not always easy to understand things, Karl Cullinane. Even I know that.

She doesn't know?

No, of course not. Why would I want to hurt—

You would have killed us, a few minutes ago. If you could have reached us.

A different thing entirely, no?

A different thing entirely.

Will you get me my sheep now? Ellegon asked plaintively.

Karl walked slowly to the railing and stared out at the dragon. "You two keep watch. I've got a debt to pay."

"What did it do to—"

"Shh."

Then I get my sheep!

No. He slipped out of his sandals, using their thongs to lash his scabbard to his shoulders.

No? Then you *are* like all the rest, you—*

Shh. Just be quiet for a moment.

Karl Cullinane pays his debts. That was the rule. And even if the debt came out of a window into Doria's mind, a window that he wouldn't have wanted to look through . . .

And to think I treated her like—

You didn't know. What are you doing?

Karl levered himself over the railing. Good—the rockface below was rough and cracked; there would be many finger- and toe-holds. *I took up rock climbing one summer—hey! why are you asking? I thought you could read my mind, even what I'm not consciously thinking about.*

Not now. There's an intensity—

Shh. I've got to pay attention to what I'm doing.

He picked his way carefully down the face, ignoring Doria's and Walter's shouted questions from above. *You can't turn off my sense of smell for me, can you?* he thought, as he lowered himself into the ankle-deep foul muck.

*No—you're really going to do it? Thankyouthankyouthankyou— I'll leave, I'll fly away, I will. Please, Karl, *please* don't change your mind. Pleaseplease—*

Shh. Stumbling and gagging at the stench, he started to walk toward Ellegon.

Never mind, Karl. He's been in this for three hundred years.

As he got closer, it became shallower; a harder surface beneath the ooze supported his bare feet.

The dragon loomed above him, its breath coming in short gasps, its wings curled protectively by its sides. *Lower your neck, will you? If there's a weak point in this cable, it'll probably be there, where you can't see it.*

Ellegon knelt in the filth, his huge head just inches away from Karl. His mental voice was strangely silent as he presented his barrellike throat.

It was a cable, and like all cables, made up of smaller strands. It took a moment for Karl's swordtip to snick through the first strand, and a moment longer for the next.

Easy, my friend, easy. Just a few dozen more. He had to stop to quell his gagging reflex; wading through this . . . sewer was something he'd try to forget.

And—he cut through the last strand—*done!*

Ellegon's massive head tilted at him. *Thankyouthankyouthankyou—*

Shh. Better get going. He slipped his sword back in its sheath.

Grab my neck, the dragon said, its mind muttering a background of *Free. Free. I'm Free.*

Karl reached out, and as he did so, the creature's wings flapped, blurring with speed as it eased into the air, then whirred over to the balcony, Karl dangling for a moment, then dropping to the tiles. *Free.*

One more thing, Ellegon said, landing.

"Look out, Karl, he's going to—"

The dragon's mouth opened, and a gout of flame rushed out, enveloping Karl. Just flame; no heat, although the reeking muck covering much of his body burst into fire, sparkling and burning away. *My flame couldn't hurt you, Karl Cullinane. Not you. Not now.* It tingled pleasantly, that was all. He turned in the firestream, letting it wash over him like a shower.

Free. The flame stopped.

Better get going.

With a snap of his wings, the dragon jumped skyward, his wings just a blur as he left the balcony and the pit behind him.

Free.

Fly away, my friend.

Three times the dragon circled overhead, gaining height as he flew.

Free.

"Karl," Doria said, shaking her head, "would you mind telling us just what's going *on?*"

"I think we'd all better get out of here, folks," Walter said, moving them along. "When the authorities find out about this, they aren't going to be all that pleased."

Ellegon flew off toward the north, now so high he was only a dark speck against the blue sky.

Free.

"Karl, why?" Doria asked.

He slipped one arm around her waist, the other around Walter's as they walked away. "Because I never felt this good in my Whole. Damn. Life."

Free.

That was faint now; did he hear it, or just imagine it?

It really didn't matter.

Not at all.

Free.

CHAPTER TEN

The Inn of Quiet Repose

We may live without poetry, music and art;
We may live without conscience, and live without heart;
We may live without friends, we may live without
*   books;*
But civilized man cannot live without cooks.

—Edward Bulwer-Lytton, Earl of Lytton

Walter Slovotsky suppressed a chuckle at Andrea's bubbly enthusiasm as she led the group down a broad street toward the Inn of Quiet Repose.

"You should see it," she said, hurrying them along. "And I got a *fine* deal for the suite—it's going to cost us just one hundred gold for the next ten days."

A hundred gold? By local prices, that wasn't much at all. Walter shrugged. Either she had landed them in some horrid hovel, or her Charm spell had been awfully effective.

Apparently, Ahira had the same idea. "If you charmed whoever's running it, won't—"

"Nope." She took a smug, prancing step. "The owner has an amulet around his neck, one he thinks wards that kind of spell away." She spread her hands. "But it doesn't have any kind of aura at all—either it's dead, or it's a phony. But here we are."

The inn was a three-storied edifice, a marble mansion like a stone

version of something out of *Gone with the Wind.* Tall fluted pillars
guarded the broad staircase; the foyer was a vast, soundless room,
with deep, blood-red carpets that seemed to suck the weariness out of
Walter's legs. He smiled as he tilted his head back to enjoy the mural
that spanned the high ceiling: chubby nymphs chasing unicorns
through a green glade.

He started to lower his pack to the floor, but six young women in
filmy white kimonos descended on them, relieving them all of their
burdens as others arrived bearing silver trays laden with steaming
cloths to bathe their hands, feet, and faces, and yet others carrying
thick towels to pat them dry, and tall, frosty glasses of ice and wine.

And all this when they were barely inside the door. Walter nodded. *I think I'm going to like this.*

And then, for a moment, he had his doubts. A huge man, yards of
yellow silk caftan barely containing his oversize belly, stepped from
behind a curtain. "Well, it seems as though you were correct, my
little friend." He scowled down at Andrea, easily half again her
height. Walter tried to guess his weight; three-fifty, four hundred
perhaps? "I wouldn't have believed that there was so scruffy a group
if—but never mind, pay no attention, Tommallo is but ranting,
again. And these are guests; their way has been pai—" He stopped
himself, rubbing a finger against his almost impossibly aquiline nose,
then shook his head. "My guests: Will you go to your suite now, or
would you care to dine first?"

Ahira spoke up. "Is there a bath—"

"You insult me!" The owner stood back, his hands on his hips.
"This, my dear sir, is the Inn of Quiet Repose. Nowhere, I say,
nowhere in glorious Pandathaway will you find an establishment so
well kept, so replete with every facility necessary to provide a guest
ease or comfort. *Every* comfort."

Walter looked the nearest of the serving girls up and down. Quite a
difference from the ugly, unbathed serving girls of Lundeyll. Then he
glanced at Karl. On the other hand, maybe the stupid swordsman
would give him trouble over that—couldn't he see that there was a
difference between here and home? When in Pandathaway . . .

The owner was still talking. ". . . you will even discover—perhaps I should save this? No, no—you will find that your suite's bath
is complete with running water, requiring only the merest turn of a
valve for its use." He stamped his bare foot soundlessly on the carpet. "And you will find your rooms to be quiet; your sleep will be
deep and sound and filled only with light, pleasant dreams. Our table

is the finest, with food—" He smacked himself on the forehead. "But I forget my manners! I am Tommallo, your host for the next ten days —and at an unusually low fee." Again, his forehead wrinkled, as though he were trying to figure out why he had agreed to such a relatively small charge. He glanced at Andrea and Aristobulus, in their gray robes. "It's as though—but no," he murmured. "I've a token to ward that away. But perhaps its potency has fled? No, no; pay attention, Tommallo, for you have guests, and yet to find out what their pleasure is, you old fool. Letting your mouth run free when—"

Ahira held up a hand. "I'm for the bath, first. I suppose everybody else is, too."

"Not me." Those were the first words out of Karl since they'd left the sewage pit. *The stupid—but never mind. I've got to help Jimmy contain the damage. Not sure what kind of police force they have here, not really—but whatever kind they have is going to be looking for Karl. And they'll be bloody unlikely to overlook his accomplices.*

"I managed," Karl went on, "to get myself cleaned up earlier. Right now, I could use some food. Anyone else?"

Well, that might have been true for Karl, but Walter hadn't been cleansed by fire—and had no desire whatsoever to try it out. He scratched at his arm; the itching from lack of bathing had subsided into a dull background of irritation, but now there wasn't anything he wanted more than a bath.

Except survival. And that means I'd better keep an eye on Mr. Cullinane. "I need some food, too." Walter patted at his stomach. "Been a long time since breakfast. Tommallo?"

"Yes?" The innkeeper beamed at him. "Snacks—I have a fresh, pungent beetlepaste—or would you prefer something more substantial?"

"Beef?"

"Ah . . . the cooks have a wonderful roast in the pit. Hindleg of a virgin heifer, marinated in wine and herbs for a week, then cooked in a vat with—"

"Enough." Aristobulus held up a hand. "Let us get to it, shall we?"

Andrea nodded, as did Doria.

Ahira shook his head. "The rest of you go along—I'll head up to our suite, and get myself a bath and a nap."

Tommallo snapped his fingers. A buxom blonde led the dwarf

away. "And for the rest of you—would you care to dine in the common room, or—"

Walter shook his head. "We need some privacy."

The innkeeper tilted his head, smiling knowingly. "Ah—and will you require an additional wench or—"

"We're fine the way we are."

Tommallo nodded, and conducted the five of them down a hallway, to a staircase, then up two flights to another hallway, and finally to a room at the corner of the building, two walls composed mainly of open windows and bead-curtained exits to the veranda outside. He bowed them in, waiting until everyone was seated on a bench at the massive oak table before clapping his hands together. "Wine for my guests!" he commanded the air.

As though they had been waiting behind the curtains, three women stepped out, bottles in hand, along with heavily laden trays. Bowls and small sharp knives were set in front of them, along with serving dishes of buttery corn, served on the cob with a tangy brown sauce, small fowl—squab, perhaps?—the skin broiled to a perfect golden crispness, a purple paste that was somehow sour and hot and sweet, all at the same time, and delightfully so.

Tommallo bowed. "Enjoy yourselves, my guests. If you have any desire at all, you need merely snap your fingers, or when in your room, pull a bellrope." He left, but the servitors kept bringing platters of food, setting them down, and leaving.

Walter sampled a knobby sheet of bread. The bulges turned out to be a cheesy orange filling. A strange combination of flavors, but a delightful one; he debated for a moment whether to reach for another helping or sample the steaming slices of beef and lamb or the silver tureen of leeks floating in a clear broth before deciding to take all three, *and* more of the bread.

There was no sound for minutes, except for the noises of chewing and frequent oohs and ahhs as all sampled the fare. *Do we talk here or—stupid!*

"Everybody," he said in English, "no Erendra—just keep the talk in English, understood?"

Aristobulus shook his head. "No," he said around a mouthful of fowl, "I don't understand—we've got nothing to hide."

"We do now." Walter jerked his thumb at Karl, who was silently chewing on an ear of corn, careless of the way the sauce was dripping on the tabletop. "Genius, here, decided to ruin the city's sewage system." He looked over at Andrea. "And besides, we don't want the staff here to overhear how we got the cut-rate price on the lodgings, do we?"

Andrea shook her head. "I wouldn't worry about it. As I said, Tommallo isn't the sort to talk things over with his employees, and—"

"*Not* employees," Karl growled. "Let's at least keep it honest."

"They are *so* employees, stupid. Slephmelrad, to be precise."

Slephmelrad. Fealty servants. Walter shrugged. It had taken a while to get used to the way that oddities of the Erendra language awakened knowledge that he hadn't known he'd had, but it had become a frequent phenomenon. *And, come to think of it, when I get some spare time it'd be worthwhile to run through every Erendra word I know, and try to integrate all that.*

"Oh." Karl shrugged, smiling awkwardly at a slender girl who looked to be about thirteen; she deposited another clay bottle of wine on the table before leaving. "Just women?"

"No." Andrea smiled broadly. "Male servants, too. And one of them—"

"Enough." Walter rubbed at his temples. Granted, the two of them had had a good time together aboard the *Ganness' Pride,* but it hadn't been *that* good. And the way she rubbed Karl's nose in her right to—something had to be done about that.

You're a fine one to talk, Walter Slovotsky. You've never made any pretense with Doria that she was your one-and-only. "We'll talk about it later." Then again, that was different. For one thing, unless he was totally misreading Karl, *and* Andrea was a liar, those two had never gotten together. And, dammit, he didn't rub Doria's nose in it. Ever.

Complications . . . everything's got complications. And Jimmy was probably at the heart of one of the worst of them. Why hadn't he made a play for Doria? It was as clear as anything that the little guy wanted her—and here, it might work. Or would that be some sort of perversion, come to think of it? What would you call it, humanality?

He shook his head. It'd probably take Jimmy a while to work things out. If he slept with Doria, was he, Ahira, being queer for humans? And if he made it with a female dwarf, was James Michael—

The trouble with me is that, way down deep, I'm shallow. My best friend is finally in a situation where he can be a whole person, and all I worry about is whether that's a perversion of some sort.

And whether I have to sleep alone tonight. He caught Doria's eye, tilting and raising his chin in an unvoiced question. She glanced at

Karl, then at Andrea, frowned, and nodded. *Well, at least that's taken care of. That's the trouble with me, though—I'm just a slave to my hormones and digestive juices.* He reached out and speared another slice of red, rare beef.

"Sewage system?" Aristobulus looked over. "You mean that little dragon?"

"How'd you hear about it?"

"I spent some time in the wizards' section of the Library, chatted with a few guild members taking a break from doing some research. Found out some . . . interesting things, between my reading and talking."

"Well?"

"Hmmm, I think I'll save it for later. There are some calculations I want to recheck. But for now . . . did you realize that this whole Guilds' Council thing is a sham?"

Karl frowned. "Wait a minute. I—"

"You didn't spend the afternoon with some of the people who really run Pandathaway, Karl. It's the wizards—the rest are just window dressing. Which is why we don't have to worry about To—about our host's getting angry, even if he does find out what Andrea did." Aristobulus smiled smugly. "Assaulting any wizard is a capital crime—ditto an authorized cleric, member of any of the five recognized sects. Including"—he nodded to Doria—"the Hand, by the way." The wizard frowned and shook his head. "I'd leave you all right now, if it wasn't . . ."

Damn me. I've got a mind like a sieve. Ever since he had learned about the Great Library, Walter had worried that Aristobulus might choose to leave the group in Pandathaway. He hadn't said anything; nothing could be done about it. If Aristobulus wanted to go, he could. "And why won't you?"

Aristobulus took a long swig of wine before answering. "It's the damn spell books again." He drained the mug and slammed it down on the table. "I may be good, but I'm not a Wizards' Guild member."

"So?"

"So, if and when I apply for membership, I'll be better off having a set of books of my own. Otherwise, I've got to *apprentice,* of all things."

Walter chuckled. The notion of Aristobulus apprenticing to some other wizard was almost absurd. Ari was pretty far along as a wizard; it was unlikely that there were many others in Pandathaway as powerful as he was. But it was a certainty that there were plenty of wizards who could gang up on him and make him toe the line. "How long an apprenticeship?"

He scowled. "Until my—get this—my *master* decides that I'm worthy." He shook his head. "And that's not the worst of it. All apprentices in the guild have to submit to being put under geas."

Now that was bad for Aristobulus, but good for the rest of them. A geas would rob him of his ability to disobey his master's orders. And it was unlikely that any master wizard would want to dispense with the services of someone with skills as developed as Ari's. Normally, the tradeoff between master and apprentice—in any profession—was that of training in the craft for doing all the trivial gruntwork. But Ari was capable of doing much more than preparing a potion under supervision; whatever guild wizard he'd be apprenticed to would quickly find his services indispensable.

But it was good for the group, at least. With a lifetime of apprenticeship to look forward to if he stayed in Pandathaway, Aristobulus was certain to stay with the group. At least until they reached the Gate, and Deighton. "You're assuming that Doc'll furnish you with another spell book or two."

"*Very* good." The wizard popped a ball of deep-fried prawns and garlic into his mouth. "And then I'll come back here, apply to the guildmaster, and live off my earnings and the stipend guild members get, just like all the others." He chuckled. "Including the extra earnings from selling phony charms, like the one that Tommallo has. The fool—why would the wizards bother to sell him a real protection when he can't tell the difference?"

As Karl reached for his third helping of beef, the wizard cocked his head. "I thought you're supposed to go light on food, before?"

"Before *what?*"

"The Games, stupid—the every-ten-days ones are tomorrow, aren't they? I thought that's what—" Aristobulus wrinkled his brow. "You mean you didn't bother asking anyone about them? I thought—"

Walter held up a hand. "We got distracted." *And it's just as well that the Games are tomorrow, at that. The cops are going to be looking for Karl, Aristobulus is probably trying to figure out a way to swipe a set of books from a local, and—*

And the simple fact is that I'm scared. He rubbed a thumb against the spot where Lund's henchman had cut him. *I know I won't stop being scared until we get home. But will it stop, even then?*

He stood. Somehow, the food didn't taste so good anymore.

Rubbing at his hair with a thick flannel cloth that served as a towel, Ahira decided that Tommallo hadn't been bragging. Their suite in the Inn of Quiet Repose was broad and spacious, oozing comfort from the deep crimson carpet that tickled his ankles, all the way to the chandeliers overhead, scores of candles burning almost smokelessly, dripping only a sweet fragrance into the common room. Beeswax, perhaps?

He sighed. And there was even half-decent plumbing—superior, by local standards. Granted, the hot water for his bath had been taken, bucket by bucket, from a copper kettle, but at least it had been hot.

He dropped to the floor next to his weapons and stretched out on his back, pillowing his head on his hands, letting his eyes sag shut. With a bit of luck, he could catch a nap before the others returned from dinner.

And it was good to be alone, without having to worry about where the others were, what the others were doing. . . .

The world slowly faded away into the warm twilight of oncoming sleep.

"Shh." Hakim's whisper boomed. "Don't wake him; he needs his rest."

Ahira opened his eyes. "Thanks for the thought, anyway."

As the others filed into the room, he shrugged, deciding against slipping away to one of the sleeping rooms. There was much to talk about; they had to figure out what the next move was.

Karl stretched out on a fur-covered couch and patted at his belly. "Sorry. Hey, you missed one hell of a good meal, though. I don't think I'll be able to eat for hours. How was your bath?"

"Restful." Ahira forced himself to sit up. "Very restful. You all should try it, a bit later."

Doria sat beside him, hugging her knees. "Why not now? You go get some sleep. We've got a long day tomorrow, what with the Games and all."

"Tomorrow? Then never mind." He rubbed at his eyes. "All right, everyone, gather around. Let's get this over with."

Hakim sat down next to Doria, followed by Karl, then Aristobulus, then Andrea. Ahira could almost see bands of tension flowing between her and Karl; it was evident in the way he avoided looking at her, and in the curious little pursed-lips headshake that she would give every time she looked at him. Probably there was some intelligent thing to do, to get the two of them to agree to better than a coldly hostile coexistence.

Trouble is, I don't have a single idea what that intelligent thing to do is. Oh well—what cannot be cured, must be endured. "I'll go first," he said. "I know where the Gate is; I've got it right here"—he tapped a finger against his temple—"and I'll sketch out a map sometime tomorrow. Somebody pull a pencil and some paper from their pack. I don't have any."

"I do." Andrea nodded. "But how far is it?"

"Looks to be a fairly long haul from here—a month of traveling, easily."

Karl cocked his head to one side, a faint smile playing across his lips. "And once we get to Bremon, it'll be tougher, maybe. Almost certainly."

"What do you mean?" Ahira hadn't mentioned Bremon; he hadn't said anything about it since they'd all met at the fountain.

Karl rubbed his hand across his face. "I . . . had a talk with a friend. He says there's a big mother of a dragon under the mountain, guarding the Gate. Sleeping."

"A *friend?*" Andrea snapped. "What sort of friend?"

Hakim raised a palm. "Best not to talk about it—he's talking about the baby dragon that is—that used to be a part of Pandathaway's sewage system. But it's best to keep quiet about it. We'd just better get ourselves together and get out of here. Could be the authorities are looking for us, even now."

Karl shook his head. "I don't think so. We were down in the slums. The folks who live there probably won't be eager to talk to the . . . cops. Even if they saw us."

Walter sneered. "You ever live in the slums, genius? Sometimes you *have* to talk to the cops, even when you don't want to."

Aristobulus nodded his agreement. "And when the sewage starts rising around their ankles? You *know* who's going to have to take care of it, and they won't like it. Not at all."

Ahira didn't know what they were talking about, but the fact that Karl knew about Bremon—apparently knew more about Bremon than he did—was something that had to be explained. The best way, probably, would be to wait, to escape the worry of being overheard if they spoke in Erendra, or being labeled as strange if they talked in an unknown language like English. But too many precautions, too much paranoia, was in itself a chancy thing. "Just talk, Karl. Keep your voice low, by all means, but please tell me *what the hell you're talking about.*"

Karl nodded slowly. "Fine. They have a funny sort of sewer system here. It dumps out into a pit, where the sewage used to be flamed into ash by a dragon, a young one."

"Used to be?" Andrea arched an eyebrow. "I take it it—"

"Doesn't anymore." Karl smiled. "They had the dragon chained there. I didn't like that, so I let him loose. End of story." He shrugged. "Probably not a big deal; all they'll have to do is get some high-ranking wizards down there, every now and then, to Fire the slop into ash."

Ahira shook his head. *The brainless—* "How long ago?"

"An hour or so before we met at the fountain. Why?"

Andrea spoke up. "Because probably the news is all over Pandathaway by now, and somebody is going to be looking for whoever did it, stupid. I thought that Walter was just joking before. Tell me, Karl, have you *ever* thought about the consequences of—"

"Shut up." That was from Doria, oddly enough. Her defending Karl made little sense. "Tell me, Karl: Did you think about the consequences?"

Karl didn't answer for a moment; he sat there tailor-fashion, his body relaxed and loose, his eyes misty like an absurdly overmuscled Buddha. "To be honest, I didn't. It . . . it was important enough that . . . consequences just didn't matter. I'm sorry if you're upset—"

"*Upset?*" Andrea was almost hysterical. "If they find out who did this, we all could get *killed.*"

Doria's face clouded over. "He said that it was important enough, didn't he? I don't understand why—but maybe I don't have to. We all—"

Andrea threw up her hands. "That's the trouble with you," she shrilled at Karl, ignoring Doria, "you're always so damn *intense* about everything. That's why—never mind." She shook her head slowly, rubbing at her eyes. "It's done."

Ahira picked up on that. "Right. It's done." He turned to Karl. "Did anyone see you three?"

"No." Karl chewed on his lower lip. "And besides, around here, the three of us aren't all that unusual-looking. Maybe even if someone did see us, and somebody else links that to Ellegon getting away—"

"—it might not matter," Ahira finished. Well, that wasn't likely, but at least it was a possibility. "But let's not take chances. I don't want you three to be seen together in public until we're gone from Pandathaway. And we'd better arrange to get out of here soon. Soon as possible. And that means that you and I'd better do well enough in the Games tomorrow so that we can buy what we need *quickly,* and get out of here." He considered that for a moment. "Better: We buy just what we need to get to Aeryk, and finish outfitting ourselves there."

Aristobulus cocked his head to one side. "I'll still need another two days in the Library, at least. I've gotten one of my spells back, but I need the Fire spell, and I think, with a bit of effort, I could puzzle out the spell that would let me bring writing materials past the Glyph—"

"No." Ahira made that as final as possible. "We don't have time for all that. You and Andrea each have one spell to relearn—you do that tomorrow morning while we get ready to leave after the Games."

Hakim lifted his head. "I've got a better idea. We could have Ari Glow a blade or two—we ran into a smith who might pay nicely for it, if Doria handles the negotiations. And then he can relearn both that and his Lightning spell. That way . . ."

"Good." Ahira nodded. "And that's the way we do it. Where are these Games taking place?"

"Mmmm." The thief spread his arms, embarrassed. "To be perfectly honest, we got kind of dis—"

"At the Coliseum," Aristobulus snorted. "North side of the city. The oddsmakers set up their tables at dawn; contestants have to be there by midmorning. Anything else you need to know? It's fortunate that at least one of us spent some time asking questions—"

"Enough." Ahira cut him off. "Spilled milk. Doria?"

"Yes?"

"You and Walter take care of placing the bets on us. Don't go deep into our money, but if Karl and I are as good as I think we are, we shouldn't have any problem winning. And since we're new here, I bet—"

Doria nodded. "—that you'll be undervalued. Fine. How much should we put down?"

Karl spoke up. "That's not the way you gamble. Not if you know what you're doing. Figure out what we need, find out what the odds are, and *then* you'll know how much to bet."

Andrea stood and stretched. "Well, unless you've got something for me to do, I'm going to wash up"—she put her hand over her mouth to stifle a yawn—"and then get some sleep. That meal's going to my head." She started to walk away, then stopped and turned. "One thing—what if you and Karl don't win?"

Ahira shook his head. "You're looking at it the wrong way.—Now, Doria and Hakim, I want to go over what you've got to buy tomorrow, just at a minimum. That way, you can price it out, and know what you'll have to bet in order to make the kind of money we need."

Andrea scowled down at him. "What do you mean, I'm looking at it the wrong way?"

He sighed. She still hadn't worked it out? "Karl, tell her."

The big man shrugged. "Look at it this way: We don't have enough money to buy what we need to get out of Pandathaway, and this is the only way I can see of making it in a hurry. And whoever's in charge of this place is probably looking for me right now, and isn't likely to think all that highly of the rest of you. So . . ."

"So?"

"So we'd damn well *better* win, hadn't we?"

CHAPTER ELEVEN

The Games

A man cannot be too careful in his choice of enemies.

—Oscar Wilde

Karl frowned. The place felt normal, but the chatter was strange. The swordsmen's pit beneath the right-hand limb of the Coliseum was a large bare room of gray stone, lit only by a few flickering oil lamps that dangled from the ceiling. The air was cold and damp; the reeking sawdust that covered the dirt floor should have been changed long ago.

But the conversation was positively merry.

"Bet I get past the second round without two marks on my hide, and you—"

"You serious? I put down a couple of silver on myself, but I only got thirty-to-one I make it to the finals. Who you betting with? I've been going to Antrius, that slimy son of a dungfly—"

"Well, of course Ohlmin's going to grab first. Nobody else can move near that fast. So I'm not holding back anything in the early rounds; I'll be satisfied if I can just get into the finals—"

"You're *dreaming,* friend. Or crazy. Dwarves are no damn good with longbows; they're just too short. Although the little buggers—"

A pinch-faced elf waved the hundred or so swordsmen—humans, elves, dwarves, and curious mixes that Karl couldn't quite identify—to a semblance of silence. Standing on a waist-high stone block in the center of the high-ceilinged room, he wore a light-blue tunic with matching leggings, a gold headband that marked him as an official of the Games, and a bored expression that proclaimed that being around a bunch of ill-washed swordsmen was not his ultimate pleasure in life.

"I am," he intoned, "Khoralt ip Therranj, Wineseller's Delegate to the Guilds' Council—"

"So bring us some wine!" a mocking voice called out from the crowd.

The elf sighed. "If you will all keep silent for a few moments, just a few moments, this will be over, and you can proceed to the winning of some money." He made as though to step down, but moved back toward the center of his pedestal as the rush of noise diminished somewhat. He went on: "I will be the chief official of the swords competition. The top prize will be two hundred pieces of gold; lesser prizes in the usual ratios."

The same voice called out, "If it's as usual, then why are you wasting our time telling us?"

Karl looked over at him. He was a thin, dark man, dressed—like all the other contestants—only in sandals, leggings, and tunic; armor was not allowed in Pandathaway's Games. Karl had a flash of dislike; the swordsman's crossed-arms slouch, his thin smirk, his whole manner suggested that he was slumming, that he was too good to be here, with ordinary warriors.

Khoralt sighed. "Perhaps not everyone here is a veteran of the Games, Ohlmin. I see some new faces; perhaps there are some men who would not even recognize you."

The thin man—Ohlmin—shook his head. "If they don't now, they will soon." He smiled thinly. "Business has been slow, lately—I've an order to fill in Aeryk, and if I don't win today, I won't have enough coin to make my purchases."

The elf shook his head. "Your business concerns are not germane, but . . ." He shrugged, raising his head to address the crowd. "Ohlmin, here, has won the swords competition every time that he has entered it, whenever his selection of slaves has dipped low enough that he's needed the extra coin." He turned back to Ohlmin. "Now, is that sufficient acknowledgment?"

Ohlmin paused. "For now." He smiled.

In another setting, Karl would have wanted to wipe the smirk off Ohlmin's face, but drawing attention to himself for no profit hardly seemed to be a good idea.

"Before I begin," Khoralt continued, "an announcement. Our sewer dragon, as most of you know, escaped yesterday. It is not known if he managed to free himself, or if he was aided. If necessary, the Wizards' Guild will discover which. But in any case, there is a standing reward of three thousand pieces of gold for the capture of the one or ones responsible, if any."

"Dead or alive?" someone called out.

"Alive. Two hundred fifty for the body or bodies, with proof." The elf pursed his lips together. "We want the culprit for a Coliseum execution. Now, as to the rules of this competition: This will be a single-elimination event, and will begin just as soon as the axe-and-hammer contest is over. You can choose your weapons just as soon as I finish; we have a broad selection; there is no reason to push. Two critical hits constitute a win, and there will be *no* arguments as to whether a blow on a non-sword arm is a critical hit: It is *not*. Decisions of the judges will be just short of final. Any dispute of the judges' decisions will be settled by bowmen in the stands, at the judges' discretion." He smiled thinly. "And that *will* be final. Are there any questions? If not, then let—"

"Wait!" A new voice called out. "Who won the bows? I had a bit of coin riding on it, and the damn armsmen say if I leave to find out, I can't get back in."

Khoralt sighed, examining a slip of parchment which he drew from his sleeve. "I will give you all the winners. Wrestling: Gronnee of the Endell Warrens. Crossbows: Edryncik, Pandathaway's Chief Man-at-Arms—" A ragged cheer went up. Clearly, a few of the swordsmen had bet on Edryncik as a local favorite. "And the axe-and-hammer is down to the last two: Wyhnnhyr of Aeryk, and a dwarf—umm, Ahira of the . . ." He paused to work out the next words. ". . . Len-kahn Tunnels. And no, I don't know where those are, either."

Karl smiled. Good. Ahira had made it to the finals, at least. And with a bit of luck . . .

The elf cocked his head to one side, considering the volume of the muted roar from the crowd outside. "From the level of noise, I would hazard a guess that the newcomer has won."

Karl sighed. *And now, the rest of it is up to me.* It was a long way to Bremon; getting there safely could depend on how well they were equipped. And that would depend on his winning the purse and the bets that Walter and Doria had placed on him by now.

The elf bowed quickly. "And now, it is time for you to select your weapons, and get out there. Good fortune to you all. Anyone who makes trouble gets an arrow through his liver."

Karl joined the ragged column shuffling toward the exit, stopping in his turn at the armory to turn in his sword and pick out one that was roughly the same size and heft.

Although, it *wasn't* a sword, not really: The weapon was made of wood, except for the wrought-iron crosspiece that served as a guard. But it hefted well; probably it was lead-filled. He fitted his fingers to the hilt and took a few cautious swings. The sword didn't balance too badly, but he was a bit nervous about the black tar that coated the "blade."

"Your first time in this nonsense?" The swordsman to his right let his own sword dangle, keeping it from touching his leg with an easy three-fingered grip.

Karl nodded. "Yes. This thing feels . . . adequate, I guess, but—"

The other, a short, stocky man with an easy, gap-toothed smile, interrupted him with a nod. "But you're worried about marking yourself with your own stick." He shook his head. "Don't worry about it, as long as you can keep from marking yourself before the first round; they send out slaves to rub the gunk off between rounds." He cocked his head to one side. "Are you willing to do me a favor?" he asked, as they stepped out of the tunnel, into the brightness of the Coliseum.

Karl sucked in air. He hadn't seen the Coliseum from the inside before, and it was a sight. Pandathaway's Coliseum was a huge curve, two gray stone arms reaching out toward the plains beyond the city, lined by rows and rows of cheering, shouting spectators in the stands. Near to the base of the curve, the cup of the Coliseum where the swordsmen stood, the stone of the Coliseum was dark, stained with age; beyond, toward the open mouth of the structure, the stones lightened, as though they were newer, added on.

And in the distance, the Aershtyl Mountains loomed, a massive backdrop that covered the horizon. From this distance, they seemed blue, wreathed with feathery clouds that clung to their peaks like cottony halos. The highest peaks were touched with snow, and glistening threads that twinkled on the mountainsides, combining into larger streams and rivers.

"Gives the actors one *hell* of a time," Karl's companion said.

Karl tore his eyes from the mountains. "What?"

A smile. "You *must* be new here—the Classics Festival just finished last month." He gestured at the plain, and the blue mountains beyond. "How would you like to play *Iranys* with that as your competition? It either breaks an actor, or pulls out the performance of his life."

"It would." Just a few weeks ago, just a few eons ago, Karl had been an acting student, paying less attention than he should have to memorizing his lines in *The Glass Menagerie*. But that was to be played on a proscenium stage; flats and lighting to aid the players. He shook his head. To act, to compete with that as a background, was a challenge that would frighten Alec Guinness.

"Now, how about that favor?"

Frowning at the smaller man's persistence, Karl turned back to him. "What favor?"

"Look, friend, this is your first time here; odds are, you're not going to make it past the first round." He jerked his chin toward the slaves raking the sands. "As soon as they finish, we have to square off —for the first round, it's pick-your-opponent. You have any objection to taking me on? I could use an easy first round."

Karl smiled. "I just might win, you know."

The other gave a slight shrug and a doubting grin. "I'll take my chances. Let's move out, now—I want to get a spot well away from the stands; sometimes they throw things."

Karl followed him out to a playing area near the center of the field. Like the fifty or so others, it was square, the corners marked by four iron poles. There would be two ways to lose a round, and any chance of advancing in the competition: either be hit by two blows that the judges deemed critical, or leave during play the five-yard-square area marked by the poles.

As the other swordsmen settled into their places, sound in the playing areas died down, except for bitter grumbling from several swordsmen, unhappy that they had not snagged weaker opponents.

Karl put that out of his mind, trying as well to tune out the increasingly loud roar of the crowd. He had to win; there was too much riding on it to let himself be distracted.

And if he was going to win the event, he would need to conserve his energy for the later rounds. He hadn't counted the contestants, but it was vanishingly unlikely that their number was exactly a power of two—and that meant that some would be awarded byes, now or in the later rounds. Likely the byes would go to contestants with winning records; in order to be ready for the last rounds, Karl would have to win the early ones quickly and easily so that he wouldn't be winded in the later ones.

From behind him and to his left, Khoralt's voice boomed, *"Prepare to fight!"*

Karl gripped his sword carefully.

And then, *"Fight!"*

Karl's opponent moved in cautiously, his sword weaving, ready to block or strike. The smaller man lunged—

Karl dropped flat on his back, his right foot kicking up toward the other's hands. The sole of his sandal connected with his opponent's wrists; Karl was rewarded by a cry of pain and the sight of the other's sword flipping end over end out of their playing area.

As he bounced to his feet, Karl's own sword lashed out, drawing a big, black X across the front of his opponent's tunic.

The other sighed, raising his hands in mock surrender. "Damn *me!*" He shook his head. "Not as clumsy as you look, big man—that should teach me to try and take advantage of a tyro." As Karl accepted his extended hand, he brightened. "Although, now that I'm out of it, I might put down a coin or two on you. Think you can make it to the final round?"

Karl shrugged. "I think I might manage to do that."

"It gets harder from here on, you know." He walked away.

Karl counted the remaining contestants, as the losers walked off the field. Sixty-two were left. One of the judges beckoned to Ohlmin and a beetle-browed dwarf, giving them byes, as Karl squared off with his assigned opponent, a tall elf, almost half again Karl's height. He was light-skinned and blond, almost an albino. But not nearly as frail as he appeared; it took several tiring minutes of sparring for Karl to work his way inside the other's guard and smack the sword out of his opponent's hands.

Thirty-two left. Karl was paired off with the dwarf who had been given a bye the previous round. The dwarf fought with a sword longer than Karl's, and with physical strength much greater. Fortunately, he was just a bit slower, and a sucker for a false opening.

Karl came out of that match limping. Before he'd been able to mark the dwarf twice, the little bastard had connected with a wicked slash to Karl's right knee.

Sixteen left. Karl favored his injured knee as he limped over to the playing area a judge indicated. This time, his opponent was a human, a long-haired, smooth-shaven man who fought in a bizarre two-swords style. It took a bit of time for Karl to weave his sword in between the long slashing sword and the short parrying one—and it cost him another blow to his knee.

He ended that round with a stroke to the other's temple; the man dropped as though he had been a puppet, his strings slashed.

As the harried slaves ran out to daub the remaining contestants off, Karl forced himself to breathe slowly, shallowly. With a bit of luck, he would have three rounds left—and that goddamn Ohlmin hadn't even worked up a sweat. Karl snatched the slave's rag, wiping the dripping sweat from his forehead. He set his sword down for a moment and rubbed at his swollen knee. It would support his weight, but just barely.

Eight contestants left. His opponent was a hulking creature, seemingly a dwarf-human hybrid: He had the heavy brows, huge jaw, and oversize joints of a dwarf, but he stood almost six feet tall, grinning with yellowed teeth as he raised his sword in a mocking salute.

Too tired. I'm just too tired. At the command to begin, Karl swept up sand with his bad leg; his opponent ducked under the spray—

—right into Karl's stroke. The blow to the hybrid's jaw knocked him out of the playing area, out of consciousness, and out of the competition.

Four. Facing an elf, Karl staggered under a preemptive slash, then barely connected with a backhanded stroke that had been aimed at the elf's midsection, but connected with his throat. Gasping for breath, the elf stumbled into a pole, and then into Karl's winning stroke.

Karl turned to see Ohlmin grinning at him, from a playing area only a few yards away. "Nicely done," Ohlmin called out. "But you're up against me, now. Care to concede, or don't you believe in accepting fate?"

Easy—he's just trying to bait you, to get you angry. Possibly that was how the smaller man had won all of his matches without working up a sweat? He certainly didn't look sturdy enough to wear his opponents down. Could he be that good? "No," Karl said, forcing himself not to pant. He drew himself up straight, not moving from his spot. No need to show Ohlmin how badly he'd limp. "Why don't you come over here and persuade me, *little man?*"

A slave ran up with a dirty cloth; Karl snatched it to scrub at his knee, making sure that he rubbed more of the oily tar on it. Best to try to hide from Ohlmin just how much the battered joint was swelling.

Karl dropped the rag to the sand. "I don't see you moving. Maybe you're not so good with that stick after all."

Anger creased the other's dark face for a moment. "I wouldn't, if I were you." Superior smile back in place, Ohlmin walked over to Karl's playing area, taking up a position at the far corner of the square.

"Wouldn't what?" Karl moved back a step, wincing at the pain shooting through his leg. As it kept swelling, the pain got worse. *Damn.*

"Wouldn't make it personal." Ohlmin's face grew somber; he shook his head slowly. "The last one to make it a personal thing, well, he's chained to a mill in Sciforth." He pinched his nostrils with the fingers of his free hand. "By the nose." Ohlmin dropped his hand and smiled. "After I beat him on the field." He stretched out his tar-covered wooden sword, the point almost touching Karl's chest. "So don't make it personal."

Karl pushed the point away with his own sword. "Just—"

Ohlmin slashed at Karl's right knee. Fiery pain shot through it, and Karl's leg buckled beneath him. He fell to the sand.

"Foul!" Khoralt shouted, running up. "That is a foul!"

Ohlmin eyed him slyly, while Karl struggled back to his feet, his knee burning as though it were on fire.

"My apologies." Ohlmin gave a quick bow. "I thought I had heard your command to begin."

Khoralt hesitated for a moment, then shook his head and pointed toward the exit. The crowd responded with a wave of hissing and shouting. The elf crossed his arms across his chest. "As I was about to say"—he gave Karl a sheepish half-smile, probably the only apology Karl would get—"I am tempted to disqualify you. But that would be too harsh, since you made only a simple mistake," he added quickly. "Instead, your penalty will be that it will take three hits for you to win, Ohlmin; your opponent will need but the usual two."

Karl opened his mouth to protest, then shut it. It wouldn't do any good. The crowd wanted to see the final match, and the elf wasn't going to deny the crowd. *So let's try to buy a bit of time, give my knee a chance to stop throbbing.* "I'll need a little time, to wipe this mark off."

Khoralt shook his head sadly. "No, we must let the match go on. We will remember that there is a false mark on your leggings." He backed out of the square. "Prepare to fight."

Karl flexed his knee. If he didn't put too much weight on it, it would support him. Probably.

"And . . . *fight!*"

Ohlmin smiled, and moved in.

In the first few seconds of the match, Karl saw that he was hopelessly outclassed—and would have been even if his knee weren't swollen. Ohlmin's weaving sword deflected Karl's swings effortlessly, and forced him back, back—if Karl hadn't backed into one of the poles marking the playing area, he would have stumbled out of the square.

The tip of Ohlmin's sword slithered in and drew a light line across Karl's chest; Karl batted the sword out of the way, slashed—

Stepping back, Ohlmin parried easily. "Try again, big man." He spat. "I have time."

Khoralt called out: "One point for Ohlmin, none for the challenger. Both require two to win."

Ohlmin paused for a moment. Karl lunged; Ohlmin dodged to one side.

I can't beat him. I'm good with a sword, but he's faster and better. But damned *if I'm going to let him walk all over me.*

Ohlmin moved in. "Give up. You're not good enough; nobody is." He launched an attack that brought the two of them together, *corps-à-corps.* Karl tried to push him back, but the smaller man was stronger than he looked.

With a sneer, Ohlmin spat in Karl's face, then whirled away. "I'd be more frightened of a novice than I am of you. A novice might get in a lucky shot," he sneered. "You won't."

"Shut up and fight." Although the other was right; a novice might throw his sword or something, or accidentally bounce Ohlmin out of the—

Got it! Karl threw his sword at the smaller man, flipping it end over end.

Ohlmin stepped smoothly to one side. The sword bounced off a pole and out of the playing area. "And that is—"

Karl lunged at him barehanded, receiving a wicked slash to the temple before he was able to fasten his left hand on Ohlmin's sword arm, just at the wrist.

Karl *squeezed.* Ohlmin screamed.

Bones crackled beneath his palm; Karl seized the front of Ohlmin's tunic with his free hand and lifted him off the ground, and—

"—*two points for Ohlmin, none*—"

—wobbling on his good leg, Karl raised the twitching form of the other man above his head and threw him as far as he could, out of the playing area. Ohlmin landed with a thump and a strangled moan.

Khoralt smiled at Karl. *"Ohlmin is disqualified, for leaving the playing area. The winner of the swords competition is—*what *is* your name?"

Karl stood up straight. "My name is Cullinane. Karl Cullinane."

"The winner of the swords competition is Karl Cullinane." The elf leaned over. "And if you want some advice, Karl Cullinane, I would suggest you get yourself and your winnings out of Pandathaway."

Karl smiled. "Just what I had in mind."

Whistling to himself, Ahira bounded up the stairs to their suite in the Inn of Quiet Repose, his battleaxe strapped to his chest, and a leather sack well weighted down with gold slung over his shoulder. Between his winnings, Karl's winnings, and what Doria and Hakim would have from having bet on them, it wouldn't be a problem to equip themselves right. And with a bit of luck, the others would soon be through the Gate, and home.

As he pushed through the curtains and into the common room of the suite, he saw Hakim, Aristobulus, and Doria sitting on the rug, coins, jewels, and finger-size bars of gold bullion scattered in front of them.

"Where are the other two?"

Hakim shrugged, a strangely sheepish smile creasing his face. "Karl hasn't gotten back yet, and Andrea's still in the Library, working on her spell." He looked from the wizard to the cleric, then shook his head.

Aristobulus nodded; Doria frowned, then snorted.

What was this? From the looks passing between the three, it seemed as though they were sharing some private joke. "Want to let me in on it?"

Aristobulus considered it for a moment. "I might as well. I didn't go into this last night; I wanted to recheck my calculations first." He pursed his lips, rubbing withered fingers against his temples. "Unless I'm sadly mistaken, the Gate Between Worlds won't work quite the way Deighton thought—*thinks* it does."

"It's not going to get us home?" Ahira almost staggered. *You mean that all this has been for nothing?*

"No, no—not that. It's just that magic doesn't work the same way in . . . our native universe. A Gate on this side won't create a . . . doorway between worlds, but more of a trapdoor. We can go through —belongingness will bring us back there—but we can't get back here through it."

For Ahira, that was no problem. He flexed his shoulders and tensed his thigh muscles—going back to being James Michael Finnegan was something that had no appeal, be it permanent or temporary.

But for the wizard, it was different. And if Aristobulus couldn't get back, he wouldn't go to the Gate—no, better: If Aristobulus didn't *think* that he could get back to this side, *with* spell books, he wouldn't go.

"I wouldn't worry about it," Ahira said, unfastening his axe, then seating himself with the other three. He cupped a pile of gemstones in his hands, then let the rubies, opals, and round-cut diamonds trickle through his fingers and bounce on the rug.

Responsibilities, responsibilities—we never would have translated across, if it weren't for me. None of the others wanted it as badly. Not even Aristobulus. I've got to get Hakim, Karl, Doria, and Andrea home. "Deighton sent us all across once; I'm sure we can persuade him to do the same for you. With spell books."

"Persuade? Even though it won't help him any? I don't remember you having so *persuasive* a manner about you, back on the other side." The wizard snorted. "And you hardly had the physique—"

"I have," Hakim said. "Maybe I'm not quite as strong back home as Karl is here, but . . ."

"You'll help?" The wizard looked hopefully at Hakim.

"I promise." The thief smiled. "If he doesn't send you back—fully equipped—then I'll break a finger at a time until he does. And in the meantime, you'll keep your mouth shut in front of K—"

"*What* is going on?" Ahira spread his hands. "I thought you two had settled that, back on the *Pride.*"

"Not that." Hakim picked up a diamond that was almost the size of his eye, and held it up to the light. "This one has a small flaw, dammit." He dropped it, and smiled. "But we still have enough, what with yours and Karl's winnings, and—"

"And your winnings, betting on us—we should be able to outfit ourselves more than well enough. Matter of fact, I want the two of you to take some of this gold, go out, and pick up all the healing draughts you can. We just may—"

"Not quite *winnings,*" Doria interrupted, holding up three gold bars and a small leather sack. "This is what we won by betting on you. We got good odds—it averaged out to be about eighty to one."

"And the rest from betting on Karl? What were they, a hundred to one?"

"*Two* hundred." Hakim shook his head. "Everybody thought that Ohlmin was such a sure winner that you couldn't even bet on him— the little bugger's won every single time he's entered. So . . ."

"So?"

"*So I didn't bet on Karl.* I thought it'd be just throwing money away, dammit." Hakim threw up his hands. "And you saw what he had to go through to win that competition—he was sweating, and limping, and—"

"So how did you?—you *didn't.*"

Hakim smiled sheepishly. "Actually, I did. I spent most of the morning and a good part of the afternoon picking pockets. Lots of money in Pandathaway."

Ahira sighed. If Karl found out that he'd worked that hard to win, but the others hadn't had enough faith in him to bet on him at those odds . . . "He'll break your neck."

"Only if one of you tells."

"We won't. But if it happens to slip out . . ."

Hakim nodded. "I'd better work on my sprinting."

Ahira shook his head. "No, make that long-distance running." He stood. "Well, let's get to it—I want us to outfit ourselves and be out of Pandathaway by sundown. Doria—you, Hakim, and I are going shopping; Ari, you wait here for the other two."

Out of Pandathaway by sundown—that had a nice ring to it. Then up the road through the Aershtyl Mountains, pass through Aeryk, skirt the edge of the Waste to Bremon.

And the Gate. And no more responsibilities for the rest. No more worries about the others getting themselves killed.

He sighed.

Hakim nodded knowingly. "It's hard on you, isn't it, m'friend?"

"At best."

PART FOUR

Bremon

CHAPTER TWELVE

The Waste of Elrood

A heap of broken images, where the sun beats,
And the dead tree gives no shelter, the cricket no relief,
And the dry stone no water. Only
There is shadow under this red rock,
(Come in under the shadow of this red rock),
And I will show you something different from either
Your shadow at morning striding behind you
Or your shadow at evening rising to meet you;
I will show you fear in a handful of dust.

—T.S. Eliot

Ahira called a halt at midmorning, easing himself painfully out of his fore-and-aft peaked saddle, then turning the horses and his pony loose under a spreading elm. He squatted on the ground, rubbing at his aching thighs. *Someday, I'd like to get my hands on whoever invented the horse. For five minutes, that's all. Just five minutes.*

"Ahira?" Hakim called out, from his perch on the bench of the flatbed wagon. "You want me to turn these critters loose, too?" He jerked his thumb at the two scraggly mules hitched to the wagon.

Ahira shook his head. "No. I'm tired enough of fighting them back into harness every morning. Set the brake, twist on the hobbles, and slip their bits—you can feed and water them where they are."

Climbing down from his gray mare's saddle, Aristobulus shook his head. "You wouldn't have so much trouble with them," he said, "if we had decent harnesses. Those stupid straps half-choke—"

"Enough." Ahira waved the wizard to silence. Granted, the strap harnesses they had bought in Pandathaway weren't nearly as good as even medieval horsecollars. Given, under Ari's direction—or, more accurately, Lou Riccetti's direction—putting together an efficient horsecollar with a trivial feat of design and engineering, but—

—*But do I have to put up with his constant whining about it?* "No," he said, "we're not going to turn the mules loose. They might run off again, and we don't want to waste the time chasing after them." Maybe Hakim got along well with the two snorting creatures—Ahira chuckled; even *mules* got along with him—but there was no sense in taking chances.

Not when you didn't have to. Take the caravan behind them, for example. In the twenty days it had taken them to get from Pandathaway to Aeryk, and the week since they had stopped overnight in Aeryk to finish outfitting themselves and stock up on food and water, the caravan hadn't been more than a couple of days behind; Ahira could see them moving, even at night.

They could be reasonable people; quite possibly it would be in both parties' interests to travel together as long as they were headed in the same direction. But—

Ahira sighed, seating himself on a gnarled root. He propped his back against the tree's rough bark. —But that was only probably, only possibly. Best not to take chances. Best to keep a distance.

Andrea walked over and stretched out on her side on the ankle-high grass. "Nice." She unslung a small waterbag, took a sip, then offered it to Ahira. "I don't guess that it'll be this easy from here on in."

He took a sip and recorked the bag. "Thanks." He gestured at the long slope below them. Perhaps ten miles away, the lush grassland gave way to the Waste, the line of demarcation between dark, water-rich greenery and brown, sun-baked earth as sharp as a knife. Why hadn't the Waste claimed part of the grassland, or vice versa? Or had it—no, that couldn't be: The boundary between Waste and grass curved smoothly away in the distance; a curve as even as that had to be artificial, not natural. It could be involved with the aftereffects of the wizards' battle that had created the Waste of Elrood, but—

—*but there's no way of knowing. And it really doesn't matter.*

"No, it probably won't be this easy." He handed her the waterbag.

"And we'd better start going easy on this; I'm a bit nervous about the water supply."

Her brow wrinkled. "But we bought the two extra barrels in Aeryk. That should be enough, even at the rate Karl and the horses swill it, no?"

He gave her a nod. "It *should* be. But should isn't always enough." Ahira chuckled, dismissing the subject with a wave of his hand. "Don't pay any attention; I'm just getting cynical." For the thousandth time, he took a mental inventory of their supplies. Twelve healing draughts, sealed in gray metal bottles. Karl had wanted to use one, back in Pandathaway, to fix his sprained knee. But Ahira had overruled him; best to save the potions for emergencies, and rely on natural healing whenever possible. A sprain wasn't like a cut; it couldn't be a path for infection.

There was a score of white woolen blankets, along with the makings of an iron framework, so that they could rig a canopy over the bed of the wagon for travel in the heat of the Waste. The blankets would keep them cool during the day, and warm at night.

And then the food: dried meat and fruit, sweets for variety and quick energy, oats for the animals, a head-sized cube of gritty salt—plenty, surely, for both people and animals. No problems there.

Miscellany: a sewing kit, seven oil lanterns with twenty forearm-sized flasks of evil-smelling green oil, a flint-and-steel kit for every member of the party. A spare crossbow, with a lighter pull than Ahira's; fourscore extra quarrels for that—if Ahira didn't need it, Hakim could handle it without much difficulty. And without much accuracy, for that matter.

And then there was the one magical implement he'd bought: a clump of dragonbane, packed carefully in a soft leather pouch. If they couldn't sneak by The Dragon, perhaps the creature's allergy to the mossy stuff would give them time enough to use the Gate.

What else? Spare knives for everyone; several hundred yards of deceptively light rope—a knife could barely cut it; a few pounds of charcoal cubes, just in case they needed a fire when there was no wood available; hammers and spikes to use as pitons, if necessary. And thinking of wood . . . he raised his head. "Karl, Hakim—we're a bit short of firewood, and we're not going to find any in the Waste. Go cut some."

Hakim nodded, getting slowly to his feet; Karl stood quickly and spun around to face Ahira.

"What do we need more wood for?" There was only a trace of challenge in his tone.

Ahira cursed himself silently. Karl wouldn't have raised any objection if Andrea hadn't been nearby. Something had to be done about the relationship—whatever it was—between those two.

But now wasn't the time. Ahira forced a smile and started to raise himself painfully to his feet. "Fine—if you don't think we need it, I'll cut it myself." He unstrapped his axe and propped it carefully against the root he'd just vacated. The battleaxe was a weapon, not a tool. "Who saw where the woodaxe is?"

Doria trotted over, her robes flapping. "Some problem?"

Ahira shrugged. "It's nothing—don't worry about it."

Karl looked sheepish as he raised his palms, shaking his head. "I'm sorry. My fault—I forgot that you and your pony don't get along. I'll cut the wood." He retrieved the woodaxe from the bed of the wagon and followed Hakim out into the woods, away from the road.

Ahira rubbed gently at his thighs. Nice of Karl to remind him. Dammit, dwarves weren't built for riding horses, and that alleged pony was a dappled demon, camouflaged. Just barely camouflaged.

On the other hand, Cullinane had been getting more considerate, ever since that first day in Pandathaway. *Which reminds me—* "Doria, why don't you and Aristobulus take a waterbag and go see if there's a spring around here. You do the walking through the brush, and let him—"

Doria's brow furrowed. "I doubt that there's a spring. And why me?"

Because I think I'd better have a private talk with Andrea, and this is a convenient excuse to get you out of the way for a minute, and do I have to be argued with about every damn thing? No, he sighed, that wouldn't do. "Because of your robes." He picked up a pebble and fingerflicked it at her sleeve; it bounced off as though it had struck a solid wall. "We don't have to worry about you getting scratched by brush."

She gave him a nod and a half-shrug, then walked away.

Ahira turned back to Andrea.

She smiled knowingly, brushing hair away from her face. "Alone at last, eh? Although"—she reached out and patted him on the shoulder—"I think you're a touch too short for me. No offense."

The way she put it, it was impossible to be offended. "None taken. But that's not what I wanted to talk to you about." He hesitated.

The personal relations among the group really weren't any of his concern, not unless they affected their chances of surviving, of reaching the Gate.

Then again, anything could affect their chances. "What's the problem between you and Karl? *He* isn't too short for you, is he?"

She gave him a clearly *pro forma* grin. "No."

"Well, you don't blame him for our being here, do you? If wanting this has anything to do with that transfer's working, it's my fault, not Karl's." To Cullinane, it had always been a game, no more. And from the way Karl's demeanor kept improving, as they got closer to Bremon, it was likely he'd be happier when it was just a game once again.

"No." She looked away. "I'm not that stupid."

Ahira snorted. "You're not stupid at all. You've been treating him like a leper. I'm sure you've got your reasons; I'd like to know what they are." *Andrea, I don't care who you sleep with, or who you don't sleep with. But Cullinane's all bent out of shape over you, and that could blunt him as a warrior. I want him thinking about our survival, not about you.* "Maybe there's something I could do?"

"No." She shook her head slowly. "There's not a whole lot that can be done about it." Her fingers grasped the air clumsily. "He's kind of . . . I don't know—how well did you know him, back on the other side?"

"Not all that well. I don't think I saw him more than three, four times outside of the games." Ahira smiled. "And we didn't take any of the same classes—I don't think Karl's gotten around to majoring in computer sciences, yet."

"Not yet." She sighed. "But give him time. He keeps getting involved in different things."

"A dilettante. Can't stick to one interest."

"No. Well, yes, but it's more than that. He's . . . sort of a monomaniac, gets completely, *intensely* into whatever he's interested in. . . ." She rubbed at her temples with stiffened fingers. "And he kind of extracts whatever he got into it for, then drops it and goes on to something else." She let her hands drop into her lap, then raised her eyes to meet his. "I know I'm not expressing myself well, but do you understand?"

"It sounds like you're scared of being, err, seduced and abandoned. No?"

"I knew I wasn't explaining it well—it's not like that at all." Her pursed lips spread into a broad, self-assured smile. "Do you think

I'm the sort of woman who gets seduced and abandoned, Ahira?"
Extending a finger, she waved it under his nose. "Do you?"
Her tone was light and playful, but he sensed a serious undercurrent. "No, I don't. I think you can handle any sort of relationship,
whether it's whatever you've got going with Hakim or"—he chuckled—"something a bit more distant with a neurotic dwarf."
She laughed. "Thank you. But you and Walter aren't the problem.
It's Karl and his goddam—"
"*Ahira!*" Doria ran toward them, her robes flapping, breathlessly
waving a dripping scrap of cloth, and—
Dripping? He jumped to his feet. "What is tha—"
"We found it!" She stopped in front of him, taking a few moments
to catch her breath. "Aristobulus and I—we found the spring, back
in the brush." She shook her head. "It's amazing—it just burbles out
of a crack in the rock, and then drains back into another one. We
couldn't even see it until we were practically on top of it. How in the
world did you know that there'd be one?"
Andrea hid a chuckle behind her hand. Sending Doria and Aristobulus off to find a spring had been a distraction.
Ahira looked at her and shrugged. "Serendipity, Doria." Well,
there'd be a chance to try to straighten out Andrea later. "Simple
serendipity."
"What?"
"It's when you dig for worms, and strike gold." He raised his
voice. "Hakim, Karl—they found a spring. It's water this morning,
soup for lunch, and baths for dessert." No need to worry about the
water supply, not anymore. With seven full barrels, all people and
animals well watered, the week-long trek across the Waste should be
easy.
Well, relatively easy.
Doria shook his head. "I don't understand."
"Don't worry about it." He looked at Andrea, spreading his hands
as though to say that they'd finish the discussion later, when they
again had a little privacy; she nodded. Ahira turned back to Doria
and pulled a trick from Hakim's repertoire: He breathed on his fingernails and buffed them lightly across his chest. "Sometimes I'm so
clever I don't even understand myself."

Karl and his horse were the first to reach the Waste; Ahira had let
him range ahead a bit, and he liked that. He was relaxed, even comfortable on his large, reddish-brown mare; the fore-and-aft peaked

saddle supported him well. But it wasn't just the saddle. Karl was taking full advantage of having his Barak persona to draw on: His thigh muscles held him firmly to the seat, his hips shifted automatically to keep him firmly astride, instead of bouncing on his tailbone, the way that the rest had been for most of the trip, until they gradually learned how to ride.

Except for Walter, of course. Karl turned to give a nod to the thief, who was basking comfortably in the late-afternoon sun on the blankets he had used to pad the cart's seat, guiding the mules with only an occasional twitch of his lazy fingers. Probably some of Walter's avowed affection for the mules was honest; certainly he'd staked out the cart at least partly from concern for his own tender buttocks, leaving his swayback gelding hitched behind with little to no regret. "Enjoying the ride?"

Walter responded with a nod and a wink. No, no doubt about it at all.

Aristobulus' whine drifted forward. Complaining, as usual. Karl urged his mare farther forward. A good horse; she needed only a touch of his heels to break into a canter, and then a light flick on the reins to slow her back down to a walk.

He stroked her reddish-brown neck, solid and dry under his palm. "Good girl—you don't even mind hauling my weight, do you?" She raised her head a bit higher, and snorted.

Ahead the Waste of Elrood stretched out across the horizon; a flat brown ocean of sunbaked mud, random cracks in the hard surface covering as if it were a fine netting that had been woven by a mad giant.

Ahira's voice boomed from behind him. "Karl—wait a moment." Shrugging, Karl let the dwarf, bouncing on the back of his little pony, catch up. "Problem?"

Ahira shook his head. "No, I need some advice. The rest of these . . . animals seem to be kind of spooked by the terrain. Do you think we ought to walk them a while? Maybe that way they can get used to it?"

Karl turned to look behind. The others' horses were twitchy, all right; what with the snorting and skittish steps they were taking, it could easily tire the animals out much sooner than it should.

"I don't think so," he said. "Look at them. Hell, look at you. You're the worst."

The dwarf scowled. "What about me?"

"The purpose of riding isn't to keep as much air as possible between your backside and your saddle, you know—the reason you have to spend so much time walking your pony is that you don't have the slightest idea of how to ride him. Same for the rest, although they're not as bad."

Aristobulus' mount stepped to one side to avoid a rut; as usual, the wizard tried to overcontrol the little mare, frustrating the horse almost as much as himself.

Ahira's right hand slipped to the hilt of his axe. That was probably unconscious; Karl resisted the urge to loosen his sword from its saddle-bound scabbard. *Easy, you're among friends.*

"Dammit, Karl, have a bit of sympathy. How long did it take you to learn how to ride?"

Karl shrugged. "I just seemed to pick it up."

"Came with the territory, right? Sort of like Hakim's ability to move silently and—and my darksight, no?"

"So?"

The dwarf threw up his hands, startling his pony. "Easy, you damned little—easy, I said. *So,* it didn't come naturally to me. Or Andrea, Hakim, Doria, or Ari. Don't put on airs because you ride better than we can; it's just a lucky break. For you. It's not a virtue." Ahira reached behind himself, rubbing vigorously.

"Don't."

"Don't *what?*"

Karl sighed. "Don't twitch in the saddle like that. Your pony doesn't know what you're doing, and he doesn't like it."

Ahira opened his mouth as though to say something to the effect that he really couldn't care less what his animal liked or didn't, then shrugged. "You still didn't answer my question."

Karl thought it over for a moment. At least Ahira's idea would give the riders some time off their mounts, give them a chance to work out some stiffness. "Actually, I've got a better idea."

Ahira's mouth quirked. "Let me guess: We get the critters used to the different surface by galloping them for a few miles, right?"

"Wrong. A horse isn't an automobile; you can kill it if you push it too hard. No, how about this? We pitch camp here until dark, then travel at night. At least for tonight—we can pitch those blankets as tarps, keep the sun off. I know you don't think that water's a problem anymore, but we might as well save all we can. And this way the horses, at least the ones who need it"—he patted his mare's neck—"can take some time to get used to this surface, just by standing around on it."

"Done!" The dwarf jerked his pony to a halt and bounced to the ground. "Everybody, time for a break."

Andrea slumped in the saddle. "Thank goodness."

"About time." Aristobulus slid off his horse.

"Fine with me." Doria levered herself out of her saddle and dropped lightly to the ground.

Walter reined in the mules, shrugging. "I don't see what the problem is. But I'm easy." He tied the reins to the back of his seat and vaulted to the sunbaked earth. "What's the plan? We've got another couple of hours until sundown—shouldn't we get some traveling done?"

Now free of his pony and any necessity of following Karl's advice not to spook the animal, Ahira rubbed viciously at the base of his spine as though trying to scour the pain away. "This surface is so flat that it won't be dangerous to travel at night. So that's what we'll do, at least for tonight. We'll pitch the tarps for shade, catch some sleep, then start up again around midnight, when the ground's cooled off enough."

Doria nodded. "You're still worried about the water."

"Not worried. Just cautious." Ahira stretched broadly. "Once we hit the far side of the Waste, I want to have as much left as possible. We don't know how deep in Bremon the Gate is, and we may need all we can carry."

Karl nodded. A good point, and one he hadn't thought of. Then again, knowing how to deal with tunnels probably came naturally to the dwarf in the same way that riding came easily to Karl.

Ahira pulled the thin white blankets out of the back of the wagon. "Hakim and I can pitch these as puptents. Do we have any volunteers for first watch?"

Andrea smiled. "You sure do." She walked over to Karl and tapped him on the chest with an extended finger. "I think Karl's had an easy enough time in the saddle; time to put him to work."

The dwarf nodded. "Fine. The *two* of you are on watch until it's been dark for at least a couple of hours. Walter and Ari replace you then."

"Now wait a minute—" she started.

"The two of you."

Karl's forehead wrinkled, almost painfully. Now that was strange. Ahira *had* been keeping Andrea and him away from each other. Which made sense. But—*never mind. If I understood people, I'd have stayed in psych.*

He cast an eye at the setting sun. Well, he'd already put up with worse than a few hours of stony silence.

Andrea stared out at the Waste of Elrood. By starlight, it reminded her of the pictures the Apollo astronauts had brought back from the moon, the ones from the Mare what's-its-name, the Sea of something-or-other.

She sighed. *I was supposed to have that quiz the morning after that night at the Student Union, and that probably would have been on it.*

Stars twinkled over a scarred wasteland. Just flat, cracked ground, gray in the dark. The sorcerers who fought here must have been very powerful, and more than a bit mad; what sane person would want to turn greenery into *this?*

She turned around to look at the others. Under the bed of the wagon, Walter snored quietly. She couldn't make out his features, but she knew that his broad face would be creased with a light smile. *Still maintaining the image, eh?* The fight back in Lundeyll had scared him badly, but Walter Slovotsky wouldn't reveal that, not even in his sleep.

Doria curled next to him, tossing fitfully. *Look,* Andrea wanted to say, *I don't know what's gone on with you and Karl, but . . .*

But what? That was the problem.

Under their respective puptents, Aristobulus and Ahira slept quietly. There was something similar about the two of them. Maybe it was that they were both so one-directional. Ari just wanted to get some spell books, and this trip across the Waste seemed to him to be a way to do that. Period.

Ahira was different, though. He was just pushing to get them home. *Just the rest of us, James Michael Finnegan. And who do you think you're fooling?* The dwarf had never said so, but anyone could see that he was just along to get the rest of them through the Gate; once that was done, Ahira would turn and run. *You don't really expect any of us to believe that you're going back to being a cripple, do you?* Not when he could be healthy and strong here.

She nodded in admiration. Not for the first time. A sense of responsibility, that's what Ahira had. Ahira felt guilty about the rest of them being here. No, not guilt; she was right the first time. Responsible, that was it.

She turned back. Karl was still looking at her out of the corner of his eye, pretending to be ignoring her. Maybe that was for the best, at least for the time being.

At least, that's what I keep telling myself.

He got up from his seat on a stack of blankets and walked over. "Enough games, Andy. We've got to talk."

She jerked her chin at the plain. "Then let's move away a bit. No need to wake the others."

He smiled thinly as he followed her. "I wasn't planning on yelling and screaming. Were you?"

She shook her head. "Not really. I think this is far enough. Do you want to sit down?"

He snickered. "I'd better be sitting for this? Okay." They sat tailor-fashion on the cracked ground, Karl balancing his sword across his lap.

"Do you have to have that with you? I don't think anyone's going to steal it, out in the middle of nowhere."

He shrugged, and pulled the blade a few inches from the scabbard. "It's a fine piece of steel, isn't it?" Silvery metal gleamed wickedly in the starlight. "And I've got this habit of losing things. I guess I'm afraid that if I ever let it out of my hands, that'll be the end of it." He slipped the blade back. "But you're changing the subject. Deliberately?"

"I'm not sure. Do I have to be?"

"No. I don't make the rules. Sometimes I don't even know what they are."

She bit her lower lip. "As in what the rules for you and me are."

He nodded, looking her square in the eyes. "Exactly. If I didn't know better I'd swear you're trying to get me to hate you, or at least dislike you one hell of a lot. And I'd kind of like to know why that's a stupid idea of mine." He shrugged. "I am stupid sometimes. Ignorant, too. I have it on good authority."

"Doria?"

"Not quite." He folded his fingers behind his head and stretched back. "I have bad breath or something?"

There was a lot different about Karl now, beyond the physical changes. *We could have had almost exactly this conversation a few months ago, and Karl would have been trembling inside that I'd turn him down. He isn't anymore.*

"Did anyone ever tell you you're always too goddam intense about everything?" The violence of her own words surprised her. "About whatever you happen to be majoring in at the moment, about whatever diversion you're into, about—"

"About you?" He chuckled thinly. "Is this going to be another episode of Slovotsky's Laws?"

"What?"

Karl shook his head, his eyes closed tightly. "One of Walter's ideas about life. It runs something like: 'Whatever you want too much, you can't have, so when you *really* want something, try to want it a little less.' Is that what this is all about?"

"No. It's not that. It's just that I'm not sure I'm ready for all that intensity about *me.*" She reached out to take his hand; he pulled it back. "Can you understand that? It's not that I don't like you, it's not that I'm not attracted to you—"

"Now, that is." He raised an arm and flexed his biceps. "What with the new, improved body, and all." Karl lowered his arm. "Which is one thing I'm going to be sorry to give up, once we get back."

"You're going to be sorry to get back?"

"Don't be silly," he sneered. "I like the good things in life. Bathing regularly, television, dentistry, not having a price on my head. Stuff like that. And you're changing the subject again. Which suggests that once we get back, and I'm short, skinny Karl Cullinane again—"

"Shut *up.*" Sometimes he made her *so* mad. "It isn't that at all. Women aren't as shallow as men."

"Thank you, Betty Friedan."

"It's just that you're incapable of keeping things . . . casual. No, that's not the word. What I'm trying to say is—"

Fear touched the back of her neck. Ignoring her natural reflexes, she closed her eyes. Her aura wrapped her thinly; it was easy to see Aristobulus' glowing strongly, a few hundred feet away, blazing in the night like a red beacon.

But there was something else, too. Not quite distinct enough to see with her inner vision, but there. "Karl." She opened her eyes. He was shaking his head, as though to wake up, his eyelids sagging shut, despite himself.

"Andy, I—" He slumped over.

Invisible fingers wrapped themselves around her throat, cutting off her air. She tried to pry them away, but they were like steel bands.

"Don't let go of her, Ohlmin," a harsh voice whispered. "Not until she's safely gagged."

"And then," another voice answered, "we can enjoy ourselves."

She opened her mouth to scream, but a cottony softness filled it. A rough hand clutched at her breasts. She struggled uselessly.

"I want this one first. There's still a lot of fight left in her."

Karl awoke slowly. And that bothered him, even in his half-awake, just-a-few-more-minutes-*please* state. He brought his hand down to wipe at his eyes.

His hand stopped short; his wrist was tangled up with something cold and hard.

Wait a minute! I was just talking to Andy—I never woke Walter. His eyes snapped open. "What the hell—"

A small fist came out of nowhere and struck him on the cheekbone. Pain lanced through his skull. He brought his hands down in a practiced—

—his wrists jerked in their iron cuffs, fastened in heavy chains to something over his head and behind him.

"I told you that nobody ever beats me," Ohlmin rasped. "Ever."

Karl shook his head, trying to clear it. Slowly, his eyes focused, becoming accustomed to the gloom. Hakim and Ahira sat beside him on the narrow bench of the small room, both still unconscious, both chained at wrists and ankles.

And in front of him, leaning over him close enough so that Karl could smell the reek of garlic and wine on his breath, Ohlmin stood, smirking.

"Sleep spells are handy things, no?" He slapped Karl lightly on the cheek. "Even if the wizards are resistant to them." Ohlmin smiled. "But spells of invisibility can fool their eyes, too."

"What are you—" A boot drove into his belly; Karl gasped for air.

"You speak when you are spoken to. Understood?" Ohlmin's voice was calm now, and somehow that was more frightening than his earlier rasp. "But I won't hurt you very much, Karl Cullinane. I've got to save you for Pandathaway. You're going to make me a rich man."

Karl tried to spit at him, but couldn't muster the breath to do it. Or the saliva, for that matter. His mouth was as dry as the Waste.

Stop reacting for a moment, and think. He fingered the chains. Slight ridges along the links proclaimed that they were cast iron, not forged. And that was good, possibly. If he had enough strength, if he had enough leverage, he could shatter them. Maybe. Cast iron was more brittle than forged. Just maybe . . .

His Barak-self didn't think much of that idea. *They're far too thick. But the wall behind you is wood. You may just be able to jerk them loose from the wall.*

"Feel free to continue thinking about escaping, Karl Cullinane." Ohlmin chuckled. "They always do. But"—he tapped at the wall— "the wagon is belted with iron straps, which is what the chains are bolted to."

Wagon? It wasn't a small room, then. They were in a wagon. No advantage there.

Better find some advantage, quickly. Ohlmin was close enough, just maybe. Karl lashed out with his right foot.

The cuff scraped his ankle as his foot was jerked to a halt, inches from Ohlmin's leg.

A chuckle. "We are professionals. And, just for your enlightenment, the rest of your party is well secured. Both of the wizards and the cleric are gagged. We may have to cut out the old man's tongue, eventually, but I'm sure we'll work out something else for the women. It would be a waste, wouldn't it?" He smiled, reached out, and patted Karl's head. Somehow that was more frightening than being struck. The light pat said that Karl was a harmless nothing, well secured. No danger at all.

Karl forced himself to keep his voice level. "Are you going to tell me how you found us, or are you trying to have me die of curiosity?"

Ohlmin laughed. "Ah, you did that very well. If I didn't know better, I'd think that you weren't terrified." He shrugged lightly. "But I don't see why not. The Guilds' Council finally prevailed on one of the grandmaster wizards to bring out his crystal ball, to find out who had stolen their dragon." Again, he patted Karl's head. "And you, my friend, are worth twenty-five hundred pieces of gold to me. My wizard—Blenryth; I don't think you've met him—is charging me quite a lot for those sleep and invisibility spells we caught you with, and quite a lot more for the one that kept us on your trail. But I'll still come out ahead." He spat in Karl's face. "I always come out ahead."

Karl couldn't quite reach his hand down to his face; the gob of spittle dripped slowly down his cheek.

Ohlmin sighed. "But enough of this. I had better get back to the women. The dark-haired one was quite good; I think I'll try the other. And besides, I'd better make certain that Hyrus doesn't damage them. Must keep them in shape for the block." He frowned. "No, one more thing." Ohlmin walked to the far corner of the wagon and rummaged through a pile of swords, knives, and crossbows.

Our weapons. And just about three yards farther than I can possibly reach. They might as well have been light-years away; it would take more than a sword to cut through the chains. He felt at the cuffs around his wrists. *Damn.* Even if Walter still had a lockpick on him, it wouldn't matter; the cuffs were riveted on.

Ohlmin extracted a long black scabbard from the pile. "I believe that this is your sword?" He slipped it out of the scabbard, examining the blade in the dim glow of the overhead lamp. "Very nice work. I don't think I've ever seen a sharper edge. No doubt you value it highly?"

Karl straightened his back. *I'm not going to beg for my life. It wouldn't help, anyway.*

"Oh, no," Ohlmin said, smiling. "No need to pretend to be brave." He set one foot on top of a box, grasped the flat of the blade carefully, and brought it down on his knee.

The sword snapped.

"You don't die that easily." The two pieces clattered on the floor. "Public executions in Pandathaway take a good long time." Ohlmin opened the door. "Think about that, for a while."

The door whisked shut behind him.

"Dammit, wake up," Karl hissed. He couldn't reach Walter, and the dwarf was chained beyond the thief. Raising his voice was certain to draw attention; whispering was all he had left.

With a rattle and a shaking, the wagon started moving.

Walter opened a lazy eye. "Will you please shut up?" His voice was calm and flat. As always. "We both woke up before you did," he said, his voice barely carrying over the wagon's clatter.

"Then *why?*"

Ahira shook his head. "Because I thought that there might be some advantage in playing possum." He shrugged. "It didn't work out that way—but conceivably it might, so keep your voice low."

"But we did hear something useful, at least," the thief said. "We're not going directly back to Pandathaway. One of his men said that Ohlmin figures to make a better profit on . . ." He swallowed, his face still impassive. ". . . on the women in Metreyll than he could in Pandathaway. So we'll be skirting the edge of the Waste."

Ahira nodded. "Metreyll has a road to the Hand tabernacle, the one in the Waste. The Society might ransom Doria for a decent price."

"If she's still alive when they get there." And the same for Andy-Andy.

"Don't be silly." The dwarf scowled. "These folks are professionals, remember? They'll keep the women alive. And that's academic; apparently the Matriarch of the Healing Hand can even raise the dead. All of which doesn't do us any good here."

Karl spat. "And what else do you know that's not going to do us any good?"

Ahira shook his head. "Not a lot. There's ten to fifteen of them, including Ohlmin and his hired wizard. I also know that these chains are too damn thick, that Hakim and I are eventually headed for the block in Pandathaway. I also . . ." He trailed off, and shook his head. "I also know that either Doria's or Andrea's gag was a bit loose, for a while."

"Huh?"

"I don't know which one," Ahira said, white-lipped, "because I can tell Doria's screams from Andrea's." He raised an eyebrow. "You want me to draw you a picture? Fine. From the sounds out there, they've been taking turns before finally deciding to—"

"Shut up." Karl clenched his hands around his chains, and *pulled.* Nothing.

He tried again, holding his breath and pulling on the chains. Sweat beaded on his forehead, lights danced in front of his eyes. The skin of his right palm split open, wetting the chains with his blood.

Karl ignored the pain, ignored the way his head was threatening to break.

He pulled.

Nothing. The chains didn't shatter, didn't stretch, didn't give. Nothing.

"Stop it." Ahira rattled his own chains. "These weren't built by amateurs."

"Amateurs?"

"Yes, amateurs—like an idiot who didn't wonder why there was a caravan following us. Like a stupid amateur who let his group take a break when he knew that there was a price on one of the member's heads." The dwarf cursed himself bitterly. "But I had to leave you on watch. Let Karl and Andrea try to straighten out their relationship, I said. And while you were doing that, they snuck up on you." He snapped a glare at Walter. "You were about to say something?"

"I wasn't," Karl said. "If I hadn't freed Ellegon, if I hadn't beaten Ohlmin, none of this would have happened. It's my fault."

Off in the distance, a scream trilled, fading quickly into a muffled whimper.

Walter spoke quietly, with a calm that horrified Karl more than the scream. "I think we can save the who's-at-fault session for some other time. You didn't know, Karl didn't know, and Andrea isn't as sensitive to magic as Ari is—even if they were both paying attention to keeping watch, she might not have felt that invisibility spell being used. So the two of you just *shut up and figure out what we do next.* Understood?"

Karl and Ahira drew twin breaths. They nodded.

The dwarf pointed his chin at the door. "How long do you think it's going to take them to settle in for the ride?"

"What do you mean?" Karl found his voice becoming shrill.

"I mean," the dwarf said, from between clenched teeth, "that they're all . . . enjoying themselves right now. They're all charged up. We need them to be relaxed, and a bit tired."

What you're asking is how long it will take for fifteen men to rape Andy-Andy and Doria. "A couple of hours, probably. Why all the interest?"

Visibly, Ahira forced himself to relax. "Then we wait for a couple of hours." Another muffled scream broke through the wagon's clatter. "We wait. Not a chance otherwise."

"And then?"

The dwarf nodded. "And then, I go berserk."

Ahira sat back in the flickering light of the overhead oil lamp, ignoring the fire in his shoulders. The chains' mounting had been designed for security, not the comfort of its victims; hours of keeping his arms over his head had left his shoulder joints painfully inflamed.

We wait.

It couldn't be helped. Even if they could break out of their chains earlier, retrieve the weapons, and charge outside, the odds were just too heavily against them. Ohlmin was probably their best warrior, and almost certainly the rest weren't anything near as good as Karl or Ahira, but it was still fifteen to two—Hakim wasn't very good in a fight; he'd be needed to find and try to free Aristobulus.

And if he can do that, maybe we have a chance.

But there had to be some time for the slavers to drop their guard. Just a bit. And the screams from the wagon ahead of them? Ignore them, or try to, at least. This wasn't the time for a gesture; it had to *work.*

So we wait.

But not until dawn; Hakim's skills weren't nearly as useful in daylight. In the day, bowmen could spot them easily, fill them all full of arrows before they were halfway out the door.

In the day, a dwarf's darksight was superfluous.

So we wait. But not long, now.

In the game, going berserk would have been a simple procedure. "I'm going to try to go berserk," you'd announce, rolling a four-sided die. If it came up with a zero, one, or two, the attempt would fail. You'd try again, next turn, if you wanted to.

And if it came up with a three, it would still be simple: Your Strength would double, going well past the maximum possible for a mortal, under normal circumstances. Intelligence and Wisdom would drop drastically, as would Manual Dexterity and Weapons Proficiency. Speed would be unaffected, as would Charisma—but your Endurance level would rise to the point where only a deathblow could slow you down.

There'd be a penalty to pay later, of course. For many turns after you had slipped out of your berserk state, you would be weak as a kitten.

But until you slipped out of it, you'd destroy, and break, and smash.

Or die trying.

Ahira fondled the thick chains. Possibly he couldn't break them, even berserk.

Never mind. It's h—it's our only chance.

He raised his head. "Karl. It's time."

"Right." Cullinane nodded slowly. "Try to remember to break us loose, too."

"I will. But one thing: While I'm out of it, you're in charge. Make sure you get everyone away you can. But don't worry about me; I'll—"

"No."

"Don't argue with me." This wasn't a game anymore. Amateur heroics were fine for around a mahogany table at the Student Union. But not here. "Once I set myself off, you won't be able to reason with me. I won't run. I won't be able to run."

Cullinane chuckled thinly. "I thought you said that once you're out of it. I'm in charge."

Ahira sighed. "Hakim, reason with him."

The thief shook his head. "I won't have to. Once he's got your responsibilities, he'll see it for himself. Which is why you picked him to take over, instead of me. Eh, m'friend?"

"Sure." Ahira leaned back against the rough surface of the wall. "It's time; we've waited long enough. Take care."

There was only one way to do it. Reach deep inside, find a core of hot anger, of raging fury . . .

And let it *burn*.

Special classes—that's what they called them. As though being a feeb were some sort of prize. Special classes, exceptional children— didn't that sound just dandy?

Mrs. Hennessy—that was her name. A short, pinch-faced redhead, always dressing just a little too well, oozing the slimy unction that the best special ed courses could teach. But the courses had never been able to purge from her noble head the reflexive notion that a bent body must hold a crippled mind.

She raised her head from the desk next to him, where she'd been patiently explaining to little Jacqueline Minelli, probably for the thirtieth time, that the little purple block indeed went into the little purple hole. "What *is* it, Jimmy?"

He always hated that nickname. Even his parents had started calling him James Michael when he began first grade. And that was six years ago.

But you didn't call a retard by his proper name. A nickname, preferably one that ended in a vowel—that was the protocol. And if the retard happened to be a mentally normal boy with muscular dystrophy? Didn't that call for a different protocol?

No, of course not. "I'm done with this nonsense." With the heels of his clumsy hands, he pushed at the math problem, sending the papers fluttering to the floor.

She stalked over and wearily began collecting the scattered sheets. "Jim-my, that was a bad thing to do."

"My name is James Michael. And I've been solving simple goddam algebra problems since I was ten years old."

"That isn't a nice word to—"

"And I'm goddam tired of being treated like I was half a person. Fuck you, bitch."

She slapped him.

And, of course, clapped her hand to her mouth in self-disgust, then spent the rest of the school day apologizing.

On reflection, that slap was the nicest thing a teacher had ever done for him.

Ahira tugged lightly at the chains. Then harder, and harder. No, not yet.

There was a shout out in the dorm hallway. "Hey! Anybody want to go out for a beer?"

His roommate-slash-keeper had already tucked him into bed, then headed out to the library. Granted, he could ask someone to help him out of bed again and dress him, but James Michael had invested many uncomfortable hours in the common room downstairs, putting up with corner-of-the-eye stares and hidden shudders until some of them had started to see past the crumpled body in the wheelchair.

But his roommate was gone. And if he went out for a beer with the rest, he'd have two choices when they came back. Either ask someone to carry him to the toilet three, maybe four times until the beer worked its way through his system, or . . .

Or spend the next few hours lying in his own urine.

Not yet. Try harder. Get through the wall of fire, and into the core.

Doria dropped into a chair, visibly considered the possibility that it would seem to him to be too far away, took a half-second to fight her own fear of James Michael Finnegan, and compromised by wiggling herself a scant inch closer.

Damn it, Doria, can't you treat me like a person?

Nothing. He tugged at the chains. Not even a dwarf's normal strength could break them, and he couldn't go berserk, he couldn't do it.

Here I am, just as helpless now as I've been all my life—
Just
his heart pounded, a beat like a bass drum
as helpless
a red film descended over his eyes, a fire in his head
as I've been
his skin tingled with a rush of blood, his tendons sang a hymn of power
all my life.
he went berserk.

There was an annoyance about his wrists. Ahira wanted to bring them down, to rip, to tear, to smash. But something restrained his hands.

It was an annoyance he didn't have to bear. Not bothering to clench his fists, he brought his arms *down.*

Metal squealed and shattered, and his arms were free. *Free.* He bent and ripped his ankle chains from the floor.

Two humans were chained on the bench next to him. Why didn't they free themselves? Didn't they want to smash, to break, to destroy? Maybe they were just too stupid. He reached up, grabbed the arm chains of the nearest, and pulled. Metal squealed and snapped.

Why were his hands so wet and sticky? It doesn't matter—pull, and again, and again.

Sounds came from their mouths, but they didn't make any sense.

"Walter—take some knives, and go find Ari. He's probably in the wizard's wagon, whichever one that is. I'll get the others."

"You'll need help. I'd better—"

"Move, dammit, *move.*"

One of the humans picked something from the corner and bolted out the door. As though in retaliation, three others lumbered in.

"Ahira—take them. I've got to get Andy, Doria."

Words, they were just words. Didn't mean anything.

But the biggest of the three new humans was pulling a sword. That was something he could understand.

Ahira clutched the dangling end of his wrist chains and whipped the loop of chain across the face of the swordsman. The unshaven face shattered; bits of tooth and bone rattled against the wall, blood bathed Ahira in salty fountain.

He shoved the falling body out of the way. Two of the enemy to face. Just two humans, with swords thrusting for him.

He batted the swords out of the way with his loop of chain, then released the end of the chain from his hands. That was the trouble with the chain: It wasn't satisfying enough. And there were two left.

A few moments later, that wasn't true: There weren't any humans, just pieces of them, scattering the room. Ahira staggered out into the night, spitting out a warm gobbet of flesh.

There must be more to smash. There had to be.

Easy, Karl—you've got one chance at this, and you had better make it good. The hilt of Walter's scimitar felt odd in his hand; the balance of the curved sword was all wrong.

So don't try anything fancy. It was easy to tell which of the four boxlike wagons held Doria and Andy-Andy; the drunken laughter and muffled whimpers called him.

He sprinted across the broken ground. Three long strides brought him to the back door of the slowly rolling wagon. From behind him came the clatter of steel, the screams of the injured, and a constant, deep growl.

Never mind. Ahira can handle them. He jerked the door open and dived in.

And was blinded by the bright lanternlight. *So go by touch.* His questing fingers nested in a beard; he gripped it tightly and pulled it down while bringing his knee up, the man's jaw crumbling like a fleshy bagful of glass. *Don't go for the kill. A quick disable, then on to the next.* He threw the body behind him, out of the wagon.

Karl's eyes cleared, faster than he would have thought possible. Three left; two men rising slowly from the bruised naked bodies of—

Save it. There's one coming at you with a knife. Karl dodged to one side and chopped down with his sword, rewarded by the unmistakable feel of steel cleaving flesh, and a thump as the knife-wielder hit the ground outside.

Two more, drunkenly fumbling for their swords. He dropped the scimitar and grabbed the two men by their hair. Karl brought his hands together swiftly; two skulls shattered, as if they had been eggshells.

He seized Andy-Andy and flipped her onto her belly as though she was weightless.

Not now, his Barak-self said. *Take out the driver, first.*

No, not a second more. For either of them. His hands trembled too badly for him to deal with the knots. He searched the floor, found a sheathed knife, and slashed the leather straps that bound her hands behind her back. A moment later, Doria was free, too.

No time for the gags, best to let them handle that themsel—*wait!*

He slipped the knife between Andy-Andy's gag straps and her cheek, and twisted the knife's edge out. "Your sleep spell. Use it on the driver, then go invisible, and use this on him," he said, pressing the hilt into her hands.

Wild eyes looked back at him, out of a bruised face. Her left cheek was so purply inflamed that he could barely see that eye.

No answer.

"Doria." No, Doria was worse; either unconscious, or pretending

to be. He turned back to Andy-Andy. "I can't wait—just do it." He
shook her. *"Do it."*

She bit her lip so hard that blood began to flow. And then nodded.
He couldn't wait. There just wasn't any time. He had to find Walter and Aristobulus, and then get them all in one wagon. That was it
—they'd take *this* wagon. Easier than moving Doria.

Doria's robes lay crumpled in a heap on the floor. He picked them
up and wrapped them around his left arm before retrieving the scimitar.

"I'll be back." Walter and Ari first, then, if he could—

He dived out of the wagon, and hit the ground rolling.

Crushing a human's face with the outspread fingers of one hand,
Ahira stumbled in front of an open wagon. The two mules reared up,
hooves striking out.

He batted the hooves away with the limp form of the dead human,
using the body like a flail. Ahira moved in on the driver, letting the
other fall in a crumpled heap. The slim blond man raised a crossbow,
pulled back the string with shaking fingers, and dropped a quarrel
into the bow's groove.

Ahira laughed. And bounded to the seat of the wagon, his hands
reaching for the driver's throat.

The bowstring sang.

Time, Karl thought, *time was the problem.* Surprise was on their
side. It hadn't been more than a couple of minutes since Ahira had
freed them. The enemy would be disorganized, startled. But that
wouldn't last long. The drill was obvious: Find Walter and Ari, load
them into the wagon with the two women, and vanish into the night.

But where the hell *were* they?

He ran toward the forward wagon, but stopped short. Six—no,
seven men were hurriedly dismounting from the wagon's back door,
swords in hand. No time to waste—Walter and the wizard weren't
there.

He turned and ran, past the wagon carrying Doria and Andy-
Andy, its sleeping driver lolling on the seat. The next wagon was just
creaking along; no sign of any activity. He kept running.

"Greetings, Karl Cullinane," Ohlmin's voice rasped from behind
him.

Karl spun around. Standing next to Ohlmin was a short, fat man in wizard's robes. The wizard raised his hands, and smiled with a wine-stained mouth.

"Leave him be, Blenryth," Ohlmin said, his eyes never leaving Karl's. "This one is mine."

Ohlmin drew his sword and lunged, in full extension. Right into Karl's left arm, the one protected by Doria's robes.

The blade *tinged,* and bounced off, as though it had hit a wall.

Before Karl could strike, Ohlmin backed away. The slim man pursed his lips. "In that case, you do it, wizard."

Blenryth raised his arms higher, a rush of harsh syllables issuing from his wine-stained mouth—

The darkness shattered as a bolt of lightning crackled past Karl from behind, streaking through the air, striking the wizard square in the center of his chest.

Blenryth exploded, spraying Karl with gobs of flesh and shards of bone, knocking him to the ground, out of breath.

Move. You don't know where Ohlmin is—

Hands grasped his shoulders; Karl reached back and up.

"Easy," Walter's voice whispered. "It's just the, umm, cavalry."

Karl bounced to his feet. Standing next to the thief, Aristobulus, looking much the worse for wear, rubbed his smoldering hands together.

And grinned.

"No time for congratulations," Karl snapped, jerking a thumb in the direction of the wagon carrying the others. "They're in that one. Get in, and get moving. I'll catch up with you." He quickly scanned the vicinity. No sign of Ohlmin. The bastard was smart enough to know when to run.

For a moment, the other two stood still. *"Now,"* Karl said. A shove sent Walter stumbling in the right direction. "I've got to find Ahira." *And Ohlmin.* He clutched the scimitar tightly. *Definitely* and Ohlmin.

The world was an incredibly deep, impossibly dark pit. *Or well, Ahira?*

No, I'm not well. I'm dead, aren't I?

"Pass me that last bottle." Hakim's voice was calm. As always, or almost always. "I'm going to pour a little more in the wound before it closes altogether."

"His mouth's moving," Aristobulus said. "Pour it down his throat, instead."

"But if he doesn't swallow—if it goes down the wrong tube . . ."

"Don't be silly. Those are *healing* draughts—the only way you could hurt him with that is if you hit him with the bottle."

A gentle hand behind his neck forced his head forward; a sickly-sweet, syrupy-thick liquid washed the taste of blood from his mouth. Ahira raised a distant palm, forcing the neck of the bottle away. "Save. For later." He opened his eyes. In the dim light of an over-head lamp, Aristobulus and Hakim knelt over him. "We." He swallowed, and started again. "We are not moving."

Hakim raised a palm. "No problem. We're far enough away now." He raised his head. *"Karl—he's awake."*

Far enough away? There wasn't such a thing as far enough away. "Who," he said, his voice a harsh croak, "who says so?"

Karl Cullinane leaned in through the open door, his face splotched with dried blood and streaked with soot. "I say so. They're going to be having other problems than chasing us in the dark."

"How about . . ." He gasped for breath. "How . . ."

"Shh." Karl leaned out for a moment, then returned. "They're both . . . here, anyway. Andy's not doing too badly." He shrugged. "All things considered. Doria's still kind of . . . rocky. Not physically," he said, with a wan smile. "They've both had enough of that stuff. But they've been through a hell of a lot."

"What . . . happened?"

"Later." Karl nodded reassuringly. "The main thing is that we got away. You took a bolt in the lung; if Ari hadn't found that cache of healing draughts in a box strapped under the wagon, you'd be dead. But he did, and you aren't. How's that for now?"

Ahira tried to shake his head vigorously. It just came out as a twitch. "How did I . . . get here?"

Walter patted his shoulder, then moved away, seating himself on a bench on the far side of the wagon. Idly, he picked up a crossbow, then took a quick fingercount of the quarrels in its strapped-on quiver. "Karl found you on the ground, if that's what you mean. Carried you—on a dead run, you should pardon the expression—until he caught up with the rest of us." He looked over at the big man, who was still braced in the doorway. "Eleven bolts—that's not going to be enough, not with my aim."

"Strap another quiver to your leg. And don't forget the cloth, and the lamp oil," Karl said.

"And the flint-and-steel."

"Right." He looked over at Ahira. "The other two are outside, in case you're wondering. They . . . want to be left alone for a while. And I can't say that I blame them." Karl patted Aristobulus on the shoulder. "Are you sure that you're up to keeping guard while we're gone?"

"Count on it." The wizard clenched his fists. "I've still got my Flame spell—anybody except you two who gets close, gets burned. And speaking of burned, do you think that Blenryth's spell books are still back there?"

Karl shook his head. "I doubt it. The wagon we torched was probably his. But if we get the chance, I'll check."

"Fine. And if you don't get the chance, don't worry about it." Hakim laughed. "Ari, m'friend, I'm beginning to like you."

The wizard scowled. "Just be careful."

Ahira struggled to rise, to get his arms to push him upward. But he couldn't. *Easy*. He forced himself to relax. *It's just temporary. It's just the aftereffects.* "You two aren't going anywhere. Not back there."

Karl stepped all the way into the wagon, bending his neck to avoid bumping against the ceiling. "Out." He jerked his thumb at Hakim and Aristobulus. They stepped silently through the door; Karl sat next to Ahira. "We are going back. Just Walter and me."

"No—" Ahira tried to shout it.

"Shh. I'm going to give you the rational reasons first. One." He held up a finger. "There are two-count-them-two water barrels on the side of this wagon. That's about five too few. Two." Another finger. "We don't have our supplies here—no food, no rope, this one lamp and one oil flask—and that bottle there is the last of the healing draughts." He patted at Hakim's scimitar, which was stuck through a sash at his waist. "Three. This sword isn't worth much; I may need a decent one later on. I kind of like Ohlmin's—and once I'm done with him, he won't have any use for it.

"And lastly," Karl continued, "there's five, maybe six of them left. If they have any sense, they're not going to try to chase us, but I don't want to worry about their having any sense. Understood? We're the fox; the only good hounds are dead hounds."

"Give me the real reason. You want to play hero?"

Karl held his breath for a long moment before answering. "This isn't for show." He toyed with the iron cuffs and dangling bits of chain that were still around his wrists. "Those bastards raped two ladies I care about. Two of my *friends,* dammit. And right now, both Andy and Doria are . . . in kind of . . ." He trailed off. Cullinane closed his eyes and tightened his fists. "They're hurt, and they're scared. And if I—damn. The next time I talk to them, I'm going to be able to say that the animals that hurt them are dead." He opened his fists and rested his face in his hands. "I want to tell them that they're safe, but that'd be a lie in this goddam world. God, how I wish I were home." He took a woolen blanket from the floor and, with the scimitar, began to cut it into strips. "And if the truth be known, my little dwarf friend, Ohlmin scares the hell out of *me.* I want him *dead.*"

"No. You're not going. Can't let you." Couldn't Karl see that it was just too much of a risk? The thing to do was make a run for the Gate, not try to hunt down the surviving slavers.

"You can't stop me." Karl tied the dangling chains from his left cuff to his arm, weaving the strips of cloth through the links. He shook the arm vigorously. No sound. "And don't bother calling Walter and trying to talk him out of it." He repeated the process with his right cuff's chains, then started work on his leg irons. "You left me in charge, remember?"

"That was just while—"

"Too bad." Karl shrugged. "As far as I'm concerned, you're still out of it." He grasped Ahira's shoulder with a strong hand. "We'll be back in a while. Take care."

Two steps to the door, and Karl Cullinane was gone.

Aristobulus kept watch until dawn, sitting tailor-fashion on the flat roof of the wagon, a blanket underneath him, a waterbag at his side, his Flame spell at the surface of his mind.

At daybreak, a speck appeared on the horizon. He stood, readying himself. If it was Karl and Hakim returning, that was fine. And if not, well then that was fine, too, in another way. Out of bow range, there was no way that a small group of humans could harm him before he blasted them.

The speck grew larger, until it became their flatbed wagon, now drawn by a team of eight horses. Karl and Hakim sat on the wagon's seat, sooty but otherwise unharmed.

"Karl, Hakim," he called out, "is everything . . ." Aristobulus let his voice trail off. He couldn't think of an appropriate word.

Cullinane pulled firmly on the reins. "Easy, easy," he murmured to the animals. Taking a leather bag from the bed of the wagon, he dismounted, pausing only to pat the large mare that was his usual mount, not one of the lead horses. "No more being hitched in front of a wagon for you. It's back to the saddle, tomorrow."

He stopped on the ground in front of the wizard and craned his neck to look up at Aristobulus. "We killed all of them," he said, his voice as matter-of-fact as if he were reporting the time of day.

"You're certain?" Aristobulus asked. "Including Ohlmin?"

Cullinane reached into the leather bag. "Including Ohlmin." He pulled his hand out.

Dangling by the black hair that was gripped in a trembling hand, Ohlmin's bodiless head swayed, as though nodding in agreement.

CHAPTER THIRTEEN

To Bremon

Melancholy and despair, though often, do not always concur; there is much difference: melancholy fears without a cause, this upon great occasion; melancholy is caused by fear and grief, but this torment procures them and all extremity of bitterness.

—Robert Burton

Karl didn't know when it had happened, but he'd developed a habit: rubbing his wrists as though to reassure himself that the cuffs were gone. It had been almost a week since Ahira had used the tools reclaimed from the slavers to chisel them all free of the remnants of their bonds. . . .

Well, the physical remnants, anyway. Karl dropped his right hand to the saddle, shaking his head at the way his wrist was reddened and sore.

He shook himself, then gave a quick tug on the reins; the mare responded by prancing to a halt and letting the two wagons pass her by.

Karl stroked her neck, smiling fondly. "I'd give you a name, but we're going to have to turn you all loose when we reach the mountain. I can't quite see trying to take you through the Gate—and it'll be easier on me if I don't name you. Understand?"

She lifted her head and whinnied. Karl chuckled; it wasn't a response to his question. She was just irritated at being passed by the harnessed horses, twitchy at that insult to her, a member of the saddle-bearing gentry.

"Well, at least I understand you." He let her break into a slow walk, while he raised himself in the saddle, drinking in the cool, sweet air of the grassland beyond the Waste. An east wind brought him a faint, minty smell, presented him with the tang of sunbaked grass, and a distant suggestion of musk.

Walter, from his usual perch on the seat of the flatbed, cocked his head and lifted a waterbag. "Thirsty?"

More out of sociability than thirst, Karl urged his mare over to the flatbed and leaned over to accept the bag, while his mare kept to the cart's pace, her head held high, a bit of extra bounce to her step, as though to deny any association with the dusty, plodding drayhorses.

Idly, Karl wondered about the fate of the two mules. Perhaps they had run off, sometime while in the slavers' possession; possibly, the roast on the slavers' campfire had been a haunch of mule. He shrugged; the only people who knew were safely dead, and he hadn't had the time or inclination to quiz them about the matter.

But there could be others on our heels. We'll have to watch out, until we're safely away from this filthy world. Uncorking the bag, he took a shallow swig of the warm, leather-tasting water, then recorked it and handed the bag down to Walter. "When we stop to rest, I want to get in some sword practice. If you're game." Ohlmin's sword was a fine piece of steel, a rust-free length of basket-hilted saber, faintly curved. But it was barely half the length of Karl's sword; using it called for a totally different style of swordplay, with much more attention to parrying at close range. The sword was mainly a thrusting weapon rather than a slashing one on attack, although its edge was sharp enough to shave with. His Barak-self seemed comfortable with it; still, best to be sure, practice as much as possible.

I'm sure Ohlmin would want me to use it well, he thought sarcastically. It hardly seemed fair that that bastard was beyond pain, though. *Then again, life isn't fair.* "So, are you up for it?"

"Am I what?"

"Never mind."

From the high seat of the other wagon, Andy-Andy cursed in low tones at her team of horses. Six were probably more than the wagon required, but they had the harnesses to spare, and putting six on meant not having to stop twice a day to change teams.

Karl turned to Walter. "She's coming back from it. At least a bit."

Walter took a grimy rag from the seat beside him and mopped at his forehead. "Some do." His next sentence, unvoiced, was, *And some don't.* Doria was close to being an automaton, responding only to direct questions, and then only with monosyllables. She ate barely enough to keep a lizard alive, and left the wagon only under duress. Karl had tried to take her aside, to explain that everything was under control, that she didn't have to worry—

He'd only tried that once. Any touch set her screaming, a high-pitched wail that wouldn't cease until she collapsed with exhaustion.

Maybe, with the right kind of care, Doria would someday be well again. And maybe they should have taken a detour, to the tabernacle of the Healing Hand. But Ahira had overruled that; there was no way they could go directly there; they just didn't have enough water to make it to the far side of the Waste. And if there was another slaver team . . .

Ahira was right. The best thing to do was to go ahead, get home as soon as possible. Back home, psychiatric therapy might not be easily effective, but Karl would find a therapist to treat what was wrong with Doria, even if he had to break a few arms. Fine, let the shrink write off their history of the past few months as some sort of group delusion—but Doria would get the help she needed. For everything.

Walter looked up at him, his brow wrinkling. "You know, don't you?"

"About what?"

"Doria."

Karl nodded. "Yes."

Walter considered it for a moment, as he twirled the reins around his fingers. "It has to be . . . what's-its-name—that dragon—"

"Ellegon."

The thief shuddered. "With all she's gone through, do you think she'll ever be all right?"

Karl shook his head. "No."

"How sure . . . ?"

He shrugged. "Not very." There was something strange about this whole conversation. Walter asking *him?* "I remember when you sounded a lot more sure of *your*self."

"So do I." Walter reached back for a wine bottle, uncorked it, and drank. "So do I." He offered Karl a swig, which Karl declined with a shake of the head. "Karl? What do we do about it?"

Karl shrugged, and urged his mare into a trot. "We go home. And then we do what we can." *And I'll carry a load of guilt with me to my grave. None of this would have happened if I hadn't freed Ellegon, beat Ohlmin. And if I'd known—would I have left Ellegon chained in a cesspool? Or would I have chosen to spend the rest of my life living with that?*

"And what will that be?" Walter asked, his voice drifting forward.

Karl didn't respond. It wasn't really a day for answers.

CHAPTER FOURTEEN

The Warrens

Hence, loathed Melancholy
Of Cerberus and blackest Midnight born,
In Stygian cave forlorn,
'Mongst horrid shapes, and shrieks, and sights unholy.

—John Milton

Bremon loomed ahead, a dark, jagged mass blocking half the noon sky.

Driving the flatbed wagon, Ahira shook his head and swore softly under his breath. The damn mountain always loomed in *front* of them, even though his mental picture of Oreen's map suggested that they were finally near the known entrance. Perhaps the rough copy he had made would have differed, but that had been lost, along with much of their supplies, to the slavers.

But no, that wasn't it. Oreen's map was clear in his mind; it was just that Bremon was too large, too massive, too gently sloped to have a clear edge, a noticeably demarked base.

Next to him on the flatbed's broad seat, Hakim peered down at him. "Are we there yet?" he asked, for only the thirtieth time that morning.

Ahira jerked on the reins. The flatbed's two horses shuffled to a quick stop on the gently uphill slope.

"You little ass!" Andrea shrilled. Ahira turned to see her wrestle

the other wagon's team to a halt, the noses of the lead horses stopping scant inches behind the back of the flatbed. "You just *stay* there." She bounded out of the high seat of her wagon, and stalked toward him through the knee-high, golden grasses.

"Excuse me," Hakim said, "I just remembered something I've got to talk over with Ari." He made a quick exit, going around the opposite side of the flatbed from Andrea's approach, and disappeared into the other wagon.

Ahira didn't blame him for manufacturing a need to talk to the wizard, or Karl for cantering his horse ahead, past the flatbed. This sort of outburst was becoming more and more common.

I can't really say that I blame her, but I don't know what I should do about it. Perhaps the best thing would be to permanently relinquish leadership of the group to Karl. No, that wouldn't do; Karl and Hakim had been lucky—but wrong.

As Andrea planted herself in front of him, he rubbed at his eyes with his thumbs, then let his hands drop. "What is it now?"

She threw up her arms. "How many times have I asked you—politely, mind—to give me a bit of goddam notice before you stop? Do you really want my team climbing into the back of this little dogcart of yours?"

Her face reddened; Ahira stifled a snapped retort and raised a palm. "Just take it easy, please." *If you're so concerned about my stopping suddenly, then why don't you just let your wagon lag behind a few yards?* That was an obvious response, but a wrong one. Clearly, she was playing me-and-my-shadow with the flatbed out of an unconscious desire to speed him up, to speed them all up. To get herself away from this world, and home. "I'm sorry," he said. "My fault—it's just that—"

He'd tried to keep his voice level, but that only enraged her. "Don't you *dare* patronize me," she said, white-lipped. "I've got a job to do, driving that stubborn, idiotic team of horses—"

"I said—"

"—fighting them, more than half the time. They've got to trust me, to know that I won't lead them into—"

"No. They. Don't." He punctuated all three words by banging his fist on the wagon's seat. Ahira vaulted heavily to the ground. "We're stopping here. Now." *Enough* of this. Granted, Andrea had been through a hard time; given, it was at least partly his fault. But enough of treating her like, like . . .

. . . like everyone used to treat me. Like some sort of feeb, giving

*her the job of driving the big wagon because it gives her something to
do, not because she's best at it. Even if she wants that sort of treatment, it's the wrong thing to do. And it stops here.* "We stop here; you
can turn your horses loose, or butcher them for supper, for all I
care." He raised his head and his voice. "Karl!"

The big man urged his horse over. "Meal break?" He jerked his
thumb at the mountain behind him. "I saw some trees ahead, about a
mile or so, I think. It'd be a bit more comfortable up there."

Ahira shook his head. "No. I was telling Andrea that we're stopping here. Permanently, as far as the wagons go. Hakim's in the
other one, talking to Ari—you go get him, have him saddle a horse.
Then you two get the joy of riding out, and seeing if you can find an
entrance. *The* entrance."

"And if we can't?" Karl frowned disapprovingly.

Ahira's hands itched for his axehilt. "Then be back by sundown.
You'll try again tomorrow, at first light."

Karl's horse took a prancing step back. "I've got a better idea, I
think. Doria's got a Locate spell; have her find the entrance."

Andrea held up a hand. "Do you two want an opinion, or don't
you give a damn what I think?" Her lips pursed; she opened her
mouth as though to go on, then stopped and started again. "It would
be better to leave her alone. For two reasons. First, Location spells
are finicky; if she doesn't know exactly what she's looking for, the
spell will fasten on something else, something that fits her . . . internal description. Besides"—her shoulders twitched beneath her
robes—"I think it's best to leave her alone, in any case. Don't put
any demands on her, not if you don't have to. I . . . don't know if
trying to get her to do something might . . . push her over the
edge."

From his perch atop his horse, Karl sighed. "I guess you're right. I
. . . was just thinking that a bit of activity would be good for her,
help to take her mind off . . ." He gestured absently. ". . . everything."

"What the hell do *you* know about it?" Andrea snapped.

Karl sat silent for a moment, then shook his head slowly from side
to side. "Know? I wouldn't say that I know much about anything."
He gave a thin smile, then turned his mare away and trotted back to
the other wagon.

Ahira stared off into the distance, keeping his eyes on the mountain, off Andrea, not saying anything.

Finally, she broke the silence. "What was that supposed to mean?"

Ahira moved to the flatbed and busied himself with unhitching the horses. "Only two things that I can think of. First, that he doesn't understand you. For which I can't exactly blame him. I don't, either."

"I was trying to explain it to him when . . ." Her voice trailed off into choking sounds. "When everything . . . fell apart. And now he's treating me like I'm . . . soiled."

"Don't." Ahira spun around. "Don't even think that. I haven't always been Karl's greatest admirer, but you're dead wrong." He put out a hand; she took it with trembling fingers. "I don't think that Karl's too good at handling guilt. That's what you're seeing—not anything else. Karl knows—we *all* know the difference between a victim and . . ." He clenched his jaw. Maybe Karl hadn't been wrong in going back to finish off Ohlmin and his slavers, despite the risk. "Just take my word for it."

She nodded slowly. "You said that there were two things that he meant?"

Ahira returned her nod. "That maybe there's a difference between knowing and caring. And Karl cares about you. As if you didn't know. He once came close to killing Hakim over you, but he stopped. Maybe it was squeamishness, maybe not." He squeezed her hand more tightly. "But he didn't hold back when it came to Ohlmin, did he?"

"And for that, I'm supposed to fall into—"

"And for that," he interrupted, "you're free to do whatever you want, without looking over your shoulder." He released her hand. "I need a bit of help with these horses. Are you available?"

Slowly, she nodded.

Karl and Walter discovered the entrance on their second day of searching. A spiral search pattern had given them a horseback view of various naked, slightly wooded, and heavily overgrown slopes, a few dozen small animals that scurried for cover at their approach, and more than a few dozen birds, who were only too glad to interrupt their constant search for food to chitter and twerp at Karl and Walter.

The thief glared up at Karl from the back of his mount, a mild-mannered sorrel gelding. "I've got an idea—what say we take a break, let me get away from this vicious beast for a while." Walter patted at the crossbow lashed to the saddle in front of him. "Besides, maybe I could shoot us some dinner."

Karl chuckled and stroked at his mare's neck. It was dry, un-sweaty; probably she could go on almost forever at this slow walk. "Why not? My horse seems a bit tired," he lied. "Although I wouldn't give odds that you could hit a bird with that bow. Your aim—"

"Was good enough when it counted, no?"

That was a good point. Karl dismounted, while from the ivy-covered rockface to their right a small bird twittered its own opinion of Walter's skill with a crossbow.

Walter jerked his horse to a stop and got off with none of his usual grace, then rubbed at his back and thighs. It was his own fault, really —if the thief had taken his turn on horseback, like the others, he would at least have the minimal horsemanship of Ahira and Andy-Andy.

The bird scolded them again.

Karl chuckled as he slipped the bridle from his horse's neck. "Seems that crow doesn't think much of your riding ability, Walter."

The thief scowled as he unstrapped the crossbow. "It's not a crow. Too small." He pulled back the string and dropped a quarrel into the slot. "Possibly it's tasty." Walter raised the bow and took aim.

Now, that was unreasonable, trying to shoot a bird out of pique. Karl shrugged. On the other hand, the thief wasn't very accurate with a crossbow. The night they had killed Ohlmin and the others, it had been Walter's ability to move silently and almost invisibly in the dark that had served them well, not his indifferent aim.

On the other hand—*hell, I've run out of hands.* "Just leave it alone—"

Twing!

The bolt went low and wide, vanishing in the ivy. With a twitter and a flutter, the bird flew away.

Karl forced himself not to smile. "Well, now we can have a whole side of . . . mountain for supper. You like yours medium rare, or— hey! What are you doing?"

The thief let his bow drop to the ground and walked toward the rockface.

"Give me a hand up," Walter said, his eyes on the spot where the arrow had disappeared. "It should have bounced off, or stuck itself in, or something."

Karl went over and knelt on one knee, cupping his hands, then straightening and lifting as Walter settled a sandaled foot into his grip. The thief caught a handhold somewhere above and scrabbled up the ivy.

Karl looked up. Walter was gone. "Where—"

The thief's smiling face poked through the green curtain. "I believe that this is what we call *gin.*" His unseen hands clapped. "I don't have a light, but this thing looks as if it goes down and in for about a million miles. You want to go back for the others, or do I?"

"Dealer's choice," Karl said calmly, his heart beating a rapid tattoo. *We're going home. Where it's safe, comfortable.*

I'm going home.

Thank God.

With everyone gathered just inside the entrance, Ahira took a few minutes to check each pack, working easily in the speckled light coming through the ivy. It would have been possible to make the others check their own gear, but that would mean waiting until their eyes adjusted to the dimness. Better to get going as soon as possible.

He considered the five waterskins. Enough for four days, maybe five, if they went on a strict water ration. It would be nice to have more, but they had lost most of the waterbags to Ohlmin's group, and carrying a barrel through the tunnels would be awkward, at best.

Ahira cinched Hakim's pack a bit tighter. "No need to have things fall out," he said.

Hakim smiled. "Whatever you say, fearless leader. I've got a suggestion, though."

"Yes?"

"Ari and Doria have their Glow spells—why not save on the lantern's oil, and use one now?"

Ahira thought it over for a moment. Not necessarily a bad idea, although the wizard's spell would be good only temporarily; the light would dim, and go out. But Doria's Glow spell was more powerful; it would keep whatever it was put on shining forever. "Karl, your sword, please."

Karl lumbered over, ducking his head under a rocky overhang. "Don't you trust me with an edged weapon?"

Ahira smiled as he hefted the blade. A decent saber, actually, but not quite the luxury-class blade that Karl's broken sword had been. "No, I'm afraid that you'll slice your foot off. Seriously, I'm going to have Doria . . ." He jerked his chin at the cleric, who was sitting slumped next to her pack. "I'm going to *try* to have her Glow it for you." Leaving Doria alone hadn't improved anything. Perhaps succeeding at something would be good for her.

"The point?" Karl's forehead furrowed. "Not to be critical, but you're not putting me in the lead, are you? Spelunking isn't exactly my specialty."

Dammit, Karl, give me a minute to finish. It'd be nice not to be interrupted. It'd be a change, anyway. "You get the spot just behind me. I won't need much light. Darksight, remember?" If the tunnels were as old as Oreen and that dragon Karl had talked to had claimed, it probably wouldn't be necessary for Ahira to go first; any sections of the ceiling that were shaky at all would have already fallen.

But no sense in taking chances. Besides, this was going to be easy for Ahira. A dwarf was built for easing through tunnels. Without adequate light, these humans would probably trip over their own feet.

The sword clutched in his hand, Ahira walked over to Doria and squatted in front of her. "Doria?"

She just sat there, her robes gathered loosely around her, eyes staring blindly through him.

"Doria, I need your help."

No response.

"Please?"

Nothing.

He reached out a hand and laid it gently on her shoulder. "Doria?"

Her face came alive, creasing into a wide-eyed rictus of terror. She inhaled violently.

And screamed.

And kept screaming, until Ahira's ears rang, and Doria lay curled on the floor of the tunnel, whimpering as she gasped for breath.

Ahira looked behind him. Aristobulus, Hakim, Andrea, and Karl stood shoulder to shoulder, glowering in unison.

I had to try. We may need her later. No—make that: "I have to try," he said to Doria, pretending to ignore the way four pairs of eyes were trying to bore holes into his back. "And so do you." *I've got to do something, I have to do something.* "Doria, I'm sorry I touch—"

"Leave me alone." Her voice was low, just one step above a whisper.

"No." He said that as firmly as he could. Maybe if he acted as though she were all right, she might be. *If I close my eyes, does the*

world go away? "I need you to Glow this sword. Make it give off light." As if of its own volition, his hand moved toward her; he jerked it back. "You're part of this group; you're one of us. And we need your help."

"Ahira." Karl's hand grasped his shoulder, urging him away. "Not now. We'll use the lanterns for a while. Maybe she'll be up to it later."

"No!" He shrugged the hand off. *You can't help a, a cripple by ignoring the disability. That just makes things worse. You compensate for it, but you don't ignore it.*

He shook his head to clear it. *But isn't that what I was trying to do, just a few moments ago? Maybe it isn't easy to deal with someone else's handicap, either.* "Doria, I'm not going to stop bothering you until you do it." Careful not to touch her, he grasped the sword by the blade and slid the hilt between her hands. "Take it. Make it glow."

Her lips moved fractionally, without sound.

"Do it."

At first, her voice was a whisper, a quiet, distant rustle of breath. Then the sound grew louder, nearer, stronger, a rush of airy syllables that vanished as they touched his ears.

And the sword began to glow. Faintly; the dim blue of the sky before dawn.

Then brighter; the color of a robin's egg.

And brighter, until it fell from Doria's fingers, glowing like the flame of a bunsen burner, bathing her face in blue light.

Ahira reached out a hand, halting his fingers an inch from the blade. No heat, although it shone with a blue-hot fury. No heat at all —he extended a quivering finger and touched his finger to the metal.

No heat; his finger touched only cool steel.

Ahira smiled. "That's beautiful. I wish I'd gone along with Ari, to see him glow the blade for that smith, back in Pandathaway." He picked up the sword and handed it to Karl.

In the light from the blade, Aristobulus smiled. "You still would be impressed. If I'd tried to get that blade this bright, the glow would have lasted for only an hour or so."

"Doria," the dwarf said gently, "how long will this last? It's beautiful." He knew the answer, but he needed to hear her say it.

Her head nodded fractionally, her hands trembling as she knitted her fingers together. "Always."

Karl's hand fell on his shoulder. "I think it's time we got going."

"Yes," Doria whispered. "Home."

The sword held high to scatter the light as widely as possible, Karl picked his way behind Ahira, the muscles in his shoulders burning like hot wires. It was as though they were walking through the insides of some gargantuan stone worm; the tunnel twisted and turned, leading downward all the way, but never losing its tubular shape, or branching off.

His arms hurt, but he couldn't let both hang at his sides, except when they stopped to rest. The last time had been a while ago. But how long? Who could tell?

Just for something to do, he *tinged* the point of the sword against the ceiling overhead.

"Stop it," Ahira snapped from in front of him.

"Why? I just—"

"Stop it." The dwarf had gotten nastier the farther down the tunnel they went.

"Ahira?"

The dwarf didn't turn around. "What is it *now?*"

"How long—"

"How long until *what?* Until we get there? I don't know."

"No," Aristobulus called from behind. "How long until we stop to rest?" His voice was ragged; the wizard wasn't holding up well.

From the rear of the group, Walter's baritone drifted forward. "I've got a better question—how long until the water gives out? And what do we do then?"

"Relax," the dwarf said, sounding anything but relaxed himself. "I've figured that out." He paused to pick his way around a pile of rocky rubble that was echoed above by a gap in the ceiling. "We go along until we either find the Gate or use up just over half our water."

Karl squeezed through between the rubble pile and the wall, barking his shin in the process. He waited on the other side, extending his hand to help Aristobulus through.

The wizard nodded his thanks.

Andy-Andy was next; she hesitated for a moment before accepting his help. "Thank you." Her voice dripped insincerity.

My, aren't we getting formal. "And you are most welcome, m'lady."

She turned away, but not before he caught a trace of a smile.

Karl shrugged, moving aside to let Doria make her own way through. Figuring out *why* Andy-Andy did *what* wasn't certain to be a waste of time and effort. But close enough.

The trouble with women is that they're too damn intelligent.

Walter moved easily through the narrow passage, balancing himself like a dancer. "Want to switch for a while?"

Gratefully, Karl handed him the sword, accepting the thief's scimitar in return. He slipped it under his belt, then folded his arm across his chest and rubbed viciously at his shoulders. Forcing someone to keep an arm overhead would make a fine torture. And probably had been used as such.

Perhaps in the Coliseum of Pandathaway? No, probably not. Too gentle; people who would chain Ellegon in the middle of a cesspool would have much worse than that in store for someone they were angry at.

But we're going home. All we have to do is tiptoe by a dragon—The Dragon.

"Karl?" Andy-Andy's form was just a silhouette in the light of the sword beyond her. "Are you going to fall asleep standing up? Or would you be so kind as to come along with the rest of us?"

He didn't bother with a sarcastic smile. She probably couldn't see it anyway. Still massaging his shoulders, he set off after the others.

Once we get to the other side, Andrea Andropolous, you and I are going to talk this out, without interruptions. And then yours truly is going to see if he can drink Walter Slovotsky under the table.

Ahira was the first to see the skeleton, of course, because of both his position at the front of the group and his darksight.

But he came close to stumbling over it; a distant, obscene reek had him distracted. It was a strange odor, far different from the cool, moist smell of the unending tunnel.

Probably just imagining it. He shook his head and sniffed twice. Nothing. He shrugged, and started to move on.

And caught himself in midstep, the blackened skull barely an inch beneath the sole of his sandal. Ahira teetered on one leg for a moment, like an aerialist on a high wire.

"Hold it." He regained his balance and motioned Hakim forward, stepping aside to bring the skull out of his shadow.

It lay on its side in the middle of the tunnel, hollow eyesockets staring blindly, open jaw leering, loose bones arrayed behind it in a charred trail.

"What the—"

"Shh," Ahira whispered. "Nobody say anything. Just stay where you are." He knelt on the rough stone beside the skull, Hakim moving the glowing sword closer without any need to be asked.

The skull had lain there a long time; dust on the upper surface was so thick that Ahira's probing finger sank into the feathery surface past his fingernail, almost to the first joint. Years, certainly. Possibly centuries.

He rubbed his finger against his chest.

Beyond the skull, a charred ribcage lay, armbones to the side, the pelvis and the long bones of the legs arrayed as though the victim had sprawled out before its flesh had vanished.

To the left of the ribcage, a round shield lay, its concavity cupping the floor of the tunnel. No design on its face, just blackness.

Blackness, and charred bones—that didn't make any sense. Unless . . . Ahira wiped his hand across the surface of the shield.

It came away black, leaving behind a dirtied outline of the design that had once decorated the shield's face: three golden circles.

Ahira wiped his other hand against the wall. It, too, came away sooty.

Hakim smiled, and leaned close. "My friend," he whispered, his lips a scant inch from Ahira's ear, "it seems to me that we're almost there."

Ahira nodded. *Take it slow, now.* "Pass the word down. Everyone is to take his pack off, and leave it. Sandals, too—we go barefoot from here on in."

And quietly, quietly. But as he turned to look into the others' fear-whitened faces, he knew that there was no need to say that.

Ahira's heart pounded. *I can send them home. And if I don't make it out of here in half the time it took to get in, I deserve to die of thirst.*

Hakim turned back from his whispering to Andrea. "I think we can quit the pretense, James. This is the end of the line for you, no? You aren't coming with us."

Ahira smiled. "I'll see you to the Gate—I'll see you *through* the Gate. But . . ." He trailed off, shrugging.

Hakim nodded. "I understand. Do you explain it to the others, or . . . ?"

"I'll leave the explanations to you. For the other side." *It's almost done, over. And how can I say goodbye to all of them?* His eyes started to mist over. He caught himself. This wasn't a time to get sentimental. "Oh," he whispered, as gruffly as he could, "we won't want that sword anymore. Drop it right here."

Hakim smiled, shrugged, and dropped the glowing blade, snatching it out of the air scant inches before it would have clanged on the stone. His smile, and his wide-armed shrug, said, *Sorry, I couldn't resist it.*

Ahira's glare answered, *Try real hard, next time.*

CHAPTER FIFTEEN

The Dragon at the Gate

> From generation to generation it shall lie waste, none
> shall pass through it for ever and ever. But the cormorant
> and the bittern shall possess it; the owl and the raven
> shall also dwell in it; and he shall stretch out upon it the
> line of confusion, and the stones of emptiness . . .
> . . . and it shall be an habitation for dragons.
>
> —Isaiah Ben-Amoz

As the distant glow of the abandoned sword faded behind, a rain-bow phosphorescence fingered the walls of the tunnel ahead.

Karl furrowed his brow. Just a lucky coincidence, or had Ahira spotted it back at the skeleton?

He clenched the hilt of the scimitar. It probably didn't matter. If it hadn't gotten brighter ahead, Ahira would have sent him back for the sword. Stumbling around in the dark was almost certainly more dangerous than a bit of light. The other choice, of course, would have been for all of them to link hands, but—

—no, that wouldn't have been another choice. Not unless they left Doria behind.

The tunnel curled like the coils of a snake, winding downward, ever steeper. He was glad that Ahira had forced them all to rid themselves of their sandals; any grip less sure than that of bare feet, and Aristobulus, at least, would have fallen.

Just in front of him, Andy-Andy stumbled; he whipped his free arm around her waist, catching and lifting her before she could fall. As he set her on her feet, she gave his hand a quick squeeze and favored him with a slight nod.

Now isn't the time to work that *out,* he thought. *There'll be plenty of time when we're back, on the other side. Home.*

Ahead, Ahira motioned for a stop, then beckoned to Walter. A few whispered words passed between the two, and then the thief crept on hands and knees downward, around the next bend in the tunnel.

Seconds passed. Karl was sure it was only seconds; he counted eighty-nine of his own heartbeats before Walter returned, and Ahira urged them all back away from the bend, and into a kneeling circle.

Chance put Karl between Andy-Andy and Doria; he pressed away from the cleric, noting that Walter, on the other side of her, was similarly squeezing up against the smaller form of Aristobulus.

"I saw it," Walter whispered, so quietly that Karl had to strain his ears to hear the thief, over the beating of his own heart. "It's about a hundred yards away from where the tunnel dumps out. At about ten o'clock, if your back's to the tunnel—understand?" Karl nodded in unison with the others.

"And The Dragon is sleeping," Walter continued. "But we've got to pass in front of It, to get to the Gate. And I don't know if we'll need Ari to operate it for us." He raised a quizzical eyebrow.

The wizard shook his head. "Either we're in a very bad way, or it's as I think: It's automatic. Does it look like water? Good. Then we're safe."

"One more problem," the thief whispered. "There's only enough room for us to go single-file—or just one at a time."

Ahira rubbed at his temples with blunt fingers. "One at a time— Hakim first."

"No," Karl shook his head, pointing to Andy-Andy. "She goes first, it's—"

"We do it my way!" the dwarf hissed.

Well, it made sense, in a way: The thief was best at moving silently. Karl nodded slowly. "But she's next." *I got her into this; I've got to see that she gets out of it.*

The dwarf hesitated for a moment. "Agreed. Then Doria."

You're not thinking, Ahira. Doria could easily turn out to be a problem. "No, then Ari." *You and I can take Doria out, if need be. And, each in our own way, you and I are responsible for her.* But he couldn't say that, and didn't need to. A few seconds of thought would let the dwarf reach the same conclusion.

Ahira sighed. "Perhaps you're right. Hakim, get going."

"See you." Walter briefly clasped hands with Karl, then Aristobulus, then chucked Andy-Andy under the chin. She jerked her head away and grabbed his hand.

"Just be careful," she whispered. "I'll be along."

Walter took a slow, long look at Doria, then threw his arms around Ahira. Karl couldn't make out Walter's whispered words, except for the last two: "Be well."

The thief crawled away, then rose silently to the balls of his feet and disappeared around the bend.

Silence.

Ahira tapped Andy-Andy's shoulder. "Go."

Karl smiled. "See you in a little while."

Her chin trembled; a stray lock of hair fell across her nose.

Karl brushed it away. "Go."

She nodded, and left.

Ahira beckoned at Aristobulus. "Get ready."

Aristobulus started to rise, then stopped. "No. All at once."

"No," the dwarf said, shaking his head. "You next—Karl and I will take care of Doria."

Aristobulus shrugged and seated himself carefully on the floor, a study in simulated nonchalance. "I'll wait."

We've all grown, Karl thought. *I think he's wrong to pull this, but it's not coming from that damn self-centeredness that I used to hate in him.* "No time to argue." He reached for the wizard—

—and found his wrists caught in Ahira's huge hands. The dwarf's mouth quirked; he dropped Karl's wrists and spread his arms, shrugging, as though to say, *What can we do?*

"Fine," the dwarf said, unlimbering his axe from his chest. "Single-file—first Karl, then you, then Doria, then me."

The wizard nodded, and stood.

Karl rose silently to his feet, as did Aristobulus. Ahira urged Doria to stand. Sullenly, clumsily, she did.

Karl took the lead, and tiptoed around the bend—

—and into a brightness that stung his eyes, and a silent, moldy reek that ached in his nostrils. It smelled of age, and cruelty, and hatred . . . and Dragon.

The Dragon lay sleeping in the huge chamber, a cavern lit by glowing rainbowed crystals that lined the walls arching hundreds of yards above the rough floor. Its huge head, wickedly saurian, rested on crossed forelegs the size of centuries-old oak trunks.

Ellegon had been right. He *was* just a baby, a miniature, smoother version of *This*. The smallest of The Dragon's mottled scales was easily Karl's height; Its mouth could have swallowed an elephant.

And the teeth sent chills running down Karl's back. They stood tall and sharp, threatening yellowed edges through which The Dragon's fetid breath whistled, like a wind through a horrid forest.

He wrestled his eyes from The Dragon and looked around the cavern. Beyond the creature's left shoulder, a mirror gleamed, a surface rippled.

The Gate. Karl tiptoed slowly forward, his feet numb on the cold stone floor.

The Gate hung unsupported in the air, just above a narrow ledge. Its surface rippled, shimmering in the cavern's light, as the Gate stood, silently waiting, like a pool of water tipped on its side.

A stone ramp led up to the Gate, tapering from a wide base to where it became a stone ledge. There was no way that more than one person could stand on that ledge; it couldn't have been more than two feet square. They would have to go through one by one.

He turned and waved for Ahira and Aristobulus to bring Doria forward.

Both of them beckoned to her.

Come on, Doria. Just a little farther.

No response. She stood still, staring wide-eyed at The Dragon, her jaw clenched and quivering. A trickle of blood ran out of the corner of her mouth and dripped, one drop at a time, onto her white robes.

Ahira shook his head as he turned to face Karl. *No good,* he mouthed. *We need a diversion. Diversion.* He pointed to Karl, then Aristobulus, and then the Gate. *You two wait at the ramp. I'll bring her.*

Karl nodded, then walked slowly by The Dragon's head, Aristobulus at his side. The hundred-yard walk to the ramp took him past The Dragon's bulging midsection. If only he had a decent sword he could—

—*what? A mosquito could do more harm to me than I could do to That.* He gripped the hilt of Walter's scimitar. *Not unless I stuck It in the eye. And I couldn't reach that with a stepladder.* And perhaps he wouldn't even be able to stick this sword through Its lids. Then again—

Doria screamed, shattering the thick silence.

HUMANS. A roar shook the cavern, sending light-bearing crystals tinkling to the floor, knocking Karl off his feet.

Slowly, ponderously, the head lifted and turned, the man-high eyelids retracting.

"Over *here*," Aristobulus shouted, his voice breaking. "The eyes, Karl, the eyes—"

Karl bounced to his feet, the scimitar held in his right hand. "I know. I'll . . ." His voice caught in his throat as the head turned, two immense liquid eyes staring directly at him.

Behind Karl, Aristobulus' voice murmured harsh syllables, spoken and then gone, while over at the entrance, Ahira threw Doria's struggling body over his shoulder and broke into a sprint.

The Dragon's mouth opened. *BURN.* Its eyes gleamed—

"And done!" Aristobulus clapped his hands together.

—and shone, brighter and brighter until they flared with the light of a thousand suns.

Ari's light spell—The Dragon was blinded!

Karl ducked to one side as a gout of flame scoured the stone where he had stood. Aristobulus hiked up his robes and wordlessly sprinted up the ramp, not slowing as he reached the top, dived through the Gate, and was gone.

A heavy, limp mass knocked Karl off his feet. Doria!

"Over here! Burn *me*, you son of a pig," Ahira shouted, his battle-axe drawn. He raced away from the Gate. The Dragon's head following him. "Get through—take her. *Move.*"

Karl snatched up Doria as though she were a piece of fluff and ran with her up the ramp, to the Gate. A quick one-handed throw, and she was gone.

He turned. Ahira ducked a flamebreath, and dashed for the tunnel's opening. Like a felled tree, The Dragon's tail slammed down in front of the hole, the impact on the floor of the cavern knocking Ahira over.

"Over here, now," Karl shouted. "We'll take turns with your attention, Dragon."

The light in The Dragon's eyes was already beginning to dim; Aristobulus' light spell was wearing off. A few seconds more, and Karl and Ahira would be trapped in the cavern, The Dragon's sight restored.

YOU WILL BURN.

Ahira ran toward Karl, The Dragon's head following him.

Karl hesitated in front of the Gate. Ahira couldn't run fast enough; it didn't seem to take The Dragon long between flamebreaths, and the gaping mouth was coming to bear on the dwarf.

"Not him!" Karl shouted. "Try and burn *me,* Dragon."

At the base of the ramp, the dwarf stumbled, and started scrabbling up it on all fours. "Karl, *go."*

A rush of flame caught Ahira. The force of the gout of fire slid the dwarf up the ramp as he crackled and screamed in the flame, his arms waving aimlessly.

Karl turned and dived for the Gate, his legs burning behind him. A searing mass struck him in the back . . .

. . . and the world dissolved into a white-hot nightmare that faded only slowly into utter black.

PART FIVE

And Beyond

CHAPTER SIXTEEN

The Way Back

It is easy to go down into Hell;
night and day, the gates of dark Death stand wide;
    but to climb back up again, to retrace one's steps
to the upper air—there's the rub, the task.

—Publius Vergilius Maro (Virgil)

Walter Slovotsky's huge hand shook him, while the damp night grass pressed against his shirt and bare feet.

"Karl, we're back." The big man wept almost silently. "We're back."

Bare feet? That made sense; they had left their sandals behind. But why did his back hurt so? As if he'd been sunburned. Worse.

"Easy, now." Her hand at the back of his neck, Andy-Andy propped him up to a sitting position.

Karl opened his eyes, moonlight off the water in front of him hitting him like a slap. Moonlight? "We did it."

Lou Riccetti knelt in front of him, barefoot in now-tattered work-shirt and jeans. "Not quite." His voice was somber, his round cheeks were wet. "We don't even have Jason's body with us, and . . ."

"And what, *dammit?*" Karl peeled back the right leg of his jeans. No wonder it ached so; it was covered with blisters.

"Look over there." Riccetti pointed. Doria lay curled on the grass, her eyes wide and unblinking, her chest barely moving. "She's gone, Karl. Catatonic."

Karl shook himself. And it was himself; smaller, skinnier. *Barak? Help me?*

Nothing. No answer, not even the feeling of the presence of his other persona. *Then I'll do without.* "Where's Ahi—James?"

"Later," Andy-Andy breathed. "Just take a moment. You need—"

"Show him." Riccetti's voice was firm.

She caught a breath, and held it for longer than Karl would have thought possible. "Look to your right."

Walter Slovotsky knelt weeping over the dead body of James Michael Finnegan. The third-degree burns that had killed James Michael still smoldered, sending up light traces of mist and smoke.

Ohgod. "He didn't change enough."

Walter wept unashamedly, his huge hands reaching out as though to shake little James Michael Finnegan awake, then drawing back.

Just think for a minute. Mirror Lake spread out in front of him in the moonlight, the Commons all around. "We're on campus." A chill wind blew across the lake, sending a rush of leaves tumbling around him. "How long?"

Riccetti shook his head. "Deighton didn't lie about the different time rates. I snuck into a dorm; we've been gone just about eight hours—it's four in the morning. Jase is . . . gone, James Michael is dead, Doria is—"

Karl backhanded him across the face. "Shut *up.*" Shaking off Andy-Andy's helping hands, he got to his feet, ignoring the shooting pains from the blisters on his soles. "We've got to get moving."

"And do *what?*" Andy-Andy shrilled.

"*Shut up,* I said." He hobbled over to where Walter knelt weeping over the burned body that had been James Michael Finnegan. "And you, stand up and clear your head. Now. We don't have time for this shit."

Walter bared his teeth and growled, "You leave me alone. You—"

"No time for that. Where do you keep your car?"

"Car?"

"Yes, car. Automobile—where do you keep it parked?"

The big man's forehead crinkled. "Over in B-Lot. What are you—"

"Not close enough. *Lou?*"

Riccetti trotted over, a faint smile peeking through the grimness of his wet face. "Yes? Are you thinking what I think—"

"You've got it. S-Lot's closest—get there, find a big car, and steal it. Spare key under the front fender, cross some wires, do whatever you have to, but get a *big* car, and get it here. *Fast.*"

"Got it." Riccetti nodded and ran off.

"Karl?" Walter looked up at him. "What's going on?"

"Lou worked it out. You should have listened more closely to Ahira. The Matriarch of the Healing Hand may be able to raise the dead. Now, we don't have Jason's body, but we do have James Michael's. And we have Doria." He took a deep breath. "So we're going back. You know where that bastard Deighton lives?"

"Faculty Row—third house from the—"

"Fine. Run up there—act like you're out for a jog, or something—and cut the phone lines. Don't go in, but if he notices you and tries to get out, *stop him.*"

Slovotsky stood. "Are you sure we should handle it this way?"

Karl grabbed him by the front of the shirt. "Ahira's out of it, and I'm in charge. Understood?"

Slovotsky smiled and nodded. "You really think we'll be able to get away with all this?"

"No. But we're going to try. Get moving." Karl released his grip. Slovotsky turned and jogged away, not looking back.

"Karl?" His feet aching hideously, he turned to face Andy-Andy. "What have you got for me?"

"Diversion." He jerked his thumb toward the road. "If anybody comes this way, you distract them. Particularly if it's Security. If we get stuck on this side, James'll get buried, Doria gets committed to some nice funny farm, and that's it. So make it good."

She nodded. "But if it's Security, and I get busted?"

"Then you stay here. So make sure you don't. If we lose you, meet us up at Faculty Row. Third house from the west end." He forced a grin. "It'll be the one with the big stolen car in front of it. Now get up to the road, and keep watch."

She nodded and started to walk away, then turned back to face him. "But what if Deighton won't send us back? Or can't?"

Karl crossed his arms over his chest. "He will. Believe me, he will."

They huddled in the bushes next to Deighton's back porch. A light shone through the drawn curtains, casting their faces into yellow shadow.

"Last chance," Karl said quietly. "We've all got family and friends on this side. Our lives are here. I promise I'll do my best to bring anybody back who wants to come back. . . ." He shrugged.

Walter smiled. Not amiably. "But there's no guarantee we can slip by The Dragon again." The big man shrugged, not noticing how that split the shoulders of his shirt. "I'll take the chance. For James."

Riccetti rubbed at his face. "I've got no problem. I've always wanted out, wanted to make some miracles." He spread his hands. "And what am I here? A ninth-semester engineering major with maybe enough money for another semester. Haven't spoken to my parents in—" He shook himself. "I just want to know how we're going to do it."

"In a minute. Andy?"

She laid a hand on his arm. "We'll talk about it later. Right now, I'm more worried about Doria and Ahira. You said that they can help them on the other side?"

I don't have time for explanations. No, that wasn't true. It wasn't a matter of time, but of nerve. *If we don't do this quickly, I don't know if I can do it at all.* "Somewhere in the Waste is the home tabernacle of the Healing Hand Society. Doria's sect."

She nodded. "And she's one of their own, so they're likely to help her. Probably." She paused for a moment, fingering the bend in her nose. "But only probably—what if their . . . records don't show her? I mean, on this side there's institutions—maybe Doria would be best here?"

"No." Karl forced a smile. "I'm an ex-psych major, remember? The prognosis for catatonia is bad. Insulin therapy, shock treatments —none of it has decent odds. That's one.

"Two. If she could be brought out of it here, what do you think her chances are of ever getting out of the rubber-room set? Even a good shrink will diagnose her as having heavy delusions—and the rest of us won't be around to back her up, not if we're going to try to get James brought back. I can't see a chance that she could persuade anyone that what happened, well, happened. As far as I can see it, we're her only chance." He turned to Riccetti. "You crack a window in the car?"

"As per instructions. The . . . bag is still in the trunk, Doria's safely under a blanket in the back seat, and after I dropped you two off, I parked it well away from a streetlight."

"Fine," Karl said. "Go back to it, start it up, and pull it into the driveway when you see the light on the front porch blink three times. If that doesn't happen within, say, fifteen minutes, get going. Take care of them, and make another try when you think it's right. Got it?"

"Got it." Riccetti walked away, stooping low as he passed under Deighton's kitchen window.

Walter straightened himself. "What have you got for me?"

"Free safety. If the bastard gets past Andy and me, stop him. Don't kill him, don't give him a concussion—but stop him. On the three blinks, you come in, too. And if we blow it, you get back to your dorm and play Football Hero until you hear from Riccetti— Andy and I will keep our mouths shut. You weren't at the Student Union tonight, you didn't know anybody was missing or dead— understood?"

"Understood. We could just *ask* Deighton, you know." Walter held up a hand. "I know—but if he tells us to go to hell and starts screaming for the cops, we're in trouble."

Karl turned back to Andy-Andy. "You still haven't said whether you're in or out."

She gripped his shoulder. "In. Idiot."

He took a deep breath. It wasn't all that bad, not here. If something had gone wrong on the other side, he would have ended up as the main feature at a Coliseum torture session; here, the worst possibility was being arrested for kidnapping, assault, and first-degree murder.

No, make that second-degree. No way any prosecutor is ever going to prove my motive, show that I premeditated it.

Karl exhaled, forcing himself to relax. "Anybody got anything else to bring up? Then let's do it, people." He stood. "Now."

Ten minutes later, Arthur Simpson Deighton sat bound to a kitchen chair, glaring at Karl with his left eye. He couldn't quite glare with the right one; it was swollen shut.

Karl finished the last knot on the ropes that bound the old man's left ankle to the chair, then stepped back to admire his handiwork. Deighton was secure: His wrists were tied tightly with two of his own neckties, and the gag was letting little else besides muffled groans through.

He walked over to the sink where Andy-Andy stood, her right hand under the cold running water. "Nice shot," he said.

"Thanks." She winced. "I wish you could have taken him down a bit faster; I think I broke my thumb."

"You shouldn't make a fist with the thumb inside. Besides, that looks like a sprain to me. You want to go down to the infirmary, have it X-rayed?"

"And miss all the fun? No thanks. And no thanks for the sympathy, either."

He shrugged, then turned as the kitchen door swung open. No problem; just Walter.

"Everything okay in here?"

Karl nodded. "Just fine. You two go out and sit in the living room with the rest. Doc and I have a couple of things to talk over."

He checked three of the kitchen drawers before he found the one with the knives. Selecting a long, thin skinning knife, he looked around for a whetstone. No luck.

And that was too bad. Sharpening the knife in front of Deighton would have been good theater.

Still, Deighton's unbruised eye widened as Karl, knife in hand, pulled up a chair, spun it around, and seated himself ass-backward, his arms resting on the chair's back, the knife held lightly between thumb and forefinger.

"Deighton," Karl said, in his best Charles Bronson monotone, "I'm going to make this short." *And as frightening as possible; I don't want you thinking about anything except that you're terrified of me.* "You used us as a bunch of guinea pigs; everything that happened on the other side was your fault. Agreed?" *And what does he know about what happened on the other side? He said in his letter that his visions were erratic, that the time differential makes it hard for him to follow what happens—does he know that Jason is dead?*

Deighton shook his head violently.

Karl smiled. "Relax. You may just have a way out of it. As I was saying, when you shoot craps with people's lives, you're responsible for the result. It's a sound legal principle—take my word for it. Say, if you torch a building for the insurance, and someone dies in the fire, you don't just spend a year or two in jail for the arson. It's murder one." Karl raised a palm. "I'll give you this: You tried to see that we were well enough equipped. You didn't know that Ari—that Riccetti was going to blast the treasure chest." He set the point of the knife under Deighton's chin, sliding the blade through the gray goatee until it touched flesh. "But that doesn't make any difference, professor. Agreed? *I said, agreed?*" He drew the knife back, just enough for Deighton to move his head.

Slowly, Deighton nodded.

"And how many times a murderer does that make you, Art? Blink once for each."

Deighton's left eye closed, then opened. He looked toward the door from the kitchen to the living room, then back at Karl.

Good. He's not sure if I want him to count Doria, but he doesn't know about Jason. Karl forced himself not to breathe a sigh of relief. *He doesn't know that Jason is dead.*

"Now," Karl went on, "it's your fault that James Michael is dead, and Doria's . . . in bad shape. If killing you would bring them back, I'd do it here and now." He touched the blade to Deighton's neck, just over the jugular. "A little push, and it would be all over." He dropped the point of the blade. "But that wouldn't bring them back, would it? It's too bad that the only way I can see to fix things requires that you stay alive."

Hope brightened Deighton's lined face. Karl went on: "So, you're sending us back. Can you do that? I mean, because it worked once with us, can you be sure that it'll work again?"

Deighton nodded.

"Good. Next question—and in case you haven't guessed, the answer had better be yes—can you transfer us from here to that green spot in the Waste of Elrood, the home tabernacle of the Society of the Healing Hand? Better nod, Art. Otherwise"—Karl touched the knifepoint to the center of Deighton's forehead—"we go to Plan B."

Deighton drew his head back.

"You don't want to know what Plan B is, do you?"

Deighton shook his head as though he were trying to shake his ears loose.

Good. Because I don't know what Plan B is, either. That was the trouble with threatening Deighton; what if he called Karl's bluff? There was no way to get back to the other side that didn't require Deighton's cooperation, and Karl wasn't sure that he had either the stomach or the knowledge to cause Deighton enough pain to make him cooperate—without killing the bastard.

So we keep him too scared to think of calling my bluff. "One more thing: Only six of us are going back; Parker is staying behind. I've got him safely away from campus, holed up in a motel. If we don't get back in a reasonable time . . ." He let his voice trail off; Deighton's imagination would work better than an explicit threat.

Karl shrugged. "Are we agreed? Good—I'm going to free your mouth now." He slipped the knife between Deighton's cheek and the cloth strips that held a balled-up dishtowel in Deighton's mouth. "Go ahead and yell. Once." Karl sliced the strips.

Deighton spat out the dishtowel. "You . . . misunderstood me." His voice quavered only a little. "I didn't mean for any of this—"

"Shut up. What equipment do you need?"

"I haven't said that I'd do it."

Karl shrugged. "Got a pair of pliers around here? I bet you'll do it after I've pulled a few teeth." He started to rise.

"Wait. There's a wood box in the living room. Oak, approximately two feet by one, six inches deep. I'll need that, and I'll have to have my hands free."

Karl reached out and patted the old man's cheek. "No problem. But if you try to free your legs before we're gone, I'll break them. At the kneecaps." He couldn't resist adding, "Shweetheart."

"You are lying in the short grasses of the well-kept lawn surrounding the tabernacle of the Society of the Healing Hand, a group of six adventurers, seeking the revivification of one of your number, the healing of the soul of another, and fleeing the shame of a distant wizard, who regrets with all his heart that you were hurt. That *any* of you were hurt.

"The tabernacle towers above you, several hundred yards to the west, blocking the setting sun. In the harsh glare, it is difficult to make out the details, but you see that it is of the same general shape as the Aztec pyramids, although easily twice their height.

"The wind is hot and dry; blowing across the Waste of Elrood, it has lost almost all of its moisture. . . .

CHAPTER SEVENTEEN

Payment

*I have always thought that all men should be free; but if
any should be slaves, it should be first those who desire it
for themselves, and secondly those who desire it for others.
Whenever I hear anyone arguing for slavery, I feel a
strong impulse to see it tried on him personally.*

—Abraham Lincoln

A white-robed acolyte led them inside, with Karl in the lead, carrying the sewn-leather bag containing Ahira's remains. A distant
uneasiness kept his right hand on the hilt of his new sword, a longish
saber with a strange leather grip that sucked all the sweat away from
his palm. Having the steel quickly available comforted him—just as
well he'd kept that skinning knife in hand while Deighton transferred them; it had translated well.

Behind him walked Andy-Andy and Aristobulus, both clutching
their leather-bound spell books as tightly as Karl held his swordhilt.

One thing you can say for Deighton, he doesn't equip us poorly. The
packs they had left outside lacked only magical implements—
Deighton had claimed that he hadn't any left, other than the spell
books, and Karl hadn't wanted to argue the point. But they did bear
food, and additional weapons, and several pup-tents, along with
other necessities.

Last in their ragged line was Walter Slovotsky, Doria's limp form held chest-high in his arms. Karl turned to see Walter nodding reassuringly to Doria, as though she could see him.

Dark corridors led to a vast, high-ceilinged hall, where the sounds of their footsteps echoed off marble walls and the smooth gray floor. Lit dimly by three ornate candelabra that hung from the ceiling, it was empty, deserted save for a high-backed throne on a white stone pedestal, three-quarters of the way across the room. Beyond the throne, a narrow slit of a window gave them a view of the greenery on the east side of the tabernacle. In the morning, no doubt, it brought more light into the room, but not now, at sunset.

Karl lowered the bag to the floor.

The acolyte nodded. "The Matriarch will see you here," she said, extending her arms for Doria. "And I will see to my sister."

Walter looked over to Karl. *Well?* his half-shrug said.

We're on their turf, but . . .

"Really," the acolyte said, a half-sneer passing across her smooth face, "do you trust us so little? If so, then why are you here, Karl Cullinane?"

We haven't exchanged a single word, but she knows my name. I'm not going to ask her how; undoubtedly, that's what she's expecting.

"We will heal her, and take care of her. Doria is one of us, now—not one of you," the acolyte said. "I must warn you that you are now prejudicing your case."

That sounded ominous; he quelled the warrior's natural response to a challenge. "Go ahead, Walter," he said. "If they're as powerful as we hope they are, we couldn't put up much of a fight anyway."

The acolyte accepted Doria's slack body, not straining with the effort. Clearly, she was stronger than she looked.

"The Matriarch will be with you shortly," she said, walking easily toward the hall's entrance. And then she was gone.

Andy-Andy put a hand on his shoulder. "Take it easy, Karl—they won't hurt her. Besides," she sighed, "what could they *do* to hurt her, the way she is?"

Walter chuckled grimly. "And if the little bitch was lying, we can still try and take her apart later. Or frighten the hell out of her, like you did out of Deighton. Nice bit of acting, that—or *would* you have carved little pieces out of him until he gave in?"

Karl smiled. "I'll never tell." *And I'll never know. I know that I could have killed him without any regret; torture is something else.* "Apology time, Ari—if I'd leaned on him a bit harder, we might have been able to get better out of him than a couple of spell books."

Clutching the leather-bound volume tightly, Aristobulus' lined face broke into a smile. "You haven't heard me complaining. For someone with no talent for leadership, you haven't done a bad job. Besides, *I'm* not the one who's wanted in Pandathaway—now I can go back, and qualify for the guild, and—"

"Not necessarily," a low, reedy voice said from behind Karl's back.

Karl turned, his weight on the balls of his feet, forcing himself to move slowly. The throne wasn't empty anymore.

An almost impossibly thin woman sat there, faintly glowing white robes gathered about her. The collar of her garment was different from Doria's or the acolyte's; it covered her head as a sort of cowl, casting her face into shadow, her features, if any, hidden as well as if she were masked. *"Greetings. You may approach me."* There was an eerie quality to her voice; it had the airiness of an old woman's, but no hint of fragility or weakness. And it was loud; if this was her normal speaking voice, her shout could well shatter stone walls.

Karl bent to pick up the bag containing Ahira's body, then straightened. They all walked across the floor, Karl carrying the bag in cupped arms. "We're here to—"

"I know why you are here."

They stopped in unison, ten yards from her throne. Karl's forehead wrinkled; she hadn't given a command, she hadn't said anything or made the slightest gesture, yet all four of them had stopped suddenly, as though responding to a compelling order.

"The issue at hand," the Matriarch said, *"is whether or not we shall honor your wishes. Clearly, the Society is in debt to you to some extent; you have done us a service by protecting one of our own, and bringing her here."*

"Then—" Karl started.

"But that is not sufficient payment for what you ask. Reviving the dead is immensely difficult, immensely draining. We require further payment."

Aristobulus took a half-step forward, then stepped back. "What sort of payment? I've still got some spells in my—"

"That is insufficient. Your spells are trivial by my standards, wizard. Did you look about our preserve? Once, the entire Waste was that lush, that fine. I protected this tabernacle against the magic of greater than you."

Walter raised his hands. "Look, Lady—instead of telling us what isn't enough, why don't you just tell us what you want? You want gold? I'll go steal you a few tons. You want diamonds? I'll—"

"Be silent." The Matriarch raised her hands to her face, the first motion they had seen her make. *"The one who spoke of you, Karl Cullinane, was correct. You are not terribly bright. But this one, this Walter Slovotsky, is worse."* She lowered her hands. *"Then again, that is hardly your fault. You are, after all, merely a human."*

And what are you, old lady? Karl thought. *God? Or is it just that you think you—*

"No. And yes. It's simply that . . ." Her voice trailed off into gibberish. She sighed. *"But you do not understand the High Tongue, and that is the only language in which I can clearly explain myself. My requirements are so necessary and so obvious—but this Erendra and this English of yours . . . the words do not cover the territory. So I shall speak as simply as I can, so that you each can understand what I require of you, if not why I require it—*

"Aristobulus."

The wizard shook himself. The voice was somehow different now, less . . . diffuse?

"True. I speak only to you, wizard. Only one of the others can hear me, and will know if you decline to offer your portion of the payment."

Aristobulus nodded. *Very well,* he thought. *You don't want what my spells can do for you—what do you want?*

"Your magic. All of it. Your . . . Aristobulus-ness. Your portion of the payment is to be but Louis Riccetti evermore. An ordinary human, unable to even read a word—to even see a word—in that book you clutch so tightly. Agree to that, and Ahira may live again. Decline, and he will surely stay dead."

How could she be sure of that? Certainly, the Healing Hand wasn't the only sect in the world; possibly there was some other cleric, somewhere, who could raise the dead.

"No. There is not. And soon, there may be none at all who can."

His aura wrapped him tightly, seething. For James Michael, could he give that up?

"Your reasons don't matter to me. It's . . . the distance between us that makes our communication so difficult, just as you could never teach your cat to fetch. You may give up your magic for whatever reason you wish. Or not. She sighed. *"But I see that you will not. You do not see enough worth in your other life, in that engineering nonsense you used to almost worship—"*

"Nonsense? Listen to me, you: There's more magic in a suspension bridge than in all these books, and—"

"Then you agree?"

To hell with her. "Engineering nonsense" indeed. "Yes," he snarled. "I'll give it up." *And I'll build bridges,* here. *I will. And horsecollars, and steam engines—*

"As you wish." She gestured lightly with one hand, murmuring words that could only be heard and then forgotten.

He *changed.* Aristobulus's slim form bulged out, the old, dry skin of his body becoming once more firm with youth. It dizzied him, he stumbled . . .

. . . and Lou Riccetti, clad in workshirt and blue jeans, picked himself up off the floor to glare at the Matriarch. He crossed his arms defiantly over his chest. And, to his own surprise, found that he was grinning from ear to ear.

"Andrea."

"Yes?" Why was *she* first? That didn't seem fair. After all—

"One of the others has the same reaction. Curious."

Andrea tried to turn her head, to see which one of the others the Matriarch was talking about, but she couldn't move.

I'm not even breathing. She tried to force her lungs to draw in air, and couldn't. Panic burned her throat.

"Be still. Do you need to breathe?"

Well, no—and that was strange. Why didn't she need to?

"You stall. Which is typical of you. You lack commitment, Andrea Andropolous. You wait, and you see, and you never decide until you absolutely have to. Your payment is this: You must agree to decide about something important. Yes or no; in or out; together or apart."

Fine. But what "something important"? I have to say yes without knowing?

"No. You never have to say yes, nor commit yourself without knowing. But an important promise will be made here, perhaps. Your payment is to agree to participate, or to reject participation in that promise. Without hesitation; without time for contemplation; without stalling. Will you make payment? Or will Ahira remain dead?"

She shrugged mentally, irritated at the way her shoulders refused to move. *I can't see that that's such a big sacrifice—and I can't see what you're getting out of it.*

"True. Will you make payment?"

Yes, but—The thought cut off as she heard the Matriarch and Walter.

"Walter Slovotsky."

I'm first. I knew I'd be first.

The Matriarch chuckled. *"You are always first, are you not? The center of your pitiful little universe. Your portion of the payment will be that egotism, that idiotic notion that everything centers on you, that as long as all is right with you, all is right with the world—and that always, all is right with you."*

He wanted to reach up and scratch his head while he puzzled that out, but his arms hung limp by his sides. No, not limp—unmoving, that was all.

"Time works somewhat differently around me, when I so command it. Your mind is free, but the nerve impulses won't reach your arms until we have finished our conversation."

Well, then, we can finish it quickly. I gave up on seeing myself as some sort of superman back in Lundeyll. I'll tell you—a knife in the shoulder can do wonders for your perspective. Is that what you wanted to hear?

"No. That is what I wanted to know.*"*

Karl's ears buzzed with the sounds of the Matriarch carrying on three conversations at once; with Riccetti renouncing his wizardy, Andy her indecisiveness, and Walter his self-centeredness. But it was as though Karl had three separate sets of ears, three separate minds: The words didn't jumble together; each word, each thought, stood out from the others, with crystal clarity.

"Karl Cullinane," the Matriarch said. *"It is your turn to offer payment. Or not."*

Payment? How was all this payment? What possible benefit could she get from this? *I just don't see what she's gaining from—*

"True. You do not see. And, quite probably, you never will. Are you prepared to make payment, or will Ahira remain dead?"

Of course he was prepared to do something for her—but what did she want? Some of his possessions?

"No."

The sacrifice of some of his abilities, like the way she had made Aris—

"No."

A portion of his psyche, as with Walter?

"No."

That left some sort of commitment, like the way she had made

Andy agree to decide about something or other. *Does that have something to do with this?*

"*Correct. And what will you commit yourself to?*"

What do you want, Lady? Why don't you just come out and ask?

"*Because I have limitations that you can never understand. I am far wiser, far more intelligent, than you can ever hope to be, but the perspective . . . limits me.*"

Wonderful. Power doesn't just corrupt, it limits, too. Eh?

"*You stall, dilettante. You delay. Answer my question.*"

There was something strange about this whole payment business, as though the other three had gained, instead of lost—

"*True.*"

Lou Riccetti had always been sort of an oddity, a misfit. No real self-respect, back in the days when he used to trail around behind Jason Parker, like some sort of obedient spaniel. But that had changed when he was transferred over to this side, when he became a wizard.

No. It hadn't. Aristobulus was just the other side of the same coin, seeing himself as worthwhile through his magic. *Only* through his magic.

And that was it. Lou Riccetti hadn't seen *himself* as worthwhile until the moment that the Matriarch had required he give up his wizardry, turned him back into a normal human being.

"*Again correct. Go on.*"

Now, Walter was a different case. Slovotsky had always seen himself as worthwhile, perhaps too much so. Until Lundeyll, Walter hadn't understood his own mortality, his own limitations.

And the Matriarch wanted Walter to know that mortality, to see those limitations.

But what did that imply? So what if Walter knew he could hurt?

"*Perhaps he can now truly understand that others can hurt, as well.*"

Karl nodded mentally.

And then there was Andy-Andy, who forestalled committing herself. *Which sounds a lot like me, actually. Psych major, soc major, bridge player, gamer, et cetera and ad nauseam. If she's got a mild case of indecision, then I'm close to terminal.*

"*Precisely.*"

Then what do you want me to decide to do? I can see that you want me to agree to do something, but what?

"*That which you have enjoyed most. That one thing which has made you feel most alive. To agree to do that, for the rest of your life, is your payment."*

Karl let his string of former majors and hobbies run through his head. No, none of those. The Matriarch had hardly gone through all of this to get him to agree to finish his acting degree.

But she said that I have to take up—what was it—"that one thing which has made you feel most alive."

And then, it all clicked into place. Normality. Commitment. Lack of self-centeredness. The commitment to understanding that there were others out there, that they had feelings, and that those feelings *counted.*

Jefferson's words swam in his brain: "We hold these truths to be self-evident, that all men are created equal—"

And in this world, they *didn't* hold that self-evident. Ellegon was a person, if not a human, and he had been left chained to a rock in Pandathaway just for the convenience of the rulers of that city. And in the slave markets, whips cracked and flesh parted. Ohlmin and his slavers had chained and abused them, because people were property here.

And the last piece: *The two things in my life that I enjoyed most were the time that I freed Ellegon and when I got us away from Ohlmin and killed those bastards.*

Matriarch, that's to be my payment. Free all the slaves. But how? Slice up all the slavers? Break all the chains? How?

"That is your problem. Do you commit yourself?"

"Of course." Karl tried to spread his hands, and found to his surprise that he could. "But that isn't a sacrifice."

"But it is payment, in the only coin I will accept."

The others stirred around him. Andy-Andy glared up at the Matriarch. "And you can count me in on it, too. Is that a quick enough decision for you?"

"Yes." The Matriarch's voice held a hint of amusement.

Lou Riccetti, arms crossed over his chest, smiled. "I'm in."

Walter Slovotsky raised his hands and shrugged. "You'll probably get us all killed trying, but . . ."

Karl threw an arm around the other's shoulder. "But he's in, too. Now, about Ahira . . . ?"

"We have accepted payment. It will take slightly more than a year to effect his revivification."

Walter shook his head. "We can't hang around here; there's a price on Karl's head, at least, and the Pandathaway Guilds' Council has already managed to nail him with a Location spell once—"

"That could not happen here. This preserve is . . . defended. But," the Matriarch sighed, *"I could hardly have the four of you within the tabernacle for that length of time, making noise and—ahh. Of course. Length of time, indeed."* She gestured, and spoke, the words vanishing as they left her mouth.

Through the window beyond the throne, night fell, the darkness only momentary as the sun rose like a glowing balloon across the sky.

And darkness, again. And light, and darkness. And light and darkness. Andlightanddarkandlightanddark as the days strobed past.

And then it slowed, until a brilliant sun hung motionless, casting bright light into the hall, with its empty throne.

Karl brushed a year's accumulation of dust from his shoulders. "Is everyone all—"

"I'm fine, in case anyone's interested," Ahira's voice rasped behind him.

Ahira?

Karl turned. The dwarf glared up at him, hands on hips, head cocked to one side. "Well," Ahira said, "don't I get a hello?"

"James!"

It was physically impossible for all four full-sized humans to hug the same dwarf at the same time, but they tried.

"And I have arranged some company for you."

Karl turned to look at the empty throne. He had heard her voice, but the Matriarch was nowhere to be seen. *"Nor will you see me again."*

"Now wait—" he started. "What if we need some help? Won't you—"

"No," the voice answered, coming at him from every direction. *"Never will the Hand aid you again. I'm . . . sorry, Karl Cullinane, but we . . . can't."*

"I don't understand."

True. I told her you were a decent person—for a human, that is —but I never claimed you were intelligent.

"As I said, I've arranged some company for you."

A huge, triangular head peeked in through the door.

"Ellegon!"

Yes, I'm Ellegon. And you are Karl Cullinane. A paw slapped against stone. *And this is a floor . . .*

"Enough. I take it you're the company."

Very clever. I am also transportation. We will camp on the edge of the forest tonight. Just in case you're interested, I've spent a good part of the past year ferrying some of your possessions here, things you left at the base of Bremon. Including one red mare that emptied her bowels all the way across the Waste. I don't think she likes me. But she does look tasty.

We are not eating my horse. And are you certain you can carry all of us?

No. Actually, I just want to see how high I can get before we crash. Any other stupid questions?

"Well, I wanted to ask the Matriarch about—"

She wouldn't answer. You are on your own.

"Isn't that *we?*"

No. Not until you introduce me to the other three. I already know Walter Slovotsky.

"And then?"

Karl, it took me three centuries of being chained in a cesspool to learn what you found in months. You just may be able to do it.

"You call that an answer?"

The dragon's head cocked to one side. *As a matter of fact, I do.*

CHAPTER EIGHTEEN

Profession

Give me where to stand, and I shall move the world.

—Archimedes

Karl walked a few hundred yards from the fire before spreading his blankets on the damp grass.

Slipping out of his leggings and tunic, he slid between the blankets and lay back, pillowing his head on his hands. High above, a coal-black sky winked its million eyes.

How the hell are we going to do it? Where do we start? With Pandathaway's Slavers' Guild, I suppose, but . . .

He shrugged. Slavery had been alive on this world for millennia. He wasn't going to figure out how to end it tonight.

But tomorrow was another day.

And besides, I've been told that thinking isn't my strong suit. He chuckled, and then sighed deeply.

Well, you're correct for once.

Thanks.

He sighed. Doria was gone, now. He probably wouldn't see her again. Would she be happy with the Society?

They take care of their own, Karl.

"Probably. Do me a favor; get out of my mind for a while. It's been kind of a tough day—"

Year.

"—year, then. I could use some rest."

I was just going to ask if you minded if I hunted up some food.

"Not my department; take it up with Ahira. Where are you, anyway?"

Down by the stream. I thought I might snatch up a few fish while I'm on watch. I can see Walter and Ahira and Riccetti from here, sitting around the fire, arguing. And Andrea's worrying—

"Arguing and worrying? About what?"

Riccetti's talking about going back to the other side for a book of tables, of all things. Why he's so interested in furniture, I don't know.

"Engineering tables, Ellegon. Different sort of thing." Although Karl had had quite enough of Riccetti's arguing about books. First the spell books, and now this. "What's Andy worried about?"

Parents, relatives, friends. How they'll miss her, not know what happened to her. And—

"Hmm—remind her about the time differential on this side. It's a problem for all of us, but we've got a few years to figure out what to do about it. It'll be at least a day or so, on the other side, before we're seriously missed. And that'll stack up to . . ." He trailed off, too lazy and too tired to worry over the calculation. *Save it for morning. Save it all for morning.*

But I was wondering about the food. I'll keep alert, I promise. Young dragons don't sleep much at all, you know.

"Young dragons also don't stop bugging the hell out of me."

True.

Ellegon went silent. Karl let his eyelids sag shut, his muscles unkink. Loosen the neck, slow the heart, rest the mind . . .

Silently, she slid into his arms. He sat up with a jerk, bowling her over. "What the *hell*—"

Andy-Andy propped her chin on one hand. "If you're going to bounce me around the meadow, I'll go elsewhere." A loose strand of hair fell across her nose. She blew it off and moved closer to him, brushing the blankets aside.

No, there weren't any bikini marks. Amazing.

After a while, she pushed him away. But gently, and only a few inches. "Looks like you finally found yourself a profession—"

"*This?*"

"—hero."

"Don't talk dirty."

Whether he reached for her, or she for him, he was never quite sure.

But he couldn't have cared less.

THE SWORD
AND THE CHAIN

for Harry Leonard
who, thankfully, still doesn't know when
to stop haranguing me

Acknowledgments

I'd like to thank the people who helped me through this one: Kevin O'Donnell, Jr., who insists that I think it through before I write it; Mary Kittredge, who demands that I get the words written, and then worry about whether or not they're the right ones; Mark J. McGarry, who swears that both of them are leading me astray; Jim Drury, who makes me feel that I know what I'm doing; Robert Lee Thurston and Judy Heald, whose support is always invaluable; Bob Adams, whose timely advice on blacksmithing was not nearly so important to me as his friendship; Darrell Sweet, cover artist extraordinaire; Susan Bissett, who, for the second time, has turned my barely legible scribblings into a fine map; my editor, Sheila Gilbert, who has the good grace to trust me; and Cherry Weiner, my agent for this work, who asked for more of Ellegon.

And, most particularly, I'd like to thank my wife, Felicia Herman, who not only gets more beautiful every year, but knows how to separate what's important from what isn't.

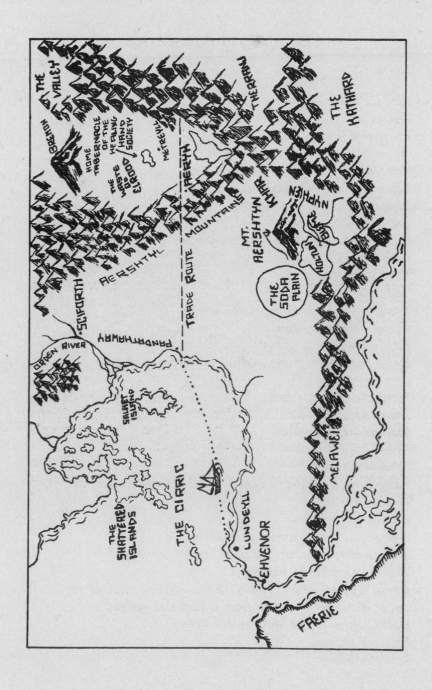

DRAMATIS PERSONAE

Karl Cullinane—warrior
Andrea Andropolous—novice wizard
Ellegon—a young dragon
Walter Slovotsky—journeyman thief
Ahira Bandylegs—dwarf warrior
Louis Riccetti—ex-wizard/engineer
Rhêden Monsterhunter—hunter
Teerhnus—blacksmith
Ch'akresarkandyn ip Katharhdn—warrior, soldier of fortune
Orhmyst—master slaver
Kirah—freed slave
Aeia Eriksen—freed slave
Tennetty—freed slave, apprentice warrior
Chton—freed slave, farmer
Ihryk—freed slave, farmer
Fialt—freed slave, farmer, sailor, apprentice warrior
Ahrmin—slaver
Wenthall—master wizard
Zherr, Baron Furnael
Sammis—master wizard
Hivar—man-at-arms
Enna—fealty-servant
Rahff Furnael—heir to barony Furnael, apprentice warrior
Thomen Furnael
Beralyn, Lady Furnael
Bren Adahan—heir to barony Adahan
Avair Ganness—captain and owner of the *Warthog*
Thyren—journeyman wizard
Jheral, Hynryd, Raykh, Lensius, Fihka—journeyman slavers
Seigar Wohtansen—Clan Wohtan wizard and warleader
Estalli, Olyla—Seigar Wohtansen's wives
Peill—elf warrior
Jason Cullinane

I find that the great thing in this world is not so much where we stand as in what direction we are moving; To reach the port of heaven, we must sail sometimes with the wind and sometimes against it—but we must sail, and not drift, nor lie at anchor.

—Oliver Wendell Holmes

Introduction

It started as a game. Just a quiet, pleasant evening for seven college students.

Karl Cullinane, Jason Parker, James Michael Finnegan, Doria Perlstein, Walter Slovotsky, Andrea Andropolous, and Lou Riccetti sat down for an evening of fantasy gaming. It was going to be fun. That's all it was supposed to be.

But then gamemaster Professor Arthur Deighton somehow transferred them to the Other Side. Without warning, they found themselves in the world they thought existed only in their imaginations, in the bodies of the characters they had been pretending to be. Short, skinny Karl Cullinane became a tall, well-muscled warrior; crippled James Michael Finnegan became the powerful dwarf, Ahira Bandylegs. All seven of them changed into different people with unusual talents.

Suddenly it wasn't a game anymore.

Jason Parker was the first to die. He spent the last few moments of his life kicking on the end of a spear.

The others survived, but now they weren't playing, they were fighting to stay alive, to escape the wrath and weapons of warriors and wizards, slavers and lords.

They had to find the Gate Between Worlds and return home.

They had to, and they did—but in the doing, they lost far too much. Ahira died at the Gate. Doria went catatonic. Nothing could be done about that at home. But, back on the Other Side, the Matriarch of the Healing Hand Society could bring Ahira back to life, could cure Doria's shattered mind.

So they returned to the Other Side. And, yes, the Matriarch was willing to help them, just this once.

But nothing is ever free. There were prices to pay, and promises to make. Promises that would be kept.

No matter what the cost.

PART ONE

Metreyll

CHAPTER ONE

Profession

"Where we do go from here?" Karl Cullinane asked, sitting next to Andrea Andropolous on the largest of the flat stones surrounding the ashes of supper's campfire. He squinted at the setting sun as he sipped his coffee.

Andy-Andy smiled. Karl always liked that smile; it brightened up what had been an already bright day. "Do you mean that metaphorically?" she asked, tossing her head to clear the wisps of hair from her face. Extending a slim, tanned forefinger, she stroked his thigh. "Or are you asking where the two of us can slip off to, to get some privacy?" She looked up at him, her head cocked to one side. "I would have *thought* that last night would have been enough for a while. Let's wait until dark, shall we?"

He laughed. "That wasn't what I meant—I was talking about how long we're going to stay here on the preserve. The Hand Society isn't going to let us live here forever." *And I was also wondering how the hell we're going to keep our promise to the Matriarch.* "But . . ." He took her hand. "As long as you've brought the subject up, I wouldn't mind—"

A firm, reedy voice sounded in Karl's head: *This is ridiculous.*

Lying on the grass twenty yards away, Ellegon opened his eyes. Then, raising his head from his crossed forelegs, the dragon glared at the two of them. *Can't you think about anything but sexual intercourse? I know you're only humans, but must you *always* be in heat?*

Curling and uncurling his leathery wings, he rose to all fours, sending a flock of birds fleeing from their perches in a nearby elm and into chittering flight. Ellegon was small, as dragons go: He measured barely the length of a Greyhound bus from the grayish-green tip of his pointed tail to the saucer-sized nostrils of his saurian snout.

His cavernous mouth closed, then opened, releasing wisps of smoke and steam. *I would think that people who were recently college students could have other subjects on their minds. Now and then, at least.*

Ellegon, Karl thought. *You're not being reasonable. I—*

No, never mind. Pay no attention. Don't bother with me. I'm only a dragon, after all. The dragon turned and lumbered away.

"Ellegon," Karl called out. "Come back here."

The dragon didn't seem to hear.

Karl shrugged. "I wish he'd be a bit less—"

"—of a pain in the butt," Walter Slovotsky finished, as he walked up. "But it's your own fault, you know." He was a big man, although not quite as tall, broad-shouldered, or well muscled as Karl. Here, at least. Back home, Walter had been a half a foot taller than Karl, and much stronger. But Karl had been changed in the transfer between worlds, receiving added height and muscle, as well as skills that he hadn't possessed at home.

There had been changes, but not everything had changed; Walter still could figure things out faster than Karl could, most of the time. And that still rankled.

"What do you mean?" Karl asked, irritated.

"Tell you in a moment; I need some coffee." Picking up a rag to protect his hand from the heat of the battered coffeepot's handle, Slovotsky poured himself a cupful. He seemed oblivious to the chilly wind that blew across the meadow, despite the fact that he was shirtless, as usual, dressed only in blousy white pantaloons and sandals, a tangle of knives and straps at his hip.

With his free hand, Slovotsky rubbed at the corners of his eyes. Their slight epicanthic folds gave him a vaguely oriental appearance, although his features were clearly Slavic, and his black hair was slightly curly. "You're just asking for a hard time, Karl. There's no reason for it. He's jealous, that's all."

"Jealous?" Andy-Andy arched an eyebrow. "Of me? Why? I wouldn't think—"

True.

"—that dragons would get jealous," she finished, as if she hadn't been interrupted. Perhaps she hadn't been; Ellegon could easily have tuned her out.

Karl turned to see the tip of Ellegon's tail vanish as the dragon disappeared into a stand of trees on the far side of the meadow.

Don't eavesdrop. You want to join the conversation? Fine. Come on back and chat. Otherwise, keep out of it.

No answer.

Walter shrugged, the corners of his mouth turning upward in an amused grin. "It's just a matter of attention from Karl. Which you're getting, and he's not."

He jerked a thumb toward Lou Riccetti, who sat propped against the base of a tall elm, his arms crossed over his blue workshirt, lost in thought. "Slovotsky's Law Number Thirty-seven: Some people need less attention than others." He shrugged. "Some want more. It all depends on—"

"Ohgod." Perched in a high branch of a dying oak, Ahira the dwarf shook his head. "*Everyone,* get your weapons; Lou, you take my crossbow. Karl, on your horse. *Move.* There's a bunch of riders galloping toward the preserve—I think we're about to be attacked."

As he spoke, Ahira was already climbing clumsily but quickly down the tree, supporting himself by the pressure of his blunt fingers against the rough bark, not bothering to look for branches to hold on to.

Karl dropped his cup as he jumped to his feet. With a quick, reflexive pat at his swordhilt, he ran across the meadow to where his chestnut mare stood, idly grazing in the ankle-high grasses.

Unless Ahira was jumping at shadows, there probably wasn't time to saddle her. He took the bridle down from the branch where it hung and quickly slid the bit between her teeth as he slipped the crownpiece over her poll and tightened it behind her ears. Reins in his left hand, he grasped her rough mane in his right and eased himself to her back, swinging his right leg over and seating himself firmly.

He flicked the reins and dug in his heels. *What the hell is going on?* he thought.

I can see it a bit better, and—

Make it quick. We're about to be attacked.

No, we are not. This is what is going on. Ellegon opened his mind.

Craning his long neck to see over a rocky outcropping, Ellegon stared out over the Waste of Elrood. Off in the distance, five shapes moved quickly across its cracked, dusty surface.

He concentrated on them; they zoomed into view. All five were filthy humans, mounted on horses. Quite possibly tasty horses.

Three of the humans rode together as they pursued a fourth, a half-naked, skinny one, wearing a metal collar with a dangling length of chain. The fifth rider, dressed like the other pursuers in matching green tunic and leggings, galloped in toward the quarry from a different direction.

Thanks, Ellegon, Karl thought. *The fifth one probably took a different route than his friends; he's trying to cut the slave off before he reaches the tabernacle grounds.*

He will. His horse is much fresher than the other four.

"Andrea!" Ahira shouted. "Get up to the bluff. Hide in the bushes, and when they get close enough, hit as many as you can with your sleep spell. We'll sort it out later. Right now, I just want to—"

"No," Karl said, reining in his horse next to the dwarf. "They're not after us. It's four soldiers, chasing an escaped slave. They're not going to come close to the clearing. Andy, how far can you reach with your sleep spell?"

She waved her hands helplessly. "Two, three hundred feet. At best."

Ellegon, do any of them have bows? You didn't notice before, and I couldn't tell.

Two of them do. Karl, we've got to talk about—

Save it for later. He turned to Andrea. "No good. They'd cut you down before you got in range. Ellegon and I'll take care of it." *Get airborne, and give me a hand.* Karl had the only horse among the five of them; depending on how far away the hunters and their quarry were, he might have to hold the fort all by himself for several minutes before the others could arrive.

Karl had a great respect for his own fighting skills, but a single man successfully taking on four or more was a longshot, no matter how handy that one man was with a sword. But with Ellegon overhead, there probably wouldn't be a fight at all; few people would risk being roasted in dragonfire.

No.

What?

I thought I made that clear. No, I will not get airborne. They have bows. I'm scared.

That was bizarre. Ellegon's scales were as hard as fine steel; he was almost immune to any nonmagical threat.

But there was no time to discuss that. "Ellegon's out—I'll show them up. Catch up with me as soon as you can."

Andrea reached out and grabbed at his leggings. *"Wait.* I've got a—"

"No time, didn't you hear me? *They're chasing an escaped slave.* Stay out of it; I don't want to have to worry about your getting hurt." He jerked his leggings out of her grasp.

Ignoring Ahira's shouts from behind, he kicked his horse into a canter. Galloping her down the incline to the edge of the Waste was tempting, but Karl wasn't used to riding bareback; best to ensure arriving rather than take the chance of being bounced off his horse's back.

He cantered down the slope toward a break in the trees. Beyond it, touched with the red light of the setting sun, the Waste of Elrood lay in harsh, bright flatness. Long ago, what now was the Waste had been covered with lush greenery like the wooded sanctuary surrounding the tabernacle of the Healing Hand. A thousand years ago, a death duel between two wizards had ended that; now a vast ocean of sun-cracked earth spread across the horizon.

A quarter of a mile ahead, a dustcloud roiled. At its head the lone rider, keeping a bare hundred-yard lead on three others, dodged his horse to avoid the fourth rider coming from the side.

Four on one. I hate four on one. But that was the way it had to be, at least for a while; it would take Walter, Ahira, and Riccetti a good five minutes to catch up. Karl would be hard pressed to hold off four warriors for that length of time. A five-minute swordfight would be an eternity.

Then again, the dragon's voice sounded dimly in Karl's head, *you might just be able to talk to them.*

Bets? He dug in his heels.

As he neared the quarry, the man swerved his horse away. A half-naked, skinny wretch with a badly scarred face, rivulets of sweat running down his dust-caked chest, he jerked on the reins with his cuffed hands, the dangling links of chain tinkling in bizarre merriment.

"N'vâr!" Karl called out in Erendra. *Don't run.* "T'rar ammalli." *I'm a friend.*

No good. The man obviously figured that Karl was with the others; his clothing was similar to theirs. To him, it must have looked like a trap, as though yet another horseman had appeared to cut him off just a few hundred yards away from the sanctuary of the tabernacle grounds. A low moan escaped his lips as he cut perpendicularly across Karl's path.

As though he had waited for just this chance, the fourth pursuer let fly a whirling leather strap, weighted at both ends. Twisting through the air, it spun across the intervening yards and tangled itself in the rear legs of the quarry's horse. Whinnying in pain and fear, the horse tumbled to the ground, sending the rider flying. He tumbled head over heels on the rough ground, and then fell silent.

There wasn't time to see to the fallen man. If he was dead, there wasn't anything to do. Injured, he probably could keep for a while; Slovotsky, Ahira, and Riccetti would be along with the bottle of healing draughts.

Reaching across his waist, Karl drew his saber. "Easy, now," he whispered to his horse, while he settled the reins in his left fist. "Just stand easy." He waited for the four soldiers.

As their horses pranced to a panting halt, he took a quick inventory of their weapons. All four were swordsmen, wearing the wide-bladed shortsword popular in the Eren regions. Karl could probably handle that, on horseback. His ruddy mare was a large and powerful animal; likely he could dance her around that tired assortment of lathered geldings while his saber's greater reach took its toll.

But the two at the rear of the group had crossbows strapped to their saddles. That could be bad.

Very bad.

But . . . crossbows? If they had them, why hadn't they used them?

Stupid. Dead . . . isn't worth . . . much. Ellegon's voice was dim now that Karl was on the very edge of the dragon's range; worse, the flow of words had developed gaps when Ellegon wasn't concentrating.

Right, he thought, wondering if the dragon could hear him. He faced the four men. "Ryvâth èd," he said, letting the guttural Erendra r roll off his tongue. *It stops here.*

The leader, a burly, bearded swordsman, answered him in the same language. "This is none of your concern," he said, moving his horse closer to Karl's. "The slave is the property of Lord Mehlên of

Metreyll, whose armsmen we are—laws regarding abandoned property do not apply."

Karl could just barely hear Ellegon. *Stall. Just stall.*

He couldn't stall for long. The younger of the two bowmen had unstrapped his crossbow and was fumbling for one of the bolts in the wooden quiver strapped to the cantle of his saddle.

But it was at least worth a try. "You," he said in Erendra, "if you touch that bowstring, I'll take it away from you and wrap it around your throat." The largest of the four was almost a head shorter than Karl; perhaps he could intimidate them for a few minutes, until the odds evened up.

The bowman, a blond youth who looked to be in his late teens, sneered. "I doubt that," he said. But his fingers stopped their search for a bolt.

Good. Just a few more minutes. "Now, we can talk," he said, lowering the point of his sword.

He listened for sounds from behind him. Damn, nothing but the clattering of hooves as the quarry's horse got to its feet. The escaped slave was, at best, feigning unconsciousness.

At best . . .

To hell with it. "He is *not* a slave. Not anymore. He is under my protection." It was only fair to give them a chance; Karl had made a promise to the Matriarch, but he could hardly fulfill it by killing everyone in this world who tolerated—or even supported—the ownership of people. It wouldn't work, even if Karl was willing to wade through a sea of blood.

Dammit. There had been a time when the most violent thing Karl could remember doing was blocking too hard during a karate lesson.

But there have been some changes made. "You're not going to take him."

The leader snorted. "Who are you?" He raised an eyebrow. "You don't look like a daughter of the Hand. You're ugly as most of them, granted, but—" He cut himself off with a shrug. "What do you suggest we do? We have chased him a long way—"

"Turn around and ride away," Karl said. "We will just leave it at that."

The leader smiled, his right hand snaking across his body toward the hilt of his sword. "I doubt—"

His words turned into a bubbling gasp as the point of Karl's saber sliced through his throat.

—

One down. Karl kicked his horse over to the next swordsman, a pock-faced beardless one, who had already drawn his sword.

There was no time to waste; he had to take this one out and get to the bowmen quickly. As the other slashed down at him, Karl parried, then thrust at the man's swordarm.

No-Beard was ready for that; with a twitch of his arm, he beat Karl's sword aside, then tried for a backhanded slash to Karl's neck.

Karl ducked under the swing and used the opening to thrust through to his opponent's chest, the flat of his blade parallel to the ground. The point slid through the leather tunic as if through cheesecloth.

Karl jerked his saber out. Wine-dark blood fountained, covering his sword from its tip to its basket hilt and beyond, staining Karl's hand and wrist. He had gotten through to either the aorta or the heart. It didn't much matter which; No-Beard would be dead in seconds.

Karl spun his horse around to face the others. Like mirror images, the two bowmen turned their horses and galloped in opposite directions.

He hesitated for a moment. At close quarters, he could take both. But with just a few yards between them, one of the bowmen could drill him through while he killed the other.

There was no choice. He would have to take out one, and worry about the other later.

The bowman to the left wheeled his horse about. Two tugs at his saddlestraps unlimbered his crossbow; he reached down to his waist for a three-pronged beltclaw.

Forty yards of broken ground separated Karl from him. Karl dug in his heels and kicked his horse into a gallop. If he could get to the bowman quickly enough . . .

Thirty yards. Bracing the butt of the crossbow in a notch in his saddle, the bowman slipped the claw over the bowstring and pulled it back, locking the string into place. The beltclaw fell from his fingers.

Twenty yards. With trembling hands, the bowman drew a foot-long feathered bolt from his quiver, slipped it into the crossbow's groove, and nocked it with a practiced movement of his thumb.

Ten. He raised the bow to his shoulder and took aim, four fingers curled around the crossbow's long trigger.

With an upward slash, Karl knocked the crossbow aside, the bolt discharging harmlessly overhead. As the bowman reached for the dagger at his belt, Karl speared him through the chest.

The sword stuck.

Damn. Karl had been in too much of a hurry; he hadn't made sure that the flat of his blade was parallel to the ground—the damn sword had wedged itself in between two ribs. As Karl tried to jerk it loose, the blood-slickened hilt twisted out of his fingers.

The limp body of the bowman slipped from the saddle, carrying Karl's sword with it. He swore, and—

Agony blossomed like a fiery flower in the middle of Karl's back. His legs went numb and lifeless. As he started to slip from his mare's back, he tried to hold on to her mane, but a spasm jerked the rough hairs from his fingers.

He landed on his side on the hard ground, his body twisted. From the corner of his eye, he glimpsed the fletching of the crossbow bolt that projected from his back.

He felt nothing, nothing at all from the waist down.

My spine. Ellegon, help me. Please.

No answer.

Nothing.

Through a red cloud of pain, he saw the other bowman still his horse's jittery prancing and reload his crossbow, taking the time to aim carefully. It was the blond boy he had threatened before. Beyond him, Ahira, Walter, and Riccetti ran across the sun-baked plain, weapons carried high. But there was no way that they could reach the bowman in time.

The point of the bolt drew his eyes. Shiny though rust-specked steel, glistening in the ruddy light of the setting sun. It bore down on him; the bowstring—

—snapped, sending the bolt looping end over end in the still air. A long red weal drew itself across the boy's leg; as he lowered his hands to protect himself from his invisible attacker, he was jerked out of the saddle.

He collapsed in a heap as Walter Slovotsky ran up and took up a position standing over the boy, one knife in each hand.

"Go take care of Karl," Slovotsky addressed the air. "I'll see to this . . . trash."

A staggered line of dust puffs drew itself across the ground toward where Karl lay. "Easy," Andy-Andy's voice murmured. "Lou has the bottle of healing draughts. It won't hurt much longer." Gentle, invisible fingers cradled his head.

Quietly, she spoke harsh, awkward syllables that could only be heard and forgotten while Karl watched Lou Riccetti puff and pant his way across the plain, an ornately inlaid brass bottle cradled in his arms.

And then, as her dismissal of the invisibility spell began to take effect, the outline of her head appeared, superimposing itself over his view of Riccetti.

The image solidified: first the brown eyes, faintly misted with tears. Then, the slightly too-long, slightly bent nose, the high-boned cheeks, and the full mouth, all framed with the long brown hair that was now touched with red highlights in the light of the setting sun. Karl had always found Andy-Andy beautiful, but never more so than now.

"Andy, my legs—"

"You stupid *shit.*" She slipped an arm under his shoulder and clumsily flipped him over onto his belly. "Quick, give it here." A cork popped.

A wrenching pain forced a scream from his mouth as the bolt was drawn from his back. But, horridly, the pain still vanished in mid-back. He was paralyzed.

No. Please God, no. He tried to talk, but his mouth was as dry as the Waste.

And then a liquid coolness washed the pain away. It vanished, as though it had never been.

"Twitch your toes, Karl," she commanded.

He tried to.

And they moved.

He was all there; he felt *everything,* everything from the top of his aching head all the way down to where his right great toe throbbed. *Probably sprained it when I fell.* "Thanks." He tried to get his arms underneath him, to push himself to his feet.

"That will be enough of *that,*" Andy-Andy said. "We're running short of the healing potion. I had to give you most of it to take care of the hole in your back. We can't afford to have you swallow any more just to take care of the shock to your system. So you just lie there. I've got to go see to the man that got knocked off his horse."

"Don't bother," Ahira said, his voice a low rasp. "Must've snapped his neck in the fall. He's dead. *Damn.*"

But, Ellegon's voice sounded in Karl's head, *he died free. You gave him that gift.*

Wonderful. Tears welled up. He hadn't done anything right. He should have listened to Andy-Andy: If he had only waited a few moments, she could have cast her spell of invisibility on him; the

escaped slave would never have been scared into turning aside; the
bola would have missed. And Karl would never have been shot, not
while he was invisible. It could have all been done so easily, if only
he had waited.

And, now, it's all a waste.

No. It was not.

That's easy for you to say. Coward.

*Listen to me, Karl. He was too far away; I couldn't hear much of
his mind as he tried to escape; I don't even know his name. But I did
hear one thing, when he saw you, and mistook you for one of the
pursuers. I heard him thinking, "No—I'd rather die than go back."*

And if I'd waited—

*He still would have died, sometime soon. Perhaps ten years from
now, perhaps fifty. No time at all; you humans are so . . . ephem-
eral. But he might not have died free. Always remember that he died
a free man.*

And was that so much?

He thought so. What right have you to dispute it? The dragon's
mental voice became gentle. *You've had a difficult time. Go to sleep
now. Lou will rig a travois, and we'll bring you back up to camp.*

But—

Sleep.

Weariness welled up and washed him in a cool, dark wave.

Ahira looked down at the bound form of the blond bowman and
swore softly under his breath. "What the hell are we going to do with
this?"

The youth didn't answer; he just stared listlessly at the ground.

The dwarf rested his hands on the hilt of his double-bladed battleaxe. The axe was the simple answer, and probably the best one. But
possibly not. In any case, there was enough time for a leisurely decision whether or not to kill the bowman; with his hands tied to the
roots of an old oak, he wasn't going anywhere.

Walter stooped to check the knots. "It'll hold him. Do you want
me to have Ellegon keep an eye open?"

Ellegon. That was another matter. If that damned dragon of
Karl's hadn't turned coward suddenly—

*Two points. I belong to myself, not to Karl Cullinane, or anyone
else. Secondly, I did not suddenly "turn coward," dwarf. I am a
coward, James Michael Finnegan. I have been, for more than three
hundred years.*

Don't call me that. My name is Ahira.

Now it is. And what scares you the most?

"What does that have to do with anything?"

I will show you, if you insist. But I suggest you save it for later, Ahira. For the time being, let it rest that there is one thing that frightens me just as much as the thought of being crippled James Michael Finnegan frightens you.

Slovotsky chuckled. "I'd take him at his word, were I you, little friend. You weren't around when he gave Karl a taste of what being chained in Pandathaway's cesspit felt like. Check with Karl before you let him show you." He raised his head and addressed the air. "Ellegon? Do me a favor and tune us out; I want a private conversation with the dwarf."

Very well. The dragon's mental voice went silent.

Slovotsky shook his head. "Not that I trust him to keep out of our heads. It's just that since he's agreed to, he probably won't let the cat out of the bag to Karl. Cullinane's going to be a problem."

Ahira looked over to the far side of the meadow. Under a pile of blankets, Karl Cullinane lay sleeping in the twilight. A few yards away, Andrea and Lou Riccetti sat talking quietly.

"Cullinane's going to be a problem," Ahira echoed, as he and Slovotsky walked to the far edge of the clearing, away from the bound bowman. "Big deal."

Slovotsky cocked his head. "You don't think so?"

"Cullinane's the least of my worries, Walter, We've got bigger ones." Ahira jerked his head at the bound form of the blond bowman. "Like what we're going to do with William Tell here. Or how long we can stay on the preserve before the Healing Hand Society kicks us out." He shrugged. "Right now, I'm more worried about Riccetti. I told him to take my crossbow. All he ended up doing was bringing along the healing draughts for after. Not exactly a big help. If we'd really needed him in the fight, we would all have been in deep trouble." Ahira pounded his fist against a tree, sending chips of bark flying off into the night.

"Don't get so bent out of shape about Riccetti; you're missing the big problem." Slovotsky laid a hand on his shoulder. "But take it easy. Try and deal with one thing at a time, as you used to when you were writing computer programs—just one step, one problem at a time.

"Take Riccetti. So what if he wasn't any good in a fight? Can't blame him. The rest of us have the abilities we gained in the transfer.

I've got *this.*" With a smooth, flowing motion, he pulled one of his four throwing knives from the tangle of straps at his hip, caught the tip of the blade between thumb and forefinger, and threw it at a nearby tree. It quivered as it sank into the trunk five and a half feet above the ground.

Slovotsky patted at his hip. "And while I'm not in Karl's league, if we can get a sword for me, I could use it reasonably well. Not to mention my thieving skills." He walked over and pulled the knife from the tree, taking a moment to clean it on a fold of his blousy pantaloons before replacing it in its sheath. "You've got your strength, your darksight, and your skills with crossbow and battle-axe. Karl's damn good with his sword; Andy-Andy has her spells."

"But Riccetti's got nothing." Lou Riccetti had been a wizard; he had given up his magic as his part of the payment to the Matriarch of the Healing Hand Society for bringing Ahira back to life.

Which means that I'd be an ungrateful ass if I gave him hell for not getting involved in the fight. If it wasn't for me—

No. That wouldn't do; recriminations wouldn't be any help. The question, as usual, was what to do next. "Any ideas on what we do with Riccetti?"

A shrug. "We hand that problem to Karl. Let him work it out; he knows more about weapons and martial arts than both of us put together. For all I know, he might be able to turn Lou into a decent swordsman, if the two of them work at it." Slovotsky seated himself on a waist-high boulder. "Leave that one alone for the time being. As you pointed out, we've got bigger problems staring us in the face. Like what we're going to do with the bowman there. If we let him go, we're just asking for trouble. On the other hand, slicing his throat in cold blood doesn't exactly thrill me."

"I don't think it matters whether or not it thrills you. Not if—and I say *if*—we have to do it. He'll keep for a while. . . . You were saying I missed the big problem?"

"Yup." Slovotsky nodded. "Have you taken an inventory of our supplies lately? It's not just that we're down to our last pound of coffee and last fifth of Johnny Walker—if we don't get some food, and soon, we're going to be eating bark in a little while."

"Good point. Make a list tonight, and we'll talk it over in the morning, all five—"

Six.

"—all six of us." He spun around, startled at the interruption. "I thought you agreed to let us talk privately."

Sorry. The dragon's mental voice held no trace whatsoever of sincerity.

Tell me, do you give Karl as much trouble as you do me?

More. I like him better.

Slovotsky threw back his head and laughed. "I told you he'd eavesdrop." His face grew somber. "But I'm still worried about Karl. What the hell are we going to do about him? He could easily have gotten himself killed today, dashing off like that. And in case you weren't paying attention, the Matriarch said that she won't help us anymore. Any further deaths are as final as . . ." He furrowed his brow as he searched for an analogy.

"A temporary rate hike from the phone company?" Ahira suggested.

"Right."

"As for Karl," Ahira said, shrugging, "I've got to try to get him to show a bit of restraint. He has this thing about freeing slaves—and it's already put a price on our heads. We can't have him just rushing off and slashing away every time he sees someone in a collar."

Not that Ahira had any complaint about Karl's feelings; as James Michael Finnegan, Ahira had been raised in a world where slavery was generally considered a wrong. Or, at least, the prerogative of governments, not individuals.

But slavery had been the way of things in this world for millennia; they couldn't change things overnight, no matter what Karl had promised the Matriarch, as his part of the payment for Ahira's revivification.

You can be sure that Karl won't be restrained, Ahira.

Oh? And why is that?

Mmmm, just call it professional pride.

Walter Slovotsky nodded. "The dragon's got a point." He rubbed the back of his hand over his eyes and yawned.

Ahira clapped Slovotsky on the arm. "It's been a long day. Ellegon, you keep an eye peeled on the Waste; Walter, I'll take first watch. Go get some sleep; I'll wake you in a couple of hours. We'll worry about all this tomorrow."

"At Tara?" Slovotsky didn't wait for an answer; he walked off, whistling the theme from *Gone With the Wind*.

CHAPTER TWO

"That Isn't Much, Is It?"

We should be careful to get out of an experience only the wisdom that is in it—and stop there; lest we be like the cat that sits down on a hot stove lid. She will never sit on a hot stove lid again—and that is well; but also she will never sit down on a cold one anymore.

—Mark Twain

Back when he was in school, pursuing one of his many majors, Karl Cullinane had avoided the sunrise religiously; he saw the dawn only accidentally, unintentionally, through cigarette-smoke-tearing, caffeine-aching eyes after a night spent among a pile of books and papers, throwing together a last-minute term paper, or cramming for a final exam.

Whenever he could, he arranged his classes—the ones he didn't intend to skip regularly; the others didn't matter—to let him sleep as late as he could. Often he rose at the crack of noon.

Back then, he could sleep through anything.

Seems there've been some changes, he thought, sitting tailor-fashion beside Andy-Andy's sleeping form, blankets piled around him as protection against the dawn chill.

The sun rose across the Waste, touching the sky with pink and orange fingers. When he looked at the Waste through half-closed eyes, it was almost beautiful.

I see you're awake, the reedy voice sounded in his head. *Finally.*

"I'm awake," he whispered, rubbing at the middle of his back. No pain; none at all. It wasn't pain that kept him awake. When a distant breeze had wakened him, Karl had been afraid to let himself fall asleep again; his sleep had been filled with visions of himself as half a person, chopped off at the middle of his stomach. And nightmares of wading through unending pools of blood and gore.

"Just leave me alone, Ellegon." He lay back, pillowing his head on his hands. The dragon had deserted him yesterday; Karl felt no inclination to talk to him now.

You're being very immature about this, the dragon said petulantly.

"Leave me *alone.*"

"What is it, Karl?" Andy-Andy whispered, her breath warm in his ear.

"Nothing. Go back to sleep." He closed his eyes. "That's what I'm going to do."

But I have to talk to you.

No.

Andy-Andy cuddled closer, her long brown hair covering his face with airy, silken threads. Karl put his arms around her and held her to him.

He drew in his breath to sigh, then spent several long seconds trying to spit out her hair without waking her.

God, how I hate mornings. He opened his eyes. *Then again . . .*

Andy-Andy lay sleeping, the blanket's ragged hem gathered around her neck, her features even more lovely in repose. Her long lashes, the olive tone of her skin, the slight bend in her slightly too-long nose—an inventory of parts didn't do her justice.

Then again, maybe I'm prejudiced. He reached out a hand to pull the blankets down—

And, then again, maybe you should give both your hormones and your mammary fixation a rest, and talk to me. You don't understand. Maybe I should make you understand.

Don't. Ellegon's mindlink could carry more than the dragon's phantom voice or images; it could also transmit feelings, experiences. And not just pleasant feelings, either.

Will you listen to me, then?

Carefully brushing her hair away, Karl sighed. *Just give me a minute.* He untangled himself from Andy-Andy's sprawling limbs and slipped out of the blankets, taking a moment to slip his breech-clout on, step into his sandals, and strap their laces around his calves. He eyed his leggings and tunic, debating with early-morning laziness whether or not to put them on now.

Later. After coffee.

Absently, he picked up his scabbarded saber and slipped the belt over his left shoulder, resting his right hand for just a moment on its sharkskin hilt. Karl had a tendency to lose things, one way or another, but here, in this world, losing his sword could quickly mean losing his life.

Near the downhill edge of the clearing, Riccetti and Slovotsky slept under their blankets, their snores barely reaching Karl's ears.

Beyond them, on a flat stone next to the smoldering remains of last night's fire, Ahira sat, drinking a cup of coffee, keeping watch over the sleeping form of the captive bowman. His head turned, and he lifted an aluminum Sierra cup in a silent invitation.

Nodding gratefully, Karl walked down the gently sloping clearing, the morning dew clutching at his feet with damp, chilly fingers. That felt good, in a strange way; the clammy cold was a physical confirmation that his legs weren't numb.

He glanced at the ashes of the fire as he seated himself on a flat rock, silently accepting a hot cup of coffee from Ahira.

He shook his head. Ahira shouldn't have been so careless with the fire. Maybe, by adding enough tinder and kindling, they could tease the embers back into a roaring fire, but maybe not. And they had only a couple of books of matches left. Once those were gone, the only way they would have to light fires would be with flint and steel. Which was a pain, no matter how easy his old Boy Scout manual had made it look.

I imagine it is. But if I were you, I wouldn't worry about it. Consider for a moment the fact that the fire is dead, but the coffee is hot. Beyond a stand of trees, a gout of orange flame roared skyward. *Think it through.* Another blast of fire cut through the lightening sky.

Karl sipped his coffee. It was just the way he liked it: too sweet for most people to stomach, with just a touch of creamer. "Ellegon? Just take it easy on me, please? I don't think all that well in the morning."

Ahira chuckled. "Who does?" He sobered. "Sleep well?"

"No." He looked down at his right hand. Somebody had washed the blood from it while he slept, but there were dry, reddish-brown flecks under his nails and in the hairs on the back of his hand. "Had a few bad dreams."

"I can't feel too sorry for you; I was up all night."

"Slovotsky didn't relieve you?"

The dwarf shrugged his improbably broad shoulders. "I didn't wake him. He's going to need his sleep. You, too—you've got a long trip ahead of you. We're short of almost every kind of supply, and somebody's going to have to go into Metreyll and do some shopping." He furrowed his heavy brows, peering up at Karl. "And scouting—we've got to figure out what to do when the armsmen are missed. To do that, we've got to know what the situation is, in Metreyll. Yes?"

"Not really. We really have a way to fix things so we don't get blamed: We leave the dead men where they are, and put a sword in the hand of the dead slave." *I wish I knew your name. I'm sorry, whoever you are, but you don't have any further use for that body. As a decoy, it might help to save our lives.* "If anyone comes around to investigate, he'll have to decide that the slave had turned to fight, driving one off, killing the other three; their horses just wandered away."

Ahira snorted. "You *do* wake up slow—the locals are going to think that an unarmed, half-starved slave killed three swordsmen?"

"As long as there aren't any other suspects around, they will. Either that, or they'll have to decide that somebody, for no apparent reason, came from God knows where to the slave's defense."

"Hmm. That doesn't sound likely."

"No, it doesn't. Happens to be true, that's all. Occam's Razor, Ahira. Most people use it all the time, even if they can't tell you what it is." Karl drank some more coffee. "Got another idea?"

"No."

"Then let's give mine a try."

"Agreed." The dwarf nodded. "Andrea, Riccetti, and I will take care of it. We'll keep their horses, yes?"

"Yes." Not that the poor assortment of fleabags would be of much use. "But there's something you're missing," Karl said. "We're low on healing draughts. Someone has to go over to the tabernacle and see if we can pry some loose. Besides, I want to see how Doria's doing."

Ahira nodded. "I'll give it a try. Tomorrow. Although . . . the Matriarch did say we're on our own. No more help. And that could mean—"

"That they won't *give* us any. Not that they won't *sell* us some. We do have the coin Walter and I took off Ohlmin—"

Only because I brought it here. You abandoned it near the Gate Between Worlds.

Karl ignored the dragon and spoke to Ahira. "We should be able to meet their price."

"You hope. I'll check it out. *And* see how Doria is. If I can. You get the Metreyll shopping trip."

"Agreed." Karl stood. "I'd better go saddle up my horse and get going."

"No." Ahira shook his head. "Not until dark. You're taking Walter with you."

"I know," Karl said, irritated, "that you don't know much about horses, but putting two men our size on one isn't good for a horse, even when there's no hot sun beating down. And we can't take one of the new horses; they might be recognized. So I'd better ride in alone, just me and my horse. I *like* her. She did good, yesterday."

Meaning that I didn't.

Exactly.

Ahira scowled. "First of all, you're not taking your horse; Ellegon's going to fly both of you over tonight, and drop you off outside Metreyll. I want Walter to go along, to keep an eye on you. You've got a tendency to get into trouble." He swigged the last of his coffee, then set the aluminum cup down gently on a flat stone. "As far as Ellegon goes, Karl, I wish you'd learn to be a bit more patient with the people you care about.

"I had a long talk with Ellegon last night. He had his reasons. Dammit, Karl, that dragon may be more than three centuries old, but by dragon standards, he's still a baby. You don't expect a child to do the right thing, not when he's scared out of his wits."

"And what the hell did he have to be scared about? All those soldiers had were bows and swords. Nothing for him to be afraid of."

*There was *so*. I'll *show* you.*

"Don't." Karl stood. "Stay out of my mind." Ellegon had opened his mind to Karl before, letting Karl feel what it had been like to be chained in a Pandathaway sewer for three centuries. A dragon's mind couldn't edit out familiar smells the way a human's could. Three centuries of stench. . . . "Maybe you had a good reason. Just *tell* me, for God's sake."

Very well, then—

"No." Ahira shook his head slowly. He lowered his voice. "Karl

has to learn not to make snap judgments, Ellegon. It could get any
number of us killed. Show him. Now."

Don't—

Ellegon opened his mind . . .

. . . and flew. *That* was the secret, after all: Alone, his wings
weren't strong enough to lift him; he had to reach inside and let his
inner strength add itself to the lifting power of his fast-beating wings.

Slowly, he gained altitude, as he circled around the craggy vast-
ness of Heiphon's reaches until the ledge where he had been born
was far beneath him, the hardened shards of his shell only vague
white flecks, barely discernible.

Ellegon worked his wings more rapidly, until the wind whistled by
him. He began to tire, and let the frantic beating of his wings subside
until they barely kept him flying. Then it occurred to him that if his
wings weren't sufficient, possibly they were superfluous; perhaps his
inner strength alone could support him in the air. So Ellegon curled
his wings inward, and lifted even more with his inner strength.

And dropped through the sky like a stone.

In a panic, he spread his wings against the onrush of air and
worked them, scooping air from in front and above, whisking it
behind and below.

For a moment, it seemed as though his frenzied effort had no
effect, but then the craggy peak slowed its menacing approach,
stopped, and began to fall away.

Another lesson learned, he thought. It seemed that his inner
strength couldn't support him all by itself, either. It would have been
nice if there were someone to tell him that, instead of letting him
learn by trial and error.

But that is the way it is for dragons. We have to learn for ourselves.
It didn't occur to him to wonder how he knew that, or how he knew
that he was a dragon.

A mile below him, a gap in the clouds loomed invitingly. He eased
the frantic beating of his wings until he started to lose altitude and
dropped slowly through the gap, letting the cottony floor of clouds
become a gray ceiling.

Below him, lush greenery spread from horizon to horizon, broken
only by the brown-and-gray mass of the mountain called Heiphon, a
blue expanse of water to the south, and a dirty brown tracing that
wormed its way across the grassland, through the forest.

What was that brown line? It cut across the forest and dirtied the tops of the rolling hills, sullying the greenery. It had to be unnatural, as though someone or something had deliberately chosen to make the land ugly.

He couldn't understand that. Why would anyone spend time on the ground soiling the greenery, when one could fly above it and enjoy it?

Ridiculous. He eased back with his inner strength, spreading his wings as he glided in for a closer look. There was something moving on the dirt line. . . .

There. A strange sort of creature, indeed. Six legs and two heads; one head long and brown and sleek, the other pasty flesh only partly hidden by greasy fur.

No, he was wrong. It was *two* creatures, not one. Both four-legged, although the smaller one's forelegs were stunted. If it got down on all fours, its backside would stick up in the air. No wonder it chose to ride on the back of the other; even a creature as ugly as that would not want to look more foolish than necessary.

But why did the larger one carry it? Perhaps the smaller was the larval form, and the larger its parent.

He flew closer, and as he did, their minds opened before him. Ellegon began to understand. The smaller creature was a *Rhêden Monsterhunter;* at least, that was what its small mind said. And the larger had no choice about carrying it; it was compelled to, under threat of leather and steel.

Another absurdity. No matter; Ellegon would end the silliness, by eating them both.

As he stooped, the Rhêden Monsterhunter's head snapped up. It reached for a strange contraption: two sticks, one bent, the other straight. That was a *bow and arrow,* but what was *dragonbane?*

The Rhêden Monsterhunter pulled back the arrow, and then released it. The stick flew toward Ellegon.

He didn't bother flaming it, and there was no point in dodging it. He was a dragon, after all; surely this puny stick couldn't hurt him.

Its oily head sank into his chest, just below the juncture of his long neck. A point of white-hot pain expanded across his torso.

Ellegon fell.

He crashed through the treetops, branches snapping under his weight, not slowing his fall. The ground rushed up and struck him; his whole body burned with a cold, cruel fire that faded only slowly to black.

When he awoke, a golden cage surrounded his face, a golden collar clamped tightly around his neck. He lay on his side on the hard ground, his legs all chained together. Tentatively, he tried to flame the chains, using just a wisp of the fire of his inner strength. He screamed as his neck burned.

Safely beyond his reach, the Rhêden Monsterhunter stood smiling. "It'll take me some days to rig a cart for you, dragon. But it will be worth it; they'll pay a fine price for you in Pandathaway."

Karl shook his head, trying to clear it. So, that was why Ellegon hadn't helped him. It wasn't really cowardice. It was sheer, unreasoning terror. Definitely unreasoning; if Ellegon had looked into the bowmen's minds, he would have seen that none of their arrows were tipped with extract of dragonbane. Dragons were nearly extinct in the Eren regions; the cultivation of dragonbane was a dying skill.

But he couldn't. As a young dragon—no, as a *child*—he had been so badly hurt by that crossbow bolt that the thought of facing another dragonbane-tipped arrow chased all rationality from his mind. The pain of the bolt cleaving through his chest . . .

*Yes. It *hurt.**

Karl looked down at his own chest. A wicked round weal over his heart stared back at him like a red eye.

Karl, I'm . . . sorry. I was just so scared.

It hadn't been fair to expect the dragon to leap to his aid. Ellegon wasn't an adult, not really. Applying adult standards to him was wrong. The dragon was a curious mix of infant and ancient: By dragon standards, three and a half centuries of age put Ellegon barely out of babyhood, but Ellegon had spent almost all of that time chained in a cesspool in Pandathaway.

How do you handle a child who's frightened? *Not* by shutting him out of your life; that was clear. Maybe there wasn't a hard-and-fast rule, but the answer had to start with listening.

Karl nodded. *So I'll start listening now.* "It's okay, Ellegon. My fault; I should have known you had your reasons. Are you sure that you're willing to fly us into—*near* Metreyll, once it gets dark?"

I'll try, Karl. I'll try to do better, next time. I will.

He sighed. "See that you do," he said out loud, while his mind murmured, *I know you will.*

Ahira stared up at him, his heavy brow furrowed. The dwarf sat silently for a moment. "I've written down a shopping list, some of the things we're going to need. All of us had better go over it."

"No problem. Something else on your mind?"

Ahira nodded. "What are we going to do about Riccetti? He's practically helpless in a fight, and I'm willing to bet that we're going to go through more than a couple before this is all over."

"Sorry, but there's no easy solution to that one. As soon as I get back, I'll start him on swordsmanship. But I can't make a swordsman out of him overnight. At best, it'll be months before he develops any kind of proficiency. Mmm . . . he's not left-handed, is he?"

"No. why?"

He sighed. "It doesn't matter, then. Lefties have an edge in swordplay, just as they do in tennis, back home. The rest of us aren't used to having the blade come from the other side. It's—" He stopped himself. Of course. An opponent's unfamiliarity was a huge advantage; it had helped a Japanese police society disarm numerous samurai at the end of Japan's feudal era. But the name of the weapon they carried—what the *hell* was it called?

It hovered just at the edge of his mind. A length of chain, weighted down at both ends—

Manriki-gusari.

Thanks. But how did you know?

I read minds, fool.

Ahira laughed. "Get some breakfast. And take it easy for the rest of the day; you'd better be on your toes in Metreyll. Karl?"

"Yes?"

"I want your word on something. No fighting unless it's in self-defense."

"Fine." Self-defense was a loose term, one that could be applied to almost any situation by a sufficiently flexible mind. "That sounds reasonable."

Hypocrite.

Huh?

You have nightmares about wading through blood, and then the next day you try to wiggle out of Ahira's suggestion that you not shed more unless you really have to.

Ellegon—

"Excuse me," the dwarf said. "I wasn't finished. You've been known to have a liberal imagination; *Walter* decides what constitutes self-defense, not you."

"Understood."

"Do I have your word?"

"You're not leaving me a lot of leeway." Karl sighed. "Yes."

"Good." Ahira spread his hands. "Just stay out of trouble. That's all I'm asking. That isn't much, is it?"

That, friend Ahira, depends.

CHAPTER THREE

Metreyll

I was never attached to that great sect,
Whose doctrine is, that each one should select
Out of the crowd a mistress or a friend,
And all the rest, though fair and wise, commend
To cold oblivion, though 'tis in the code
Of modern morals, and the beaten road
Which those poor slaves with weary footsteps tread
Who travel to their home among the dead
By the broad highway of the world, and so
With one chained friend, perhaps a jealous foe,
The dreariest and the longest journey go.

—Percy Bysshe Shelley

The preserve was miles behind. Half a mile below, the Waste of Elrood lay in the starlight, a solid expanse of baked, cracked earth, the blankness relieved only by an occasional stone outcropping.

Shivering only partly from the cold, Karl clung to Ellegon's back. The cool night air whistled by, whipping through his hair.

He looked down and shuddered. Even if the Waste had not held bad memories, it would still have been unpleasant; a landscape like something out of the pictures the Apollo astronauts had brought back, with none of the charm of accomplishment those pictures carried with them.

Behind him, Walter Slovotsky chuckled. "I wouldn't worry about it, Karl," he called out, his voice barely carrying over the rush of wind. "It's an advantage—as long as we're at the preserve, anyone who wants to give us trouble would have to cross forty miles of the Waste to do it."

He has a point, Karl. And, powerful as they are, I'm willing to bet that the Hand clerics are grateful for that protection.

That was probably true. And it pointed up one of the troubles in this world: Anytime you had anything, be it a piece of land, a horse, a sword—even your own life—you always had to consider the possibility that someone would try to take it away from you.

Just because he wanted it.

And is that so different from your world? For a moment, Karl's head felt as though it were being stroked by gentle fingers—from inside. Then: *Or don't you consciously recall the Sudetenland, Lithuania, Wounded Knee, or—*

Enough. You made your point. Just leave it at that, eh?

But, dammit, there *was* a difference. Back home, there was at least an acknowledgment that the strong preying on the weak was wrong. It was reflected in laws, customs, and folktales, from fables about Robin Hood to the legends of Wyatt Earp.

He chuckled. Well, it was the *legend* that counted, anyway. Back when he was majoring in American history, Karl had found several accounts that suggested that the Earp brothers were just another gang of hoods, as bad as the Clantons they had gunned down—from ambush—at the O.K. Corral. The Earps had managed to wangle themselves badges, that was all.

And when you think about it, quite probably Robin Hood robbed the rich to give to himself.

Which made sense; in the holdup business, robbing the poor had to be easier than robbing the rich—but it was bound to be financially unrewarding.

That's why they call them "the poor," Karl. If it was rewarding to rob them, they probably would be known as "the rich."

Funny.

Only to those with a sense of humor.

The boundary of the Waste loomed ahead, a knife-sharp break between the scarred ground and the forested land beyond. In the starlight, the huge oaks would normally have seemed to be threatening hulks, but by comparison with the Waste, their dark masses were somehow comforting.

You don't have to go any farther. Set us down anywhere near here.

Just a short way. Ellegon's flight slowed. *Let me put you a bit closer; this way, you won't have so far to walk.*

Why the sudden concern for my sore feet?

I have my reasons, the dragon responded, with a bit of a mental sniff. *But since you're so eager to be on foot . . .*

The dragon circled a clearing among the tall trees, then braked to a safe, if bumpy, landing.

Karl vaulted from Ellegon's back, landing lightly on the rocky ground. Reflexively, he slipped his right hand to his swordhilt as he peered into the night.

Nothing. Just trees in the dark, and a mostly overgrown path leading, he hoped, toward Metreyll.

Walter climbed down to stand beside him. "My guess is that we're about five miles out," he said, helping Karl to slip his arms into the straps of a rucksack. "We *could* camp here and walk into town in the morning, I guess," Walter said, frowning. He brightened. "Or maybe we should just walk in now."

Karl slipped his thumbs under the rucksack's straps. "Do I get two guesses which you'd rather do?"

Be safe. Take three.

"Well?" Slovotsky jerked a thumb toward a path.

"Why not?" *Ellegon, you'd better get going. But do me a favor: Circle overhead, and see if the path leads to the Metreyll road.*

I didn't set you down here by accident, fool. Of course it does.

As Karl and Walter moved away, the dragon's wings began moving, beating until they were only a blur in the darkness, sending dust and leaves swirling into the air. Ellegon sprang skyward and slipped away into the night, his outline momentarily visible against the glimmer of the overhead stars.

Be careful, he said, his mental voice barely audible.

And then he was gone.

"Let's walk," Karl said.

They walked in silence for a few minutes, carefully picking their way along the dirt path through the trees. Finally, Walter spoke.

"I've got a suggestion, if you don't mind."

"Yes?"

"Look, this is just a supply trip." Slovotsky patted at the leather pouch dangling from his belt. "Right?"

"You have a keen eye for the obvious." Karl shrugged. "What's your point?"

"Hmm, let me put it this way: I'm not going to take the chance of lifting anything. Granted, as long as we're based in the sanctuary, we've got a nice buffer zone between Metreyll and us, but there's no need to push it. We don't want to get the locals angry at us. Too risky."

"Fine. So you're not going to use your skills." That made sense. There was enough to do in Metreyll, and with all the coin they had, money wouldn't be a problem for a long while. They had to buy provisions and supplies, as well as some hardware. And weapons; the party was short of spares.

"That wasn't what I meant." Walter ducked under an overhanging branch, then made a show of holding it out of the way so that Karl could pass.

Sometimes, it seemed as though Walter made too much of Karl's being larger than he was. Then again, maybe that was understandable; Slovotsky had long been accustomed to being the biggest man in almost any group.

"What I meant," Slovotsky went on, "is that *you* have to watch it. There's liable to be some sort of slave market in Metreyll. Not as big as the one in Pandathaway, granted, but something—the whole economy of this region is based on slavery."

"So?"

"So we give Metreyll a bye. No interfering with local . . . customs, no matter how repugnant. At least for the time being. My guess is there's still a reward out for you in Pandathaway. We don't want reports getting back there about your still being alive."

"Thanks for your tender concern about my health."

Slovotsky snorted. "And thank you for the sarcasm. I don't particularly care if you believe it, but I *am* worried about you. As well as me. If you start swinging that sword in Metreyll, we're both in deep trouble."

"Walter, where did you get the idea that I'm some sort of bloodthirsty monster?"

"Mmm . . . yesterday was kind of a clue." He held up a hand to forestall Karl's objection. "Okay, that was a cheap shot. Look—I'm not saying that you really enjoy slicing open someone's gut. With the exception of the time we killed Ohlmin and his men, I don't think you've ever liked violence.

"But it doesn't bother you the way it used to. What it comes down to, Karl, is something you said in Pandathaway, after you freed

Ellegon. Something about if what you're doing is important enough, you worry about the consequences later."

"Wait—"

"No, you wait. Slovotsky's Law Number Seventeen: Thou shalt *always* consider the consequences of thy actions. You could make a lot of trouble for all of us, if you don't keep your head on."

He understood Walter's point. And it did make a kind of sense; the time he had freed Ellegon had cost them all much. But to commit himself *not* to do anything about people in chains . . .

Karl shrugged. "I gave Ahira my word. Just leave it at that."

Walter sighed deeply. "Unless I can convince you that I'm right, I wouldn't trust your reflexes, Karl. I've seen the way you clap your hand to your sword whenever you're irritated about anything. When you know there's no reason to cut someone up, you're safe to be around, granted; I'm not worried about your stabbing me if I don't put enough sugar in your coffee. . . . The trouble is, you're thinking as if you were the only one who can suffer from your actions, dammit."

"You sound scared."

"I am." Walter snorted. "Not just for my own tender hide. I didn't want to tell you this, but . . . Ellegon told me something, on our way over; he tuned you out. Wasn't sure whether you should know or not. He left it up to me whether and when to clue you in."

"And what's this great secret?"

"Well, you know his nose is more sensitive than ours." Walter shook his head slowly. "It must have made it hell for him in the sewers. But the point is, he can pick up on things that you and I can't. Even things that a medical lab back home would have trouble with. Slight biochemical changes, for instance. Hormones, like that."

A cold chill washed across Karl's back. *"Whose* biochemical changes?"

"Andrea's. Nobody knows it but you, me, and Ellegon, Karl. She's pregnant, although only a couple of day's worth. I guess congratulations are in order, no?"

Ohgod. "You're lying." He turned to face Slovotsky. "Aren't you?"

"Nope. Now, did that drive the point home? If you screw up, you're not just endangering you and me—and Andy, for that matter. You get yourself killed or put the rest of us on another wanted list, and you're putting on unborn child's life in danger. Yours." Slovotsky snorted. "So are you still interested in playing Lone Ranger right away? If you call me Tonto, I swear I'll stick a knife in you."

His head spun. *A baby?*

"Karl, you—"

"Okay. You made your point." *I'm going to be a father.* He rubbed his knuckles against the side of his head. *There's going to be a baby depending on me.*

"Hope so." Slovotsky said solemnly. Brightening, he clapped a hand to Karl's shoulder. "Hey, can I be the godfather?"

"Shut up."

Slovotsky chuckled.

"You want what?" The blacksmith turned from his forge, bringing the redly glowing piece of metal over to his anvil, holding it easily with the long wrought-iron pincers. He picked up his hammer and gave the hot metal a few tentative blows before settling down to pounding it in earnest.

Wary of flying sparks, Karl moved a few feet back. "I want a length of chain," he said in Erendra, "about this long." He held his hands about three feet apart. "With an iron weight on either end— those should be cylindrical, about half the size of my fist. If you can do that sort of thing."

"It wouldn't be difficult," the smith said, returning his worked iron to the forge. "I can have that for you by noon, if you're in a hurry."

Sweat running in rivulets down his face and into his sparse red beard, he pumped the bellows for a few moments before pausing to take a dipperful of water from an oaken barrel. The smith drank deeply, clearly relishing every swallow. He took a second dipperful, tilted his head back, and slowly poured the water onto his upturned face, then shook his head to clear the water from his eyes.

"What do you want it for?" he asked, offering Karl a dipperful of water with a gesture of his hand and a raised eyebrow.

"Religious artifact." Karl accepted the dipper and drank. "I'm an apostle of the metal god."

The smith cocked his head. "There isn't a metal god."

"Then I'm probably not one of his apostles."

The smith threw back his head and laughed. "And Teerhnus is liable to get his proud nose cut off if he puts it where it doesn't belong, eh? Very well, have it your way. Now, as to the price—"

"We're not done yet. I'll want two of them. And I'll also want to buy some of your other equipment. I'll need . . . a general-purpose anvil, some basic tools—hammer, tongs—and a hundred-weight of rod, sheet, and bar stock, a bit of—"

The smith snorted. "Granted, there is enough work for another smith in Metreyll, but you don't look the type." He set his hammer down and reached out, taking Karl's right hand in both of his. "From this ridge of callus I'd say you've spent much time with that sword in your hand, but none with a hammer. And you're too old to apprentice."

Karl drew his hand back. "It's for a friend. Now, what sort of coin are we talking about for all this?" It was hard to concentrate on the transaction with the back of his mind shouting, *A father—I'm going to be a father!*

Teerhnus shook his head. "You don't know what you're talking about." He gestured at the seven different anvils scattered around the shop, each mounted on its own treetrunk stand. They ranged dramatically in size and shape, from a tiny one that couldn't have weighed more than thirty pounds to an immense, almost cubical monster of an anvil that Karl probably couldn't have lifted. "Even a brainless farrier needs at least two anvils to do any kind of work at all. If your friend wants to be able to do more than shoe horses, he'll need at least three. And I'll need quite a bit of coin for each. *Damn,* but it's a pain to cast a new anvil. You are planning to travel with them?" He peered at Karl from under heavy brows. "I'd be a fool to help you set up a friend of yours in competition with me, no matter what the price."

Karl shook his head. "That's not what I'm planning to do. I swear it."

The smith nodded. "On your sword, if you please."

Karl slowly drew his sword, then balanced the flat of the blade on his outstretched palms. "What I have sworn is true."

The smith shrugged. "I guess that settles it. Nice piece of workmanship, that sword. Are those Sciforth markings?"

"I don't know. Would you like to see it?"

"Of course." Teerhnus accepted the hilt in his huge hands. He held the sword carefully, stroking a rough thumbnail along the edge. "Very sharp. Holds the edge well, I'll wager." He flicked the blade with his finger, smiling at the clear *ting!* "No," he answered his own question, "that's not a Sciforth blade. They make good steel in Sciforth, but not this fine. Could be Endell, I suppose; those dwarves know their alloys." He rummaged around in a wooden bin until he found a soft wool cloth, then handed sword and cloth to Karl. "Where did you get it?"

Karl shrugged as he used the cloth to wipe the blade; he replaced his sword in its scabbard. He couldn't answer honestly; the smith wouldn't believe him. Or possibly worse, he might. Back home, on the Other Side, the sword had been a skinning knife; it had translated well. "I just found it somewhere." Better an evasion than to be caught in a lie. "Now, when can you have the anvils and such ready?"

"Hmmm . . . you're planning to be in Metreyll long?"

"Not past sunset. I'm en route to . . ." Visualizing Ahira's map of the Eren regions, he picked a city at random. ". . . Aeryk. I plan to be out of Metreyll by nightfall."

"Can't be done." The smith shook his head. "I do have work to do. I could spare some rod stock, I suppose, but I don't have any spare hammers, and casting anvils is just too much trouble to bother with."

Karl produced a pair of platinum coins, holding one between thumb and forefinger. The obverse showed the bust of a bearded man, the reverse a stylistic rippling of waves. "Are you sure?"

"Pandathaway coin, eh?" The smith spread his palms. "Well . . . those two are fine as a down payment, but I'll need six more on delivery."

"This *is* platinum, after all—and Pandathaway coin, at that. I thought you'd be happy to take these two, and give me some gold back, as well as the iron."

"I doubt that." The smith grinned. "I wouldn't call that thinking at all. Let's agree on seven platinum, and we'll both be happy."

The money wasn't really a problem, but there was no need for Karl to draw attention to himself by seeming to have too free a purse. "Three. And you will give me five gold back. Pandathaway coin, not this debased Metreyll coinage."

"Six platinum and six gold. And *you* will stay in Metreyll, along with your strong back, long enough to help me cast three new anvils."

Karl sighed, and resigned himself to a long bargaining session. "Four . . ."

Five pieces of platinum, six of gold, four of silver, and a bent copper poorer, Karl waited for Walter Slovotsky in the town square, near the lord's palace.

Metreyll was laid out differently than the other cities they had seen. Unlike Lundeyll, the city itself had no protecting walls. Unlike Pandathaway, it was both landlocked and apparently unplanned; Metreyll's streets radiated out from the central palace like a misshapen web, woven by a demented spider.

Although calling it a palace might have been too generous an assessment: It was a cluster of nine two-storied sandstone buildings, surrounded by narrow, crumbling ramparts. The raised portcullis showed its age: The timbers were splintering, the pulley chains and spikes so rusty that it was clear that the portcullis was lowered rarely if ever.

Two mail-clad guardsmen at the gate eyed him casually as they sat on three-legged stools, their spears propped up against the wall nearby, but well out of reach.

Karl nodded to himself. Ill-kept, unattended defenses were a clear sign that Metreyll hadn't known warfare for a while, and the lack of challenge from the bored guardsmen meant that the locals were used to the presence of strangers.

"Are you going to sleep just standing there?"

Squinting in the bright sunlight, Walter smiled down at him from the bench of the half-filled flatbed wagon. "You'll be glad to hear that beef is cheap—seems the ranchers had too good a year. I picked up about four hundred pounds of jerky for a song." He snorted. "Not exactly 'This Way to Cheap Street,' but a song."

He set the brake and dismounted, patting the two hitched mules in passing. "Although horseflesh—even muleflesh—is at a premium. I bought a stallion and another gelding—the hostler will hang on to them until dark—but they set me back a nice piece of change. Apparently it's going to be another bumper crop of cattle this year, and the tributary ranchers are paying nice prices for labor—all kinds of labor."

Karl smiled as he took off his rucksack and tossed it into the wagon. "I almost wish we needed a bit of money. When I was a kid, I fully intended to be a cowboy." He shrugged. "Maybe we could look into all of us hiring out as hands, anyway. Just for a while." Of course, they would have to figure out how to keep Ellegon out of sight.

No, that probably wouldn't do. He had responsibilities now. Fulfilling childhood fantasies was something he would have to set aside.

Walter shook his head. "I don't think that's such a good idea. All the hiring is for a cattle drive—and guess where that's headed."

"Pandathaway?"

Slovotsky nodded. " 'Everything comes to Pandathaway'—except us, I hope. I doubt they go easy on felons' accomplices."

"Good point. So you keep your eyes open, too."

"They never close, Karl. Now, how'd you do at the smith's?"

"Fine, I guess. Although he struck a hard deal. Come to think of it, I probably was taken. But he did throw in a couple of used swords." He shrugged. "In any case, we can pick up that gear at sunset, too. West end of town." He eyed the noon sun. "Any ideas on what we should do until then?"

Slovotsky raised an eyebrow. "Joy Street? Or whatever they call it. It's down this way—" He held up a palm. "You don't absolutely *have* to cheat on Andy, you know. Just a few beers, while I see what's available. Prisoner of my hormones, I am."

Karl laughed. "Why not? I could use a beer." He boosted himself to the bed of the wagon and sprawled on a sack of grain. "You drive."

The unpaved street twisted gently through the markets, past a drab tarpaulin where a sweaty grain seller hawked his muslin sacks of oats and barley, a ramshackle corral where a well-fleshed hostler groomed his tattered assortment of swaybacked mares and half-lame geldings, an open-air workbench where a squinting leatherworker and a bewhiskered swordsman haggled angrily over the price of a fore-and-aft peaked saddle.

Wagons creaked through the street, as farmers and their slaves brought sacked grain and caged chickens to market. Some wagons were drawn by dusty mules, or slowly plodding oxen; others were handcarts, pulled by slaves.

Karl gripped his sword. He fondled the sharkskin hilt for a moment, then sighed and let his hand drop. *Damn* Walter for being right. This wasn't the time or place to get involved in a swordfight. *And besides, I can't solve the problem by chopping up everyone who owns a slave. That just wouldn't do it.*

That thought didn't make him feel any better. "Goddammit."

"Just keep cool," Slovotsky whispered, urging the mules on.

The street widened as the slave market came into view. Surrounded by a hundred bidders and spectators, a noisy auction proceeded in front of a boxlike wagon bearing the wave-and-chain insignia of the Pandathaway Slavers' Guild.

The auctioneer accepted a handful of coins from a farmer, then, smilingly, snapped the farmer's chains around the wrists of a skinny, bearded slave before removing his own chains. "You should have no difficulty with this one; he has been well tamed," the auctioneer said, as the farmer looped a hemp rope around the slave's neck. As the slave was led away, Karl shuddered at the old scars that crisscrossed his back. *Well tamed . . .*

"Easy, Karl," Walter whispered. "There's nothing you can do about it."

One of the slavers brought the next slave out of the wagon. This slave was a short, dark man in a filthy cotton loincloth. His whip scars were fresh; livid red weals were spattered randomly over his hairy torso and legs. Lines around the edge of his mouth and eyes suggested that he used to smile often. But he wasn't smiling now; chained at his neck, wrists, and ankles, he stared sullenly out at the crowd.

A cold chill ran up Karl's spine. "Walter, I know him."

"No kidding?" Slovotsky's expression belied his calm tone; he looked as if he had been slapped.

"The Games in Pandathaway—he was my first opponent. Took him out in a few seconds."

This was horrible. An expectant father had no business risking his own life, forgetting the danger to the others, but this man was somebody Karl *knew.* Not a close friend, granted; he didn't even know the other's name. But someone he knew, nonetheless.

He turned to Slovotsky.

The thief shook his head. "Karl, do us both a favor and get that expression the hell off your face. You're starting to draw stares." He lowered his voice. "That's better. We're just a couple of travelers, chatting idly about the weather and the price of flesh, got it? I don't know exactly what harebrained scheme you're working on, but we're not going to do it. No way. Remember, you gave Ahira your word."

"Walter—"

Slovotsky raised his palm. "But this isn't the time to put your honor to the test. We've got plenty of coin. We'll *bid* on him. Sit tight for a moment." Tossing the reins to Karl, he vaulted from the wagon and moved into the crowd.

The bidding was stiff; several of the local farmers and ranchers forced the price from the initial twelve gold up to more than two platinum. The most persistent, a stocky man in a sweatstained cotton tunic, followed each of his bids with a glare at Slovotsky, as though challenging him to go on. When the bidding topped two platinum, the stocky man threw up his hands and stalked off, muttering vague curses under his breath.

Finally, the auctioneer raised the twig above his head, holding it delicately between his thumbs and forefingers.

"Will anyone challenge the price of two platinum, three gold for this man?" he asked the crowd in a practiced singsong. "A worthy, well-mannered slave, no doubt useful both in the field and as breeding stock. Both he and his sons will work hard, and require little food. No? I ask again, and again, and——" He snapped the twig. "The slave is sold; the bargain is made."

He nodded down at Slovotsky. "Do you want to claim him now? Very well. No chains? Two silvers for the ones he wears, if you want them. I'd advise it; this one hasn't quite been broken to his collar. Yet. And watch the teeth—he's nasty."

Walter reached into his pouch and handed over the money, accepting the slave's leash and an iron key in return. A few cuffs and curses moved the man down the platform's steps and over to the wagon.

The slave's eyes widened as he saw Karl. "You're Kharl—"

Slovotsky backhanded him across the face, then drew one of his knives. "Keep your tongue still if you want it to stay in your mouth." The point of his knife touching the smaller man's neck, he urged him onto the back of the wagon. The auctioneer smiled in encouragement before calling for the next slave to be sold.

"Just keep quiet," Karl whispered. "And relax. Everything's going to be fine."

"But—"

"Shh." With a clatter, the wagon began to move. "I know a smith on the edge of town. We have to make a stop first, but we'll have the collar off you in just a little while. Just be patient."

"You mean—"

"He means you're free," Walter said, giving a flick to the reins. "It just won't show quite yet."

The little man's mouth pursed, as though he were bracing himself for a slap. Then he shook his head, puzzled. "You mean that, Kharlkuhlinayn." It was half an unbelieved statement, half a terrified question.

At Karl's nod, his face grew somber. And then his gap-toothed mouth broke into a smile. A special sort of smile.

Karl didn't say anything. Nobody else would have understood how beautiful that smile was.

Unless they had seen it on the face of someone they loved. Or in a mirror.

"Ch'akresarkandyn ip Katharhdn," the little man said, as he sat on a sack of wheat in the bed of the wagon, rubbing at the lesions left by his chains. The sores were infected, oozing a hideous green pus in several places. Undoubtedly, his wrists and ankles ached dreadfully, but the light rubbing was all he allowed himself. "It's not so hard to pronounce, not as difficult as Kharlkuhlinayn."

"Call me Karl."

"You can call me Chak, if you'd like. You can call me whatever you want." Chak nodded slowly. "I owe you, Kharl. I don't understand why you freed me, but I owe you."

Walter chuckled. "So your only objection to slavery is when you're the slave."

Chak's brow furrowed. "Of course. It's the way of things. Although . . ." he shook his head. "There's times when it turns my stomach. Then again, it doesn't take much to turn my stomach. I'm a Katharhd; we've got delicate digestion."

"What happened to you?" Karl asked. "When we met, you were living off your winnings in the Games, but—"

"You put an end to that, Karl Cullinane, and I've spent many an hour cursing your name. When you knocked me out of the first round, I was down to my last couple of coppers. Fool that I was, I signed with this shifty-eyed Therranji; said he was taking on guardsmen for Lord Khoral. Damn elves can't help lying.

"In any case, fourteen of us rode out of Pandathaway. Took a while until we were past Aeryk and clear of the trade routes. One night, we camped and had dinner—with an extra ration of wine. Spiked wine; we all woke up in chains, got sold off in small lots. Seems the Therranji was a clandestine member of the Slavers' Guild, not a recruiter for Khoral." Chak shrugged. "He was just trying to get us clear of Pandathaway. That way, chaining us wouldn't bring the Guilds Council down on him for ruining the damn city's reputation as a safe place to be." His eyes grew vague. "Not that it'll stay safe for him."

A clattering came from around the bend, accompanied by a distant snorting and whinnying of horses.

Chak's nostrils flared. "I know that bloody mare's whining. It's the wagon of my former owners." His right hand hovered around the left side of his waist. "Wish I had a sword." He eyed the two scabbarded weapons lying on bed of the wagon. "Would you be willing to lend me one?"

Karl nodded. "Sure."

"*No.*" Walter shook his head. "We don't want any trouble. Karl, give him your tunic. I don't want them to see Chak out of his chains; we don't need loose talk about two strangers who bought and freed a slave."

Karl shook his head. "I never gave my word about not—"

"Karl. It comes down to the same thing. Now, is your word good, or not? Give him your tunic, please."

Nodding slowly, Karl complied. "Just sit tight for a moment." He tossed the tunic to Chak, who slipped it on without comment, although the hem fell well below his knees. Chak sat down, tucking a loose blanket around his legs to hide them, and began a careful study of the contents of a muslin sack.

Karl snatched the rapier from the bed of the wagon and tossed it to Walter.

Slovotsky raised an eyebrow; Karl shook his head. "I'm not looking for trouble," Karl said. "But slip this on anyway. We don't need to look helpless, do we?"

"Well . . ." Walter conceded the point, belting the rapier around his waist. "Let's look busy."

Karl jumped down from the wagon and busied himself with offering bowls of water to the mules, while Walter checked the leads of the trailing horses.

The slavers' wagon passed without incident, although the two slavers riding beside it gave practiced glances at Karl's and Walter's swords. Karl nodded grimly; when the smith had agreed to throw in a pair of swords, Karl had deliberately picked a slim rapier for Walter, one with a well-worn, sweat-browned bone hilt. Since Slovotsky wasn't good with a blade, it had seemed a sound precaution to pick a weapon that advertised a nonexistent expertise.

Several grimy faces peered out through the barred windows of the boxy slave wagon. Chak kept his face turned away, although he couldn't resist sneaking a peek.

As the wagon pulled away, he sighed. "Damn." The word was the same in Erendra as in English, something Karl occasionally wondered about.

Karl took his hand off the pommel of his sword. Walter and Ahira were right; they couldn't afford to draw attention to themselves here and now. But . . .

But that doesn't excuse it.

Walter peered into his face. "I'm sorry, Karl." He spread his palms. "Slovotsky's Law Number Nine: Sometimes, you can't do anything about something that sucks." He sighed. "No matter how *much* it sucks," he murmured.

Chak was already pulling off Karl's tunic. "That child is what bothers me. Just too young."

Karl raised an eyebrow as he slipped on the tunic.

"She's only eleven or so. But Orhmyst—he's the master; the rest are just barely journeymen—likes his women young. Says they're more fun. He's had this one for better than a year, ever since he raided Melawei; kept chattering about keeping her, even after they get to Pandathaway. Said she wouldn't bring much coin, compared with the pleasure."

Karl's heart thudded. *"What?"*

Walter's face whitened. "He's raping an eleven-year-old girl?"

Chak rubbed at the back of his neck. "Every night. And she spends her days whimpering, and begging for some healing draughts to stanch her bleeding; Orhmyst isn't gentle." Chak pounded his fist against the bed of the wagon. "In the Katharhd Domains, we'd cut off his balls for that, and not worry about whether the girl was slave or free."

"Walter," Karl said, "we can't—"

"Shut up, dammit. Give me a minute." Slovotsky brought his fist to his mouth and chewed on his fingers for a long moment.

Then he threw up his hands. "Cullinane, if it were possible that you set this up . . . never mind." He glared at Karl. "You remember what I was saying, about how you sometimes can't do anything about some things that suck?"

Karl nodded slowly.

"Well, you can just forget it. Sometimes I don't have the slightest idea of what I'm talking about—"

"We agree on something, at least."

"—but for now, how do you want to handle this? You're the tactician, not me."

"I promised Ahira I wouldn't get in any fights, unless it was a matter of self-defense." He chuckled, knowing what Walter was going to say.

"And you also agreed that I'd decide what constitutes self-defense. This does." Walter flashed a weak grin. "We'll work out an appropriate rationalization later. Tactics are your department: How are we going to do it?"

Karl smiled. "We'll follow them, but lag behind. Until it gets dark. Then you get the pleasure of skulking around, doing a nice, quiet recon." He turned to the little man. "Do you want in on this? You can have a share of their coin."

Chak shrugged. "I wouldn't mind. Always could use a bit of extra coin. Particularly," he said, patting at a phantom pouch, "now." He took the other sword from the wagon and drew it partway out of the scabbard. It was a wide, single-edged blade, more of a falchion than anything else. Chak nodded. "As long as my share includes this, it might be worth it."

Karl raised an eyebrow. "And maybe you've a score to settle with these folks?"

"That too." Chak smiled grimly. "There's always that."

Karl sat back against the base of a towering pine, his sword balanced across his lap. Deliberately, he twisted the chain of the manriki-gusari between his fingers. It helped to keep his hands from shaking.

Overhead, the branches and pine needles rustled in the wind, momentarily revealing, then hiding the flickering stars. A cool breeze blew from the west, sending a shiver across his chest. Half a mile down the road, almost hidden by a stand of trees, a campfire burned, sending gouts of sparkling ashes soaring into the night sky.

Chak grunted. "That friend of yours is taking too long," he whispered. "Probably tripped over his feet. Got himself killed." He tested the edge of his falchion's blade, then sucked at the cut on his thumb for the twentieth time. At least. "Good blade."

Karl shook his head. "No, we would have heard something."

"We would have heard that it's a good blade? Truly?"

"No, if he'd gotten into trouble—" Karl stopped himself, then gave Chak a sideways look. The little man's face was a caricature of puzzlement. "Seems you're getting your sense of humor back."

Chak smiled. "I always joke before a fight. Helps to steady the nerves. Now, my father, he always used to drink. Claimed it sharpened his eye, tightened his wrist. And it did, at that."

"Oh." Karl was skeptical; he let it show in his voice.

A snort. "Until the last time, of course. His wrist was so tight it was still straight as an arrow after a dwarf chopped his arm off." He bit his lip for a moment. "Which is why I don't drink before a fight

—joking keeps the arm looser." He looked over at Karl. "Now that you know all about me, tell me where you're from. The name is unfamiliar, although you look a bit like a Salke. A tall Salke, but they do grow them high."

Karl shook his head. "It's kind of complicated. Perhaps I'll go into it sometime."

"As you wish." Chak took one end of the manriki-gusari. "But you *will* tell me about this metal bola you're holding. Please? Never seen one like that before; doubt even you can throw it far."

"You don't throw it, usually. And as to what it can do, I suspect I'll have a chance to show you, in a while."

"Damn sure of yourself, Kharl."

"Of course." He smiled genially at Chak as he knitted his fingers together to keep them from shaking. *In fact, it's all I can do to keep my sphincters under control.* But he couldn't say that. "We were talking about that valley of yours."

"Not mine. Not really; I just passed through it once. But it is pretty. And not occupied, as far as I was able to tell. At least, not as of a few years ago. It's just too far away from any civilization; if anyone wanted to settle there, he'd have to travel for ten, twenty days to get to the nearest cleric. And since it's in Therranj, it'd be a bitch for humans to do business. Damn elves'll take you, every time."

"But people could live there."

"Sure." The little man shrugged. "Like I said, if they were willing to do without civilized necessities. I'm—"

"Making far too much noise," a voice hissed, from somewhere in the darkness.

Karl leaped to his feet, his sword in one hand, the manriki-gusari in the other.

Walter Slovotsky chuckled as he stepped from the shadows. "Relax. It's just your friendly neighborhood thief."

Karl quelled an urge to hit him. Dammit, he had asked Walter, more than once, not to sneak up on him. And Walter was usually good about it.

Just nerves, I guess. "How are they set up?"

Slovotsky squatted and picked up a twig. "This is the wagon," he said, making an X on the ground.

"The road runs here." He drew a gentle arc to the left of the X.

"Campfire here, on our side of the wagon; throws light on our side of the road. Chak, there are four of them, no?"

"Yes."

"Well, I could only see three. One's on watch on top of the wagon, a bottle of wine and a cocked crossbow to keep him company. There's a huge one sleeping on our side of the fire—he's got a bow, which isn't cocked." Slovotsky shrugged. "But he's sleeping with his sword in his hand. The third one's in a hammock strung up *here,* between two trees."

He spat on the ground. "Couldn't find the fourth. He could be out in the brush relieving himself, but if he is, he's either got the runs or is constipated as hell. I gave him plenty of time to show up; no sign."

"Maybe he's in the wagon?"

Walter shrugged. "Could be."

Chak shook his head. "They don't sleep in the wagons. Too dangerous. And if one of them was with the women, you would have heard. They don't use gags. But I wouldn't worry about it; they've only got the two bows, and we've accounted for those. As soon as the fight starts, the fourth one will pop up, and we'll cut him down."

"So?" Walter asked. "How do we do it?"

Karl stood. "We'll play it as we did with Ohlmin and his friends, with a bit of the way we handled Deighton thrown in. Conceal yourself close to the wagon—close enough to be sure you can get the watchman with your knife—and wait. Chak and I will work ourselves in, as close as we can. Give us plenty of time to get into position, then start things off by throwing a knife, taking the watchman out. That'll be the signal for Chak and me."

"Fine," Walter said. "But we don't know what their watch schedule is. What if they switch off before we get there?"

"Good point. If all they do is change places, don't worry about it; just take out whichever one is on the wagon. On the other hand, if the crossbow moves from the wagon, or if the slaver by the fire cocks his bow, we'll need to know that before we take them. If that happens, just slip away; when enough time has passed and Chak and I haven't heard anything, we'll head back here, rethink the attack, and try again."

He turned to Chak. "You kill the one in the hammock. I'll take the one by the fire."

The little man nodded. "Should be easy. What do I do after?"

"Just grab one of their bows, see if you can find the fourth one. Or help me, if I'm in trouble."

"Walter, when you take the watchman out, try for the chest—but any good disable is fine. Don't expose yourself to go in for the kill; as soon as you get the watchman, look for the fourth man."

He clapped a hand to Walter's shoulder. "Remember, football hero, you're free safety. We've got to be damn sure we get them all; if one of the bastards escapes, we're in deep trouble. We don't need for word to get back to Pandathaway that I'm still alive."

Walter's mouth quirked into a smile. "Bloodthirsty, aren't we?"

"You got any goddam objection?"

"That wasn't an accusation. I did say *we,* after all."

CHAPTER FOUR

On the Aeryk Road

Those who know how to win are far more numerous than those who know how to make proper use of their victories.

—Polybius

Walter Slovotsky crouched in the tall grasses surrounding a huge oak, his belly hugging the ground, one of his four teak-handled throwing knives in his right hand. His palm concealed the blade; a reflection from the steel could alert his target, twenty yards away.

Beyond the boxy slave wagon with the sleepy-eyed guard sitting cross-legged on its flat roof, the campfire burned an orange rift into the night. From where he lay, Walter couldn't see beyond the wagon to where Karl and Chak were—

—*should be,* he reminded himself. *Should be.* They were supposed to have moved silently into place by now, but Walter had long ago learned that things didn't go the way they should around Karl. Not that things always went badly, just differently.

Too bloody much of the time.

He slipped his thumb along the cool slickness of the blade and decided to wait just a few more minutes, to make sure they had gotten to the right places.

This had to work just right.

If it didn't, the fact that Karl was still alive would soon be common knowledge, even if a surviving slaver caught only a glimpse of him. No other men six and a half feet tall made a habit of taking on slavers on the trade routes of the Eren regions. Come to think of it, no shorter men got into that habit; the Pandathaway guilds had long made that an ill-advised profession to get into.

So why the hell am I in this? Not because of some eleven-year-old girl I've never even laid eyes on.

It was because of goddam Karl Cullinane. As usual. Walter could have tolerated knowing that somewhere, some little girl was being mistreated, even raped. People were being mistreated everywhere; cutting the number by one or two wasn't going to change that.

You had to take the long view. Maybe there was a way to change things, but it couldn't happen overnight. Risking everything for a moment's gratification just didn't make any sense at all.

So why did I agree to this?

He sighed. *Goddam Karl Cullinane. If I had just shrugged and dismissed it, he'd have looked at me as if I were a piece of shit.*

And was that such a big deal? Was Karl Cullinane's opinion so important?

Yes. Ahira was Walter's best friend, and Karl had worked out a way to bring Ahira out of the grave. That counted for something.

That counted for a lot.

And Karl's growth over the past months counted for more. When they had arrived on This Side, Karl had been a directionless flake; Walter had watched him grow, seen him strip away his shield of not caring, of choosing not to understand others, not to commit himself.

It all added up to respect. The simple fact was that Walter respected Karl, and wanted to receive the same in turn from him. Walter Slovotsky had always been respected by everyone whose opinion he cared about, and he wasn't about to learn how to live without that.

He shook himself. *If I don't pay attention to what's going on, I may have to learn how to live with a bunch of crossbow bolts in me.* He rubbed at a slim scar that curved around the left side of his collarbone. A knife had left that as a remembrance of Lundeyll; it hadn't been any fun at all. One of his own knives, and it had cost quite a bit to get it replaced in Pandathaway. In fact—

Enough. It was time to stop stalling, and get it done.

One way or the other.

He set the knife down with the bulk of the oak's trunk between it and the view of the watchman, and raised himself on his toes and fingertips, inching slowly, silently into the cover of the tree. *Aim for the chest*, Karl had said. Very well; the chest it would be.

Picking up the knife between the thumb and first two fingers of his right hand, he stood and moved quickly to his right. Raising the knife to shoulder level, he threw, then dove for the cover of the grasses.

With a flicker of steel, the knife tumbled end over end through the night air.

The guard must have seen the sudden movement; with a grunt, he jerked back and to the side. The knife's hilt caught him a glancing blow in the left arm, then fell away in the dark.

"Datharrrrti!" the guard called out as he reached for his crossbow and jumped to his feet. *Raiders!*

Oh, shit. Karl had said to hide in the shadows, but he hadn't been counting on this. With a functioning crossbowman on the roof of the wagon, the fight would be over before it began.

The bowman, a blocky little man, leveled his crossbow at Walter.

Ignoring the rustle of branches overhead, Walter broke into a staggered sprint, snatching another of his knives from his belt and throwing it, still on the run. At least it might distract the bowman for a second or two.

With a meaty thunk, the knife sank into the watchman's thigh. His leg crumpled; he fell to the roof, a sound halfway between a scream and a groan issuing from his lips. Clapping his hands to his leg, he dropped the crossbow.

Walter reached the side of the wagon. Without a pause, he grasped the edge of its roof and pulled himself up.

Below, steel clashed against steel. Karl fought with the gigantic swordsman who had been sleeping next to the campfire. Swords flashed in the firelight; screams and shouts filled the air.

Groaning, the watchman pulled the knife from his thigh, rose to his knees, and lunged at Walter, stabbing downward.

Walter caught the descending arm with both hands, stopping the razor-sharp point just inches from his left eye. A clout to the side of his head set the world spinning, but he held on as they rolled around the rough wood.

The watchman's free hand clawed at Walter's throat; the rough fingers fastened on his windpipe. Walter tried to drag air into his lungs as they struggled face to face, gasping as he drew in the foul reek of wine on the other's breath.

Inexorably, the knife moved toward his face, the point seeking his left eye, as if on its own volition.

Walter pushed against the knife arm. The blade's progress slowed; the point stopped four inches from his eye.

His hands started to tremble. The point moved closer. Three inches away, then two, then—

With a heave, Walter lurched on top of the slaver, driving his knee into the open wound on the other's thigh.

The watchman screamed; his fingers loosened from Walter's throat. Just for a moment, the watchman's right arm lost its strength.

Walter didn't wait for him to recover; he twisted the knife arm behind the watchman's back and up, past the hammerlock position, until he felt a sickening, wet pop as the arm separated from the shoulder socket, the knife falling from the slaver's limp fingers.

The slaver whimpered; feebly, he kicked at Walter, trying to slide away on his belly.

With one smooth motion, Walter snatched up the knife and stabbed downward into the other's kidney. He pulled the knife out and stabbed again, and again, and again, as the blood poured from the slaver's wounds.

With a muffled scream, the slaver twitched, then fell still.

Walter's stomach rebelled; he fell to his hands and knees, sour vomit spewing from his mouth. Wiping his mouth with a bloody hand, he willed his body back under control.

Below, Cullinane sliced down at his huge opponent's swordarm; as the other parried, Karl whipped the manriki-gusari around the slaver's blade and jerked, sending both the manriki-gusari and his enemy's sword flipping end over end into the night. He lunged in full extension; his blade slid into the slaver's throat, almost to the hilt. Blood fountained as Karl kicked the slaver off his blade; the giant gave a bubbling groan and fell face down onto the campfire.

As he lay there motionless, the fire hissed, sending up clouds of smoke and steam. A reek of scorched flesh reached Walter's nostrils. He gagged, but quelled the urge to vomit again.

"Walter," Karl shouted, "are you okay?"

Walter nodded.

Chak walked slowly into the dwindling firelight, his falchion dripping with blood. "Mine's taken care of. But where's Ohrmyst?"

Walter vaulted to the ground, letting his knees give to absorb the shock. "We've got to find him. *Quickly!* If he gets away—"

"I know, dammit. I know." Karl looked from side to side, his face a snarling rictus. "Chak, you go that way, I'll—"

He stopped, lowering the point of his sword.

Cullinane smiled. He scanned the ground for a moment, then walked over to the fire and picked up a water bucket and a soft cloth. Ignoring the body that lay smoldering in the ashes, he dipped the cloth in the water and started washing his hands. "There's another cloth here—clean yourself up. You can use it."

What was this nonsense? This wasn't any time to relax. "Karl—"

"I wouldn't worry about the fourth man," Karl said, cleaning, then resheathing his sword. "Wouldn't worry about him at all."

A distant flapping of leathery wings sounded from the direction of the road. "Although," Cullinane went on, "next time, I wish you'd look a bit more closely; Orhmyst was sleeping in a hammock slung way up high in that oak tree." He pointed at the tree Walter had hidden under. "When the alarm sounded, he lit out."

A dark, massive bulk came into view overhead; the wind whipped up dust and burning embers from the campfire.

Chak shouted and dove for the concealment of the woods.

Relax, Walter. Ellegon hovered overhead. *I don't think Ohrmyst will be talking to anyone. And would you tell your friend that I'm harmless? Please?* He landed on the ground with a thump, then lowered his massive head so that Karl could reach up and pat it.

Karl's laugh sounded forced as he scratched vigorously against the dragon's jaw. "Only relatively."

True. Ellegon burped.

"What are you doing around here, anyway?"

I told you I'd do better this time. And Ahira figured you might get into trouble; he sent me out to check the road from the sanctuary to Metreyll. When I didn't spot you, I started checking this road.

Walter nodded, then knelt over the water bucket, looking away from the body sprawled over the coals. He splashed water on his face; the sudden cold helped quell the last traces of his nausea.

"That was nice timing, Ellegon," he said.

A clattering from inside the wagon jerked his head around. "Karl, what say we free some people?"

Karl shot a glance toward the woods. "Chak, it's safe. You can come out now."

No answer.

Don't worry; he'll come out when he calms down. Then, accusingly: *You didn't tell him about me, did you?*

"Well, no. It didn't exactly come up. I wasn't thinking ahead."

Not thinking ahead. That was Karl, all over. In fact—

Ohmygod. "Karl—we're going to free these people, no?"

Cullinane cocked his head, puzzled. "Of course. That's the purpose of the exercise, after all. What—"

"Bear with me a minute." A cold wind sent a shiver up his spine. "There's fifteen, sixteen slaves in the wagon, right?"

"Not slaves anymore." Cullinane stooped to pick up his manriki-gusari, then twirled it easily. "Not anymore."

"And, I assume, some of them will want to join up with us. At least for a while."

Cullinane nodded as he pulled the smoldering body of the dead slaver from the campfire. He dragged him a few feet onto the bare dirt before riffling through his pouch. "Gin," he said, dangling a brass keyring. "And you're right, but so what? We've got enough food."

"And some might *not* want to come with us. They might want to go home."

"So what?"

"So," Walter said, impatient, "we give them some coin, maybe a horse if we can spare one, and wave as they go on their merry way. Right?"

"Right." He lifted his head and raised his voice. "Stand easy in there," he said in Erendra. "You will be free in a moment."

"Dammit, Karl, listen to me. What happens when they start talking about the nice, big man who—teamed with a dragon, of all things —took on a bunch of Pandathaway slavers, and then *freed* them? Word gets back to Pandathaway, somebody puts two and two together, and—"

Cullinane's face went ashen. "And the hunters are on our tails again."

Including Andy-Andy's rather pretty one, which isn't going to be all that mobile in a few months. I care about her, too, Karl. "Exactly what we've been trying to avoid. So what do we do?"

Karl Cullinane drew himself up straight. "We free them. Period."

Walter shrugged. "Fine. And what do we do about the aftermath?" *Karl, if you aren't scared shitless, you don't understand the situation.*

"We work it out. Somehow. Just like we work out what to do with that Metreyll armsman." He started toward the wagon, then caught himself. "Of *course.*" As he turned back to face Walter, his face was creased in a huge smile. "Did you ever study economics?"

"No." What the hell did that have to do with anything?

"I did. For a while." A mischievous grin replaced the friendly smile. "And economics is, my dear friend, the answer."

"Well?"

"I'll tell you later. C'mon, we've got some locks to unlock, some chains to break. I think I'm going to enjoy this. You coming?"

"Sure." Why not? Besides freeing them, the only choice was to leave them as slaves, and Cullinane wouldn't accept that.

Probably have to cut their tongues out, as well. And I wouldn't stand for that.

So I might as well get what pleasure I can out of this; sure as anything I'm going to be in front of the blades when the shit hits the fan.

As they walked toward the wagon, Karl threw an arm around Walter's shoulder. "You know, there are times when I enjoy this profession. A lot." A half-shudder went through Cullinane's body, but his smile remained intact.

Understandable. It was one thing for Karl to feign shrugging off his revulsion for violence, but another matter to truly take bloodletting for granted. *The day you can kill without any twinge of conscience, Karl, is the day I want to get as far away from you as I can.* "You've really got a solution?"

"The solution, Walter." Cullinane smiled. "By the way, in case I didn't mention it, you did just fine. If the watchman had been able to use his bow, all three of us would have been in deep trouble. The rest of it doesn't matter." With a sniff, he dismissed Walter's vomiting as irrelevant.

"Thanks." Respect; that felt good. *Next question: is Cullinane's respect worth going through* this *again? Next answer: I'll duck that issue for as long as I can.* "But this idea of yours—you're not going to tell me yet, are you?"

"Nope. A little frustration is good for the soul."

"I'm not going to like the answer, am I?"

Nope. Ellegon snorted. *Not one little bit.*

CHAPTER FIVE

The War Begins

If ever there could be a proper time for mere catch arguments, that time surely is not now. In times like the present, men should utter nothing for which they would not willingly be responsible through time and in eternity.

—Abraham Lincoln

Ahira sighed, shaking his head. *I should have known better,* he thought. *I really should have.*

Correct.

Thank you, Ellegon. The dwarf spat. *Thank you very much. Any sign of trouble on the Waste?*

I would have mentioned it if there were.

"Is. There. Any. Sign. Of. Trouble. On. The. Waste?"

No. There is nothing visible on the Waste.

Good. Stay on watch. The dragon didn't answer; Ahira decided to take that as an assent. "Karl?"

"Yes?" The big man turned from his conversation with Andrea and the grimy little girl.

"We need to talk. Take a walk with me."

"Sure. Give me a minute." Karl patted Andrea on the arm and smiled down at the silent little girl, who clung to Andrea's arm as though it were a lifeline. "See if she'll let you give her a spongebath —and dig up something else for her to wear." He switched to English. "Push for the bath," he said in a low voice, "and give her as thorough a going-over as you can. She's been through a rough time, and we'd better know if there's anything physically wrong with her."

Andrea pulled the girl closer. "Why not just give her more healing draughts? We've still got some left from what you found in the slavers' wagon, no?"

"Only three bottles. I don't know how long they'll have to last. We can't afford to dispense the stuff when it isn't necessary, just as a precaution."

"And if she does need some?"

Ahira grunted. "Then we give to her. Karl, I do want a word with you. Now."

"One more thing." Karl switched back to Erendra and raised his head. "Chak,- keep an eye on the bowman. It won't be for much longer."

Sitting across from the bound youth, Chak nodded, then jerked his thumb at a large wooden trunk next to the boxy slave wagon.

"Yes, Kharl, but do you mind if I go through this trunk while I do? I might find something. Maybe another bottle or two of the healing draughts; maybe some more coin."

"How do you plan on opening it?"

Chak smiled. "I think I can find a key."

"Go to it, then."

Across the clearing, five other former slaves sat talking with Walter and Riccetti. Three men, two women, all of them filthy, although none were apparently injured; despite his protestations, Karl had been generous with the bottles of healing draughts he had found in the slavers' wagon.

There wouldn't be more of that coming their way, at least not from the Healing Hand Society; the Hand acolyte had been more than clear on that point.

"Well?" Karl raised an eyebrow. "What is it?"

"I sent you into Metreyll to pick up provisions and supplies, not six—no, seven more mouths to feed."

He shrugged, his shoulders threatening to split the seams of his worn leather jerkin. "I would have brought back all of them, if most hadn't wanted to—

Crunch!

Ahira snatched his battleaxe from his chest, tearing the handle right through the straps that bound it to him. A thumb-flick sent its leather sheath spinning away.

Cullinane drew his sword and spun around into a crouch. "What the—?"

"Sorry," Chak called out, as he stood over the shattered trunk. He hefted the sledge. "But I told you I'd find a key."

Ahira looked down at the torn leather thongs that had secured his battleaxe to his chest. "Nice friend you've got there, Karl."

He chuckled. "Take it easy, Ahira, you're all tensed up."

Ahira stared pointedly at Karl's naked blade. "And, of course, you're not."

"Well . . ." He slipped the saber back into its scabbard.

"Never mind." Ahira raised a palm. "Never mind. What *is* this insane plan of yours?"

Karl shook his head. "In a while. First, how's Doria doing?"

Ahira spat. "They wouldn't let me see her. The acolyte I spoke to said that she's being 'fully integrated into the body of the Society,' and that any contact with outsiders—*outsiders*—was forbidden." *Be well, Doria. May you find with the Hand all that eluded you with us.*

"You think she's okay?"

"Hope so. If she isn't, there's not a damn thing we can do about it." Frustrating, but true. The Matriarch of the Healing Hand Society had protected the Hand preserve against the powers that had devastated the Forest of Elrood, turning it into the Waste. Handling a few warriors and a novice wizard wouldn't cause her to work up a sweat. "Unless you feel like storming the tabernacle."

Karl snorted. "Fat chance. As to how I think we ought to proceed, how about you gathering everyone around, while I have a talk with Andy, so that—"

"Kharl! Kharlkhulinayn!" Chak ran toward them, a long, thin piece of metal held high in his hands. "Look!" He jerked to a halt and handed it to Karl, holding it carefully as though it were a fragile piece of glass. Chak smiled broadly, as though he had just presented Karl with the Hope diamond.

Ahira looked at it. It looked like an oversized butterknife, actually; the flat blade was almost three feet long. He reached over and tested the edge against his thumb. Dull as a butterknife, too. "What is this?"

Chak stood back. "You don't know? *That*, Ahira, is a woodknife."

Karl cocked his head to one side. "I'm no wiser; what is a woodknife?"

"Look." Chak lifted it from Karl's outstretched palms and walked to a nearby sapling. Holding the handle with just thumb and two fingers, he slashed at the trunk, as though in slow motion.

The blade passed through the trunk as though it weren't there. With a rustling of leaves, the sapling crashed to the ground.

"See?" Chak said, bouncing the blade off his own neck. "It cuts only through wood. Nothing else. Quite a find, eh? I expect we're going to find quite a bit of use for this, where we're going."

What the hell did that mean? "Karl? Would you please tell me what you're—"

Cullinane raised a palm. "Tell you what: Why don't you gather everyone around, so I only have to go through this once. No rush; I've got to talk to Andy first, soon as she's finished bathing the girl. Private matter."

What's going on with the two of them now? I thought they'd worked things out. Ahira opened his mouth, then closed it. *None of my business.* He nodded. "Fair enough, but this had better be good."

"It will be. I hope."

Karl led Andy-Andy well away from the camp before sitting both of them down on a fallen log. "How's she doing?"

"Not too bad, at least physically. A few bruises, some abrasions were all I could find. But I'm not up on anatomy . . . it's too bad you can't check her over." She left the obvious unspoken; a little girl who'd gone through that particular kind of hell didn't need any man poking and prodding at her.

He chuckled thinly. "Two weeks of premed doesn't make me an internist. If you can't find anything wrong with her, I probably couldn't. Well . . . just keep an eye on her; we can always dose her again later if she needs more.

"But that's not why I needed to talk to you." *I wish I could put this off a bit longer, but—*"I've got a question for you."

She smiled up at him. "I can guess what it is. I've heard that fighting hikes up the ol' hormones, eh? Well . . ."

"Shh." He shook his head. "This is serious. I've got something to ask you, then something to tell you." *And I hope I'm doing this in the right order.*

Her face matched his somber tone. "Okay, Karl. You are serious. About something."

He took a deep breath. "The question is this: Will you marry me?"

Her eyes opened wide. "Will I *what?*"

"You heard me." All of a sudden, he didn't quite know what to do with his hands. They clutched aimlessly at the air in front of him. "I know we don't have a priest around, but we could improvise some sort of ceremony. Marry me—you know: live together, have kids, the whole bit."

She threw up her hands and laughed. "Karl, just 'cause we've slept together a couple of times . . ."

"It's not that." *Not just that,* he amended silently.

"If it's not that, then it has to be something else, something that's pretty impor—*no.*" Andy-Andy paled. "I'm pregnant? I must be, but how do you know?"

"Ellegon. He can detect the pheromonal changes. But how did you guess?"

"It's the only thing that makes sense. We haven't discussed this before. . . ." She shook her head. "Dammit, Karl, I'm not *ready* to be a mother, and—"

He raised a palm. "And we can take care of that. If necessary."

"How?"

"Do I have to go into details? Just take my word, please. It can be done."

"How?"

He shrugged. "This isn't exactly the way this was supposed to go, you know . . . Okay, think about it: We've got a lot of healing draughts, and I think I can improvise the tools for a D&C. I know I'm not a doctor, but we've got room for error. It'd hurt, but the draughts can protect you from any risk of infection, any permanent damage. If you want an abortion, you can have it. Up to you," he said, trying to sound casual, failing miserably. The thought of himself performing the abortion bothered Karl, not the notion of an early abortion itself. He'd never bought the idiotic notion that a microscopic blastula was a human being.

Doing a primitive abortion here isn't the only choice. We could try to sneak you back home, through the Gate. But I really don't want to try getting past The Dragon again, and I'm sure as hell not going to suggest that.

She tented her hands in front of her mouth and chewed on a forefinger. "Let me think, okay?"

"Fine. Take your time. Is . . . is there anything I can do?"

"Just leave me alone for a while."

"Andy—"

"Please?"

He stood. "Okay—but I've got to go talk to everybody else. Ahira's on my back. Join us in a few minutes?"

"Maybe. Just . . . just give me some time."

He nodded. "I love you, you know."

"I know." She smiled weakly. "Now get lost for a while."

"Please listen," Karl said in Erendra, as he stood in the center of the circle of faces. "I've got something to say." He paused to look at them. With one exception, all of the former slaves still looked scared. The exception was Chak. His smile almost radiated trust as he sat tailor-fashion, his right hand never straying far from the hilt of his falchion.

Lou Riccetti's round face beamed up at him. Trust to Lou to work things out, if they involved numbers. And those economics courses he'd taken didn't hurt either. Riccetti nodded reassuringly.

Ahira scowled. As usual. He didn't like being kept in the dark. Probably he wouldn't like what came next any better.

And then there was Slovotsky. *Walter, if I can ever figure you out, I'll admit to being a genius.*

Actually, Walter's easy. He's—

Shh. Karl went on: "For those of you who don't know, there are people after my head. When I met Ellegon, he was chained in a cesspit in Pandathaway. I didn't like that; I freed him.

"The Pandathaway guilds didn't like *that.* They sent slavers out after me. After all of us. They caught up with us in the Waste.

"We managed to get away, and then kill all of the bastards. By now, Pandathaway probably thinks that I'm dead." The Matriarch had said that he couldn't be located while on the Hand preserve, and certainly a location spell couldn't have spotted him during the period that he had been home, on the other side of the Gate. "They will soon be hearing that I'm alive.

"There's probably nothing that we can do to prevent that." Twenty yards behind Ahira, the bowman glared over at him. "Even if we killed him; the other freed slaves will talk.

"I propose that we don't even try. Instead, I suggest that we do two things. First, Chak knows of an uninhabited valley in Therranj. I propose that we move there, and settle down; raise food and cattle, everything. We'll have to send another party into Metreyll to pick up some more supplies and animals, cattle, sheep, goats, chickens, whatever we need. The trip will take a while; and building houses, clearing fields, planting crops, all of it will be hard work. But once we're settled in—"

Walter shook his head. "That won't do it. Pandathaway is ticked at you, Karl; they won't let a bit of distance stand between them and revenge." He shrugged. "It might buy us some time, but that's all."

Notice the "us"?

Yes. Now, shh. Karl held up a hand. "No. I'm not going to spend much time there for the first couple of years; certainly not enough to be located and found. Instead . . . Lou: Explain a bit about supply and demand, and how that effects economic utility."

Riccetti picked up his cue as though they had rehearsed it. Which they had, of course.

He stood. "The price of anything depends on two things: how much of it is available, and how badly people want it; supply and demand. If anything—*anything*—gets too expensive, then people start to find substitutes. That applies to swords, to grain, to cattle— and to slaves. Karl's talking about making slaves too expensive."

"Exactly." Karl folded his arms across his chest. "And we'll do that by making slave-taking too expensive, too risky a business. I'm talking about doing the same thing that we did yesterday, but on a larger scale. We'll hit every caravan we can, force the Slavers' Guild to beef up their caravans, adding more and more guards, cutting down on the profits from slaving. And we'll *keep* doing that until the system starts to collapse."

Shaking his head, Ahira spat. "That's just plain silly. There are a lot of slaves, Karl; you won't affect the price of slaves one whit. Figure that Pandathaway alone imports, say, three, four thousand slaves per year. Right now, they get them via raids on Therranj, Melawei, and so forth. Let's say that each caravan has twenty slaves, and that you hit—and free—one caravan each tenday. And let's assume that every one of the freed slaves either joins us in this valley of yours or finds his or her way home.

"That's only a thousand or so freed slaves each year." He shrugged. "It'll drive up the price a bit. But that's all."

Smiling broadly, Walter Slovotsky nodded. "Beautiful, Karl. Dammit, James, you're wrong; it'll do more. Once we've demonstrated that *we* can take on slavers and get away with it, others will start doing it, too. Everyone has shied away from crossing the Slavers' Guild because of the fear of retribution. Once we show that we can get away with it, most of that fear will be gone.

"It's a sure bet that some of these unemployed mercenaries will try to get into the business. And since they'll have stolen the slaves, they'll be afraid to sell them. They'll have to free them, making their profit off money that the slavers carry. Just as we did." He hefted his now-full purse. "A nice bit of thinking it through, Karl. That is what you're talking about, isn't it?"

"Yes."

From across the clearing, Andy-Andy's voice called, "It's crazy, you know." She walked quickly toward the group.

How did she hear?

I echoed your words. A mental smirk. *And if you're really nice to me, I won't relay your thoughts without permission.*

I didn't know you could do that. Although it really wasn't all that surprising, come to think of it.

You didn't ask.

He scowled. *Well, then, relay this.* He stopped himself. *Never mind.* "Andy—"

"Later." She smiled. "We'll have plenty of time, on this trip to that valley of yours. But we'd better move quickly." She placed the flat of her hand on her stomach. "Before I start to swell."

Karl couldn't help smiling.

Ahira shook his head. "This is insane, you know, but . . ."

"But what?" Riccetti frowned. "It makes perfect sense."

"But let's try it." The dwarf bounced to his feet and stuck out his hand at Karl. "You can count me in." As they shook hands, Ahira shrugged. "It's worth a try." He turned to the freed slaves. "You may either come with us, or leave. Anyone who wishes to leave us should see me later."

Slovotsky smiled. "All we have to do is take on a few thousand slavers."

Andy-Andy shook her head. "There's one other thing."

"Oh?" Ahira cocked his head. "What am I missing?"

"We've also got to stay alive."

Karl nodded. "That *is* the keystone of the whole plan, after all." A gout of fire roared into the sky. *Nice keystone.*

Ellegon at his side, Karl smiled down at the bowman. "I'm going to turn you loose. We'll give you a waterbag and a knife; start across the Waste tonight. I want the extra time to get clear of here." As the youth glanced over at the string of horses, Karl shook his head. "If you try to leave before then, or raise a hand to any of us, or steal a horse, I'll have Ellegon eat you."

The dragon leered. *Please try to leave early. I could use a snack.*

The bowman glared up at Karl. "The Pandathaway Guilds Council will hunt you down like an animal. They will find you, Karl Cullinane. And, my Lord Mêhlen willing, I will travel to Pandathaway to watch you die."

Karl smiled. "Have Lord Mêhlen give them a message from me. Tell them: Karl Cullinane is alive, and . . ." He let his voice trail off.

Did this make any sense? *Here I am, an expectant father, and I'm asking for trouble. Ahira was right; this is absolutely insane.*

You made a promise to the Matriarch. And though she will not help you further, will you keep that promise, or not?

Karl looked across the clearing to where the little girl was smiling at Andy-Andy over a bowl of stew. Not much of a smile, but a smile nonetheless. And a very special sort of smile. . . .

Yes. Hell, yes. He cut the bowman loose. "Tell them this: I'm hunting *them.*"

PART TWO

The Valley

CHAPTER SIX

Settling In

All things are artificial, for Nature is the art of God.

—Sir Thomas Browne

The valley took Karl by surprise, although that morning Ellegon had told him they would reach it shortly after noon.

He led his mare up a gentle incline, through the charred remains of what once had been a stand of trees. There was no way of knowing what had caused the fire that had burned a black slash across the surrounding miles; possibly someone's carelessness, possibly a lightning strike.

The fire had been years before; rain had since reduced the burned trees to a flat ash surface that allowed easy passage for both the flatbed and the former slave wagon.

Life was starting to return; impudently, thumb-thick saplings rose chest-high, as though in a promise that this area would be wooded once again. In the light breeze, leafy ferns nodded their agreement.

In further confirmation, the grasses had started to reclaim the ground at the top of the hill.

His horse snorted, nudging him from behind.

"Dammit, Carrot, we're moving fast enough." He turned to stroke her neck before resuming their slow pace through the rubble. "You take it easy, hear? I don't want you breaking a leg."

She whinnied as if she understood, and agreed that breaking a leg was, indeed, not the ultimate goal of her horsy life.

Hmmm, *would* the healing draughts work on a horse?

Possibly. Quite possibly.

But would Ahira object to his experimenting, even if it meant the difference between preserving and having to kill the horse?

Certainly; the dwarf and the horses had something less than a deep and abiding affection for each other.

Behind him, Ahira grunted as he pulled on the reins of his gray gelding. "Move, you filthy little monster. *Move,* I said." The small horse towered above the dwarf, drawing back its head to the limits of the reins and snorting at Ahira as it gave ground, inch by inch.

Quite a horseman, eh? The mental voice was faint.

Quite.

Following Ahira, Slovotsky sat in his usual place on the bench of the flatbed, with blond Kirah close beside him. A few weeks of freedom had done Kirah's appearance good; she actually was quite pretty, although a bit too skinny for Karl's tastes.

Deep in quiet conversation, Walter smiled, and patted her knee. Karl found that vaguely reassuring, and was ashamed of himself for feeling that way.

Walter's my friend, dammit. I should be happy he's found someone, not relieved that I don't have to worry about him and Andy-Andy anymore.

To the best of my knowledge, Walter has never been accused of practicing exclusivity.

Ellegon!

If you're going to trust either or both of them, then do so. If not, don't. But whipping yourself with worry suggests that you don't think you have enough real problems to worry about. Would you like to hear my list?

No thanks, Ellegon. . . . I can always turn to you for a spot of reassurance, eh?

Think nothing of it.

I won't.

Behind Slovotsky and Kirah, Lou Riccetti napped under a light blanket, with a sack of grain for his pillow. The wind carried his snores to Karl's ears.

Hmph. Riccetti was *supposed* to be keeping an eye on the bull, who was secured to the flatbed by a length of rope tied to his brass nose ring. Karl thought about waking Riccetti, then dismissed the idea. No need, the lumbering beast followed without complaint.

From its high seat, Andy-Andy drove the former slave wagon, little Aeia huddled next to her, the five chicken cages tied down on the flat roof. The bars were gone from the wagon's windows, having joined the other rod stock in the back of the flatbed.

Trotting along beside the wagon, the two goats voiced their unflattering opinion of the whole party. Aeia turned to give them a few reassuring words. She liked the goats, although the smelly creatures didn't return her affection.

Aeia was still a problem; she had yet to make it through a night without waking up crying, not going back to sleep until Andy-Andy held her for at least an hour.

What it came down to was simple: Aeia was homesick. There was a solution to that, but Andy-Andy wasn't going to like it; she had practically adopted the girl.

Spread out behind the wagon, Tennetty, Chton, Ihryk, and Fialt led their horses, occasionally switching the five cows to make them keep the pace. The cattle were brakes on the whole procession; they could barely walk fifteen miles on a good day. Goddam splay-footed beasts—

Stop worrying; the trip is almost over.

Last was Chak, who insisted on riding his horse through the charred rubble, swearing at her when she balked.

Karl stroked Carrot's neck as they walked up the hill. "Easy, now."

A carrot works better than a stick, most of the time. This time Ellegon's voice was louder, clearer.

Karl looked up. High overhead, the dragon circled, a dark speck against the blue sky. *True. Which is why I finally got around to naming my horse Carrot.*

A suitable name. She is probably very tasty.

"Ellegon, you are *not* eating my horse. Case closed."

Hmph. I would have thought I deserved some sort of reward for finding a route you can take your wagons over. The mindlink grew tighter for a moment, then loosened. *Lewis and Clark didn't have aerial reconnaissance. Neither did Cortez, or Pizarro. You may have noticed that you haven't had to turn around and try a different route once over the past three months.*

"I noticed. Honest. And I noticed it the first day, even before you mentioned it. So would you please—" He cut himself off. Snide comments were not the way to handle a child asking for praise. *You've done one hell of a job, in case I haven't mentioned that recently.*

You haven't.

The crest of the hill lay just a few yards ahead; the slope steepened. On an impulse, Karl dropped Carrot's reins and ran up, onto the summit, and over the hill.

And into wonder.

The valley opened up below him, trees and grasses spread out in a welcoming green embrace. In the distance, silvery threads of streams wove their way down from the far, snow-peaked mountains, tumbling through stands of pine and maple, finally emptying into the mirror-bright lake that cupped the valley floor.

Half a mile below, seven deer drank at the lake's edge. The water was still, mirroring the fluffy clouds and blue sky. A five-point buck looked up at him; then the group sprinted gracefully into the forest, leaping high over the grasses as they ran.

The wind blew across the valley, bathing him in the warm tang of sunbaked grasses, and the cool scent of pines.

He didn't notice Chak walking up. One moment, Karl was all alone; the next, the little man stood beside him, Carrot's reins in one hand, the reins of his own gray mare in the other.

"Like it?" Chak smiled, handing him the reins.

Karl didn't answer him.

It wasn't necessary.

"Ready, Lou?"

Riccetti nodded, smiling inside. *Ready? I've been waiting my whole life for a moment like this.*

Ahira beckoned him to his feet. "You go first."

Riccetti rose and walked to the campfire. He turned to face the others, his back to the crackling flame.

"The two main considerations in this sort of construction," he said, "are water supply and defense."

All the others looked at him, listening intently.

Which was nice; Lou liked being the center of attention. For once.

Slovotsky nodded. "Good point, but what does that do for us?"

The fire was hot; sweating, Riccetti moved away from it, the heat still pressing against his back. "Form follows function, Walter," he said. "What we've got to do is figure out what sort of complex to make, given our present limitations of materials and the lack of power tools. I wish we had a few dozen tons of concrete mix, steel girders, PVC pipe, and such. But we don't."

Both Chton and Fialt frowned, while the other new people stared back blankly; Riccetti realized that he had lapsed back into English.

Item, he thought, *English, teaching of. Discussion: Many useful concepts are not available in Erendra, absent a great deal of neologism or circumlocution. Examples: concrete, suspension bridge, gunpowder, steam engine, railroad. Question: Should we actually teach English, or settle for supplementing Erendra vocabulary?*

Sprawled on the ground behind the others, Ellegon raised his head. *Noted, Louis. I will remind you of this later, when you have time to consider it.*

Don't forget.

Dragons don't forget, stupid. We leave that sort of thing to humans.

"My apologies," he said in Erendra, both to Ellegon and to the natives. "I was saying that we don't have many different materials to work with, nor do we have . . . magical tools, other than the woodknife."

Chak spat. "And you should be grateful for that, instead of complaining that we don't have any other magical tools. Woodknives are rare, Richetih; takes a master wizard to make one, and it takes him *years.* I don't know where Ohrmyst bought—or, more likely, stole—his. I've traveled far; only heard of a few in existence. Only seen one other, in Sciforth, and that one heavily guarded. You couldn't have bought that knife for a wagonload of gold."

Cullinane raised a palm. "Stand easy, Chak. Lou was just commenting, not criticizing."

That seemed to settle the matter for the little man; Chak listened to Karl the way Riccetti would have listened to Washington Roebling himself.

Riccetti went on: "How and what we build has to be planned with that limitation in mind. We also have to consider the problem of the water supply."

Tennetty shrugged, sending her straight black hair flipping about her face.

She was a slim woman, with an almost impossibly thin nose, and a permanent expression of distance on her drawn face. The daughter of a poor farmer on one of the Shattered Islands, on her fifteenth birthday she had been sold to a slaver's ship. The ten intervening years hadn't treated her kindly, as she passed from owner to owner; it showed in her lined face.

Riccetti found her profoundly unattractive, even when her mouth was closed. Which was usually, but nevertheless all too seldom.

"What problem?" She gestured at the lake, which lay shimmering in the starlight. "If we build our houses close to the lake, then we have a short walk for water. If we are stupid enough to build them far away, then we have a long walk for water. What is so complicated about how far you have to carry a bucket?"

Sitting on the other side of Andrea from little Aeia, Cullinane shook his head, grinning. "I'd really like to have running water, myself. Taste of home, and all that. You've got a way?"

"Yup." Riccetti smiled. "I took a quick look this afternoon, while the rest of you were lolling around camp. So far, I've counted seven streams that feed into the lake. I've found one with a waterfall." He pointed. "About a quarter-mile that way. The waterfall's small—it's not much taller than Karl is. But if we set up the compound over part of that stream, surrounding the waterfall, we can divert it, and still have a bit of flow to play around with. We'll want a mill, for one thing . . . and in the future, I might be able to rig up some sort of water heater."

"Hot showers," Andrea said, sighing. She bent her head toward Aeia's. "Have you ever had a hot shower?"

She shook her head. "What's a shower, Andy?"

"But in the short run, we can have flowing water inside, for washing, cooking, and for privies."

Ahira's forehead furrowed. "How are you going to build a flush toilet?"

Riccetti shrugged. "That's years away. For now, you're going to have to settle for a constant-flow one, sort of like an outhouse with some water from the stream running underneath. Open pipes like the Romans', but we'll use wood instead of lead."

Slovotsky nodded his approval. "That's not bad. Constant-flow toilet, eh? It's so simple, it'd be hard to think up, if you didn't already know about it. I guess you weren't wasting your time in your engineering courses."

Cullinane threw back his head and laughed.

The dwarf glared at him. "What's so funny?"

The big man shook his head. "Never mind." His expression went vague.

*Louis, Karl has asked me to tell you that he remembers lending you his copy of *Farnham's Freehold*, and that he's glad he did.*

That's nice.

*And he also said to mention that he won't tell anyone that you swiped the notion of constant-flow toilets from Heinlein. *If* you build the first one for him and Andrea.*

Tell him to go to hell. I'm running the construction here, and I'll do as I see fit. He waited for Ellegon to relay the message. Cullinane glared at him for a moment, then relaxed, his hand miming tipping a hat.

Good. It was best to start things off by letting everyone—Cullinane particularly—know who was in charge of the building.

"In any case," he went on, "that's the first part of it. The other thing is that the waterfall is in a stand of pines. We can save a lot of effort by building there; even green, pine is good to build with. It's a bit tricky, but I've read about how to use it."

I'd give any digit you care to name for one-tenth of the library Farnham had. Or even for Robertson's Green Wood Construction. Or the Britannica, or the Rubber Handbook, or anything.

All that stood between him and all of those books was about five hundred miles of forest, plains, mountains and Waste, plus the warrens surrounding the Gate Between Worlds.

And The Dragon, guarding the Gate.

Ellegon snorted. *You had best learn to live without those books, Louis. He is still awake. And will be, for much longer than you will live.*

Riccetti shuddered. No *way* was he ever going near The Dragon again. "So we build there," he said. "Agreed?"

"Sounds right to me," Cullinane nodded. "You were talking about defense. Some sort of castle?"

"No. We don't have the tools or the manpower for stonework, even if we could find stone worth quarrying. My suggestion is that we go for something like a western fort. It'll look a bit crude, but—"

Fialt spat. "I am *from* the west. I was born and raised on Salket. We build with stone there; we are civilized." He was the oldest of the group, a grizzled graybeard of fifty or so.

Slovotsky chuckled. "Not your west—ours. But it sounds like a lot of work, Lou."

"It will be. But it should give us some defense. If the colony grows a lot, we won't be able to put all the houses inside, of course, but it still makes sense to have some sort of fortification to retreat to, if necessary. We may not need it, but . . ."

Chak nodded. "Kharl's plan should keep us relatively safe, as long as he doesn't spend too much time here. But you're right, Richetih: no sense in taking a chance for no payoff."

Ahira cocked his head to one side. "That's easy for you to say— you're going on this first expedition with Karl; little of the sweat will be from your brow. Not more than a tenday's worth, at best."

"Damn, but I like your positive attitude, Ahira." The little man smiled. "Pointing out another nice part of Richetih's plan."

Riccetti spread his hands. "That's the broad outline. If we do it this way, I'll mark out the boundaries in the morning, and we can get right to work. Should be able to have three walls of the palisade up within a—"

"Palisade?"

"The outer wall. We'll put a walkway around the inside, around the top. As I was saying, it should be done within two, maybe three tendays. Ahira, you're still the leader. It's up to you." *And if you don't want to do it my way, I'd like to hear what idiocy you have in mind.*

Andrea raised an eyebrow. "Why just three-quarters of the wall? It seems to me it'd be more efficient to do the whole thing at one time."

"No. The gate will be the hard part; by leaving that wall for last, we can have a way of bringing wood in to build the houses and such. We could do the houses first, but I think we'll save some effort by using the palisade as the fourth wall for some of them, and for the grainmill, when we build it. Besides, we'll want to set up a smithy and make some nails before we do the houses; we can build the palisade walls with just wood and leather.

"And sweat, of course." He turned to Ahira. "That's my proposal. There'll be lots of details to work out, but it seems to me this is the best way."

"Any objections?" The dwarf waited silently for a moment. "We'll do it. Lou, you're in charge of construction. Complete charge; you don't ask anyone, you tell them, unless you think you need another opinion. Refer any discipline problems to me." He tapped his thumb against the blade of his battleaxe.

Cullinane snorted. "That include you?"

"Lou, if I give you any trouble, you can refer it to Karl."

Or me.

"Or Ellegon." The dwarf turned to Slovotsky. "Now, Walter, what are your thoughts about crops and animals?"

Riccetti sat down, barely listening as Slovotsky stood and began to talk about slash-and-burn agriculture, and where he wanted to put the first field.

For more than four years, Lou Riccetti had been an engineering student in a world that really didn't want things built. The days of great construction had passed from his world; the future of engineering was with piddling little electronic circuits, not big structures, not great things. There would be no more Brooklyn Bridges built, no more Hoover Dams.

But here, it was different. A world to conquer.

He smiled.

I'm going to be building things, he thought, his heart beating audibly in his chest. *It's a small start, but it's a start.*

He shook his head. This was ridiculous. Getting all excited about putting together a bunch of log cabins and some stockade fencing? And some sort of smithy, come to think of it. That would have to be done early; the flatbed contained fifty or so pounds of thin nail stock, but no nails. Then again, nailmaking shouldn't require a full-fledged smithy; a hot fire, a bellows, a hammer, and the smallest of the anvils would do. And—

Ridiculous. It had to be done, granted, but getting excited about it?

I disagree. Ellegon lifted his head from his crossed forelegs, curling and uncurling his wings. *It is not ridiculous, friend Louis. Not if it makes you feel this good.

Build and enjoy.

The first wall went up much more quickly than Karl would have believed possible.

It wasn't just because of the woodknife's ability to turn the felling, stripping, and shaping of a tall pine from a tedious affair into something that took only minutes, helpful as that was.

And it wasn't just Ellegon's great strength, although that certainly helped, too.

Ellegon would seize the blunt end of a stripped log in his massive jaws and drag it from where it fell to where the empty post hole was. That made harnessing the horses unnecessary, although Riccetti could and did rig a block, tackle, and twenty-foot-tall tripod. With that, and with the aid of the mules and the cannibalized harnesses from the flatbed, Karl, Walter, and Ahira could raise the upper end of a log into its proper position and lower the flat end into its hole, before packing dirt around the now-upright log to keep it steady.

And it wasn't just that all of them worked hard, although they certainly did.

Ellegon hauled logs, beginning work when the sky grew light, not quitting until well after dark. Fialt, Kirah, and Chak took turns with the woodknife, felling and stripping pines, keeping a constant supply of twenty-foot posts coming, as well as stacking the scraps for the cooking fires. Karl, Walter, and Ahira dug the holes and raised the posts. Andy-Andy and Aeia kept bowls of hot stew and pitchers of cold water coming from dawn to dusk. Ihryk and Tennetty hunted deer, duck, and rabbit, gathered wild garlic, onions, chotte, burdock, maikhe, and tacktob for the stewpot, stretching the supply of dried beef and putting off the time when it would become necessary to start converting the chickens from egglayers into roasters.

What really made it all work was Riccetti.

Lou always seemed to be at Karl's elbow, any time he needed a bit of advice or instruction. At times, he wondered if there weren't really three or four Lou Riccetti's; others reported the same.

Riccetti was the one who knew how to lash together a tripod of logs and throw together a wooden block and tackle to raise and support a pole, or turn a dozen saplings and a few hundred yards of rope into a double-lock bridge across the deep-bedded stream.

He was the one who withheld a portion of the scrap wood, for Ellegon to roast slowly into wood tar, to be later distilled down to creosote, which would protect the palisade against insects and rot.

Riccetti showed them how to lash the poles together at the top of the wall with wet leather strips, so that as the leather dried, it shrank and linked the individual poles together solidly.

More important, he knew how to apportion the work so that no bottlenecks developed; Karl, Walter, and Ahira always had just enough poles to work with, without worrying about falling behind while unused ones accumulated, or letting valuable time go by while they waited for the next.

Riccetti was, finally, in his own proper environment; Karl smiled at the little swagger his walk had developed.

The sounds and smells of the dying were far away; the days passed quickly, filled with the sweet smell and unwashable stickiness of freshly cut pine, the stink of his own sweat, and the deep sleep brought on by hard labor.

CHAPTER SEVEN

Moving On

Now hollow fires burn out to black,
And lights are guttering low:
Square your shoulders, lift your pack,
And leave your friends and go.

—Alfred Edward Housman

It was a clear night. Andy-Andy lying still beside him, Karl stared up at the dome of stars.

Downslope from them, halfway between them and the palisade wall, little Aeia huddled in her blankets, asleep at last. It had been a rocky night for the girl, filled with bad dreams and loud screams.

If there is a hell, Orhmyst, you are surely there.

"Andy," he whispered.

"Yes?"

He quirked a smile. She hadn't been sleeping either.

"I've got to leave, for a while."

She sucked air through her teeth, then rolled over on her side, facing him. She stroked his forehead with gentle fingers. "I know. You're worried about Pandathaway."

"Not worried: terrified. If I stay here too long, I'm not just endangering myself." He patted her barely distended belly. "There's others involved, too."

"Like Karl, Junior?" She grinned at him.

"Even if it is a boy, we're not naming him after me. With a mother as pretty as you, he'll have enough of an Oedipus problem without saddling him with his father's name. Besides, it's probably a girl."

"It will be a boy, Karl." Her face grew somber. "We women know about these things."

"Bullshit." He snorted. "I think we know each other a bit too well for you to give me that sort of nonsense."

"We *do* know about these things," she said, shrugging, "and we're right about, oh, fifty percent of the time."

"Funny. Very funny. But you're changing the subject. Or trying to."

"I'm starting to get fat, is that it? You're going to run off and find some sixteen-year-old—"

"Shh." He put a finger to her lips. *"Shh.* Not even in jest. Please." A long pause. "How long will you be gone?"

"Don't know for sure. Six months, at a minimum. Maybe closer to a year."

"When?" she asked, her voice a low whisper.

T'were best done quickly. "In a day or two, I think. It won't take long to pack. I don't know if you've noticed, but Chak's getting itchy."

"And so are you."

There was more truth in that than he cared to admit. "No, it's not that. But this vacation has gone on long enough; it's time to get back to work."

She rolled onto her back and stared up at the sky, her head pillowed on her hands. "Slicing up people. Some work."

"Slicing up *slavers.* Or, if you want to be more accurate, my work is murdering slavers. But it isn't the words that matter, Andrea. You know that." *Please, Andy, don't ever let the blood come between us. Please.*

She sighed deeply, and then closed her eyes. She lay quietly for so long that Karl began to wonder if she had fallen back asleep. "Who are you taking with you?"

"Well, Chak, for one. He's seen more of the Eren regions than any of the rest of us, and he's pretty handy with a sword." *Besides, he rankles at taking orders from anyone except me. I'm not leaving a time bomb behind.* "I'd like to take Ellegon, but he's just too conspicuous." *And he's also the most deadly being I know. He stays here, and keeps an eye on my wife and unborn child.*

I am honored, of course. But I will miss you, Karl. Don't do something stupid and get yourself killed. Please?

Just as a favor to you.

Thanks.

"Who else?" she asked, a decided edge to her voice.

"Well, I can't take Walter, not this time; somebody's got to run the farm." *And if I did take him along, I'd never know whether it was because I wanted him along, or because I didn't trust both of you enough to leave him here.* "I think I'll invite Ahira to come along; he'll want to go. He's just as good in a fight as I am—"

Better.

"—and he's got a fine strategical sense. His darksight might come in handy; it's even better than Ellegon's."

"How's he going to take your being in charge, Karl?"

"Huh? Who said anything about—"

"As Walter would say, think it through. You've always thought he was too conservative, too eager to avoid a fight. So you're going to let him be in charge when you're going out *looking* for trouble?"

He snorted. "We'll work it out. What we're doing is too important to let who's-in-charge games screw it up. And . . ."

"And? I don't recall your mentioning *my* name."

He snorted. "Don't be silly."

"Silly?"

"This isn't a time for reflex pseudo-feminism. We're going to be gone for six months, at least. If you think I'm going to let a woman at term bounce along on the back of a horse, try thinking again. Case closed; you stay here, where it's safe."

"Always the diplomat, Karl." She dismissed the issue with a wave of her hand. "But I guess you're right. It's just going to be you, Chak, and Ahira?"

"Can't expect any of the new people to do any good in a fight. The best is Fialt, and he wouldn't last ten seconds against a real swordsman. On the other hand, he's trying hard to learn. If he wants in, he's got it. Chton, Kirah, Ihryk, and he are happy here, or I'd escort them somewhere safe. Tennetty, though . . ."

"Tennetty wouldn't be happy anywhere."

"Exactly. But she's hot to kill some slavers. I can't say as I blame her; she can come along if she wants to. Which she will."

"Is that all?" She frowned. "It sounds like an awfully small group."

"It is. But I think it's the best one, for now." *I may as well get it over with.* "There's one more person we're taking along, Andy."

"Karl, you are *not* taking Aeia."

"We're taking her home." He shrugged. "Might as well swing through Melawei. The hunting should be good; there've been slaving raids all along that coast." Mainly by sea, according to Chak; to the best of his knowledge, Ohrmyst had been the only slaver to try the difficult overland route to Melawei.

Question: How does one take on a slaver's ship?

Answer: very carefully. Do you have any more stupid questions?

No.

"No!" Andy-Andy said, echoing his response to Ellegon. "You can't. She's getting used to being around us; she'll adjust. I'll take care of her."

"We're not her family, Andrea. She's been through hell. You should know that, better than I do; let's let her grow up in her own country, with her own people."

Andy-Andy sat up, angrily pulling the blankets around her. "What good did *they* do her? Tell me. Her *people* let her get caught by slavers, raped. Karl, you can't take her back to them. I won't let you."

He tried to put his hand on her shoulder, but she shrugged his arm away.

"Shall we leave it up to her?" he asked.

"She's too young to decide. She needs someone to take care of her." She looked away from him, toward where Aeia slept.

"Like you?"

"Yess," she hissed, "like *me.* Don't you think I'm good enough to take care of her? *Don't you?*"

He shook his head. "No, I don't."

Her head spun around. "You bastard." Tears filled her eyes.

"Andy, it's not that there's anything wrong with you. The thing of it is this: She's a little girl. Somewhere, she has family. And they probably miss her as much as she misses them."

She sneered. "Just as our families back home will be missing us? You didn't seem so worried about *that.*"

"Different case. For one thing, we're adults; we have to make our own decisions. For another, with the time differential between here and home, the fact that we're gone hasn't even been noticed yet; at home, we've only been gone a few hours.

"But, again, you're dodging the issue. Think about this: If someone stole little whatever-her-name-is from you, you'd want her back." He laid a palm on her belly. "Wouldn't you? Or would you think that some stranger could take better care of her?"

She didn't answer for a long time.

Then: "Leave it alone, Karl. You're right, as usual. Bastard." She daubed at her eyes with a corner of the blanket. "But it's going to be a boy." Gathering her robes about her, she rose and walked down the slope toward where Aeia lay sleeping. She seated herself beside the girl and took one of Aeia's small hands in both of hers.

And sat there, watching her, until the night fled, and the sun sat above the treetops.

PART THREE

The Middle Lands

CHAPTER EIGHT

Ahrmin

Revenge is a dish that tastes best when eaten cold.

—Sicilian proverb

The windowless room was dark and musty, redolent with the smells of aging paper and parchment; the only illumination was a single overhead lamp. In a dark corner, a tall brass censer burned, sending vague fingers of smoke feeling their way into the air. His eyes stung.

Ahrmin repressed a shudder. He never liked being near wizards at all, but it was even worse to confront one on the wizard's own territory. That was one thing his father had always said: "Stay away from the wizards, son, whenever you can." In Ahrmin's nineteen years, he had never seen a reason to doubt that advice.

He stood motionless in the middle of the blood-red carpet, not daring to interrupt Wenthall's unblinking study of the crystal ball.

Though why the thing was called a ball was something Ahrmin couldn't understand. The "ball" was a head-sized crystal model of a human eye, the iris and pupil etched on its front, complete down to a spoke that projected from the back, to symbolize the cords that connected the eye to the brain.

The fat wizard gripped the spoke as he held the crystal before him, staring at the back side of the ball as if he were sitting behind a giant's eye, looking out through it.

Finally, he shook his head, sighed deeply, then carefully set the ball down on a wooden stand before turning to Ahrmin. "Good. I see you received my summons."

"Yes, sir." *Why me? I'm just barely a journeyman. If you have a need for my guild, why not send for a master?*

He didn't say that; Slavers' Guildmaster Yryn had spent most of his tenure trying to improve the often uneasy relations between the Slavers' Guild and the Wizards' Guild, and was known to have little patience with any apprentice or journeyman who did anything to offend wizards.

If the apprentice or journeyman survived. The rapprochement between the slavers and the wizards, while tentative, had paid well; it had opened up both Therranj and Melawei for frequent slaving raids. The Wizards' Guildmaster was thought to be lukewarm about the loose alliance; Yryn tolerated no action that might change that indifference to opposition.

Wenthall walked to a water bowl and splashed water on his face, drying his black beard with his gray robes. "You recall that there is a reward out for the one who stole our sewer dragon," he said, seating himself on a stool, his hands folded over his bulging belly.

"Of course." Despite himself, Ahrmin voiced it almost as a question. After all, the reward had gone unclaimed for more than a year. Undoubtedly, the culprit was dead somewhere, or had fled the Eren regions, past the range of even Wizards' Guildmaster Lucius' location spells. "But hunting dragons isn't something I can do, Master Wenthall; I don't have that kind of experience. Even if there are any small ones left."

The wizard's eyes flashed. "Just listen, fool. I do not want you to hunt a dragon—you and I have further grievances against the one who freed our sewer dragon. The same one believed responsible for the deaths of both Blenryth, of my order, and Ohlmin, of yours."

Ohlmin? That had to mean—no; it was impossible. "But Karl Cullinane has to be dead, or must have fled the region, at least, sir. None of you wizards has been able to locate him."

Wenthall rose to his feet, sighing. He walked over to a scrollrack set into the nearest wall.

"There is one other possibility," the wizard said, rummaging through the scrolls, finally selecting one.

He unrolled it; it was a well-worn map of the entire Eren region. "He could have been in the one place in the region that is protected from both the erratic sight of my crystal ball and my more reliable spells of direction. And a message I've received from Lord Mehlên of Metreyll suggests that that must be the case. He was . . ." The wizard tapped at a spot on the map. "*There.* The home tabernacle of the Healing Hand Society. That is where Cullinane hid. He is not there right now. But he has been. Protected by the Hand."

"You're certain?"

"*Yes,*" Wenthall hissed, "I am certain. I haven't been able to see him with the ball, but there is no doubt that Karl Cullinane is alive, boy. He is *alive.* Look."

Puffing from the exertion, the wizard reached up to a high shelf and brought down a chamois-wrapped parcel, almost a foot high. He unwrapped it carefully before gently setting it down on a table, a baked-clay statue of a bearded man, holding a long sword.

Ahrmin looked closer. The statue was incredibly detailed, down to individual hairs carved into the head. "Karl Cullinane?"

"Karl Cullinane." Wenthall rewrapped the statue and put it away. Then, from the folds of his robe, he produced a strange device: a hollow glass sphere the size of his fist, containing a murky yellow oil. "Look here."

Reluctantly moving closer, Ahrmin peered into it.

A mummified finger floated in the sphere's center. The finger had been messily severed from its owner's hand; a shard of bone projected from its hacked-off end, and shreds of skin and tendon waved slowly as it floated.

"Hmmm." Walking quickly to a compass on its stand in the corner of the room, the wizard took a sighting. "He's moved again. Not far—but south and west. *Still* south and west. . . ."

"Your pardon, Master Wenthall, but I don't understand."

For a moment, the wizard's nostrils flared. "Stupid little—" he stopped himself. "Never mind. Listen closely.

"This device works like a location spell. After much effort, I have managed to attune it to the body of Karl Cullinane." As the wizard slowly spun the sphere in the palm of his age-withered hand, the dismembered finger maintained its position, pointing unerringly to the southeast. "Too much effort; getting that statue accurate enough for the spell to work was the most precise, most finicky work I've had to do in ten years. But never mind that.

"As long as Cullinane remains within range, this will show you in which direction he is. If, as you turn the ball, the finger fails to point consistently in one direction, there are four possible explanations. First, he has fled the Eren regions. Second, he is inside the Hand sanctuary." Wenthall grimaced. "Third, he is otherwise magically protected. Or, last," the wizard said, smiling thinly, "he is dead."

"Will it tell me where he is? Not just the direction, but how far?"

"Yes." Wenthall nodded. "But only indirectly." The sphere disappeared in the folds of his cloak. Two quick strides brought the wizard across the room. He shuffled through a pile of papers and parchment on his desk and produced a map of the Eren regions, spreading it out on a low table.

"We know," he said, picking up a charstick, "that he is in this direction. But where on this line?" Wenthall shrugged, then drew a solid line that stretched from Pandathaway into the Middle Lands, through Holtun and Bieme into Nyphien and beyond. "We can't be certain. And there is no way of knowing, at any given moment, whether he is moving or stationary; the device is not as precise as we would wish. That could be critical. Were he on his way to Aeryk, your task would be easy; were he traveling to Therranj, it would be more difficult. Your guild is not in the good graces of the western Therranji these days."

"True." Ahrmin smiled; slave-taking raids did have a way of making one's guild unpopular with the locals.

"But I have been tracking his progress for the past tenday. It seems that he is traveling through the Middle Lands, possibly bound for Ehvenor."

"Ehvenor, Master Wenthall? Could he have dealings in Faerie?"

"That seems unlikely," the wizard said, scowling. "It's too risky for humans. Particularly normals. But there are other reasons for going to Ehvenor besides trying to beg passage into Faerie. As you should know, slaver."

"Melawei. He's bound for Melawei."

But why? There were only two reasons for traveling to Melawei: copra and slaves. Neither seemed to apply to Karl Cullinane.

"Quite possibly," Wenthall said. "But possibly not; it's conceivable he has dealings in the Middle Lands. I suggest you begin by taking passage to Lundeyll—here." He tapped the map. "Take another sighting, with both ball and compass. If Cullinane hasn't moved, the two lines will intersect at his location.

"Now"—the wizard raised his finger—"if ever you do lose him, you can use that technique to locate him precisely.

"In any case, from Lundeyll you can take the southern route through the Aershtyls, if he is still in the Middle Lands. There is a land route to Melawei; that could be his intention. If so, you should be able to beat him there by ship, no?"

"Certainly, Master Wenthall. The overland route is said to be very difficult."

"Fine. I will speak to your guildmaster later today. See him before you leave Pandathaway; he will give you a writing that will allow you to commandeer a raiding ship. If, that is, Cullinane is bound for Melawei."

"Perhaps he'll take ship to Melawei." *I could catch him at sea. If the* Flail *or* Scourge *are in Lundeport . . .*

"Perhaps." The wizard extended his hand, the sphere cradled in his palm. "Treat this device carefully; it is the product of far more time and effort than I would like to recall. A finger from a freshly killed maiden elf is difficult to obtain these days."

Accepting the proffered sphere, Ahrmin nodded grimly. "I'll find him, sir, and bring him back to you," he said. He started to turn away, but caught himself.

No. His father wouldn't have wanted him to leave it just at that; by profession, slavers were supposed to be cold and bloodless. "The reward still stands? There will be expenses in this, Master Wenthall. I'll have to hire a team. And if I commandeer a ship in Lundeyll, I'll have to pay the seamen's wages. That is the law, master."

The wizard chuckled thinly. "Quite your father's son, eh? Very well, the reward is doubled. Trebled, if you bring him back alive." The wizard smiled. "I have a use for his skin, but it must be taken while he lives."

Despite himself, Ahrmin shuddered. But he forced a smile and a nod. "You will have it, sir. I swear." With a deep bow, he turned and left the wizard's room.

So Karl Cullinane was alive and well. Probably, Cullinane often snickered over killing Ohlmin. He wouldn't be snickering soon.

You killed Ohlmin, Karl Cullinane. You shouldn't have killed my father.

CHAPTER NINE

Baron Furnael

When we are planning for posterity, we ought to remember that virtue is not hereditary.

—Thomas Paine

"Relatively speaking, I'm beginning to like the Middle Lands," Ahira said, looking up at Karl from the back of his dappled pony. "Bieme in particular."

"Relatively speaking," Karl answered, tired.

Ahira nodded. "We've seen a few slaves, but neither slavers nor whips. By local standards, this isn't bad."

"By local standards."

Ahira snorted. "What are you today? A Greek chorus? Like you and Slovotsky in Chem?"

Karl laughed. "I didn't know you knew about that."

"Walter told me. Swore me to silence, until the statute of limitations runs out. Not that it matters anymore." His smile faded. "What's bothering you?"

"A touch of homesickness, I think."

"You miss Andrea."

"Yes, but . . . actually, I was thinking about home-home, not the valley-home." Karl loosened his tunic to scratch at his ribs. "I think I'd trade a finger for a bar of Lifebuoy, or a pound of Kenya double-A coffee, or a case of toilet paper . . . hell, even for a pizza."

"You complain too much. Why let it get to you? At least we're not camping out every damn night, for now. The beds may not be Posturepedics, but they are soft."

Karl nodded. The dwarf had a point. In the forty days of traveling since they had left the valley and worked their way into the Middle Lands, they had gone through some hard times.

Not dangerous, particularly; the only slaver caravan they had run across had been easy pickings, so much so that Karl didn't consider the encounter a proper shakedown for Fialt and Tennetty.

The slavers hadn't even bothered to set out a watchman. The *late* slavers.

Karl had been able to send seventeen former slaves toward the valley, one of them carrying a letter to Andy-Andy. He hadn't worried that the group might not find the valley, as long as they passed nearby. Ellegon would be flying watch at night. Once the dragon spotted them and flew close enough to read their minds, they would be met and guided in.

No danger there, not for anyone.

The closest Karl and the rest had come to real danger was when Fialt accidentally slashed Tennetty across the belly during a fencing lesson. Two quickly administered healing draughts had taken care of that; a switch to wooden swords for training purposes ensured that they wouldn't again have to use up more of their small supply of expensive healing draughts for that sort of accident.

It wasn't the danger that bothered Karl. It was the drudgery.

Moving camp every day had been fun during the summer when Karl's Scout troop had gone up to Manitoba to canoe down the Assiniboine, but part of the fun of that had been knowing that the primitive life-style was temporary, that hot showers, clean clothes, fast food, and air conditioning awaited them at the end of the trip.

But that wasn't true here. The endless grind of stopping to camp, finding firewood, lighting a fire with flint and steel, cooking, cleaning pots and pans with dirt clods, pitching their tents, watering the horses, breaking camp in the morning—all of it had started to wear on him, bringing him almost to the breaking point.

Perhaps crossing the border from Nyphien into Bieme hadn't saved his sanity, but sometimes it felt like it.

Bieme was possibly the oldest of the Middle Lands; certainly it was the best developed. Tilled by drayhorses and oxen, the farmland produced an abundance of grains and legumes, one-tenth of the fields lying fallow under strict rotation. The productivity of the land and its people had brought both wealth and trade to Bieme; grain sellers and hostlers came from as far away as the Katharhd and Lundeyll to do business there.

Few armsmen were evident, and then only singly, or in small groups. They functioned primarily as a constabulary, rather than a standing army. While there was no love lost between Therranj and any of the Middle Lands, an attack on Bieme would have to go through one of the surrounding principalities first, giving the Biemei ample time to prepare; there was no need to have a large nonproductive soldier class standing by, although all freefarmers were required to produce a well-honed sword for inspection on two different holidays each year.

The best thing, though, was the inns along the main thoroughfare. By law, each community of five hundred or more along the Prince's Road had to sponsor a well-kept inn, the high standards maintained through frequent inspections by the local baron's armsmen—where there was a local baron—and infrequent but potentially more penalty-bearing ones by the Prince's.

Throughout most of the Prince's Road, the village inns were no more than a day's ride apart. In the few places where villages were more widely spaced, there still was an inn, directly supported by the crown. And the Prince's Inns were the most luxurious and least expensive of all.

"There's a trick to all of this," Karl said, as he reined in Carrot, forcing her to keep close to the rest of the group. "Easy, girl." He stroked the rough hair on her neck. She was still dry, even after half a day's ride. His only complaint about her was her tendency to go at her own quick pace, her sneering disdain for the slower pace of the other horses.

"A trick?"

Karl nodded. "Remember Kiar?"

"That inn with the marble floors? Not quite as lush as the Inn of Quiet Repose, but a nice place." The dwarf nodded. "This sour beer isn't all that good, but that cook really knew how to use it as a marinade. Although," he added under his breath, "I guess I do miss some things from home. I'd kill for a Genesee, or a Miller. Or even a Schlitz."

Karl raised an eyebrow. "Kill?"

Ahira shrugged. "Well, maim. I really do love a good beer."

"Don't remember you being much of a beer drinker back home."

Ahira frowned. "I had to be careful about when I drank. It used to really start my kidneys going."

Karl shot a glance over his shoulder. That had become a reflex, and one that he didn't intend to give up, even in the relative safety of the Prince's Road.

But there was no problem. Tennetty, Fialt, and Aeia rode behind, Chak bringing up the rear. The little man favored him with a friendly nod and a slight, open-handed wave.

"So?" Karl asked. "Beer does that to everyone."

Ahira chuckled. "You're forgetting." He raised a thick arm and flexed it, the chainmail tightening around his biceps. "I wasn't just anyone. Muscular dystrophy, remember?"

"I know, but—"

"What does that have to do with it? Karl, I couldn't go to the *john* by myself; couldn't even lift myself out of my wheelchair and onto the toilet. Going out for a drink with the guys wasn't something I could do, unless I had my roommate-slash-attendant with me, to drag me off to the bathroom. I used to envy the hell out of the way all the rest of you were so mobile."

"You don't anymore."

"Well, no," the dwarf said, unconvincingly.

Karl nodded to himself. There was something he had that Ahira didn't, and that was the memory of always being sound of body, of being able to take for granted something as trivial as going out for a few beers.

As if he were reading his mind, Ahira cocked an eyebrow. "Let's leave it alone. 'What cannot be cured . . .' You were talking about the inns?"

"Right," Karl said. "There's a trick there. If you notice, a lot of the inns were originally built by the crown. Back in Kiar, they'd taken down the Prince's coat of arms, but the outline was still on the stone. A prince built it, and supported it for a while."

"And then?"

"People moved nearby, probably got a good deal from the Prince on the land, and such; the crown brought in a cleric, probably sponsored a smith or two."

"Cute. And then, when the population was large enough, the Prince gave the territory to a baron, and made the locals support the inn."

"Right." Karl nodded. "At least, that's the way I read it." And, if it had worked that way, it spoke well for the local form of government, despite Karl's admitted bias against feudalism. There was nothing wrong with a bit of economic encouragement. It was coercion that was the problem with feudal societies.

"Hmm." Ahira considered it for a moment. "Possible. And it's not as oppressive around here as we've seen elsewhere. That why you haven't signaled for a fight?"

Karl shook his head. No, that wasn't it at all. The plan didn't call for them to attack every slaveowner they ran into; that would quickly result in their being buried under a flood of bodies: Anyone who either owned a slave, wanted to own a slave, or had owned a slave would see them as the enemy.

Attacking slavers was different. Outside of the markets, slavers were unpopular; locals always knew that in a slaver's eye, everyone was potential merchandise.

"No," he said, "we fight slavers, and in self-defense."

"Liberally construed." Ahira threw back his head and laughed. "Like the way you and Walter decided that attacking Orhmyst was self-defense."

"Well, it felt like self-defense." Karl dismissed the subject with an airy wave. He stood in the saddle and turned, raising his head. "Chak?"

"Yes, Kharl?"

"Where are we stopping tonight?"

"Furnael." Chak dropped his reins to rub his hands together. "Best inn in the Middle Lands. We might even meet Baron Furnael himself."

Tennetty snorted. "What a thrill."

"Time for some practice, Fialt, Tennetty," Karl said, gesturing at them to follow him out of the common room and into the courtyard. Chak was ready; he had the bag of practice swords slung over a shoulder.

Ahira yawned and stretched. "I'm going to get some sleep. See you folks in the room."

Aeia put down her rag doll and lifted her head. "Me, too?"

"Well . . ."

"Please, Karl? You didn't let me, last time. Please?"

He smiled down at her as he nodded genially, then gently rubbed his fingers through her hair. "Sure." *Sure, little one, I'll be the gracious father substitute and teach you a bit more about how to disembowel a rapist.*

Goddam world. An eleven-year-old girl should be thinking about dolls and boys and stuff like that. "Let's go."

Wordlessly, Chak followed, carrying the canvas bag of wooden swords.

The courtyard of the Furnael inn was a large open square, surrounded by the windowed walls of the inn proper. Slate flagstones checkered the ground, well-trimmed clumps of grass separating them.

Heavy with fruit, evenly spaced orange trees dotted the courtyard. Karl unbuckled his sword and hung it on a low branch, then reached up and pulled down a couple of oranges, tossing one to Chak before quartering the other with his beltknife.

Nothing for the other three; they would get theirs later, as a reward for a good session. If at all.

He ate quickly, not minding that some of the juice dripped down his chin. The fruit was cool and sweet. He tossed the peels to Chak, who stashed them under the equipment bag. "Now," he said, wiping the remaining juice and pulp from his chin, "we're going to start with a bit of hand-to-hand today." Karl slipped out of his jerkin and unlaced his sandals, stripping down to breechclout and leggings.

It promised to be a hot session; he slipped out of his leggings, awkwardly balancing on each foot alternately.

Already down to his breechclout, Chak hung up his sword and nodded. "This keeohokoshinkee stuff of yours?"

"Kyokoshinkai. And yes."

"Good." Chak nodded his approval.

Fialt frowned, rubbing a finger through his salt-and-pepper beard. "Rather do swords," he said. Which was, for Fialt, being unusually talkative.

Tennetty recoiled in mock horror—and probably a bit of real disgust. "Not around me. Not even with a wood sword. Liable to put my eye out while you're trying for a thrust to the kneecap."

"Fialt," Chak said, "you'll do swords with me, later. After Kharl's done with you." He shot a grin at Karl. "I'll make him sweat a bit. A bit more."

Karl nodded. When it came to fencing, Chak was the better teacher. There was a good reason. Karl had gained his skills with a sword as part of the transfer to this world. He'd never had to go through the long hours of learning. There was no deliberate method to his swordplay; his arm and wrist just *did* it, as of their own volition.

A gain? Well, yes; his instantly acquired fencing skills had saved his life on more than one occasion. But it was a loss, too; he'd never had the experience of learning, of knowing how to improve his skills. While he had run into only one swordsman more adept than himself, there were undoubtedly others.

The loss went beyond his inability to teach. Without knowing how to learn swordfighting, his skills were frozen at their present level. He would never get better.

Guess I'll have to live with it.

But with his karate skills, there was the possibility of improvement, enhanced by the innate agility, balance, and reflexes of his body on this side. Here, he could easily have won enough in competition—if they had competitions here—to qualify for a brown belt; back home, the best he had been able to do was green.

"Loosen up, first," Karl said, breaking into a series of bends and stretches. The others followed his example; working out without first warming up was an invitation to wrenched muscles and torn tendons.

After his joints and tendons stopped protesting and settled down to a nice, quiet ache, he straightened. "Enough. Let's start."

Tennetty, Fialt, and Aeia lined up opposite him, bowing Japanese-style, their eyes always on his. Karl returned their bows.

Were the traditional customs irrelevant here? he wondered, not for the first time.

Possibly. Quite possibly the customs of the Japanese dojo were out of place; probably they had been silly back home. Probably it would be easier for him to use simple or compound Erendra names for punches, kicks, blocks, and strikes.

But the traditions seemed to have worked back home; there was no sense in violating custom without a compelling reason.

"Sanchin dachi," he said, swinging his right foot past and slightly in front of his left and planting his feet a shoulder width apart, toes canted slightly in. *Sanchin dachi* was the best practicing stance for strikes and punches, as well as snap-kicks. Not necessarily the best fighting stance—Karl had always favored *zenkutsu-dachi,* a split-legged, forward-leaning stance—but a natural one that could be assumed without triggering a violent response.

"We'll start with a few *seiken.*"

"Chudan-tsuki, sensei?" Chak asked, as he took his position at the end of the line, next to Tennetty.

"Fine. Start with your right hand." As always, he began by demonstrating. *Seiken chudan-tsuki,* a punch to the midsection, began with the nonpunching hand extended outward as though it had just been used to block, the punching hand pulled back, the fist inverted, resting at his side, just under the pectorals.

He moved slowly, pulling his left hand back as he brought his right hand out, turning his wrist so that the back of his hand faced upward, tensing his entire body just at the moment that the blow would have made contact, had there been a real opponent.

"And now the left." He demonstrated, then dropped his hands. "Now . . . on my count, *seiken chudan-tsuki;* groups of four." He moved closer to them. "*One*—keep it slow, now; follow the pace. *Two*—better, better. *Three. Four.* Speed it up a bit, now. One, two, three, four. Full speed, just as if it were for real. One-two-three-four. Keep going."

Chak was doing it properly, as usual; his stance easy, he punched smoothly, his arms moving like greased pistons.

Karl passed behind the little man and moved to help Tennetty. "No, keep your wrist straight," he said, adjusting her hand. "Mmm . . . better. A bit more tensing of the belly when you strike. *Don't* rise to the balls of your feet. Flat-footed blows have much more power." He moved on to Fialt.

Fialt was still throwing the shoulder of his striking arm forward. Standing in front of him, Karl reached out and grasped his shoulders. "Try it now. Ignore me." With Karl's much longer reach, Fialt's punch wouldn't land.

Fialt punched the air in front of him, pushing his shoulder forward against Karl's hand. "No good," Karl said. "You've got to keep the shoulder steady, Chak?"

"Not the knives, again?" The little man frowned.

"Knives, again. Tennetty, Aeia, keep it up."

Chak walked over to the tree where his clothes and equipment hung and drew his two beltknives, tossing them hilt-first to Karl. Karl caught them, then rested the knifepoints gently against Fialt's shoulders. "Now try it."

Fialt scowled, and punched timidly.

"That was better. At least your shoulders didn't move. But," Karl said, increasing the pressure of the knives against Fialt's shoulders, "you didn't have any force behind the blow. Wouldn't have squashed a bug. Do it right, now."

Still a timid punch.

"Do it better or I swear I'll stick you," he said, just as his karate

teacher had once said to him. Karl wondered for a moment if Mr. Katsuwahara had been lying, and dismissed the notion as blasphemous.

This time, Fialt struck properly, his shoulders rock-steady, his body tensing at the moment of impact.

"Nice." Karl nodded, handing the knives back to Chak. He turned toward Aeia, and—

Fialt struck, a perfectly executed *seiken chudan-tsuki* that landed just below Karl's solar plexus, knocking him back.

Blindly, Karl brought his right arm around to block Fialt's second blow, then swung his right leg into a fast but gentle roundhouse kick that bowled Fialt over.

"Very pretty," a voice called from the balcony overlooking the courtyard. Karl glanced up. A man stood, looking down at them, his hands spread on the balcony rail.

"Chak. Handle it." Karl jerked his thumb in the direction of the voice as he stooped to help Fialt up. "Nicely done, Fialt."

Fialt's grizzled face broke into a smile. "I did it right?"

"Very. You hit me legally, and hit me hard. If you'd really been aiming here,"—Karl tapped himself on the solar plexus—"you would've had me." He clapped a hand on Fialt's shoulder. "Keep it up and we'll make a warrior of you yet."

"Just a man who can protect himself and his own. That's all I ask." Fialt nodded grimly. "That's all."

"I said, *very pretty, sir.*"

"And who are you?" Karl turned.

"Zherr, Baron Furnael, sir." He bowed. "May I join you?"

At Karl's nod, Furnael walked back into the building, reappearing just a few moments later at the door into the garden, two armsmen and an old man in gray wizard's robes at his side.

Baron Furnael was a tall man in his early fifties, perhaps an inch or so over six feet. Despite his age, he seemed to be in good shape: His thick wrists were heavily muscled, his leggings bulged with well-developed calves and thighs, only a small potbelly puffed out the front of his leather tunic.

Furnael's face was deeply lined, and stubble-free enough to suggest that he shaved himself both carefully and frequently, or else had someone else shave him. On his upper lip, a pencil-thin mustache was heavily streaked with gray, although his short-cropped hair was as black as a raven.

Karl kept his chuckle to himself. That bespoke a bit of vanity. But why hadn't Furnael dyed the mustache, too? A bit of self-honesty? Or was it just that whatever dye they used here would have stained his lip?

"Baron." Karl bowed slightly, Fialt, Tennetty, and Chak following suit.

Aeia glanced up at him, looking ready to break into tears. Strangers often affected her that way. Particularly male strangers. Which was understandable.

"Easy, little one." He smiled. "I think it's time for your nap."

She nodded and ran away, her bare feet slapping the flagstones.

Furnael smiled. "A pleasant child. Yours?"

"No. But in my care. She's a Mel. I'm not."

"So I see." Furnael turned to the armsman at his right and snapped his fingers. The armsman produced a bottle of wine, and uncorked it with his teeth before handing it to Furnael. "A drink for luck?" Furnael asked, his voice making it clear it was more a command than a question. He tilted back the bottle and drank deeply. "Zherr Furnael wishes you luck, friend." Smiling thinly and wiping his hand on a purple silk handkerchief he produced from a sleeve, Furnael handed the bottle to Karl. "Enjoy."

In the Eren regions, a drink for luck was a custom that was invariably followed by an introduction, whether the drinkers already knew each other or not. Typically, a drink for luck would take place between two strangers meeting on a road, the provider of the wine drinking first to assure the other that it was unpoisoned.

The fact that Furnael had suggested—ordered—a drink for luck in a situation where the custom wasn't really appropriate was suspicious. The fact that his armsman had an opened bottle ready was more so.

Karl drank deeply. The rich, fruity wine was icy cold. "Karl Cullinane thanks you, Baron."

Furnael's smile broadened. "So. I was wondering if it was you, in this company; it's said that you travel with a Hand cleric and another warrior from a land called Seecaucuze. Not a Mel child and a Katharhd."

Secaucus was Walter's hometown. So it was only known that Karl had been traveling with Doria and Walter. Which suggested that someone had seen the three of them at the cesspit when Karl had freed Ellegon, or that some spell had been able to look back, into that time and place. But how would anyone on this side have known that

Walter came from New Jersey? Slovotsky hadn't mentioned it, as far as Karl knew.

Probably Walter *had* mentioned it to some local, at some time, and that local had talked to someone else about the stranger he had met, and someone in Pandathaway had started putting two and two together. That didn't sound good at all. Too damn many unknowns.

"There has been a price on your head for more than a year, friend Karl," Furnael said. "It seems that Pandathaway wants you."

Chak started to edge toward his sword; one of Furnael's armsmen, hand near the hilt of his shortsword, moved between the little man and the tree where Chak's falchion hung.

Even if Furnael meant them harm, this wasn't the right time to do something about it. The odds were poor, with the wizard right there, behind Furnael. "Stand easy, Chak," Karl said. "Stand easy. That goes for you, too," he said, holding up a palm to forestall any move by Tennetty or Fialt. "I don't think the Baron is out to collect the reward."

Furnael spread his hands. "You are wanted in Pandathaway, friend Karl. This is Bieme. And here we have no love for the Guilds Council." He gestured at the wizard who stood behind him. "Sammis, here, once was a guild master, studying daily in the Great Library. Today, he uses his death spells to kill corndiggers; he was thrown out of the Wizards' Guild, forced to flee Pandathaway."

"What'd he do, give out a spell for free?"

Furnael cocked his head to one side, his forehead furrowed. "How did you know?" He shrugged. "In any case, it is fortunate for you that my Prince is neither allied with Pandathaway nor particularly hungry for coin," he said, laying his hand on the hilt of his sword. "Even if you are as good as they say, we do have the advantage."

"That depends on how you look at it, Baron." Ahira's voice came from the balcony above.

About time. Karl glanced up. Beside Ahira, little Aeia stood, the spare crossbow held clumsily in her arms, leveled at one of Furnael's armsmen.

Ahira held his own crossbow easily, the bolt lined up not on Furnael, but on the wizard. "Aeia can't cock the bow, but she can put out a sparrow's eye at sixty paces."

Karl suppressed a smile. Aeia could probably hit a *cow* at *five* paces, if the cow was big enough. The little girl tried hard, but she had no talent for bowmanship at all.

Ahira went on: "And I'm not too bad with a crossbow, myself. We're generally peaceable folk. How about you?"

As usual, Ahira had picked his potential target correctly. If the wizard opened his mouth to use a spell, Ahira could put a bolt through his back before the first words were fairly out.

Karl folded his arms across his chest. "You were saying, Baron?"

Furnael smiled broadly. "Again, very pretty, sir. I was saying that I must have a word with my chief man-at-arms; he didn't tell me about the others, just you. And I was also saying that you simply must be my guests at dinner, at my home. We dine at sundown. And . . ." Furnael let his voice trail off.

"And?"

"And, as long as you break no law, harm no one, do not offend my Prince, you are safe here. Within my barony, at least. You have my word on that, Karl Cullinane."

And even if you're eager to try to collect the reward, you'd rather do it over my dead body than yours. Karl hesitated. If they had to take on Furnael, there probably wouldn't be a better time.

But he couldn't kill everyone who *might* present a threat. "We are honored, Baron. And accept."

The baron's smile made Karl's palm itch for the feel of his saber's sharkskin hilt. Furnael gestured at the nearer of his armsmen. "Hivar will conduct you to the estate." He turned and walked away, the other armsman and the wizard at his side.

"What was that all about?" Chak asked, his swordbelt back around his waist.

Karl shrugged. "I think the Baron wants to know what we're up to. What I'm up to. Seems that freeing Ellegon has gotten me some interesting word-of-mouth. It also seems that word about what we're doing hasn't gotten to Bieme yet."

"So? How do we handle it?"

"We'll see." Karl turned to the others. "Well, what are you all standing around for? This practice isn't over. You, there. Hivar, is it? These aren't Pandathaway's Games. If you want to stay around, then strip down and join in."

Sitting in the honored-guest position at the foot of the long oaken table, Karl wiped his mouth and hands with a linen napkin. *Just what are you up to, Zherr Furnael?* he thought. Lifting the wedge with both hands, Karl took another nibble of the sweetberry pie. He ate carefully; the dark filling was bubbly hot.

"I must admit to a bit of embarrassment," Furnael said, pushing his high-backed chair away from the table. "I've never had a guest go hungry at my table before. And two?" He daubed at his mustache and the corners of his mouth with a purple silken napkin, then dropped the napkin back to his lap as the white-linened servitor at his side held out a washing bowl for his use.

"I wouldn't have thought it possible," he said, drying his hands on a towel, gesturing at the servant to continue down the table to Fialt, Tennetty, Aeai, and Karl.

Karl considered another helping of pie, but decided against it. Overeating any further wasn't the way to cap the best meal he'd had in months. *Whatever your flaws may be, Zherr Furnael, you do set a fine table.*

"Normally it wouldn't be possible, Baron," Karl said. A fresh washbowl was presented to him; Karl washed the meat juices and berry stains from his fingers. "At least as far as I can imagine."

With a slight nod and a vague frown, Furnael sat back, knitting his fingers over his belly. His face a study in concern, he cocked his head at Chak and Ahira, who sat side by side, across from the others, their silver plates clean and empty in front of them. "Is there anything you would eat? Anything?"

Ahira shook his head. "My apologies, Baron, but it's a religious matter. It's the fast of St. Rita Moreno, you know. My ancestors would never forgive me if I let food or water pass my lips today."

Furnael furrowed his forehead. "I must admit I'm not familiar with your faith, friend Ahira. Which warrens are you from?"

The dwarf frowned at the question, as though surprised at Furnael's prying. "The Lincoln Tunnels. Far away." Ahira sighed, the picture of a dwarf far away from home, missing the comfortable familiarity of his own warrens.

Furnael opened his mouth as though to ask just exactly where, and how far away, then visibly reconsidered. Dismissing the subject with a wave and a shrug, he turned to Chak. "Surely a Katharhd doesn't have religious objections to my food."

Chak glanced at Karl. For once, the little man didn't seem pleased with him. Chak didn't relish having had to pass on the Baron's fare. Platters of juice-dripping roast beef, the slices crisp, brown, and gar- licky around the edges, purply rare in the middle; spit-roasted pota- toes, so hot that they had to be nibbled carefully from the end of a knife; tiny loaves of warm, pan-baked bread, each with a dollop of sweet, icy butter at its core; bowls of a pungent mixture of chotte and burdock, sauteed together in wine and fresh garlic—it had been a delightful meal, much better than Karl had had since Pandathaway.

But I don't think we're going to trust you any too far, Baron Zherr Furnael. You reek of hidden intent. Never did like people who do that.

Furnael had politely sampled all of the food first; eating from the same table as the baron probably wasn't risky.

But only probably.

The cover story, such as it was, had more than a few holes in it. But for all of them to trust Furnael's food was too much of a chance. Best to keep up the pretense.

Karl nodded.

"My apologies," Chak said, glancing with apparently real regret at the silver platters, still well laden with food, that lay invitingly on the table. "But this western food doesn't agree with me. Haven't been able to stomach what you eat here; I've been living on my morning meals of oat stew and greens for more tendays than I like to recall."

"Oat stew?" Furnael shrugged. "Well, if that's what you desire . . ." He gestured to one of his servitors, a short, plump, round-faced woman. "Enna? Would you—"

"No," Chak said. "Please."

The Baron's face clouded over. "And why not?"

Good question. They hadn't worked out what to say if Furnael was able to provide such a bizarre and disgusting dish.

Ahira spoke up. "With all due respect, you're not thinking it through, Baron."

"Well?"

"If all you were able to keep down was oat stew, how eager would you be to eat more than once a day?"

Karl chuckled. "Or even that often." He looked over at the dwarf. *Nice going, Ahira.* "Baron?"

"Yes?"

"It was a wonderful meal and all, but what's this really all about?"

"What do you mean?"

"What I mean is this: I'm wanted in Pandathaway; there's a large reward on my head. You say you're not interested in collecting that reward. Fine; I'll accept that."

The Baron lifted a razor-sharp eating knife and considered its bright edge. "Although you are not convinced of it." Furnael smiled thinly. "Perhaps that's wise under the circumstances; perhaps not." He tested the edge of the knife against his thumbnail, then replaced it on the table, the point, perhaps by chance, aligned with Karl's chest.

"What I'm not convinced of," Karl said, "is that you invite every-one who stops in the Furnael inn into your home. And it'd be impossible to believe that you'd provide this sort of wonderful fare—"

"I thank you, sir." Furnael inclined his head.

"—for all guests of the inn. It seems to me that there has to be something else on your mind."

"Point well taken, Karl Cullinane. I do have a business proposition for you. If you are as good with that sword as your reputation suggests."

"I doubt I'd be interest—"

"Would you at least listen to it, as a courtesy?" Furnael stood, dropping the napkin on his chair. He lifted his swordbelt from the rack next to his chair and buckled it on. "Let's take a short ride together and talk about it privately. These days I get little enough chance to ride just for the pleasure of it. Enna, see to the needs of our other guests, if you please."

Karl stood and buckled on his own sword. "Very well." He walked with Furnael toward the arching doorway.

Ahira cleared his throat. "Baron?"

Furnael turned, clearly irritated. "Yes, friend Ahira?"

The dwarf steepled his hands in front of his chin. "It's occurred to me that you may have a fallback position in mind, if Karl turns you down. And, since you are a wise man, that fallback position is undoubtedly something terribly wise, such as wishing us well, as we go on our way."

"And if my, as you put it, fallback position isn't so wise?" Furnael gestured vaguely. "As an example only, what if the alternative I present Karl Cullinane with is my taking possession of a young girl who is manifestly an escaped slave, and returning her to her proper owners?"

"Aided by, no doubt, your full complement of twenty or so armsmen, some of whom you have stationed outside, as a precaution."

"No doubt." Furnael smiled.

"Baron, may I tell you a story?"

"This hardly seems the occasion."

"Please?" The dwarf smiled thinly. "At least listen, as a courtesy to a guest? It's a very short story, Baron. And it might amuse you."

Furnael gave in, seating himself on the empty chair next to Ahira. "Since you insist."

"Good. Let me begin it like this. There once was a slaver named

Ohlmin. A master of the blade, Ohlmin won the swords competition in Pandathaway's Games every time he entered. With one exception.

"One man defeated him. Karl Cullinane, fighting in his first competition, ever. As you perhaps can understand, Ohlmin resented that."

Karl quelled a smile. That was true, as far as it went, but Ahira's rendition left out a few critical facts. For one thing, Ohlmin had been a better swordsman than Karl; Karl had won only by a judicious application of a hole in the rules of the swords competition.

Ahira went on: "For that reason and others, Ohlmin hunted our party down, and caught us in the Waste of Elrood. Along with a hired wizard, Ohlmin had fifteen slavers with him, all good with their swords.

"Ohlmin put Karl, Walter Slovotsky, and me in chains. He spent a bit of time working Karl over with his fists, as well. After a number of hours, we managed to break free."

"How?" Furnael raised an eyebrow. "Slavers' chains are too strong to be broken, even by a dwarf."

Ahira smiled. "Trick of the trade. In any case, break free we did. I managed to account for four of the slavers before a crossbow bolt struck me down. The wizard who was with us killed their wizard. For the sake of the injured among us, Karl put us all in a wagon and fled, leaving one of their wagons aflame, and half of the slavers dead."

"Most impressive," Furnael said. "But I already knew that Karl Cullinane is a great swordsman."

"I'm sure you did, Baron." The dwarf inclined his head. "What you didn't know is this: Eight of the slavers were alive when we fled. Ohlmin was among them."

Ahira sighed. "I wanted to leave it at that. We were away, and free, and alive. We all hurt a bit. Karl had used the last of our healing draughts to save me. And Karl wasn't at his best; having your arms chained over your head for hours leaves your shoulders weak and stiff. I wanted to call it a day, leave the slavers behind."

The Baron cocked his head to one side. "But Karl Cullinane didn't." The pallor of his skin belied his calm tone.

"No. With another of our party, Karl went back for Ohlmin and the rest. Two against eight."

"I suppose Karl Cullinane and his companion gave a good account of themselves."

"Karl left seven of them lying dead on the ground. All save Ohlmin."

"But Ohlmin got away." Furnael started to rise. "Nevertheless, a very impressive feat. I thank you for telling me, friend Ahira. Now, Karl Cullinane, if you would walk this way?"

Ahira laid a hand on the Baron's arm. "No, Baron, I said that he left seven of them. He didn't leave Ohlmin; Karl brought Ohlmin's head back, as a remembrance." The dwarf removed his hand, and smiled amiably. "Have a nice talk."

The night was bright, lit by the shimmering of the million stars flickering overhead and the score of smoking torches along the ramparts of Furnael's keep.

Sitting comfortably in Carrot's saddle, Karl rode beside Furnael. The Baron was mounted on a slightly smaller, snow-white mare whose black marking over her right eye made her look like an equine pirate.

As they rode slowly along the narrow dirt road outside the keep, Furnael paused beneath each of the four guard stations. At each station the noble silently raised a hand to greet the watchman peering out through an embrasure, leaning lazily against a jutting stone merlon. Each guard nodded and waved in response.

By the time they reached the Prince's Road, Karl was tired of Furnael's silence.

"Baron?"

"Bear with me awhile longer, Karl Cullinane." With a flick of the reins, he turned his horse east onto the Prince's Road, Karl following.

Soon, the walls of the keep were far behind; Furnael picked up the pace as they topped a hill, then started down toward a cluster of low wooden buildings, half a mile away, wisps of smoke rising from their chimneys and twisting into the night. "Those are the slave quarters of my own farm," Furnael said. On both sides of the road, fields of chest-high cornstalks waved and whispered to themselves in the light breeze. "I have been keeping loose security," he said, with a deep sigh. "No passwords; I have a few armsmen, and no soldiers at all. But that's going to have to change. Everything's going to change."

"Things look peaceful enough, Baron," Karl said. "If you'll forgive the contradiction."

"If I wouldn't forgive being contradicted, would that make things look one whit less peaceful?" Furnael smiled. "Enough of this formality: if I may call you Karl, I would be honored if you would call me Zherr. When we are by ourselves, that is." At Karl's nod, Furnael smiled, then pursed his lips, shaking his head. "And it is truly said that looks can be deceiving. Do you know the Middle Lands well?"

"Not at all."

"Except for some problems with the Therranji, it's been peaceful for most of my life, and unless the Therranji push much harder than they have been, they're not going to threaten Nyphien, much less Bieme.

"It's been peaceful for a long time. For all of His Highness' reign, for that matter. His father and mine settled the boundary disputes with Nyphien to the west; our grandfathers fought Holtun. Most of His Highness' soldiers have long settled down to their farms. In all the country, it'd be hard to find a score of Bieme-born men who've been blooded in combat. Displaying a shiny, well-honed sword on Birthday or Midsummer doesn't make a man a warrior."

Furnael indicated the keep behind them with a wave of his hand. "I have forty armsmen. Only Hivar is native to Bieme—his father served mine, as did his grandfather. The others are slephmelrad, too, but originally outland mercenaries. I'd thought we could grow fat and happy through my life, and that of my sons. I'd thought that. And I still hope so."

"But you don't believe it anymore?" Karl shook his head. "The reasons don't show, Baron."

"Zherr."

"The reasons don't show, Zherr. I haven't seen any signs of war or any sort of deprivation in all of Bieme."

"Ahh, you see war and deprivation as linked?"

"Obviously, Zherr. War causes deprivation."

"True. But it can be the other way around, as well." Furnael pursed his lips. "There is danger in wealth, even if it's only enough wealth to keep your people well fed, clothed, with perhaps a bit more to pay the cleric. What if your neighbor isn't wealthy?

"The border wars with Nyphien started because of a two-year case of dustblight that hit western Nyphien and part of Khar. The first year, they paid the Spidersect to abate the blight, but barely recovered half their corn, less of their wheat, and none of their oats or barley; the second year, there was no money left for the Spiders, and the Nyphs tried to push their borders east, into Bieme.

"By the third harvest, the war was fully underway." The Baron shook his head. "I've heard tales of it. Not a pretty war. Not pretty, at all."

"And that's happening again?"

"No, not exactly. Mmm, hold up a moment." Furnael stopped his horse, then bent to pick a fist-sized stone from the road. He threw it onto the road's rough shoulder, then remounted. "A different direction; a different problem. Less than a day's ride to the east, both barony Furnael and the Principality of Bieme end, and Holtun and the barony of my good friend Vertum Adahan begin. And Vertum Adahan *is* a good friend, though I've never crossed his doorstep, or he mine."

"Why?"

The Baron shook his head sadly. "There was a blood feud between our families. Depending on which side you believe, my great-grand-mother was either stolen from her husband, Baron Adahan, or left him voluntarily. The Baron took another wife, but Adahan men raided into Furnael throughout the rest of my great-grandfather's rule, and into my grandfather's."

"Which side do you believe?"

Furnael smiled thinly. "Sir, I will have you know that I am a dutiful great-grandson; of *course* great-grandmother left her husband of her own free will to go to my lecherous great-grandfather, and even insisted that he give her a room in the keep that locked only from the outside, in order to reassure him that she didn't want to go back to Adahan." He shook his head. "I'll show you her room, if you'd like. You can decide for yourself.

"But, as I was saying, while the feud died down during my father's time, the old feelings still run deep; there are family graveyards on many of my freefarmers' holdings with tombstones that read 'mur-dered by the swine Adahan.' I'd hoped that in the next generation . . ." He caught himself. "But I talk too much. I hope you'll forgive me, Karl, but it's so rare that I see anyone who isn't either one of my slephmelrad, or slaves, or a foreigner trying to grub a few extra wagonloads of corn for his coin; it's a pleasure to speak freely."

"I . . . appreciate that, Zherr." Karl didn't believe for a second that Furnael was speaking freely. The Baron was trying to gain his sympathy. Why? Was it just that Furnael didn't think he could intim-idate Karl into taking on whatever job Furnael had for him? Or was there something more?

As they neared the cluster of wooden shacks, each about twenty feet square, the door of the nearest swung open and a woman and three children walked out, smiling and calling out greetings.

Though calling them all children might have been an overstatement; the tallest was a black-haired boy of sixteen or so, who looked much like a younger version of Furnael, although he was, like the other two children, dressed in a farmer's cotton tunic and loose drawstring pantaloons, instead of leather and wool. He ran up and took the reins of Furnael's horse in hand, gesturing to another to do the same for Carrot's.

Furnael dismounted, urging Karl to follow him. "Karl Cullinane, it is my honor to present my eldest son: Rahff, the future Baron Furnael. Rahff, this is Karl Cullinane. Yes, son, *the* Karl Cullinane."

What was the son and heir of a baron doing in the slave quarters, dressed like a peasant, his face streaked with dirt and sweat, his hands blistered?

Karl didn't ask; when Furnael was ready, he'd tell Karl whatever he wanted Karl to know.

Rahff bowed stiffly, his eyes wide, his jaw sagging. "The outlaw, sir? Really?" An expression of awe flickered across Rahff's face.

Karl was uncomfortable; he'd never had to deal with a case of hero worship before. "That depends on your definition of outlaw," Karl said. "But I'm probably the one you're thinking of."

"It is a . . . pleasure to meet you, sir," Rahff said, the formality of his manner in comical contrast to his humble dress and grimy face.

The smallest of the children, a boy a year or so shy of Aeia's age and a few inches short of her height, ran up and threw his arms around Furnael, burying his face against the Baron's waist. With a warm smile, Furnael ran his fingers through the boy's hair. "And this is Rahff's brother, my son Thomen. Don't be offended at his silence, Karl; he is always shy around strangers."

"Of course, Baron. I am pleased to meet you, Rahff. And you, Thomen."

"Not 'Baron'—Zherr, please," the baron said, picking Thomen up with a sweep of his arm. "This isn't a formal occasion."

"Zherr."

The woman walked over. She looked something like a slightly younger female version of Furnael, with the same high cheekbones, though she had a more rounded jaw. Her hair was the same raven black.

"Karl Cullinane," Furnael said, "my cousin, wife, and the mother of my sons: Beralyn, Lady Furnael." Furnael's voice was more formal now, carrying in it a hint of distaste. Or anger, perhaps.

"Karl Cullinane," she said, taking his hand in both hers. In the light streaming through the open door, her hands were red and swollen; some of the blisters on her fingers had broken open. "I hope you will forgive me for not greeting you at our home."

"Of course, Lady." He bowed over her hands. "Of course." *What the hell is a baroness doing here?*

"And," Furnael went on, casting a quick frown at Beralyn, "the youngster holding your horse is Bren Adahan, son and heir of Vertum, Baron Adahan, of whom I have spoken." Furnael set Thomen down and walked over, clapping a hand to Bren's shoulder. "Good to see you, Bren. Is your tenday going well?"

"Very well, Baron." Raising an eyebrow to ask for permission, Bren reached up to stroke Carrot's neck the moment Karl nodded. "A fine horse, Karl Cullinane." He ran sure hands over her withers, patted at her belly and flank, then gently felt at her left rear hock.

All the while, Carrot stood proudly, her head held a bit higher than normal, her nostrils flared, as though daring Bren to find any hint or trace of a flaw.

"She's Pandathaway-bred, isn't she? What's her name?"

"That's where I bought her. And her name is Carrot," Karl said. "I take it that you like horses."

"Oh, very much." Bren was a sandy-haired boy of about Rahff's age, with a broad, easy smile. "My father has a stallion I'd love to see cover her. Has she foaled yet?"

"No. She's been a bit too busy to take time out for that." Like an assassin in the night, longing for Andy-Andy stabbed at him. *God, how I miss you.* It was hard to think of her visibly pregnant, her belly swollen, and know that he wouldn't see her, wouldn't touch her for months. At best.

In the back of his mind he could almost see her standing in front of him, hands on hips, her head cocked to one side, a whimsical smile playing over her lips. *So? Who told you this hero business was supposed to be easy?*

Bren went on: "If we have time, later, would you listen to some advice? I think breeding Carrot with a Katharhd pony might produce a—"

"Your manners, Bren," Furnael said, shaking his head, a warm smile making his stern tone a lie. "You're forcing me and my guest to stand outside in the cold wind." He shivered violently, although the breeze from the north was only refreshingly cool. "Would you like to unsaddle and curry the horses, and then join us inside?"

He turned to Karl. "May I? Please?"

"Certainly. No need to tie her; she'll stay around as long as she knows I'm inside."

"Of course," Bren said disapprovingly, miffed at being told something so patently obvious.

Furnael led him into the shack. It was small, but well kept: The stone floor was smooth and clean; the spaces between the wallboards had been filled with fresh clay by a careful hand. No draft disturbed the fire that blazed merrily in the stone hearth, with its cast-iron stewpot bubbling as it dangled over the flames.

Furnael unbuckled his sword and hung it on a peg before pulling a stool to the rough-hewn table that stood in the center of the room, beckoning Karl and the others to join him. There were only three remaining stools; Karl, Rahff, and Thomen sat, while Beralyn stood next to her husband, frowning down at him.

Furnael chuckled. "You must forgive my wife. She doesn't approve of this."

"And why should I?" Beralyn sniffed. "It's nothing but nonsense. My beloved husband," she added, her voice dripping with sarcasm.

The Baron threw his arm around her waist and patted at her hip. "You'll forgive me. As usual."

"Until the next harvest."

Rahff frowned; Furnael caught the expression and turned to the boy. "And none of that, not in front of our guest. You will show proper manners, boy." He gestured an apology to Karl. "This is a family tradition. Before each harvest, the sons of the Baron spend three tendays in slave quarters, working the fields as hard as the slaves—"

"Harder, father," little Thomen piped up. "Rahff says we have to show we're better."

"—eating the same food, wearing the same clothes as do the field slaves. Gives a sense of proportion. Vertum thinks well enough of it that he's sent Bren to join our boys this year. I think Bren is profiting from it."

"Nonsense," Beralyn said. "You should listen to your children. When Rahff is the Baron, he won't put his sons through this."

Furnael snorted. "Which is exactly what I said when I was his age. Karl, feel free to wander around, later; you'll see that this cabin is no better than any of the others. We treat both our fealty-servants and slaves well, here."

"This cabin is worse," Beralyn said. "You sent your men down to chip the clay out of the walls. Again."

"As I *will*, each and every time you clay the walls for the boys. If Rahff or Thomen want to do it for themselves, that's fine. I've tolerated your living with them to cook for them; don't test my patience further."

He shook his head. "Karl, my wife thinks to blackmail me into giving up the tradition, by living down here when our sons do."

"Zherr, you wanted to talk about some problem?" Karl asked, uncomfortable at finding himself brought into a family argument.

"Indeed." Furnael leaned on the table, steepling his fingers in front of his face. "There have been raids into Holtun. A band of outlaws has taken up residence somewhere on the slopes of Aershtyn. Perhaps two, three hundred of them. They ride down at night, punching through the idiotic line defense the Holtish—" He cut off as Bren opened the door.

The boy shook his head sadly. "Please don't stop on my account," he said. "I don't have any delusions about Prince Uldren."

Furnael smiled a thank-you at the boy. "They carry off women and food, killing any who raise a hand against them. Behind them, they leave the farms ablaze, cutting the throats of all the cattle and sheep, like a dog covering with vomit that which he can't eat. It seems they've found a large cache of salt, somewhere, and they have lately taken to salting the ground behind them."

He shook his head. "I've talked to Sammis about it, and there is nothing his magic can do. He could kill the weeds, of course, as he does for the farms in my barony. But salted land will grow no grain, whether the weeds are left standing or not.

"If this goes on, Holtun will find itself in the midst of a famine. To the west lies the soda plain; they will have to turn east. They will have to invade Bieme, just as the Nyphs did in my father's time. These two friends"—he gestured at Bren and Rahff—"will find themselves blood enemies. And not just in theory, but in fact."

"And you can't take on the raiders yourself." Karl nodded. "Holtun wouldn't stand for it."

"At the first sign of Biemei soldiers crossing into Holtun, the war would start. Already, there have been a few clashes along the border. I know that this sounds disloyal, but if only the raiders had ventured

into Bieme . . . perhaps Prince Uldren would have swallowed his
pride and seen the wisdom in some sort of alliance."

"I doubt it, Baron," Bren shook his head. "His Highness is, as my
father says, a pompous ass. And one who'd be as likely to grip his
sword by the blade as by the hilt. Fancies himself a great general,
though."

Furnael nodded. "Karl, I'd like you to stop that. I hope you'll see
that we are good people here. And we are people who are willing to
pay, and pay well. Perhaps you could pretend to join the raiders, lead
them into an ambush? Or track them to their lair, take them on
yourselves, chase them into my barony, where we could deal with
them? Or something—anything."

Karl closed his eyes. The strategy wasn't a problem. Not Karl's
problem, in any case. Ahira could probably work something out.

Still, three hundred against five was not Karl's idea of good odds.
Then again, they wouldn't have to take on all three hundred at once.

But that wasn't the issue. *The question isn't can we, it's should we.*

And that was harder. Granted, Zherr Furnael was—or at least
appeared to be—a good man for this world; given, any war between
Bieme and Holtun would be bad for everyone concerned, including
the slaves of both sides.

But . . . I'm Karl Cullinane, dammit, not Clark Kent. I can't do
everything; *I've already made a promise I'm not sure I can keep; I
can't let other things divert me.*

His conscience pricked him. How about Aeia? Taking her home
didn't constitute carrying the war to the slavers.

No. Aeia's case was different. Melawei was suffering from slave
raids; it was reasonable to take her home, since that path would lead
to some good opportunities to strike at the Slavers' Guild.

What would helping Furnael have to do with ending slavery? Anything?

No, there was no connection.

I'll have to turn him down. I—

Wait. "There . . . is a price, Zherr. A large one."

Furnael spread his hands. "We do have money, Karl."

"I don't really need money. But, in return for me and my friends
solving your problems, would you be willing to give up all your
slaves?"

Furnael smiled. "That's a high price, Karl. It'd cost me much time
and coin to replace all the slaves in my barony. Perhaps we could
consider—"

"No. Not replace. Your payment would be to give up the owning of slaves throughout your barony. Forever."

For a moment, the Baron's face was a study in puzzlement. Then Furnael sighed. "I . . . I thank you for the politeness of not turning me down directly. But it wasn't necessary; I understand. You don't want to make our battles yours."

"Baron, I'm completely serious."

"Please. *Don't* insult my intelligence." Furnael held up a hand. "Let it be, Karl Cullinane, let it be."

Karl opened his mouth, then closed it. It wouldn't work. To Furnael, the concept of slavery was so normal that he couldn't take at face value any suggestion he give up owning people. It wasn't really offensive to Furnael, just incomprehensible. But trying to explain further could only be an affront.

Furnael's face grew grim. "I'd thought to try to frighten you into serving me, you know. Threatening to hold that little girl—Aeia, is it?—as hostage against your success." He drummed his fingers on the wood. "You do seem to care about her welfare."

"That wouldn't leave me any choice, Baron."

Furnael nodded. "Then—"

"No choice at all. I'd either have to take on three hundred raiders, relying on your word to release Aeia if I did, *or* I'd have to take on you and your forty or fifty armsmen, none of whom seem to have done much recent fighting." Karl let his hand fall to the hilt of his sword. "That would be an easy decision, Baron. Granted, my friends and I would probably all die, but we'd take some of you with us. And how would that leave you in the war that's coming?"

"It was just a thought. But a silly one." He sighed deeply. "The sort of warrior I need wouldn't be frightened into doing something unwillingly." The Baron shook his head as he rose to his feet and walked to the peg where his sword hung. "But, as your friend Ahira put it, I have prepared a fallback position. A ruler, even a lowly baron, should always keep an option ready."

"Baron, you—"

Furnael lifted the scabbard and drew the sword.

Karl leaped away from the table, sending his stool clattering on the floor. Drawing his own sword with one fluid motion, he spun around into a crouch. *Got to be careful. Can't let the woman or the children get behind me; they might grab my swordarm.*

The sword held loosely in his hand, Furnael drew himself up straight. "Karl Cullinane," he said, his voice dripping with scorn, "put up your sword. You are in no danger here, not from me. I swear that on my life, *sir.*"

What the hell was going on? First Furnael had tried to buy his services, then intimidate him, then he had gotten ready to attack Karl. "I . . . don't understand." Karl lowered the point of his sword.

"On my life, sir," the Baron repeated.

To hell with it. I've got to trust somebody, sometime. Karl slipped his sword back into its scabbard.

The Baron turned to Rahff. "Hold out your hands, boy."

Silently, Rahff shook his head.

"Do it." The Baron's shout left Karl's ears ringing.

Slowly, Rahff extended his palms. With exquisite gentleness, Furnael laid the flat of the blade on the boy's palms, then untied his pouch from his own waist. Carefully, Furnael tied the leather strands about the middle of the blade. "There are ten pieces of Pandathaway gold here."

White-faced, Beralyn laid a hand on Furnael's arm. "Don't do this. He's just a boy."

Furnael closed his eyes. "This gives us a chance, just a chance, Bera. If Rahff survives, he may be strong enough to see the barony through the coming years, through the war. I . . . I don't see any other way. Please, please don't make this any harder."

He opened his eyes and turned back to Karl, tears streaming down his cheeks. "Karl Cullinane. I offer my eldest son to you as apprentice, sir, to learn the way of the sword, bow, and fist. I offer as payment my horse, this gold, this sword, and the services of my son, for a period of five years."

Karl looked down at Rahff. The boy's whitened face was unreadable. "Rahff?"

"It's not his choice, Karl. I'm the boy's father."

Karl didn't look at Furnael. "Shh. Rahff? Do you want to be my apprentice?"

Clenching his lower lip between his teeth until the blood flowed, Rahff looked from his mother, to his father, and back to Karl. Slowly, he walked over and extended the sword and pouch, his arms shaking. "It's . . . my father's wish, sir."

"But is it yours?"

Rahff looked from his father, to his brother, to his mother, to Bren. Hero worship was one thing; agreeing to leave his home and family was another.

Bren nodded. "Do it. If you stay, we'll soon be enemies, be after each other's blood."

"And if I go? Will that make any difference?"

"I don't know. But it will give us five years' grace, five years until I have to kill you, or you have to kill me." Bren clapped a hand to Rahff's shoulder, gripping tightly. "Five years, at least."

Rahff swallowed. Then: "Y-yes. Will you accept me as apprentice, Karl Cullinane?"

Karl looked at Baron Zherr Furnael with a new sense of admiration. It took a certain something for a man to see his own limitations, to accept the likelihood of his own destruction, while planning to protect at least a part of his family from the storm of arrows and swords that would certainly leave him dead.

Not necessarily just part of his family; perhaps Furnael had other plans for Thomen and Lady Beralyn.

Apprenticing Rahff to an outlaw was a cold-blooded act, but that didn't make it wrong. If Rahff survived an apprenticeship, he might be strong enough to hold the barony, perhaps even all of Bieme, together through the coming year.

And what if he dies, Zherr Furnael? We're heading into danger; what if he's not quick enough or lucky enough to live through it?

Karl didn't voice the question. The answer was clear: If Rahff couldn't survive a five-year apprenticeship, then he wasn't the ruler that the barony needed.

Zherr Furnael would either have a worthy successor, or a dead son. Not a pleasant gamble.

But what other choice do they have? Karl accepted the sword and pouch on the palms of his hands. "I accept you, Rahff, as my apprentice. Spend some time saying goodbye to your family and friends; we leave in the morning. Oh, and you can sleep at the inn, if you'd prefer." He untied the pouch from the sword, then accepted the scabbard from the Baron.

"I'd rather stay."

"You're his apprentice, boy." Furnael's low voice was almost an animal's snarl. "You will sleep at the inn."

Karl drew himself up straight. "I'll thank you not to interfere with my apprentice, Baron. I gave *him* the choice, not you." He took two copper coins from his pouch and dropped them on the rough table. "This should cover his lodging; he'll spend the night here, as he chooses."

Slipping the sword into the scabbard, Karl handed it to the boy.

"Take good care of this, Rahff. You're going to be spending many hard hours learning to use it."

And may God have mercy on your soul.

The boy nodded somberly.

"But I think you'll do just fine."

A smile peeked through Rahff's tears.

And through Furnael's.

PART FOUR

Melawei

CHAPTER TEN

To Ehvenor

Practice is the best teacher.

—Publilius Syrus

As they rode down the shallow slope toward Ehvenor, the fresh-water sea called the Cirric lay below them and ahead of them, rippling off across the horizon. Off in the distance, Karl could see the rainbow sails of a wide-beamed sloop, tacking in toward the harbor.

Ten, perhaps twelve small ships huddled around Ehvenor's docks, as seamen bustled like ants to load and unload their cargo. Just harborside of the breakwater, three large ships lay at anchor, attended by half a dozen small launches that swarmed around them like pilotfish around a shark.

The low stone buildings of Ehvenor cupped the harbor, flat and ugly. The streets were narrow, crooked, and strewn with refuse; the town of Ehvenor looked like one large slum.

There was only one exception. A cylindrical building, seemingly three or four stories high, stood in the center of town like a rose on a pile of dung. It shone whitely.

Karl rubbed his eyes. It was hard to make out the details of that building; the edges and details fuzzed in his eyes, as though he couldn't focus on it.

"Ahira?"

The dwarf shook his head. "It doesn't seem to suit my eyes, either."

"You think that's the Faerie holding, or embassy, or whatever they call it?"

The dwarf snorted; the snort was immediately echoed by his pony. "Not likely to be anything else; I doubt the locals build out of mist and light."

Karl nodded. "I'd like to know how they do that."

"Ever hear of magic?" Ahira fell silent.

After a reflexive check to see that the others, riding behind him, were doing fine, Karl patted at Carrot's neck. "I wonder how you're going to take to being on a ship."

Did horses get seasick?

And how about the others? Chak, Tennetty, and Rahff had never been on a boat before. Fialt wouldn't be a problem; he was a Salke, and apparently everyone on Salket spent a good deal of time at sea. Ahira wouldn't be a problem, fortunately. A vomiting dwarf wouldn't be any fun to be around. And Aeia was a Mel; according to Chak, everyone in Melawei was practically conceived at sea.

Well, at worst, we're going to have four upchuckers among us. Probably including me.

Karl rubbed at his belly. *Maybe this time will be different. God, please let this time be different.* His only other time at sea had been on the *Ganness' Pride.* The trip from Lundeyll to Pandathaway on the *Pride* was not one of Karl's fondest memories; he had spent the first few minutes throwing up his breakfast, the next couple of hours vomiting up food he didn't even remember swallowing, and most of the rest of the trip with the dry heaves.

Ahira chuckled.

"What is it?" Karl looked down at the dwarf. "You think seasickness is funny?"

The dwarf shook his head. "No. I wasn't thinking about seasickness at all."

"Oh. So it's my nervousness about going on a boat again that's funny?"

Ahira scowled. "*Your* nervousness? Karl, you don't know what nervousness about being on a boat is."

That was strange. Ahira hadn't shown a trace of nausea while they'd been aboard the *Ganness' Pride.* "Iron-guts Ahira, that's what we'll have to call you. You hid your seasickness well."

"No, I wasn't seasick. There are other problems than seasickness," the dwarf said, scowling. "Think it through, Karl."

"Well?"

"How much do you weigh?"

"Huh?" What did that have to do with anything?

"A simple question, actually. How much do you weigh?"

"Mmm, about two-twenty or so, on This Side. Back home, about—"

"How much do I weigh?"

"About the same, I'd guess." A dwarf was built differently than a human. Ahira's body wasn't just shorter and disproportionately wider than Karl's; his muscles and bones were more dense. *More dense.* "Oh. I hadn't thought about that." A human's body was, overall, less dense than water. But the dwarf . . . "If you fell overboard, you'd sink like a stone, chainmail vest or no."

"Exactly. I could easily drown in five, six feet of water. A bit more serious than a spot of projectile vomiting, no?"

"But what was so funny about that?"

Ahira smiled. "You were the one thinking about boats. I was thinking about towns."

"Well?"

"Think about it. What was the first town we ever dealt with on This Side?"

"Lundeyll. We just barely got out of there with our lives." Not all of them had gotten out alive. Jason Parker had died in Lundeyll, spending the last few moments of his life kicking on the end of a spear. *Someday, if I can find the time, I think I'll look up Lordling Lund and feed him his fingers, one joint at a time.*

"Exactly. We left Lundeyll just about ten seconds ahead of the posse. The next town was Pandathaway. We got out of there a couple days before Ohlmin left, chasing us. We didn't spend any time worth talking about in a town until you and Walter went into Metreyll. And look at the time frame there: From the time you killed Lord Mehlên's armsmen until Metreyll found out must have been . . . at least a week, maybe a tenday." The dwarf held out a stubby finger. "One: ten seconds." Another finger. "Two: three days." A third finger. "Three: a full week." Ahira shot a glance at Karl. "Now, think about Bieme, and Furnael. For once, we left a town without anybody after us, even though the Baron wasn't pleased about your turning down that job. I was a bit nervous about that for a couple of weeks, but now that we're almost in Ehvenor, it's clear that he's not coming after us."

"So?" Karl didn't see the point of it all.

"So, it seems to me it's sort of a progression; looks like we're learning to get along better and better with the locals. If this keeps up, eventually we might even make friends somewhere, be invited to stay. *If* this keeps up . . ."

"Well?"

"Well, yonder—I'm starting to like saying yonder—lies Ehvenor. All we have to do there, all we *want* to do there, is book passage to Melawei."

"Do you always have to belabor the obvious before you ask me a favor?" Karl couldn't help returning Ahira's smile. "Try just asking."

"Fair enough: While we're in Ehvenor, try to avoid sticking any locals through the gizzard."

Karl shuddered. *You're talking as though I like bloodshed.* He opened his mouth to protest, then closed it. *Keep it light, just keep it light.* "That's asking a lot. What'll you do for me?"

Ahira thought about it for a minute. "Ever hear of positive and negative reinforcement?"

"Of course. Use to be a psych major."

"Good. Let's use both. Negative reinforcement: If you get us into trouble here, I'll bash you with my axe."

"And the positive reinforcement?"

"If we do get out of Ehvenor without any bloodshed, I'll give you a lollipop. Fair enough?"

"Fair enough." Karl chuckled a moment, then sobered.

Even though it was hidden by the banter, Ahira was serious.

And he had a point. If they ran into slavers in Ehvenor, the city wasn't the place to take them on. The locals wouldn't like it; Karl had no illusions about his group's ability to take on a slaver team *and* a large detachment of local armsmen.

Though the group was shaping up nicely, come to think of it.

Tennetty was getting better and better with a sword. She didn't have the upper-body strength to parry more than a few solid thrusts without tiring, but she did have an almost instinctive feel for the weak points in an opponent's defenses.

Rahff was coming along well, although he didn't seem to have Tennetty's natural bent for swordplay. The boy had to work at it.

But he did work hard. A good kid, although the way Rahff hung on Karl's every word was quickly getting tiresome.

Fialt's swordsmanship was still lousy, but his hand-to-hand skills had come a long way, and he had developed a nice feel for both manriki-gusari and staff.

Chak was a good man. Not a fancy swordsman, but a reliable one. With Chak on watch, Karl could sleep peacefully; with Chak bringing up the rear of the group, Karl could concentrate on what lay ahead, with only an occasional glance behind. Chak was . . . solid, that was it.

Even little Aeia's bowmanship was coming along. She wasn't as good as Ahira had told Furnael, of course. But not too bad, either. Aeia and a cocked crossbow could be a nice hole card in a fight.

Wait a minute. "Ahira?"

"Yes?"

"I've got one question, though. If you don't mind."

"Well?"

"Where are you going to get the lollipop?"

CHAPTER ELEVEN

Ehvenor

Remember that no man loses other life than that which he lives, or lives any other life than that which he loses.

—Marcus Aurelius

Him? Karl started. The aging, wide-bellied ketch tied at the end of the narrow dock didn't look familiar, but the man in the sailcloth tunic, directing the loading crew, did. *Avair Ganness, what the hell are you doing here? And if you're here, where's the* Pride?

It had to be him. While sweat-stained sailcloth tunics weren't at all rare around the docks, there couldn't be a whole lot of short, dark-skinned sailors with waist-length pigtails and thick, hairy legs who carried themselves with the rolling swagger and easy confidence of a ship's captain.

"Captain Ganness?"

Avair Ganness shouted a quick command at a seaman, then turned.

His swarthy face paled. "You? Not *again.*" He opened his mouth to call to one of the bowmen at the foot of the dock, then pursed his lips and shrugged, beckoning to a crewman. "Quickly," he said, "finish loading and prepare to cast off."

"But we don't sail until—"

"*Smartly,* now. We may not have to, but I want to be able to cast off and up sails in half a score heartbeats. We may need to show Ehvenor a fast set of heels. Understood?"

"Aye, sir." The sailor shrugged and vaulted over the splintered railing, calling out to crewmen to halt the loading process and prepare for casting off.

Ganness turned back to Karl, a tragic smile spreading over his face. "What is it now, Karl Cullinane?" He spread his hands. "If you've managed to get the Ehven as angry as you did Lord Lund, I'd at least like to know why I'm going to die on this wretched dock."

Karl raised a hand. "I'm not wanted here. Pandathaway, yes. But I understand that Ehvenor isn't interested." As Chak explained it, there was no love lost between Pandathaway, the center of trade, culture, and magic of the Eren regions, and Ehvenor, dominated by the outpost of Faerie.

Ganness nodded, conceding the point. "True enough. As far as official Ehvenor goes. But not all Ehvenor is official Ehvenor."

He pointed a blunt finger shoreward. At his motion, a group of filthy, rag-clad men scurried for the shadow of a warehouse, all the while gibbering at each other in strained, high-pitched voices. "Watch your back, Karl Cullinane. Being around faerie too long does strange things to some humans; drives them crazy. I don't keep bowmen at the foot of the dock for the pleasure of it; in the past, crazies have fired boats—with themselves aboard, more often than not. Some of them would slit you open, throat to crotch, just for the fun of it." Ganness smiled. "Instead of the money."

Karl rested his hand on his swordhilt. "Perhaps you'd like the money?"

Ganness sneered. "Me?" He spat on the dock. "Of course. But while the notion of carrying your head back to Pandathaway thrills me, the idea of becoming a side attraction in the Coliseum doesn't. I don't dare set foot in Pandathaway or Lundeyll, not anymore. Not since I was fool enough to carry you from Lundeyll to Pandathaway. The wizards have long memories. I won't have any further dealings with them, for as long as I live." He laughed ruefully. "And that's a safe claim, come to think of it. Now," he said, drawing himself up straight, "what are you doing here?"

"I'd heard that a ship called the *Warthog* was leaving for Melawei tonight. Is this it?"

"Yes. And she's mine, such as she is."

Karl looked the ketch over, from the gashed bow all the way to the stern, where a pair of seamen worked a bilge pump, sending a constant stream of brown water over the side and into the harbor. "Not quite the *Ganness' Pride,* eh?"

"Not quite."

"What happened?"

"Lund wasn't pleased with my carrying you from Lundeyll; he hired himself a brace of pirate ships to hunt her down. They caught up with me just off Salket. The *Pride* went down; I barely escaped with my life. All thanks to you." Ganness sighed. "But you haven't answered my question."

"I think I have. I need to buy some passages to Melawei: seven people and two horses going, six and two coming back. Are you willing to carry us?"

"The same you were with before?" Ganness brightened. "Including Doria?"

"No, the only one you'd know is Ahira. The dwarf."

"Too bad." Ganness pursed his lips. "I may regret asking this, but are any of the others good with a sword or bow?"

"All of us. You might be able to use an extra sword or two. There's been a bit of trouble on the Cirric, I hear." That was a bald lie. Karl hadn't heard anything of the sort. But, given that slavers were raiding Melawei, it was reasonable to assume that they might pounce on a few merchantmen. And if Ganness was even considering carrying them, it was certain that the captain was afraid of just that.

"True enough." Ganness stood silently for a moment. "Are you sure that you're not wanted here? I'm not about to let you close another port to me."

Karl patted the hilt of his saber. "I'm certain. I'll swear it on this, if you'd like."

Ganness nodded. "Fine, then. I can put the horses in the hold, but the only other accommodations I've got are deck passage—unless you'd prefer to sleep with your animals?"

"No thanks."

"Very well, then. It'll be six gold for each human, five for the dwarf, two for each horse. Each passage, each way. Payable now." He held out his hand.

Karl raised an eyebrow. "On this? That's almost ten platinum. I could almost buy this ship for that."

"No, you couldn't. I wouldn't sell." He smiled. "Besides, *Warthog* is faster than she looks. In some ways, she's better than the *Pride* was."

Karl held back a laugh. The *Ganness' Pride* had been a lean, shapely sloop, not a floating leak. The only way this scow was better than Ganness' former ship was that it would hurt Ganness less to lose her. "Well, at least she's here."

One hand on his hip, Ganness held out a palm. "The coin, if you please."

Karl heft the pouch. "I don't have that much with me." But should they take passage on Ganness' ship? Maybe it would be better to wait for the next one.

No. It could be a long time before another Melawei-bound ship left. And if he turned Ganness down, the captain might be tempted to let it be known there was a wanted man around, for whose head Pandathaway would pay well. The threat was implicit in Ganness' ridiculously high price for passage.

Karl opened the pouch and counted out six gold coins. "You can have this as a deposit; I'll have the rest for you at the time we sail."

"Agreed. And I will see you then."

Karl started to turn away, but Ganness' shout stopped him. *Wait.* "Aren't you forgetting something?" Ganness asked.

"What?"

The captain gestured to Karl's sword. "I think there's still a bit of swearing to be done. On your sword, if you please. If, that is, you do want passage."

Karl hesitated.

"Truly," Ganness went on, "she is a good ship. Seaworthy and fast."

"Of course." Slowly, Karl drew his sword then balanced it on his palms. *I may as well get this over with. Next thing I know, he'll be telling me she made the Kessel run in three parsecs.*

Ahrmin clung to one of ten rope ladders secured to the dock, restraining a shiver.

The Cirric was cold this late at night, but it and the darkness provided good cover for Ahrmin and his ten men. He had spent several hours considering how many of the forty men from the *Scourge* to take with him. Too small a group wouldn't be able to take on Cullinane and his friends; too large a group would be impossible to hide. The element of surprise was always a huge advantage, and Ahrmin believed in having every advantage available.

Ten seemed about right. Enough to overpower Cullinane's group; not too many to hide.

It would take sharp eyes to see their heads and the few inches of rope that had been tacked to the side of the dock. The dock was a thick and sturdy one, rising more than two heads' height above the smooth black water.

Near the ship, sandals slapped against wood and voices called out orders, as the crew made the final preparations for the *Warthog* to sail.

Clinging to the ladder next to Ahrmin's, Jheral nudged him. "Shouldn't you check that ball again?" he whispered. "Or are you afraid of losing it?" Jheral shook his head to clear the water from his eyes and his long, pointed ears.

Ahrmin rewarded him with a scowl. The damned elf was more trouble than he was worth. Jheral had been a journeyman slaver for more than twenty years, and made no secret of his strong distaste for Ahrmin's promotion to master.

Not that Guildmaster Yryn had had any choice; he couldn't place Ahrmin in authority over senior journeymen without promoting him, and this job was clearly too much for Ahrmin and a group of junior journeymen and apprentices.

Probably Jheral and the others could have taken that. But the guildmaster had gone further, taking the unusual step of expressing his confidence in Ahrmin in the Writ of Mastery, by way of trying to avoid any conflicts. Normally that would have settled the matter; Guildmaster Yryn was known for being stinting in his praise.

It hadn't settled it; in fact, Yryn's strategy had backfired, acting as fuel to the journeymen's resentment—Jheral's in particular.

"We could have just waited for them at sea," Jheral went on, "instead of floating here like a bunch of silkies."

"Be quiet. Do you want them to hear us?" That suggestion was ridiculous; it just couldn't work. In a sea battle, it would be impossible to capture Karl Cullinane alive. Stealth was the only chance.

But Jheral's first idea did make sense. Grudgingly, Ahrmin reached over to the inflated pig bladder that was tied loosely to the ladder and reached underneath, pulling on the slim rope to haul up the fine-mesh net bag containing the device Wenthall had given him.

"Light," he whispered.

Jheral drew his knife, cupping his hands around the blade to prevent the bright glow from shining through the cracks in the dock. Thyren, the *Scourge*'s wizard, had refused Ahrmin's request to help them catch Karl Cullinane, saying that he had signed on only to neutralize the Mel wizards during the slaving raid. But he had agreed to Glow a knife . . . in return for Ahrmin's promise of share of the reward.

The finger floated in the yellow oil, pointing unerringly toward the city, toward Karl Cullinane.

Ahrmin waited, watching the finger.

With agonizing slowness it moved, until it came to rest parallel to the dock.

Silently, Ahrmin pushed himself away from the ladder, pulling the bladder with him, beckoning at Jheral to follow.

Like a compass needle, the finger swung. Karl Cullinane was nearing the dock; he was somewhere in the shadows of Ehvenor. Somewhere near.

"He's almost here." Ahrmin tugged on the netting to make certain that it still secured the ball, then checked the rope fastening the netting to the bladder. The knots were still tight; he let the ball sink below the surface, then beckoned to the others bobbing in the dark water. "On my signal, we move," he whispered. "Remember, we can kill the others, but I want Karl Cullinane alive. And, Jheral—put that knife away."

"For a moment." Jheral smiled. "For a moment."

At the foot of the dock, Karl held up a hand and climbed down from Carrot's saddle. "Rahff, has Pirate ever been on a boat before?"

The boy shook his head. "No." The white horse snorted and stamped her feet, pulling back against the reins as Rahff tried to lead her. He stroked at the horse's neck with his right hand as he held the reins in his left. "And she's getting a bit skittish. I'm sorry, Karl."

"Don't apologize, Rahff. You do just fine with the horses."

Rahff drew himself up straight, standing proudly.

Karl suppressed a pleased chuckle. A few words of mild commendation did wonders for the boy's posture. Whatever his virtues, Zherr Furnael had clearly never been unstinting in his praise.

Karl tried to calm Pirate down, but the horse snorted and snapped at his fingers.

It was just as well that they had sold the other horses, instead of trying to bring them on board. While Carrot wasn't a problem, Pirate's skittishness could quickly have become contagious.

Chak tapped Karl's shoulder. "Let me try."

"Go ahead."

The little man reached into his sack and produced a strip of cloth.

With a quick motion, he whipped it around Pirate's eyes, fastening it in place as a blindfold.

The blindfold worked; Pirate calmed instantly, as though someone had thrown a switch.

Fialt hoisted his bag to his shoulder. "You should keep the horses toward the middle; gives you a bit of room for error if the animal gets twitchy."

Tennetty threw an arm around Fialt's waist. "Hmm." She smiled. "I guess you are good for something, clumsy. Something else, that is."

Ahira raised an eyebrow; Karl shook his head. Something else? Apparently both of them had missed what had been going on between Fialt and Tennetty.

"Can't put the two of them on watch together anymore," Karl whispered. "They'll be paying too much attention to each other to keep a proper lookout. That's probably been going on for a while."

"Happens." Ahira nodded. "But don't be too critical, eh? Let he without sin cast the first stone, and all that."

"Right." Karl raised his head. "Let's go. Slowly, now."

As he led Carrot onto the dock, Aeia skipped ahead, her little feet flying across the wood. She stopped just a few yards from the *Warthog,* nervously eyeing the strangers on board the ship.

Ganness held out a hand. "Welcome aboard." He raised his head and called out, "You have the coin?"

"As agreed," Karl called back. "Go ahead, Aeia. Get on. We'll be there in a moment." After the slightest of pauses, she walked up the ramp and onto the deck.

Karl pulled on Carrot's reins. "Easy, girl. It'll just be another—"

A hand reached out of the water and fastened itself on Karl's ankle. Another hand stabbed a glowing knife into his calf.

Pain cut through him; he fell, landing hard on his side, his left arm caught beneath him. A shrill scream forced its way through his lips.

Swords and knives in their hands, eleven men slipped out of the water, surrounding them all in a circle of steel points and edges.

Karl reached for the hilt of his sword, but the same glowing knife stabbed through his right wrist, pinning his hand to the wood.

His fingers writhed; his nails clawed at the wood.

Another hand grasped his hair. "Don't try to move." An elf's thin face leered inches from his. "That will only make it hurt more."

"We only want Karl Cullinane," a low voice rasped. "The rest of you can go. Or die."

Karl couldn't move his head, and the reflexive twitching of his right hand sent red-hot currents of pain shooting through his arm. He could only see Carrot's rump, Fialt, Tennetty, and two swords, just at the edge of his vision, menacing them.

Fialt raised his hands. "We don't want any trouble—"

He slapped at Carrot's hindquarters, sending the horse galloping down the pier. He snatched the manriki-gusari from his belt, then leaped out of Karl's vision.

Fialt staggered back, blood fountaining from between his hands as he clutched his chest, while Carrot's pounding hooves set the dock shaking.

"Chak," Ahira shouted, *"now."*

Karl struggled to free his left arm as the elf's fist pounded against his face.

Blood filled Karl's eyes. Blindly flailing his arm, he managed to fasten his left hand on the elf's throat.

Karl squeezed, ignoring the pain, ignoring the clatter of steel and the splashes of bodies falling in the water. The only thing that mattered was his left hand, and his grip on the elf's throat.

Karl squeezed.

The blows grew more frantic.

Karl squeezed. The flesh of the elf's neck parted beneath his fingers, bathing his arm in blood.

The blows eased, then stopped.

"You can let go of him now," Ahira said, bending over him. "He's dead. And the rest are gone." A sudden stab of pain, and the knife was wrenched from Karl's hand. "Rahff, the healing draughts. Quickly, now."

Karl shook his head, clearing some of the blood from his eyes. "No." Pain pounded redly in his hand and calf, making each word a hideous labor. "First. Get on board. All of us. Take off. Then."

The dwarf pulled him up, helping Karl balance on his good leg. The dock was slippery with blood. Three bodies lay face down on the wood.

Tennetty knelt in a pool of Fialt's blood. Her fists drummed a rapid tattoo on his back. "You *idiot,*" she trilled. "Never were any good against a sword. Never." She beat against his back as though trying to pound him back to life, tears streaming down her face.

Chak sheathed his sword and grasped her hands in his. "There's nothing more you can do for him," he said gently. "We have to go."

He pulled her to her feet, then stopped to pick up Fialt's body and threw it over his shoulder.

Ganness ran over, two bowmen at his side. His face was ashen, his lips white. "I thought you said—"

Rahff reached over and grabbed the front of Ganness' tunic. "You heard Karl. Just shut up. We'd better get out of here; they may come back."

"But—"

Rahff raised his bloody sword. "Shut *up.*"

Karl tried to listen, tried to keep his eyes open, but the darkness reached out and claimed him.

It was a long swim back up to the light. The water rocked him, and tried to force itself into his mouth.

He gave up and let himself sink into the darkness, but a hand reached out and grasped his face, pulling him to the light.

"Karl," Ahira said, forcing more of the sickly-sweet liquid between his lips, "we're safe now. For the time being."

Karl opened his eyes. He was lying on a narrow bunk, sunlight streaming through the oversized porthole and splashing onto his chest. The ship was canted, sailing close to the wind.

"Where?" He struggled to get the words out. "Where are we?"

"Ganness' cabin." The dwarf smiled. "Ganness started to object when we brought you down here, but he took one look at Rahff and changed his mind. That's one loyal apprentice, Karl. Good kid."

Karl nodded. He brought his right hand up, in front of his face.

The wound from the knife was just a pinkish scar on the back of his hand, mirrored on his palm. As he stared at the scar, it continued to fade. Soon it would be gone. It would be just as if nothing at all had—

No. "Fialt."

The dwarf shook his head. "Nothing we could do for him. Healing draughts can't help a dead man. But Chak brought the body on board." He bit his lip. "I . . . I thought you'd want to say the words over him, before we bury him in the Cirric. Tennetty says that's the way they do it on Salket."

Karl raised himself on an elbow. "I'd better go see to every—"

The dwarf planted a hand on Karl's chest and pushed him back. "Everybody else is fine. I've put Rahff and Chak on watch; the horses are safe in the hold." A crooked smile played across Ahira's lips. "Although I'd better bring Aeia in. She's been crying. Thinks you're dead. Rahff and Chak have been telling her you're unkillable, but I don't think she believes them."

"*I* sure as hell don't. How many of the bounty hunters did we kill?"

Ahira shrugged. "Three for certain; another four wounded and pushed into the water. The rest dove and disappeared."

"And Ganness. How is he taking all of this?"

With a weak smile, Ahira picked up his battleaxe from where it lay on the floor. "I talked to him for a while, and he stopped squawking." He lowered the axe and sighed. 'But he got away, dammit."

"He? Who?"

"You didn't notice who was leading that group?"

Karl snorted. "I was sort of busy. What's the mystery?"

"The leader looked to be about eighteen. Dark hair, dark eyes, slim nose. Good with a sword; it took him half a second to spear Fialt through the chest and return to the on-guard position. Had one hell of a familiar-looking and very cruel smile. And that voice . . ." The dwarf shuddered. "Didn't he sound like someone we know?"

Karl tried to remember the voice. No, he had been in too much pain to pay attention. But that description—except for the age, that sounded just like—"Ohlmin? But he's dead." *I cut his head off, and held it in my hands.* There were times that violence bothered Karl, but killing that bastard had been a distinct pleasure.

Ahira nodded. "But maybe he has either a son or a younger brother who isn't."

Karl elbowed the dwarf aside as he pushed himself to his feet. His legs were wobbly, but they would support him. "How would you feel about fixing that?"

"At our first opportunity. In the meantime . . ."

"We bury our dead."

Karl stood at the rail, Rahff and Aeia next to him.

In front of him, Fialt's body lay shrouded on a plank; the plank was supported at one end by the starboard rail, supported at the other by Tennetty, Chak, and Ahira.

Karl laid his hand on the rail. "I never knew Fialt as well as I would have liked to," he said. "Guess it's because I never took enough time. But he wasn't an easy man to get to know. Quiet, most of the time. A private person, our Fialt was.

"I never really understood why he came along. He didn't seem to have the . . . fire in him that Ahira, Tennetty, and I do. And it wasn't a matter of practicing his profession, as it is for Chak. Or of learning through doing, as it is for Rahff.

"But that doesn't tell us much about him. What do we really know about this quiet man? We know that he was awkward with a sword, and none too good with his hands. Although he was learning, and no one ever tried harder. We know that he was a Salke, and a sailor, and a farmer, and a slave. And, finally, a free man. But that was about all.

"About all . . ." Karl gripped the rail, his knuckles whitening.

"There were only two times that I had even a peek through the wall he put up between himself and the rest of the world. It seems to me that Fialt wouldn't mind my talking about those two times. And I hope he'll forgive me being frank.

"The first was during a lesson. He had done something well, for once—damned if I can remember what, right now—and I'd said something like, 'We'll make a warrior of you, if you keep this up.'

"He turned to me and shook his head. 'Just a man who can protect himself, his friends, and his own. That's all I ask. That's all I ask. . . .'

"The other time was last night. Fialt must have known that he wasn't good enough to take on a swordsman by himself; he should have waited for a signal from Ahira.

"But he didn't wait. It didn't make *sense,* dammit." Karl gripped the body's stiff, cold shoulder. "You should have waited, Fialt, you should have. . . ." Karl's eyes misted over; his voice started to crack. He took a deep breath and forced his body back under control.

"I . . . guess that tells us something important about our friend. Both virtue and flaw. I will miss that virtue, that flaw, and Fialt, whose body we now surrender to the Cirric." He patted the shoulder and stepped back.

Their faces grim, Tennetty, Chak, and Ahira raised their end of the plank. The body slipped from the plank and splashed into the blue water below, falling behind as it sank.

Chak drew his falchion and raised it to his forehead in salute. Ahira unstrapped his battleaxe, mirroring Chak.

Tennetty stared at the ripples, her eyes red, her face blank.

Karl drew his own sword and balanced it on his palms. "I promise you this, Fialt: You will be avenged." He slipped the sword back into its scabbard.

"Maybe I'm wrong, but I like to think you'd want it just that way."

CHAPTER TWELVE

The Guardians of the Sword

I have been here before,
But when or how I cannot tell;
I know the grass beyond the door,
The sweet keen smell,
The sighing sound, the lights around the shore.

—Dante Gabriel Rossetti

Karl stood at the *Warthog*'s bow, holding tight to the railing as the ketch lumbered slowly across the gently rolling sea toward the small inlet and the lagoon beyond. Overhead, the jib luffed merrily in the wind; below, water foamed, splashed, and whispered against the hull.

Gentle waves lapped against the sandy shore. High above, a slim-winged tern circled in the royal blue sky, then stooped to pluck a small fish from the blue water, bearing its wriggling prey away.

Karl rubbed at his belly, once more enjoying the taut feel of a full stomach. It had taken him time to adapt to being at sea, but his body had made the adjustment. And in less time than it had taken before.

Only six days of feeding the fish this time. Hmm. If this goes on, in a few years I'll only be vomiting for the first few seconds I'm at sea.

A vision of himself stepping on board, immediately vomiting, then smiling and feeling fine rose up unbidden. He laughed out loud.

Aeia looked up at him, raising one eyebrow just the way Andy-Andy did.

"It's nothing," he said. He reached into his pouch and drew out a half-dried orange, peeling it with his thumbnail. Popping a section into his mouth, he waved a hand at the shoreline. "Look familiar?"

"Yesss . . ." First she nodded, then she shook her head. "But I don't see my house."

Little one, as I understand it, Melawei stretches out across about two hundred miles of shoreline, with scads of inlets, beaches, islands, and lagoons. We're not going to bump into your hut. "Don't worry. It may take a few day, but we'll find it."

Her forehead creased. "Are you sure?"

Standing next to her, Rahff elbowed the girl in the shoulder. "Karl promised, didn't he?" With a derisive snort, Rahff elbowed Aeia again.

That had to be stopped, nipped in the bud. Not that the boy had done anything terrible, but the point had to be made. "Rahff."

"Yes, Karl?"

"We don't hit the people we're supposed to protect."

Aeia looked up at him. "He didn't hurt me, Karl."

"Doesn't matter. A man whose profession is violence must not commit violence on his own family, or on his friends. You and I are supposed to watch out for Aeia, protect her, not hit her, or bully her."

Rahff thought it over for a moment. "How about you and Ahira? You and he threaten to hit each other all the time."

"Think it through, Rahff. We play at threatening each other; we don't actually hit each other. See the difference?"

"Yes." The boy cocked his head. "But how about practice? We've all gotten bruises from you." He rubbed at his side.

"Good point. That's instruction, not violence. Anyone can back out of practice at any time. That includes you, apprentice. No more training or no more hitting. Understood?"

"Understood. I'll stay with the training." Rahff turned back to the rail.

Karl smiled his approval. A good kid; Rahff took criticism and instruction as a lesson, not as a blow to his ego.

At Ganness' shouted command, the helmsman brought the ship about again, maneuvering it between two outreaching sandspits. The hull rasped against a sandbar; the ship shuddered free, and swung into the placid water of the lagoon.

Karl shook his head. No wonder the hull was as watertight as a sieve, if this was the way Ganness treated it. Even given Ganness' explanation that the Mel would deal with a ship only after it had grounded itself, there had to be a simpler way than bouncing the boat across sandbars until it got stuck at low tide in the lagoon.

Still, Ganness' seamanship and his confidence in it were noteworthy; on This Side, there was no moon, and the weaker solar tides made for only a slight difference between high and low water. It took guts for Ganness to dare a deliberate grounding; breaking free would be tricky.

Karl turned to Ahira, noting that the dwarf's one-handed grip on a cleat on the forward mast wasn't quite as casual as Ahira tried to make it seem. A casual grip didn't leave the knuckles white. "Any problem?"

Ahira didn't turn around. "No."

Karl switched to English. "Hey, it's me, remember? James, are you okay?"

"I'm fine. I just don't like it when the boat jerks around."

Another bump swung Karl around, sent his hands flying back toward the railing as the ship rocked once, then fell still, grounded. Aeia and Rahff exchanged indulgent smiles over Karl's poor sense of balance.

Look, kids, when you've got a couple hundred pounds of mass to carry around, it isn't as easy to keep upright as it is for you.

But never mind. Let them have a few private chuckles. He scanned the shore, trying to see if there was anyone or anything in the dense greenery. Nothing. Ganness had said that the locals would meet them, but—

"Karl?" Ahira's voice held a hint of amusement.

"Yes?"

"Don't turn around for a second. I've got a question for you."

Karl shrugged. "Sure."

"This shoreline looks like Hawaii, no?"

"I was thinking Polynesia."

"Hawaii's part of Polynesia, Karl. And this is the same thing. Not Diamond Head; it looks more like Lahaina. Palm trees, sandy beaches, almost no rocks, warm, blue water, even though it's fresh and not salt."

"Right." Karl started to turn.

"Hold it a moment," the dwarf snapped. He chuckled. "Now, given all that, when the natives show up, you wouldn't be surprised if they were paddling dugout canoes—outrigger types—would you?"

"It wouldn't surprise me at all."

A similar environment would tend to produce similar artifacts. The simplest, most convenient road—and hunting ground, for that matter—would be the sea. If the Mel didn't have the resources to build large sailing ships, they would build canoes. And if they didn't have animal skins or birch bark to build the canoes with, they'd have to make dugouts. Dugout canoes were inherently more unstable than other sorts—therefore, outriggers. All logical.

"Is that what this is? The natives have dugouts?"

"It makes sense to you, right?"

"Right."

"Then turn around and tell me why their canoes look like miniature versions of Viking longboats."

Karl turned.

Three canoes floated in the lagoon's mouth, each five or six yards long, with an outrigger mounted on the port side, each manned by oarsmen.

And each with a wooden carving of a dragon's head rising from the prow.

After checking on Carrot and Pirate in the hold, Karl climbed back on deck. He gathered Ahira, Aeia, Chak, Rahff and Tennetty around him, keeping the group well away from Ganness and the three sarong-clad Mel, who were busy at the bow, haggling over the price of Melawei copra and Endell steel.

The locals spoke Erendra with a curiously lilting accent, far different from the flat half-drawl of Metreyll or the clipped speech of Pandathaway. A familiar accent. . . .

"Hey, Karl?" Ahira looked up at him.

"You hear it, too?"

"I sure do. You got any explanation of why these folks talk like the Swedish Chef?"

Chak frowned. "It might help," he said, scowling, "if you would either teach me this *English* of yours, or just keep your conversation in Erendra. At least when I'm around."

"Good idea." The dwarf nodded. "I'll give it a try."

Karl gestured an apology. "We were talking about the accent these Mel have. It sounds familiar. Like something from home."

"Home?" Rahff shook his head. "Not my—"

"Our home." Karl waved his hand aimlessly. "The Other Side. A region called Scandinavia." That was very strange. Differences between here and home were to be expected; he had grown used to them. On the other hand . . . coupled with the dragon-headed canoes, the familiarity of the local accent was vaguely frightening. It had to mean something.

But what?

It couldn't be just a transplanting, as had happened with their group. After all, the Mel didn't look like Scandinavians, not at all: Their hair was black and straight, their skin dark; they had slight epicanthic folds around their eyes.

Chak shook his head. "That doesn't make sense. I thought you were the only ones to cross over."

"That's what I thought, too."

The largest of the Mel, a deeply tanned, broad-shouldered man in a purple sarong, walked over. His lined face was grim as he stopped in front of Karl, planting the butt of his leaf-bladed spear on the deck in front of him.

"Are you from Arta Myrdhyn?" he asked, his accent still sending chills up and down Karl's spine. "Has he sent for the sword?"

Karl shook his head. "I'm sorry, but I don't understand."

The Mel gave a slight shrug, as though that was the answer he had expected, but it had disappointed him nonetheless. "Avair Ganness," he said, "says that you are a man from a land strange to him. He says that your name is Karl Cullinane, and that you are someone for whom the slavers have offered a large reward. Is this true?"

I'm not sure whether it's the slavers or the whole Guilds Council that's offering it, but you're close enough. Karl nodded, gesturing to Chak to take his hand off the hilt of his sword. This didn't sound like a prelude to an attack. And even if it was, the Mel still in the boats were too far away; Karl, Tennetty, Chak, and Ahira could easily handle the three spearmen on board. "Yes. It's true."

"And why do they hunt you?" The Mel's face was flat, unreadable.

"Three reasons. First: I freed a dragon that Pandathaway kept in chains. Second: I killed slavers and a wizard who hunted me for doing that. Third: It is my . . . profession to kill slavers and free slaves." *And there's a fourth reason, it seems. One—at least one—of the slavers has made it a personal matter.*

He laid a hand on Aeia's shoulder. "This is Aeia; one of your people. We have brought her here. Home."

"I see. And if slavers were to raid Melawei while you are here?"

Before Karl could answer, Chak snickered, drawing his thumb across his throat, sucking air wetly through his teeth.

Karl nodded.

The Mel's face became even grimmer as he slowly rotated his spear, planting the point deeply in the wood of the deck until the spear stood by itself. Placing his calloused hands on Karl's shoulders, he drew himself up straight. "I am Seigar Wohtansen, wizard and warleader of Clan Wohtan. Will you and your friends do me the honor of guesting with Clan Wohtan while you are in Melawei?"

Karl looked past Seigar Wohtansen's shoulder to Ganness, who stood openmouthed in amazement. And down to Aeia, whose eyes grew wide. Clearly, this wasn't the standard way to greet visitors from other countries.

Back when he was minoring in anthro, Karl had learned something of the vast range of acceptable behavior, and the way it varied from society to society. But the notion of host and guest was close to universal. Except for the Yanamamo, of course, the only culture known by the anthropologists who studied them as "those bastards." The Mel didn't seem like a This Side version of Yanamamo.

Wohtansen stood silently, waiting for Karl's answer.

"I am honored," Karl said. "And we accept."

Wohtansen dropped his hands and ran to the railing, calling down to the men in the dugouts. "There are guests of the clan here, who require help with their animals and baggage. Why do you just sit there?"

Aeia let out a deep breath.

"What is it?" Karl asked. "Glad to be home?"

She shook her head. "No, it's not that."

"Why? Afraid I'd turn him down and hurt his feelings?"

The girl shook her head. "If you'd turned him down, he would have had to try to kill you."

Ahira cleared his throat. "I think we'd all better be careful with our pleases and thank-yous. No?"

Setting down his wooden mug on the grass-strewn floor, Seigar Wohtansen sat back on his grass mat, leaned on his elbows, and shook his head. He sighed deeply. "An acceptable meal, guests of my clan?"

"Not acceptable." Karl smiled. "Excellent." The others echoed him as they reclined on their mats.

The guesthouse of Clan Wohtan was the largest of the seventeen huts in the village, and the most luxurious. It was a long, low structure, somewhat like a bamboo version of a quonset hut, the wrist-thick poles that formed the framework bent overhead, rising to about six feet at the center. Long, flat leaves were woven among the closely spaced poles. The light wind dryly whistled through them.

There was no fireplace in the hut; the slightest spark could easily set it aflame. Their dinner of grilled flatfish and deep-fried balls of coconut milk had been cooked over the firepit twenty yards in front of the open end of the guesthouse, the food brought in on plantain leaves.

The cook—and a good one, at that—had been Estalli, the younger of Seigar Wohtansen's wives; she was a slim, attractive girl who looked to be about sixteen. Now, she knelt attentively beside Wohtansen, the hem of her sarong tucked chastely under her knees while her naked breasts bobbled above, refilling his mug from a clay jug of fermented coconut juice while Wohtansen's seven sons and daughters served Karl and the rest.

Wohtansen's other wife, Olyla, a hugely pregnant woman in her late thirties, presided over the tail end of the meal from the single piece of furniture in the hut, a cane armchair.

Illumination was provided by seven head-size glowing stones, each suspended in an individual net bag hung from the centerpole that ran lengthwise down the roof of the hut. The light from three of the stones had begun to fade; Wohtansen had spent much of the meal reassuring Olyla that his promise to refresh the spell still stood, and that he would do so tomorrow. Her knowing smirk said that this wasn't the first time he had made that promise.

Understandable. Life in Melawei was lazy and easy; it would always be tempting to put work off to tomorrow.

Karl had another swig of the coconut juice. It was dry and crisp, like a light Italian wine. But how did they get it so cold?"

He shrugged. Well, if Romans could make ice in the desert, maybe the Mel could chill a bottle of wine.

He looked over at Aeia, who was sprawled out on her grass mat, sated after the heavy meal, half asleep. "Good to be home, little one?"

She frowned. "I'm not home yet."

Wohtansen smiled reassuringly. "We're not too far from Clan Erik, little cousin. No more than two days by sea." He closed his eyes tightly for a full minute. "If your horses can take just a bit of water, you should be able to ride straight there. And in less time. We can start out in the morning." He shrugged. "I've got to go that way myself. I'll need to arrange for Ganness' copra to be picked up, and I'll have to visit the cave."

Estalli reacted to the last two words as though she had been slapped. "Seigar—"

"Shh. Remember Arta Myrdhyn's words. 'He will be a stranger from a far land.' I'll have to take Karl Cullinane there. And if he's not the one, the sword can protect itself. It has before."

That was the second time Wohtansen had brought up this sword. Karl spent a half-second debating with himself whether asking might offend the Mel. Then: "What sword is this?"

Wohtansen shrugged. "The sword. I wish Svenna—he was the Clan Speaker—hadn't been taken by the slavers; he could tell you the story, word by word." He raised his head. "Though Clan Erik still has its Speaker. Do you want to wait until you can hear it properly?"

"To be honest, I'm itching with curiosity."

Not particularly about this sword, though. What were a group of Mel men doing with Scandinavian names and Scandinavian accents?

And more.

The figureheads on the dugouts looked like the dragons on Viking longboats; they were stylized, almost rectangular, not saurian like Ellegon.

The huts were bamboo-and-cane versions of Viking lodges.

That didn't make sense. A climate and environment similar to Polynesia could have given rise to a culture similar to the Polynesian culture, complete with loose, wraparound clothing, outrigger canoes, and a loose and easy life-style based on the bounty of the sea. But where had the Scandinavian elements come from?

It was possible that the dragon-headed canoes *or* the accent *or* the similarity of some of the names could have been a coincidence, but not all three.

Seigar Wohtansen sat up, then drained his mug, beckoning to Estalli for a refill.

"Very well. My father's father's father's . . ." He knit his brow in concentration as he counted out the generations by tapping his fingers against his leg. ". . . father's father's father's *father,* Wohtan Redbeard, was called a pirate, although he truly was a just man. He sailed his boat on a sea of salt, as he raided the villages of the wicked landfolk, taking from them their ill-gotten grain and gold."

As Wohtansen spoke, the children sat down on the mats, listening intently, as if to a favorite, often-repeated bedtime story.

". . . he and his men would appear from over the horizon, beach their boat, then . . ."

One of the little boys leaned over toward an older sister. "How could they sail on salt?" he asked, in a quiet whisper.

She sneered down at him, holding herself with the air of superiority possessed by older sisters everywhere. "There was salt in the *water.*"

"That doesn't make sense. Why would they waste salt by putting it in the water?" he pressed. "Father says salt is hard enough to find as it is."

"They didn't. It was already there."

"How?"

"Shh, Father's talking."

". . . but this night was dark, and a storm raged on the sea, sending his ship leaping into the air, then crashing down into the troughs between the waves. . . ."

"Why didn't they just land?" The boy nudged his sister again.

She sighed. "Because they were too far out at sea."

"Didn't they know that they weren't supposed to go out of sight of land?"

"I guess they forgot."

". . . and just as he thought that his ship would founder and sink, the sky cracked open around him, and the ship found itself on the quiet waters of the Cirric. . . ."

"But how did it *get* here?"

"Weren't you listening?" She gave him a clout on the head. "The sky cracked open."

He rubbed at the spot where she had struck him. "I've never seen that."

"You will if you don't be quiet."

". . . standing at the prow was an old man. White-bearded, he was, dressed in gray wizard's robes. Clutched tightly in fingers of light, a sword floated in the air over his head.

" 'I, Arta Myrdhyn, have saved your lives and brought you here,' he said, in a tongue they had never before heard, but somehow understood, 'to take this to a place I will show you.' His voice was the squeak of a boy whose manhood was almost upon him, yet his face was lined with age. 'You and your children will watch over it, and keep it for one whom I will send.'

"A man named Bjørn laughed. 'My thanks for the sword,' he said. 'But I will take it for myeself.'

"As he sprang across the deck at the wizard, lightning leaped from the wizard's fingers, slaying Bjørn instantly. . . ."

The boy looked up at his sister. "Bjørn? What kind of name is Bjørn?"

"An unlucky one. And a stupid one. Now, *shh.*"

". . . brought them to the cave, and left the sword there, amid the writings that only two of them could see, and none of them could read. 'Watch for strangers,' Arta Myrdhyn said. 'One day, a stranger will come for the sword.'

" 'But how will I know him?' my many-times-great-grandfather asked.

"The wizard shook his head. 'You will not, and neither will your children, or their children. It is not yours to know, but to watch, and wait. The sword will know. . . .' "

"How can a sword know anything?"

"It's a magical sword, stupid."

"Hmph."

". . . accepted them gladly, and offered their daughters as wives." Wohtansen raised his head. "And so, they settled down to an easier life, raised their children, and grandchildren, down the nine generations." He thumped his hand against his mat. "And here we are." He tapped the jug. "More juice?"

Ahira caught Karl's eye. "What we've had has already gotten to my bladder." He elbowed Karl in the side.

"Oof. Me, too. If you'll excuse us for a moment?"

"Did you catch all that, Karl?" Seating himself on a waist-high rock, the dwarf drummed his heels against the stone.

Karl's head swam. It made sense, but it didn't. All at once. "I don't understand it. Part of it makes sense, but . . ." What Wohtansen had said boiled down to the sort of story a group of conquering Vikings might tell to their children and grandchildren. "But eight, nine generations? When were the Vikings? About eleventh century, no?"

Ahira nodded. "Something like that. And with the faster time rate on This Side, if a bunch of eleventh-century Vikings crossed over, they should have been here for far more than two centuries."

Karl nodded. That was what Deighton had said, and what they had observed. Their trip from Lundeyll to the Gate Between Worlds had taken a couple of months on This Side, but when they had used the Gate to return home, only a few hours had passed. Once, he had sat down with Lou Riccetti to figure it out: For every hour that passed at home, about four or five hundred flew by here.

"It can't be something as simple as Deighton lying," Karl said.

"No." The dwarf scowled. "Deighton has lied to us more than once, but not this time. We know he was telling the truth. This time. The time rate is faster here, relatively."

"Maybe not." Karl shrugged. "Maybe the time differential fluctuates. That'd explain some things."

"Like what?"

"Think it through." Karl stamped his foot. "Wish I'd had the sense to, before." He gestured around them. "If this side really was four hundred times as old as Earth, that'd make it about sixteen hundred billion years old, no? It'd be that much more worn; most of the atmosphere would have escaped, probably; all the mountains would have worn themselves down."

"Huh?" Ahira's forehead furrowed. "You're telling me that mountains wear out? Too much dry-cleaning?"

"Give me a break. Mountains tend to wear down, just like anything else. The Appalachians are older than the Rockies, which is why they don't rise as high, not anymore. In another couple of billion years, they'll be the Appalachian plains, if tectonic forces don't raise a whole new set of mountains. Entropy."

The dwarf pounded his fist against the rock. "Deighton lied again."

"Maybe; maybe not." Karl shook his head. "So, the time differential fluctuates. But maybe Deighton didn't know that. After all, the time rate could have worked just the way he said it did during his whole life. He could have been telling the truth."

"I doubt it." The dwarf shook his head. "I didn't think you caught it. Remember the wizard's name: Arta Myrdhyn. Sound familiar?"

"Myrdhyn. Well, that kind of sounds like Merlin." Karl shrugged. "I guess it's possible that Arta Myrdhyn inspired the legends about Merlin."

That wouldn't be surprising; he had already seen evidence that happenings on this side had leaked over the boundary between worlds: elves, dwarves, wizards throwing bolts of lightning, the silkies of the northern Cirric, the notion of fire-breathing dragons, the cave beneath Bremon that was echoed in the writings of Isaiah—

"No. Or maybe," the dwarf corrected himself. "But that's not the point. Remember how Wohtansen described the wizard? 'White-bearded . . . his voice was the squeak of a boy whose manhood was almost upon him, yet his face was lined with age.' Doesn't that sound like someone we know?"

Ohgod. "And the name: Arta—Arthur. Arthur Simpson Deighton. But he said—"

"That he had only seen this side, but never had been able to bring himself across. That's what he *said,* Karl. Doesn't make it true."

Karl shook his head. "I don't see what this all adds up to."

"Me neither." The dwarf shrugged. "And I've got a hunch we're not going to for quite a while. If ever. Unless you want to try to slip past The Dragon, again, then go quiz Deighton."

"I'll pass, thanks."

"Thought so."

"I don't see you volunteering."

"I'm not." Ahira flexed his arm, his biceps bulging like a huge knot. "I like it here. No, I think we just keep thinking about it. Maybe Walter or Andrea or Lou Riccetti will have some idea; maybe Ellegon knows more than he's telling. We'll just have to wait until we get back to the valley."

"Well, what do we do in the meantime?"

Ahira smiled. "That's easy. We live. Eat. Breathe. Kill slavers. All the usual stuff."

Karl snorted. "Well, let's get back inside, then. Got a lot to think about."

Ahira raised a finger. "There is one more thing we'd better do."

"Yes?"

"I think we'd better have a look at this sword of Wohtansen's."

"Right."

CHAPTER THIRTEEN

The Scourge

Her beams bemocked the sultry main,
Like April hoarfrost spread;
But where the ship's huge shadow lay,
The charmed water burnt away
A still and awful red.

—Samuel Taylor Coleridge

"I still say we should have taken them while they were at sea," Lensius muttered to Hynryd, his voice pitched so that Ahrmin could hear him, but only barely. Lensius shook his head, his long, greasy ringlets of hair waggling in counterpoint. "And we would have, were I in charge."

Hynryd nodded. "That's what Jheral thought, too."

"I know. He—"

"*Enough.*" Ahrmin's fingers tightened on the hilt of his sword. Lensius and Hynryd fell silent.

Ahrmin sighed. The fiasco at the dock hadn't done anything to improve his standing with his thirty-seven remaining men. What had once been only a silent resentment had become open doubt, sometimes verging on mutiny.

But that didn't matter. Only one thing mattered.

So I failed, Karl Cullinane. This first time. That's not so important;

even Father couldn't beat you the first time. But it isn't the first time that counts, Karl Cullinane. It's the last time.

He looked around the *Scourge*'s cramped forward hold. Of the thirty-odd faces, the only one that didn't bear a frown was Thyren's; the wizard held himself above both the sailors and slavers. In contrast to the grubbiness of the rest, the wizard's gray robes were clean and unwrinkled, his drawn face freshly shaved, his thin lips holding a disdainful smile.

"Ahrmin?" Raykh scratched at his head. "I think we should consider letting this Karl Cullinane go. There's enough gold to be had picking up a few dozen Mel." He rapped on the bulkhead behind him. "Enough space in the hold for one hundred and fifty, two hundred, if we pack tightly enough."

Ahrmin's irritation rose. He'd had enough of the tight-pack fanatic. Of all tight-pack fanatics.

It had been proved, over and over again, that there was more money to be made by delivering a smaller number of healthy slaves than by tight-packing them, chaining them all closely together in the hold, leaving them to stew in their own wastes during a sea voyage, having to throw away those who didn't survive, then treat the others with expensive healing draughts before a sale.

Tight-packing was a particularly stupid way to handle Mel. Mel didn't take easily to their chains; many would refuse to eat. Tight-packed, they could lose more than half of the slaves. Even loose-packed, the trip from Melawei to Pandathaway would kill ten, maybe twenty percent of the cargo, and leave the rest sick as dogs.

Of course, they could always sell the surviving slaves as-is. But in Pandathaway—or anywhere else along the coast, for that matter—there was little demand for sickly slaves who had to be either healed or nursed back to health before they would be any use to their new owners. Tight-packing would kill much profit.

Besides, tight-packing the women would remove one of the great joys of the profession.

Ahrmin snorted. "And what would you do? It would take several tendays in a good port to refit the *Scourge* for tight-pack."

Raykh shrugged. "It seems a bit late to point that out. We could have—"

Thyren cleared his throat; Raykh fell silent.

"I believe that was Ahrmin's point," the wizard said. "We're not in Pandathaway. Nor are we in Lundeyll, or Port Salke, or even Ehvenor. To be precise, we're off the coast of Melawei. Even if you wanted to take the time and money to refit the slavehold, I doubt that the locals would be willing to help you."

Fihka spoke up, his low growl barely carrying over the rush of water. "We could always make them help us."

The wizard eyed him for a moment, then carefully spat in Fihka's face.

Fihka reddened, but kept his white-knuckled fists at his sides, not even daring to raise his hands to wipe the spittle from his cheek. The others near him turned their faces away, not wanting to be next.

"Fool," Thyren said, smiling gently. "Who do you think I am? Grandmaster Lucius? Arta Myrdhyn? I can easily hold off any one of these Mel wizards and his apprentices. I could probably take on two, perhaps as many as three. But if I were stupid enough to allow you to anchor the *Scourge* offshore for—a tenday, did you say? two? —we would quickly find the ship surrounded by every Mel wizard and apprentice that could run, paddle, swim, or crawl. There is a limit to how many spells I can intercept."

Thyren rose. "But enough of this nonsense; I have better things to do than listen to more squabbling." He rose and left, all of the men glaring in unison at the door as he closed it behind him.

You would be able to dispel more if you didn't insist on keeping other spells in your head, wizard. Like your lightning bolt, or flame spell, Ahrmin thought. *But then you wouldn't be able to abuse everyone with impunity, would you?*

Then it occurred to him that Thyren had, albeit unknowingly, done him a favor. By acting as a lightning rod for the men's discontent, the wizard had given Ahrmin a chance to ingratiate himself with the others.

But how?

He thought for a moment, and an idea that had been in the back of his mind suddenly jelled.

"Raykh," he said. "You should trust me more."

Raykh's head snapped around. "What?"

"You assumed that I had no reason for not taking the *Warthog* at sea."

The other sneered. "I know your reason. You want to take Cullinane alive."

"And you'd rather take a share of a much smaller reward? Never mind. There is another reason. One that will fatten all of our pouches, as well. As much as a tight-pack would if all the slaves survived. And . . ."

"And?" Raykh leaned forward, interested.

"And my plan will ensure that we can come upon Karl Cullinane unaware. It will be tricky, granted; and we have to assume that Cullinane has business in Melawei that will take him at least a day's ride away from where they've beached the *Warthog.* I'll be happy to share my idea, if you're interested." Ahrmin lay back on his bunk, cradling his head on his arms. "But my major concern is Cullinane. If you don't mind forgoing some extra slaves, some extra coin . . ." He closed his eyes.

"Wait," another voice piped up. "Don't keep it a secret, Master Ahrmin."

He sat up, making sure that his smile didn't reach his face. *"Master Ahrmin," eh? I like the sound of that.*

"Very well." Ahrmin nodded. "The timing will be tricky, but I'm sure we can do it." He pulled the glass ball from his pouch, unwrapped the soft leather sheets that covered it.

Ahrmin cradled the ball in the palm of his hand. "It all depends on this."

The finger floated in the center of the sphere, bobbing slowly in the yellow oil. From the finger's hacked-off stump, threads of tendon and shreds of skin waved gently, while the slim fingernail pointed unerringly toward the north.

"Listen carefully, now. We'll lie offshore, out of sight, until we're sure that Cullinane has gone a fair distance away, then . . ."

CHAPTER FOURTEEN

The Cave of Writings

The great brand
Made lightnings in the splendor of the moon,
And flashing round and round, and whirled in an arch,
Shot like a streamer of the northern morn,
Seen where the moving isles of winter shock
By night, with noises of the northern sea . . .

—Alfred, Lord Tennyson

There are times, Karl thought, *when I like this business a whole lot.* He rode Carrot at the edge of the water, sometimes kicking her into a canter, urging her a short way into the surf. Her hooves kicked up spray, bathing both of them in a cool shower.

"Stop that, Karl. Get back on the beach." Aeia laughed, wiping the spray from her eyes. To his left and a few yards behind, she bounced along on Pirate's back, her feet barely reaching the shortened stirrups.

She patted Pirate's white neck. Aeia had grown fond of that horse; it occurred to Karl that she would probably have a harder time saying goodbye to Pirate than to him.

Almost three hundred yards offshore, four dugouts kept pace with them. The first one held Tennetty, Chak, Ahira, Seigar, Wohtansen, and two other Mel paddlers; the other two, each manned by three Mel, were piled high with trade goods from the *Warthog.* In a couple of days, the men of Clan Wohtansen would free the boat from its sandbar, so that Ganness could sail down to collect his copra.

Ahead, a small island grew closer. Perhaps a quartermile offshore, it was heavily wooded and roughly conical, rising to a height of almost a hundred feet at its peak.

Aeia's eyes grew wide. "Karl." She pulled Pirate to a stop and stared at the island, her eyes filling with tears.

He guided Carrot over to her side. "What's wrong?"

"I *remember.* My parents' house is . . ." Her pointing forefinger wavered, then straightened. "That way. Along that path." Her arm trembled; she lowered it.

He dismounted from Carrot's saddle and helped Aeia down from Pirate. "Let's walk, shall we?"

Taking Pirate's reins in her left hand, she clasped Karl's right hand as they walked along the sand.

From the top of a slanting palm tree, a rough tattoo of drumbeats issued, then echoed as they were repeated along the path into the forest.

As the three dugouts were beached, Karl smiled down at Aeia. "Let's wait a moment."

"But—" she tugged on his hand.

"But nothing." He smoothed down the sides of his sarong. "I may be dressed in local costume, little one, but I don't think anybody grows quite this tall or hairy around here. I'd rather your clan finds out that I'm friendly *before* we meet them, rather than after I've gotten a spear through my chest."

Seigar Wohtansen spoke a few quiet words to one of his men; the Mel sprinted across the sands and disappeared into the forest, as Wohtansen and the rest walked over to where Karl and Aeia stood.

They were all dressed in local costume. Karl laughed at the way Chak's sunburned potbelly protruded over the waist of his sarong, although Rahff wore his with dignity. On the other hand, Tennetty actually looked kind of nice in a sarong, if you could ignore the scars along her belly and back. And the way that her right hand never strayed far from the hilt of her sword.

I guess I've been away from Andy-Andy far too long, if Tennetty's starting to look good.

Ahira looked ridiculous. The hem of his sarong brushed the sand, and it didn't really go with the chainmail vest that he wore over a thin under-shirt. Dwarfs weren't built to wear sarongs.

But who except me would tell him that?

As always, the dwarf had his battleaxe with him, strapped across his broad chest. While Ahira really wasn't as touchy as his scowling face suggested, it was unlikely that anyone would risk finding that out.

Wohtansen tapped Karl's shoulder. "The Eriksens will be down to pick up their goods in a short while. And, I suspect, celebrate their surprise." He ran affectionate fingers through Aeia's hair; his face grew somber. "Which means that you and I had best be getting on to the cave. I know Clan Erik; likely you won't be able to leave the celebration for days without offending someone."

Aeia's lower lip trembled; Karl dialed for a reassuring smile, relieved to find that at least some sort of grimace spread across his face.

It would be hard leaving Aeia here. Karl had never had a little sister before.

"I guess we'd better," he said, handing Carrot's reins to Chak. "Keep an eye on everything."

"No sweat, kemo sabe," Chak said in English, his thick accent leaving a lot to be desired.

Karl raised an eyebrow. *"Kemo sabe?"*

Chak nodded, then turned to Ahira. "I said that properly, no?"

"Close." Ahira shrugged an apology to Karl. "Well, he *asked* to be taught some English. And so did Rahff."

"I can see you started them with the important stuff first."

"Of course."

Wohtansen was getting impatient. Karl turned to accompany him. "Coming, Ahira?" Karl asked.

The dwarf shook his head. "You have to swim to get there. I think you'd better count me out. But I will want to hear about it, later."

"Swim?"

Wohtansen nodded. "You'd better give your sword to one of your friends. You'd have trouble swimming with it."

Karl unbuckled his swordbelt and tossed the scabbarded sword to Rahff. "Don't lose it, now."

"Of course, Karl." His apprentice nodded gravely. "And . . . up your nose with a rubber hose," he added in English, bowing slightly.

Karl laughed. "Ahira, you cut that out." Karl unstrapped his sandals, then kicked them off, absentmindedly spraying Ahira with sand.

The dwarf chuckled; Karl and Wohtansen dropped their sarongs on the sand and jogged away.

The water was warm and clear; Karl kept to Wohtansen's pace as they swam toward the island.

But it had been a long time since Karl had been swimming, and a quarter of a mile was more distance than he was used to; by the time Wohtansen pulled himself up onto the flat top of a jutting boulder, then offered Karl a hand up, Karl was grateful for the help.

He mimicked Wohtansen, stretching out on a rock, resting while the hot sun dried his skin. His breath came in short gasps; Karl forced his breathing to slow down. "Any reason we couldn't just take a canoe over?"

Wohtansen smiled tolerantly at Karl's panting. "Yes." He thumped a fist on the boulder. "Whole island is rocky, like this. No place to beach it. Besides, it's better not to draw attention to this place. Just in case." Wohtansen rose to his feet. "This way."

The narrow path twisted sharply upward through the bushes, until they arrived at the summit of the island, a rocky outcropping overlooking the seaward side. A single palm grew there, projecting out of a crack in the rock. A sparkling in the leaves caught Karl's eye; he glanced up. A glass ball, only slightly larger than a lightbulb, hung in midair among the palm's fronds, bobbling slightly in the breeze.

Wohtansen smiled. "A gift from Arta Myrdhyn; you can see what it does when we get below."

Below?

The Mel brought him to the ledge and pointed downward. A few yards from where the waves broke against the rocks almost a hundred feet below, the water burbled. "There's a spring that feeds into the Cirric down there. It will help us coming out, but it does make it difficult to go in.

"Listen closely: After I strike the water, count forty breaths, take as large a breath as you can, then follow me. Dive directly for the rough water, then swim down, as far as you can. The tunnel goes deep, very deep. Don't hesitate, just keep swimming down. It will be difficult for you, but it can be done.

"You must keep your eyes open; when you see light, swim toward it. I'll meet you and help you the rest of the way. Do you understand?"

At Karl's nod, Wohtansen walked away from the edge, took a running start, and leaped outward, away from the edge, his body arching into a classic swan dive, then straightening a scant pulsebeat before he hit the surface.

Wohtansen struck the dark water cleanly; he vanished, only a small splash marking his passing.

Karl took a deep breath and began counting.

One breath. *I don't like this, not at all.* But he kept breathing and counting.

Ten. *Well, at least we know why someone as young and vital as Wohtansen is the wizard around here. Not a job for an old man; one misstep and he'd shatter himself on the rocks.*

Twenty. *If I remember right, the cliffdivers in Acapulco dive more than a hundred feet from La Quebrada—if they can do it; why the hell can't I jump a bit less?*

Twenty-five. *Because I'm not trained for it, that's why the hell I can't do it. Or why I shouldn't, if I had a brain in my head.*

Thirty. *But do I have any choice?*

Thirty-five. *Not if I want to see this sword.*

To hell with it. He began hyperventilating, forcing air in and out of his lungs. He counted out five quick breaths, added another fifteen for good measure, eyed the distance from the rocks to the bubbling water, ran, and dove, his hands forming into fists of their own volition.

The air clung to him like a rubber sheet; the scant three seconds that he fell felt like a long hour.

He hit.

The water slammed into him like a brick wall, knocking the air out of his lungs, as he sank into the smooth tunnel, scraping his right shoulder against the stone. For a moment, he considered returning to the surface, giving up for now, trying again later. But he knew that if he backed away now, he would never regain his nerve.

So he swam down, into the black water, kicking his legs as frantically as he worked his arms.

The pressure in his chest grew; his lungs burned with a cruel fire; his diaphragm ached to draw anything, anything into his lungs.

And just when he finally thought his head and chest would split wide open, a horizontal channel appeared beside him, marked by a flickering light. Karl swam toward the light.

A hand grasped his outstretched arm; Karl went limp and let Wohtansen pull him through the horizontal tunnel, then up through another vertical one.

Two yards above him, the surface rippled invitingly. Desperately, he kicked himself from Wohtansen's grasp and stuck his head through to the surface.

His first breath was the sweetest one he had ever taken.

Karl pulled himself out of the water and lay gasping on the rough stone floor.

Seal-like, Wohtansen slipped from the water, then handed Karl a thick, soft blanket. "Here. Take a moment to dry off. It gets cold in here." Following his own advice, the Mel took another blanket from a cane drying rack.

As he dried himself, Karl looked around. They were in a small, almost spherical room, the stone floor concave to accommodate the pool in the center, the walls rising to a height of perhaps five yards. Glowing crystals speckled the walls.

Just like the crystals in the Cave of The Dragon. An icy chill crept along his spine; he rubbed himself harder, but the chill remained.

A long, jagged crack ran along the ceiling on the far side of the room, letting in shreds of noon sunlight through the green foliage that grew over the outside of the wall.

That wall couldn't have been more than a few inches thick; chiseling a doorway wouldn't have been difficult. Still, it was understandable why the Mel hadn't created another, more convenient way into the caverns. If this was the source of their magic, it would be best to keep it hidden.

On the far side of the cavern, a tunnel stood as the only exit other than the pool.

Wohtansen helped Karl to his feet, and they started to walk toward the tunnel. Low enough that Karl had to stoop to walk through it, the tunnel was only ten feet long, opening up on another cavern. "You won't be able to see the magical writing on the far wall, but I think you'll enjoy . . . *this.*"

Karl started. On the wall beside him, a huge picture window looked down on the sea.

Window? How can there be a window? They were inside the island; a window on that wall would open on rock, not look down on the Cirric. And it wasn't a painting; the waves in a painting didn't ripple; the clouds in a painting didn't move.

"That's just not possible. We're at sea level."

Wohtansen smiled. "Remember the Eye you saw above. Arta Myrdhyn left it there, and this here, so that we would never have to leave this place without knowing what lies outside."

Wohtansen at his side, Karl walked to the window and ran his fingers over the cool glass.

The view spun.

"Gently, gently," Wohtansen said, pulling Karl's arm from the glass. He put his own fingers on the left side of the glass, and pressed gently for a moment.

Like a camera panning to the left, the picture moved. Now the glass revealed a distant view of the beach, where perhaps a dozen people stood.

"It seems that some of the Eriksens have arrived on the beach," Wohtansen said. He pressed his fingers to the center of the window, holding them firmly against the glass. The field of vision narrowed, zooming in until it could hold only four figures, all of them with the flat appearance brought on by a telescope or binoculars.

Ahira stood smiling, while a fiftyish Mel couple, their faces dripping with tears, hugged little Aeia so hard that Karl thought they might squeeze the air out of her.

Wohtansen removed his hand from the glass, then lightly touched it on the right side, again removing his hand when the seaside view slid around. "But this is what it's for." He jerked his head toward the exit tunnel. "Come."

They walked into the tunnel. This one was longer than the other, forty yards of twisting turns. As they neared the tunnel's mouth, the brightness grew. But it was a different sort, a whiter, purer light.

Karl stepped up his pace. He reached the final bend in the tunnel and stepped out into brightness.

"I don't—" the words caught in his throat; his head spun.

Above a rough stone altar, gripped tightly by ghostly fingers of white light, the sword floated in midair.

CHAPTER FIFTEEN

The Sword

Once more unto the breach, dear friends, once more;
Or close the wall up with our English dead!
In peace there's nothing so becomes a man
As modest stillness and humility;
But when the blast of war blows in our ears,
Then imitate the action of the tiger;
Stiffen the sinews, summon up the blood,
Disguise fair nature with hard-favored rage;
Then lend the eye a terrible aspect.

—William Shakespeare

Karl's breath caught in his throat. His hands trembled.

But why? In and of itself, the sword didn't look unusual.

It was a fairly ordinary two-handed broadsword, three inches wide at the ricasso, tapering at first gently, then suddenly, to a needle-pointed tip; a cord-wound grip and long, thick brass quillons proclaimed it a sword for use, not for dress.

The blade was free of nicks and rust, granted, but Karl had seen many swords just as good. Perhaps a sword like this was worth sixty, seventy gold. No more.

So why was just looking at it like an electric shock?

"Part of the spell." Wohtansen chuckled thinly. "It affects everyone that way."

Karl tore his eyes away from the sword and the ghostly hand gripping it. He turned to face Wohtansen. "What . . . ?"

The Mel shrugged. "I don't know much more about it than I've told you. There are two charms on it that I can see." He tapped the middle of his forehead. "With the inner sight. One holds it there, waiting." He gestured at the bands of light clutching the sword. "For the one whom Arta Myrdhyn has intended to have it."

"The other?"

"A charm of protection. Not for the sword, for the bearer. It will protect him from magical spells."

Karl couldn't keep his eyes off the sword any longer; he turned back. His palms itching for the cord-wound hilt, he took a step forward.

"Wait." Wohtansen's hand fell on Karl's shoulder. "What do you read on the blade? What does the blade say?"

The blade was shiny steel, lacking any filigreed inscription. *"Say?* Nothing." Karl shrugged the hand away.

"Nothing? Then we may as well go; the sword was not left for you." Wohtansen stared intently into Karl's face. "I'd hoped you were the one," he said sadly, then bit his lip as he shook his head. "But hoping never did make it so."

Karl took another step toward the sword. It vibrated, setting up a low hum that filled the cavern. As Karl leaned toward it, the humming grew louder.

He reached up and fastened both hands on the hilt, while the radiance grew brighter, the humming louder. The fingers of light dazzled his eyes; they gripped the sword more tightly.

His eyes tearing, Karl squinted against the light and pulled. The vibration rattled his teeth, but he gripped the hilt tightly and pulled even harder. The light grew so bright that it made his eyes ache even through closed eyelids, but the sword didn't move at all.

Goddam it, he thought. *Here I am, trying to grab a magical vibrator when I should be home with my wife and child and—*

The sword gave a fraction of an inch, then stopped, frozen in place.

"Karl." Wohtansen's voice was shrill. "It's never moved before. Pull harder, Karl Cullinane. Harder."

He pulled harder. Nothing.

He gripped the hilt even more tightly, then braced his feet against the stone altar, and pulled on the sword until his heart pounded in his chest, and the strain threatened to break his head open.

Move, dammit, move.

Nothing. He set his feet back on the floor and released his grip.

The light faded back to its original dimness; the vibration slowed, then stopped.

"I can't do it." Karl shook his head. Wohtansen tugged at his arm.

"A pity," Wohtansen said. "When it moved, I was certain you were the one."

He pursed his lips, then shrugged, as he led Karl back through the tunnel, the radiance diminishing behind them. "But it's not the first disappointment in my life; it won't be the last."

Wohtansen waved a hand at the window and walked to the far wall. "I do have to reimprint some spells; if you'd like, amuse yourself with the Eye while I study." He seated himself tailor-fashion in front of the wall opposite the glass, folded his hands in his lap, and began reading the invisible letters, moving his lips as he studied it.

Karl stared intently at the wall. No, it was just a blank wall to him; since he didn't have the genes that allowed him to work magic, he couldn't even see the writing.

That hardly seemed fair.

Then again, damn little was fair; damn little even made sense.

Although some things were beginning to. Arta Myrdhyn and the sword, for one.

Things on this side were often reflected as legends on the other side, at home. A great broadsword, somehow involved with the plans of a powerful wizard, held immobile until the right man appeared to claim it . . . that sounded like the story of Excalibur. The legend had been garbled, granted, but that wasn't unexpected.

The Excalibur story had never made sense to Karl; if whoever could remove Excalibur from the stone were automatically to become king of England, England would quickly be ruled by the first stoneworker to happen along and chisel it loose.

No spell could prevent that; magic worked erratically back home, when it worked at all.

But what does all this add up to? Deighton had brought a group of Vikings through to this side, not primarily to guard the sword, but to guide the right one to the sword, a sword that protected its bearer against magic.

And the right one was supposed to take it. To use it. To use it for *what?*

Karl shook his head. He couldn't follow the thread any further.

What are you really up to, Deighton?

He shrugged. Ahira was right. It would be a long time, at best, before they knew.

Karl turned to the window that looked out on the sea. He pressed his fingers against the left side of the glass and spun the view shoreward. A procession of Mel was engaged in bringing canvas sacks down the beach and depositing them on the sand just above the high-water mark. The pile was already well over six feet high.

Karl shrugged. Ganness' copra, no doubt. Too bad for Avair that he couldn't bring it directly to Pandathaway, but would instead have to sell it in Ehvenor to some Pandathaway-bound merchant. The dried, unpressed coconut meat would bring a high price in Pandathaway; after it had been run through presses, what oil the wizards didn't need would find its way into gentle soaps and balms, while the remaining meat would end up in breads and cakes.

But why were they bringing it down to the beach now? Ganness and the *Warthog* weren't due until tomorrow. Right now, the Eriksens should be celebrating Aeia's return.

Karl spun the view seaward. Just over the horizon, a black speck grew. A ship.

That explained it. Ganness was on his way a day early, and the Clan Erik coastwatchers had spotted the *Warthog*. Undoubtedly, the watchers had sounded the alarm, which had then been canceled when Wohtansen's men explained that there was a friendly ship en route.

Karl opened his mouth to tell Wohtansen about it, but changed his mind; the Mel was still studying the wall, his whole body tensed in concentration.

Wish I'd asked how long this was going to take. Idly, he centered the ship on the screen and pressed his fingers to the center of the glass.

The *Warthog* grew in the screen as it seemed to sail directly toward Karl. The ship rode high in the water, since most of its cargo had been unloaded in Clan Wohtan. As it moved closer, Karl could make out Ganness at the prow.

That was unusual; Ganness generally ran the ship from the main deck, where he was midway between the lookout in the forward mast and the steersman at the stern. That way, he could lounge in his chair while still able to hear warnings and give commands easily.

Only when the ship needed careful handling did he act as either lookout or steersman himself. Beaching the ship in the lagoon had needed that careful handling; beaching it here should just be a matter of sailing the *Warthog* slowly toward shore until it wouldn't go any farther.

Ganness' figure grew in the screen. Trembling, he raised a hand to wipe sweat from his brow.

What's Ganness nervous about? I guess there could be underwater boulders near the shore, but that shouldn't scare him like this.

Karl moved his finger to scan the rest of the ship, but his control wasn't fine enough; the *Warthog* scudded out of the Eye's field of view.

Damn. He removed his finger from the screen, centered the ship as soon as the field widened, and zoomed in carefully, making fingertip corrections to the aim of the Eye.

Standing next to Ganness was a young man. His face was dark and thin, his hair straight. A cruel smile flickered across his lips as he examined a dark glass ball, slipped it into his pouch, then turned to say something to the men behind him.

He looked for all the world like a younger version of Ohlmin.

Karl's heart pounded.

"Wohtansen, look."

The Mel wizard scowled at him. "Not now, please. This is difficult."

"Shut up. This is important. That's the slaver who tried to take me on the docks at Ehvenor. He and his men have taken the *Warthog.* They're going to be sailing right up to the damn beach, and the Eriksens won't know—"

"—that they are slavers." Wohtansen whitened. "We've told them to expect friends."

"Right." Karl's right hand ached for his sword. *Got to figure out exactly what they're going to do.* The slavers had the element of surprise. How would they use it?

They would probably drop anchor or beach the ship, and let some Eriksen dugouts come out to meet them, just as if this were a normal trading session. Then the slavers would kill or capture the Mel in the canoes, and use the canoes to go ashore, their wizard protecting them all the while from the Mel wizard's spells.

They would work it something like that. The slavers had clearly gone to some trouble to gain the advantage of surprise, and they would make good use of it.

"Karl," Wohtansen said, his voice shaky, "they must have already raided my clan. Otherwise someone would have chased after us, to warn us."

"Be quiet for a moment." That was true, but there wasn't anything that could be done about it right now. "We've only got one edge. You and I know what's going on, but they don't know that we know."

But how could they use that single advantage? Karl and Wohtansen couldn't take on the slavers all by themselves. "You swim to shore, and quietly warn my people, *only* my people. Tell Ahira to get into the treeline with his crossbow; have Chak take Tennetty and Rahff, and hide themselves along the path to the village."

"But the Eriksens—"

Karl shook his head. "If we let them know, they'll sound the alarm. All that would do is turn this into a standard raid, with Clan Erik taking to the hills, and the slavers scooping up a few dozen stragglers. We've got to stop them; that wouldn't do it."

The Pandathaway wizard, he was the key; Karl would have to take the wizard out. "Just keep quiet until you hear from me. If you raise a fuss, all you'll do is bring their wizard down on your head. Now, *move.*"

"But you can't take on the wizard, not by yourself. You don't have a chance."

"I won't be by myself. Get going."

Wohtansen ran toward the tunnel that led to the entrance pool.

Karl didn't wait for the splash; he turned and sprinted toward the cavern of the sword.

He seated himself tailor-fashion on the cold stone. "Deighton, can you hear me?"

No answer.

"I know you put this sword here for a purpose."

Still no answer. Nothing. Held firmly by the fingers of light, the sword hung silently in the air. "Arta Myrdhyn, talk to me. *Say something.*"

Nothing.

He stood and walked over to the rough stone altar and gently laid his hand on the sword's hilt. As though he were holding a baby's arm, he pulled on the sword, as gently as he could.

It didn't move.

He pulled harder, harder; the light brightened, the sword vibrated.

Karl loosened his grip. Force wasn't the answer. Reason had to be.

Why would Arta Myrdhyn create or procure a sword that rendered its user immune to magical spells? What was such a sword good for? The answer was obvious: It was good for killing wizards. That was Arta Myrdhyn's intention.

Not all wizards, of course. Myrdhyn wouldn't go to all that trouble to wipe out his own kind; he wanted a specific wizard killed.

So. The sword had been left here for a purpose, and that purpose was for the right person to take it, to use to kill an enemy of Deighton's. That made sense.

But why would a wizard as powerful as Arta Myrdhyn need to do this in such a roundabout way? Why not just kill the wizard himself?

There was only one answer: Deighton wasn't sure that he could win, not in a fair fight.

Unsummoned, a vision of the Waste welled up. It had been lush green forest, until a battle between two wizards had scarred the land forever.

And the Shattered Islands lay across the northern part of the Cirric. Legend had it that they once were one island, one kingdom. But the name of that island had been lost.

Lost? That didn't make sense. There were records of *everything* in the Great Library of Pandathaway; knowledge couldn't be lost as long as the library stood. Unless . . .

Unless the name had been excised. Not just from paper, but from minds. And who could do that better than the grandmaster of Wizards' Guild?

Hypothesis: Deighton fought the grandmaster; their battle created the waste and shattered the island.

And while Deighton wasn't killed, he had lost, and had either created or found the sword, brought some Vikings across to guard it, then fled to the Other Side.

And, eventually, brought us across.

That had to be connected. If this was truly part of his battle with the grandmaster, Karl and the rest being sent across had to be some sort of attack on his enemy.

Then why hadn't Karl been able to take the sword? If all that was true, then the sword should have practically jumped into his hand. All it had done was move a little.

Then I can't take the sword because, for some reason, I'm not the one who is supposed to kill the grandmaster. But I am somehow connected with the right one, or the sword wouldn't have twitched.

No! Deighton hadn't sent them across until the night Andy-Andy joined the group. That was what triggered it. "Connected with? As in 'the father of' ?"

He rested his hand on the sword's hilt. "And if I were to agree to take this for the purpose of bringing it back to the valley, giving it to my son when he's ready—"

Black shapes flickered across the silvery blade, forming themselves into thick black letters.

Take Me.

Karl blinked. The letters were gone.

The ghostly fingers faded, then vanished; the sword clanged on the stone.

Quickly, he stopped to pick it up; the steel was blank, unmarred.

"Okay, Deighton, you've got yourself a deal." *There's going to be an accounting between you and me, one of these days.*

But, in the meantime, I'd damn well better work out how I'm going to use this.

CHAPTER SIXTEEN

Blood Price

*The world breaks everyone and afterward many are strong
at the broken places. But those it cannot break it kills. It
kills the very good and the very gentle and the very brave
impartially. If you are none of these you can be sure that it
will kill you, but there will be no special hurry.*

—Ernest Hemingway

Keeping all of himself except his eyes and nose below the waterline, Karl clung with both hands to a half-submerged boulder.

The sword, wrapped tightly in a blanket from the cavern, was
slung across his back with two strips Karl had torn from another
blanket.

Hiding in shadow, he kept motionless as the *Warthog* passed, no
more than two hundred feet away. At the bow, the boy who looked
like Ohlmin stood next to Ganness, one arm around the captain's
shoulders in false comradery, the other resting on a scabbarded dagger.

All over the ship, thirty, possibly forty strangers worked in sailcloth tunics, never straying far from their swords and bows.

So, that's the way they're playing it. All of Ganness' crew had been
replaced by slavers. Probably the crew was chained below. More
likely, they were held captive in the slavers' own ship. Or, conceivably, they were dead.

With excruciating slowness, the *Warthog* passed the island. There was no lookout at the stern; Karl pushed off the boulder and swam after the ship, struggling against the weight of the sword to keep his head above water.

The ship slowed still further; its huge jib luffed, flapping in the wind, while crewmen doused the mainsail. But they didn't bring the ship about or drop the anchor; the *Warthog* drifted in toward the sandy shore.

So that was the plan: The slavers would ground the ship just as though this were a normal trading session. Then wait until enough of the men of Clan Erik came down to the beach to load the cargo, charge shoreward through the shallow water, and attack the unprepared Mel.

Let's see if I can put a few holes in that plan.

It would have been nice to have Walter Slovotsky around; Walter could have figured out some way to get aboard without alerting anyone, then taken out half the slavers before anyone realized there was an intruder among them.

Hell, Walter would probably have been able to steal all their pouches, file their swords down to blunt harmlessness, then tie all the slavers' sandal laces together without being spotted.

Karl would have to confront all of them, take out the wizard quickly, then do his best to hold on until help arrived.

And that just plain sucks. Too much had to go right. It would work just fine, *if* Karl could take out the slavers' wizard quickly, *if* he wasn't too tired to hold off a score of slavers, *if* the Eriksens arrived quickly enough.

Too damn many ifs.

He gave a mental shrug. *I'm not Walter Slovotsky, but let's see if I can do a bit of Walter-style recon.*

He reached the stern of the *Warthog* and clung desperately to the massive rudder, his breath coming in gasps. His back and thighs ached terribly; the tendons in his shoulder felt like hot wires. Swimming with the sword on his back had taken more out of him than he had thought.

The rudder was slippery, overgrown with some sort of slimy green fungus. The ship's railing and deck loomed a full ten feet over his head. It might as well have been a mile. There was nothing to grip; even rested, he wouldn't be able to pull himself up by his fingernails.

But halfway up the blunt stern was Ganness' cabin. In the *Warthog*'s long-ago better days, the captain's cabin had been a light, airy place, the light and air provided by a large sliding porthole made up of glass squares. Or was it a window? Didn't something have to be round to be called a porthole?

The glass had long since broken, and the window was covered by boards, but the window sash might still slide, if he could get a grip on it without stabbing himself on the points of the rusted nails that held the boards in place.

Panting from the exertion, Karl pulled himself up onto the rudder and rose shakily to his feet, balancing precariously, his hands resting on the splintered wood of the windowsill.

He tried to slide the boarded-up window to one side.

It didn't move. Years and years of the wood swelling and contracting in the hot sun and cool spray had welded the window in place.

If he pushed harder, he'd likely lose his footing and splash back into the water. Either that, or his hands would slip and open themselves up on the nails.

The nails—of course! His balance growing even more hazardous, he reached over his shoulder and unslung the sword, then unwrapped it, dropping the blanket and strips of cloth into the water. He held the sword hilt-up.

Careful, now. And I'd better pray that there's nobody inside the cabin. Using the pommel like a hammer, he tapped lightly against the point of a nail, flattening it. It didn't make much sound; no one on the *Warthog* would be able to hear it over the whispering of the wind and the quiet murmur of the waves.

His free hand held flat against the wood to dampen the vibration, he hit the flattened nail harder, driving it back through the wood.

The second nail took less time; the third, only a few seconds.

Soon, he pried the board away, dropped it carefully into the cabin, and went to work on the second board. Within a few minutes, he had cleared an opening large enough to accommodate his head and shoulders.

The slavers were using the cabin as a storeroom; it was piled high with muslin sacks, rough wool blankets, cases of winebottles, and chains.

Karl slid the sword into the cabin and followed it in.

For a moment, he lay gasping on the floor. *No time. Can't afford this.* He rose to his hands and knees, then crawled to the cabin's door, putting his ear to the rough wood. No sound. Good; that meant that the slavers were all on deck.

Using a rough blanket to towel himself off, he took a quick look around the room. Over in a corner was his own rucksack. He opened it and drew out his spare sandals and breechclout, quickly donning them before picking up the sword. *I always feel better when I'm dressed, and a fight is no time to worry about splinters.*

But there was no armor in the room. That was bad; tired as he was, he could easily miss a parry. This was one time that he would have liked to have his boiled-leather armor, no matter how uncomfortable it was over bare skin.

As he moved again toward the door, a familiar-looking brass bottle under a bunk caught his eye. Propping the sword against the bunk, he stooped to examine the bottle, and found that there were eight other, similar ones, all marked with the sign of the Healing Hand.

Healing draughts. Thank God. He uncorked a bottle and drank deeply, then splashed the rest of the bottle on his face and shoulders. The sweet, cool liquid washed away his muscle aches and exhaustion as though they never had been.

Reclaiming the sword, he straightened. *Good. My chances of getting out of this alive have just gone way up.* He tucked another bottle of healing draughts under his arm. It might come in handy.

Next to the stacked bottles of healing draughts were five other brass bottles. These were plain, unengraved.

He unstoppered one and sniffed. Lamp oil. Not necessarily any use, but—

I'm still stalling, he thought, suddenly aware that the dampness on his palms hadn't been caused by either the splashed healing draughts or the water of the Cirric. *I'd better get to it.*

Both of them standing aft of the forward mast, Ahrmin smiled genially at Thyren. The wizard looked silly in a sailcloth tunic, but Ahrmin wasn't about to tell him that.

"Have you spotted their wizard yet?" Ahrmin asked, as he stooped to check Ganness' bonds and gag, then rolled the captain through the open hatch, enjoying the thump and muffled groan as Ganness landed in the hold.

Thyren smirked. "Wizards."

"Wizards?"

Thyren closed his eyes. His forehead furrowed. "There's one on the beach." He opened his eyes. "And another, some distance away, beyond the treeline."

"Are you sure?"

"Yes. My inner sight sees their glow." He raised a palm. "But they can't see me; my own glow is damped. They won't be able to see it until it's too late. I *have* done this before, you know."

"Good." Ahrmin turned to glare at Lensius and Fihka. Lensius was fondling a hooknet, while Fihka had taken his bolas from the rack beneath the mainmast. "Put those *down,*" he hissed. "We don't show any weapons until we're ready."

"And when will that be?" Lensius muttered.

"When enough of them gather on the beach." A simple plan, but a good one: The crossbows would kill twenty or thirty of the Mel men, cutting the locals' ability to defend themselves down to almost nothing. That, and the element of surprise, would make it easy to gather up scores of women and children.

The nice part of it was that once Thyren had killed the Mel wizards and Ahrmin's men had gotten down to work, Ahrmin would be able to take Thyren and a few others out in search of Karl Cullinane, leaving the rest of his men to the boring task of chasing down the Mel.

Thyren waved a hand at Ahrmin's pouch. "Best to see where Cullinane is."

Ahrmin shrugged. The last sighting he had taken, before they had steered around the tiny island, had shown that Cullinane was in the direction of the Mel village. Since he wasn't on the beach, he was probably up at the village.

Resting comfortably, I hope. It will be the last time you will ever be comfortable, Karl Cullinane. I've put away four bottles of healing draughts, so that I can keep you alive on our trip back to Pandathaway, while I amuse myself with you. I have to deliver you unmarked to Wenthall, but that doesn't mean I can't spend hours cutting you open, then healing you up.

"Take a sighting," Thyren repeated. "If he's within range, I'll put him to sleep before I deal with the Mel wizards. That way, he won't have the chance to run."

Ahrmin sneered. "Run? And abandon his friends? Leave slavers alive behind him?" He turned to Lensius. "Now, if you please."

Lensius smiled, and beckoned to the milling throng on deck. With merry whoops, all except five of the slavers vaulted over the side and charged toward the beach.

Thyren caught Ahrmin's arm. *"Take a sighting."*

Ahrmin shrugged and reached for his pouch. "Since you insist

. . ." He pulled the glass sphere from his pouch and unwrapped the soft leathers that covered it. "Although we don't have to—"

His breath caught in his throat. Bobbing in the yellow oil, the dismembered finger pointed straight down.

"Ganness!" Karl hissed, pulling the other away from the light streaming down through the hatch. When both of them were safely in shadow, Karl shook the captain's shoulder with one hand while he wielded the sword with the other, slicing through the ropes that tied Ganness' hands behind his back.

His face ashen, Ganness shook his head. His eyes cleared. "Cullinane, they want you."

"Shh. Drink this." Karl unstoppered the bottle of healing draughts, then forced the mouth of the bottle between Ganness' lips. Immediately, color started to return to Ganness' face. "You'd better get out of here. Things are going to get very nasty in just—"

"Greetings, Karl Cullinane." A familiar face leaned out over the edge of the hatch. "Please don't move a muscle." Four crossbowmen looked down at him, their bows cocked, the bolts pointing directly toward his heart. "I've been waiting to meet you. If you'll be kind enough to stay where you are, I'll be down in a moment."

There was no doubt in Karl's mind that Ahira was right: The face was Ohlmin's, only younger, smoother. Perhaps the eyes were a bit sharper, maybe the smile was a trifle more cruel, but that was all.

Another man joined the five above. "Don't be foolish. Let me put him to sleep. Then you can chain him at your leisure."

The boy shrugged. "Very well."

The other raised his hands and began to mutter harsh words that were forgotten as soon as they were heard.

Ganness' eyes sagged shut, but Karl only felt a momentary faintness.

He held the sword tighter, while the wizard paled.

"It's not working," the wizard shrilled. "Something's interfering with—"

Karl didn't wait for the wizard to finish; he dove for the companionway, bolts thudding into the deck behind him. He ducked through a door, and looked around, while feet pounded on the deck above him.

There was no way out. They would have the aft hatch covered before he could get to it.

The captain's cabin, the way I came in. He ran to the cabin, slammed the door behind him, and threw the bolt.

On the other side of the door, voices shouted, feet thudded. *I can dive out through there, and*—no. If the slavers' wizard hadn't already taken out Wohtansen, he would be doing that at any moment. There just wasn't time to get off the ship and then warn Wohtansen to get away.

I'll have to take them out quickly, then get to the wizard. It's either that or make them come to me. His eye fell on the bottles of lamp oil next to the healing draughts.

I've got to try it. As hard blows shook the door, he uncorked all except one of the bottles of oil, then slathered their contents around the room, soaking himself with the lamp oil in the process. He lunged for his knapsack, jerked it open, then extracted a piece of flint before dropping the knapsack and opening a bottle of healing draughts.

The pounding grew louder.

Another few seconds and they'll be inside. A quick, hefty swig of the sweet liquid for luck, then he poured the rest of the bottle over his head, careful to keep both sword and flint dry. He made sure that the healing draughts covered him from head to toe, then tossed the empty bottle aside before opening another, putting it to his lips, and draining it.

He uncorked the last bottle of lamp oil and held it in his left hand. A quick thrust to the oil-wetted wood stuck the sword into the wall beside the door. He coated most of the sword with the oil, then dropped the empty bottle to the floor.

He retrieved another bottle of healing draughts, and waited, while the slavers pounded against the door.

The wood held solid, but the bolt began to give, protesting the punishment with the squeal of metal strained beyond its limits.

As the door crashed inward, Karl took a deep breath and stroked the flint along the sword's length.

One spark caught the oil.

The cabin burst into flame.

Fire seared him; his skin crackled in the flames, the pain taking his breath away. But he healed instantly, only to be burned again.

The fire burned brighter, hotter. As the flames seared his eyeballs, Karl screamed, jamming his eyelids shut.

He smashed a bearded face with the bottle of healing draughts, then jerked the sword from the wall and swung one-handed, slicing through a slaver's neck.

A lancing pain shot through his belly accompanied by the cool slickness of a steel blade; Karl fell back, batting the blade away. He switched grips and threw the sword like a javelin, driving it into a slaver's chest to its brass quillons.

Another hand fastened on his bottle of healing draughts.

No. The bottle was Karl's only chance to come out of this alive. He bit the other's hand, his teeth rending muscle and tendons, a rush of salty blood filling his mouth.

The pain stopped as his wound healed, but the fire still roared, still burned him. Karl reached out with his free hand and caught hold of a slaver's ear. While the slaver screamed, Karl brought his hand down and his knee up, the man's face shattering against his knee like a bagful of eggs.

Screams still filled his ears, but now they were only his screams. Karl staggered through the shattered door and into the companionway beyond, his whole body on fire.

His right hand fumbled at the bottle's cork, but he couldn't control his fingers. He brought the cork to his mouth, clamped his teeth on it, and jerked it loose.

As he drank the sweet healing draughts, he inhaled some of the fluid. Doubled over in a coughing spasm, he splashed the healing draughts over his body, making sure to get some into his eyes.

The pain receded. He opened his eyes. At first, his vision was cloudy; it was as if he had opened his eyes underwater.

Then his vision cleared. He poured some of the healing draughts onto the smoldering spots of his breechclout, feeling the burns on his thighs and buttocks subside.

The pain was gone. Tossing the empty bottle aside, he let out his breath, then sucked in sweet, fresh air. Behind him, the fire was spreading beyond the cabin. Through the wall of flame he could see unmoving bodies, scattered across the room, crackling in the flame.

Beside him in the companionway, a dead slaver set against a bulkhead, propped up by the sword stuck through his chest, unseeing eyes staring up as Karl jerked the sword from the body.

The stench of burning flesh filled his nostrils. He gagged, stumbling back through the companionway.

Ganness lay unmoving on the deck.

"Ganness." Karl slapped Ganness' face lightly, then harder. *"Wake up."*

Ganness' eyelids fluttered, then snapped open. He grabbed at Karl's arm.

"Ganness, the ship's burning. Get over the side. Quickly, now."

"My ship—"

"Your life—move." Karl jerked Ganness to his feet, then pushed him toward the companionway. "Get out through the rear hatch; I've got to get to the wizard."

Karl ran to the forward ladder, then climbed it, his feet touching every other rung. He broke through into daylight.

On the beach, a battle raged.

No time for this. Where's—

At the bow of the *Warthog,* the wizard stood, wind whipping through his hair, rippling his tunic, as he raised his hands over his head, murmuring words that Karl couldn't make out.

Lightning crackled from the wizard's fingers, the sunbright bolts shooting shoreward.

"Wizard! Try me!"

The wizard turned, his sweaty face going ashen as his eyes widened. "Karl Cullinane. *Wait."* He raised his hands. "Please don't. We can talk—"

Karl took a step forward.

The wizard murmured another spell. Again, lightning crackled from his fingertips, streaking across the few feet that separated Karl and the wizard.

Inches from Karl's chest, the lightning shattered into a stream of sparks that flowed around him, never touching him.

Karl took another step.

"The *sword*—it's the sword of Arta Myrdhyn."

"A sword made to kill wizards."

And another step.

Again, the wizard threw up his hands. *"Wait.* I surrender to you. There's much I can do for you, Karl Cullinane, much I can tell you. Wait, please."

Karl stopped three feet away and lowered the point of the sword.

The wizard relaxed momentarily, a relieved smile spreading across his face.

Karl returned the smile, then slashed. Once.

The smile was still on both of their faces as the wizard's head rolled across the deck and splashed overboard, leaving his body behind to twitch in a pool of blood for a moment, and then lie still.

On the beach, the battle stopped. Slavers and Mel alike staggered, then dropped to their knees, and to their bellies, unconscious.

Except for one man. Seigar Wohtansen stood at the waterline and lowered his arms. The sand around him was dotted with smoldering black patches.

He sprinted across the sand to the nearest Mel man and kicked him awake, holding a hand across the man's mouth to prevent him from crying out. "Quickly, before they wake." Roughly, the Mel woke another of his fellows, and then another, until all the Mel men stood among the sleeping bodies of the slavers.

And slowly, cold-bloodedly, they picked up swords and knives, cutting the slavers' throats as they slept.

Karl shuddered, but the roar of the fire behind him suggested that the *Warthog* wasn't the place to be right now; he levered himself over the side and dropped into the water, wading toward shore.

As he reached the beach, Wohtansen ran up. "This way—some got by us. Going up toward the village."

They ran up the path, under the overhanging branches. "Just put them all to sleep," Karl said, panting as he ran.

Wohtansen shook his head. "Can't. All out of . . . spells."

Scattered across the trail ahead, the pieces of several dead slavers lay, already covered with a blanket of flies. Karl nodded to himself as he leaped over a part of a leg. Looked like Ahira's handiwork; nothing but a battleaxe could dismember someone so thoroughly.

That boded well.

A break in the trees loomed ahead. Through it, Karl could see the tops of Mel lodges.

Karl picked up the pace, leaving Wohtansen behind.

The lodges of the village were set in a wide circle, surrounding a grassy common area, cleared patches with grids and stones for cooking fires on the near side, water vats on the far side.

Thirty or forty bodies littered the green. Slavers and Mel men, women, and children lay across the grass, some dead, some moaning from their wounds.

But the battle wasn't over. Tennetty parried a slaver's thrust, then lunged in perfect extension, spitting him on her sword. She jerked the sword out and turned to help Chak with his opponent.

A few yards away from Tennetty and Chak, Ahira ducked under his enemy's swing, then swung his battleaxe. The axe didn't slow as it cut through the slaver's torso.

But Rahff was in trouble. Karl ran toward the boy, hoping he'd make it in time, knowing that he wouldn't.

Rahff stood between Aeia and a tall, long-haired swordsman. The boy's bloody left arm hung uselessly; a long, bloody gash ran from elbow to shoulder.

The swordsman beat Rahff's blade aside and slashed.

Rahff screamed. His belly opened like an overripe fruit.

Karl was only a few yards away; he dropped the sword and leaped, his arms outstretched.

As the slaver pulled back his sword for a final thrust, Karl landed on him, bowling him over. Before the slaver could bring his sword into play, Karl grabbed the man's head and twisted, neckbones snapping like pencils.

He pounded the slaver's face with his fists, not knowing if the man was already dead, not caring.

"Karl." The dwarf's face was inches away from his. Ahira gripped Karl's hands. "Rahff's *alive*. He needs help."

Karl turned. The boy lay sprawled on the grass, his head cradled on Aeia's lap, his hands clawing at his wounds, trying to hold his belly closed.

"Tennetty," Karl snapped. "Find my horse—healing draughts in the saddlebags."

"On my way," she called back, her voice already fading in the distance.

Rahff's arm was badly gashed; a long, deep cut ran from the elbow almost to the shoulder. His whole left side and much of the ground underneath it was soaked with dark blood.

Rahff smiled weakly, trying to raise his head. "Karl, you're alive," he said, his voice weak. "I told them you would be."

"Shh. Just lie there." Karl ripped a strip of cloth from his breechclout and slipped it around the upper part of Rahff's left arm. He tied a quick slipknot, then pulled it as tight as he could. That would keep him from bleeding to death from that wound. But what about the belly?

There was nothing he could do. Direct pressure would just spread the boy's intestines all over the meadow; there was no way to clamp all the bleeding veins and arteries shut.

Just a few minutes. That's all he needs. Just a few minutes. Tennetty would be back with the healing draughts and then—

"Chak, Wohtansen's somewhere around. He should know where the Eriksens keep their healing draughts."

Without a word, Chak ran off.

Rahff coughed; a blood-flecked foam spewed from his lips. "Aeia's fine, Karl. I took care of her. Just as you said we were supposed to."

"Shut up, apprentice." Karl forced a smile to his face. "If you'll just keep still for a moment, Tennetty or Chak will be back with a bottle, and we'll fix you right up."

"I did right, didn't I? She's fine, isn't she?" He looked up at Karl as though Aeia weren't there.

"She's just fine, Rahff. Shh."

Ahira laid a hand on Karl's shoulder. "The boy was overmatched. That slaver went for Aeia, and Rahff couldn't wait for me to finish off mine."

"How the *hell* did they get by you?" Karl snarled. "I told Wohtansen to tell you to hide on the path."

Ahira shrugged. "Just too many of them. Six of them engaged Chak, Tennetty, and me, while the others ran past. By the time we killed ours off and got up to the village . . ." He shook his head. "They went crazy, Karl. Most of them didn't bother trying to capture anyone, they just started hacking. Mainly trying to wound the Mel, it seemed. I guess they figured we'd be so busy treating the injured that we wouldn't have time to chase after them. A lot of them got away, Karl. After they had their fill of killing."

Their fill of killing. They're going to learn what a fill of killing is. "Just take it easy, Rahff. Just another moment or two."

Rahff's hand gripped Karl's. "I'm not going to die, am I?"

" 'Course not." *Hurry up, Tennetty, Chak. Hurry. He doesn't have much time.* "Ahira, find the Eriksen wizard. Maybe he knows—"

The dwarf shook his head. "Pile of cinders; the slavers' wizard got a flame spell through to him."

Rahff's breathing was becoming more shallow. Karl laid a finger on the boy's good wrist. His pulse was rapid, thready.

Come on, *Tennetty.*

At a cry of pain, Karl looked up. Coming around from behind a hut, Chak ran toward him, an uncorked brass bottle cradled in his arms.

White-lipped, he knelt beside Karl, pouring the liquid into the boy's open belly.

The healing draughts pooled amid the blood and the gore.

It's not working. Karl slipped a hand behind Rahff's head, prying the jaw open with his other hand so Chak could pour healing draughts into the boy's mouth.

It puddled in Rahff's mouth. The overflow ran down the boy's cheek and onto Aeia's lap.

Chak lowered the bottle. "He's dead, Karl. It won't do him any good."

"Keep pouring." Gripping Rahff's arm tightly, Karl couldn't feel a pulse. He slipped a finger to the boy's throat.

Nothing.

Karl spread the fingers of his left hand across Rahff's chest, and pounded the back of that hand with his fist, all the while cursing himself for never having taken a CPR course.

Live, damn you, live. "I said to keep pouring. Drip some on his arm." He put his mouth over the boy's, pinched Rahff's nostrils with his left hand, and breathed in. And again, and again, and again . . .

He became aware that Ahira was shaking him. "Let him go, Karl. Let him go. He's dead." The dwarf gathered Karl's hands in his and pulled him away.

The boy's head fell back, limp. Glazed, vacant eyes stared blankly up at Karl. Slowly, Chak knelt down and closed Rahff's eyes.

A drop fell on Rahff's face, then another. Aeia wept soundlessly, her tears running down her cheeks and falling onto Rahff.

Karl rose and led Aeia away from the body. At Chak's low moan, he noticed for the first time that the little man was clutching the side of his waist. A bloodstain the size of a dinner plate spread out across Chak's sarong.

"Drink some," Karl said quietly, motioning toward the bottle. "Then give the rest to the wounded. And give them whatever Tennetty comes back with, if it's needed."

"Fine." Chak raised the bottle to his lips, then poured some of the healing draughts into his own wound.

The wound closed immediately. Visibly getting stronger, Chak gripped his falchion. "Can I kill Wohtansen, or do you want to?"

Karl jerked around. *"What?"*

"I'd better show you. Take that sword. You'll be wanting it."

Karl walked over to where the sword lay and stooped to pick it up. "Aeia, go find Tennetty."

"No. I want to stay with you." She clung to him, her tears wet against his side. "But what about Rahff?"

Ahira sighed. "I'll take care of him."

"There's . . . no rush, Aeia." He blinked back the tears. "It doesn't hurt him anymore." He turned to Chak. "Take me to Wohtansen."

Behind a hut, Wohtansen was ministering to a wounded woman, pouring healing draughts down her throat and into a deep gash in her belly.

"Tell me," Karl said.

Chak spat. "He found *two* bottles of the stuff, but he couldn't be bothered to bring one for Rahff. I had to pry it from his fingers."

Karl stood over Wohtansen and spoke quietly. "Stand up, you bastard."

Wohtansen didn't glance up. "I'll speak to you in a moment."

Karl reached out a hand and lifted Wohtansen by the hair, dropping the sword so that he could slap the Mel's face with his free hand.

In the back of his mind he realized that hitting a clan wizard and war leader might possibly trigger an attack by the remaining Mel; certainly it would make Karl *persona non grata* throughout Melawei.

But he didn't care.

"Why didn't you bring it over there? We could have saved him," he shouted, punctuating every word with a slap. "Why didn't you—" He caught himself, letting Wohtansen's limp form drop to the ground.

Chak felt at Wohtansen's neck. "He's still alive." Laying the edge of his blade against the Mel's neck, he looked up at Karl. "Should I fix that?"

"You leave him alone!" The Mel woman shrilled up at Karl. "That boy was a stranger. Not one of ours."

Aeia launched herself at the woman, pounding her little fists into the woman's face until Karl pulled her off. "Come on, Aeia, let's go."

They gathered on the beach, half a mile away from the sands where the bodies lay. Off in the distance, the *Warthog* still burned, sending sparks and cinders shooting hundreds of feet into the night sky.

A few yards from where they sat, Rahff's body lay, wrapped in a blanket.

I won't have him buried in Melawei soil. I won't have his body polluted that way. Rahff would be buried in the Cirric. Not here.

Karl looked from face to face. All were grim, although Tennetty's expression was a mix of satisfaction and frustration. Karl could understand the first; after all, she'd gotten her quota of slavers. But the frustration?

"Tennetty? What is it?"

She shook her head, her straight hair whipping around her face. "I can't find him. The one that killed Fialt. I've looked at all the bodies, but . . ." She pounded her fist on the sand. "He got *away*."

"No, he didn't." Karl waved a hand at the burning wreck. "The one who killed Fialt was the leader, right? Black hair, thin smile—"

In light from the burning ship, a smile flickered across her sweat-shiny face. "You killed him?"

"Yes. He and some of his friends trapped me in Ganness' cabin. So they thought."

She looked at him for a long moment, her face blank, unreadable. Then: "Thank you, Karl." She gripped his hand in both of hers for just a moment, then dropped his hand and turned away. She walked a few yards, then stopped, watching the burning wreck.

Aeia stared down at a spot in front of her, picking up sand and letting it dribble through her fingers. Soundlessly, she rose, walked over to the pile of driftwood where Carrot and Pirate stood hitched, and stroked Carrot's face. The horse snorted, then nuzzled her.

Karl walked over and stood beside her. "You're going to miss Carrot, eh?"

"No." Carrot, lowered her head. Aeia put her cheek against the horse's neck. "I can't. I can't stay here."

He stroked her shoulder. "They didn't understand about Rahff. They didn't know he was your friend." His words sounded false, even in his own ears. But he couldn't try to push her into leaving home.

"No. They just didn't *care*. I . . ." her voice trailed off into sobs. Aeia turned and threw her arms around Karl, burying her face against him. Tears wet his side.

"Go talk it over with your parents, with your people. If you want to come with us, you can." He ran his fingers through her hair. "You know that."

"No. I won't talk with them. They let Rahff die. I want to go with you."

"Think it over."

"But—"

He pried her arms away. "Just think it over." He turned and walked back to the others.

Ganness sprawled on the sand, visibly relieved to be alive. In a while, he'd once again start regretting the loss of his ship. But it wouldn't hurt him as much as losing the *Ganness' Pride* had.

Chak had been through all this before. Just another day in the life of a soldier of fortune.

Sure.

"Ahira?"

The dwarf looked up at him, not saying a word.

"What the hell do we do?"

Ahira shrugged. "I think it's time we go home. At least for now."

"I know. It's just that I wish . . ."

"But you wish this victory had been bloodless, at least for our side. And you wish that Wohtansen had had as much concern for one of us as for one of his own. And you wish that the world were a fine and simple place, where every problem you can't solve with your head you can solve with one simple blow from your sword. Right?"

Ahira shook his head. "Doesn't work that way, Karl." Ahira pushed the hilt of his battleaxe into the sand and scooped up handfuls to scour the congealed blood from its head. "Just doesn't work that way. You're trying to start a revolution; one that will shake this whole damn world, turn it upside down. Didn't Thoreau say something about revolutions not being hatched in a soft-boiled egg?

"Before we're done, rivers of blood will flow. And not just the blood of slavers, either. A lot of good people are going to die, and die horribly. That's a fact, Karl. Yes?"

Karl nodded. "Yes."

Ahira sat silently for so long that Karl thought the dwarf was finished.

Just as Karl was about to speak, Ahira shook his head. "Karl, what it really comes down to is whether you think the end justifies the means." Ahira chuckled. "Sounds hideous, doesn't it?"

"It does, at that." Still, Ahira was right. The world was not full of nice, clean, easy choices. And wishing that it was would never make it so.

The battleaxe now clean, the dwarf rose to his feet and strapped the axe to his chest.

He flexed his hands, then finger-combed his hair. "You asked where we go from here. I think we take off and walk back toward Clan Wohtan. Ganness says the slavers' ship is there, with only a skeleton guard. We'll take the ship, kill the slavers, and free the Mel and Ganness' crew. Then we can give Ganness the ship—"

"We do owe him a ship."

"Two, actually. We'll have him drop us off as close to the Pandath-away-Metreyll road as he can. We buy a few more horses, and ride back to the valley."

Chak joined them. "Except for losing Rahff, we haven't done too badly here. The wizards lost one of their own; maybe they won't be so eager to send guild members along on slaving raids into Melawei."

To hell with that. Who cares if—He caught himself. So the Mel weren't all nice people. Did that make it okay to clap collars around their necks?

Aeia clutched at his hand. "I'm coming with you. I won't stay here."

Tennetty pulled her away. "Nobody will make you stay here." She patted the hilt of her sword. "I swear it."

"But what do we do about Rahff?" Aeia shrilled.

There wasn't any answer to that. Killing Wohtansen wouldn't change it. Rahff was dead, and he'd stay dead. Like Jason Parker, like Fialt.

And probably like me, before this is all over. He stopped and picked up his own sword, belting it around his waist. He gripped the shark-skin hilt for a moment. It felt good, comfortable, familiar in his hand. "Ganness, you sure that the slavers don't have another wizard with them?"

"Yes." Ganness nodded. "But why do you care? You have the sword."

Karl didn't answer. He lifted the sword of Arta Myrdhyn, holding it with both hands. The bright steel caught the flicker of the *Warthog*'s flames.

Once more, dark shapes moved across the blade, forming sharp letters. **Keep me,** they said.

No.

Karl walked to the edge of the beach, then into the Cirric until the water rose to his knees.

He held the sword over his head, the hilt clenched in both hands. *Okay, Deighton, you've got me to do your dirty work for you. I'll probably die with my blood pouring out of me, as Rahff did.*

"But not my son, Arta Myrdhyn. *Not my son.*"

He swung the sword over his head three times, then threw it with every ounce of strength he had left.

It tumbled end over end through the air; Karl turned back toward the beach, not caring where the sword fell.

Ahira's eyes were wide. "Look at that."

Karl turned back. Ghostly fingers of light reached out of the water and caught the sword, then pulled it underwater. A quick glimmering, and the sword was gone.

For now.

It doesn't matter if you keep the sword here for him. Karl shook his head. *Not my son.* "Okay, people, let's get going. We've got some traveling to do before we reach Clan Wohtan."

Chak nodded. "A couple days' travel, a quick fight, a day or so getting the pirate ship ready for sea, a tenday at sea, and quite a few more tendays' ride, and then we're home."

Tennetty shrugged. "Sounds easy to me."

PART FIVE

Home

CHAPTER SEVENTEEN

Jason

Home is where one starts from. As we grow older
The world becomes stranger, the pattern more
*   complicated*
Of dead and living. Not the intense moment
Isolated, with no before and after,
But a lifetime burning in every moment . . .

—T. S. Eliot

Tennetty kicked Pirate into a canter, coming even with Karl, then slowing her horse down to a walk.

Carrot whinnied, lifting her feet a bit higher as Karl rode her through the tall grasses.

"Easy, Carrot." He patted her neck, then glared at Tennetty. "Don't do that—she likes to be out in front."

She shrugged. It was possible that Tennetty could have cared less about something than she did about what Carrot wanted or didn't want, but only barely. "How long?"

Fine. On this trip, I didn't have Slovotsky asking "Are we there yet?" all the damn time. Instead, I've got Tennetty asking "How long is it going to be?" Three times in the morning, four in the afternoon, twice when we're sitting around the campfire in the evening. I could set my watch by her. If I had a watch.

It had taken a couple of weeks on the newly named *Ganness'*

Revenge to arrive at the little fishing village of Hindeyll, then weeks of travel on the Pandathaway-Metreyll road to get to the Waste, another month to skirt the Waste and cross into the outskirts of Therranj.

Of course, we could have cut out some time if we hadn't jumped those slavers near Wehnest. Backtracking to chase them down must have cost us a week. At least. Not a bad raid, though; it had added a sackful of coin, three horses, and another member to their party.

Peill was a nice addition to the group; Karl had never met anyone with such a talent for tracking as the elf.

He turned to see the tall elf riding next to Ahira's pony, Chak and Aeia on the dwarf's other side, while Ahira continued the English lesson.

Guess this stuff about elves and dwarves not getting along doesn't apply when the dwarf is the one who shatters the elf's chains.

Peill's skills with a longbow could come in handy, particularly if he could teach others to use it. The trouble with the crossbows was that their rate of fire was just too damn low, although they did have the advantage of greater accuracy.

But from ambush, a few good longbowmen might be able to finish off a group of slavers before they even knew that they were under attack.

Then again, it would be hard for a longbowman to conceal himself; a crossbowman could shoot while prone, or from a perch in a tree. . . .

Well, it was something to think about, anyway. Maybe talk over with Chak.

But I can do that later. We're almost home, and we all deserve a vacation.

"I asked you, 'How long?' " Tennetty glared at him. "If you're going deaf, you can damn well count me out of the next trip."

Perhaps twenty miles across the plain, the ground sloped upward into an area of blackened, burned ground. Beyond that, the valley lay.

"I figure we'll get there sometime tomorrow."

It was almost over. For now. But only for now.

Karl sighed. *I'm never going to be done with blood. Not until the day I die.*

Then again, if you don't learn to keep your eyes open while you're feeling sorry for yourself, that could be anytime now.

"Ellegon!" He scanned the sky. Nothing but clouds, and a few birds to the east. *Where are you?*

Try behind you.

Karl turned in the saddle; above and behind him, a familiar shape dropped out of the blue sky.

I usually come this way on the returning leg of my patrol, the dragon said.

Both Carrot and Pirate snorted and held their ground as the dragon landed; the other horses galloped away in different directions, their riders vainly trying to control the animals' panic.

Tennetty swore as she struggled with Pirate's reins. "Easy, now. Easy, damn you. The idiot dragon's just trying to scare you, not eat you."

Good to see you too, Tennetty.

"Try giving a little warning next time."

"Cut the crap, both of you," Karl snapped. "Ellegon, how is Andy-Andy? And the baby?"

A gout of fire roared into the sky. *Took you long enough to ask.*

Don't play games with me, Ellegon.

Both your wife and son are fine.

My son. Karl shook his head. *If ever anyone wished for a daughter* . . . "You stay away from my son, Deighton," he whispered. "Just leave him alone."

Across the plain, Aeia and Chak had reined their horses down to a canter, while Ahira's and Peill's mounts still galloped away.

"Just as well," Tennetty said. "Might teach them all something about keeping their animals under control." She patted at Pirate's neck, then held out a hand to Karl. "Give me your reins."

"Huh?"

She jerked a thumb at the dragon. "I think you might be able to persuade Ellegon to give you a ride the rest of the way home. I'll gather the others together and bring them all in sometime tomorrow."

It was tempting, but . . . "I'd better stay." The group was Karl's responsibility, until they got home. He could relax then.

Idiot.

"Idiot," Tennetty echoed. She rolled her eyes, looking toward heaven for reassurance. "Ellegon, explain to Karl how his wife would feel about his being gone a day longer than necessary."

Well . . . I don't think Andrea would exactly appreciate it. She's been a bit worried; she was hoping you'd be back by now.

"You sure things are safe around here?"

I was just finishing my patrol, Karl. The dragon pawed at the grass. *Though you could be right, come to think of it. I smell a nest of rabbits somewhere around here; maybe your whole party will get eaten if you're not here to protect them. If it will make you happy, I'll be willing to fly back and baby-sit Ahira and the rest after I drop you off at home.*

"The reins, please." Tennetty snapped her fingers. "Get moving."

He laughed. "You win." He jumped from Carrot's saddle, tossing the reins to Tennetty. "See you tomorrow," he said, climbing up to Ellegon's back.

The dragon's wings began to beat, moving faster and faster until they were only a blur, whipping so much grass and dust into the air that Karl had to close his eyes.

Ellegon leaped skyward. *I've got strict instructions about where to set you down,* he said, as the ground dropped away beneath them.

As they passed over Chak and Aeia, Karl returned their waves. *Ellegon?*

Be quiet for a while; I'm going to put on some speed. His wings began to work even faster, the wind drawing tears out of Karl's eyes.

Karl put his head to the dragon's rough hide and held on.

Almost home. The rush of wind slowed.

Karl raised his head. They were flying over what had been a burned rise leading to the valley. It had become even more green; soon, the evidence that a fire had once burned would be gone.

The valley spread out below. When Karl had left, the encampment had been one wooden wall, a stone fireplace, and two wagons.

There had been some changes. More than thirty log cabins spread out along the shore of the lake, several of them with split-rail corrals for horses and cattle.

Children scampered around a wooden dock that jutted out from the shore, pausing momentarily in their play to wave to Ellegon as the dragon passed overhead.

Where there had been only forest, there now were fields, stalks of corn, and seas of wheat waving in the breeze.

The fortifications had been completed; they now enclosed a group of five houses, one with a slow-turning waterwheel. Ellegon dove toward the bare-dirt courtyard, braking with his wings.

Mill?

Yes. Riccetti has done well, no?

No. You've all done well.

Deftly avoiding the network of hollowed half-logs that piped water to the five houses, the dragon landed inside the walls. Karl dismounted.

Welcome home.

To his right, a familiar face peeked out of an open-sided cabin whose chimney puffed smoke into the air. Walter Slovotsky, wearing a leather apron and carrying a smith's hammer, ran into the courtyard, dropping the hammer as he ran.

"Karl." Slovotsky stuck out a hand, drew it back, shaking his head. "To hell with it." He threw his arms around Karl.

"Dammit, you're breaking my back," Karl said, untangling himself.

Slovotsky chuckled. "Fat chance." He turned. *"Kirah!* They're—" He caught himself. "Is everyone—?"

"We lost Fialt, but the rest of us are fine." *Except for Rahff. I wish he'd gotten the chance to—*

Later, Karl, later. Homecoming is supposed to be a happiness.

You know a lot about happiness?

I'm learning, Karl. Walter, take him to her.

Slovotsky led Karl toward a cabin on the far side of the courtyard, talking nonstop as they walked. "I wish we'd known you were getting back today. Lou's taken a party to the far side of the valley. He found a cave full of bats a couple of months ago, and we're finally getting them all cleared out."

"Bats?" Karl removed his hand from the hilt of his sword. "Some sort of trouble?"

"No." Slovotsky laughed. "Just garden-variety fruit bats. They can give you a nasty bite, but Thellaren—he's our cleric—can fix you right up."

"Cleric?"

"Spidersect. Showed up one day, half starved; seems he had some trouble with the Therranji. Does one hell of a business, although Andy and I had to reason with him about rates. The bastard was charging—"

"Then why clear out the bats?"

Slovotsky smiled knowingly. "Think about it. What are bats good at making?"

"Baby bats, and bat sh—" *Of course.* Karl raised a hand. "Never mind. I take it you've found some sulfur, too."

"You got it. No willows around here. But oak seems to work okay."

Take the crystals of saltpeter from underneath any well-aged pile of excrement, add sulfur and powdered charcoal in the right proportions, and *voila!*—gunpowder. Well, it was probably a bit trickier than that, but not much.

Maybe I'm not going to be needing longbows, after all.

"It was Riccetti's idea. He remembered reading that Cortez used bat guano to make gunpowder."

"I didn't know Lou was a historian."

"Only when it comes to making things." Slovotsky nodded. "He's already made some gunpowder—stinks to high heaven when it burns —and I'm working on a flintlock right now."

Slovotsky caught himself as they stopped in front of the cabin's door. "Later; we'll have plenty of time. She's in there, Karl." Slovotsky waved as he jogged off. "I'd better go see Kirah. We've been fattening a calf."

Karl opened the door and walked in.

The cabin was well kept, from the burnished wood of the floor to the ceiling timbers, hung with unlit oil lamps. A beaded curtain covered a doorway on the opposite wall.

On the right-hand wall, a rough table stood beneath a mottled glass window. On the left-hand wall, a pot of stew burbled merrily in the stone fireplace.

Two huge wooden chairs stood side by side in front of the fireplace, both with blankets padding their seats. The arms of one chair were stained with nicks and sweat marks; the other looked new, unused.

He unbuckled his sword and hung it over the back of the newer chair.

"Who is it?" She pushed through the curtain, a wicker basket filled with clothes in her arms. Her eyes grew wide. "Hi."

"Hello."

He wanted to reach out, to run to her, but he couldn't. There was an almost palpable distance between them. The months of separation had changed her, changed both of them.

Worry lines had begun to form around her eyes. Her hair was tangled, matted down. It wasn't just that she looked more than a few months older. Her smile was strained.

He could see her looking at the changes in his face, not sure that she liked what she saw.

There had been a time when Karl took the world lightly, even while he took it seriously. A time when he could push the darkness away, when he could dismiss it, if only for a while, not merely pretend that it didn't exist. There had been a time when Karl had been basically a gentle man, sometimes forced into doing violent things, but always, deep inside, untouched by the violence.

That time was gone. Forever. It could never be the same between them.

The thought cut at him like a knife.

"Andy, I—" He fumbled blindly for the words. For the right words, the ones that would make everything right between them.

He couldn't find them. Maybe they didn't even exist.

"*No,*" she shrilled. She threw the basket aside and ran to him.

As he gathered her into his arms and buried his face in her hair, he knew that he was both right and wrong. Yes, there had been changes. No, things could never be the same.

But they could be better.

After a while, he took a loose sleeve of her robe, wiped first at his own eyes, and then at hers.

She looked up at him, her eyes still tearing, still red. "Karl?"

"Yes?" He ran his fingers through her hair.

"If," she said as she rested her face against his chest, "if you *ever* give me another look like that, I swear I'll hit you. Don't you—"

"Shh."

Stupid humans. Ellegon's massive head peeked through the open door. He snorted, sending ashes from the fireplace swirling around the room.

Karl raised his head. *What is it now?*

You always have to make things more complicated than necessary, don't you?

"What are you getting at?"

Tell her you love her, idiot.

She pushed away from him and smiled. "Yeah. Tell me you love me, idiot." She grabbed his hand. "But later. I've got someone for you to meet."

She pulled him through the beaded curtain and into the bedroom.

Under the murky window, a cradle lay. It was a plain wood box, mounted on two wooden rockers.

He peered inside.

"Don't wake him," she whispered. "It's a pain to get him back to sleep."

The baby, wrapped in a gray cotton diaper, slept peacefully on the soft blankets. Karl reached out a hand and gently touched the child's soft cheek. Still asleep, the baby turned his head to nuzzle Karl's fingers.

Karl pulled his hand back. "He's so . . . small."

"That's *your* opinion." She snorted. "He sure as hell didn't feel that way when I was flat on my back in labor. But he'll grow."

"How old is he?"

"Just under two months." Andy-Andy slipped an arm around Karl's waist. "I named him Jason, after Jason Parker. I hope that's okay; we didn't decide on a name before you left, so . . ."

"The name's fine."

"I did good?"

"Andy, he's beautiful."

He takes after his mother. Fortunately.

CHAPTER EIGHTEEN

The Flickering Candle

. . . the bravest are surely those who have the clearest vision of what is before them, glory and danger alike, and yet notwithstanding go out to meet it.

—Thucydides

Walter Slovotsky walked quietly around the bonfire and tapped him on the shoulder. "Karl, take a walk with me," he said, his voice slurred. He snagged a bottle from one of the merrymakers, bowing an exaggerated apology.

Andy-Andy leaned over and whispered in Karl's ear, "He's drunk again."

"I noticed. Has this been happening a lot?"

"Yes." She nodded. "Ever since Kirah started to show. But I don't think it's just the expectant father jitters. Maybe you should go see what's wrong. I haven't been able to get him to talk about it. Neither has Kirah." She cast a glance across the clearing. "And I'd better go check on the baby."

He chuckled. "Between Ellegon and Aeia, I'm sure he's okay." Ellegon had told him that there were bears and pumas up in the mountains. Probably the animals would continue to avoid the village.

But if they didn't, Ellegon could always fit an odd bear or puma into his diet.

"Still . . ."

"Okay. See you later."

"Not too much later, I hope. Kirah's going to keep Aeia and Jason tonight. No interruptions." Her eyes smiled a promise at him.

Karl rose and followed Walter off into the dark, leaving the bonfire behind them. The welcome-home party was in its twelfth or thirteenth hour, but it hadn't let up. Some of the revelers kept the music going with their flutes and drums; others loitered around the cooking fire, slicing off sizzling pieces of roast calf from the slowly turning spit.

Tennetty, Chak, Peill, and Ahira looked road-weary, having arrived only that morning. Still, the four of them held court, a few dozen meters from the fire, standing in a circle of fifty listeners, taking turns relating the story of Karl Cullinane on the *Warthog*.

Six of the listeners drew Karl's attention. A group of battle-scarred men, they listened raptly, occasionally interrupting Tennetty or Chak to press for more details. Karl had been introduced to them, but had forgotten their names. But he hadn't forgotten the fact that they were former mercenaries, now engaged in the profession of taking on slavers.

Which means, he thought, *that the whole world doesn't rest on my shoulders anymore.*

And it also means I'm becoming a legend, he thought, and smiled. *Probably have more volunteers than I can use, next time.* He sobered. That possibility might have its pluses, but it sure as hell had its minuses.

As they walked, Slovotsky passed him the clay bottle; Karl took another swig of the tannic wine that already had his head spinning.

The fire and sound far enough behind them, Karl seated himself on a projecting root of an old oak, gesturing at Slovotsky to join him. "What's bothering you?"

"Me?" Slovotsky snorted. He tilted back the bottle and drank deeply. "Nothing's bothering me, Karl. Not a damn thing." Slovotsky was silent for a while. Then: "How soon are you planning on going out again?"

"Eager to get rid of me?"

"How about an answer?"

"Mmm, I don't want to leave too soon. Maybe six months or so. I suspect it'll take Pandathaway a while to put another team together. If they don't just write off killing me as a lost cause."

Karl folded his hands behind his head and leaned back against the bulk of the trees. "Besides, I think that the Slavers' Guild is going to be a bit too busy to go looking for me." He closed his eyes. "How many people have we got here?"

"Just over two hundred, as of the last census. Seems to grow every day, practically. But it's not going to get any easier: The size of the slavers' caravans keeps growing. They're running scared, Karl. Which isn't good; I'd rather have them fat and self-satisfied."

Karl shrugged. "So we'll take bigger raiding parties."

If this scheme of Riccetti's to make some rifles panned out, he might not need a much larger team. Granted, the manufacture of cartridges was probably decades away, but even a few flintlocks and blunderbusses would give them a huge edge.

"Think it through, Karl. Think it through."

He opened his eyes to see Slovotsky shaking his head. Karl grabbed his arm. "What the hell is bothering you?"

"Take a look at the silo?"

"No, but what does that have to do with anything?"

"It has to do with *everything*. We're getting a damn fine yield for the acreage. Better than any of the locals have ever seen. And this is just the first real harvest. Wait until next year."

"This is doom?"

"Yup. Free societies . . ." Walter interrupted himself to down the last of the wine. He flipped the bottle end over end, then caught it by the neck, setting it carefully on the ground. "Free societies *produce*. You should see how hard these poor bastards work, once they understand that what they grow or make is theirs."

"Didn't Riccetti say something about taxes?"

"Sure." Slovotsky shrugged. "Two percent of production or income, payable to the town treasurer—that's me, for now. We've been using it to sponsor public works like the mill, pay Riccetti and your wife for running the school, grubstake new arrivals. Matter of fact, I'm going to have to assess what you've brought back. Quite a bit of gold and platinum, no?"

"A bit. Just net, right?" Idly, he wondered what the tax on the sword of Arta Myrdhyn would have been.

"Net. No tax on what you make and spend outside. Only what you bring back, or make here. Keeps things simpler. But can we leave all that for tomorrow?"

"Sure. But would you just come out and tell me what the hell has got you running scared?"

"Running scared is right." Slovotsky snorted. "You still don't see it, do you? Free societies produce more than slave societies. Always have, always will. Right?"

"Right. So?"

"*So,* that means we're going to continue to flourish and grow. *So,* eventually we're going to attract some notice. *So,* when we do, some bright baron or prince or lord is going to work out that we just might overflow this valley and spread out, and eventually, challenge his power." He shook his head. "*So* . . . how long do you think that the slave societies are going to let us get away with it? A year, almost certainly. Five, probably; ten, possibly; twenty, maybe. But not forever, Karl. Not forever."

Dammit, but that made sense. The only reason they had gone unmolested so far was the small size and remote location of their colony.

"*So,*" Walter went on, "we're in a race. We have to grow large enough, strong enough, quick enough, so that we can take on all comers. Or . . ."

"Or? You've got an alternative?"

"Or your kid and mine grow up as orphans. If they're lucky. We're going to have to keep our wives pregnant all the time, rescue and arm as many slaves as we can, and work our butts off to have a chance at winning the race. Any chance at all." Slovotsky smiled in the dark. "Let me ask you again: How soon are you planning on going out again?"

Karl sighed. "Give me ten days." *Dammit.* "I need to spend some time with Andy."

Slovotsky echoed his sigh. "Take twenty. I'd better break in a new treasurer, and I've got some smithing to finish before we go."

"We?"

"We. Slovotsky's Law Number Forty-three: 'Thou shalt put thy money where is thy mouth.'" He rose and held out a hand. "Count me in."

Karl accepted the hand and let Walter pull him to his feet.

"So what do we do now, Karl?"

"We?" Karl shrugged. "*We* don't do anything now. I'm going to let my wife drag me off to our bedroom. You're going to finish getting drunk tonight, because you're going back into training tomorrow." He threw an arm around Slovotsky's shoulder. "And after that . . ." he let his voice trail off. The words escaped him. *Ellegon? Can you hear me?*

No, not at all. Not one—

Please. Give me the words.

No, Karl. You don't need me for that. You already know the words.

But I don't.

Try.

"We . . . survive, Walter. We . . ."

Gentle fingers stroked Karl's mind.

". . . we protect ourselves, our families, our friends, and our own." Fialt had said that, and Fialt was right. But there was something more. "We keep the flame of freedom burning, because that is why we all are here."

"Fair enough."

I told you that you knew the words.

And you're always right, eh?

Of course.

CHAPTER NINETEEN

The Hunter

I am in blood,
Stepped in so far, that, should I wade no more,
Returning were as tedious as go o'er.

—William Shakespeare

He lived like a jackal, sleeping during the day in a hollow under a palm tree, feeding at night at the garbage pits behind the village, always running for cover at the slightest sound.

He never tried for his own kills; anything that could betray his presence had to be avoided. There were just too many of them.

All of his burns and cuts had long since healed, but the scars remained. The bottle of healing draughts he had managed to drink while the fire burned around his bleeding body had kept him alive, although only barely; it had not brought him back to unmarked health.

He waited, feeding and gathering his strength for the hard trip over the mountains. That was the route he would have to take. The sea was closed to him; even were another raiding ship to come this way, they would hardly recognize him as one of their own.

But he always kept his pouch with him.

And every once in a while, Ahrmin would unwrap the glass sphere and watch the dismembered finger floating in the yellowish oil, pointing unerringly to the north and east.

And smile.

THE SILVER CROWN

For Tim Daniels
in memoriam, dammit

Acknowledgments

I'd like to thank Mary Kittredge, Mark J. McGarry, and most particularly Harry F. Leonard, all of whom helped to make this a better book than it otherwise would have been. This is both my fourth book and the fourth time I've thanked all of them in print; that isn't coincidental.

I'd be more than a little remiss if I didn't also thank my agent, Richard Curtis; my editor, Sheila Gilbert, for her advice, support, and patience; my favorite policeman, Officer William T. Badger, NHPD/VSU, for creating the quiet; and Felicia, for the usual—and more.

There is nothing more difficult to take in hand, more perilous to conduct, or more uncertain in its success, than to take the lead in the introduction of a new order of things.

—Niccolò Machiavelli

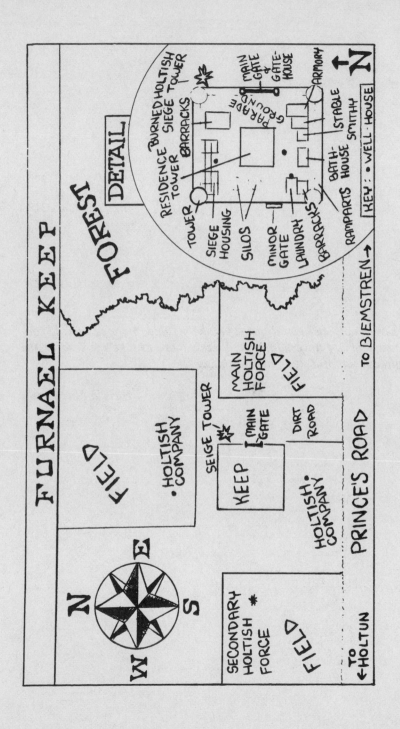

FURNAEL KEEP

DRAMATIS PERSONAE

Ahrmin—master slaver

Fenrius, Danared—journeyman slavers

The Matriarch of the Healing Hand Society

Doria—Hand acolyte

Karl Cullinane—warrior, raiding-team leader

Tennetty, Ch'akresarkandyn ip Katharhdn, Piell ip Yratha—squad leaders in Karl Cullinane's raiding team

Walter Slovotsky—Karl Cullinane's second-in-command; thief, warrior, smartass

Wellem, Erek, Therol, Donidge, Hervean, Firkh, Restius—warriors, members of Karl Cullinane's raiding team

Gwellin, Gerrin, Daherrin—dwarf warriors, members of Karl Cullinane's raiding team

Sternius—master slaver

Jilla, Danni—slaves

Ellegon—a young dragon

Henrad—novice wizard; Andrea's apprentice

Andrea Andropolous Cullinane—wizard, teacher, Karl Cullinane's wife

Jason Cullinane—Karl and Andrea's son

Aeia Eriksen Cullinane—Karl and Andrea's adopted daughter, teacher

Mikyn—freed slave

Alezyn—Mikyn's father

Ahira Bandylegs—Home Mayor

Louis Riccetti—ex-wizard, the Engineer

Ranella, Bast—apprentice Engineers

U'len—cook

Thellaren—Spidersect cleric

Kirah Slovotsky—Walter Slovotsky's wife

Jane Michele Slovotsky—Walter and Kirah's daughter

Ihryk—farmer, houseman

Pendrill—stableman

Werthan—farmer

Anna Major—Werthan's wife

Anna Minor—Werthan and Anna Major's daughter

Afbee—assassin

Nehera—dwarf blacksmith

Daven—warrior, raiding-team leader

Wraveth, Taren—warriors, members of Daven's raiding team

Jherant ip Therranj—elf warrior

Dhara ip Therranj—emissary from Lord Khoral of Therranj

Beralyn, Lady Furnael

Thomen Furnael—heir to barony Furnael

Chton—farmer, leader of Joiner faction

Petros—farmer, of sorts

Harwen, Ternius—farmers

Valeran—guard captain in the service of Lord Gyren of Enkiar

Halvin—Valeran's second-in-command

Norfan—one of Valeran's warriors

Prince Harffen Pirondael—ruler of Bieme

Aveneer—warrior, raiding-team leader

Frandred—Aveneer's second-in-command

Theren, Thermen, Migdal—warriors, members of Aveneer's raiding
  team

Zherr, Baron Furnael

Garavar—a captain of the House Guard

Taren—warrior of the House Guard

Arthur Simpson Deighton/Arta Myrdhyn—lecturer in philosophy,
  master wizard

Introduction

It had long since ceased being a game. Friends didn't really die in a game.

But . . . it had been just a game, years before. Professor Arthur Simpson Deighton was the gamemaster. Karl Cullinane, Jason Parker, James Michael Finnegan, Doria Perlstein, Walter Slovotsky, Andrea Andropolous, and Lou Riccetti had sat down for an evening of fantasy gaming. The game suddenly, without warning, became real: James Michael became Ahira Bandylegs, a powerful dwarf; skinny Karl Cullinane turned into Barak, a massive warrior; Lou Riccetti became Aristobulus, wielder of powerful magicks; Andrea became Lotana, novice wizard.

It had become real, every bit as real as the pain Jason Parker felt in his last moments kicking on the end of a bloody spear, every bit as real as Ahira's fiery death, and his resurrection by the Matriarch of the Healing Hand Society.

But there was a price to be paid for that resurrection: Karl and the others promised to fight to end slavery. They declared war on the Pandathaway-based Slavers' Guild, the dealers in human flesh who traveled across the Eren regions, securing and selling their cargo.

Attacking the slavers was one thing—but what to do with the freed slaves? Some could be sent home, but some had no home to go back to. That was easily solved: They built Home, a new kind of society for the world they found themselves in.

Aeia Eriksen did have a home to go back to, a village in Melawei. While returning her there, Karl discovered evidence that Professor Deighton was actually the almost legendary wizard Arta Myrdhyn, who had left a magical sword in a cave, clutched in fingers of light, waiting.

Waiting for whom? For Karl's son, it seemed; Deighton/Arta Myrdhyn had plans for Karl's son. . . .

Not my son, Karl said. He left the sword of Arta Myrdhyn in Melawei and returned Home, continuing to venture out and attack Slavers' Guild caravans wherever they could be found.

It had long since ceased being a game.

A revolution is never a game; it is, in more senses than one, a bloody mess.

PROLOGUE

Ahrmin

"You may enter, Ahrmin," the acolyte said. She was a slim woman, dressed in the long white robes of the Healing Hand Society. Her long blond hair shimmered in the sunlight as she stared coolly at him out of the yellow-irised eyes set exotically but not unpleasantly far apart in her high-cheekboned face.

Idly, Ahrmin estimated that she was easily worth thirty gold; he could remove that air of superiority within a tenday, perhaps less. Perhaps much less.

She shook her head as though in response to his unvoiced comment. "You, and you alone. The others shall remain outside. It is unpleasant enough to tolerate their presence on the preserve; I will not have their breath fouling the air of the tabernacle itself."

She started to turn away, but spun back as Fenrius growled and started toward her. Fenrius towered menacingly over her slim form, but the huge man froze in place as the acolyte raised her hand, all the while murmuring soft words that Ahrmin could hear clearly, but never recall. As always, he tried to remember them, but he couldn't; they vanished as the sounds touched his ears.

As the spell ended, the cleric gripped the air in front of her; Fenrius' arms flew down to his sides, his leather tunic wrinkling as though he were in the grip of a giant invisible hand. Muscles stood out cordlike on his unshaven cheeks; his mouth worked silently, lips drawn wide in a soundless gasp as sweat beaded on his forehead.

"No," she said, smiling gently, almost affectionately. "Not here.

Here, you are within the grasp of the Hand. In more senses than one." She began to tighten the grip of her straining fingers. Leather squealed in protest; Fenrius' breath whooshed out of his lungs.

His mouth worked frantically, but no sound escaped.

Ahrmin's five other men stood stock-still, Danared shaking his head in sympathy. But even he was not foolish enough to make a move toward the acolyte.

Just as Ahrmin was sure that Fenrius' chest would cave in beneath the pressure, the acolyte stopped, cocking her head to one side, as though listening to a distant voice.

"Yes, Mother," she said, with a deep sigh. She raised her hand and twitched her wrist; Fenrius tumbled end over end through the air, landing on the grass with a thump.

"You may follow me, Ahrmin," she said.

Ahrmin limped after the acolyte down dark corridors to a vast, high-ceilinged hall, the drag-slap of his sandals a counterpoint to her even steps. They walked through a high arch and into the hall, halting in unison before the high-backed throne, as though obeying an unspoken command. Later, he couldn't recall whether the room was crowded or empty; his eyes were drawn to the woman on the throne.

If the acolyte was thin, this woman was positively skeletal. He always remembered the tissue-thin skin on the back of her hands, skin as white as a dead man's, unmarked save for the bulges caused by underlying bones and sinews.

But despite the funereal slimness of her form, she radiated a sense of power as she sat there, her face hidden by the upswept cowl of her faintly glowing white robes.

"Greetings, Ahrmin, son of Ohlmin," she said. *"I have been expecting you."*

Her voice was like nothing he had ever heard. Though she seemed to speak softly, her words rattled his teeth.

"Then you know what I want."

"What you . . . want is obvious," the acolyte hissed. "Karl wrecked your body—he should have killed you. He should have—"

The Matriarch raised a hand. *"Be still, daughter. We shall take no side in this matter."* She turned back to Ahrmin. *"Which is precisely the point. You were injured in combat with Karl Cullinane—"*

"Injured?" He raised a fire-twisted hand. "You call this *injured?*" Had it not been for the bottle of healing draughts he had drunk while the ship burned around him, Ahrmin would have died. As it was, he had never fully recovered from the burns or the long trip over the mountains from Melawei to Ehvenor.

"Yes. Would you not agree?" She gestured, her long fingers twitching spastically as she spoke words that could only be heard and forgotten.

The air to one side of the Matriarch shimmered, solidifying into a mirror.

"Look at yourself," she commanded.

He did, forcing his shoulders back and standing tall.

It wasn't a pretty sight; it was never a pretty sight. The hair on the right side of his head was gone, the skin permanently browned and puckered, save for the few fleshy spots where his trembling hand had splashed enough of the healing potion to restore those patches to normal health.

The left side of his face was normal enough; the fire had only singed him there, and the healing draughts, combined with his body's natural healing ability, had brought that back to normal.

But the right side of his face was a horror. The flames had seared away his ear and most of his lips; it had burned his cheeks down to the bone. While the draughts had healed what remained, their power was not great enough to bring flesh back from ashes.

Surely, the Matriarch was powerful enough to do that; she was said to be able to raise the dead. Surely—

"No." She dismissed the thought and the mirror with a wave of her hand. *"I do not expect that you will understand this, but there are forces involved here that even I would not wish to involve myself with again. I have done so three times. Once, many years ago, to protect the tabernacle and its preserve, and twice again,"* she said, laying a gentle hand on the acolyte's arm, *"for reasons that do not concern you. I will not do so now."*

"But I've brought gold." He waved a hand toward the door. "Sacks of it."

"Gold?" The acolyte sniffed. "Bring a mountain of gold, and we still won't help you. Right now, you wouldn't have a chance against Karl. But if we healed you—"

"I'll hunt the bastard down and kill him. He murdered my father —and did this to me." *I'll hunt him down whether you help me or not,* he thought. *I'll hold his head in my hands.*

The Matriarch folded her thin arms across her chest. *"That is entirely a matter of opinion."* She extended a skinny arm, her sleeve rippling. *"Now, go."*

There was no point in staying. He couldn't fight the Hand, not even if he had the entire guild behind him.

He spun on his heel and limped away. Their words echoed down the marble halls after him.

"We have to help Karl, Mother. Or at least warn him."

"Ahh. Your skills have improved, daughter. You read beyond Ahrmin's surface thoughts?

"Yes—Karl must think he's dead. He doesn't know—"

"Nor can we tell him. Our responsibilities lie elsewhere. And elsewhen. To interfere now, to involve the Hand further at this juncture . . . it would ruin everything. As well you know."

"I do know, but . . . Forgive me, Mother—I was lying. He just might be able to kill Karl, or have him killed. It's—"

"You are forgiven. You are not the first of our order to tell a lie."

"He could kill Karl, if he took him by surprise—"

"I think you perhaps underrate this Karl Cullinane of yours. In any case, my decision stands, daughter."

"But what can we *do?*"

"For now, nothing. We must wait. Waiting is a difficult skill; I commend its practice to you, Doria. . . ."

PART ONE

The Forest of Wehnest

CHAPTER ONE

The Hunter

Out of the darkness of the tent, a hand reached out and gently grasped his shoulder. "Karl, ta ly'veth ta ahd dalazhi." *Karl, it is time to wake up.*

Karl Cullinane came awake instantly. He clamped his left hand around the slim wrist and pulled, slamming the other into the tent pole, almost dislodging it. He brought his right hand around to block a possible knife thrust—

—and stopped himself when he realized who it was.

"Ta havath, Karl." *Easy, Karl.* Tennetty laughed, her breath warm in his ear. She switched from Erendra to her thickly accented English as she pushed away from him, rubbing at her shoulder. "I don't think Andrea would approve. Besides, if you move around much more, you'll bring the tent down around both our heads."

He released her and sighed. He would have preferred Tennetty to be a bit more nervous about waking him, a bit less trusting that he would recognize her before doing something sudden and fatal.

"What is it, Tennetty?" he asked in Erendra. "Is the dragon here?" *Ellegon?* he thought. *Can you hear me?*

No answer.

"Wake *up*, Karl—you're a full day off. He isn't due until tomorrow."

"Slovotsky, then?"

She nodded. "On his way up," Tennetty said, smiling faintly in the dim lanternlight as she untangled herself from his blankets. "Gerrin spotted him—and a small caravan, camped down by the fork."

"Slavers or merchants?"

"He couldn't tell, not from here." She shrugged. "But if they are slavers, it would explain Slovotsky's return." She rose to her knees and took up a piece of straw from his bedding, using it to carry fire from her lantern to his, idly pausing to straighten his tent pole in passing. Tennetty was a slim woman, but not a soft one; beneath her ragged cotton undershirt, strong muscles played.

"I've had my team's horses saddled and ordered a general weapons inspection." She flashed a smile at him, then dropped it. Tennetty seemed to have a permanent sneer, which somehow started with her narrow eyes and continued down her thin, broken nose, all the way to her cracked lips. A scar snaked around her right eye; a black patch covered the remains of the left.

"You take a lot on yourself, don't you?"

"Perhaps." Picking up her lantern, she rose smoothly from her half-crouch and held the tent flap for him. "Let's go." She hitched first at the wide-bladed shortsword on the left side of her belt and then at the crude flintlock pistol on the right side.

"I'll be a minute," he said, his hand going to the spider amulet secured around his neck by a leather thong.

That was a long-standing reflex, its source back in his long-ago college days. Karl Cullinane had always had trouble keeping track of things; pens, pencils, books, lighters, change, and keys always seemed to vanish from his possession, as though they had turned to air. The amulet was too important; it couldn't become part of that pattern of lost valuables.

"If you see Slovotsky, tell him to get up here. In the meantime, give the order to break camp, then have your team wait by their horses—and tell Restius to keep the animals quiet this time, even if he has to slit the throat of that idiot mare of his."

"You want me to have your horse saddled?"

"Fine. But make sure the bellybands are tight—no, forget it." He shook his head. "No, I'd better take care of Stick." No reason to put someone else to the trouble when Karl would have to check the work himself.

"Anything else?"

"Mmm—tell Chak I want to see him when he gets a chance. That's all."

She nodded and left.

Tossing his blankets aside, Karl dressed quickly, first donning skintight knit-cotton pants and a thick under-shirt. He pulled on a pair of rough leather trousers before slipping on his socks and forcing his feet into his tight steel-toed boots.

Vibram, he thought, for the thousandth time. *How much would I pay for one pair of Vibram soles?* Certainly a hundred pieces of gold; definitely his third-best horse. But would he trade, say, Carrot or Stick for a good pair of soles? Probably not, but it would be a close call. Not that he'd ever get the chance; such synthetics were easily a hundred years away on This Side.

He uncorked a jug of water and drank a scant mouthful, then splashed some on his face, drying it with a dirty towel. He slipped his leather tunic over his head before belting his sword around his waist, reflexively checking to see that it was loose in its scabbard.

Forming his hands into fists, he stood and stretched broadly, trying to loosen the almost permanent knots in his neck and shoulders.

Dammit, he thought, *this doesn't get easier.*

He stooped to retrieve two unloaded pistols and a small pouch from his saddlebags, tucked the pistols crossways in his swordbelt, and tied the pouch to a small brass ring mounted on the right side of the belt. He gave his hair a quick fingercombing before blowing out the lantern and stepping out into the night.

Above, a million stars winked at him out of a coal-black sky. The faerie lights were active tonight. Sometimes, when they changed slowly, it was difficult to distinguish them from stars, but not tonight. Hovering halfway between forest and sky, they flickered on and off, pulsing through a chromatic scale. First a series of deep reds, then a quick flash of orange before they worked their way through the yellows, greens, and a chorus of blues, turning indigo and vanishing, only to reappear in a few moments in a flash of cerulean.

"Lights are bright tonight," Wellem said. He stood sharpening a dagger and staring up at the sky. His hands moved in a smooth, practiced motion, stroking the stone lightly, evenly across the blade. "Awfully bright."

"That they are."

"Makes me feel like I'm back in Ehvenor, almost." He sighed. "Not used to seeing them so far north."

"What do you think they are, really?" Karl asked idly.

"I haven't learned anything new, Karl Cullinane." Wellem shrugged. "I can still only give you the faerie answer: 'Sometimes they are, and sometimes they are not.' Tonight they are." He turned away, still whisking the stone against the dagger.

There had been a time when a younger, less jaded Karl Cullinane would have stood and admired the clear sky, the many colors blinking in the night—

But that time, that youth, was gone. Now he simply saw a sky clear enough, a night bright enough to provide little cover for either the slavers or for Karl's people. Too bad—were it cloudier, the darksight of his six dwarf warriors would have given their side an extra edge. Karl always took any advantage that came his way. He saw no sense pushing his luck further than necessary; as it was, it was necessary to stretch it awfully far.

The encampment spread out around him on the mesa. His hundred warriors were breaking camp. Some brought down the tents and stowed the noncombat gear; some gave a final cleaning to a crossbow or flintlock rifle; others took a few moments to touch up the edge of a sword or a Nehera-made bowie. The tiny cooking fires had long since been doused; a few stray flinders might have betrayed their presence to slavers en route from Pandathaway to their hunting grounds in the east.

All made their preparations quietly, with only an occasional grunt or muttered comment. Before a battle was always a quiet time. By dawn, even if everything went well in the forest below, some would surely be injured or dead.

The bushes behind him rustled. He reached for his sword.

" 'Yea, though I walk through the valley of death, I will fear no evil . . .' " a familiar voice said.

Karl let his hand drop. " '. . . for I am the meanest son of a bitch in the valley,' " he finished. "That's too long, Walter; not a good password. Besides, I'm the one already in camp; *I'm* supposed to give the challenge, not you. Cut the crap and come on out. And be more careful next time—Gerrin already spotted you."

"Damn dwarf has good eyes," Slovotsky said, pushing his way through the brush. As usual, he was dressed only in sandals and a blousy pair of pantaloons, his throwing knives strapped to his right hip, a shortsword belted to his left. His chest, arms, and face had been blackened with a mixture of grease and ashes, and his chest and belly were scraped bare in spots, but his cocky, all-is-right-with-the-world-because-Walter-Slovotsky-is-in-it smile was intact, although just barely so.

"Welcome back," Karl said. "I've missed you. I've been getting a bit nervous; it feels like it's been a long time."

"Sure does. It's good to be back." The corners of Slovotsky's mouth lifted into a knowing smile. "You're not the only one. But thanks, anyway." He fondled his own spider amulet between thumb and forefinger. "You're not going to like this, Karl," he said. "This thing started flashing red—the slavers have a wizard with them."

"Damn!" Karl spat. That was surprising, but not unprecedented. Usually, only the largest Slavers' Guild raiding parties would spend the money on the services of a wizard. "Well, we can handle that—just have to take the wizard out first." Wizards were just as subject to a surprise attack as anyone else, after all.

"That was the *good* news. Karl, they have guns."

"What?"

"Guns. I spotted three, and there're probably others. Could be rifles, maybe smoothbores—they look just like our flintlocks, as far as I could see. I didn't want to get too close; I've always thought I look better without bullet holes."

This was bad. And it shouldn't be happening. The secret of making gunpowder was something that Karl, Walter, Ahira, Andy-Andy, and Lou Riccetti guarded carefully. Riccetti had yet to share the secret with any of his Engineers, though undoubtedly most of them suspected what the ingredients were. But Engineers didn't talk.

To the best of Karl's knowledge, no guns or powder had fallen into unauthorized hands during the five years they'd been using guns on This Side.

They'd known it wouldn't last forever, but Lou Riccetti's guess was that it would take a minimum of ten years for the secret to get out, and Karl had thought Lou's estimate conservative, if anything. While there was room for error, the mixture had to be close to the traditional ratio of fifteen parts saltpeter to three parts sulfur to two parts powdered charcoal for it to be usable gunpowder. It would take a long time for others in this world to work out the ingredients and proportions, given only descriptions of the weapons that the Home raiders were using to supplement their bows and blades. The construction of rifles that didn't blow up in a user's face should have slowed the locals down, too.

It *should* have taken a long time. . . .

"Damn," he said. "You're sure? Never mind." He gestured an apology. If Slovotsky was willing to make the absurd claim that the slavers had guns, then the slavers had guns.

Karl beckoned to the nearest of his warriors, a gangling teenager whom he often used as a message runner.

"Yes, Karl?"

"Erek—message for Tennetty. No attack yet; tell her to have the horses hobbled. I want a staff meeting, right away. I'll need the squad leaders up here, and fast. And I'll want some fire for the lantern in my tent. Repeat."

Erek closed his eyes. "Attack postponed indefinitely; Tennetty to order the horses hobbled. Chak, Piell, Gwellin, and Tennetty to report to you, here, immediately. Your lantern to be lit."

He opened his eyes, looking questioningly at Karl. At Karl's nod, Erek smiled and ran off.

"Good kid," Slovotsky said. "Too bad he's such a lousy shot."

"Guns aren't everything." Karl snorted. "I wish you were as good with a sword. Little Erek can outscore Chak almost a quarter of the time." He beckoned Slovotsky into his tent as Wellem arrived with a lantern.

"You want it now?" Slovotsky asked, seating himself tailor-fashion on the rug.

"Save it. The others will be along in a minute."

Being in charge, Karl thought, all too often required listening to silly arguments. It wasn't enough to command obedience; he had to earn it—not once, but over and over again. And one of the things that meant was giving his warriors room to be wrong, at least when being wrong wouldn't hurt anything.

"Why all the fuss?" Gwellin shrugged. "They might not move on in the morning—"

"They will," Slovotsky put in. "Why would they stay?"

"Come nightfall tomorrow, we'll have the dragon to help out. Bullets can't hurt it."

"Idiot!" Tennetty spat. "What if they have dragonbane? Besides, do you really think we can take them by surprise with a *dragon* in the sky?"

"So who says we have to surprise them? Ellegon should be able to roast all of them."

"*Fine* idea. I'd love to see that." She turned to Walter. "Roasted gunpowder is kind of noisy, isn't it?"

"Yup. Not a good idea, not if I'm going to be anywhere in the neighborhood—and most particularly not if we want a sample for analysis. Try again, Gwellin."

"Then," the dwarf said, pounding a fist on the ground, "I'd say we just let this group go." Gwellin and his six dwarves were serving with Karl's team only temporarily, saving their shares of the loot, building up their savings so that they could return to Endell well laden with both captured valuables and acquired knowledge. Karl liked having Gwellin around; it was good to have the advice of someone who could be more objective, more businesslike about the business of killing and robbing slavers.

"Go on," Karl said. "Why do you think we should let them go?"

The dwarf stroked at his craggy face. "They aren't pulling a chain of slaves, so all we could get out of this would be a bit of blood, whatever money they have on them, and maybe this powder of theirs. I don't think they'll be carrying a lot of gold, not a group this size. And I don't want to face guns, not if we don't have to." He hefted his oversized mace. "I can't move this faster than a bullet."

"Don't be stupid." Ch'akresarkandyn shook his head. He was short for a human, only a head taller than the dwarf. The movements of his head and hand were slow and lazy, but Chak was neither; the dark little man was a good swordsman and an energetic and effective teacher of both blade and gun. "Do you know how to make gunpowder?"

"No, do you? What's the point?"

"The point," Tennetty put in, her usual sneer firmly in place, "is that they shouldn't, either." She looked over at Karl, her forehead momentarily wrinkling, as though she was wondering why he let this discussion go on. Tennetty's squad was run without dissension; her warriors could either do exactly what she said, when and how she said it, or they could find someone else to lead them on the next raid. "And we have to find out how they got it, and—if possible—cut it off at the source."

Idly, she brought her right index finger up and slipped it underneath her eyepatch, scratching. Karl made a mental note to have Thellaren look at the socket, once they got back to Home. Or maybe he'd try to push her into getting the glass eye that the cleric had been trying to sell her on.

Gwellin shrugged. "That is your concern—the fire burns in your belly, not mine."

"You're right about that," Tennetty agreed grimly.

"But how did they get the powder?" Piell asked. The elf steepled his overlong fingers in front of his face, considering. "It must be that Riccetti. He must have sold out."

"Piell," Slovotsky said, with a loud snort, "there is an old saying, back on the Other Side—"

"Not again." Chak threw up his hands. "There's *always* an old saying back on the Other Side. And for some reason, they're always called Slovotsky's Laws. Which one is it now?"

"The one I was thinking of goes something like this: 'When you know not whereof you speak, your mouth is best used for chewing.' Forgetting the fact that Lou has never even had the opportunity to sell out, there's about as much chance of his betraying a friend as there is of your falling in love with a female dwarf." He pulled a piece of jerky out of his pouch and tossed it to the tall elf. "So try this."

Piell batted the jerky aside and glared at him. "Walter Slovotsky—"

"Enough." Karl raised a palm. Not that he had any objection to a little bickering among his squad leaders, as long as it was confined to a war council. A bit of argument helped to blow off steam, helped to keep everyone's nerves from growing wire-tight before the battle. But enough was enough. "You see the problem: If they do have guns—"

"I saw—"

"Shut *up*, Walter. If they do have guns, we have to find out how and why. Most likely, the wards aren't as good as Thellaren says they are."

And there was another possibility, and that one chilled his insides: Home had paid the Spidersect a great deal of money to install and maintain the wards that both served as a magical burglar alarm and hid the valley from the view of Pandathaway wizards' crystal balls. Both Thellaren and Andy-Andy had said that it would have taken a wizard close to the level of Grandmaster Lucius to pierce the spell.

What if they were up against someone like that?

He let the thought drop. No, there was no reason to worry about that. If they were up against a wizard as powerful as Lucius or Arta Myrdhyn, they would already be dead.

"In any case," Karl said, "we've got to rethink the attack."

Gwellin shook his head. "Even if what you say is true, there isn't that much difference. If we can take them by surprise, maybe—"

"—we can kill them all," Karl finished for the dwarf. He shook his head. "And that's no good. We can't afford to have just dead slavers on our hands. Not this time: Dead bodies can't talk. I'll want at least one of them alive, preferably two."

"Make it three." Tennetty studied the edge of her knife. "I am likely to use them up quickly." She raised an eyebrow. "I do get to do the interrogation, don't I?"

"Maybe. We'll also need to capture one of their rifles—"

"That's no problem, not even if we—"

"—*and* at least a pouch of their powder for analysis. I'll want to get as much as we can. So, the original plan is off. We can't just have a horseback attack to draw them out so the rifles can get at them. We're going to have to get a bit more tricky."

Chak smiled. "I like it when you get tricky."

"Sorry, Chak. Not this time."

His face fell. "I have to stay with my squad?"

"Yup. Walter—"

"Now wait a minute, Karl. *I'm* not the one who likes it when you get tricky."

"You're going to like this even less than usual, Walter. How good are you with a crossbow these days?"

Slovotsky frowned. "Not very, as you know."

"Right." Karl could count on Slovotsky for a good recon. Slovotsky had made his way into and out of places that Karl would have sworn a stray leaf couldn't have invaded without notice. Walter was also a reliable knifeman and a passable swordsman; he was also one of Home's better rifle shots. But he wasn't good with a crossbow, and taking out at least one watchman without alerting the slavers might require a crossbow's range and silence.

He sighed regretfully, trying to decide if he was being hypocritical. *But I can't trust this to anyone else, dammit. It's my responsibility.* "You've just gotten yourself an assistant."

"Who?"

"Me."

Karl finished rubbing the greasepaint over his bare chest, then stood motionless while Walter tended to his face.

Slovotsky nodded. "That should do it. Remember to keep your mouth closed—don't want to flash those pearly whites at them. Also, if he starts to look your way, close your eyes as much as you can—the whites can stand out."

"Got it." Karl turned back to the others. It wasn't really necessary to give the final orders himself—Tennetty or Chak could have handled that—but Karl didn't allow himself to hold the others distant. They weren't just his warriors, they were his friends. This could easily be the last time he'd see some of them alive. He owed them at least the remembering.

Morality didn't prevent mortality. There was probably some sort of epigram in that, too depressing to be converted into one of Slovotsky's Laws.

But it wasn't just true, it was important. Good people could die fighting on the right side in a just war. It had happened at Gettysburg, and at the Somme, and at Anzio, Normandy, and Entebbe.

It had also happened in Ehvenor, when Fialt's death had bought Karl and the others a few seconds. And in Melawei, where Rahff Furnael's lifeblood had poured on to the sandy ground. And outside of Metreyll, and Wehnest, and . . .

"Chak?" He turned to the little man who stood quietly by his side.

"Yes, Kharl?" Chak was tense; his accent was slipping. "You were going to tell me about why you assigned Erek to my squad. It isn't because he's any good with a rifle or shotgun. Must be because you want me to keep an eye on the boy, eh?"

"Stop trying to read my mind. Ellegon's the only one who can do that."

"Sorry. What did you want?"

"Well . . ." Karl smiled. "As it happens, I was going to ask you to keep an eye on the boy. Eh?"

Chak returned the smile. "It's too bad that I can't read your mind."

Karl laughed.

Chak sobered. He opened his mouth, closed it, then shrugged. "He reminds me a bit of Rahff, too." He fastened a hard hand on Karl's shoulder. "But," he said in his thick English, "I want to turn the two-guns squad over to Wellem. He can handle this kind of slaughter as well as I can—and I've already told him to watch out for Erek."

"So—"

"So, I want to keep an eye on your back. It has a tendency to sprout holes when I'm not around." Chak raised a palm to forestall Karl's objection. "Think about it, please—Jason told me to watch out for you, and I don't like disobeying Cullinane orders."

Karl hesitated for a moment.

"One more thing to say, and then I'll be quiet: Three have a greater chance of getting a sample of this powder out than two do. Is that not so, Kharl?"

"It is so." Karl sighed. "Strip down—you won't need the paint."

He picked Wellem out of the crowd and caught his eye. "Wellem, do you want it?" he asked.

At Wellem's nod, Karl gave him a thumbs-up sign. "Very well. Two-guns squad is yours for this one."

Wellem nodded again, then turned to the rest of his group and began whispering.

"Listen up, people," Karl said. "For those of you who haven't heard, the slavers have guns. At least three, although we're going to assume that there are more. We also know that there's a wizard with them. Before all hell breaks loose down there, Walter and I are going to try to kill the wizard, then make a grab for a slaver or two, a gun, and some of their powder. It's our job to pick out the slaver and keep him alive—don't worry about killing the wrong one.

"There are two things I *do* want you to worry about. The first one is that Walter, Chak, and I are going to be out in front. Watch where you point your guns. I don't want a repeat of that Metreyll fiasco." He rubbed his back, just above the kidney. "It's not that I mind the pain, you understand, it's just that bullets and powder are too expensive to waste on my hide."

A rough laugh ran through the crowd. Good; that would loosen them up a bit.

"The second thing I want you to worry about is the fact that there are shortly going to be about thirty very scared slavers down there, all of whom will know that they're under attack, all of whom know that we're not interested in taking them prisoner. And they're not going to be too thrilled with Walter or with Chak or with me."

He nodded to Slovotsky. Better for Slovotsky to give them a first-hand description than for Karl to give them a secondhand one.

Walter Slovotsky knelt in the light of the shrouded lantern and smoothed the dirt. "Here's their campfire, right smack dab in the middle of the meadow, just east of the fork." He made an X on the ground. "Three wagons—here, here, and here. This one is the most ornate; I'm assuming it's the wizard's. The two—the three of us are going to make our move in from the southeast, parellel to the main road, here.

"That leaves two more watchmen. They were, umm, right about here and here. All of the watchmen have rifles. We have no way of knowing if there are other rifles located inside the circle of wagons, or in the wagons themselves." He shrugged. "Since they're coming out of Pandathaway, it's not surprising that they aren't carrying slaves; clearly, the wagons are all being used to hold their supplies. It could be just food—but, for all I know, they could be loaded with guns and powder. So watch out."

"Hear that, folks?" Karl said. "A barrel of powder can produce one nice explosion. So keep your eyes open. If you see any fire going into any wagon, yell 'Fire.' If you hear anyone yelling 'Fire,' try to get some cover between yourself and the wagons. Everyone got that? Fine. Gwellin—your turn."

The dwarf stood. "My squad stays as close behind you as we can, making sure we're far enough back enough so that we can't be seen or heard. If you come under attack, I light my rocket. Then we support you with a volley in the direction of the wizard or his wagon, and switch to crossbows for a second, third, and fourth volley. After that, we move in with axes, maces, and hammers. If you're not spotted, we wait for your signal, then do the same."

"Good. Piell?"

The elf nodded. "My group stays behind the dwarves, and becomes the second wave. Our objective will be to get the slavers to run away, into Chak—into Wellem's squad. If that is not possible, I will light off another rocket. Yes?"

"Yes. Tennetty?"

"I'm what you always call a free safety. My squad is the reserve; we wait with our horses on the road, making sure we're out of earshot until the attack is well under way. Then we mount up. If they're running, we help chase them into the two-guns squad. If they hold fast, we try to scatter them, then pick off the stragglers. We're also responsible for killing the two other watchmen, if Gwellin's or Chak's people don't get them first. It's simple stuff: If they run, we chase them. If they don't, we make them run, and *then* we chase them."

"And?"

She sighed. "And if everything goes bad, we rescue whoever we can, and pull out. We also pick up our wounded, carry them out of danger, and treat them with healing draughts, then haul ass back up here and wait for Ellegon. I'd rather—"

"—be in the thick of it." Karl repressed a sigh. Tennetty had spent ten long years as a slave; there was nothing she enjoyed more than bathing in a slaver's blood. *Lady, you're a psycho. But fortunately for the both of us you're one hell of an effective psycho.*

He looked from face to face. "Enough talk, people. Let's do it."

Down the road, the slavers' campfire burned an orange rift into the night. With Chak bringing up the rear, Karl kept himself two yards behind Walter, mimicking the other's half-stoop as he eased his way through the woods, parallel to the road, stepping carefully across the damp floor of the forest, a cocked but unloaded crossbow held in his left hand. Occasionally he patted the top of the quiver strapped to his right thigh.

A leather pouch slapped silently against his left thigh as he walked; his swordsheath pressed reassuringly against his back; a manriki-gusari, cloth strung through its links to prevent rattling, was slung across one shoulder. He let his hand rest against the two oil-skin-wrapped flintlock pistols stuck crossways into his belt.

Goddam walking arsenal, that's what I am, he thought. *But there's always—*

"*Down,*" Slovotsky hissed, his voice pitched low enough to carry only a few feet, no more.

Karl stepped behind a tree and dropped to the ground. Half a dozen feet behind him, Chak dropped to the ground and froze in place, motionless as a statue.

The skin over his ears tightening, Karl strained to hear whatever had alarmed Slovotsky.

It didn't make any difference. The wind still whispered through the trees, and the flames of a campfire crackled somewhere off in the night, but that was all. Or were there distant voices? Maybe.

Slovotsky beckoned for Chak to move forward, then crabbed himself backward to join them, his mouth only inches from their ears. "Something's wrong. Hang on for a minute," he said. "I'm going to do a quick recon."

"Problem?"

"Maybe. Back in a jiffy. Watch my stuff." Slovotsky laid the oil-skin containing his own pistols on the roots, set his scimitar down next to it, and crept off.

He was gone a long time; Karl stopped counting his own pulse-beats at three hundred, and lay quietly, waiting.

Dammit, hurry up, Slovotsky, he thought.

Chak patted his shoulder. "You worry too much, kemo sabe."

"It's my job, dammit," Karl whispered back. He couldn't wait forever; there were just too many people involved. Eventually, Tennetty or Wellem or Gwellin would get too nervous to wait for a signal and trigger the attack. If Walter and Karl hadn't taken out the wizard by then, the odds would quickly switch from their favor to the slavers', despite the advantage of surprise, despite the fact that they had the slavers outmanned. "And don't call me 'kemo sabe.' "

"Whatever you say, kemo sabe."

The thing about Chak that Karl depended most on was the dark little man's rock-solid trustworthiness when it came to anything serious; one of the things about Chak that he liked best was his unwillingness to take anything seriously except when necessary. Chak always liked to joke around before a fight; he said it kept his mind calm and his wrist loose.

"Karl," Walter's voice whispered out of the darkness, "it's me."

"What—"

"Relax—we got a break, for once. The wizard was off away from the wagons and the fire. Seems there's a bit of a gang-bang in progress, and I guess it must have offended his delicate sensibilities. He'd walked at least a hundred yards into the woods to relieve himself, so . . ."

"What did you do?"

"I slit his throat. Stashed the body under the roots of an old oak. Getting a bit bloodthirsty in my old age, eh?"

"Never mind that—you said something about a gang-bang?"

"Yeah. They've got a couple of women. Taking turns. Strange, no?"

"Yes." That *was* bizarre. These slavers were coming from Pandathaway. Pandathaway was where guild slavers brought slaves to, not from. Bringing slaves out wouldn't mean just the extra expense of feeding them or the lost income of not selling them, it would also cut down on the available space for human cargo on the slavers' return trip.

"What do you make of that?" Slovotsky asked. "It just doesn't make sense."

Chak shook his head. "Yes, it could make sense—if they are not on a raiding mission but doing something else. If they're not planning on bringing slaves back, they might bring themselves some company. Or it could be some sort of purchase. If they're bringing back a big chain from somewhere, the added expense of bringing along a couple of women for pleasure wouldn't matter to them."

A buy? That meant that the slavers would have a lot of coin on them. Unless—

The guns. Maybe they were taking guns somewhere, planning to sell them. But where? Why? Now they needed a captive to question more than ever.

"Change of plans," Karl said. "We don't kill the guard—we snatch him."

Chak rolled his eyes heavenward. "You don't always have to complicate things, do you?"

Walter shook his head. "I don't like it. The guard's still where he was when I was here before—about a hundred yards ahead, but across the road from us."

"Which way is he facing?"

"Sort of sideways, looking down the road."

"Fine. You go back and tell Gwellin to bring his people up closer, just the other side of the bend in the road. Have him send Daherrin back with you."

"No good—you can't move that many people silently, Karl. The watchman would hear them from there."

"We'll have him tied down by then. After you bring Gwellin's people around, you and Daherrin hurry back to where the watchman is now. That's where we'll be. Daherrin hauls the watchman away, then the three of us work ourselves close to the fire, before the shit hits the fan. We've got to try to get the slaves out."

"I knew it." Chak looked knowingly at Walter. "That's what the change of plans is about." He shrugged. "I guess there's no need for me to get much older—how about you?"

"*Cut the crap,*" Karl hissed. "Once the attack's fully under way, it might not be possible to get them out alive. How's all that sound to the two of you?"

Chak shrugged. "Not bad, not really."

"I don't like it, Karl. He's got kind of a thicket of brambles behind him; you'll have to come right across the road to get him. And I'm quieter than you are. I should take out the watchman while—"

"No." Walter might be quieter than Karl was, but Karl was stronger. That might be important. "Eventually, someone's going to check on the wizard. *Do it.*"

Slovotsky clapped a hand to Karl's shoulder. "Good luck—"

"Thanks."

"—you'll need it."

Karl crouched behind a bush, peering through the dark at the watchman sitting across the road on a waist-high stone, staring blankly out into the night.

He would have to cross the road under the eyes of the watchman in order to get his hands on the other. And even then, he'd have to move quickly, in order to silence the watchman before the slaver could raise an alarm.

Not good odds. The deeply rutted dirt road was only about five yards wide at this point, but those would be a long five yards.

Maybe too long.

At times like these he could almost hear Andy-Andy's half-mocking voice. *Looks like your mouth has gotten you into trouble again. Okay, hero, how would Conan do it?*

Well . . . Conan would probably sneak up quietly behind the watchman and club him over the head, knocking him unconscious.

Then why don't you do it that way?

Because I'm Karl Cullinane, not Conan. Because things just didn't work that way. Even assuming that he could get within clubbing range, it was much more likely that such a blow would either draw a scream out of the watchman or simply crush his skull.

Better think of another way, then. He edged back into the woods, his fingers searching the ground until he found a small stone, one about the size of a grape. He worked his way back to the brush until he was beside Chak. Setting his crossbow, quiver, and pistol down carefully, Karl unslung his manriki-gusari and draped it carefully around his neck, then reached over his shoulder to loosen his sword in its sheath. He took a wad of cloth and several thongs from his pouch and held them in his left hand.

"Here," Karl whispered, handing Chak the stone. "Give me a slow count to fifty, then throw the stone over his head and past him."

Chak nodded. "One . . . two . . . three . . ."

Matching the count silently, Karl crept back to the road and waited. . . . *twenty-three . . . twenty-four . . .*

The watchman stood for a moment to stretch, then scratched at his crotch before seating himself again.

. . . *thirty-five . . . thirty-six . . .*

Karl braced himself, clenching his jaw to keep his teeth from rattling as he hefted his manriki-gusari.

. . . *forty-two . . . for—*

The stone whipped through the brambles; the watchman jerked to his feet and spun around, bringing his rifle to bear.

Karl eased himself up to the surface of the road, swinging and throwing the manriki-gusari in one smooth motion.

The meter-long chain whipped through the night air, wrapping itself around the watchman's neck, bowling the man over, his rifle falling into the bushes. Karl drew his sword and lunged at the other, slapping at the watchman's hands with the flat of his blade when the slaver reached for the knife at his belt.

Karl set the point of the blade under the other's chin. "If you cry out," he whispered, "you die. Be quiet, and you live. You have my word."

"Who—"

"Cullinane. Karl Cullinane."

The slaver's eyes widened. Karl toed him in the solar plexus, then stuffed the wad of cloth in the other's mouth while the slaver gasped for breath.

"I didn't say you wouldn't hurt—I just said you'd live."

CHAPTER TWO

Battleground

First say to yourself what you would be; and then do what you have to do.

—Epictetus

As he had grown older, Karl had learned to deal with the fear. He'd had to.

Deal with it, yes, but not well. That would have been too much to ask of himself. Karl Cullinane had spent twenty-one of his twenty-nine years as a middle-class American, living safely in the last half of the twentieth century. Deep inside, he still wasn't used to having lost that safety, that comfort. The only way he could handle that was to push the fear away, if only for a time.

The quiet moments before a fight were always the worst. Too much time to think; too much opportunity to let himself be scared.

His heart pounding, Karl checked the slaver's knots and gag once more before turning him over to Daherrin.

"And take this, too," Karl said, handing the slaver's rifle and pouch to the dwarf. It was a strange-looking rifle: The lock, if any, was inside the stock; the trigger looked more like a miniature pump handle than anything else.

But there wasn't enough light or time to examine it fully; that would have to be saved for later. If there was a later.

Karl clenched his hands into fists. It wouldn't do for Walter, Chak, or Daherrin to see his fingers tremble.

Grasping the slaver by the front of his tunic, the dwarf swung him to his right shoulder, balancing the man easily, then accepted the slaver rifle and powder kit in his oversized left hand. Dwarves weren't just shorter and more heavily built than humans; their joints were thicker, their muscles denser, far more powerful.

"And remember," Slovotsky said, "if everything blows up in our faces here, this stuff has to get back—"

"—to Home," Daherrin finished. "Including this useless piece of meat," he said, bouncing the slaver up and down on his shoulder. "It will be done."

The dwarf turned and walked away.

Karl finished unwrapping his pistols from their protecting oil-cloth, then primed their pans. He tucked the vial of fine priming powder and oilcloth in his pouch before sticking the pistols back in his belt, making sure that the barrels pointed away from his feet.

Chak had done the same with his two pistols; he patted their curving butts and flashed Karl a quick smile.

"Gwellin had a couple of spares," Walter said, handing each of them one of the three shotguns he'd brought back, along with the dwarf. "Hope you don't mind my supplementing things a bit."

Chak hefted his shotgun easily. "I don't mind at all."

"Me neither." Karl propped the butt on the ground while he slipped a bolt into his crossbow and nocked it with a practiced motion of his thumb. "Is the gun loaded?"

"Standard shotgun load. Everything but the pan. Gwellin did it; I watched him myself."

"Good." Handing the crossbow to Chak, Karl picked up the shotgun. He took the vial of priming powder from his pouch and primed the pan, bringing the frizzen down and locking it into place with a quiet click. He handed the vial to Chak and waited while the dark little man primed his own shotgun.

Karl was a bit vain about the shotguns; they were his own innovation. Normally, when the lands inside a rifle barrel had worn down to uselessness, the weapon had to be rebored and rerifled, which changed the caliber, making standard rounds useless. Karl had come up with the notion of doing a more thorough reboring of the barrel, until the bore was a thumb's width, then cutting it down, turning the weapon into a smoothbore shotgun.

Walter gave the crossbow back to Karl, then clapped a hand to his shoulder. "It doesn't get any easier, does it? You want me to do a quick recon?"

"No. Let's get this over with." He gave a quick glance down the road. Five dwarf warriors waited off in the distance, just on Karl's side of the bend.

He waved at them to follow, then started walking down the road, Walter on one side, Chak on the other, the campfire growing closer with every step.

"Here we go," Karl said.

Chak sucked air through his teeth; Walter brought his shotgun up.

Ahead, the road forked. In the dark, three boxy wagons stood around the campfire. While more than a dozen slept under their blankets, ten grizzled men sat around the fire, drinking and talking. Beyond them, several others stood over a huge blanket on which lay the moaning forms of the two women. The men called mocking words of encouragement to their friends while waiting their own turns.

Walter turned to beckon to the dwarves. With all the noise from the camp, they wouldn't be noticed for the next few seconds. "Ready when you are," he whispered, his voice faltering momentarily.

Chak brought his shotgun up to his shoulder.

Karl's hand grew tight around the crossbow's stock. He raised it to his shoulder, curled his fingers around the trigger as he took aim at the nearest of the slavers around the campfire, and squeezed.

Ffft! The slaver lunged forward, clutching at the feathers that just barely projected from his chest.

The crack of Chak's shotgun split the night. Three of the slavers screamed in pain as they caught some of the scattering pellets; a fourth clapped both hands to what had been a face.

As the other slavers leaped to their feet, Karl dropped the crossbow to one side, transferred the shotgun to his right hand, braced it against his hip, and fired.

Another man lunged for a rifle, but the blast from Slovotsky's shotgun opened his belly as though it were an overripe melon; he fell to the grass, vomit pouring from his mouth in a bloody torrent.

Others dashed across the meadow, running for the road. Chak raised a pistol and sighted down his arm.

"No!" Karl shouted. "Leave them to the two-guns—follow me." He dropped the empty shotgun and sprinted for the blankets, snatching his pistols from his belt and cocking them.

The slavers were beginning to react to the attack. Several of them made a mad dash for the nearest of the boxy wagons, only to be cut down by two quick volleys of gunfire.

Piell's signal rocket screamed into the night.

"Down!" Karl threw an arm across his eyes and looked away as it exploded above the meadow, a white flash that momentarily dazzled his eyes.

The nine slavers around Karl, Chak, and Walter hadn't been prepared for it. They screamed, blinded, if only for a few moments.

One of the slavers, clad only in his leather tunic, was pawing around the ground for his sword. Karl kicked him in the face, bones crunching beneath his boot. He turned to shoot another who was trying to bring an unsteady rifle to bear on Chak. With his left-hand pistol, he quickly gutshot a third, then reached over his shoulder to draw his sword as a blocky man, his teeth bared in a snarl, lunged for him, a foot-long dagger clutched tightly in his white-knuckled fingers.

Karl's sword was barely out of its scabbard when a heavy mass slammed into his back, a hairy arm snaking around his throat.

There wasn't time to think about it. He could deal either with the enemy clinging to his back or with the one charging from the front.

Instinct took over. Ignoring the slaver on his back, he parried the other's knife with the flat of his blade, then thrust the point of his sword into the knife wielder's throat, twisting savagely as he pulled the blade back.

Crack! Impact shook the slaver on Karl's back as the pistol shot rang out. The slaver shuddered, and the arm around Karl's throat went limp. Karl grabbed the thick wrist, spun, and twisted, bringing his knee up into the man's chin, bone shattering like glass.

Two yards away, Chak favored him with a brief smile as he dropped his smoking pistol to the ground, then drew his falchion to parry the attack of another slaver.

Walter's scimitar clanged against the ninth slaver's steel. It looked as though Walter could handle the man, but it didn't occur to Karl to play fair: he skewered Walter's opponent through the kidney, then spun around into a crouch.

Chak's opponent was down, clutching at a wounded arm. The dark little man didn't waste any more time on the slaver; he drew his remaining pistol and shot him in the chest.

With a clatter of hooves, Tennetty's horsemen galloped through the meadow, sending the last of the uninjured slavers into flight. Therol detached himself from the rest of the group, leaping off his horse to dispense healing draughts to two injured dwarves, the only casualties on Karl's side. So far.

Karl breathed a sigh. It was over for him, at least for now. Piell's and Gwellin's squads had knocked down all of their targets, and the now combined squad was working its way through the scattered bodies, administering deathblows to the wounded.

Down the road, shots echoed, horses whinnied, and men screamed.

"Karl!" Gwellin called out, standing over the body of a slaver, a bloody battleaxe in his hands. "Do you want us to—"

"No. Not until the shots die down." Killing the rest was the job of the two-guns squad and Tennetty's horsemen, not Gwellin's dwarves or Piell's squad. For them, the fight was over. Unmounted men rushing the slavers from behind would risk being mistaken for slavers in the darkness. Karl had lost far too many of his warriors in his time, but not one had been killed by friendly fire, and he didn't intend that any ever should.

A low moan from the ground drew Karl's attention. The half-naked slaver that Karl had kicked in the face was starting to move, holding the shattered remnants of his jaw together.

Over his cupped, blood-dripping hands, the man's eyes grew wide as Karl approached him.

"*Karl,*" Walter snapped. "We want another live one, remember?"

Karl kicked the man in the shoulder, bowling him over, then stooped to bring the slaver's hands behind his back and tie them tightly with a leather thong from his pouch.

"Therol, check the wagons for healing draughts, and treat this one. A few drops from every bottle, eh?" It was always necessary to test captured healing draughts on someone expendable; two years before, Karl had lost one of his warriors to what had looked to be a bottle of Healing Hand Society draughts, but had actually been poison.

"Done," Therol called back. "And how about you?"

"Me?"

"Don't talk about it, Therol," Chak shouted. "Just get your ass over here. Karl's hurt."

"Chak, I'm *fine.*"

"Right." Slovotsky snorted. "Sure you are." Walter's hand slipped down Karl's back. When he brought it in front of Karl's face, blood dripped from the fingers.

"It's not too bad, Karl. Just a nick—but you'd better get it healed before your adrenaline level drops and it starts to hurt you."

What had been a dim, distant pain suddenly cut across his back like a whip. He gasped, then willed himself to ignore it. *There's no danger. Therol will have me healed up in a minute.* Pain was just a biologically programmed warning of danger. There wasn't any danger here, so the pain should go away. It was logical, but it didn't help.

It was best to keep busy, try to keep his mind off the pain. "Chak, you and Gwellin's people check out the wagons—except for the wizard's wagon. Just put a guard on that one and leave it alone."

"Do you think there's anyone in there?"

"I don't know, so assume that there is."

"I was just asking." Chak sniffed. "I *have* done this before."

"Sorry. Put it down to nerves."

"Yes, Karl." Chak ran off, calling for Gwellin.

Every motion making the wound on his back cry out in agony, he turned to face the two women huddling in the blankets. He took a step toward the nearest one, a blonde, her almond eyes and high cheekbones betraying a mixed heritage, with forebears from both the Kathard and the Middle Lands.

"No." Her eyes grew wide. "You're *Karl Cullinane*. Don't kill me, please. Please. I'll do anything you want. I'm very good, really I am. Please—"

"Ta havath." *Easy.* Karl tried to smile reassuringly. "T'rar ammalli." *I'm a friend.*

Therol arrived with the bottle of healing draughts and slopped some of the icy liquid on Karl's back. As always, the pain vanished as though it had never been. He worked his arms for a moment, relishing the comfort.

The blonde was still pleading with him. "Please don't hurt me. Please . . ."

Damn.

"Those *bastards.*" Slovotsky shook his head. "Again?"

"Yeah."

Slovotsky held out a hand; Karl exchanged his saber for two of Slovotsky's knives.

The women edged away from him as he slowly approached, holding the knives out, offering them the hilts.

"Everything you've been told is a lie. I'm not going to kill you. I'm not going to hurt you—you're free, as of now." It was a calculated gamble, but one that hadn't yet failed, although he still had a scar on his right cheek from the time that it came close to failing.

The blonde took the proffered knife, holding it awkwardly at arm's length. The brunette mimicked her.

"Karl," Walter said in English, his voice pitched low, "either I've been away from Kirah too long, or both these ladies are gorgeous."

"Ta havath," he murmured. "So what if they are?" With the way they were huddled in their blankets, he couldn't see much of them, but what he could see looked good.

Awfully good, which was privately embarrassing. It wasn't just that he intended to remain faithful to Andy-Andy—he should have been feeling only sympathy for these two poor wretches, not noticing the swell of a full breast or the smoothness of a shapely thigh.

He switched back to Erendra. "Nobody's going to touch you. We'll get some clothes for you in a little while, just as soon as things settle down."

"So," Slovotsky continued in English, "we're looking at prime stuff, here. I could see the slavers taking some culls out of Pandathaway, but these two would go for a hell of a lot of money there. Or anywhere else."

Slovotsky was right, of course. As usual. But what did it mean?

The pounding of a horse's hooves spun Karl around, his hand reaching for the hilt of a sword that wasn't there.

It was only Tennetty. She slipped from Pirat's back, her face creased in a broad smile. "Everything's fine, Karl," she said. "Three casualties on our side."

"How bad?"

"I *said* that everything's fine. Wellem was the worst. He caught a round in the gut, but we got the draughts into him in plenty of time. Mm, I got a capture, too." She eyed the slaver that Therol was treating. "That makes three, yes?"

"Yes."

"Good. So—"

"Would you take care of the women, first? Later there'll be plenty of time to stick a knife in these bastards and get them to talk."

"Agreed. But I'll take care of the women my way, since we have a spare slaver. Unless you're really set on stopping me?" Tennetty carefully kept her hand away from her swordhilt. "I'm asking nicely, aren't I?"

Karl shrugged. "Go ahead."

She took a shrouded lantern down from her saddle and slipped the baffles, then elbowed Therol out of the way and urged the slaver to follow her into the woods by the simple expedient of grabbing the man by his hair and pulling him to his feet.

"Follow me," she ordered the two women, smiling gently. "And bring your knives. Relax—this is the best thing in the world for you." The slaver safely in hand, she led the two women into the woods, her voice trailing off in the distance. "Now, you can take your time with him, but Karl doesn't like it, so it'd be better if you start with . . ."

Slovotsky started to object, but Karl quelled him with a sudden chopping gesture.

"She's been there, Walter. And we haven't."

"I don't have to like it. I don't have to like any of it, and I don't, Karl. I've gotten used to killing, but—"

"*No,* you don't have to like it." Karl shrugged. "What you have to do is not let it get to you," he said, looking Walter square in the face as he forced himself not to shudder at the screams coming from the woods. "Let's check out the wagons."

"Right."

"So?" Walter asked, squatting in front of the blanket Karl had spread on the grass. "What do you make of all this?"

"Trouble." Karl stood and stretched, squinting at the noon sun. He rubbed the back of his aching neck and sighed, then held out his hand for the waterbag.

Walter tossed it to him. Karl drank deeply, then splashed some on his face before recorking the bag and handing it back.

Walter uncorked it and took a sip. "Speaking of trouble, not only did I find three bottles of dragonbane extract in one of the wagons, but Daherrin has been checking out their crossbow bolts. A lot of them seem to be absolutely coated with the stuff. Looks like the slavers are still interested in offing Ellegon."

That wasn't surprising: Ellegon was awfully useful for the Home forces to have around.

"Are you sure you burned it all?" Karl asked. Once thoroughly burned, dragonbane was every bit as harmless to Ellegon as burned pollen would be to a pollen-sensitive human, no matter how serious his allergy.

"Of course. Dumped the bottles in the hottest part of the fire; threw in every suspicious bolt."

Karl looked over to the slavers' campfire, now barely smoldering. "Have Daherrin build up the fire, just to be sure."

"Right."

Karl looked around. The aftermath of the battle wasn't pretty. It never was. But it had, in its own gruesome way, become almost routine.

Just beyond the campfire, two piles of bodies lay, gathering flies. The smaller pile was a haphazard arrangement of fully clothed slavers; it continued to shrink as Daherrin and two assistants frisked the bodies, reclaiming both valuables and whatever clothing was sufficiently unbloodied to be usable, then stacking the corpses like cordwood.

By Karl's orders, the wizard's wagon had been left completely alone. There hadn't been any complaint; wizards had been known to leave hidden glyphs.

While the two remaining wagons had been left intact, their contents had been unpacked, sorted, inventoried, and repacked. Piell had removed the inlaid brass wave-and-chain insignia of the Pandathaway Slavers' Guild from the wagons' sides and propped up the plaques facing the road.

Standard operating procedure—slavers were always left for the vultures, along with some means for passersby to identify them as slavers. It was important that everyone know that only slavers had to worry about unprovoked attack by the Home forces; it took most of the steam out of pursuit by the locals.

"Well?" Walter raised an eyebrow. "What have we got?"

"A puzzle. I don't like puzzles." The guns weren't guns, and the powder wasn't gunpowder. What the slavers had been using was a fine-grained powder that looked more like ground glass than anything else. The gunlocks fired what appeared to be water through their breechholes and into the barrels. The water had to be loaded with something, but what?

Whatever it was, it worked. Loaded into one of the slaver's smoothbores, the powder could sink a lead ball a full two inches into a block of pine, only a quarter-inch less than a Home-made rifle firing Riccetti's best powder.

"Take a look." Karl unlooped his amulet from his neck and held it over the glass vial containing the slaver powder. The amber gem came alive: It pulsed with an inner light, first a dark red, then a greenish blue, then red, then blue again. "There's a charm involved."

"Well, your wife should be able to puzzle that out. What's bothering me is that it doesn't stink when it's lit off—however the hell their guns light it off. You try tasting it?"

"Tasting it?" Karl raised an eyebrow. "Do I look stupid?"

Slovotsky smiled. "Answer me first." His face grew grim; he shook his head. "We know that it works—somehow—and that it's charmed."

"Or the pouch is charmed, or something." Karl eased the cork out of the bottle and sniffed at it again. No scent at all. "Could it be cordite? Or just plain guncotton?"

"Not cordite. I've seen smokeless powder; it's darker, and it stinks when it's lit off, not like this stuff. But I've never been around pure guncotton, although I think it *is* white like this." Slovotsky stood, stretching in the bright sunlight. "It can't be guncotton, though— you use fire to set off guncotton, not water." He jerked a thumb in the direction of the woods where Tennetty had gone off with the two surviving slavers in tow. "Maybe Ten'll have something more. She's taking her time with the prisoners."

"Maybe they've got a lot to say."

"Don't count on it. We killed the master in the fight, and master slavers don't tell their journeymen a whole lot."

"So? Where do we go from here?"

Slovotsky thought it over for a moment. He pursed his lips. "Go back to first principles. What would you have wanted Daherrin to do if he'd gotten out with that one pouch and gun, the rest of us left behind, dead?"

"Get it back to the valley; have Riccetti analyze it." Karl nodded. "Which is what we'll do—although we'd better include Andy-Andy and Thellaren in on the group."

Tennetty's slim form appeared through a break in the trees. Karl beckoned her over.

"How are they doing?"

"Just fine." She nodded. "Chak and I got them drunk; they're sleeping it off. I think Chak likes Jilla—the blonde."

"Really?"

"She could do worse," Tennetty said. "It's going to be a major adjustment for both of them. They were raised as room servants in the Velvet Inn in Pandathaway. Sternius picked them up at a foreclosure sale, for a bit of diversion during the trip." She jerked her thumb over her shoulder. "I gave them your tent; didn't figure you'd mind."

"Must have taken you quite a while to do all that."

She shook her head. "Not really. I spent most of the time interviewing the two slavers."

"What'd they tell you?"

She smiled thinly. "Everything they knew." The smile fell. "Which wasn't much. You were right; this wasn't a raiding party. It was some sort of a trade. They were on their way to the inn in Enkiar to deliver guns and powder to whoever the buyers are."

"Any idea how much they were going to be paid?"

"Sure. Each of them was to get—"

"Not that—how much were they going to get for the cargo?"

"They didn't know. I do know what they were going to be paid in: a chain of slaves. How many?" She shrugged. "Your guess is as good as mine."

"Or as bad." Thirty or so slavers could handle a chain of anywhere from about one hundred to well over a thousand slaves, perhaps as many as two thousand. It all depended on how closely chained and how well tamed their human merchandise was. "What else have you got?"

"Not much, and most of it negative. These two don't know where the guns and powder were supposed to go from Enkiar. They don't know who made the powder in the first place; Sternius had all the barrels loaded in his wagons before he put together his team."

"How about the guns?"

She shrugged. "They picked them up at a smith's in Pandathaway, just before they left. Arriken the Salke—he has a medium-big shop on the Street of Steel." She chewed on her lip for a moment. "You know, we could go into Pandathaway and look him up."

Karl nodded. "Not a bad idea. Although the idea of entering Pandathaway makes me a bit nervous." He fingered his beard. "I guess I could lose the beard, maybe dye my hair. Dressed as a sailor—"

"No way." Slovotsky shook his head. "Thousands of people in Pandathaway saw you win the swords competition; a lot of them must still be around."

"I wasn't suggesting that Karl do it. But me, well—"

"Right, Tennetty." Karl snorted. "And there are a whole *lot* of one-eyed women warriors wandering around."

"Well, there's that glass eye that Thellaren has been trying to sell me. Maybe it won't look natural, but . . ." She fingercombed her bangs to half-cover her eyepatch. "But if I wear my hair like this . . ."

"Hmmm." Slovotsky nodded. "It might work. But why not take it from the other end? Pandathaway is too risky—but we could try it from the Enkiar side. I'm more than a little curious about who the guns and powder were going to, and why. And particularly how much they were paying. There's a technical term for the kind of trouble we'll be in if this stuff is relatively cheap."

"What's that?" Karl asked.

"Deep shit." Slovotsky smiled.

"But how would we do it?" Karl rose and stretched. "We don't know who we'd be looking for. The leader might have, but—"

"But what if he got himself killed? What if, say, the group was jumped by that evil, wicked Karl Cullinane and his raiders? And what if they lost, say, a quarter of their number before their guns drove that wicked Cullinane character off?"

Karl nodded. "Not bad." He turned to Tennetty. "How soon are they due in Enkiar?"

She shrugged. "Whenever they got there. Sternius wasn't rushing, but he wasn't lollygagging, either. I figure they're due in about three tendays, but I doubt that the buyer'd be worried if it took four. Only one problem."

"Well?"

"We need the right . . . props. By the time we get to Enkiar, I'm sure we'll be able to handle these slaver rifles, but that's not going to do it, not all by itself."

"So? What's the problem?"

"The first is the wizard. The buyers will be expecting one; apparently this stuff is too valuable to trust to such a small party without having a wizard around for the extra protection. Even if we put one of us into wizard's robes, that might not fool them."

"That's easy," Walter said. "Ellegon's due tonight; we'll have him fly back Home, bring back Henrad. Time the kid earned his keep."

"That's not enough." Tennetty shook her head. "What if the buyers are expecting the slavers to have a couple of slaves with them? I don't think we could expect Jilla and Danni to play along."

"No," Walter said, "we couldn't. Besides, if everything blew up in our faces, they wouldn't be able to fight their way out. No, we'll do it this way: What happened is that one of the slaves got killed in the fight, and the other tried to escape. We flogged her seriously, then healed her up when infection set in and it looked like it was going to kill her. Left a few scars. . . ."

Tennetty finally got it; she gasped, her face paled. "I *can't*. No—nobody's putting a collar around my neck."

"Easy, Ten." Karl laid a hand on her arm. "You don't have to. Maybe it won't be necessary for the disguise to work. The thing is, though . . ." He let his voice trail off.

"Well?"

"Who else could do it? Who else could look the part—and fight her way out, if all hell breaks loose?"

Slovotsky nodded. "As it always seems to. The only other choice I can think of is Andy."

"No." Karl shook his head. *"No.* Not if I'm going to be around. And not if I'm not. Clear?" When Andy-Andy was endangered, it was hard for Karl to concentrate on anything but her safety. He owed the others better—he owed himself better.

Tennetty looked him straight in the eye. "So I'm expendable, but Andrea isn't. Is that the way of it?"

"If you want to think of it that way, then go ahead. It's your choice." He folded his hands over and cracked his knuckles. "But damned if I'm going to justify myself to you, or to anyone else. You got that?"

She grunted.

"I asked if you got that."

"Yes."

"I can't hear you."

"Yes, dammit."

"Fine." He closed his eyes for a moment. He was missing something.

Ahh—if they were going to impersonate the slavers, then this raid didn't happen. And if it didn't happen, then what were all these bodies doing littering the meadow?

He raised a hand and beckoned Erek over. "I want Stick saddled and brought to me; I'm going up to the mesa to wait for Ellegon."

"Messages?"

"Two. First is to Chak. Begins: You and Slovotsky are going to pick a thirty-man team to impersonate some slavers; report to Walter. I want the wagons cleaned up and the insignia remounted; they're to be ready to roll by morning—but keep everyone out of the wizard's wagon; it's to stay sealed up until we have Henrad check it out. Ends. To Gwellin. Begins: Report to Tennetty, immediately. Ends. Go."

Erek nodded and ran off; Karl called Daherrin over. "Change of plans—I want the slavers buried in the woods."

"Buried? What for?"

"Practice."

Daherrin snorted, then broke into a deep-chested laugh. "I *will* get an explanation eventually, won't I?"

"If you live until dark. Bury them deep; I don't want any wolves digging them up. This raid didn't happen. Got it?"

"Yes, Karl Cullinane." The dwarf walked away, bellowing for his assistants.

Karl turned to Slovotsky. "Walter, I want you to pick the team carefully. No dwarves, and go light on elves."

"Of course."

"Compare notes with Tennetty and Chak. This could easily turn out to be messy; anybody who was even a bit off his game last night goes back Home."

"How about Donidge? I hear he was damn good last night."

"So?"

"So, his wife's due in a few tendays. I think it would be nice if he was around for it."

"Good point—count him out. Same for anybody else with pressing business back Home." He lowered his voice. "Exceptway orfay oinersjay; Ahiraway's avinghay enoughway oubletray, as it is. Ka-pish?" Pig latin wasn't exactly an elegant code, but no adults from This Side spoke English well enough to puzzle it out.

"Sí, señor. Gwellin's going to lead the overland group?"

"Right. Also, I want you to have the team work out with the slavers' guns, but make sure everyone's damn careful with that powder until we know more about it. Turn in your own guns to Gwellin; he's to have them broken down and loaded onto the flatbed."

"Can I keep a couple of pistols?"

"No—and none of our bullets or powder, either. We're going to play slaver until we get to Enkiar, and I don't want any slipups." Karl turned to Tennetty. "You're to supervise the stowing of the slaver powder. I want a little taken out of each barrel and put in a flask. Carefully, now—this stuff might be poison; make sure you don't get any on you. Then seal the barrels back up tight and leave them alone."

"Fine." She nodded. "Who's going back Home with the powder?"

"You are. If Ellegon's brought the basket, you'll take Jilla and Danni with you. Otherwise they'll go back overland with Gwellin. Prepare them for both possibilities. Also, take three of the slavers' guns for analysis—put them with the powder. You're to take slaver rifles and powder to Riccetti and Andy-Andy; have them run an analysis. I'll want Ellegon to catch up with us somewhere this side of Enkiar; we'll set up a rendezvous when he gets here. He can bring Henrad along with him."

"And me?"

"Look—if you want in, you've got it. If you don't, you may as well take some time off at Home. If you do want in, you'll have to get yourself outfitted with that glass eye."

"Very well," Tennetty said. "You can count me out of this one, Karl. I don't want to wear a collar again. *Ever.*"

That was too bad, but he wasn't going to try to push Tennetty into doing something that she really wasn't willing to do. "Fair enough. We'll have to do without."

Walter opened his mouth, then closed it. "Fine."

Erek arrived, leading Karl's horse. Karl pulled himself to Stick's broad back. "Anything else?"

"Yes." Tennetty jerked her thumb at the woods. "I've still got those two slavers."

Damn. Karl had forgotten about that for a moment—forgetting wasn't a luxury he could allow himself. "What kind of shape are they in?"

She shook her head. "Not too bad. Just a few cuts and bruises. I mean, I hamstrung them, of course—"

"Of course."

"—but they're not near dead. Should I fix that? Or do you want to?"

"The watchman lives. I promised him."

"Oh, *great.* 'Karl Cullinane's word is as good as gold'—is that it?"

"Yes."

"No!"

Stick took a prancing step backward; Karl reined in the stallion with difficulty. "Easy, damn you. . . . Yes, Tennetty. My word counts for something."

"What do you want to do? If we're going to try to impersonate a slaver team, we can't afford to have him wandering around, working his mouth. Do you want me to turn him *loose?*" she shrilled, her hand resting on the hilt of her saber.

Walter moved behind Tennetty; Karl waved him away. "No, Ten. Take a bottle of healing draughts—one of theirs. Fix up his legs, and one arm. We'll take him back Home, keep him locked up. He won't see any more than traders already have. Once we come back from Enkiar, we'll turn him loose. I promised that he'd live."

Tennetty took a deep breath. "And the other? You didn't promise every bloody slaver his life, did you?"

"No, I didn't. Kill him. Walter, go with her; take charge of the prisoner. I won't want a *ley de fuga,* kapish?"

"Got it."

Karl gave a light tug on the reins; Stick broke into a canter.

CHAPTER THREE

Ellegon

I am a brother to dragons, and a companion to owls.

—Job

The night passed slowly, filled with the chirping of crickets, the whisper of wind through the trees, the flickering of the stars, and the pulsing of the faerie lights overhead. The faerie lights were more subdued, tonight changing slowly, as though the bloodshedding of the preceding night had shocked them into sullen dimness.

Karl finished laying the fire, spread his blanket near the edge of the mesa, then sat down, watching the sky, leaving the wood unlit.

Be here tonight, he thought. *Please.*

Stretching out on the blanket, he pillowed the back of his head on his hands and let his eyes sag shut. It could easily be a long wait.

Karl wasn't on the watch list—rank hath its privileges; and he could have allowed himself to fall asleep in his own tent—but if he wasn't up on the mesa waiting for Ellegon, he would have to put up with the dragon's nagging complaints until Ellegon took off for the trip back Home.

Ellegon was reliable within his limitations, but he did have limitations. It usually took the dragon three days to make it from Home to this particular rendezvous, but any number of things could throw him off schedule. Sometimes, innocuous things—Riccetti might have delayed him to fire a load of soft-pine charcoal, or Nehera might have been working on a batch of high-alloy steel.

Occasionally, Ellegon would be late because the dragon had been delayed at another resupplying stop, helping a hunter team out of trouble.

More than once, Ellegon's arrival had meant the difference between victory and death. A fire-breathing dragon was a nice hole card; standard doctrine, whenever possible, was to schedule a raid just before one of Ellegon's resupplying runs.

Karl smiled, remembering the expression on the face of the slavers who had trapped his team just outside of Lundeyll. Everything had gone wrong that time. A sudden rainsquall had come up, making it impossible for his team to reload their weapons, and it turned out that most of the supposed slaves chained behind the wagons had really been slavers. His back to the Cirric, Karl had resigned himself to a fight to the death, until a familiar voice sounded in his head.

So he had surrendered. Sort of.

Thermyn had been very pleased with his catch, until the moment Ellegon's massive head snaked out from behind a rock outcropping and bit off his legs, leaving an expression more of surprise than pain on his face. . . .

Usually, though, lateness was just a result of Ellegon's trying to avoid people. Dragons were close to extinct in the Eren regions; humans seemed to have an almost instinctive fear of the creatures.

Ellegon didn't fly over populated areas during the day. While the dragon was immune to almost any nonmagical threat, a dragon-baned crossbow bolt could cut through his scales like a hot knife through butter. And though he could fly far, far above the range of any bow, he did have to land eventually. It was best that nobody know when he was in the area, the dragon said.

That was true, but Karl had long suspected that fear of being attacked was only part of the reason the dragon avoided coming within range of strangers; Ellegon simply didn't like reading the hate and fear in their minds.

They had worked out a routine for Ellegon's resupplying trips. The dragon would leave the valley during the afternoon, flying throughout the night and reaching his first resting place just before dawn. He and his human assistant would rest during the day, taking to the air at night, flying as high as possible, crossing the land in night-long hops, finding another resting place before morning, then sleeping, eating, and talking during the day.

Karl had long ago noticed that the more Ellegon liked whoever had been assigned to assist him, the later the dragon tended to be. Extended conversation with adults was a rare pleasure for the dragon; the few Home citizens who really liked Ellegon and felt safe around him were usually too busy to spend much time with him.

Karl lay back, occasionally nodding off, until a vague reassurance touched his mind, bringing him quickly out of his light sleep.

A familiar voice sounded in his head. *Well? I brought the fatted calf—where are the party hats?*

"Ellegon!" A smile spread across Karl's face; he jumped to his feet. *Where are you?*

Just out of sight. I'll be there in a moment. Hang on, stupid.

The flapping of leathery wings sounded from below. Ellegon's massive form rose above the edge of the mesa; the dragon folded his wings against his sides and landed on the flat surface like a sparrow rising to a perch on a rooftop.

A very massive sparrow—the shock of his landing knocked Karl off his feet.

Hello, clumsy, Ellegon said. He was a huge beast, fully the length of a Greyhound bus from the tip of his twitching tail to the end of his saurian snout. He loomed above Karl in the dark, gouts of smoke and steam issuing from nostrils the size of hubcaps.

Would you help Henrad down? The ride seems to have disagreed with him. He's been like this for the whole trip.

"I can't imagine why," Karl said. *Light the fire, if you can reach from here.*

No problem. Ellegon snaked his head out and carefully flamed the wood, while Karl walked around the dragon's side and climbed halfway up the rope ladder to help Henrad unbuckle his riding harness and dismount.

Even in the flickering firelight, the apprentice wizard was almost green. Karl brought Henrad over to his blankets and helped him sit down. The boy gratefully waved Karl away, then leaned forward, his head between his knees.

We ran into a bit of turbulence—rain clouds are moving in. I'll want to take off fairly quickly, if I'm going to outrun it.

Fine. But why Henrad?

Objection?

No, as a matter of fact, he should come in handy. In the morning, the boy could check out the wizard's wagon and disarm any magical glyphs, leaving any physical traps to Slovotsky. *But you didn't answer my question.*

Your wife's idea. His crush on her is getting a bit out of hand— stop that.

Stop what?

Stop reaching for your sword. Andrea can handle him; if she couldn't she would have let me know. She just thought she could use a break from his roving hands and from him "accidentally" bumping into her at every opportunity.

Karl glared at Andy-Andy's apprentice. *I'd better have a word with him, anyway.*

I don't remember you being tolerant of other people messing with your apprentices. Leave it be, Karl, leave it be.

As you did?

Me? The dragon's mental voice was all innocence. *What did I do?*

I suppose that you didn't make the ride as rough as possible. Karl snorted. *I guess I'm just overly suspicious.*

You should watch that tendency of yours. It's not one of your prettier failings.

Others had already arrived to help unload. They began by removing the saddlebag-slung leather sacks, then untied the huge wicker basket cupping the rear half of Ellegon's back and unloaded the burlap sacks underneath it.

Tennetty led the two former slaves up to the dragon, muttering reassuring words, while Daherrin carried the bound, blindfolded, gagged slaver over and unceremoniously dumped him in the basket.

"Daherrin," Karl called out, "sling the basket and rig the tarp. It might get a bit wet up there." *What did you bring?*

Lamp oil, salt, dried beef, mutton, vegetables, bread—the usual. Open that wooden box first. Lou sent along a dozen bottles of the latest batch of Riccetti's Best.

Oh? How good is it?

What does a dragon know about corn whiskey? I can tell you that Ahira swears by it, although I think he's been using a bit too much, of late.

Karl walked over to the dragon's head and reached up to scratch the fine scales under Ellegon's chin. It was like trying to pet a granite wall.

Mmm . . . nice. Harder. It was the thought that counted; Karl would have had to use a hoe for the dragon actually to feel it.

It's good to see you, he thought. *I'm sorry you can't stay long.*

Don't be too sorry. You'll be seeing a lot of me over the next few days. Chton and his Joiners have petitioned for a town meeting; Ahira said to tell you that he is—and I quote—"looking down the barrel of a vote of confidence" and that you are to—quoting again—"hie your ass Homeward, on the double." He's worried, Karl.

How about you?

I think it's going to be close. And with two hunter teams away, he could lose. Pity you didn't think to allow for proxy voting in the Constitution.

Well, if Thomas Jefferson didn't think of it, how would you expect me to?

I have higher expectations of you—

Thanks—

—despite the fact that you are a constant disappointment, and—

—a whole lot. Karl beckoned Chak over. "Which would you rather do: take a side trip Home with me, or run the team until Enkiar?"

"Run the team?" Chak opened his mouth, then closed it. "Why me? Why not Slovotsky?"

"I thought you don't like taking his orders."

He doesn't, but he didn't think you noticed that.

It's not polite to peek into somebody's mind without his permission.

True. Then again, dragons aren't particularly polite.

I've noticed.

Observant, aren't you?

"Well, Chak?"

The little man shrugged. "I'd just as soon go Home with you, all things being equal."

Why are you bringing him Home?

Peep better. Tennetty says that he likes one of the new women. I want to give him a good shot at her, so to speak. It's about time Chak settled down and started a family. Can you reach Slovotsky?

Mmm . . . got him. He's on his way up.

Good. Relay, please: Nothing to worry about, Walter, but I've been called Home.

Ellegon's mental interpretation of Walter's voice was even more animated than usual. *"Trouble? Please don't let there be trouble—"*

Honest. No real trouble. It's just politics. I've got to kick some tails—

Metaphorically, for once, Ellegon put in.

Right. How would you feel about running the team until Enkiar?

"No objection, other than the obvious one . . ."—he wants to go Home, is what he's saying, Karl—". . . but why not Chak?"*

Relay: Because he's not married, and you are, and there are a couple of possible candidates that will be going home with Ellegon and me.

"Good idea. No problem; I'll keep things together."

Good. Hurry up and get up here. We're going to make this a quick turnaround.

Don't you want to know about your family?

There's nothing wrong with my family.

The reason Karl hadn't asked Ellegon about his family wasn't that he didn't care—it was just the opposite. The dragon knew that giving him news of anything wrong with Aeia, Jason, or Andy-Andy took precedence over everything else; since Ellegon hadn't said anything, there wasn't any problem.

True.

He turned back to the dragon. "Any chance of Walter's running into any of our teams between here and Enkiar?"

None. The last of Daven's team have returned Home, and Aveneer is working the edge of the Kathard. Hmmm, I'd better play mailman. If you'll excuse me?

"Sure."

Ellegon raised his head. *Personal messages,* he announced, *for the following: Donidge, Ch'akresarkandyn, Erek, Jenree, Walter . . .*

Karl always liked to watch people get their mail, although Ellegon was scrupulous about turning him out. As the dragon relayed each message from home, the recipient's face would light up like a beacon.

Chak's dark face broke into a wide smile as Ellegon gave him the message. He nodded three times, then sighed, a far-off look in his eyes.

Karl waited until Chak's eyes cleared. "What's the news?"

The little man shook his head, still smiling. "Your son says that I should be real sure not to get my fool ass killed. I think he's been spending too much time around U'len."

"Probably."

Walter arrived, almost breathless.

Karl stuck out a hand. "We're taking off. Run things as you see best."

"I always do."

"But if you don't mind taking some advice . . . Ellegon says that you can't get jumped by any of our teams, but don't take chances. There may be some independents working the road between here and Enkiar. I'd rather you avoid them. Use roving point men, okay? Next, I want you to fill Henrad in, and have him go over the wizard's wagon, for magical traps, and—"

"Hey, if you're leaving me in charge, you'd better trust me not to stab myself in the foot, eh?"

"Right." He clapped a hand to Walter's shoulder. "Take care of things, okay?"

"Sure. Kiss my wife for me—and kiss yours for me, too."

Karl glared at him.

Walter spread his hands. "Face it: I'm irrepressible."

"Right." Karl helped Chak into the basket, then climbed up the rope ladder to the saddle on Ellegon's back and strapped himself in. "Everybody clear. Daherrin, are the straps okay?"

"Tight and strong," the dwarf called back, as he finished belting Chak, Tennetty, and the two women into the basket, then tied down the tarpaulin, leaving only their heads peeking out.

You ready?

Home, James.

My name is Ellegon. The dragon's wings blurred; he leaped skyward.

PART TWO

Home

CHAPTER FOUR

Karl's Day Off

If a man insisted always on being serious, and never allowed himself a bit of fun and relaxation, he would go mad or become unstable without knowing it.

—Herodotus

Almost Home. Close your eyes.

As they passed through the invisible barrier of the Spidersect wards, the air around the dragon shimmered and sparkled, reacting to Ellegon's partially magical metabolism.

Even through his tightly closed eyes, Karl was dazzled, although the momentary discomfort was reassuring. The ragged circle of wards enclosing the valley didn't only prevent outside wizards from peering in, it also prevented anyone from carrying anything magical inside. Soon after Thellaren had set up the wards, three different assassin teams had tried to slip through, but even when they had no other magical implements, their healing draughts had tripped them up.

Word had gotten out; there hadn't been an assassin team in the valley for more than three years.

The light faded; Karl opened his eyes as Ellegon banked and turned, circling in.

The valley spread out beneath them, the fields of corn and wheat a patchwork blanket, ragged toward the edges. Roads crisscrossed the valley like a spider's web, most of them crossing near the compound at the south end of the valley or just outside of Engineer Territory in the north.

Ellegon lost altitude as he swooped across the lake, circling in toward what once had been the original compound and now housed the grainmill, silo, Karl and Andy-Andy's first house, and the former smithy, now used for receiving and settling new arrivals.

The basket barely missing the sharp points of the compound's palisade, the dragon slowed, then hovered, lowering the basket to the ground with a gentle thump, then landing beside it.

Karl unstrapped himself from the saddle, then turned to untie the basket's straps. He quickly slid down the dragon's side to help Chak, Tennetty, and the two women out and onto the ground. They left the slaver inside. There was no rush about him.

"Solid ground," Tennetty breathed. She favored Karl with a smile. "I think solid ground is one of my favorite things in the world."

Chak stretched broadly. "I know what you mean."

"Hey," Karl said. "No complaints. Next time Ellegon'll let you walk."

"Karl's Day Off. I don't see you," Tennetty said, jerking her thumb toward the Old House. "I'll take Jilla and Danni through Receiving and see that the prisoner is properly guarded—my word."

"I can finish up—"

"Karl's Day Off," Chak said, nodding. "Go."

"But the powder. I've got to get that to—"

"The Engineers," Chak said. "And you want Riccetti briefed. Consider it done, kemo sabe. It's Karl's Day Off—begone!"

Chak and Tennetty turned and walked away as though Karl simply weren't there.

You seem to have difficulty winning arguments with people you care about. Ellegon chuckled mentally.

"Really? I never noticed," Karl said.

Sarcasm doesn't become you. School will be letting out shortly. I'm going swimming.

"But there's . . . I give up." Karl threw up his hands. "You win. I'll go change, then join you." He jogged over to the Old House, deliberately ignoring the three millworkers who were deliberately ignoring him.

Early on, Andy-Andy had insisted on a few luxuries for Karl, for fear that if he didn't claim them firmly enough, he'd never get even a taste of them. One of the most important was Karl's Day Off.

The rule was this: Despite whatever was going on at Home, regardless of the fact that there were usually five to ten people who wanted to see him the instant he got back, Andy-Andy had made it clear that Karl was not to be bothered by anyone except members of his immediate family for a full day after returning Home.

It had become almost ritualistic; citizens would pretend not to see him, treating him as though he were invisible.

Shutting the door behind him, he unbuckled his swordbelt and hung it on a peg, then untied the amulet from his neck, stowing it safely behind the top door of a crude bureau. It wasn't necessary to keep the amulet on his person at Home; the entire valley was under the wards' protection.

Hopping on alternate legs he loosened his boots and kicked them toward a corner, then stripped, slipping on a pair of shorts and tucking a towel, shirt, a pair of drawstring jeans, and sandals under his arm before exiting the Old House and jogging the few hundred yards to the lake.

Down the beach, Ellegon had already set down in the water just beyond the end of the schoolhouse's dock. Only his huge head and a portion of his back rose above the clear, cold water, and both were almost concealed by the crowd of half-naked children swarming over him.

Relay, please: Andy?

She knows you're home, but she's busy. Leave her alone while you get clean.

Good idea. Karl dropped his bundle of clothing to the hot sands and dashed for the water.

As always, it was far colder than he'd remembered. The lake was fed by the icy streams that trickled down from the mountains; as he entered the water, he wondered for the thousandth time if it was possible that ice melted at minus forty on This Side.

He forced himself to run into the water until it reached his waist, then dove headfirst and set off with a clumsy but powerful breaststroke toward the dock and the dragon.

If God had ever set out to create the perfect swimming companion for adult or child, Ellegon would have been it. With the dragon around, there was no need for a buddy system to ensure that any head going under the water surfaced with a live body attached. Ellegon would simply order any overtired child—or adult—out of the water, and *nobody* was interested in flouting his orders.

Well, almost nobody; Jason was a special case.

But Ellegon wasn't just a lifeguard.

Care for a dive?

As Karl reached the dragon, he set his feet against Ellegon's right forward knee and stood, rising half out of the water. He shook his head to clear the wet hair from his eyes, making a mental note that he'd better get another haircut, and soon.

I asked if you would care for a dive.

"Sure."

Ellegon carefully shook a pair of twelve-year-olds from his head, then craned his long neck so that Karl could step onto it.

Gently, this time. Wouldn't do for the kids to see me scream in terror.

The scales slippery beneath his feet, Karl stood gingerly and flexed his knees, balancing himself just behind the dragon's eye ridges. Ellegon quickly straightened his neck and tossed his head, sending Karl flipping head over heels forty feet into the air. Karl stretched out his arms, air-braking into a swan dive as he fell; he pulled himself into a tuck, then straightened as he slammed feet first into the water, slipping down into the dark iciness, rebounding gently off the sandy bottom of the lake.

As his head broke the surface, a slim arm snaked around his neck, a hand pressed hard against the back of his head, and a pair of firm young breasts pressed against his back, while powerful thighs scissored his waist.

"Hi!" Aeia said, kissing him on the back of the neck while firmly endeavoring to force his head underwater. "You're back."

"I noticed." *She's getting a bit too old for this,* he thought, far more conscious of her young body than was comfortable. He took a quick, deep breath, and dove.

Do you want to know what's really going on in her head?

No. Don't peep my family for me.

He'd caught her by surprise this time, diving before Aeia had the chance to grab a breath; she released her grip before he ran out of air.

He surfaced, blocked her next try, then grabbed her by the wrist and spun her around, pushing her toward the dock. "Go put on your halter."

"For *swimming?* Don't be such a—"

He forced a grim expression to his face. "Do it. Now."

She pouted and swam away, slipping seallike out of the water and onto the dock, then padding sullenly toward the schoolhouse, adjusting her shorts as she did.

What am I going to do about this?

As I understand it, a bit of repressed sexuality between father and daughter is normal, whether the daughter is adopted or not.

Where did you get that bit of bullshit?

From the usual place: your head. Psych 101. Remember?

Oh.

One bit of advice, if you don't mind?

Yes?

It would be best for everyone if it's kept repressed. Adopted daughter or not, a husband really shouldn't cheat on a wife who can turn him into a toad.

Well, Andy-Andy couldn't really turn him into a toad, but the dragon had a point.

"Right." He looked around, then quickly submerged to avoid the outstretched hands of three boys and two girls who had apparently decided that it was time to drown Karl Cullinane. He swam underwater, ducking under Ellegon's broad belly, then surfaced on the other side. *Is she still busy? Where's Jason?*

She kept him after school. If you ask my opinion—

Which I didn't. But I have a hunch I'll receive the benefit of it anyway.

Good guess. I think she's too strict with him. Karl, he's only six years old. Just—

Ellegon was interrupted by the pounding of feet on the dock and a sudden splash.

Not again! The dragon ducked his head underwater and came up with the wriggling form of Jason Cullinane in his mouth, then carefully spat the coughing boy onto the pier.

Clearly forcing himself to stop coughing, Jason straightened.

He says that he's fine. I'm giving him a bit of hell.

Good for you.

With the sole exception of Jane Michele Slovotsky, Karl had never really been impressed with children. The so-called special things about them were clearly parents' illusions, born of parents' need to feel special.

Jason, on the other hand, was special. It wasn't just that he had Andy-Andy's knowing brown eyes and smooth olive skin, or that the boy's straight brown hair was somehow finer than hair had any right to be. Even at six, Jason Cullinane had developed his own skewed ideas about what was right and wrong, which tended to be resistant to anything short of *force majeure,* and were completely immune to a father's attempts at reason.

What was simultaneously convenient and completely infuriating was that Jason, who could give a donkey stubbornness lessons as far as Karl was concerned, was easily influenced by his peers, and would obey Ellegon almost readily.

*You're *not* old enough to keep the water out of your nose when you jump unless you hold your nose. Until I tell you otherwise, I want you to hold your nose when you jump into the water. I am not going to pull you out again,* the dragon threatened.

I am lying through my many teeth, he said to Karl in a mental aside.

I know.

Jason wiped his nose and sniffed; his brown eyes grew vague.

Talk with your mouth. I want your father to hear you promise.

"I'm sorry, Ellegon," he said. "I won't do it again."

Karl swam over to the dock and pulled himself onto the hot wood. "Hi there."

"Hi, Daddy." Jason walked over to where Karl stood and stuck out a tiny hand.

"What's this?"

"Wanna shake hands."

"What? Jase—"

"Too old to kiss. Only babies do that."

"Who says?"

"Mikyn says."

"He does, does he? Well, whoever Mikyn is, he's wrong. He—"

"Is *not.* Shake hands."

Karl shrugged and sadly accepted the boy's hand in his. "Well, if you're too old, you're too old. What's new?"

"Can I go play?"

Karl could almost have cried. Well, when he was six years old, a lake with a dragon in it would have been a lot more interesting than talking with a father. "Sure."

Before the word was halfway out of his mouth, Jason was already jumping into the water, this time holding his nose.

Karl sighed, then turned and walked down the dock to the school-house. It was a single-roomed building, the classroom roughly the same size as those that had been used on the Other Side since the Sumerians invented schools. While the walls were of good pine, and the benches and desks solidly built, the windows were of smoky, barely translucent glass. Glassmaking was one of the crafts that Home was still deficient in.

At the far end of the room, Aeia and Andy-Andy were crouched in front of a young boy, perhaps two years older than Jason, who was seated on Andy-Andy's chair, shaking his head.

Seeing her always brought it back to him: A smile really could brighten a room. She fingered the bend in her ever so slightly too large nose as she listened to Aeia talking with the boy.

Andy-Andy's frown spoke volumes: She was unhappy, but not with either Aeia or the boy.

She tossed her head, sending her shoulder-length black hair whipping about her face as she turned to glance at him, rewarding him with that smile.

Lady, you still take my breath away.
Should I relay that?
Don't bother. If she doesn't know . . .

He cleared his throat. Aeia, now wearing a halter, turned to wave him to silence.

Karl raised an eyebrow. He'd never been shushed by Aeia before. He walked over and laid a gentle hand on Andy-Andy's shoulder. She turned her face upward, giving him a quick peck.

"What is it?" he asked. "This all I get?"

Old saying: When you don't know what you're talking about, your mouth is best used for chewing.

"Mikyn?" Andy-Andy shook her head. "Please take off your shirt." She turned to Karl. "He's been holding his side all day; he almost couldn't get out of the chair."

"Can I help?" *Ellegon, please relay: Maybe he's a bit shy about taking off clothes in front of you two. Mikyn apparently has some funny ideas—it seems he told Jason that only babies can give their fathers a kiss.*

She says, "Karl, I think this is a bit more serious."
Ellegon, why don't you just peep him?

She already asked me to. There's a block—a lot of emotion going on under the surface, but I can't read it at all. I'm not perfect, you know. Sometimes, when you get too intense, I can't even read you.

Okay; back to basics. Relay: Let me give it a try. What's to lose?

She nodded, then rose, giving him a quick peck on the lips before taking Aeia out of the room.

Karl chuckled thinly. *Some welcome.* "Hi there," he said in English, then switched to Erendra when the boy didn't answer. "What's the problem?"

No answer.

"You know who I am?"

"J-Jason's father."

"Right. You can call me Karl. Andrea says that your side hurts. Can I take a look?"

Mikyn shook his head.

"You don't have to." Karl nodded. "We'll do it your way. Do you mind talking for a while?" Karl pulled over Andy's chair and seated himself ass-backward, folding his arms over the chair's back.

"No."

"I don't remember seeing you around. Are you new here?"

"Yes."

New here. Well, if Karl hadn't brought the boy in, then somebody else had; Jason was the oldest person to be born in Home, Jane Michele Slovotsky second by half a year.

Relay: Tell me about the boy.

She says, "Not much to tell. Sad story, but typical. Daven's team brought him and his father in, about tendays ago. They're cropping for the Engineers until they earn their grubstake. They're from Holtun—used to be owned by some baron or other who got burned out by the Biemish; apparently got scooped up early this year, after some battle or other. The mother got sold off. This isn't the first time he's been hurt; Mikyn bruises easily. I think one of the older boys may have been beating him up. But Ellegon can't peep out who—"

No need, dammit.

You know what it is?

I know what it sounds like. He dialed for his command voice. "Take the shirt off, *now.*"

Wide-eyed, the boy started to comply, then remembered that he wasn't supposed to take his shirt off and pulled it back down.

But not before Karl saw the huge bruise across his ribs. "Aeia, get in here." His jaw clenched. *So much for my day off.*

He forced a smile to his face. "I'm going to have Aeia take you over to Thellaren. You won't have to take off your shirt for him to fix you up. And then you can go right home."

That last hit Mikyn like a slap. The boy's face whitened.

Karl smiled reassuringly. "No, not your home. Jason's and mine. You don't have to go back to your father, if you don't want to. But when you do, he's not going to hurt you anymore. I promise."

You want me to send for a sword?

No. Drop Ahira off at the Old House. Then find Mikyn's father and probe him. If I'm right, scoop him up and bring him, too.

He nodded to Aeia. "Take Mikyn to the cleric. When you're done there, find him a bed in the New House; he's staying with us tonight. I'll see you later."

He walked to the door and walked back to the Old House, his hands balling themselves into fists.

Leathery wings flapped outside the Old House, followed by a solid thump.

Limping slightly, Ahira swung the door open and walked into the room, his forehead creased in irritation.

The dwarf was barely half Karl's height, but fully as wide. That, combined with his heavy brows and overmuscled body, always made him look as though nature had intended Ahira to be a tall man, but his body had never gotten the hint.

Despite the situation, Karl had to repress a smile. He always had to, whenever he saw Ahira wearing a pair of Homemade jeans and a blue cotton workshirt. Somehow the dwarf looked more natural in chainmail and leather.

Karl gestured him toward a chair. "Good afternoon, Mr. Mayor."

The dwarf remained standing. "Cut the crap—I'm busy. I *was* busy, that is, until that damn dragon of yours swooped down out of the sky and scooped me up without so much as a by-your-leave."

"What's the problem?"

"Territory dispute. Riccetti's complaining that Keremin's encroaching on a field that belongs to the Engineers."

"Well? Is Lou lying?"

"Fat chance."

"So? What's the big deal?"

"Well, Keremin's a Joiner, but he's been a quiet one, lately. I'm trying to smooth it over, without getting him all that angry at me just before the town meeting."

"Any chance of giving Lou a substitute parcel?"

Ahira shrugged. "It's the lot just west of the cave." He sighed and sat down. "And it's his. Politics is thirsty work—hint, hint."

"Sure." Karl found two clay mugs in the near cabinet, then took a bottle down from the shelf, uncorked it, and poured each of them three fingers of Riccetti's Best. "You missed something kind of important."

"What is it now?" Ahira sipped his whiskey, then made a face. "This isn't too bad, but have you tasted the beer lately? I could swear that it's getting worse. I'd give my kingdom for a Miller, my empire for a Genee Cream."

"Ahira, we've got a case of childbeating, I think."

"Shit. Who?"

"New folks. The kid's name is Mikyn. I don't know the father's."

The dwarf's free hand clenched into a fist. "You want me to handle this? I don't like childbeaters any more than you do."

"Sure you do. You feel a lot of sympathy for the poor, misunderstood bastards. Matter of fact, you're the only thing that's standing between big, bad Karl Cullinane and this particular poor, misunderstood bastard."

"Really? You're sure about that?"

"Yup."

Leathery wings flapped overhead. *We are here. And you were correct about Alezyn. I'm sorry, Karl.*

Why?

Dammit, this is the sort of thing I'm supposed to spot, and prevent. It's just that I hate probing people I don't know, and it's really—

Shh. We're not required to be perfect. We're just required to do our damnedest.

But what do we do when that isn't enough?

There wasn't an easy answer to that. Karl lifted his head. "Alezyn, get in here. *Now.*"

The door swung tentatively open, and Ellegon nudged Alezyn into the room. Alezyn sprawled face-first on the floor, then picked himself up.

The trouble was, Alezyn didn't look like a childbeater. He was a short, balding little man, with a round face and wide eyes; his expression was half hostile, half frightened; he looked far more like someone beaten on than the sort of brute who would take his frustrations out on a child.

"What is this all about?"

"We want to talk with you," Ahira said.

"Yes, Mr. Mayor." Alezyn started to tug on his forelock, then caught himself.

"And," the dwarf went on, "either we're going to have a very productive talk, or . . ." He let his voice trail off.

"Or?"

Ahira turned to Karl. "Show him."

Karl stood. He grabbed the smaller man by the front of his tunic and easily lifted him off the ground.

"We haven't met before. My name is Karl Cullinane. And what I want is for you to understand why I'm going to start with *this.*" He bounced Alezyn off the nearest wall, then took a step forward as the other lay on the bare wood floor, gasping for breath.

Ahira caught his arm. "No, don't kill him."

Ellegon poked his head through the door. *No, I have a better idea. Let me eat him. I've always wondered how a man who beats children would taste.*

Karl wouldn't have thought it possible for the little man's eyes to grow wider. He was wrong.

"Never mind, Ellegon," Karl said. "It'd probably poison you."

From Ahira: "You're planning to put the fear of God into him, right?"

No, the fear of me. *Sometimes God doesn't follow through.*

"Too risky. He might take his frustrations out on the kid, then panic and kill him."

So?

"So follow my lead." "Put him down, Karl."

"But—"

"Put. Him. Down." As Karl complied, the dwarf helped Alezyn off the floor, and threw an arm around the man's shoulder. "Let's talk, just you and me."

Alezyn made an abortive attempt to shake the arm off, but he might as well have been trying to pry away a steel bar.

"I understand what you've been going through," Ahira said gently. "Captured, enslaved, your wife sold off. And now, you're in a new country, and we don't do things the way you did them at home. Frustrating, eh?" He helped Alezyn to a chair, then offered him a sip of whiskey. "Go ahead. It'll be good for you."

The little man took a shallow sip. "Yes, b-but—can I talk freely? Without *him* hitting me again?"

"Of course. You're under my protection while you're in this room." The dwarf turned to glare at Karl. "You hear that?"

"Yes."

"Yes, *what?*"

"Yes, Mr. Mayor."

"Better." Ahira turned back to Alezyn. "You were saying?"

"Mikyn is my son. When he disobeys, I have the right to punish him. He's *my* son. *Mine.*"

"That's right. And what you're going to have to learn is that here, 'my son' or 'my wife' or even 'my horse' means something different than 'my shovel.' Or . . ."

"Or?"

"Or I'll kick your ass out that door and let Karl slice you into breakfast for Ellegon," the dwarf bellowed, his face a mask of rage.

"As I was saying," he said in a calm voice, "you've got a lot to learn. And I don't think you're going to learn it cropping for the Engineers. I've got just the schoolroom in mind. Karl."

"Yes, Mr. Mayor?"

"Escort Alezyn over to the parade ground. Daven's team is running some maneuvers." He switched to English. "The other day, I was telling him some stories my father used to tell me about Marine boot camp. He'll understand when you tell him that Alezyn is to be treated as a boot." He turned to Alezyn and spoke in Erendra. "Karl will take care of your son until you're done training."

"Training?"

"Yes. We're going to make a warrior out of you."

"A warrior?" Alezyn's face whitened.

"Yes. It's either that, or banishment. You can start running right now, if that's what you want. Or . . ."

"Or?"

The dwarf chuckled. "Whenever I end a sentence with an *or,* you really should hold on to your curiosity. We're going to make a warrior out of you, or we're going to kill you trying. You can either get your stupid butt out the door and wait for Karl, or . . ." His voice trailed off.

Alezyn didn't ask; he bolted for the door.

Karl chuckled. "Ahira, I like your style." He sobered. "We've got lots to talk about. Why don't you bring Kirah and Janie over to the New House for dinner?"

Ahira picked up his cup and drained it, then looked inside. "I seem to be out of whiskey." Karl passed him the bottle; ignoring the cup, the dwarf uncorked it and tilted it back. "Mmm . . . dinner sounds good—want to include Riccetti?"

"Sure. Can you put him up for the night, though? I'm putting Mikyn in our guesting room, and I wouldn't want to slight Lou."

"Damn well better not. And sure, he can have my room. I don't get much use of it, lately."

"Really? I didn't know that your social life had picked up."

"Very funny. Janie's been having nightmares again. I have to sleep with her most nights." The dwarf snorted. "At least, she says she has bad dreams; I think maybe she just wants some more attention."

"You're spoiling that kid."

"You think so, eh?" Ahira cracked his knuckles. "You want to try to stop me?"

"Me?" Karl raised his hands in mock surrender. "I wouldn't dare —but I'd better get over to the house; U'len will have my hide if I don't give her a bit of warning. And we'll add Thellaren, too. Get some work done tonight."

"How about Karl's Day Off?"

"Screw Karl's Day Off." He walked out into the square, where Alezyn stood waiting.

CHAPTER FIVE

Dinner Party

No medicine can be found for a life which has fled.

—Ibycus

Karl considered the last thick wedge of blueberry pie on the earthenware serving tray, then decided that the remaining shards of Karl's Day Off entitled him to it.

He slipped it onto his plate and brought a spoonful to his mouth. Damn, but it was sweet. Fresh-baked goods were what he missed most when he was on the road.

At the other end of the table, Andy-Andy smiled a promise at him.

Well, maybe fresh-baked goods weren't exactly what he missed most.

Sometimes, life is almost worth living. He folded his hands over his belly and sat back, letting his eyes sag half-shut.

Reaching for a piece of cornbread, Ahira accidentally elbowed a knife from the table; it clattered on the floor.

Karl leaped out of his chair, his hand going to his waist for the hilt of the sword that wasn't there.

"Karl!"

He stopped himself in midmotion, feeling more silly than anything else. Gesturing an apology, he took his seat, feeling every eye in the room on him. "Sorry, everybody. It's . . . just that it takes a while, after you've been out. I kind of need to . , , decompress."

"You're not the only one," Chak said from the doorway, chuckling as he sheathed his falchion. The little man walked over to the table and took a piece of cornbread from the breadboard. "When I heard the clatter, I rolled, drew my sword, and was halfway down the stairs before I realized that it was probably just some eating ware."

"How are the children?" Andy-Andy asked.

"Wonderful." Chak smiled. "Jason and Janie are snoring, and I was finally able to get Mikyn to fall asleep."

Karl snorted. "You didn't have to play baby-sitter, you know. You're allowed to come up and eat with the rest of us."

"I never see enough of Jason and Janie," Chak shrugged. "I've seen you eat more than often enough, Karl. It's no thrill."

"Thanks." Karl gestured to a chair. "Do you want to join us, or would you rather go watch the children sleep?"

The dark little man pitched his sheathed falchion into the sword-stand in the corner and sat, pulling himself up to the table next to Aeia. "U'len, I'll have some beef," he called toward the kitchen.

The answer came back immediately: "Then go bite a cow!"

A chorus of quiet chuckles sounded. Karl looked around the long table. Except for Chak, everyone seemed satisfied, although Aeia's plate was closer to full than he liked to see. Was she eating so lightly because of some teenage pickiness, or because she was afraid to appear less than grown-up in the way she handled a knife and fork?

Well, either way, she could always snack later, he decided. U'len wheedled easily.

In the seat of honor at Karl's left, Lou Riccetti had pushed his chair away from the edge of the table and loosened his trousers' drawstrings, accepting the offer of a damp cloth from the teenage junior apprentice Engineer who waited attentively behind his chair, one hand always resting on a holstered pistol.

More than once, Riccetti had privately offered to waive the body-guard when he was visiting, but Karl had vetoed that. For the next few years, Lou Riccetti would be the most valuable person in the valley, and the rituals that Riccetti and Ahira had developed for the Engineers were too useful to allow for weakening exceptions. Karl wasn't necessarily going to remain the only target of guild-inspired assassination attempts.

He frowned; Riccetti's weight bothered him. Karl had always secretly suspected that Riccetti, pudgy before they'd been transferred to This Side, would run to fat, but he'd been dead wrong. Lou was almost skeletal these days; he claimed he was just too busy to eat, and while his junior Engineers cooked for him, none was ever presumptuous enough to tell the Engineer to slow down or eat more.

"I should send U'len over to cook for you," Karl said. "Got to get some meat on your bones."

"I'm doing fine."

"I'll tell you when you're doing fine, asshole. Eat regularly, put on some weight, or I'll tell U'len to keep the stew coming while I hold you down and force-feed it to you."

The apprentice—Ranella, that was her name—kept her pimpled face calm only with visible effort. In Engineer Territory at the north end of the valley, nobody spoke to the Engineer that way. Ever.

"And I get no say in the matter?" U'len said with a sniff, as she bustled through the curtains covering the arched doorway that led from the kitchen to the dining room, two fresh pies balanced on a wooden slab next to a platterful of roast beef that overflowed, dripping red juices. She was a profoundly fat woman of about fifty, her face perpetually red from the heat of the stove.

"You think I have little enough work to do here, that you can make me cook for those filthy Engineers as well? You should lay off your sword practice for a few tendays, and exercise your mind. If you have one." She handed Chak the platter of beef, then set one pie down gently on Andy-Andy's end of the table and slammed the other down on Karl's. "Always making problems for me, for your wife, for everyone and everything . . ."

"Easily solved—at least as far as you're concerned," Karl said. "You're fired."

"I am *not*. You wouldn't dare, you brainless son of a—"

"*Enough.*"

"*I* will tell *you* when I've said enough," she called over her shoulder as she vanished back into the kitchen. "Damn fool swordsman. I'd say he had droppings for brains, except that'd be unfair—to droppings. . . ."

Well, U'len was the best cook in the valley, although her tongue was just as sharp as her kitchen knives. Karl was secretly pleased with her irritability; U'len had come a long way from the cringing wretch in the slave markets of Metreyll.

Sitting on Riccetti's left, Thellaren brushed a few stray crumbs from his black robes and smiled as he reached for a piece of pie, his hands seemingly immune to the hot drops of bubbling blueberry filling.

"You seem to collect irritating people around you, Karl Cullinane." The fat Spidersect priest shook his head. "One would think that you like it that way." Thellaren broke off a crumb and blew on it before feeding the tarantula-sized spider on his shoulder. The creature grabbed the morsel in its mandibles, then scurried away, hiding itself somewhere inside the priest's ample robes.

"True enough." Ahira grinned slyly. "After all, look who he married."

The dwarf had timed that just right, just as Andy-Andy had lifted her goblet and begun to drink. Water spurted out of her mouth and onto her plate.

Riccetti flashed a brief smile. "Two points, Ahira."

Andy-Andy glared at both the Engineer and the dwarf, then broke into a fit of giggles.

Karl sighed happily. He hadn't heard her actually giggle for years.

After a brief glance at Ahira for permission, Kirah joined in the general laughter. Walter's wife was still, even after all this time, reserved, almost silent, around Karl. The dwarf was a different case; since Ahira lived with her, Janie, and Walter, she had come to take him for granted.

Karl pushed his chair back from the table and folded his hands over his navel. "So? Where do we stand?"

"Which?" Riccetti downed the last of his water. "Politics or powder?"

"Dealer's choice."

Ahira bit his lip. "It's the politics that worries me. Even if the locals—"

"The slavers."

"—even if the slavers have figured out how to make powder, we have quite a few tricks in reserve. Nitrocellulose," Ahira said with a sigh. "If necessary."

Riccetti snorted. "Fine. *You* figure out how to keep it stable."

Karl raised an eyebrow. "How's the research going?"

"Not well. It's still averaging around ninety, ninety-five days before the damn stuff self-detonates." He threw up his hands. "It could be that I've got to figure out a better wash—or maybe just bite the bullet and admit that I can't do it with the kinds of impurities we're getting in the sulfuric. Or maybe I should just tell you to find yourself another jackleg chemical engineer."

"Hey, Lou—"

"Don't heylou me, dammit. If I had *wanted* to major in chemical engineering instead of civil engineering, I would have. You know how I was taught to procure explosives?"

"Well—"

"I was taught to *order* them. Out of a *catalog.* You get a *license,* you fill out the *forms,* you write a *check . . .*" He chewed his thumbnail. "And really pure chemicals—"

"Wait." Ahira held up a hand. "Lou, with all due respect, do we have to go through this again? We all know that you're going to keep working on guncotton, and everybody in this room believes that you'll lick the self-detonating problem, eventually."

"*Sure* I will. Ever read that Verne book about a trip to the moon?"

"The one where they shot them out of a cannon? No. Why?"

Riccetti spread his hands on the table. "Observe—at no time do the fingers leave the hand. I like it that way." He drummed his fingers on the table. "Most of the book was nonsense. But ol' Julie had one thing right. Most of his characters—people who spent a lot of time dealing with explosives—were missing a few body parts. If I had to start making explosives in quantity, God knows what'll happen."

"So don't make any quantities until you're ready to."

"I guess I should have studied chemical engineering. Or brought along a few pounds of PYX, maybe."

"There is a . . . nastier alternative." Andy-Andy's face grew grim. "I could put in the work to learn transmutation of metals, instead of just doing this agricultural kid stuff. How many pounds of uranium would it take to—"

"Forget it." Riccetti shook his head. "Three problems. First, without good explosives for the lenses, setting off a fission bomb isn't easy. Second, it isn't only uranium you need, you need uranium that's ninety-seven plus percent U-two-thirty-five. Third, you won't live to get good enough to do any kind of transmutation. It's not like rainmaking. Aristobulus wasn't far enough along for transmutation, and you're still not half the wizard . . . he was."

"Delicately put." Ahira raised his eyes to heaven. "But Lou's right, although for the wrong reasons. We're not taking that route."

Thellaren raised an eyebrow, but didn't ask. "Mr. Mayor, what do you think we ought to do about the political situation? You are not willing to consider Lord Khoral's new offer?"

"New offer?" Karl asked. "Something I don't know about?"

"Yeah." The dwarf shook his head. "We've got another emissary from Khoral due between now and the town meeting, and I expect he's going to go up the ante. More serfs; titles enough to go around—how would you like to be Karl, Baron Cullinane?"

Karl snorted.

"All he wants is your fealty, Karl. And, just maybe, he wants Lou to give him the secret of gunpowder."

"What he wants, Ahira, is both Lou and a bargaining chip to bludgeon the Slavers' Guild with."

"It's not the bludgeoning that bothers you. It's the possibility of *not* bludgeoning. C'mon, now, there's never been a human baron in Therranj," the dwarf teased. "Wouldn't you like to be the first?"

"No, thanks." It was partly a matter of ego, partly a matter of dignity. But mainly it was a matter of independence.

Karl didn't like the idea of being told what to do by anyone, and he most particularly didn't like the idea of becoming a second-class Therranji. Elves had ruled in Therranj forever; the present Lord Khoral claimed to trace his ancestry back for thousands of years. Humans were second-class citizens in Therranj, and though most of them were as native-born as the elves, descendants of immigrants from the Eren regions, humans were forbidden to own land, ride horses, or practice half a score of professions.

And despite the fact that Khoral had already offered full Therranji citizenship to everyone in the valley—humans, elves, and dwarves alike—Karl was more than sure that that wouldn't quite take. Racial prejudice was different here, but still every bit as firmly entrenched on This Side as back on the Other Side.

Maybe worse, in a way; here, there was a sound basis for at least some of it. While Karl didn't have anything against dwarves or elves, he wouldn't want Aeia to marry either; any children would be sterile, mules.

And then there was the matter of the Slavers' Guild. Western Therranj was a prime raiding ground for the slavers, and certainly that was a common interest between Home and Therranj for now—but that could change. There was no doubt that Khoral wanted to hold the threat of Karl Cullinane over the slavers' heads, promising to restrain him if the guild would lay off the raids on Therranj.

What bothered Karl was that Khoral just might persuade the guild. The spreading war in the Middle Lands increased the supplies of slaves in its wake; it was becoming increasingly easy for the guild to trade in Bieme and Holtun rather than raiding into Therranj.

There was an even darker side to it. What if Khoral was sincere? What if he really would make Karl some sort of baron?

That was a trap for both ruler and ruled. Karl's authority over his warriors flowed from respect and choice—both theirs and his. There might come a time when he could give up that authority and what went with it, when he'd be able to say that he'd never again have to see friends' intestines spill onto the grass.

But that could only happen as long as he remained free. Not trapped by a title.

"The town meeting is the problem," Karl said. "At least for now. It might get a bit dirty—"

"Karl—" Andy-Andy started.

"—*politically,*" he went on. "No bloodshed. I'll handle it. Just make sure that the envoy's kept busy until the meeting. Give him a full, in-depth tour, excluding Reserved caverns. Hell, you can have Nehera discourse for a couple of hours on alloys. Hmmm . . . I don't see any need for the envoy to be muttering with the Joiners—so be careful." He turned to Lou. "Anything outside of the caverns that shouldn't be seen?"

"Well, nothing critical, but yes," Riccetti said, frowning. "There's a charcoal heap still smoldering—that's no problem. But we've got a few pots boiling over wood fires. I'll draft Ellegon to hurry the job, but getting them inside before they cool would be a problem. Andrea, would you levitate them for me?"

"After that crack about how easy rainmaking is, I shouldn't—but I will." She wrinkled her brow. "I hope they're covered, though. You did know I'm rainmaking tonight?"

"I knew," Riccetti said. "The pots are under flies. As for getting it out of sight . . . I can have everything inside by tomorrow night if you'll come over after school and give us a hand."

"Sure."

He didn't say what was in the pots, but Karl assumed it was dirt from the cave floors, saltpeter being crystallized out of the bat guano as an ingredient for gunpowder. There was no need to be overly secretive. Everyone in the valley either knew or suspected that the making of gunpowder involved boiling something. Exactly what would be hard to guess, but there was no need to take extra chances.

Karl nodded. "Sounds good. As far as the emissary goes, he can say what he wants to; I just want the last word. Both with the elf and before the voting."

"Karl, you're treating this too lightly," the dwarf said, shaking his head. "I really think you ought to go around and talk to people."

"Too obvious. The Joiners will be expecting me to do some politicking for you."

"Hell, *I'm* expecting you to go around politicking for me."

"Guess again." Karl shook his head. "You're thinking like a politician."

"Which you're not."

"Precisely. We living legends do things differently." Karl blew on his fingernails and buffed them on his chest. "By now, it's common knowledge from here to the caverns that I'm back because you sent for me. And since I've always hated to do the expected, I'm going to do nothing political, say nothing political, until the town meeting."

"And then?"

"And then I . . . transcend the political."

Ahira chuckled. "The last time I was around when you 'transcended the political,' you beat the hell out of Seigar Wohtansen. Hope you don't end up as unpopular around here as you are in Melawei."

"Don't mention Melawei." Karl slammed his fist down on the table, sending plates and silverware clattering. *"Ever."* It wasn't just that Melawei was where Rahff had died; Melawei was also where the sword of Arta Myrdhyn lay waiting in a cavern beneath an offshore island, clutched in fingers of light.

It's not waiting for my son, you bastard. You keep your bloody hands off Jason. He rubbed his fingers against his eyes until sparks leaped behind his eyelids. "I'm sorry, Ahira—everybody." He opened his eyes to see Lou Riccetti standing, his fingers clutching the apprentice's wrist. Chak stood behind her, one hand gripping her hair, his eating knife barely touching the wide-eyed girl's throat.

"Easy, Chak," Karl said. "Let her go."

Eying the apprentice suspiciously, Chak let go of her hair and took his seat again, carefully examining the knife's edge.

"Ranella," Riccetti said quietly, releasing the girl's arm. "We have discussed this. You may pull a weapon on *me* before you threaten Karl. Understood?"

"But I was just—"

"An excuse? Did I hear an *excuse?*"

"No, Engineer."

"Am I understood?"

"Yes, Engineer."

Riccetti held out his right hand; the apprentice laid the pistol gently in it. "Report to the officer of the watch as quickly as possible, and ask him to send me a pair of *decent* bodyguards; I'll remain here until they arrive. You won't need to use your horse; the run will be good for you. Begin now. Dismissed."

"Yes, Engineer." Her face a grim mask, the girl spun on her heel and sprinted from the room.

Riccetti turned to Karl. "I . . . understand about some things making you angry, but I really don't want you to ever force me to do that again. Ranella's a good kid; I don't like having to punish her."

Riccetti was right. At Karl's original insistence, Engineers were trained always to be careful of Riccetti's safety, and anything that might dull that training was wrong.

Karl raised a hand in apology. "Sorry, Lou—you, too, Ahira. My fault, again. I've been out too much lately; I really should spend more time at Home."

Thellaren cleared his throat. "I believe we were discussing the political issues?"

"Right." Karl smiled a quick thank-you at the cleric. "There's two sides to the problem: the Joiners and Khoral's emissary. We've got to pry enough votes away from the former to make sure you stay in office, while letting the latter know that Therranj is better off with us as a friendly neighbor than they would be if they decide to get nasty. So . . ."

"So?"

"So, trust me."

The dwarf sat silently for a moment. "Done."

Karl picked up the handbell from the table and rang it. Footsteps sounded on the stairs; Ihryk stepped into the room.

"Hell, Ihryk. I didn't know you were working." Ihryk worked part-time for Karl and Andy-Andy as a houseman, using the income to supplement his work on his own fields. He could have expanded his fields and supported himself and his family entirely by farming, but he seemed to like the variety almost as much as the pay.

"We finished planting my wheat two days ago; I start my tenday tonight."

"It's good to see you. How are things upstairs?"

"The children are fast asleep."

"Good. Aeia, why don't you say goodnight to everybody and let Ihryk tuck you in."

She frowned. "But Karl—"

"Enough of that," Karl said. "If you don't get enough sleep, the kids'll run you ragged tomorrow."

"Uh, Karl?" Andy-Andy raised a finger. "With all due respect, buzz off. While you were on the road, Aeia and I decided that she's old enough to pick her own bedtime."

"Right. Sorry, Aeia." Karl added another entry to his ever-lengthening list of things to do. He'd have to get Aeia married off. Not that he could force her into anything. God knew where she'd picked up that stubborn streak, but she had.

One way to do it might be to pick someone appropriate and forbid Aeia to see him. But who? Karl couldn't see turning her over to some ex-slave farmer who didn't know one end of a sword from another, but the idea of Aeia ending up as a warrior's widow didn't thrill him, either. Besides, Andy-Andy wouldn't stand for that.

Maybe an engineer. He'd have to talk to Riccetti, have Lou keep an eye out for someone who might be right for Aeia.

Well, I'm not going to solve that one tonight. Karl turned to Kirah. "It would be a shame to wake Janie. Why don't you let her spend the night here?"

It wasn't just that he liked having Janie around, although he did. Mainly, he was thinking of the morning; Jason thought of Jane Michele as a sort of younger sister who required a good example in order to stay out of trouble, and that tended to suppress Jason's natural inclinations to get himself into trouble.

She nodded.

"Good," he said, standing and stretching. "Sorry to interrupt the party, people, but I've had a long day, and I've got to turn in."

Andy-Andy rose. "Ahira, Lou, Thellaren, I'll give you enough time to get home before I start the rain."

Riccetti frowned. "Do you have to do it tonight?"

"I promised. Ihryk isn't the only one who's planted in the past few days; a good rain will give those fields a nice start." She smiled at Karl. "I'll help them all on their way. Why don't you go up and stretch out?"

He opened the door slowly. Karl stepped into Jason's room, moving quietly, softly, like a thief in the night.

Barely visible in the dim starlight that streamed in through the open window, the three children slept together, Mikyn's and Janie's bedding rumpled, but empty.

Janie was snoring, as usual. How a cute little girl like Jane Michele had developed such a snuffling snore was something that escaped Karl.

Mikyn huddled on his left side, curled into a fetal position, his breathing shallow, ragged, as though he didn't dare relax, not even in his sleep.

Maybe I let Alezyn off too lightly, Karl thought. Well, if so, that would be easy to fix. Then again, killing somebody just because he was a bastard was probably not the best way to handle things—the world was so damn full of bastards.

He had to chuckle at the way Jason slept between the other two children, stretched out flat on his back, one little arm thrown protectively around each of the other's shoulders.

Karl seated himself tailor-fashion next to the bed as the rain began, falling softly, a gentle benediction on the ground outside. He reached out and gently cupped the back of Jason's head with his hand. Jason's hair was fine, silky . . . and clean, for once.

Little one, he thought, *I don't see nearly enough of you.* That was one of the troubles with this damn business. It took Karl away from home too much, and left his nerves frazzled too much of the time that he was home. Normally, it wasn't as bad as it had been tonight; usually, the trip back gave him a chance to decompress. But riding Ellegon back had cut that time short. Too short.

Slowly, gently, Karl bent over and carefully kissed Jason on the top of his head. *Arta Myrdhyn,* he thought, *you're not going to get your hands on Jason. Not my son.*

He heard Andy-Andy's footsteps on the stairs, and waited to hear her walk to their room, and then, seeing that he wasn't there, turn around and look for him with the children.

She surprised him; she came directly to Jason's room. She stood in the doorway, the light of the hall lantern casting her face into shadow. A stray breeze touched the hem of her robes, swirling it around her ankles.

"Everything okay in here?" she whispered.

"Fine," he answered, rising. "Come take a look."

"No." She touched a finger to his lips. "You come with me." She blew out the hall lamp and led him down the hall to their room.

Wind whipped at the curtains, sending their hems fluttering over the bed. Andy-Andy pulled the covers aside.

"Well, well." He raised an eyebrow. "Andy, what do—"

"Shh." She shook her head slowly. "Don't say anything." She

pulled her robes over her head, tossed them aside, and stood naked in front of him. "Your turn."

He returned her smile, pulled off his shirt, and stooped to unlace his sandals.

Ellegon's roar cut through the night. *. . . assassins,* his distant voice said. *With crossbows, dragonbane . . .*

Karl could barely hear the dragon. *Where?* he thought, trying to shout with his mind.

The mental voice cleared. *Better. Werthan's farm. They have taken the house, but they aren't planning on staying inside. I'll have to get closer to read them better.*

"You said they had dragonbane. Get the hell up in the sky. I want you on high sentry. Do not get within range of the bows. How many of them are there?" And what the hell was wrong with the wards? They should have picked up the assassins' healing draughts, even if they weren't carrying anything else magical.

They don't have any healing draughts—and dragonbane isn't magical. It just interferes with the magical parts of my metabolism.

Never mind that. How many of them are there?

Three. I couldn't get much out of their minds, but they're headed this way.

"*Thryk!*" he shouted. "Unlock the guncase and get me two pistols. Move." He saw that Andy-Andy was already struggling back into her clothes. "Chak! To me!"

He turned to his wife. "We'll play it just like a drill, beautiful," he said, forcing a calm voice to come out of his throat. "You get the children into the cellar."

Andy-Andy was capable of giving him a hard time, but not in this sort of situation; she dashed for Jason's room.

Karl ran to the top of the stairs. "U'len, bring the maids; I'll send the stableboy and Pendrill."

Until and unless he knew better, Karl was going to assume that the assassins were after him; the first thing to do was to see to the safety of his family and servants.

At the bottom of the stairs, Chak had already retrieved Karl's saber as well as his own falchion. He tossed the scabbarded sword up to Karl, then gave a quick salute with his falchion. "You have a better second in mind?"

Karl was about to answer, but a shout from outside interrupted him.

"Karl! It's Ahira. I have Lou and Kirah with me."

Karl ran down the stairs and swung the door open. The three of them were half naked, although Ahira had his battleaxe clutched firmly in his hands.

"Get in here—*move it.* Kirah, help Andy get the kids to the cellar. Ahira and Lou, get down there. Chak, you go with them. I'm going to take Tennetty, if she's available, or go it alone."

"But—"

"My family comes first. I'm counting on you and Ahira to keep them safe for me. I need to worry about my own neck."

Chak opened his mouth to protest, then shrugged. "Yes, Karl. Nobody will get past me."

The dwarf nodded grimly. "Understood." Handing his battleaxe to Chak, he helped Andy and Kirah usher the three sleepy-eyed children down the stairs to the basement.

Karl paused to think. Reinforcements, that was the first order of business, but the New House was between where Ellegon reported the assassins were and where Daven's encampment was. Not good.

Ellegon—where's Tennetty?

She'll be outside in a moment. She plans on having Carrot saddled for you.

"Good. I want Daven's team surrounding this house. Light bonfires. Nothing and *nobody* gets inside until you sound the all-clear."

On my way. The dragon's mental voice began to fade in the distance.

"*Wait*—this all could be a feint. After you alert Daven, I want you to fly a spiral search pattern."

Over the whole valley? That will take—

"Just do it. Then back to high sentry over the assassins, but not until you're sure that we're clear."

I believe that the three of them are alone—

Ellegon—

But I hear and obey. Luck.

Ihryk arrived with two pistols from the downstairs weapons case, plus a beltpack containing powder, bullets, and swatches for bullet patches.

Karl nodded his thanks as he belted on his saber, tucking the pistols in his belt. He'd better get outside immediately and let his eyes begin to adjust to the dark. He glanced down at his naked chest, drawstring jeans, and open-toed sandals. Not a good idea. His scabbarded sword in his hand, he ran for the door and up the stairs to his bedroom.

He stripped quickly in the dim light of the overhead glowsteel, then dressed himself in black suede trousers and a black wool shirt, drew a black wool half-hood over his head, pulled on his steel-toed boots, belted on his sword, and ran down the stairs.

The barn was less than a hundred yards from the New House; Pirate, Tennetty's usual mount, stood properly ground-hitched in the light drizzle.

Despite everything, he almost laughed. Pirate was a snow-white mare, her sole marking a black patch over right eye—sort of a horsy equivalent of Tennetty, although Pirate's patch was only a marking.

He stepped inside the barn. Assisted by sleepy-eyed Pendrill and the stableboy, Tennetty had already bridled Carrot and slipped a horse blanket onto the chestnut mare's back.

Karl jerked his thumb toward the house. "Both of you, get into the cellar, and tell Ahira I said to bar the door. *Run.*"

As Pendrill and the stableboy exited the barn at a trot, Karl took his western-style saddle down from the rail and saddled Carrot, matching his strength against the mare's as he pulled the cinch tight, then tucked the pistols into the top of his pants before he slipped his scabbarded sword into the boot and lashed it into place.

He felt very much alone. There were three of the others, and unless he wanted to wait for reinforcements, it would be only him and Tennetty facing them. Not that he despised Tennetty's or his own skills, but three against two was not good odds, not when the three could be waiting in the bushes for the two. Too bad Slovotsky wasn't here; this was definitely Walter's sort of party.

"Chak?" she asked.

"With the family."

"Good." Tennetty nodded. "I wish Slovotsky were here," she said, as though she were reading Karl's mind. "Do we wait and pick up some of Daven's crew?"

His first inclination was to say no, but he caught himself. "What do you think?"

She shook her head as he led Carrot out of the barn and onto the dirt of the yard. "I don't like working with new people. Daven's may be good, but we're not used to them. And in the dark? They'd just as likely shoot us as them. Besides," she said, patting her saddlebags, "if any of Werthan's family are still alive, they might need some healing draughts, and soon. I say go."

He pulled himself to Carrot's back and settled the reins in his left fist. "We go." He dug in his heels; Carrot cantered over to the back porch, where Ihryk stood, waving at him.

"Karl, you said to get into the cellar, but—"

"Your family." Karl nodded. "If Ahira can't handle things here, you won't matter much. Take one of the horses."

Tennetty kicked Pirate into a full gallop; Karl spurred Carrot to follow.

The east road led directly toward Werthan's farm; they galloped side by side down the muddy road, the drizzle soaking them down to the skin, rain and wind whispering through the cornfields.

No, he thought. This didn't make sense. An ambush wasn't a strategy Karl and his people had a patent on. If he was going to set up an ambush for someone moving between Werthan's farm and the New House, he'd set it up along the road. No guarantee that the assassins weren't at least that minimally clever.

"Wait," he called out, pulling Carrot to a halt. He wiped the rain from his face and shook his head to clear the water from his hair.

Tennetty braked Pirate fifteen yards ahead, then waited for him to catch up.

"We can't stay on the road—we're too vulnerable. This way." He urged Carrot off the road and into the fields, Tennetty following. It would slow them down; the horses couldn't move as quickly between the rows of corn and across the wheat fields as they could on the road. But galloping full-speed into a hail of crossbow bolts would slow them down even more.

Less than fifteen minutes later, they were within sight of Werthan's one-room farmhouse.

Light still burned through the greased-parchment windows, but everything was deathly still. Even the normal night sounds were gone; all Karl could hear was the panting of the two horses and the thudding of his own heart.

He vaulted from Carrot's back, landing clumsily on the soft, wet ground.

Tennetty dismounted next to him. "Do you think they're still inside?" she asked in a low whisper. "Damn silly way to run an assassination."

"It won't be so damn silly if you and I are stupid enough to knock on the door and walk in. No chances; we'll assume they're inside, maybe with one hidden outside, on guard."

"And if that's not the way it is?"

"If they're not, we'll work out what to do next. Right now I want your cooperation, not your temperament."

He untied his scabbard and slipped it out of the saddle boot. "Keep your blade sheathed—got to watch out for light flashes." He'd hold his scabbarded sword in his left hand, a pistol in his right. If necessary, he could fire the pistol, drop it, then draw his sword in little more than a second, tossing the scabbard aside. Much faster than the time it would take to draw a sword by reaching across his waist.

Tennetty went to Pirate and took saddlebags down. She slung them over her shoulder, lashing them tightly against her chest with leather thongs.

Karl dropped Carrot's reins carefully to the ground and stepped on them. "Stay, girl," he said, then beckoned at Tennetty to follow as he walked away in a half-stoop, dropping to his belly and crawling when he reached the edge of the fields.

They worked their way around to the back of the house, and waited there, crouched silently on the hard dirt, listening.

Werthan didn't have a proper barn, just a smaller shack that served as a toolshed and chicken coop. Whatever had happened in the house hadn't left the chickens awake.

Tennetty pressed her lips against his ear. "Do you know the layout inside?"

"No. Do you?"

She shook her head. "Sorry."

"Then I'll take it." He handed her both of his pistols and slipped his saber from his scabbard, laying the scabbard gently on the ground. In the cramped quarters of the shack, a sword would be a better weapon than a pistol. The pistols would be more useful in Tennetty's hands.

"Work your way around to the front, then make some noise—nothing too obvious. I'll move when you do. If I need your help, I'll call out—otherwise, stay outside. But if I kick anyone out the front door or window, he's yours."

She nodded and started to rise.

He grasped her shoulder. "Watch your back—they may not be inside."

Tennetty shook his hand off. "You do your job, I'll do mine."

Karl stood next to the rear window, waiting. The shack could easily be a trap, but so what? Let it; let the trappers become the trapped.

Tennetty was taking her own sweet time. She should be making some—

Crack!

The snap of a twig sent him into action; he kicked open the rear door and then moved to one side and dove through the greased-parchment window.

He landed on his shoulder on the dirt floor and bounced to his feet, his sword at the ready.

All his precautions were unnecessary. Nobody was in the shack. Nobody living. The room stank of death.

Karl forced himself to look at the three bodies clinically. Werthan lay on his back, staring blindly at the ceiling, the fletching of a crossbow bolt projecting from the left side of his chest. His wife and daughter lay on their sides, their limbs and clothing in disarray, the pools of blood from their slit throats already congealing on the floor.

It wasn't hard to reconstruct what had happened. Werthan must have heard a noise outside and gone to investigate, expecting that perhaps a weasal had gotten in with the chickens. The assassins had killed him, then murdered his wife and daughter to prevent them from raising an alarm. Scratches on Werthan's heels showed that they had dragged him inside the shack.

He couldn't bear to look closely at the little girl. She was only about three.

I won't let myself get angry, he thought, willing his pulse to stop pounding in his ears, failing thoroughly. *Anger leads to reaction, not thought. My anger is their ally, not mine. I won't be angry.*

"Tennetty," he said quietly. "I'm coming out." He walked to the front door, opened it, and stepped through, closing it gently behind him. The rain had stopped; the damp night air clung to him.

"Well?"

"Dead. Werthan, his wife, and his daughter."

I have them pinpointed, Karl.

He tilted his head back. High in the sky, Ellegon's dark form slid across the stars. "Where are the bastards?"

Alongside the road, a quarter-mile from here, just beyond that old oak.

Karl nodded. He could barely see the tree in the dark.

They've spotted the glow from the bonfires around the New

House and are trying to decide what to do next. The leader suspects that somebody may have raised an alarm, but he isn't sure. And they *are* after you, in case you were curious. You ought—*

"Weapons?"

Two crossbows, plus swords, knives. Karl, I can get one of Daven's squads, and—

"No." He stuck two fingers in his mouth and whistled. "They're mine."

"What are you whistling for?" Her eyes wide, Tennetty snatched his hand away from his mouth. "They're not that far away; they'll hear you."

"That's the idea." He pulled off his shirt. "And they'll see me, too." He raised his voice. *"Did you hear that? Can you hear me?"*

No answer.

"You're crazy, Karl, we can't—"

"No." He stopped the back of his hand a scant inch from her face. "They're all mine," he said quietly. "Each and every one."

"At least take your pistols—"

"No." He shook his head slowly. "I want to feel them die. I want—" He stopped himself. *Save the feeling for later. When they're dead.*

He raised his sword over his head and waved it as he ran down the road toward the old oak.

"My name is Karl Cullinane," he shouted. "I've heard you're looking for me, you bastards. I'm waiting for you. If you want me, come and get me."

As he neared the tree, a dark shape rose between two rows of cornstalks; Karl hit the ground and rolled as a bolt whizzed overhead.

Karl sprinted for the man. But the assassin didn't simply wait for him; he ducked back down in the corn and ran. He was in too much of a hurry. Karl could plot his progress by the rustling of the stalks. He leaped through a row of corn and crashed into the assassin, both his sword and the assassin's crossbow tumbling away somewhere into the night.

It didn't matter; he was half Karl's size. As they rolled around on the ground, Karl kneed the other in the crotch, then slammed the edge of his hand down on the assassin's throat, crumpling his windpipe.

The assassin lurched away, gagging with a liquid awfulness as he died.

One down.

Karl rolled a few feet away before rising to a crouch and looking around, the skin over his ears tightening.

Nothing. No sound. The other two weren't stupid enough to flail around in the cornfield in a panic.

And Karl was unarmed, his sword lost somewhere in the darkness.

Not good. He regretted his stupidity in charging blindly into the field and ordering Tennetty to stay away, but there was nothing he could do about it now. If he raised a voice to call for help, all that would do would be to pinpoint his position for the two remaining assassins, one of them still armed with a crossbow.

Then again, you might want to use me, no?

Right. I'm missing two—where's the nearest one?

For a moment, Karl felt as though distant fingers stroked his brain.

I can't go deep enough, not without getting closer. I can't tell which way you're facing. Where is the bonfire in relation to you?

Karl raised his head momentarily above the cornstalks. Down the road, a distant glow proclaimed that the bonfires surrounding the New House were still going.

Got it. The one with the crossbow is two rows behind you, just about halfway between you and the road. But he's looking in your direction, and you're not going to be able to sneak up on him.

And the other one?

You're not going to like this. He's running alongside the road, about halfway between here and the New House. No crossbow, but he's carrying more throwing knives than Walter does, and I think one or two of them may be dragonbane-tipped.

He's Tennetty's—you spot for her. I'll take care of things here.

The dragon swooped low over the cornfields toward the house.

Karl cursed himself silently. His temper could yet be the death of him. Kill the slavers—hell, yes—but letting his anger instead of his intellect control the means was something that he should have outgrown.

The first thing to do was to find his sword.

He searched around the soft ground, finding nothing but weeds and dirt. Come daylight, finding it would be no problem, but daylight was hours away.

Let's test his nerve a bit. Karl lifted a dirtclod and pitched it off into the night, aiming roughly where Ellegon had said the assassin was.

It whipped through the cornstalks, and then . . .

Silence. Nothing, dammit. This one knew his business; if he'd fired blindly, Karl would have been able to attack before he reloaded his crossbow.

On the other hand . . .

Karl walked back to the dead assassin and relieved the man of his beltknife. Not a bad weapon; it was a full-sized dagger, with almost the heft of a Homemade bowie.

He hoisted the corpse to his shoulder, then walked opposite to where Ellegon had said the remaining assassin was and crashed through one row of cornstalks, propelling the body ahead of him through the next row.

The bowstring twanged.

Karl stepped through the stalks, the knife held out in front of him.

Kneeling on the ground, the slaver was using a beltclaw to pull back his bowstring.

"Greetings," Karl said.

CHAPTER SIX

Mindprobe

*He who has a thousand friends has not a friend to spare,
And he who has one enemy will meet him everywhere*

—Ali ibn-Abi-Talib

At the sound of a gunshot down the road, Karl spurred Carrot into a gallop.

Everything is under control, Ellegon said, momentarily probing deeply. *As I see it is for you.*

Sure. Fine. Three more innocents dead, their throats slit. Just fine.

He eased back on the reins; the horse settled into a gentle canter.

You take a lot on yourself, Karl Cullinane.

There was no answer to that; he didn't try to find one.

He rounded the bend. In the vague glow of the distant faerie lights, Ellegon stood over Tennetty and the prostrate corpse of the last assassin.

No—not a corpse. While Tennetty's shot had opened the assassin's belly nicely, the bastard's chest was still slowly moving up and down.

The dragon lowered his head.

"What's going on?"

"Shut up—Ellegon's busy." Tennetty turned to glare at Karl, her fingers fastened on the assassin's wrists. "It might be a good idea to find out what this one knows, if anything."

Too much pain. I can't get through.

"Damn." Tennetty spat as she pulled the bottle of healing draughts from her pouch and sprinkled a bit of the liquid on the assassin's wounds, then dribbled some more in his mouth. "I hate wasting this stuff." She raised her head. "How about a hand here?"

Tennetty had already frisked the assassin and relieved him of his knives and pouch. Karl gripped the assassin's right wrist and pressed it firmly against the ground while Tennetty did the same with his left.

Better. Shh—no. He's blocked too thoroughly. I can't go beyond his conscious mind.

She shrugged. "No problem." She picked up his knife and flicked the scabbard away.

The assassin's head started to stir; his eyes opened.

"Who sent you?" she asked. "Tell us, and you'll live."

The round-faced man clenched his jaw. "I tell you *nothing.*" He struggled, uselessly.

"Thank you." She smiled as she set the knifepoint against the side of his face, just over the trigeminal nerve, barely breaking the skin.

Stop that, Tennetty. It was not necessary. Try another question, but don't distract him this time. He has to think of the answer for me to read it.

Karl shrugged. There was always the obvious question. "What do you know that you don't want us to? What are you hiding?"

"Ahrmin. He wants to know about Ahrmin."

Ahrmin? Karl almost lost his grip.

Ahrmin was dead in Melawei, burned in the *Warthog.*

Guess again. He hired these three in Enkiar less than a hundred days ago. They're not slavers, they're mercenaries . . . I've broken through, Karl. Give me another moment, and . . . I have it all. Ahrmin, Enkiar, the Healing Hand, everything.

The Hand?

It seems Ahrmin requires major reconstruction. I'll give you his face later. For now . . . stand back from him, and move away.

"No!" Tennetty drew her beltknife with her free hand. "He's my kill."

You will stand aside, Tennetty.

"Why?"

Ellegon's mental voice was calm, matter-of-fact. *You will stand aside, Tennetty, because the little girl's name was Anna. They called her Anna Minor, as Werthan's wife was Anna Major.*

*You will stand aside because I had promised to teach her how to swim. And you will stand aside because she always called me Ehgon, because she couldn't manage the l-sound.

*And you will stand aside because this is the one that smiled down at her to quiet her as he opened her throat with his knife.

And if you don't understand any of that, you will stand aside, Tennetty, and you will do so now, because if you do not stand aside I will surely burn you down where you stand.

Tennetty moved away.

Gently, Ellegon picked up the struggling assassin in his mouth and leaped skyward, his mindvoice diminishing as he gained altitude and flew away. *There are balances in this world, Afbee. And while there is no justice, some of us do our best. I see you have a strong fear of falling. . . .*

"Karl? You want me to finish up here?"

"Can't. I lost my sword somewhere, and then there's—"

"I'll find it. You go home." Tennetty's face was wet. "Go."

Karl lay back in the huge bed, his head pillowed on his hands. Homecoming was supposed to be a joyous time, a passionate time for him and Andy-Andy. No matter what happened on the road, this was separate, different. Home.

But not tonight. He just couldn't—

"You're not sleeping," Andy-Andy whispered.

"I can't." His eyes were dry and aching. *You'd think, after all I've seen, after all I've done, it would get easier.* He patted her shoulder and slipped out of bed. "You've got school and some crops to deal with tomorrow—better get some sleep. Don't wait up."

"Karl—"

"Please."

Ahira was waiting in the hall. The dwarf was in full combat gear, his battleaxe unsheathed, his chair propped up against the door of Jason's room, his feet not reaching the floor.

Karl raised an eyebrow. "Trouble?" he asked in a whisper.

"Not at all," the dwarf answered him quietly, shaking his head. He cradled a clay bottle in the crook of his arm. "Everything's quiet. Chak and Ellegon are doing a search out over the plain, although I'm sure it won't turn up anything. It's just that . . ." He rubbed his hand down the front of his chainmail vest, then tinged his thumbnail against the axeblade. "Sometimes I forget what we're all about. I get caught up in the politics so much, sometimes . . ." He let his voice trail off, then smiled sadly. "Tomorrow, I've got to raise a burying party, to go out to Werthan's place and put him and his two Annas in the ground, and that hurts.

"But that's tomorrow." Ahira uncorked the bottle and took a sip, then offered Karl the bottle. "Tonight I'm going to drink a swallow or two of Riccetti's Best.

"But mainly, I'm going to sit here in my armor, with my axe at hand, and keep in my mind the simple fact that there are three children sleeping safely in that room there—two of whom I couldn't love more if they were blood of my blood and flesh of my flesh—and that nothing and nobody is getting past me to hurt them."

"Damn silly thing to do," Karl said, his eyes misting over.

"Isn't it, though? Mmm . . . you want me to find you a chair?"

"I can find my own chair."

CHAPTER SEVEN

The Bat Cave

It is always good
When a man has two irons in the fire.

—Francis Beaumont and John Fletcher

The best way, maybe the only way, to deal with the pain was to get to work, whether or not the work was pleasant. Riding into Engineer Territory at the north end of the valley was a mixture of the two; it was something Karl always enjoyed, the pleasure dimmed only by the awkward necessity of stopping to see Nehera when he did.

The weathered Erendra sign on the split-rail fence was unchanged; it translated to "Proceed further only with permission"; it was amply decorated with the glyph for danger.

Karl laughed. Riccetti had changed the English part of the sign again, or at least had had it changed.

ENGINEER TERRITORY
Louis Riccetti, Prop.

Screw the rest—we work REAL magic here.

The smithy interrupted the miles of fence; huge doors like those of a barn stood on both sides of the line, although the eight half-sheds containing wood, charcoal, and iron stock were on the Engineers' side of the fence.

Nehera was a quasi-Engineer; his services and those of the apprentice Engineers learning smithing from him were needed by everyone in the valley: There were always horses and oxen to be reshod, plow blades to be sharpened and straightened, nails to be drawn from thin nail stock, tools to be made and repaired, horsecollars forged, and so on.

Not all of his work was secret, nor did he do all of the secret work. While Nehera did virtually all of the barrelmaking, the rest of the gunsmithing was done deeper in Engineer territory, in the two other smithies.

Better get it over with, Karl thought, as he dismounted from Carrot's broad back, then stepped on her reins for a moment, ignoring the hitching post in front of the smithy. *If Nehera hears that I had someone else do the work, I'll have to put up with more sniveling than usual.*

But dammit, why couldn't the dwarf be more like U'len? Just once, couldn't he snap at Karl, or tell him to go to hell?—anything that showed a bit of spine.

The civilian-side door was closed, indicating that something secret was going on inside. Karl walked toward the apprentice Engineer outside the guardhouse at the gate.

The boy was well trained. "Vhas!" he called out, bringing his rifle almost in line with Karl's chest. *Halt.* "Who goes there?"

Karl obediently halted, keeping his hands well away from his sides. "I am Karl Cullinane. Journeyman Engineer," he added, with a smile.

The boy nodded and smiled. "You are recognized, Journeyman Engineer Karl Cullinane, and welcome to Engineer Territory. I have a message for you from the Engineer: You are to join in the cave at your convenience."

"Thank you." *Might as well have some fun,* Karl thought. "Your name and orders, apprentice?"

"Journeyman!" The boy drew himself into a stiff brace. "I am Junior Apprentice Bast. My general orders are as follows:

"My first general order is: I am to remain at my post until properly relieved.

"My second general order is: I am to challenge anyone who approaches the fence or the gate, calling for them to halt as they do so.

"My third general order is: I am to allow no person to cross through the gate or over the fence into Engineer Territory within my sight unless and until he has halted for my challenge, and I am satisfied that he is authorized to do so.

"My fourth general order is: Should any situation not covered by the first three general orders arise, I am to send my second for the senior apprentice of the guard."

"And what would you have done if I had advanced after your call to halt?"

The boy sobered. "I would have sent my second for the senior apprentice of the guard, Journeyman," he said, pointing his chin toward the guardhouse.

"What for, Bast?"

There were only two answers; the boy picked the right one.

"To haul away your dead body, Journeyman," he said with utter seriousness.

"Good." Fortunately, there had never been a case in which an innocent citizen had tried to cross the fence after being hailed. It was just as well; many Home citizens resented the Engineers' patent arrogance.

Karl vaulted the fence and walked into the smithy.

Nehera was busy at work at the forge, two apprentices working the bellows while the smith held the long-handled tongs, occasionally pulling them back to check the color of the work.

From where he stood, Karl couldn't be sure, but it looked as if Nehera might be working on another sword. Homemade blades weren't popular only with Home warriors; they were slowly becoming a major trade item. Nehera had taken Lou's and Karl's scant knowledge of how Japanese swords were made and added his own considerable knowledge of steelworking; the result was finer blades—lighter, stronger, better able to hold an edge without chipping—than could be found elsewhere.

As the dwarf pulled the bright-red iron out of the fire and spun on his peg, bringing it over to the blocky anvil, Karl's guess was verified: Nehera sprinkled a scant spoonful of carbon dust over the steel, then hammered the iron bar over double, the anvil ringing like a bell.

He stuck the dull-red bar back in the fire, then turned to splash water on his face.

As he shook his head to clear his eyes, he spotted Karl for the first time.

Here we go again.

"I crave pardon, master." Nehera dropped to his knee, his peg skittering out sideways at an awkward angle. "I did not see you."

Karl didn't bother to tell Nehera that he didn't have to go through this every damn time; the dwarf still didn't get it, couldn't get it. Somewhere, somehow, Nehera's spirit had been broken, beyond Karl's ability to repair it.

That was the pity of it all: Nehera couldn't understand that he wasn't property anymore. The deep scars that crisscrossed his face, back, arms, and chest showed that he had been hard to break; the peg that served as his right leg confirmed that he had once too often tried to run for his freedom.

"Rise, Nehera," Karl said. "You're forgiven, of course."

"I thank you, master." The dwarf's puppy-dog smile almost made Karl vomit.

Dammit, you don't have to kneel in front of me, you don't have to beg me for forgiveness for not kneeling immediately, and you sure as hell don't have to look at me like that for forgiving you for not cringing quickly enough.

But what was the use? He could, once again, explain to Nehera that he didn't have to do that—he could even make it a command—but neither explanations nor commands of that kind had any effect. Whether Karl liked it or not, Nehera felt that he belonged to Karl, and that this was the way a slave was supposed to act; he simply refused to comprehend orders to the contrary.

The strange thing was, there were actually people in the world who liked this sort of thing, who felt that some other person cringing in front of them was their right, and their pleasure.

At that thought, Karl's fists clenched.

Nehera's face blanched.

"No, no," Karl said, forcing a smile to his face, "it's not you. I was thinking about something else. How goes the work?"

"I work hard, master. I swear it." The dwarf snuck a sideways glance at the forge, caught himself, then gave the slightest shrug Karl had ever seen.

Karl raised a hand. "Please, don't let me interrupt. We can talk while you work. I wouldn't want you to ruin something."

"I obey." Nehera momentarily drew the steel out of the fire, then replaced it, gesturing at the apprentices to pump the bellows harder. He treated them with a distant sort of superiority. After all, though they were free men, Nehera's owner had put him in charge. "It will take some time, master. Is there something I can do for you?"

"Three things, actually." Karl unbelted his scabbard. "First, this edge needs a bit of touching up. Do you think you might be able to do that for me sometime today?"

"Immediately."

"No rush, Nehera. I have to visit the Engineer, and I'll hardly need a sword here."

"May I speak?"

"Of course."

"I humbly crave your pardon, master, but you should always carry a sword." He limped quickly to the wall and brought down a scabbarded saber, pulling it a few inches from the scabbard, then offering it to Karl. "If you would care to test the edge?" Nehera extended his arm.

"No. I'm sure that it's fine."

"But, master—"

"No, Nehera," Karl said, cursing himself immediately for raising his voice as the dwarf dropped to his knee again.

"I have offended you again, master. I am sorry."

Karl sighed. "Forgiven, Nehera. Rise."

The dwarf got back up with irritating speed. "You said that there were three things, master?"

You make my teeth itch, Nehera. "Yes. Number two: I know you'd rather work in steel, but I need a golden collar made—human size. You can melt down some Metreyll coin."

The dwarf bowed his head. "Yes, master. That will be done before the next time I sleep."

"No, it won't—take your time. But I do want it before the town meeting. There is one other thing, Nehera. I've been hearing stories about how you've been working yourself too hard. That is to stop. When you are too tired to work, you must rest."

"As you command, master."

Damn. Enough of this; I'm going to go see Riccetti.

Karl accepted the clay bottle and took a light swig, then washed down the fiery liquor with a long drink of water. "Thanks, Lou. I needed that."

Still, the whiskey didn't wash the bad taste out of Karl's mouth. Which was perhaps just as well. Life was full of bad tastes.

He sat back in his chair, enjoying the coolness of the cave.

Well, this section of the warrens wasn't a proper cave, but a relic of the long-ago dwarven inhabitants, driven away, so legend had it, by

Therranji elves. But it looked like a cave, and that was what they called it.

Caves were supposed to be damp and musty places—and most of the caverns were—but Riccetti's quarters were different, almost homey.

Riccetti's apprentices had cleared out the dirt, all the way down to the bare rock. Then they had installed four wooden walls and built a massive oak door to block Riccetti's quarters off from the rest of the tunnel, chiseled the floor smooth, and then finally bored openings through the rock to the outside to allow both for airflow and for the pipe venting Riccetti's Franklin stove.

Glowsteels hung from pulleys set into the arching ceiling above, fitted with ropes and winches so that they could easily be lowered and removed for Andy-Andy to recharm.

It was very much a Lou Riccetti type of place: rows of wooden worktables stood along two of the four walls, well laden with bottles and vats of various and sundry preparations, steel pens, bottles of ink, and stacks of notes awaiting copying and filing by apprentices.

But it was Riccetti-type homey: the sleeping and socializing part of the room consisted only of a pile of bedding in a corner and two armchairs, now occupied by Karl and Lou.

"Try the beer," Riccetti said. "I think it's the best batch yet."

Karl set down the whiskey bottle, lifted his mug, and sipped at his beer, forcing himself not to make a face. Ahira was right: While Riccetti's corn whiskey was usually good, his beer was a crime.

"Drink up," Riccetti said, chuckling. "You're being awfully patient. It isn't like you."

"I'm not like me. Not today." There were things that a human being just couldn't get used to, not if he wanted to remain a human being.

Riccetti *tsk*ed. "I should give you hell, for once. You're the one who's always saying that instead of getting worked up over something you don't like, you should do something about it." He snickered. "Not that I've always been a fan of how you've handled things. But you usually do well enough."

Yeah, Lou? And how am I supposed to bring a murdered baby back to life? But he didn't say that. "Any progress on the slavers' powder? I know you'll need help from Andy and Thellaren, but—"

"Guess again." Riccetti smiled. "Nope. It's all done. I stayed up part of the night, doing a few simple experiments. I finally figured out how they were doing it this morning. I'm going to have Andrea check my results, but—"

"What? And we've been sitting here making idle chatter for—"

"Take it easy, Karl. I'm sorry. It's just that . . ." Riccetti's voice trailed off.

Karl nodded his understanding. It was lonely, constantly dealing with people who were subordinate to you, even when some of those people were friends. Riccetti rarely could make the time to visit Ahira or Andy-Andy at the south end of the valley; last night had been an exception. "Sorry. So, what is it? Some sort of explosive?"

"Nope." Riccetti set down his own beer mug and rose from his chair. "Just let me show off for a minute."

He walked to the worktable and took down a small glass vial and a stone bowl. "This is slaver powder." He uncorked the vial and tipped about a quarter-teaspoon into the bottom of the bowl. "And this," he said, taking down another vial, "is distilled water—about the only really pure substance I can make. Stand back a second." Riccetti tilted the bowl to point against the naked wall, then dribbled a careful drop of water onto the bowl's lip. "It'll take a moment for it to work its way down to—"

Whoosh! The backblast of heat beat against Karl's face.

"Just plain water did that? What the hell kind of compound—"

"No, idiot, it's not a compound, it's a mixture." Riccetti poured more powder on a marble slab, then beckoned Karl to come closer. "Take a good look at this—and don't breathe on it; it's already sucked up some water from the air."

Karl looked closely. Mixed among the white powder were tiny blue flecks. "Copper sulfate?"

"Yup. Heat it up, and it becomes cupric sulfate—plain white. Add water—even let it pick up some from the air; it deliquesces nicely—and it sucks it right up; turns blue. Which is what it's in there for."

"Now, wait a minute. Copper sulfate isn't an explosive. You use it for—"

"—blueing rifles. Right. But in this, it's a stabilizer. It's there to absorb the water, and prevent the real stuff from being exposed to too much. Visualize this," Riccetti said, cupping his hands together. "You've got a hollow iron sphere, filled with water. Got that?"

"Yeah."

"Okay, now, heat it over a fire, a damn hot one. What happens?"

"The water starts to boil."

"Right. But since it can't escape?"

Karl shrugged. "If it gets too hot, it blows up, just like a pressure cooker does if it isn't vented right."

"Right." Riccetti frowned. "But what if you're cheating? What do you get if you're using some sort of spell to hold the iron sphere together?"

"Huh?"

Riccetti snorted. "Pretend that the sphere is absolutely, unconditionally unbreakable—doesn't break, doesn't bend, doesn't stretch, doesn't warp. Nothing. What does the water become?"

"Superheated steam?"

"Right—maybe even a plasma. Now, imagine that someone puts some sort of preservation spell on the contents of the sphere, forcing what's inside to remain as is. Let the sphere cool, remove the protection spell so you can cut it open, and what do you find inside?"

"Something that's very hot, but isn't." Karl's brow furrowed. "That doesn't make any sense. What would it be like?"

"This." Riccetti pursed his lips. "That's what they did, I think. Some sort of preservation spell, with a built-in hole: If the stuff gets in contact with too much water, the spell fails, and what do you have? You've got superheated steam—lightly salted with copper sulfate—which wants to expand, and fast."

"And if the only direction to expand in is along the barrel of a gun—"

"—pushing a bullet ahead of it . . . you've got it. There's nothing special about the water that their guns use—doesn't have to be."

Karl buried his face in his hands. "Then we're in for it. If they can do it—"

"Hang *on* for a second, Karl. You're not thinking it through. Look at the brighter side. These aren't easy spells. They're a hell of a lot more advanced than anything your wife can do—and she's not bad. They're even beyond what I used to do, way back when."

"All of which means what?"

"I just build things." Riccetti shrugged. "That's your department. I can tell you that it takes a very heavy-duty wizard to do this, and that there aren't all that many of them, and that they won't work cheap. My guess is that this powder cost your slavers one hell of a lot of coin.

"Take it a step further. Even in Pandathaway, there aren't more than a handful of wizards capable of something this difficult."

"So? Even, say, five or six of them, working full-time—"

"Never happen. I can tell you that from personal experience."

Riccetti shook his head. "Magic is like cocaine, Karl, assuming you have the genes that let you work it in the first place. Anyone who does can handle a bit now and then, but everybody has his limits. Once you get beyond those limits, you're hooked. All you're interested in is learning more, getting more spells in your head. Drives you a bit crazy."

That sounded familiar. That was the way Riccetti had been, back when he was Aristobulus, back when the seven of them were first transferred over to This Side. The only things that had mattered to Aristobulus were his spell books and his magic.

Come to think of it, it was reminiscent of the crazies who hung around the Ehvenor docks. *Being around Faerie too long drives some crazy,* Avair Ganness had said. Maybe it wasn't just Faerie—maybe it was magic itself.

"Now," Riccetti went on, "look at it from the point of view of whoever got the Pandathaway wizards to make this stuff. It's going to be hard to pull the wizards away from their studies to do it, and it won't be possible to do that very often. This slaver powder is going to stay rare—unless they start producing it in Faerie."

Karl nodded. "That'd do it."

"Damn straight. If the Faerie were to line up against us . . ." He shrugged. "You may as well worry about Grandmaster Lucius deciding to take us on, or somebody bringing an H-bomb over from the Other Side." He waved at the door. "In any case, compare their production of this with our production of real gunpowder. You notice any shortages?"

"No."

"Exactly."

There was something Lou was missing about all of this; it hovered on the edge of Karl's mind.

Andy-Andy! "But Andy—she's a wizard. She could—"

Riccetti threw his hands up in the air. "Of course. Idiot. Do you want more beer or would you like a whiskey?"

"But—"

"Shh." Riccetti poured each of them more whiskey. "Drink up. And for God's sake have a little faith in your wife."

Karl sipped the whiskey. "You've got a lot of respect for her, don't you?"

"Damn straight. You lucked out, Cullinane." Riccetti nodded. "But, if you'll notice, she spends most of her time teaching school, and almost all the magic she does is agricultural, bug-killing, glowing steel, the occasional levitation when somebody runs across a boulder when trying to clear a new field. It's all baby stuff; she has almost no time to learn more.

"Hell, she only picked up the lightning spell this year. She hasn't had the chance to push herself as far along as Aristobulus did. And in my opinion, deep down she's even more strongminded than . . . he was." He shook his head. "Relax. In order for her to push her skills to the addiction point, she'll have to have years of leisure time —just as Pandathaway wizards do."

Or as Arta Myrdhyn must have had, at some point. He was a wizard powerful enough to turn the forests of Elrood into the Waste, to charm a sword to protect its bearer against magic, then set up a watch-charm to hold it for its proper user.

Not my son, bastard. Karl shook his head to clear it. No more time to waste, not with Riccetti having figured out what the slaver powder was. The question was, what was going to happen in Enkiar? And how were Ahrmin and the Slavers' Guild connected with the powder?

Riccetti cleared his throat. "If you don't mind, I have to get back to work. I've got a few things going, and I'd better go chew out that idiot apprentice who tried a quarter-charge of powder in a new rifle. *Quarter*-charge—I told him to use a quadruple charge, but his English isn't as good as it's supposed to be."

Karl shrugged. "Quarter charge? What's the problem?"

"He hung the bullet, that's what the goddamn problem is. He has to take the lock off the gun and the barrel off the stock, then clamp down the barrel and unscrew the breech plug—and then shove the damn thing out with a rod—" Riccetti caught himself. "But I was forgetting!" he said, brightening. "Got a present for you."

He walked to one of the shelves and pulled down a plain wooden box, holding it carefully but proudly as he opened it.

Inside were six iron eggs, a seam running across their equators, each with a small fuse protruding from the top.

"Grenades?"

"Yup. They break up nice—jagged pieces, about the size of a dime. Cast iron does that." Riccetti took one out of the box and held it up, flicking a bitten fingernail against the three-inch fuse. "Slow fuse, burns for just about five seconds. Then, *whoom.* Use them a bit sparingly, eh? They each contain enough powder for a signal rocket." Riccetti closed the box and fastened the lid.

There was a rap on the door.

"Enter," Riccetti said.

A teenage apprentice opened the door and stepped inside. "Message from the Mayor, Engineer: The emissary from Lord Khoral has arrived, and seeks an audience with Journeyman Karl Cullinane. The Therranji are camped just outside the customs station."

Karl sighed. "Back to work. Both of us."

"See you before the town meeting tomorrow?"

"Probably not. Can I count on you, anyway?"

"Always, Karl. Always."

CHAPTER EIGHT

An Acquaintance Renewed

Slaves cannot breathe in England; if their lungs
Receive our air, that moment they are free!
They touch our country, and their shackles fall.

—William Cowper

"I don't like it. Don't like it at all." Daven shook his head, his hairless scalp shining in the sunlight. He was probably the most battered human being Karl had ever seen. His left eye was covered by a patch; half of that ear and three fingers of his right hand were missing. Long scars ran down his face and neck, vanishing into his tunic.

"Your opinion wasn't asked, Daven," Chak said.

"Be still, Chak." Karl shook his head and switched to English. "Don't irritate him, understood?"

"Yes, Karl." Sitting astride his gray gelding, Chak glared down at Daven. It was possible that he naturally had little liking for Daven, but more likely Karl's own distaste was infectious.

Karl didn't particularly like the former Nyph mercenary, not the way he enjoyed the company of Aveneer, the third raiding-team leader.

Still, Karl had to admit that Daven had a certain something. A year or so back, after a raid on a slaver caravan, one of Daven's men had gotten the bright idea of selling some slaves instead of freeing them. Daven hadn't returned Home for advice or instructions; he had hunted the bastard down himself and brought the charred bones back.

"The Mayor agreed to allow an emissary," Daven went on as though Chak weren't there, "but they've sent more than two hundred—and I wouldn't swear on my life that the only soldiers among them are the fifty wearing armor."

"Can't blame them," Karl said, fitting his boot into Carrot's stirrup and pulling himself up to the saddle. "There've been enough slaving raids into Therranj; traveling without military escort would be asking for trouble."

Daven smiled. "So why are we here?" He gestured at the log cabin that was officially Home's customs station, and the grassy slope below the cabin, where fifty warriors from his team waited, guns loaded and horses saddled.

"Because I don't like to take chances."

"No, not you." A snort. "I believe that. How many of my men do you want to take with you?"

"None. You're here for show. Period. I'm just going over to chat. I don't care what you hear, all of you stay here until and unless I send for you." Karl jerked his thumb skyward. "Ellegon covers me on this." He pulled on the reins and turned Carrot away, Chak following on his gelding.

Daven shrugged. "You have all the fun." His laugh followed Karl and Chak over the rise.

The Therranji had camped on the plain, almost a mile from the ridge that overlooked the valley. Khoral's emissary traveled in style; the encampment reminded Karl of an old-time circus, the several dozen tents ranging in size from three barely larger than a typical Boy Scout Voyageur to a mammoth red-and-white silk one that could almost have served P.T. Barnum as a big top.

Near the entrance to the main tent, a team of cooks attended to a side of beef, turning it slowly over a low fire. The wind brought the scent to him; it smelled absolutely wonderful.

Mounted elven soldiers in chainmail and iron helmets patrolled the perimeter. Three of them approached Karl and Chak as they rode toward the camp.

Don't make any unnecessary enemies.

Karl looked up. High overhead, Ellegon circled.

"Since when do I go around making enemies unnecessarily?"

Chak laughed. "How about the time you drew on Baron Furnael? That could have turned bloody. Or when you beat Ohlmin—"

"Enough. It was necessary, or I wouldn't have done it."

That's what they all say.

Karl ignored the jibe. *Tell me, Kreskin, what are the elves up to?*

My name is Ellegon. And they're all shielded. Sorry. But you might want to get on with this; your wife is already inside—

What?

—with Tennetty to keep her company. Not my idea, Karl; I told her you wouldn't like it.

Karl quelled the urge to spur Carrot past the horsemen, then forced himself to pull her gently to a halt. This was a time for negotiation, not violence.

Just keep it that way. I can recall a time or two that you've turned—

Enough. Don't you ever forget anything?

Nope. Just think of me as a many-tonned conscience. A gout of fire roared through the sky.

Chak shook his head. "I don't like it."

"Neither do I." Karl bit his lower lip for a moment. "When we dismount, hand the nearest elf your falchion—don't wait for him to ask—then go inside, quietly. When I call for you, I want you and Tennetty to bring Andy out. Move slowly, but get her on a horse and over the hill."

"And what will you be doing?"

"That all depends on them. But I don't want any potential hostages clogging the negotiations." Karl wound his reins around his saddle horn and folded his arms over his chest. He didn't even have a pistol with him; SOP was to avoid letting any foreigner see guns, although he had made several exceptions to that rule in his time.

"Greetings," the foremost of the soldiers said, in an airy voice. In full armor and padding, he looked almost fully fleshed, if exceedingly tall; elves always looked like regular people, stretched lengthwise in a funhouse mirror. But the appearance of fragility was deceptive; pound for pound, elves were stronger than humans. "You are the human called Karl Cullinane?"

I'm called Karl Cullinane because that's my name—and what do I look like, a dwarf?

Temper, temper.

"Yes, I am Karl Cullinane."

"You are expected. You and your servant will follow me."

I just might have to teach you how to say please, but this isn't the time—not quite yet. Karl unwound his reins and nudged Carrot into a walk. The speaker took the lead, while the other two rode beside Karl and Chak.

Can I trust you to keep out of trouble for a while? I have a patrol to fly, and I've got to see that Aveneer's supplies are packed.

Go ahead.

I'll be back. The dragon wheeled across the sky and flew away.

The soldiers led them toward the large tent, then stopped their own horses, waiting for Karl and Chak to dismount first.

Nodding at Chak to copy him, Karl levered himself out of the saddle.

While Chak surrendered his sword to the elven armsman and was ushered inside, Karl dug into his saddlebag and removed a carrot for Carrot. He slipped her bit, dropped the reins to the ground, then stepped on them before feeding it to her, running his hand down her neck. "Good girl."

The soldier cleared his throat. "They are this way."

Karl turned and started to follow him into the tent; one of the other soldiers reached out a hand and grasped Karl's arm.

"I'll have your sword, human."

Karl didn't answer. *On the other hand, maybe this* is *the time to teach you some manners.*

He looked down at his arm, then up into the elf's eyes, and smiled. He had put a lot of practice into that smile over the years; it was intended to frighten, to suggest that the bared teeth were going to be sunk into a throat.

The elf dropped his hand. "I will need to take your sword before you enter," he said, his voice a touch less arrogant.

"Guess again." Moving slowly, Karl walked back to Carrot and tied her reins around the saddle horn, then let her nuzzle his face for a moment before turning her around and slapping her rump. "Go home, Carrot. Git!"

He turned back. The three soldiers had been joined by six others; mounted troops were gathering around.

Good.

"Why did you do that?"

"I don't want my horse to get hurt." He raised his voice. "Chak!"

"Yes, Karl," came the distant answer.

"Get Andrea out of there."

"Understood."

I'd damn well better be doing this right, he thought. He turned back to the elf who had demanded his sword. "Now, you were going to try to take my sword away from me?" He stuck his fingers in his mouth and whistled, beckoning to all the elven soldiers in the area.

He drew himself up straight, resting his right hand on the hilt of his sword. "Listen carefully, all of you. This . . . person—what's your name?"

No answer.

"I asked your name!"

"Jherant ip Therranj, personal armsman to—"

"I didn't ask your rank." Karl sneered. "I'm not interested. Now," he said, addressing the rest, "Jherant here wants my sword. He didn't ask politely; he demanded it.

"I don't think he's good enough to take it." Karl smiled again. "Little Jherant here doesn't look quite sturdy enough." He looked from face to face as he gripped the sharkskin hilt. "Which of you wants to help him?"

An elf dismounted and tossed his helmet aside. "I will, human," he said, pronouncing the word like a curse. The elf nodded to another, who began to circle around behind Karl. Karl heard a distant whisk of steel on leather as the elf drew a dagger.

"Good," Karl said. He pointed to another. "You, too. And you, and you, and you. We're going to play a little game now. What we're going to do is to see how many of you have to die because Jherant hasn't learned a little bit of elementary politeness. I'm willing to bet my life that it's all of you." He looked Jherant straight in the eye. "But don't go away. You're going to be first. Even if your friend at my back closes—"

Karl kicked back, catching the elf in the solar plexus. As the air whooshed from the elf's lungs, Karl reached up and twisted, relieving him of the dagger, then dropping it point-first into the ground.

Karl lifted the gasping elf in his arms and handed him to the nearest of his companions. "Next?"

Jherant paled. This was ridiculous—one human against more than a dozen elven soldiers?

Slowly, Karl drew his sword, then raised it in a salute. Three of the elves copied him, while others moved away, also drawing their weapons.

He stood, waiting.

Tension hung in the air like taut wires. His sword in his right hand, Karl crooked his fingers and beckoned to Jherant. "Come here. You wanted my sword—here it is."

Another elf snickered and nudged Jherant from behind. White-faced, he drew his sword—

"What goes on here?" a firm contralto demanded. The tent flap was pushed aside and a woman walked out, blinking against the bright sunlight.

She was something from a dream: tall, slim, and fineboned, her long hair so blond it was almost transparent. Her features were delicate; most beautiful human women would have looked gross and crude standing beside her.

She looked down at the nearest of the soldiers and frowned. "What goes on here?" she asked again.

The elf ducked his head. "Your pardon, Lady. This . . . human wants to fight with us."

She looked over at Karl, one eyebrow raised. "Is this so?"

"Not necessarily. I just want to kill the ones without any manners. Improve the breed a bit for you. I might have given this idiot my sword if he'd asked politely, but he demanded it."

"You're Karl Cullinane, I take it." Her lips twitched. "I see that the stories are true. You'd take on all of my soldiers, hoping to hold out until your reinforcements arrived?"

"You don't know my husband, Lady Dhara," Andy-Andy said, as she pushed through the tent flaps and stood beside the elf woman, Tennetty and Chak to either side of her. "I don't think he's waiting for reinforcements."

"Now," Karl said quietly, "get Andy out of here. No reinforcements. Tell Daven."

Tennetty nodded and pulled at Andy-Andy's arm.

One of the soldiers reached out a hesitant arm as though to bar them; Chak grabbed, twisted the elf's arm up and behind his back, then booted him away, snatching the sword out of his scabbard as he fell on his face.

A thin smile crossing her face, Tennetty's hand snaked out and seized another elf by the trachea. Not daring to move for fear that she would rip his throat out, the elf stood there as she quickly unbuckled his swordbelt and let it drop to the ground. Looking him straight in the eye, Tennetty suddenly snapped her knee into his groin, then stooped to retrieve the scabbard. She turned around, her newly acquired sword held easily in her hand.

Nobody else moved.

"Sorry, Karl," Tennetty said. "I gave them my sword. Andrea said there was to be no trouble."

Dhara eyed Karl. "I take it that you have other ideas."

"Perhaps, Lady. It all depends on you. I've been told that you've come here to negotiate. Would you rather do it with words, or with swords?"

"Words," she said. "Definitely words." She gestured at Jherant. "You are dismissed from my service," she said, before turning to another elf. "Captain, have that fool stripped of his weapons and driven away. Karl Cullinane may keep his sword. Anyone who is discourteous to him will answer to me. If he survives." She gestured toward the tent flap. "Karl Cullinane. If you, your wife, and your two friends would be kind enough to join me?"

Karl sheathed his sword. "Delighted, Lady. After you."

You were taking a big chance.

Karl sipped at his wine. *It would have been more of a chance not to.*

You can explain that later.

"Your eyes look . . . distant, Karl Cullinane," Dhara said, reclining on the opposite couch. She held out her own wineglass for a refill.

"Just talking to the dragon." He jerked his thumb skyward. "No offense intended."

Dhara chuckled. "In your world, politeness must be much more important than it is thought to be here." She wetted a slim finger and ran it around the rim of her glass, enjoying the clear, ringing tone. "Although I must confess that I wonder how serious you were. Mmmm . . . 'No offense intended'—is that the correct phrase?"

Andy-Andy shook her head gravely. "Lady, I wish you wouldn't do that. You weren't around when he declared war on the Slavers' Guild single-handedly. I was."

From Andrea: "I could back your play better if I knew what it was." She's not thrilled with you, Karl.

Tell her I'll thrill her later. "If you'd care to find out just how serious I was, Lady, it could be arranged."

Chak sighed and got slowly, painfully to his feet. "Here we go again."

"Hold on for a moment." Tennetty drained her glass. "Can I get in on this? You always get all the fun." She tested the blade of her newly acquired sword with her thumb. "I've heard dull blades are good for cutting cheese—how's yours?"

"Another cheese cutter." Chak shook his head. "Maybe Nehera can put a decent edge on it."

From Tennetty: "You're absolutely insane, you know."

"Don't bet against Karl Cullinane, Lady Dhara," Tennetty said. "The odds are too long."

"You think he could take on my fifty soldiers? Even with your help?"

"I didn't think that was the issue. You're an emissary from Lord Khoral, and one of your men challenged Karl—doesn't that make the question whether or not Karl is going to declare war on Therranj itself?"

Dhara paled. "Are you—" She caught herself. "I find myself in an awkward position. Lord Khoral sent me to negotiate your incorporation into Therranj. I seem to find myself having to negotiate a peace treaty instead."

From Andy-Andy: "I see a method in your madness, but there's still too damn much madness in your method."

Thanks. "Sit down, Chak. Frankly, I'd rather not get involved in a war with Therranj," he said to Dhara, trying to sound as though he were considering the subject casually.

I get it. I don't like it, but I get it. If you can create the slightest doubt in her mind that Therranj couldn't take on you alone, then she's not going to have any trouble swallowing the idea that leaving Home alone is the best move—assuming that she can't get you to join up.

Right. And we've made that point. The threat is patent nonsense—
Which only makes it better.

Exactly. 'Legend' is another word for 'nonsense.' She's not sure that she believes any of this, but there have been too many stories about me being passed around, growing in the telling. Last time I heard about how I took on Ohlmin, Slovotsky wasn't in on it, and Ohlmin had a hundred men, not eight. The rest of this is just pro forma; I've made the point.

And if she had called your bluff?

Karl didn't answer. There wasn't a real answer. Years ago, it had become clear that he wasn't likely to die of old age. His situation wasn't like that of an Other Side soldier in a normal sort of war; Karl had enlisted for the duration, and the duration was sure to be longer than even his natural lifespan.

If this was where he was going to die, that was the way it would have to be. Chak and Tennetty would have been able to get Andy-Andy out in the confusion, and that would have had to be enough.

Well, as long as you don't believe your own bullshit . . .

You so sure it's bullshit?

Yup. And you are, too. Now, stop sweating and start negotiating.

The elf woman beckoned another servitor to refill their glasses. "Now, where were we?"

Karl smiled back at her. "We were discussing peace between Therranj and Home. Sounds like a good idea to me—as it should to you."

"I thought the issue was to be the incorporation of the Valley of Varnath into Therranj proper. That is its proper name, you know."

"Not anymore." Karl shrugged. "Look. We're going to have a town meeting on the question of joining Therranj. The majority will decide—"

Tennetty interrupted him with a loud snicker. "Karl's always thought that counting noses means something."

Dhara raised an eyebrow. "And you don't?"

She laughed. "Of course not. But my opinion doesn't matter—it's my loyalty that does."

"Enough," Karl said. "As I was saying, I'm voting against. I think Ahira is going to stay in office, and Home is going to stay independent. But that doesn't mean that we can't continue to trade with you. We have things you want: Riccetti's horsecollars, better plows than you're used to, finer blades—"

"Guns. And gunpowder. We want your Lou Riccetti to produce them for us."

"—and we also produce a food surplus, each and every year. That doesn't amount to much yet, but we're still growing. And as far as the guns go," he said with a shrug, "those are our secret, and are going to stay that way for the foreseeable future."

"Really?" She raised an eyebrow. "I've heard otherwise."

I don't like this, Karl.

Neither do I. Has anyone been talking about the slaver powder and guns?

Negative. Ellegon made it a blanket statement of fact.

"As a matter of fact," Dhara went on, "there have been guns operating in the war between Bieme and Holtun. I have it on good authority that the Biemish reverses have been due to the Holts' having some."

I haven't heard anything about this. Pry for more information.

"I'd have to doubt that, Lady. Your sources must be mistaken. We haven't taken sides in the war—"

"Nevertheless, there have been guns. You would like witnesses?" At Karl's nod, Dhara snapped her fingers. "Bring them in."

Elven soldiers brought three humans into the tent, guarding them closely.

"Thinking that you might demand reliable witnesses, I couldn't resist buying these, when I ran across them in a Metreyll market. Which is somewhat ironic; it seems that they were originally headed to Metreyll, although not to become slaves. They were captured by mercenaries employed by Holtun—mercenaries who used guns to kill their bodyguards."

Karl started to speak, but as the three were led in, his words caught in his throat. He didn't recognize the adult man, but both the woman and the boy were familiar.

"Rahff!" Karl leaped to his feet. "How? I saw you die—"

"Karl!" Chak caught his arm. "It's not him."

No, it wasn't Rahff. Rahff had died in Melawei, protecting Aeia. If Rahff had lived, he would have been older than this boy. If Rahff had lived . . . but he hadn't.

And then there was the woman. White streaks had invaded the black of her hair, but the high cheekbones and eyes were a feminine version of Rahff's.

They were Thomen Furnael and his mother Beralyn, the baroness.

Years ago, Karl had suspected that Zherr Furnael had a plan to get the rest of his family away from the oncoming war. Just as he had apprenticed Rahff to Karl, hoping that Karl could teach the boy enough to lead the barony through the war.

But it hadn't worked. Rahff had been killed in Melawei, and now it seemed that Furnael's plan to safeguard the rest of his family had failed.

Until now. *Ellegon, get the dwarf. I want him to take over Daven's team. Just in case.* "Thomen, Baroness," he said, inclining his head. "It has been a long time."

Dhara snapped her fingers. "Beralyn, you will tell him about the guns. Now."

"You don't understand, Lady Dhara," Karl said, his hand on the hilt of his sword. "The baroness and the boy—all three of them are here now, they're under my protection now. They're free. They're beholden to nobody, owned by nobody."

"Another bluff, Karl Cullinane?"

Tennetty was the first to move; she kicked a table toward the nearest guard, then leaped at Dhara, wrestling the elf woman from the couch, bringing one arm up behind Dhara's back in a hammerlock, setting her blade against the elf woman's throat.

One of the soldiers drew his sword and lunged toward her from behind. Chak parried, then kicked at the elf's elbow; the blade fell from nerveless fingers. He stood, smiling at Dhara's guards.

In the distance, three gunshots rang out.

Nobody's hurt, yet. I've sent for the dwarf instead of fetching him; Daven needed a bit of persuading to stay put. We compromised on a few warning shots.

"Nobody's seriously hurt yet, Dhara. Those shots were just a warning."

Andy-Andy raised her hands and wet her lips. "These are the mother and brother of Karl's first apprentice, Lady Dhara. I wouldn't push the matter."

Even with Tennetty's blade at her throat, Dhara managed a smile. "Lord Khoral intended to give the three of them to you, as tokens of our sincerity. If you wish to free them, well, that is your concern. Not mine."

Gently, she tried to push Tennetty's blade away; at Karl's nod, Tennetty let her.

"We'll have to continue this discussion later," Karl said. "Baroness, Thomen, and you, whoever you are, if you will follow me, we'll see to your needs."

The three didn't say anything; they just followed sullenly.

CHAPTER NINE

A Matter of Obligation

A sense of duty pursues us ever. . . . If we take to ourselves the wings of the morning, and dwell in the uttermost parts of the sea, duty performed or duty violated is still with us, for our happiness or our misery. If we say the darkness shall cover us, in the darkness as in the light our obligations are yet with us.

—Daniel Webster

"You expect me to be grateful, Karl Cullinane?" Beralyn sneered. "You, who might as well have murdered my son." She sat back in her chair. "Go ahead, kill me. That won't change anything."

The shack was small, but neat; originally, it had been Ahira's house, but now it was one of the three small log cabins that were used for receiving new arrivals, giving them a place to sleep and take their meals until they could adjust to Home life.

Karl bit his lip, opened his mouth, closed it. He turned to the boy.

"Thomen, I need to know something." Karl tapped at the two rifles on the table in front of them. "One of these is a Home rifle; the other is one we seized from slavers just about a tenday ago. The men who killed your guards and took you—which kind did they have?"

Karl was sure what the answer would be—but what if he was wrong? What if someone on his or Daven's or Aveneer's squad had taken up slaving?

Hesitantly, the boy started to point toward the slaver's gun, but his mother's voice brought him up short.

"Don't answer," the boy's mother snapped. "We will give your brother's killer no help."

Anything I can do?

No. Just go away. Karl couldn't even work up the strength to blame Beralyn. She had been against apprenticing Rahff to Karl from the first, knowing that it would endanger the boy.

It hadn't just endangered him. It had killed him.

There was a knock on the door, and Aeia walked in without waiting for an answer. "Greetings," she said, her face grave. "Andrea says that Rahff's mother is here. Are you her?"

Beralyn didn't answer.

"We didn't meet when I was in Bieme. But I did get to know Rahff well. You should know something about how your son died."

"I know how my son died."

Aeia shook her head. "You weren't there. I was. If it hadn't been for Rahff . . ." She let her voice trail off.

Thomen looked up. "What if it hadn't been for Rahff?"

Aeia smiled gently. "I would have been killed instead. The slavers had gone crazy; they were killing everyone they could reach. Rahff stood between me and one of them."

Karl pounded his fist against the table. *If only I'd been a little smarter, a little faster.* If he had been only a few seconds faster he would have gotten to the slaver before the bastard opened Rahff's belly. If only Karl had worked out that Seigar Wohtansen would treat his own people first, he would have been able to get the healing draughts to Rahff in time.

Aeia sat down next to Thomen. "Rahff hit me once, did you know that?"

"What for?"

She shrugged. "I doubted Karl—out loud. Rahff sort of elbowed me in the side. What did you tell him, Karl?"

"Aeia . . ." Karl shook his head. "I don't remember."

"I bet Rahff did. You said, 'A man whose profession is violence must not commit violence on his own family, or his friends. You and I are supposed to watch over Aeia, protect her, not bully her.' "

Just as I was supposed to protect Rahff. Teach him, protect him, not watch him die.

It has been more than five years, Karl. Isn't it time you stopped flogging yourself over Rahff?

"Don't you ask me that." Karl jumped to his feet. "Ask her, dammit, ask Beralyn. Tell her that it's okay now."

He pounded his clenched fists in front of his face. "There hasn't been a day gone by when I haven't remembered. He trusted me. The boy practically worshipped me." He turned to Beralyn, trying to think of the words that would soften her stony expression. "Baroness . . ." But there weren't any words.

It was too much; Karl pushed away from the table and walked out into the courtyard. He leaned against the wall of the old smithy.

High above, Ellegon's dark form passed across the stars. *Anything I can do?*

"No. Just leave me alone." Karl buried his face in his hands. "I've just got to be alone for a while."

Time lost its meaning. He never knew how long he stood there.

A finger tapped against his shoulder. He turned to see Beralyn standing next to him, her face wet. "You loved him, too, didn't you?"

Karl didn't answer.

"I've spent years hating you, you know. Ever since a trader brought us your letter, telling us that he was dead."

"I . . . understand."

"I thank you for the understanding. What do we do now, Karl Cullinane? Do we go on hating each other?"

"I don't hate you, Baroness. You've never given me any reason to hate you."

"But you don't like me much, either. You feel that I should be grateful because you freed Thomen, Rhuss, and me."

"Just tell me what you want, Lady. Don't play games with me."

She nodded slowly. "My husband sent Thomen and me away, once the Holts started using these guns and the tide of the war turned against us. He thought we would be safe. But it seems that guns are flowing out of Enkiar these days—flowing toward Holtun."

Enkiar, again. That was where the slaver caravan had been heading. That was where Ahrmin had hired the assassins. What did it all mean?

Well, he'd find out soon enough.

"Aeia told me that you're going to Enkiar. She didn't say where you would be going after that."

He shrugged. "I guess that depends on what happens there. Maybe back here, maybe on another raid." And maybe to the source of the slavers' guns. Not only was there a score to be settled there, but even light trading in slaver guns and powder had to be stopped.

"You owe me, Karl Cullinane. You owe me for my son. I wish to collect on that debt."

He looked her full in the face. "How?"

"You know my husband. Zherr isn't going to survive this war. I'm likely never to see him again. Unless . . ."

"Unless what?" Dammit, couldn't anyone speak plainly?

"Unless you take me back to Bieme. I want to go home, Karl Cullinane. And I want your word." She gripped his hand. "I want your word that if it's humanly possible, you'll take me home, after Enkiar. That's little enough payment for my son's life."

"Baroness—"

"Isn't it?"

"Yes, but—"

"Do I have your word? This . . . word of Karl Cullinane that you prize so much?"

"You have it."

"There is one more thing."

"Yes?"

"Thomen. He is to stay here, to be sent with another party. I won't have him around you."

CHAPTER TEN

Practice Session

Even if you persuade me, you won't persuade me.

—Aristophanes

Karl gobbled down the scrambled eggs, then took a last bite of the half-eaten ham steak before pushing his chair away from the table.

"And just where do you think you're taking your brainless body off to, Karl Cullinane?" U'len asked, her fists on her more than ample hips.

Suddenly he felt about eight years old, and was surprised to find that he liked the feeling.

"Gotta rush, U'len. I've got a workout with Tennetty and a couple of Daven's men, and then I've got to get ready for the town meeting."

"First things first. Eat."

"No—"

"Yes." Andy-Andy shook her head. "U'len's right. Sit down and finish your breakfast."

Jason hid a broad smile behind his tiny hand. "Daddy's in trouble," he announced in a stage whisper, addressing nobody in particular.

"Damn straight," Aeia said, the English words still incongruous coming from her. "He acts as if he's in charge here or something."

He glared at her.

"Siddown, hero," Andy-Andy said. "Out *there* you may be the legendary Karl Cullinane, but in *here* you're an all too often absent husband and father who thinks he can wolf down his food and run."

Relay, please: You didn't think I was so damn absent last night.

There was no answer: He snorted. *Question: Why is a dragon like a cop? Answer: You never can find one when you need one.*

"Give me a break, please." *Keep it light,* he thought. There were too few opportunities to have an argument that could be treated lightly, where winning or losing didn't really matter; he decided to enjoy this one. "I've got things to do."

"Exactly right. And the first heroic thing you're going to do today is to finish your ham. All of it."

"Yeah," Jason piped in. "Children of Salket are starving, and you wanna throw away good food?" he went on, in a fine imitation of his mother's voice when she got angry.

"Name two."

"Karl—"

"I'm eating, I'm eating." He pushed his chair back to the table. Somehow, it seemed that the remaining ham had grown larger in the past seconds.

Karl's workouts tended to draw crowds. Even on a morning when most people were doing their best to finish whatever they were working on so that they would be free for the late-afternoon town meeting, more than fifty had gathered around the corral to watch.

Pendrill and the stableboy chased the three horses out of the corral, while Wraveth and Taren cleared out the fresh dung, then stripped to the waist before donning padded shirts and trousers and slipping the wire-mesh masks over their heads.

Karl settled for just a mask. The practice swords' edges had been dulled, and the points had had steel balls welded to them; with the mask precluding the possibility of losing an eye, there was little chance of much more than a bruise or two, and Karl wasn't likely to get bruised. Besides, the padded practice garments tended to interfere with his freedom of movement. His overfilled belly was going to do enough of that; no need to aggravate the problem.

Tennetty was late. After a few minutes that Karl spent chatting with Wraveth and Taren, she rode up, then hurriedly slipped from Pirate's back, waving away Taren's offer of a mask and practice sword.

Her wrists were bandaged. Karl walked over to her.

"Problem?"

She shook her head. "You still want me in the Enkiar operation? I'll need some fresh scars on my wrist, and I'd rather get them from Thellaren's scalpels than by wearing cuffs a moment longer than I have to." She tapped at her patch, her lips pursed in irritation. "Thellaren's working on the glass eye, and I asked Chak to ride out and get Nehera started on trick chains—you happy?"

"It's necessary, Tennetty." But why the sudden change of mind? Karl shrugged mentally. It wasn't any of his business.

She broke into a smile. "I have a surprise for you. Remember Jilla and Danni?"

"Yes?"

"They want to join our team. Seems that they've decided to become warriors, get a bit of revenge."

Wonderful. Once Karl had let a woman join up just because she had a thing for seeing slavers' blood. That someone had been Tennetty; he had lucked out.

But he didn't want to push his luck. He'd been fortunate enough to find in Tennetty someone with a natural bent for combat, plus a personality skewed enough to be able to handle it. "How did you talk them out of it?"

"Well . . ."

"You *did* talk them out of it, didn't you?"

"No." She snorted. "They don't think it's all that hard." She set a hand on her hip and bent her other wrist. " 'It looks *soooo* easy. You pull a trigger, slice with a sword—' "

"You're joking. Tell me you're joking."

"Nope. They'll be here in a while. I made them a deal: Whoever scores on you we'll sign up. Whoever you beat has to find herself a man and settle down—and we get to pick the man."

"We?" He raised an eyebrow. "You got anyone in particular in mind?"

"Obvious: Chak for the blonde, Riccetti for the brunette. By the way, they're both good cooks, although I can't vouch for their . . . other talents. You might want to try them out—"

"Tennetty . . ."

"Think about it, Karl. Might give Chak something to come Home to, put a little weight on Lou, and maybe smiles on both of their faces."

That might not be a bad idea, provided Chak and Lou agreed to it. Not bad at all. As far as Karl could tell, none of the female apprentice Engineers were sleeping with Lou; Riccetti had always been shy around women. And while Karl trusted Chak with his life, discussing Chak's relationships with women—or, rather, the lack of them—wasn't something he was comfortable doing.

Karl raised an eyebrow. "They went for it?"

Tennetty nodded. "That they did. Remember, for most of their lives, they were owned by a Pandathaway inn. Their only real talents are over a stove and in a bed, unless you consider arranging flowers to be a major skill. I don't think that either of them would have a hard time getting Riccetti to agree. If you want, we could rig it so that Lou thinks it's his own idea. I don't vouch for Chak; he can be clever, in his own little way."

"That wasn't what I was asking. They really agreed to sparring with me?"

"Well, I had to throw in a few conditions for them to be willing to face the great Karl Cullinane."

"Such as?"

"First, they get to use real swords."

"Great. Thanks a lot." That was pushing things a bit far. Even an absolute tyro could get in a lucky slash. "I'd better send for some armor." Normally, Karl didn't like wearing a lot of armor; in combat, speed was more important, particularly if you had a bottle of healing draughts handy to take care of the occasional nick.

"Umm, that was the second condition. You don't get to wear armor. No mask. Nothing but your pants—"

"Thank heavens for small favors."

"Really?" Tennetty snickered. "I never noticed. The third handicap is that you use only a practice sword."

Karl snorted. "Anything else? Do I have to fight with one hand tied behind my back?"

Tennetty produced a leather thong. "Number four."

Look, Karl wanted to say, *this isn't a pleasant business. Don't get into it if you don't have to.*

But he didn't. It wouldn't have done any good. For some people, blood was a drug. Tennetty was that way; the killing never really bothered her.

Then again, how do I know that? Karl hid his own feelings as much as he could, even from Andy-Andy.

There were things he had to do; horrible, awful things. The only justification was that not doing them was worse. Remonstrating with himself was a luxury for late at night; he couldn't spend precious moments in combat remembering that an enemy had once been a cute little baby, bouncing on a mother's knee.

But he didn't have to like it. He didn't have to force himself to feel the pleasure that Tennetty got from the killing, and that Jilla and Danni seemed to have learned at her hands.

He worked his left hand in the leather thongs that bound it behind his back. It wouldn't be hard to work it out of the thongs, but that would take time. And it would be seen as cheating.

Not that he had anything against cheating, not if it made the difference between bleeding and not bleeding, but . . .

Damn. One of the watchers in the crowd was an unfamiliar elf, not a Home resident. One of Dhara's people, no doubt. Which upped the stakes: Karl wouldn't only have to win; he would have to win in such a way as to impress the elf. The Therranji had already been shocked by the scene Karl had pulled the day before; best to keep them impressed.

How the hell do I get myself into things like this?

Do you really want an answer? With a rustling of leathery wings, Ellegon landed next to the corral. *It's because you're egotistical, smug, stupid, foolish—*

Ellegon—

—and those are your good points.

"Thanks."

Jilla and Danni walked out through the gate from the Receiving complex, naked swords held clumsily in their hands, whispering conspiratorially to each other. Each wore a deeply cut halter and a sarong slit well up the thigh. Rather nice thighs, at that.

Naughty, naughty. And if you're thinking that's accidental, guess again. Jilla decided that if you're watching other parts of their anatomy, you won't be concentrating on the hands with the swords. By the way, the halters are loosely tied; they'll slip off with just a bit of exertion. Sort of a second line of defense.

Well, at least Andy-Andy isn't—

"Hey, hero," Andy-Andy said, tapping him on the shoulder. "What goes on here?"

"Great. Just great." He put his free hand on the corral railing and vaulted over, accepting a practice sword from Tennetty. "Let's get to it."

Naked blades didn't always make Karl nervous, but they did always make him serious. He eyed both of the women professionally as they circled him, waiting for him to make the first move.

If this had been for real, he would have tried for a quick injury to either—preferably a leg wound, some sort of disabler—and then taken out the other, finishing off the injured opponent at his leisure.

But that wouldn't work here. There was prestige at stake, as well as injury.

Why you're worrying about prestige when you're facing two swords is something I fail to understand.

He made a tentative lunge toward Danni, allowing her to retreat, the sword held awkwardly in front of her face. *Because I can't afford to lose face before the town meeting.*

In either sense. Think about it. You're not all that pretty to begin with—

Shh. He forced a casual smile to his face.

Mr. Katsuwahara had had it right, way back when.

The way to think of *kumite,* of practice, he had said, is to treat it as real, except for the last inch of your own blows. Block as though the punches really would crush your trachea, the kicks would truly rupture your diaphragm. Your strikes should be aimed just outside the kill points—the navel instead of the solar plexus, the upper thigh instead of the groin, the orbital ridge instead of the eye—and then focused just an inch away from the flesh.

That wouldn't quite do it here, but it was the right idea. Treat the swords as real—because they were, dammit—and then work out how to come up with an offense that wasn't really an offense.

Danni slashed at his leg; he parried easily, putting enough force into the move to make the steel sing.

He spun to block Jilla's stab at his left shoulder. Dammit, they had him between them, and both of them had moved in too close.

But why was that bad? In a fight, you wanted your opponents' blades to endanger each other; they had to avoid cutting into an ally's flesh, while any meat your sword met was an enemy's.

And what of someone who was foolish enough to move in too close? Why wasn't that a problem? That was supposed to be an opportunity to bring feet and elbows into play.

Because this isn't a real fight, dammit. It isn't supposed to be.

Danni poked her sword at his shoulder—

Where thought would have failed him, reflex took over.

He didn't stop to think that ducking aside brought Danni's sword into line with Jilla's face; there just wasn't time to think about it.

It wasn't thought that opened his right hand, letting the practice sword drop, while his left arm clenched, snapping the leather thongs that bound it.

And it wasn't thought that brought his two palms together, clapping his hands against the flat of Danni's blade, stopping it a scant half-inch from Jilla's left eye.

"No." Danni gasped. "I almost—"

"Right." He twisted the sword from Danni's hand, then turned and snatched Jilla's blade from her nerveless fingers.

Jilla rubbed at her left eye, although it hadn't been touched. Her breath came in short gasps; her face was ashen.

Karl forced a chuckle. "You've just had a taste of what it's really like. Just a little taste, mind." He tossed one of the swords end over end into the air, letting the hilt *thunk* into his palm. "You know what we really do? We're merchants, in the business of selling pieces of ourselves. Tennetty's eye, Chak's toes—take a look at Slovotsky's scars sometimes, or Daven's.

"Look at my chest," he said. "I picked up this scar outside of Lundescarne. A slaver had a chance to whittle on me with a broken sword while I was busy choking the life out of him. And then there's —" He stopped himself. "And we're the lucky ones."

Anger welled up and choked him. "Idiots. You don't have to see a friend's intestines spread across the grass because he wasn't quick enough with his sword. You can let yourselves sleep soundly at night, because a little sound or a light touch doesn't have to mean anything to you. You don't have to jump through a window and find three people dead, their throats cut because someone was after your blood and they happened to be in the way.

"And you don't have to keep going, death after death, killing after killing, year after year.

"But you want in on it?" He offered them each a sword, hilt first. "Congratulations. You've got it."

Eyeing the sword with horror, Danni staggered away.

"Yes, Karl Cullinane." Jilla gripped the other one tightly. "I want in. I understand what you're saying; I've spent the past tenday listening to Tennetty. And I know I'll need training, but—"

"You want in." He shrugged. "Tennetty, she's in your charge. You get to train her. I want you to start by running her until she drops." He turned and walked away.

CHAPTER ELEVEN

Town Meeting

*The deadliest enemies of nations are not their foreign foes;
they always dwell within their borders. And from these
internal enemies civilization is always in need of being
saved. The nation blessed above all nations is she in whom
the civic genius of the people does the saving day by day, by
acts without external picturesqueness; by speaking, writing, voting reasonably; by smiting corruption swiftly, by
good temper between parties; by the people knowing true
men when they see them, and preferring them as leaders to
rabid partisans or empty quacks.*

—William James

Ahira snickered. "Ever wish you hadn't freed Chton? Just sort of
let him slide by that time?"

"No." Karl pursed his lips. "Just 'cause he has clay feet like everybody else?" *Including me, for that matter.*

He bit into his sandwich, refusing the offer of a wineskin from a
passing carouser.

Town meetings were half a political event, half a valley-wide party.
Since everyone in the valley took at least the afternoon off from
work, the meetings would have been called far more often if they
didn't require a petition by twenty-five percent of the voters.

Behind the speaking platform and its chest-high ballot box, six whole sheep were slowly turning over cooking fires. A team of volunteer cooks took turns cranking the spits and basting the carcasses with wine and oil, slicing off sizzling pieces of meat, wrapping them in fresh-baked flatbread, handing out the sandwiches as they were ready.

Someone had broached the whiskey bottles and beer barrels early. Karl noted with satisfaction that none of the Engineers or the warriors joined in the throng milling around the booze, filling their mugs with the trickling liquid fire.

Good. Let the Joiners get drunk. Anyone who was passed out couldn't vote.

Like most things democratic, Home town meetings were a zoo. There were many things to be said in favor of democracy, but neatness wasn't one of them. With the exception of the absent warriors and a few outlying landowners who were too busy with their own fields, all of the voters and most of the other citizens had elected to attend.

He turned back to the dwarf. "Any landowners playing games?" Karl patted at the large leather pouch dangling from the right side of his belt. Still there; good.

Ahira shook his head. "Not that I can tell. I'll keep my ear to the ground for complaints, though—assuming I'm still Mayor by nightfall."

The law involving town meetings was explicit: Nobody was ever to be pressured not to attend, under penalty of fine, confiscation of property, or banishment, at the pleasure of the Mayor, depending on the nature of the pressure.

That applied to nonvoting citizens as well as voters; it was important that nonvoter citizens get a taste of democracy. Get someone hooked on deciding his or her own fate, and the security of cropping quickly lost its appeal. The trouble with sharecropping back on the Other Side hadn't been the basic idea of trading labor on someone else's fields for a portion of the harvest and a place to live; the flaw was that it could easily become a form of debt slavery.

In the short run, the cure for that was easy: Just make sure that there were more proven fields than there was labor to farm them. Let the landowners bid for labor, rather than letting laborers bid against each other.

"Should be straightforward, assuming things go right." Ahira nibbled at his sandwich. "Although we're likely to run into at least one challenge."

"Oh?"

"See that kid over by the barbecue?"

Karl followed Ahira's pointing finger. The subject was a boy of about twelve, dressed in dirt and rags. He was busily feeding himself, wolfing down sandwich after sandwich.

"New arrival? What the hell is going on with supply?"

"Not new; he's a voter, believe it or not. He's been here for the last quarter. Aveneer brought him in while you were gone. Umm, Peters? No, Petros—Petros is his name. Stubborn kid. He didn't want to crop and build up his grubstake, so he managed to sweet-talk Stanish out of the use of some rusty old tools, then proved a field halfway up the mountain, just above and beyond Engineer Territory. It's barely inside the wards. I don't know what he's been living on, or how he managed to clear the ground without the woodknife, but he did. Then—

"Then, he trailed a flatbed carrying seed corn out to your fields, and picked up the spillings from the road—at least, that's what he says. More likely, he stole a few pounds of seed, but just try to prove it."

"I don't think so." The theft of a few pounds of seed didn't bother Karl. But a twelve-year-old child looking like a famine victim did. "He's working a full-sized field all by himself?"

"Yup. Scraggliest-looking field I've ever seen; I doubt that there's as much as one cornstalk per square meter. The rest is weeds. He sleeps under a brush lean-to. Last time I was inspecting, I saw what he had, and it's not much: crummy handmade bow and arrows, fire-hardened spear—probably lives off weeds and rabbit. There's at least one mountain lion working that area; likely he'll wake up in its belly some morning. Pitiful."

"Damn." Karl shook his head. "You really think anyone's going to challenge his vote?"

Ahira nodded. "He says he's fifteen, but nobody believes it. I think he should be in school, but you want to argue it with him?"

"Not at all. You'll have to excuse me; this is someone I've got to meet. Go do some politicking."

Karl worked his way through the crowd around the barbecue until he was next to the boy. It wasn't much of a problem; nobody wanted to be downwind of Petros.

"Greetings," he said.

The boy's eyes widened. "Are you who I think you are?"

Karl stuck out a hand. "Karl Cullinane."

Petros' eyes shot from side to side.

"T'rar ammalli." Karl smiled. "I just want to shake your hand; no harm."

The boy extended his own hand. Karl took it briefly, then released it, forcing himself not to wipe his own hand on his tunic. "I have a proposition for you."

Petros shook his head. "I will not crop for anyone. My field is mine, and so is my vote. I don't need help."

Then why do you look more like a Biafran refugee than anything else, kid? And has anybody ever told you what a bath is? But Karl didn't say that. A twelve-year-old former slave with this kind of pride, this kind of stubbornness, was a treasure. The trick was to make sure that this particular treasure survived, its pride intact. "Maybe not, but I could use yours—and not with cropping, either. You know Nehera?"

"The smith? Of course. What of it?"

"Take a walk with me," Karl said, taking a couple of sandwiches, then urging the boy away from the rest of the crowd.

Petros shrugged and followed him.

"I have a problem with Nehera," Karl said, handing the boy a sandwich and taking a bite out of the other one. "He hasn't gotten the idea that he's free. Thinks he has to belong to someone, and he figures that someone is me."

"Poor you."

Karl let a bit of steel creep into his voice. "You think I own people, boy? Ever?"

"Well, no. I've heard about you."

"Better, then. As I was saying, I can't break him of the notion."

"Damn dwarves are supposed to make lousy slaves. That's what my mas—what someone who used to own me said."

Karl shrugged. "That's the theory. His spirit's broken, though. And I don't know how to go about fixing it. That's your job, if you want it."

"Broke spirit?" Petros snorted. "How am I supposed to fix that?"

"If I knew how, I wouldn't need you—that's your problem. I want you to play apprentice one day out of three. I'll clear it with the Engineers. While he's busy teaching you about smithing, I want you to teach him how to be free. Interested?"

"What's the pay?"

"Not much. You get to work on your own tools, and while you're playing apprentice, you eat out of Nehera's pot. Might even pick up a few skills while you're at it."

Petros shook his head. "My fields take too much time—"

"Nonsense. All you're doing between now and harvest is a bit of weeding. If you didn't have to spend so much time gathering food, you'd have plenty of spare time on your hands."

The boy considered it. "Maybe. That your best offer?"

"What else do you want?"

"Next planting, I want the use of a horse and plow."

Was that an honest counteroffer, or was the boy pushing, testing him?

Karl shook his head. "Just the horse. I've got plenty of horses. You'll have to rent a plow yourself."

"Deal." The boy stuck out his hand. "Shakeonit."

"One more thing."

"Well?" Petros eyed him suspiciously.

"You smell like an outhouse." Karl jerked his thumb toward the lake. "Take a bath. Now. You can pick up a cake of soap at the schoolhouse. Tell Aeia I said so."

"Done. But I'll be back in time to vote. Nobody taking my vote from me."

The boy walked off toward the lake, trying his best to hold back a smile.

Karl didn't bother trying; he just turned his head away. *Go ahead, Petros, think of me as a sucker.*

Standing on the speaking platform, Ahira pounded his fist against the metal gong. "Your attention please," he called out, his voice even louder than the gong. "The twenty-third Home town meeting is hereby called to order. Get the food off the fire and plug the kegs," he called out to the cooks. "There is a decision to be made."

". . . and the offer is a *good* one," Chton said, for the eighteenth time. Karl was sure it was eighteen. As he lay back on the grass, propped up on his elbow next to Andy-Andy, he hadn't had anything better to do than count.

Oh. Before I forget. Ahira says that there's a mountain lion around Petros' farm—

Such as it is.

Right. It would be kind of convenient if that lion got itself eaten.

Consider it munched.

". . . what are we here? Just a few thousand, barely eking out a living from the soil and what we have to trade our blood and dying for."

That did it. *Enough of that crap. Point of fact, please.*

Who? Moi?

Chak, please. And cut out the Miss Piggy imitation; you don't have the right intonation down.

Then you don't remember it clearly; I stole it from Andy-Andy's head, and she's got a better aural memory than you.

"Point of fact," Chak said, leaping to his feet.

Chton tried to go on, but Ahira interrupted him. "Point of fact has been called. Your claim?"

"I don't remember Chton shedding any blood. I don't know him all that well, but I thought he was just a farmer."

Correct that, and quick.

Chak's eyes momentarily glazed over. "Pardon me, I didn't mean to say something bad about farmers. What I was objecting to was Chton's taking credit for the blood that the warriors and the Engineers shed—not him."

Ahira nodded judiciously. "You may continue, Chton, but omit taking credit for prices you haven't paid."

For a moment, Karl thought that Chton was going to burst a blood vessel. *"Haven't paid?* How about Werthan, and his woman and child? Were they not farmers? Is a farmer's blood any less red than a warrior's? Would they not be alive today instead of lying in cold graves if we were under the protection of Lord Khoral?"

Karl kept his face blank, but he couldn't help how his fists clenched. A child, body sprawled on a rough wood floor, her lifeblood a pool that would stain forever . . .

A murmur ran through the crowd.

You'd better answer that, Karl. If that wasn't addressed to you, I don't know what is.

No. There wasn't an answer; there wasn't an excuse.

Ihryk rose to his feet. "I'll answer him, Mr. Mayor."

"You?" Chton sneered. "One of Karl Cullinane's hirelings?"

"I don't remember that sneer in your voice when Karl pulled you and me out of the slave wagon, Chton. I don't even remember you at Werthan's houseraising." Ihryk raised his fist. "But I'll tell you this —Werthan and Anna would have spent their lives with collars around their necks if it weren't for the likes of Karl Cullinane. And so would you and I."

"Yes," Chton shot back, "the *noble* Karl Cullinane, the *great* man.

Who just happens to be the richest man in the valley. If we join with Therranj, we'll all be as rich as he is, have as many servants as he does. Is that what bothers you, Karl Cullinane? Is that why you oppose Lord Khoral's offer?"

Karl, I think it's about time. If he calls for the vote now—

I know. Karl rose to his feet. "Point of personal privilege, Mr. Mayor."

Ahira nodded. "You may address the point."

Karl walked to the platform, forcing himself to move slowly, knowing that a hurried step might make it look as though Chton's taunts had scored.

He stepped up onto the rough wood and turned to face the crowd.

"About damn time, Karl," Ahira whispered. "This better be good."

"It will be." He raised his voice. "Chton has made a point, and a good one. I . . . guess I should be ashamed. Yes, of course, the reason that I don't want Home to become part of Therranj is that I'm afraid for my status. It's only logical, isn't it? If everyone is better off, then it only follows that I would be worse off. . . ."

He wrinkled his brow. "Wait. That doesn't make sense. Wouldn't I be better off, as well?" He nodded. "I know what Chton means, though." He picked a familiar face out of the crowd. "Harwen, I was just talking about it to you the other day, remember? I was complaining about your being out riding. I figured I'd be more comfortable riding both Carrot and your horse," he said, taking an absurdly wide stance.

A quiet chuckle ran through the crowd.

"And Ternius, you noticed me over by the cooking fire? I was glaring at everyone who was eating. After all, I can eat more than will fill my belly, can't I?" He glanced at the remaining roasts near the fire. "Well, I'll try, but I don't think I'd enjoy it.

"You know something, Chton? I just can't do it. I just can't ride more than one horse at a time, or sleep in more than one bed at once, or eat more than my belly will hold. Or lie with more than one woman at a time—"

Now.

"You had damn well better not, Karl Cullinane." Andy-Andy leaped to her feet. "Point of information, Mr. Mayor."

"Recognized. What information do you want?"

"None. It's information I'd better give. You cheat on me, Karl Cullinane, and you'll be missing something I have reason to know you're fond of." She produced a knife from the folds of her robes and considered the edge.

The quiet chuckle became a full-throated laugh.

Now that you've got them laughing, what are you going to do?

That was just the warm-up. Watch me.

Karl raised his hands in mock surrender. "You see my point, Chton."

"Listen—"

"You've had your say; I'll have mine now." He hitched at the leather pouch at his waist. "Khoral doesn't want much from us, and that's a fact. All he wants is our fealty, and he'll give us much in return." Karl untied the pouch from his belt and held it in both hands. "Very much. He'll make me a baron, and give me the whole valley as my barony. Maybe, if I turn it down—and make no mistake, I would turn it down—he'll give it to Chton.

"He'll send us serfs. All of you who have farms will have people around who will have to work your fields for you, or starve. Doesn't that sound good? Doesn't that sound familiar? Khoral will divide up the land for us, and then we can make them farm it. We won't even have to clap collars around their necks—they'll either work for us or starve.

"And what does he want for this? Stand up, Lady Dhara, and tell us what he wants for this."

She stood, but Karl didn't give her a chance to answer. "All he wants is our fealty; each and every one of us. That's all. He will give us gold, he says, and promise that our taxes will be low. All he wants is our fealty. All he wants is for us to say that he, Lord Khoral, is better able to decide how we should live than we are. You like that idea, Tivar?" He beckoned to a farmer who he knew was undecided. "You like the idea of turning your destiny over to that elf?"

"N-no."

"Wait!" Chton spun on Karl. "What's the difference between having Khoral rule and letting you and Ahira run the valley as though it were your fief? Tell me that."

Karl walked to the ballot box and slammed his hand down on it. "This is the difference, fool. The difference is *choice.* Khoral wants you to trade this in—you know what he'll give you instead of this?"

"Yes, gold—"

Now.

Don't teach your grandfather—"Gold. That's what it comes down to, isn't it, Chton? You and the rest of your Joiners want gold, and

Khoral offers gold." Karl dug his hand into his pouch. "I have some of that gold right here." He pulled his hand out.

The buttery golden collar shone in the bright daylight. "Is this what you want clamped around your neck?"

"No," several voices cried out, most of them Engineers.

"I can't hear you. Do you want this?"

"No!" The voices were stronger, although the warrior and Engineer factions were still the most vocal.

"Now," Karl said, deliberately lowering his voice, forcing them all to listen carefully, "you have a choice. You can vote your confidence in the Mayor, or you can throw him out. Even if Ahira stays in as Mayor, you can still change your minds later. But this?" He raised the golden collar over his head. "Once you clamp this around your throat, do you think you can decide to take it off later? What if it doesn't fit you, Chton?" He tossed the collar to the platform. "What if it chokes you?"

"Wait, that's not fair—"

"Fair? I'll show you fair. Lady Dhara—catch this." He kicked the collar at Dhara; she caught it automatically, then dropped it as though it were on fire. "You can take that back to Lord Khoral and tell him that Home might make a good ally for Therranj, but if he tries to swallow us, he'll choke."

He strode to the ballot box and stopped in front of the two barrels next to it. "You all can vote in privacy, if you wish," he said, selecting a single stone from the barrel of white ones, "but here's how I vote; I don't mind any of you seeing." He held it up for all to see. "I vote my confidence in Ahira—and for independence." He slammed the stone down into the ballot box, then walked off the platform.

Daven, Andy-Andy, Tennetty, and half a dozen others want to know if they're supposed to join you.

No, not yet. Let someone else go first.

Petros vaulted to the platform. "I vote with Karl Cullinane," he said, taking up a white stone. Somewhere or other, the boy had managed to procure a knife; now he brandished it. "Does anybody value his life little enough to try stopping me?" He dropped the white stone in the ballot box, then leaped from the platform, standing beside Karl.

Before Chton had his mouth half open, Ranella, the apprentice Engineer, had jumped to her feet. "The Engineers stand with Ahira," she said. "All of us."

"I do, too," Ternius said. "And I don't see any need to wait."

"And I—"

"I will—"

The trickle became a torrent, and then a flood.

"Transcending the political, eh, Karl?" Ahira smiled up at him as they walked down the road in the starlight. "Sounded to me like you were being very political, in your own way. Including lying."

"Lying? Me?" Karl stooped to pick a pebble from the road, then threw it off into the night.

"That golden collar was inspired."

Karl breathed on his fingernails and buffed them against his chest. "Thank you. I thought it made a nice metaphor. Didn't you?"

"Right. But I don't recall that as being one of Khoral's gifts."

"I never said it was, did I?"

"No. You didn't." Ahira was silent for a few minutes as they walked along the road toward the house that the dwarf shared with Walter and his family. "We make a good team, you and I. I can handle the day-to-day stuff, but I can't . . . inspire people, not the way you do." He shrugged. "Just not in me."

"Don't put yourself down."

"I'm not. It's just that if you hadn't been here, we might have lost. You might have found yourself faced with Chton as Mayor the next time you came Home."

"Stop talking around whatever it is that you want to talk about, Ahira. Just say it."

"You've got to settle down, Karl. Spend more time here, not on the road. If you'd been here, you might have been able to shame Chton into not pushing for a town meeting in the first place."

"Can't. Too much work to do. There's the Enkiar operation coming up, and I've promised to take Beralyn home."

The dwarf nodded grimly. "It might be best, in the long run. I've been talking to Gwellin; he's always thinking about going back to Endell."

"I knew that—but why you?"

"You notice a lot of dwarf women around?"

Karl nodded. "Well, it was always understood Gwellin and his people are only temporarily with us. But their word is as good as—"

"The word of Karl Cullinane." Ahira chuckled. "Quite right; no word will be said about guns. But, Karl . . ."

"Well?"

"Well, if they ever throw me out of office, I'm thinking that it might be a good idea if I went with him. I'm still not sure what I am, Karl. I've spent seven years now as a cross between a human and a dwarf, and I'm beginning to wonder . . ."

Karl stopped. "Ahira. Look me in the face. You wanted to lose today, didn't you?"

The dwarf didn't answer.

"Didn't you?"

"Karl, I . . . just don't know." Ahira pounded his fist against the flat of his hand. "I really don't know, not anymore. It's different for me than it is for you. You subordinated Barak to your own needs years ago. I'm . . . still betwixt and between. And I know that I owe my life to Walter, and Riccetti, and Andy—and most particularly to you, but . . ." He looked up. "Dammit, Karl, why can't things be clearer to me? You always seem to know what you're doing."

"Not you. Please." Karl threw up his hands. "Don't you start to buy into the legend. I'm still me, Ahira, just plain old Karl Cullinane who staggers through life, improvising as he goes." *And some of those improvisations have cost lives, Jimmy.* "I just do the best I can." He clapped a hand to Ahira's shoulder. "But once I finish with this Enkiar operation and get Beralyn back to Bieme, what say I hang around Home for a while? Would that do for the time being?"

"Let's try it." The dwarf nodded. "I think so. It wouldn't be all bad, you know. You could teach some school, spend more time with your wife and son."

"Okay. Just give me time, Ahira. It'll take a while to finish up what I've started. One favor, though."

"Yes?"

"When it's just the two of us alone, could I call you James Michael? It'd be sort of a taste of home."

"And it might remind me who I really am supposed to be, eh?"

"No. That you've got to decide for yourself."

They walked along in silence for a long time. In front of them, the lamp still burned on the porch. The dwarf climbed the steps and turned to him. "You do what you have to, Karl. And I'll hold out here just as long as I can. Who knows? This whole Joiner nonsense may subside."

But your own problem won't. "Maybe it will."

"About that favor . . ."

"Yes?"

"I think you'd better call me Ahira. It's who I am, after all. Good-night."

CHAPTER TWELVE

Parting

The voice of the turtledove speaks out. It says:
Day breaks, which way are you going?
Lay off, little bird, must you scold me so?

—Love Songs of the New Kingdom

Karl checked the third packhorse's cinch for the twentieth time as he eyed the house in the predawn light, wondering if he'd ever see it again. *I've always got to make my goodbyes count,* he thought. *They may end up being all too real.*

You're stalling. Which is probably the most sensible thing you've ever done. You should let me—

No. Case closed.

Beralyn and Tennetty sat astride their horses, waiting with patently false patience. Chak, sitting comfortably in the saddle on his gray gelding, was more phlegmatic. It didn't matter to him whether they left now or in a few minutes.

Karl shook his head. *I'd better go.*

Andy-Andy stood on the porch, watching him silently. There was nothing more to say; all of it had been said last night.

I'll miss you terribly, he mouthed. As always.

One more thing to do. He walked up the steps and into the foyer, then climbed the stairs to Jason's room.

Mikyn and Jason lay sleeping under their blankets.

Karl knelt on the floor and gently kissed Jason on the forehead. No need to wake him. *Watch over him, will you?* He tore himself away from the room, and the boy.

As always, Karl.

U'len caught up with him on the steps. "Look, you—be careful," she said, her voice a harsh whisper. "I have a bad feeling about this." She shook her head, her hands behind her back.

"You always have a bad feeling."

She snorted. "True enough. Here," she said, producing a muslin sack, then turning away. "For the road."

"But we've got plenty of food—" He stopped himself. "Thank you, U'len," he said. "See you soon."

She nodded gravely. "Maybe. Maybe this time. But one time you won't come back, Karl Cullinane. Get your fool ass killed, you will, sooner or later."

"Maybe." He forced a smile. "How about double or nothing on your salary? If I'm not back in, say, two hundred days, you get double your pay for that time—otherwise, you work for free for however long I'm out."

"I don't bet against you." She cocked her head to one side. "Although, if you'd care to give me odds?" She put her hands on his shoulder and turned him about, then pushed him toward the door. "If you're going, get out of here."

Andy-Andy was still waiting on the porch. "I still think you should let Ellegon fly you."

He shook his head. "I don't want him away from Home. Not until Gwellin and the rest are back on guard. They should be back in a couple of weeks at the outside; then he can go back to resupplying runs. But until then, I'd just as soon not have to worry about whether or not you're safe when I go to sleep at night."

"And I'm not supposed to—" She stopped and shook her head in apology. Arguing over a settled issue wasn't a luxury that Andy allowed herself. "Did you mean what you told Ahira the other night? About spending some more time around here, after this one?"

He nodded. "I think a couple of years of semiretirement would do me a bit of good—let Chak run the team for a while. Besides, if the guild keeps raiding into Therranj, I might just take a small group out for a tenday every now and then, keep them on their toes."

The whole world didn't rest on Karl's shoulders, not anymore.

With Aveneer's and Daven's teams working, with rumors of others attacking and robbing slavers, the guild was on the run.

Even if he knew that he couldn't possibly live to see the end of the work, it was fairly begun. A phrase from Edmund Burke popped into his mind: "Slavery they can have everywhere. It is a weed that grows in every soil."

Not any soil around me, Eddie. Just think of me as a weedkiller.

No. Lou Riccetti was the weedkiller, although eventually, the secret of gunpowder would get out. And that might not be a bad thing. Like them or not, guns were a leveling phenomenon, a democratizing one, in the long run. "All men are created equal," people would say. "Lou Riccetti made them that way."

He hitched at his swordbelt, then threw his arms around her, burying his face in her hair. "Be well," he whispered.

"You'd damn well better take care of yourself, hero." She pressed her lips to his and kissed him thoroughly.

He released her and walked down the steps, then over to the roan he had picked for the trip. Carrot was getting a bit too old to be taken into battle; this mare would have to serve until he was able to reclaim Stick from Slovotsky.

He levered himself into the saddle.

Tennetty tossed him a square of cloth. "Wipe your eyes, Karl."

He tossed it back. "Shut up. Let's get out of here."

PART THREE

Enkiar

CHAPTER THIRTEEN

To Enkiar

Cease to ask what the morrow will bring forth, and set down as gain each day that Fortune grants.

—Quintus Horatius Flaccus

The watchman picked them up less than a mile outside of camp.

"Two all-beef patties," a harsh voice whispered from somewhere in the trees, "special sauce, pickles, cheese . . ."

The voice fell silent.

". . . lettuce, onions on a sesame-seed bun," Karl called back, deciding that he was going to have to have a serious talk with Walter about the passwords Slovotsky was selecting.

It was a sound idea, in principle, and Karl had approved of it when Walter had suggested it several years before: The password phrases were culled out of Other Side popular culture, guaranteeing that Karl, Walter, or Ahira could answer a challenge without having been given the response ahead of time.

But this was just too much. It was too damn much. Karl had been dreaming of Big Macs and similar delicacies for years.

His mouth watering, he dropped his reins and turned to Beralyn. "Baroness, raise your hands."

"What?"

"There is someone pointing a gun at you who doesn't know you, and doesn't know that you don't have a pistol trained on my back. He will know it if you get your hands high in the air. *Now.*"

Slowly, she complied.

Piell stepped out onto the road, his slaver smoothbore carefully just out of line with the baroness' chest. "Greetings, Karl." The weapon didn't waver. "I don't recognize your . . . companion."

"Ta havath, Piell. Beralyn, Baroness Furnael, I'd like to introduce Piell ip Yratha."

"May I lower my hands now?"

"Certainly," Tennetty said. "If you really want a hole through your chest. Piell isn't going to take either Karl's or my word that you're harmless, not until he's sure that we're not under some sort of threat. You still could have a pistol up your sleeve; if you were fast enough, you'd be able to get it out before we could do anything about it. We've got to prove that you don't."

Chak snorted. "You could have warned her *before* you said 'certainly,' instead of after."

"It's more fun my way."

"Shut up, both of you." Karl slowly edged his horse over to the baroness, drew his saber, and held the point a scant few inches from her throat. "Satisfied, Piell?" He resheathed his sword.

The elf lowered his rifle. "Yes." He turned and gestured to someone hidden in the woods; leaves rustled momentarily.

Piell bowed deeply as he turned back. "Please lower your arms and accept my apologies, Baroness—*Furnael?*" He raised an eyebrow. "Rahff's mother?"

"Right." Karl nodded. "Now, I don't want to get shot on the way in. How much of a lead should we give your second?"

"He is quick on his feet, Karl Cullinane. I suggest you take a few moments to water your horses, then ride directly in." Piell eyed the late-afternoon sun. "We are camped in a clearing—you'll be met. I'd better move up and find another watch station. If you'll excuse me?" He bowed deeply toward Beralyn, then vanished into the bushes.

Karl dismounted, took a waterbag and a wooden bowl down from a packhorse's bags, and began to water the horses. "Sorry about the discourtesy," he said. "But it can save a bit of trouble. If you *did* have us covered, all we'd have to do is go along with whatever you wanted, and count on Piell to take care of things from the other end."

"There seem to be many . . . strange rituals involved in this business of yours."

Tennetty snickered.

The interior of the late wizard's wagon was elegant: The floor was deeply carpeted, the wooden walls covered with tapestries. Karl, Chak, Walter, and Henrad, Andy-Andy's apprentice, sat around a common bowl of stew, eating a late supper. Piell was busy settling the baroness in for the night, while Tennetty was off by herself, working on her disguise.

Setting down his spoon, Karl reached over to what had been the wizard's study desk, took down a leather-bound book, and idly flipped through the pages, ignoring Henrad's wince. He hadn't brought up the Henrad problem with Andy, but there was no sense in taking it any easier on the boy than necessary.

The pages of spells were just a blur to him, although anyone with the genes that allowed him to work magic would have found the letters sharp and black.

There was no sense in staining the pages; Karl tossed the book to the boy, then picked up his spoon.

"You cut it kind of close, Karl," Slovotsky said, folding his hands behind his head and lying back on a floor pillow. "I was beginning to worry. Piell, Henrad, and I have been talking about doing Enkiar without you. Why didn't you just have Ellegon fly you over? Come to think of it, why haven't you lost the beard, like we were talking about?"

Karl swallowed another mouthful of stew before answering. "I didn't have Ellegon fly me over because I'm nervous about leaving the family alone, after that last attempt. I want him guarding them until Gwellin, Daherrin, and the rest are Home, and on watch. Besides, there's another reason that I'm nervous about leaving the valley alone right now. . . ."

"Well?" Slovotsky raised an eyebrow. "Don't you trust me anymore?"

Karl forced a chuckle. It wouldn't do to go public about Ahira, and about Karl's own doubts that Ahira would want to stay on as Mayor forever. That was for Walter's ears only.

"No, not at all. It's just that . . . don't you think that this business with the baroness smells kind of funny? Supposedly, she, Thomen, and Rhuss were just witnesses that guns have been used in the Bieme-Holtun war. But why *them* in particular? Why did Khoral go to the trouble to find someone that he must have known I'd feel beholden to?"

"To get you out of the valley for as long as possible." Slovotsky nodded. "To let them push for another town meeting while you're gone. Why did you play along?"

Karl shrugged. "I think that Khoral is underestimating our people —the Engineers, in particular. I think I persuaded Dhara that they won't go along with any sort of fealty to Khoral. It's Riccetti's Engineers that Khoral really wants, not the land."

Henrad spoke up. "But what if you're wrong?"

"If we don't solve this powder problem, it doesn't matter," Chak said, talking around a mouthful of stew. "I think this slaver powder is more dangerous than all the elves in Therranj put together."

Slovotsky raised an eyebrow. "Why?"

"Ow! This is *hot,"* Chak said, his eyes tearing.

"You probably just bit into a pepper."

"Pass the water." Chak accepted the jug, tilted it back, and drank deeply. "You know, this isn't bad stew, but someone has to teach your cook that pepper's a spice, not a vegetable."

"You didn't answer my question."

Chak snorted. "I was busy being peppered to death. . . . It's a matter of status, of legend. We are . . . the feared Home raiders; we carry thunder and lightning with us. And as long as we're the only ones who can do that, local lords and princes are going to be nervous about interfering with us, no matter what the reward; as long as we don't make a habit of taking on local lords and princes, they won't feel obliged to.

"But what if they can come up with their own guns? Couldn't that change the whole balance?"

"Maybe." Karl wasn't sure that Chak had a solid point, but he didn't like contradicting him in public.

"In any case," Walter said, "you're probably right that Ellegon's the best person to keep an eye on things—including politics. Even if the elves are shielded, Chton and the rest of the joiners aren't, eh?"

"Right. But the person that they're really underestimating is Ahira, I think. He can keep a lid on Home for years." *As long as his heart is in his work,* Karl added to himself. "And then . . ."

"And then?"

He sat back in his chair and closed his eyes. "We had a huge victory; I don't know if anyone else saw it. There's this twelve-year-old kid, name of Petros. He lives in a lean-to next to what Ahira says is the scraggliest field that he's ever seen. Doesn't crop for anyone, because he wants his own land, his own vote, and he wants it *now*."

Karl opened his eyes and smiled. "You give me another hundred like Petros, and I won't ever have to worry that Home might be bought out by anyone. Ever." He waved it away. "But forget about that for now. We've got Enkiar to deal with. And Ahrmin."

"Ahrmin." Walter shook his head. "I hope Ellegon's wrong about him. His father scared me shitless. The son is probably going to be worse."

"He's badly burned and scarred, but he's still alive—and he hired the assassins. In Enkiar."

Slovotsky pursed his mouth. "If I remember right, he's the one who killed Fialt. Tennetty'll be all over him like ugly on an ape—which explains her being here. I've got to admit that her being with you surprised me."

"Dammit." Karl threw up his hands. Of course. That was why Tennetty had changed her mind, decided that she was willing to play slave. *Sometimes I think U'len's right about my lack of brains.*

Slovotsky smiled. "You missed one, eh? Happens to the best of us. You think we'll have a shot at Ahrmin?"

"Maybe. *If* he's still in Enkiar. *If* he shows his face. *If* this whole thing isn't a trap for yours truly." Karl bit his lip. "Which is why we're going to do things a bit differently than we'd planned. I don't think that Lord—what's the name of the Lord of Enkiar?"

"Gyren," Chak said. "Otherwise known as Gyren the Neutral. Trying to make Enkiar the trading center of the Middle Lands—he never gets involved in anything."

"Exactly. I don't think we have to worry about the locals being involved in some sort of guild plot, but we do have to face the possibility that the other end of this gunrunning operation is going to put us face to face with Ahrmin."

Karl rubbed a hand against his face. "Which is why I haven't shaved. He's seen Tennetty and Chak, although only for a few minutes and in the dark. He probably won't recognize them. I'm the problem. No matter what I do, if Ahrmin sees me, he's going to recognize me."

"So? What are you going to do? Sit this one out?"

"No, Walter. I want you to keep an eye on Beralyn."

"You're going to stay behind?"

"No, I'm going ahead. I'm going to be the bait. Well, half of the bait, anyway."

Chak smiled. "If I'm reading your mind correctly, I'm the other half."

"Any objections?"

"Well . . . I've always liked it when you get tricky." Chak eyed the edge of his eating knife. "I liked Fialt a lot, Karl. And Rahff." He nodded grimly. "And if you'll recall, I was the one who chiseled through Anna Major's chains."

"Well?"

"Promise to save a piece of him for me. If you can."

"If I can. I won't try too hard, though."

Chak laughed. "At least you're honest."

"Someone has to be." He turned to Walter. "We brought only half a dozen rifles and four pistols. I can't exactly hide the rifles under my cloak—so I'll take whatever pistols you have."

"Hey, you had me send all of our weapons back Home with Gwellin. Don't blame me if—"

Karl held out a hand. "I love you like a brother, Walter, but that doesn't mean I don't know you. You held out a few pistols and rifles as insurance, didn't you?"

"Well . . ." Slovotsky spread his hands. "Can't blame a guy for trying."

"Not this time, anyway."

CHAPTER FOURTEEN

Valeran

What we anticipate seldom occurs; what we least expected generally happens.

—Benjamin Disraeli

"I'm getting a bit irritated," Karl said, keeping his voice pitched low as they rode side by side down the street toward Enkiar's inn. "Nobody seems to have recognized me."

"What a pity!" Chak laughed. "So—Karl Cullinane is supposed to be the center of the world, eh? Have you been taking lessons from Walter Slovotsky on the sly? We don't have . . . teebee on This Side, remember?"

"Teevee."

"Eh?"

"Tee*vee,* not tee*bee.* Teebee is something else."

"In any case, we don't have it. As I was saying, your visage isn't all that well known. Which is just as well."

"Right." But if Ahrmin was still in the Enkiar area, he would certainly have somebody out watching, just on the off chance of spotting Karl Cullinane. The ill-feeling was mutual; Karl had killed Ahrmin's father, Ohlmin.

One of the few times I really enjoyed killing, he thought, remembering.

Whatever had happened to Ohlmin's head? They had left it behind in the wagon outside of Bremon, and the Gate Between Worlds; likely the skull was still there.

A sextet of foot soldiers approached them as they neared the inn.

"Greetings," their leader said. He was a tall and rangy man, perhaps in his mid-forties, though his hair and short beard were still coal-black. His stern blue eyes considered them carefully. "Your names and purpose in Enkiar?"

Chak spoke up first. "I am Ch'akresarkandyn ip Katharhdn—"

"I can see that you are a Katharhd, fellow." His pursed lips made it clear that seeing a Katharhd wasn't his idea of a great treat. "Your business?"

"I watch his back." Chak jerked a thumb toward Karl. "To see that it doesn't sprout knives."

"I see. And you are?"

"My name is Karl Cullinane." Karl smiled genially, raising his right hand, keeping his left hand near where the two pistols tucked into his belt were hidden by the folds of his cloak. "And I am just passing through. Have you any objection to that?"

"None. As long as you don't bring your . . . feud into Enkiar." The leader turned to the man next to him. "Though I don't believe that there are any Pandathaway guildsmen in Enkiar at the moment, are there?"

"No, Captain. There have not been for several tendays, at the least. Just the—"

"Good." He turned back to Karl. "Keep your war out of Enkiar, and you and your gold are welcome. Unless you intend to free our slaves?"

"Not today." Under special circumstances, Karl made exceptions, but a general policy of slicing up all slaveowners was a general policy of suicide. *Give us a generation, and we'll change that.*

The man next to him tugged at the captain's sleeve, then whispered in his ear for a moment.

Karl shook his head. "I wouldn't."

"You wouldn't what?"

"I wouldn't think too seriously about trying to collect the bounty that the Slavers' Guild has placed on my head, no matter what it's risen to. Not that you couldn't take me, but I do have friends; the final cost is likely to be far too high, all things considered. Best to check with your lord before taking the matter any further."

The captain smiled back at him, almost affectionately. "I will.

Assuming that he doesn't want you poisoned, would you join me for dinner?"

"And if he does want me poisoned?"

"Would you join me for dinner anyway?" He smiled with patently genuine friendliness.

"My pleasure, Captain." Karl laughed. "My pleasure."

"Ta herat va ky 'the last run' ky, ka Haptoe Valeran," Karl said. *It is called the last run, Captain Valeran.* "The notion is that none of our lives are taken cheaply. Ever."

A servant brought another bottle of wine. Valeran pulled his sleeves back before uncorking it, then splashed some wine first in his own glass, then in Karl's, then in Chak's.

Valeran drank first. "Not bad. I think you'll like it. And as for this 'last run' of yours, I have heard about it. Reminds you of the old days, Halvin, eh?" He smiled at the silent soldier standing next to the door. "It tends to take all the fun out of treating you and your people as outlaws, I suspect." Valeran nodded sagely, then sighed. "Not my sort of life, not anymore, but an . . . interesting one, I take it."

Karl chuckled. "There's an old curse, back in my homeland: 'May you live in interesting times.' " Well, that wasn't much of a lie; from here, China was as close as America. Or as far. "Not something I'd suggest, given an alternate. And it looks like you have a good one, here. You're from Nyphien, originally?"

"All my men are; we were first blooded against the Katharhds, in the Mountain Wars." He considered Chak carefully. There was a trace of hostility in Valeran's voice, although the Mountain Wars between the Nyphs and the Katharhds had fizzled out more than fifteen years before. "I've always preferred being a barracks commander to being a field soldier, even being a field soldier against the Katharhds."

The little man shrugged. "My family was in the north during the Mountain Wars, Captain Valeran. My father died fighting against the Therranji and their dwarf hirelings. Bloody work, Captain Valeran, just as bloody as the Mountain Wars."

"Yes," Valeran conceded. "It was bloody. But . . . I must confess I miss it, from time to time. There was a certain something to it, no?"

Karl shook his head. "All things considered, I'd rather be in Phil —I'd rather be bored."

"Then I beg to suggest that you could find boring employment as a soldier anywhere in the Eren regions. Although . . . perhaps Lord Mehlên of Metreyll wouldn't be interested, or Lund of Lundeyll, come to think of it—and perhaps Enkiar's neutrality would make it difficult for my lord to employ you. But, if you'd like, I could broach the subject to Lord Gyren?"

"I'm not much for giving fealty."

Chak snickered. Karl silenced him with a glance, then turned back to Valeran. "Meaning no offense, in my native land your present function wouldn't be considered a soldierly one."

"No?" Valeran raised an eyebrow as he sipped his wine. "What would they call me, a doxy?"

Karl had found himself liking the guard captain. There was an undefinable something in the captain's manner that made Karl certain he was a man to whom honor wasn't just a word, but a valued possession.

"No, not at all," Karl said. "We would call you a 'policeman'— your primary task is to maintain internal order, not protect Enkiar from invading forces."

"True, true, but it must be a strange country you come from, Karl Cullinane, where such subtle distinctions are considered important."

Karl laughed. "We had many strange distinctions. There's the color of one's skin, for example. In my land, my friendship with Ch'akresarkandyn would be thought strange—"

"—as it is here; I've no fondness for Katharhds. Meaning no offense," he said, ducking his head momentarily in Chak's direction. "Are you certain you'd care for nothing?"

"I can't eat the local food," Chak said, glaring at Karl. *Just once,* his look said, *could you be the one with the delicate digestion?*

"You were telling me why those in your land would think your friendship strange, I believe?"

"Because of Chak's skin color. Or mine, for that matter. Depending on which point of view you took, he would be considered too dark, or I too light. It was our version of racial prejudice."

"Racial? But he's every bit as human as you and I. It's not as though he were a dwarf or an elf."

"In my world there are no elves or dwarves. We have to make do with . . . peripheral distinctions."

"Skin color. *Skin* color. Skin *color.*" Valeran tried the words as though tasting them. *"Skin color."* He shook his head. "And were you and I friends, my own coloring would cause comment?" Valeran extended a deeply tanned arm.

"No, because it's acquired, not natural. You tan more thoroughly than I do, that's all. It wouldn't be a matter of import."

"And I suppose that, say, a Mel's eyefolds would be considered significant."

"Of course."

Valeran laughed. "A strange land, indeed. You were telling me in which direction it lies?"

"No, I wasn't. Although if you're interested, there is a way to get there, if you'd like to try it. You just have to tiptoe past the father of dragons, that's all."

"No, though I thank you for the kind suggestion."

They drank in silence for a few minutes.

"It must be interesting work, though," Karl said. "Few people meet many outlanders; you must encounter them all the time."

"True, true. And a strange lot many of them are." He snorted. "We have had a lot of Biemish and Holts coming through, of late— some deserters, more slaves. Vicious war—and over what?"

Valeran meant it as a rhetorical question, but Karl decided not to take it that way. "Depends on how you look at it. Last I heard, the war was started by some raiders coming down from Aershtyn into Holtun. The Holts decided that Bieme was responsible, and there you have it."

"War, and a dirty one. You can tell by the scavengers, coming through with chains of slaves. We had another one here, just a couple of tendays ago."

"Really? The guild operates regularly out of Enkiar?"

"Not a guild man, no—we haven't had one since Ahrmin was here."

Karl's wineglass snapped in his hands.

Valeran laughed again. "So. That is what this is all about. You have been prying for information on Ahrmin, eh?" He shook his head. "You won't find him here; he left . . . some time ago, to pick up another chain of slaves . . . somewhere or other. Nice fellow, actually, although it's pitiful the way he looks. Did you have something to do with that?"

"Why do you ask?"

"He was just as eager for news of you as you are for word of him."

"Understandable." Karl nodded. "I . . . burned him a little."

"I wouldn't have thought you so foolish. You should have killed him, or let him be."

Chak snorted. "He has a point there, Karl."

"I *thought* I had killed him; I'd intended to. He was bound for Bieme, you said?"

"I didn't say. And won't. He will be back here eventually, although you will be long gone by that time."

"I will?"

"I'm afraid I'd have to insist." Valeran looked him straight in the eye. "I'm really afraid I would."

At the door, a soldier thumped his hand against his breastplate. "Message, Captain," he said, entering the room at the captain's nod of permission and handing Valeran a scrap of paper.

Valeran read the message twice before cocking his head to one side and looking Karl over. "I am not one to believe in coincidences, Karl Cullinane. It seems that a group of guild slavers have just entered the town and taken rooms at the inn. I'm curious as to your intentions."

Karl sat back, pretending to consider the matter. "How many of them are there?"

"Thirty or so. And they are armed with guns, as you may have gathered. I wouldn't suggest that you attack them, not in Enkiar."

"I agree."

Valeran raised an eyebrow. "I'm surprised. You agree not to attack them?"

"No, all I agreed was that you would suggest that I not attack them."

"Thirty to two?" Chak put in. "Long odds—"

"Then you will agree to leave them alone while in Enkiar?"

"—but I guess they'll just have to take their chances."

Karl raised a hand. "I'll give you my word, Captain. This group of slavers . . . as long as they do not attack either Chak or me, we will not attack them, for as long as they remain in Enkiar." He wrinkled his brow. "Or let us say for up to a tenday. I wouldn't want them to think that they can safely set up shop permanently here, or anywhere else."

"I have your word on this?"

"You do. I'll swear it on my sword, if you'd like." Slowly, Karl drew his saber and balanced it on the flat of his palms. "As I have agreed, so will I do." He polished the blade with a soft cloth before resheathing it.

"Very well. You won't object to my posting a guard outside of your rooms, will you?"

"Do I have a choice?"

"Certainly. You may object, or you may not object." Valeran shrugged. "I'll post guards, either way."

The Enkiar inn was seven two-storied buildings of varying sizes, grouped around a common courtyard. Karl and Chak's suite was on the second floor of one of the smaller buildings. Its balcony and windows faced outward, away from the courtyard. The inn was at the edge of the town; beyond the road, a sea of wheat beckoned in the starlight.

Below, Karl could see three soldiers on watch, although there were others nearby; he knew of another three on guard outside the single entrance to the suite.

That could be trouble. Karl couldn't see a way out of the suite that wouldn't involve fighting past the guards. He drew the curtains.

"I can't think of anything useful to do," Chak said. "We're fairly neatly hemmed in for the night. Best to leave things to Slovotsky, eh? Come morning, he should have some idea of who's buying the guns and powder, and maybe what Ahrmin's connection is. We might as well get some sleep, eh?"

"Might as well."

Bare feet thudded quietly on the balcony outside. The curtains were momentarily whisked aside, and a dark shape moved into the darkness of the sleeping room. It stepped toward the nearest of the two beds and leaned over it.

Karl silently rose from the pile of blankets in the corner and tackled the intruder, grasping the other's right wrist and bringing the arm up behind the other's back, to the hammerlock point.

"It's just *me*, dammit," Walter Slovotsky said. "Leggo."

Karl released him. "Sorry. Announce yourself next time, okay?"

"Definitely. I'd have done it this time except there's a guard patrolling below, and I was sure he'd hear." Slovotsky seated himself on the bed, rubbing his right shoulder. "Do me a favor and put that down, Chak." He gestured a greeting at the little man, who sat in his pile of blankets, a cocked pistol pointed at Walter's midsection.

Chak uncocked the pistol and set it on the floor. "We weren't supposed to see you until tomorrow. And how did you get past the guards?"

"I came over the roof—that sort of thing's my specialty, remember?" He eyed the ripped hem of his pantaloons with distaste. "Got my pants caught between two shingles; had to rip them loose.

"We've got trouble. They made contact too quickly. The deal's been concluded."

"Dammit, why—"

"Because I didn't have any choice!" Slovotsky's whisper was harsh. "Because there wasn't any way to stall without making things look funny. The Holts have taken their powder and guns and left town, leaving me with the claim token to the slaves in the pens." He spread his hands. "Nothing I could do."

"Holts?"

Slovotsky nodded. "They're the buyers. Prince Uldren sent High Baron Keranahan, his nephew. We got more than three hundred slaves, all Biemish. They're apparently most of what's left of barony Krathael; the fighting there has been bloody. I tried to stall, honest, telling him about the raid by you, but that only made him more eager to finish things up and get out of here. He's a lot more interested in getting the guns and powder to Holtun and passing along word of your location than he is in trying for the bounty himself."

"Did he say who he was going to pass word along to?"

"No, but I've got a good guess. Ahrmin. I don't know exactly what's going on, but that little bastard seems to be working hand in hand with Holtun—and with the Aershtyn raiders—"

"Shut up for a second." Karl waved Slovotsky to silence.

It was finally starting to make sense. Bieme and Holtun had been at peace for two generations, until the raiders from Aershtyn had reawakened old hostilities. It was possible, perhaps even likely, that the Aershtyn raiders who had triggered the war had been encouraged by the Slavers' Guild, if they were not actually part of the guild itself.

Cui bono? Who benefits? That was the question.

The answer was simple: The war left the guild and its allies easy pickings in its wake.

Karl nodded. Guild backing also explained why the Holts were able to keep the war going, despite the incompetent generalship of Prince Uldren: With the guild supplying Holtun with guns and powder, it was possible that the Holts could win, or that the war would go on forever.

The only beneficiaries would be the guild. And the buzzards.

"There's more," Walter said. "And you're not going to like it. Tennetty went with them."

"What?"

"Her idea—she doesn't want to see the powder get to Holtun, and she had this crazy idea that she can do something about it. And

Keranahan seemed sort of interested in her, so I . . . kind of gave her to him. But she was still wearing those trick chains. She should be able to—"

"She'll get her fool ass killed is what she'll do. You spotted the reason she decided to play slave, to come along. How could you be such an *idiot?*" Tennetty wasn't going to do anything about the powder, not until she got within range of Ahrmin. She hated Ahrmin as much as Karl did; the little bastard had killed Fialt, speared him through the chest.

No. Not Tennetty, too.

Karl sat down on the bed and rubbed his hands against his eyes.

"Karl," Chak said, "we can't do anything about it tonight. We have to trust her to know what she was doing."

"Like hell we do." He stood. "Walter, get going, over the roof. You're pulling up stakes and heading out tonight. Your story is that you're nervous after hearing that I'm in town. Leave one of your knives stuck in the roof, right near the peak."

"Why—"

"Shut up. Have Piell split off and work his way around; I'll meet him east of town—tonight if I can manage it, tomorrow if not. He's to have two extra horses, healing draughts, his longbow, and all the guns and powder that you can scrape together."

"What do I do?"

Karl closed his eyes, concentrating. "One: Play slaver—take the Biemish slaves down the road to the rendezvous; wait for Ellegon. Explain to the Biemish who you are and that they have a choice of going back to Bieme or going to Home. We're going to have to split the team more, dammit.

"Two: Those who want to go to Home, send them back with the smallest group you think safe.

"Three: Drop the masquerade—"

"All *right!*" Slovotsky slapped his hands together. "You mean I can stop playing slaver?"

"Shut up and listen. I want you to wait at the rendezvous for Ellegon's supply drop. He should be there any day now, and he'll probably have some guns and powder. Tell him I'll want a massive drop outside of Biemestren—we'll use barony Furnael as a backup—every gun Home can spare, powder, grenades, the bloody works. Tell him to add Nehera and a couple of apprentice Engineers to the drop.

"Four: Once you've rendezvoused with the dragon, I want you to ride after us. With a bit of luck, you'll catch up with us this side of

Bieme. Make sure you keep Beralyn safe—she's our passport." Karl opened his eyes. "Am I missing anything?"

"I don't like this." Chak shook his head. "I thought you didn't want to choose sides in this stupid war."

"I didn't; it seems that Ahrmin's chosen them for me. The way I read it, the guild is backing the Holts. We're siding with Bieme, at least long enough to break up the guild-Holt alliance."

"And what are we going to do about Tennetty?"

Karl bit his lip. "Walter, how many of them are there?"

"Fifty or so. All armed to the teeth, now." Slovotsky spread his hands. "I'm sorry, Karl, but you know Tennetty. When she's got her mind set on something . . ."

"Just get out of here."

White-faced, Slovotsky turned to go, but Karl caught his arm. "Walter . . ."

"Yeah?"

"I'm sorry. I should have anticipated this." Tennetty hadn't had any enthusiasm for this, not until she had heard that Ahrmin was still alive, and had been in Enkiar. This was what she had been planning all along. Damn—if Karl had thought it through, or had Ellegon probe her, this could have been avoided.

It isn't Slovotsky's fault; it's mine.

"Right." Slovotsky shook his head. "I'll be telling myself that for years." He clasped Karl's hand. "You getting her out of it?"

"I'm going to try. Now get lost."

Chak looked at Karl and raised an eyebrow. "You, me, and Piell against fifty?"

"Don't forget Tennetty."

"I wasn't. But I don't know how useful she's going to be, not in this."

"You don't like the odds?"

"No. Not one little bit." Chak shrugged. "Do you see another choice?"

"Maybe." Karl pounded on the door, then swung it open. *"Hey!* I want to talk to Captain Valeran, and I want to talk to him now."

"I thought Enkiar claimed to be neutral in the war between Holtun and Bieme, Captain." Karl gestured Valeran to a chair and poured each of them a mug of water.

"Yes, Enkiar is neutral, Karl Cullinane. Anyone may trade for anything here." Valeran rubbed a knuckle against sleepy eyes, then sipped at his water. "Am I to assume that you had me waked at this hour to discuss our neutrality?" he asked acidly.

"No. I had you waked to discuss Enkiar's siding with Holtun in the war—a fact that is shortly to become *very* public knowledge, from Sciforth to Ehvenor."

"Nonsense. Lord Gyren does *not* take sides; both Holtun and Bieme are free to trade in Enkiar."

"Including for *gunpowder?* You consider allowing the Holts and the Slavers' Guild to trade here in guns and gunpowder to be neutral?"

"What is this nonsense?"

"High Baron Keranahan brought in a chain of slaves to trade with the guild—"

"Yes, yes, for gold. To pay—"

"No. For this." Karl took a small vial of slaver powder from his pouch. "A form of gunpowder, made in Pandathaway. Enkiar has been where the trade has taken place." He tipped a spoonful onto the floor—"Stand back, please"—then picked up a water pitcher, stepped away, scooped up a handful of water, and threw it.

Whoom!

"Think about this long and hard, Captain. Bieme will soon know that the Holts were able to trade for guns and powder in Enkiar, while the Biemish weren't. Do you think that they will consider that neutral?" Karl cocked his head to one side. "If you were they, would you? Do you think that *anyone* will think of Enkiar as neutral?"

"N-no. Not if . . . what you say is true," Valeran said slowly, eyeing Karl with suspicion. "How do you know all this?"

Karl smiled. "That's the first good question you've asked, Captain. Sit back and relax; this is going to take a while. Now . . . we were on a sweep through the forests near Wehnest, when I received a report that there were slavers in the meadow below with guns. . . ."

". . . and I can tell you that if you were to search Keranahan's wagons, you'd find almost one hundred guns, and eight large barrels full of this," Karl finished.

"Which *your* man sold to him, Karl Cullinane. Not the Slavers' Guild—"

"Captain. You are trying to avoid facing the simple truth that the Holts have used Enkiar as an unintentional partner in their . . . arrangement with the guild. Do you really think that tonight was the first time Enkiar has been used to trade slaves for powder?" Karl said. "Tell me, Captain, how do you think that would reflect on Enkiar's supposed neutrality?"

"Not well." Valeran shook his head slowly. "But what do you expect me to do?"

"That all depends on whether you are only Lord Gyren's puppet, or can think for yourself. You and your men are sworn to uphold Enkiar's neutrality?"

"My oath is to Enkiar; my men are fealty-sworn to me." Valeran pounded his fist on his open palm. "But I *can't* remain faithful to that oath, not and challenge Baron Keranahan at the same time. That would kill the neutrality, just as surely as if Enkiar was seen as taking sides with Holtun. It's the principle, Karl Cullinane: Once Enkiar's neutrality is shattered, it can't be restored." He pursed his lips for a moment. "Unless . . . unless nobody ever hears of how Enkiar's neutrality has been violated. The Holts could be quietly persuaded to conduct their gunpowder trade elsewhere. . . ."

"It's too late for that," Karl said. "My friend Walter Slovotsky has already been in and out of here tonight."

"So you told me." The accent on the second-to-last word was definite. Valeran eyed him levelly, as though to say, *I may well not be your match, Karl Cullinane, but that will not stop me from trying to do my duty.*

Karl nodded his understanding. "Unless I tell him otherwise, the story will soon be spread wide and far of how Enkiar has been the place where Holtun got guns and powder. And to tell him otherwise, I'll have to live."

"That would go well with some proof."

"Check the roof. You'll find a knife at its peak. Slovotsky left that as a bit of evidence that he was here. Or do you want to believe that I walked out on the balcony and climbed up the sheer face to the roof without being spotted?" Karl rose to his full height and stretched. "I don't think I can climb that quietly—do you?"

"No. I'll have it checked immediately." Valeran beckoned to the guard at the door and whispered briefly in his ear. The man ran out of the room.

"But I ask again," Valeran went on. "Assuming that you're telling the truth, what do you suggest that I do?"

"It all depends on you, Captain Valeran, you and your twenty men. *I* ask again: How loyal are you to Lord Gyren?"

"What do you mean, sir?" Valeran drew himself up straight. "Are you questioning—"

"No, I'm not questioning your honor, Captain. I'm asking if you're loyal enough to Gyren to have him put a price on your head, if it comes to that. Well?"

Valeran sat silently for a moment. "I see what you mean. And the answer is yes, Karl Cullinane. But if you've lied to me . . ."

"I know. But I haven't."

Valeran sighed. "Then I must see Lord Gyren, explain the situation, and . . . resign from his service. He will understand, Karl Cullinane. I assume you wish to employ my men and me in hunting down the Holts?"

"Obviously. You and your men have families?"

"Not I, but most do, yes."

"Chak, how are we fixed for money?"

The little man nodded. "Well enough. I've got about six pieces of Pandathaway gold on me, five sil—"

"Fine. Give." Karl accepted the pouch from Chak and tossed it to Valeran. "That is for their women and children, to maintain them until a group from Home comes to guide them. Leave one of your men; they will remain in his charge until then."

Valeran bounced the leather pouch up and down on his palm. "I may regret doing this, but . . ." He nodded, a vague smile playing across his lips. "Damn *me,* but it's good to be alive again. *Halvin!*"

The guard at the door turned about. "Yes, Captain."

"I thought I would never say this, but . . . we ride tonight."

Halvin gave him a gap-toothed smile. "Yes, Captain. It has been a while, sir."

"Put that smile away, fool. Your memory fails you." Valeran turned to Karl. "I repeat: Should I find that you have lied to me, Karl Cullinane, one of us will die."

"Understood. And until then?"

"Until then . . ." Valeran got to his feet and drew himself into a rigid brace. "What are your orders, sir?"

CHAPTER FIFTEEN

Firefight

Take calculated risks. That is quite different from being rash. . . . The most vital quality a soldier can possess is self-confidence, utter, complete and bumptious.

—George Patton

Ahead, the well-rutted road twisted and turned in the predawn light. As Stick cantered down the road, Karl reached down and patted at the stallion's neck. "Faster, Stick, faster," he said, digging in his heels and settling himself more firmly in the saddle, his hand automatically checking to see that the rifle was still secure in its boot.

Valeran spurred his large black gelding, barely matching Stick's pace. "I would like to hear your plan, Karl Cullinane, if that's permitted," he called out above the clattering of hooves. "You *do* have a plan, don't you?"

"Of sorts. Be still for now—and hang back, if you don't want to risk getting shot."

Piell was waiting around the next bend. Karl pulled on Stick's reins, swinging his leg over the saddle and dismounting as the stallion halted.

The elf was not pleased. "Ch'akresarkandyn told me what you're going to do—what you're going to *try* to do. I don't like it at all."

"I don't remember asking your opinion."

He snorted. "You're going to hear it anyway—"

"Shut *up*." Karl reached up and gripped the front of the elf's tunic. "If you want out, you've got it. Just leave the bow and guns and get the hell out of my way."

"Ta havath." Piell raised both palms. "Ta havath, Karl."

As the others rounded the bend and cantered into sight, Karl released the elf. "How many rifles do you have?"

"Five—and I have two shotguns left; I gave one to Chak. I also have my bow and just over twoscore arrows."

"Can you rig a few of the arrows for fire?" Karl asked, beckoning to Valeran and his men to dismount.

"Yes. You intend to fire the wagons?"

Karl nodded. "Think about what happens if they try to put out the one with the slaver powder in it."

"I have." The elf smiled. "Do you think we can actually get Tennetty out?"

"Oh? So you're in on this?"

"I always was."

Karl took his shrouded lantern down from his saddle, pulled back the baffles, and hung it from a knot in a tree. He turned to Valeran. "It normally takes anywhere from two to ten days to teach someone how to use a gun correctly. We don't have the time to teach reloading and safety, but I'm going to teach you and four of your men to use guns right now." He extended his hand. "Unloaded?" he asked, flicking open the pan and feeling inside.

"Yes."

"Good. Valeran, pick four of your people."

Valeran pointed at four of his men. "Over here, if you please."

Karl called out to the other fifteen. "You can listen to this, too, but those of you with crossbows, get them cocked and loaded.

"Now . . . using a rifle is simplicity itself. There are five steps. First, you pull back the hammer—that's this thing—until it locks." He thumbed the hammer back until it clicked. "Hear that sound? Second, you raise the rifle to your shoulder, selecting a target."

He aimed the empty rifle at a nearby tree. "Third, you line up your front and back sights right on the center of whoever you're going to shoot. At the range we're going to be, do not allow for drop as you would with a crossbow. Four, hold your breath and squeeze the trigger—"

Snap! Sparks flew from the lock.

Halvin spoke up. "You said that there were five steps?"

"Yes. Five: Drop the damn rifle and get your sword into your hand as quickly as you can, because there are going to be one hell of a lot of very angry Holts around you, even if you've killed your target."

He tossed the rifle to Halvin. "Practice."

Hoofbeats sounded from down the road; Karl beckoned Valeran and his soldiers over to one side, drawing a pistol and cocking it.

It was only Chak. His horse was panting, the cloths wrapped around its hooves cut to ribbons.

The little man dismounted, almost out of breath. "They're not moving too quickly; we should be able to get around in front of them by taking the north road."

"Did they see you?"

Chak snorted. "Screw you, kemo sabe," he said in his halting English. "Your nerves are making your mouth say stupid things."

"True. Sorry." Karl jerked his head toward the road. "Grab another shotgun, and a crossbow. I want you and Piell to take the north road, and set up some sort of roadblock; the rest of us will lag behind until we hear shots. Piell, listen up: When they near your roadblock, I want you to drop the lead horse of the lead wagon, then fire that wagon. Got it?"

Piell nodded.

"Go."

Valeran opened his mouth as though to say something, then changed his mind.

God, but I wish Ellegon were here. Was Valeran as trustworthy as he seemed? The dragon could have found out with a moment's effort.

Karl shrugged. No point in worrying about it; he was already committed to trusting Valeran. He lowered the pistol's hammer, flipped the pistol, and caught it by the barrel. He held it out to Valeran. "This works just like a rifle; you hold it at arm's length, pull the hammer back, then sight down your arm. Squeeze the trigger gently; don't pull at it. Or you can just press the gun against my back."

"Your back?"

"You're wondering if I've been leading you on—if I have, you can get even very quickly. In the meantime, mount up."

A single shot sounded from down the road. Karl kicked Stick into a gallop; behind him, Valeran urged the others along.

Ahead of them, the Holts had dismounted from their horses and the three wagons. The lead wagon was skewed sideways across the road, its lead horse lying on its side on the road, whinnying in pain, an arrow projecting from its chest.

Damn. "Take cover, everyone. Valeran, assign somebody to handle the horses. Make sure he keeps a good grip on their reins."

So much for Karl's original idea. Piell could have picked a worse place for the ambush, but not much worse. The Holts had already set up a line of defense behind their wagons and in the irrigation ditch along the side of the road. Rushing them would just be suicide. The worst of it was that dawn was already breaking; in the light, Karl's people, already outnumbered and outgunned, would be even more vulnerable.

Another shot sounded; a bullet whizzed overhead, snapping through the leaves.

"Don't shoot yet," Karl shouted, untying his own rifle from the saddleboot, slinging his saddlebags over his shoulder.

"Go!" He slapped Stick on the rump, sending the stallion back down the road, out of the line of fire. He ducked into the ditch on the right side of the road, tossing the saddlebags to one side.

"Piell, can you hear me?" he called out in English, knowing that Tennetty would also recognize his voice. "Fire the wagons, now. Then move; I don't want them fixing on your position." He cocked the rifle, then looked out onto the road. There were plenty of targets; the Holts weren't used to facing guns. Karl took aim at a head, took a quick breath and held it, then squeezed slowly on the trigger.

The rifle kicked against his shoulder as the Holt's head exploded in a bloody shower; Karl ducked back behind into the ditch, fumbling in his pouch for a rag and his powder horn, leaving the tallow box—here, a spit patch would serve just as well.

Coughing in the acrid smoke, he blew down the barrel to clear it, then poured a measure of powder from the horn into the rifle, spat on a patch and slipped it over the hole, then thumbed a ball into place. He drew his ramrod and shoved the ball and patch down the barrel, seating them firmly.

"Karl Cullinane," Valeran called out. "There are a group of them, moving toward us."

"On my command," he called back. "You with the rifles will rise, raise your weapon to your shoulder, pick a target, and fire—and then duck back down, quickly." He pulled back the hammer to half-cock, quickly cleared the vent with his vent pick, then took out his vial of priming powder.

"They're moving, again."

"Now!"

Gunshots thundered. Karl charged the pan, then snapped the frizzen securely into place.

He raised his head above the ditch. All of the Holts had taken cover, except for one wounded man lying on the road, cradling his belly in his hands. One out of four shots reaching a target wasn't too bad, not under the circumstances.

Another of the Holts rose, only to drop his rifle and scream as a longbow's arrow sprouted from his side.

Thanks, Piell.

But this wouldn't do. The Holts would gather themselves for a charge in a few minutes, once they realized that they had their enemy outgunned and outmanned.

"Bows, covering fire. Valeran, get that lamp to me." He untied the straps from his saddlebags, then pulled out the box of grenades, opened it, and extracted one from its padded compartment.

Valeran arrived with the lantern. "I don't like this. They have all used rifles before, and we haven't. And my men aren't used to facing these . . . guns."

"I know." Karl slid the lamp's baffle open just a crack, then stuck the end of the fuse into the flame.

It caught immediately. He raised his head above the boulder and threw the grenade high and far, directly for the spot in the ditch where he hoped the remaining nine rushing Holtish soldiers were.

"Down!" he called, following his own advice.

The grenade dropped behind the road and into the ditch, then exploded with a loud *crump!* followed by a chorus of screams.

Karl looked out. The lead wagon was burning nicely; Piell's fire arrow must have gone inside and caught something flammable. Tennetty's slim form was outlined against the fire as she worked her way behind one of the Holtish soldiers, then slipped an improvised garrote around his neck, pulling him back, out of sight.

Good. She'd worked her way free. The Holts didn't know it, but they had more to worry about than some outsiders attacking; they had a tiger among them.

More gunshots sounded. One of Valeran's men pitched forward, clutching at his throat; another stooped, uncorking a bottle of healing draughts, then shaking his head and recorking it.

This just wasn't going to make it. *There're too many of them, and Valeran's people aren't used to this kind of fighting.*

Karl didn't like it, but he would have to settle for getting Tennetty out and forget about the slaver powder.

"Withdraw," he called out. "Everybody—and I mean *everybody!*" he shouted, hoping that Tennetty could hear him over the crackling of the fire. He sneaked another glance. One of the Holts had spotted her and was bringing his gun to bear.

Karl raised his rifle to his shoulder and took aim, ignoring the *whipcrack* of bullets around him, then squeezed the trigger. The bullet caught the Holt on his chestplate; it knocked him down, his own weapon discharging toward the sky. Tennetty dove for cover, disappearing into the ditch.

"Withdraw," Karl repeated. "Piell and Chak, acknowledge, dammit."

A distant shout marked Piell's position, but where was Chak? Perhaps it was just as well. If Karl couldn't spot him, likely the Holts couldn't, either.

Chak sprang up next to the second wagon, fired his shotgun into an intervening soldier, then disappeared into the wagon's interior, a waterbag clutched in his hands.

What the hell does he think he's doing? Karl had given the order to withdraw. The main objective had been accomplished; they would just have to let the powder go by.

Three of the Holtish soldiers followed Chak into the wagon. That was probably their mistake. In the close quarters of the wagon, they would probably get in each other's way more than Chak's. *But what's he doing with a waterbag—*

"*No!*"

The wagon exploded in a cloud of steam and dust, sending pieces of horses and soldiers tumbling into the still air.

That was enough for the few uninjured Holts. Some mounted their horses and galloped away; others just ran.

Valeran grabbed at Karl's arm. "What happened?"

"Chak. He . . . took out their powder. Lord Gyren will be satisfied," he said, his voice sounding curiously flat and emotionless even to his own ears. "We have preserved Enkiar's neutrality."

"There are still some of them alive."

Karl tossed his rifle to one side, bringing his sword into his right hand and drawing his remaining pistol with his left. "Not for long. Follow me."

There is nothing quite as ugly as sunrise over a battlefield. In the dark, it is possible to ignore the spilled contents of the bags of skin, the flesh, blood, and bones that once were human beings.

During a battle, it's necessary to look beyond the carnage, in order to avoid becoming part of it.

But in the light of day, it's a different matter entirely. This battlefield had once been a wheat field. It would again be just a wheat field, someday.

But not this day. Now, it was the blood-drenched floor of a slaughtering ground, corpses already attracting scavengers.

Using his saber like a flail, Karl shooed two crows away from the body of a Holtish soldier and forced himself to look at the man's face.

No, not a man, a boy, perhaps seventeen, maybe eighteen years old, beardless. Under a shock of brown hair, his ashen face was pale, still; a casual glance would have made Karl think he was only sleeping.

Valeran cleared his throat. Karl turned to see Tennetty standing next to the captain.

"Karl—" she started, then caught herself. "We . . . haven't found any sign of Chak. Could he—"

"No." Karl shook his head. "There was only one door to the wagon. He must have set the waterbag on top of one of the powder barrels, then put his pistol right up against the bag."

He could almost see it in his mind's eye: the three Holts satisfied that they had Chak cornered; Chak quirking a smile at them as he fired, the bullet crashing through the bag and wood, driving the water into the slaver powder, then . . .

He looked Tennetty square in the face, at first not trusting himself to speak. If only she had followed orders, none of this would have happened; Karl would have let this shipment get by, rather than attack at such unfavorable odds.

And Tennetty knew that. Let her live with the guilt.

Why, dammit, Chak—why?

What happens when you decide that some objective is more important than your own life is?

But it wasn't as important as Chak's life, not this. The Holtish had gotten powder before, and would again. Not in Enkiar, though. Enkiar would now be closed to them for the trade in slaver powder, but Enkiar would have been closed to them in any case.

It wasn't worth Chak's life. But it had been, to Ch'akresarkandyn.

That wasn't enough. "Tennetty."

"Yes, Karl." She stood in front of him, her hands well away from the sword at her waist, making no movement to protect herself.

"We're moving out." He kept his voice low, little more than a whisper. He knew that if he started shouting, he would lose control completely. "I want you to start Valeran and his men on marksmanship tonight, when we camp. By the time we reach Bieme, they are to be as competent as possible. When Slovotsky and his people catch up with us, you turn the training over to him. Bieme is going to be tough; I want us up to strength."

"Yes, Karl. Although I don't know what you think a few tens of us can do in that sort of—"

He reached out and gripped her throat, the tips of his fingers resting against her trachea. He could bring his fingers together—

—but that wouldn't bring Chak back. "Shut your mouth," he said, dropping his hand. "If I want your opinion, I'll ask for it."

She started to turn away.

"One more thing, Tennetty," he said, grabbing her by the arm, spinning her back to face him. "I don't want you to get yourself killed. You're to live a long, long life—hear me? And every day, you're to remember that it was you who killed Chak, just as surely as if you'd slipped a knife between his ribs. If you hadn't gone independent, if you had just played things out as I told you to, this wouldn't have happened."

"If *you* had let me try for Ahrmin—"

He backhanded her to the ground, then booted her in the shoulder as she started to rise, sending her sprawling on the dirt. "Don't speak to me, not anymore. Not unless I speak to you first. Understood?"

Her hand slipped to the hilt of her sword.

"Go ahead, Tennetty, *please.*"

She shook her head slowly, her hand falling away from her sword. It wasn't fear that saved her life at that moment, it was guilt.

And what do I do about my own guilt? he thought.

There wasn't any answer.

"Just get out of my sight," Karl Cullinane said, as he turned to Valeran. "Have you buried your man?"

Valeran shook his head. "Not yet."

There was no real point in hurrying. *I should probably wait here for Walter, Beralyn, and the rest, instead of letting them catch up farther down the road.*

That would be the logical thing.

"Bury him, Valeran. We're getting the hell out of here."

That evening, they made camp beside a brook to wait for Walter Slovotsky and the rest.

In the morning, Tennetty and two of the horses were gone.

PART FOUR

Bieme

CHAPTER SIXTEEN

Prince Pirondael

Our fathers and ourselves sowed the dragon's teeth.
Our children know and suffer the armed men.

—Stephen Vincent Benét

Biemestren, the capital city of Bieme, reeked of a long peace, now shattered.

The castle itself was surrounded by two zigzagging stone walls, each barely shy of ten meters in height, the inner one with eight guard towers scattered around its circumference. The residence tower rose from inside the inner wall, resting on the flat top of a twenty-yard-high, almost perfectly circular hill.

But the castle itself was only a handful of buildings that housed the prince, his court, and the House Guard; the vast majority of the population of Biemestren seemed to live in the newer buildings outside the wall, clinging to it as they fanned out like a tree ear on an old oak. Beyond them were the rude encampments housing several thousand refugees from the west.

A breeze brought a foul reek to Karl's nostrils. If the local clerics weren't on the ball, vermin-spread diseases would likely do as much damage as the war.

"Nice location for a castle," Walter Slovotsky said. "That hill is the highest spot for twenty miles around."

"It's too round to be a real hill; it's a motte," Karl said. "This was probably a basic motte-and-bailey castle, originally."

"I know what a bailey is, but what's a motte?" Slovotsky raised an eyebrow.

"The hill that the castle's on." Karl searched his memory for an Erendra equivalent, but there wasn't one. "Basically just a pile of dirt. If we dug down, we'd find timbers of the original castle's foundation buried in it.

"It's an old trick. Goes back to before Charlemagne; it was how the Norman nobles held out, carved out their own fiefs in both France and Britain. Siege engines can break the walls, but the motte itself is practically indestructible. Even if invaders breach the outer wall, they have to fight their way up a steeper hill than nature would probably provide, and *then* have the inner defenses to contend with."

"And meanwhile the defenders don't have to sit on their hands. Nice bit of defense." Slovotsky nodded. "Back Home, when we were building the original palisade, why didn't you suggest a motte?"

"If you'll remember, Riccetti was running that show. Besides, we didn't have the manpower to move a whole lot of earth, not even if you include Ellegon. He's got his limitations, just like the rest of us."

"Besides, you didn't think of it."

"True."

"This is pretty damn near impregnable, though," Walter said. "Even if the Holts get this deep into Bieme, there's no law that says the Biemish have to sit tight and not shoot back, while they're working on breaking the walls. One wizard shooting out a flame spell or two a day—"

"Wouldn't do it. Not if I was running the siege, and I'm sure that the Holts know a lot more about siege warfare than I do." Karl shrugged. "Bring up ten, twelve onagers at once, and it's watch-the-walls-go-down, even if they have a garden-variety wizard and you don't."

"But you said that they wouldn't be able to break through."

"Not immediately, no. Ever hear of a siege? Breach the walls in a few places, keep the defenders too busy to plug the holes, and you can still starve them out if they don't drop their guard enough for you to take the castle any other way. If the defenders are really good, it could take years, but who's going to come to Bieme's rescue? The Nyphs? They're more likely to try to lop off a piece of the country, if they can be sure that Khar or some Katharhd bands won't move on them while they're distracted."

"Motte, eh?" Slovotsky said, clearly preferring a lighter subject. "I'll remember that. They probably just call it a mound."

"So we'll teach them the right word."

Slovotsky laughed. "Your mind is a junkpile, Karl. I know for a fact that you know squat about world history—"

"Give me a break. I never got around to majoring in any kind of history. Too much work. Always liked the soft sciences; if you had anything on the ball, they'd practically give the school to you."

"So where did engineering come in? You were going to be an electronics engineer when I first met you."

"Just that one semester; I was young and ambitious. Too much work. I switched to poli sci right after that; electoral behavior is a hell of a lot easier than electrical behavior."

The outer wall's portcullis was raised, announced by a squeal of metal on metal that could be heard for miles.

A troop of fifty armored, mounted soldiers rode through, cantering down the road toward Karl and his people.

"Pay attention, folks, we've got company," Karl said in English, repeating it in Erendra for Beralyn, Valeran, and his people. "Let's hope that Baron Tyrnael's runners got the message through. I'd rather not get mistaken for an enemy."

Once again, he found himself pausing, waiting for a cynical bit of bravado from Chak. Chak would have said something, maybe "Too bad for them if they do, kemo sabe."

Damn you, Chak, he thought. *Who said you could up and die on me?*

"Pay attention, Karl. Shall I go back for Beralyn?"

"No. Stay with her; bring her forward when I call. I want to make sure that these folks are ready to talk, not fight. Her face is our passport; I wouldn't want to get it slashed."

"Right. One suggestion, though: Your temper gets out of hand every now and then. This might be a good time to keep hold of it. Beralyn says that temper is one thing that Prince Pirondael doesn't put up with."

"Don't end a sentence with a preposition."

"Fine," Slovotsky said. He broke into a broad smile. "Temper is one thing that Prince Pirondael doesn't put up with—asshole."

Karl disliked Prince Harffen Pirondael at first sight, although he wasn't quite sure why.

It wasn't because the prince had kept him waiting for more than an hour for no apparent reason, or that his men-at-arms politely but firmly insisted on relieving Karl and Walter of their swords before they were ushered into the Presence.

The first was an irrelevant, if petty, perquisite of office; the second was an understandable precaution, under the circumstances. This wasn't the same sort of situation as he had faced with Dhara; there was no need to step on Pirondael's toes until he apologized.

So that wasn't it. Karl wrinkled his brow. Then what was it? He didn't dislike the prince simply because he had chosen to meet with them in a large, bare room in the dwelling tower that had only one chair, now fully occupied by Pirondael's sizable bulk—that was just another princely perk.

Karl didn't dislike the prince because of the way that his two guards stood just beyond springing distance, their crossbows loaded, eyeing Karl with professional caution. Quite the contrary: Karl had a profound respect for Pirondael's guards. Back home, back on the Other Side, there were people who sneered at the notion of honor. But that was clearly the only thing that kept Pirondael's House Guard faithful. They weren't surrounded, not yet; those who wanted to desert could have escaped to the west.

Those who remained with Pirondael couldn't have been expecting that Bieme would win the war, not against an army armed with Slavers' Guild guns.

Why were they waiting for the coming of the Holt army?

Because they had sworn their loyalty to Prince Pirondael, and they meant it.

Maybe that was it. Pirondael didn't look like the kind who deserved that kind of loyalty, this fat prince lolling back on his throne, wearing his purple-and-gold finery, his silver crown of office resting on his oily black curls, not a hair out of place.

And perhaps Karl resented the unnecessary formality of Pirondael's wearing his jewel-inlaid crown instead of a simple cap of maintenance.

He knew that he resented the way that Beralyn had gravitated to her prince's side, occasionally interrupting him to whisper in his ear. No, that wasn't a betrayal, even if it felt like one. Beralyn didn't owe Karl anything. It wasn't like Tennetty running out on him.

He shrugged to himself. It didn't matter why he disliked the prince, or even that he disliked the prince. This wasn't about personalities.

"There's an old saying where I come from, your majesty," Walter said in Erendra, then switched to English. " 'The first hit's free, kid.' "

"Which means?"

"Utshay upway, Walter." Karl elbowed Slovotsky in the side, then turned back to the prince. "It translates to 'A wise man accepts a gift in the spirit in which it is intended.' It's a simple proposition, your majesty," he said. "We're willing to get rid of the slavers and their powder—and we'll start by lifting the Furnael siege."

He crossed his arms over his chest. "We'll have to capture two or three slavers or Holtish officers for one of my people to interrogate; she can find out where their center of operations is. All I need is a few mercenaries, provisions, and the temporary use of enough land for our training and staging grounds. The rest is up to us."

"But as an independent force, not under my barons' command." Pirondael stroked his salt-and-pepper beard. He looked vaguely like Baron Furnael, which was understandable: apparently, all of the Biemish nobility were more or less related. "You see the problems that would cause?"

"No. I don't. And, honestly, I don't care. Before the slavers brought guns and powder into the war, you took how many baronies away from Holtun? Two?"

"Three." Pirondael smiled, remembering. "The Holtish should not have started the war. Prince Uldren isn't much of a general. Then again, neither am I. The difference is that he insists on being one, while I do not; I leave the planning to those who know war."

"And how many of those baronies do you still hold?"

The smile vanished. "None. Since they brought those accursed weapons into the war, we've lost those, plus barony Arondael, Krathael, and most of Furnael—most of them almost emptied of their people, hauled away by slavers. As we speak, Furnael Keep is under siege." Pirondael shrugged. "It may already have fallen, for all I know—"

"Your majesty," Beralyn put in, only to be quieted by a quick chopping motion.

"—and while I wish I could, I can't spare the troops holding the line in Hivael to try to break the siege. You say that you can do that, with how many men?"

"One hundred—forty of mine, sixty of your mercenaries to be released into my service. Plus a few . . . surprises that I have in mind."

"I'm told that there are more than a thousand Holts maintaining the siege."

Karl smiled. "Their misfortune."

"Or mine, if you are not sincere." Pirondael shook his head. "My men tell me that you are . . . not oversupplied with these guns of yours." He raised a palm. "No, Karl Cullinane, none of my soldiers have tried to capture any. I'm told that would not be wise. But I was asking what else you require."

"To break the siege and take the slavers out of the war? Nothing. Except . . ."

"Except? I *thought* that there would be more."

"I'll need you to get rid of any dragonbane in Biemestren and its environs. I want it all burned—by the end of tomorrow."

The prince spread his hands. "That is hardly a problem. We have not cultivated dragonbane for hundreds of years. I wouldn't know where to find any. Why is this important to you?"

"Within the tenday or so, a friend of mine is arriving. He doesn't like dragonbane."

"A friend?" The prince whitened. He started to turn toward Beralyn, but Karl stopped him with a nod.

"Yes. And if you're still thinking about trying to torture the secret of gunpowder from Walter and me, I'd caution against it. For one thing, neither of us knows how to make it," he lied. "And for another, my . . . friend wouldn't like it. Don't get Ellegon angry, your majesty. Dragonbane or not, you wouldn't like him when he's angry. Now, have we an agreement, or not?"

"Possibly, possibly. If you manage to break the siege of Furnael Keep, what then? You will require additional forces in order to attack the main guild camp on Aershtyn, no?"

"Possibly. We'll talk about it then, your majesty. Have we an agreement?"

The prince nodded.

Karl turned to Walter. "Walter—"

"I know, I know." Slovotsky raised his hands. "You want a recon of the siege of Furnael Keep, and you want the report yesterday. It'll take me a bit more than a week; you think you can live without me for that long?"

"Yup." Karl turned back to Pirondael. "Your majesty, if you'll have your soldiers lead us to our staging grounds, we have many preparations to get under way."

The prince nodded. Karl and Walter turned and walked out of the room, reclaiming their weapons at the door. Accompanied by three guards, they walked down the stone staircase of the tower and out into the bright daylight.

"I don't like it, Karl. I don't like it at all. Assume we succeed at barony Furnael and in knocking out the slavers on Aershtyn. What if Pirondael decides that's enough, once we've taken guns and powder out of the war? It could be Holtun that gets chopped up and shipped off by the slavers—after all, the guild has been free to deal in Bieme before. Would that be any better?"

"No. But I don't think he'll push for that."

"And if he does?"

Karl looked him full in the face. "Three guesses. The first two don't count." They emerged from the arched doorway, squinting in the bright sunlight.

"That's what I thought. Who've you got in mind to replace him? The line of succession passes to his sons—"

"Both of whom are dead." Maybe that was it. The death of his sons should have been bothering Pirondael. What kind of man shrugged that sort of thing off?

"And then probably to a near relative, no?"

"As I understand it, right now the legitimate succession would be pretty much up for grabs among the barons—at least one of whom is a man of honor, one who will keep any agreement we make with him. And he's under siege. For now."

"Which is why you want to break the siege of the keep, instead of going directly to Aershtyn. I don't like it when you get tricky." Slovotsky caught himself. "Sorry."

"Better get going."

"Right."

"One more thing, Walter?"

"What?"

"Don't get yourself killed."

Slovotsky smiled. "My pleasure."

CHAPTER SEVENTEEN

"One Thing at a Time"

Do not peer too far.

—Pindar

Karl spread his blankets on the ground and lay back, staring up at the night sky.

There were no faerie lights dancing in the overcast sky tonight; only a dozen of the brightest stars were visible through the haze. Across the field, the five equally spaced signal fires sparked their message up into the night. Either Slovotsky or Ellegon would recognize the signal; both of them should be showing up soon.

He closed his eyes, but he couldn't sleep.

This time I may have bitten off more than I can chew, he thought. Even if Ellegon brought enough guns and powder, the odds were just too much on the other side. The sixty mercenaries that Pirondael had released to him would have to be watched carefully; it was unlikely that they'd be worth much in a firefight. Valeran's men were coming along quickly, granted, but riflery wasn't something that they could learn enough of in only a few tendays, not when it was such a new skill. While their marksmanship was adequate, their reloading speed was pitiful even during practice; in combat, it could only be worse.

That left Karl, Walter, Piell, and their ten remaining warriors, plus

Henrad. Many Ellegon would bring along a couple of warriors, in addition to Nehera and the Engineers.

That still wasn't enough, not even with Ellegon. The dragon couldn't be risked in close combat; the slavers would surely have some dragonbaned bolts.

Reflexively, he started to curse Tennetty for deserting, but one more person wouldn't really have made any difference.

Dammit, I can't do it all by myself, he thought.

But this war had to be stopped, no matter what. The guild couldn't be allowed to trigger a war with impunity. This was even more dangerous than slaving raids: Human spoils of war could easily and cheaply supply Pandathaway and most of the Eren regions with slaves for years to come.

This wasn't how Karl and the others had planned it. Their plan to interfere with the slave trade was three-pronged: first, to make the business deadly to the slavers; second, to drive the price of slaves up, forcing the locals to invent and adopt better ways of getting things done; third, to turn Riccetti and his Engineers loose, seeing that new technology was a medium for freedom, not repression.

That last was always a real fear. The invention of the cotton gin had brought new life to slavery in the United States.

So . . . the slavers had to be stopped, and stopped here; war was too efficient a way for them to procure human merchandise.

But how?

We just don't have enough manpower, just don't have enough time.

It was conceivable that they could break the siege of Furnael Keep; possibly they could surprise and savage a slaver encampment; but ending the war was just too much to ask. Old hatreds, old angers had been awakened. How could they be stilled?

That's what it came down to: If the war couldn't be ended, the guild would profit. The Holtish and the Biemish were willing to sell each other off. It had to be stopped.

But I just don't know how to shut a war down.

He shook his head. It would have been nice to have Chak to talk to. Chak had long ago come to terms with the notion that he was going to die in battle, and had accepted it almost eagerly. Or maybe not almost.

How do you stop a war?

I don't know. But since when is not knowing an excuse?

"Hail, Caesar: We who are about to die . . ." Walter Slovotsky's voice sounded in the distance.

Karl stood. ". . . are going to take one hell of a lot of the bastards with us," he called back.

"That's not the response."

"It'll have to do, for now. When did you get back?"

"Just a few minutes ago. Valeran said you left orders I was to report to you the instant I arrived. I'm reporting."

"How does it look?"

Slovotsky rubbed at his tired eyes. "Look, Karl, I had a hard four days' ride to Furnael, a tough all-night recon, and a harder ride back. Can we let it wait until morning? I've got to get some sleep. One thing at a time, eh?"

"What did you say?"

"I asked if we can wait until morning."

"No, not that—what did you say after that?"

Slovotsky's forehead wrinkled. "One thing at a time?"

"One thing at a time." Karl nodded. "Sometimes, Walter, you're a genius."

"Huh? I don't follow."

"Never mind." Karl shook his head. "Don't worry about it." *One thing at a time. First we save Furnael Keep, then kill Ahrmin and his group, and then stop the war—somehow, dammit, somehow.* "That's my department. You get some sleep; we'll talk in the morning."

"Fine by me."

As Slovotsky stumbled off, Karl lay back down.

"One thing at a time," he said to himself.

And then he was asleep.

CHAPTER EIGHTEEN

Aveneer

*One finds many companions for food and drink, but in a
serious business a man's companions are very few.*

—Theognis

"Karl," Walter called out from the top of the low rise, "I think
you'd better get up here."

"Trouble?"

"No, but move it, anyway."

Karl handed the rifle over to Henrad. "Keep them working at it—
dry firing only."

The boy nodded, his face a sullen mask. Henrad was supposed to
be Andy-Andy's apprentice, learning magic, not teaching basic riflery.

Too bad for him. Karl started up the slope, pausing for a moment
to speak to Erek, who was busy conducting a class in speed reloading
for the benefit of Valeran and his men.

"How's it going?"

The boy smiled. "Good. Valeran is almost as fast as I am; Halvin's
a touch faster."

"Great. Keep at it." Karl broke into a jog.

Slovotsky was beaming as he stood atop the rise. "Things just
started to look up," he said, as Karl trotted over. "Check this out."

Off in the distance, a line of more than two hundred mounted soldiers rode toward them. But not Biemish soldiers; even at this distance, Karl could see that they were armed with rifles. He squinted; the man at the head was a burly redhead.

"Aveneer!" He turned to look at Slovotsky. "How—"

"I don't know." Slovotsky shrugged. "It sure wasn't me."

"Maybe Ellegon? When you met up with him west of Enkiar—"

"I just relayed your orders, Karl. As far as I know, the dragon was planning to head home and pick up the supplies and crew you ordered, then rendezvous here. If he had anything else in mind, he kept it a secret."

"I guess we'll know in a minute."

Aveneer spotted Karl and waved, then gestured to Frandred, his second-in-command, to have the men dismount. Aveneer spurred his roan into a full gallop, braking the horse to a panting halt as he neared Karl.

He dismounted heavily, then stood for a moment, oversized hands on his hips. Nature had intended Aveneer to be a towering giant of a man, but something had gone wrong; although his hands, feet, and facial features were larger than Karl's, the Nyph stood more than a head shorter.

"You look well, Karl Cullinane," he said, turning for a moment to check the leather thongs that bound his battleaxe to the side of his fore-and-aft-peaked saddle. Aveneer was the only human Karl knew who preferred a battleaxe to a sword; an axe was typically a dwarf's weapon.

"I heard," Aveneer said, his voice a slow basso rumble, "that you could use some help." He ran blunt fingers through his dirty red hair. "I hope you don't mind the presumption. But it was . . . convenient for us to ride this way."

His appearance and that of his men made his words a lie. They were all road-dirty, with the deeply ingrained filth that only a long forced ride could cause.

"No, I don't mind." Karl took Aveneer's outstretched hand in his. Aveneer's grasp was firm, although he wasn't trying for a bone-crushing grip; Aveneer wasn't much for childish games. "I don't mind at all. But—how?"

Aveneer nodded slowly. "I told her that would be the first thing you would want to know." He raised an arm; a lone rider broke off from the rest of the group. "She caught up with us in Khar."

It was Tennetty, the glass eye gone, now replaced by a ragged eyepatch that somehow looked much more fitting.

Karl didn't know whether he wanted to hug her or shoot her down as she stopped her horse in front of him and waited, her face impassive.

"Tennetty . . ." What could he say? Karl had been sure that she had deserted; it now was clear that she had decided to hunt up some reinforcements. Did that make up for her indirectly causing Chak's death? No, but . . .

Dammit, why couldn't she have stayed a deserter? That had made things so much simpler.

"Greetings, Tennetty," he said, the words sounding warmer than he had intended.

She nodded grimly, not saying anything.

"We have plenty of powder left, and a few spare guns," Aveneer said. "The pickings have been slim. We were hunting for a slave-raiding party in the Kathard, but . . . nothing."

"Well, you won't be able to say that in a while. How tired are you?"

Aveneer rubbed at his bloodshot eyes. "Bone-weary, Karl. As is obvious. And our horses—"

"Walter, have their animals seen to."

"Right." Slovotsky trotted away.

Karl turned back to Aveneer. "What I meant was, can you and your people ride with only a day and a half of rest?"

"Of course. What will we be facing at the end of the ride?"

"Slovotsky says that there are a thousand men holding Furnael Keep under siege. He guesses that there's anything from one hundred to four hundred warriors inside."

"Can we count on them? Do they know we are coming?"

"No. If Walter could have snuck inside, then—"

"—the Holts could have done so, too. Hmm. . . . The Holtish have these slaver guns I've been hearing about recently?"

"Yes. Not many, though—Walter guesses less than two hundred, about one gun for every five men."

"Most of their weapons are up north, where most of the fighting is going on, eh?" Aveneer pursed his lips and nodded. "Let me see if I understand this: You want to take less than three hundred of us against a thousand Holtish line troops—perhaps with some slavers mixed in—relying on Baron Furnael to support us, although there won't be any way for us to coordinate our movements with him. Correct?"

"Correct."

"Well." Aveneer brightened. "Then it looks like I won't die in bed after all. Now, is there someplace where an old man can sleep?"

Karl started to open his mouth, then closed it. Karl wouldn't have gone to sleep unless he was sure that his people were settled in, but there were sound arguments for doing it the other way.

It's Aveneer's team, not mine; criticizing would only be asking for trouble. "Use my tent," he said. "See you in the morning." He called for Erek, then had the boy lead Aveneer away.

Behind Karl, Walter Slovotsky cleared his throat.

"I thought you were going to see to the horses," Karl said.

"I delegated it. Just as well I did, Karl—I heard that last." Slovotsky shook his head slowly. "I don't like the idea of riding out. I thought we were going to wait for Ellegon."

"And *I* thought he'd be here by now. We can't wait forever; we move out day after tomorrow, regardless. He'll probably catch up with us en route."

I hope, he completed the thought. Though Aveneer's people had plenty of rounds and powder, that could be eaten up quickly in battle. Besides, since Chak had died, there had been nobody around who Karl could talk freely and comfortably with. Being around Slovotsky wasn't the same as being around Chak or Ellegon.

"He'd better." Slovotsky nodded grimly. "And Aveneer's team? How are you going to split them up?"

"I'm not. He and Frandred know their people better than I do, and they're all used to the way he splits them into three equal-sized teams. We're better off adapting to him, rather than the other way around. I'm going to stay in overall command—"

"Surprise, surprise."

"—and keep Valeran and his squad with me. We'll scatter Pirondael's mercenaries among Aveneer's squads."

"Sounds okay."

"One more thing: I want to get as close as possible to the keep before we're spotted. I guess that means we'll have to travel at night."

"That won't do it, not all by itself. You'll need somebody extremely talented—ahem!—riding ahead, doing recon and watcher removal."

"Can we do it?"

"Maybe." Slovotsky considered it for a moment. "They've set out watchers along the Prince's Road, so the obvious route is out. I'm sure that they've also got some in the forest, but not as many. Besides, the visibility is poor; we'll be able to slip by a lot. If you're willing to go the forest route, I'll try to clear the way, about half a day ahead. But I can't do it by myself. Not and have a half-decent chance of getting all the watchmen."

"That's the problem. If one reports back we're in trouble."

"It's worse than that. Think it through, Karl: If one of them *doesn't* report back on time, that's a warning. But that kind of warning should move slowly; we can probably outrun it." He paused, closing his eyes. "Ten. Give me Piell and nine others who can move quietly, all of us with the fastest horses available. Crossbows and longbows—if we need to use guns, then we've already blown it."

"Any chance of pulling it off?"

"Fifty-fifty. *If* Aveneer's people are any good. Do I get my choice of backup?"

"Talk to Frandred, but he'll want to clear any selections with Aveneer."

"Fine. How about Tennetty?"

"No." Karl shook his head. "She's my second."

"You'll trust her with your back?"

"Looks like it, no?"

CHAPTER NINETEEN

The Siege

He either fears his fate too much,
or his deserts are small,
That puts it not unto the touch
To win or lose it all.

—James Graham, Marquess of Montrose

During peacetime, a trip from Biemestren to Furnael Keep would have been a slow, pleasant five-day ride along the Prince's Road, their nights spent in the inns scattered along the road, each inn an easy day's ride from the next. They would have slept on fluffy down mattresses in dry, airy sleeping rooms, taking their meals at the common table along with merchants and other travelers.

But this wasn't a normal time. None of the inns were open; trade along the Prince's Road was suspended for the duration of the war.

They had to try to avoid being spotted. So they traveled at night, eating cold meals when they camped at daybreak. Daytime was for sleeping, the night for traveling, carefully, quietly, trusting to Walter Slovotsky and his scouts to kill or capture any watchers, to ride back to warn of any concentration of troops, or to tie white cloths at eye level on the proper side of forks in the paths, blazing the trail in the only way that they could follow at night.

It took a full ten days to get from the outskirts of Biemestren to where the forest broke on cleared farmland in barony Furnael. Ten days of interrupted sleep during the day, uninterrupted hours of plodding on horseback at night.

In the distance, the battered keep rose above the morning fog. From his hiding place just within the tree line, Karl could see the charred remnants of a siege tower against the south wall, the stone near it blackened, some merlons cracked, others broken and tumbled to the ground below.

The keep was battered, yes, but not broken. Several of Furnael's soldiers stood watch on the battlements, occasionally peering out an embrasure to try a chancy crossbow shot at one of the Holts below.

Slovotsky had been right: The Holts were tunneling, and that meant trouble.

Karl swore softly, then stopped himself. It could have been worse. There were basically four ways for the Holtish to lay siege to the castle. First, they could just try to starve the defenders out. That would be a long and drawn-out process, one that the Holts had undoubtedly discarded immediately.

Thank goodness for small blessings. That would have been most dangerous for Karl and his people; if the Holts were taking a passive view about attacking the keep, they would likely be ready to repel a relieving force.

The Holts' second option was to try getting over the walls, either by siege towers, ladders, climbing ropes, or some combination. The charred remnants of one siege tower showed that they had tried that, and it had failed; the lack of further tower or ladder construction suggested that the Holts had abandoned that idea.

The third possibility was for the Holts to try to break the walls of the castle or force the gate. They could do it with rams, or with siege engines like catapults and onagers.

Karl had been hoping that the Holts had switched to that. It would be the easiest technique for Karl to counter; a quick attack on the siege engines would leave them in flames.

But the Holts had chosen the fourth method: They were mining, attempting either to break into the keep at a point which they hoped would be a surprise, or simply to undermine the walls and collapse them.

The chained workers were likely captured Furnael slaves or freefarmers, now forced to work for the Holtish, which explained why the watchmen on the walls didn't simply fire their bows at the workers bringing wheelbarrows loaded with rocks and dirt from the tunnels.

Doesn't look good, and that's a fact.

Karl worked himself back from the tree line and made his way into the woods to the clearing where Walter, his outriders, and Tennetty stood waiting with their horses.

The problem was one of coordination. Between Karl's people and Furnael's warriors, they probably had force enough to disperse the Holts, despite the fact that the Holts probably had them outmanned. Home guns were more accurate than slaver blunderbusses, and a score of sharpshooters on the keep's ramparts would quickly make the notion of an active siege unattractive. Combined with a couple hundred mounted troops that could strike anytime, anywhere, the Furnael/Home forces should present a strong enough threat to scare the Holts off, or kill them all, if necessary. But in order for it to work, the keep's defenders would have to know that they had allies out here, and Furnael—or whoever was commanding the defenders, if he was dead—would have to agree to cooperate, to coordinate.

And even so, it would be bloody. "I read something once, something that concluded two armies of roughly equal strength meeting is a recipe for disaster," Karl said. "You know where that comes from?"

"Sorry," Walter Slovotsky said. "Sounds familiar, though." He raised an eyebrow. "You've got something better in mind?"

"Yup. Two things. First, we have to do some damage to the Holts, to demonstrate our credibility. Second, we've got to get someone close to the wall with a voice and a note—and that calls for a major diversion."

"So? You're going to try something tricky. Maybe a combination ambush and bluff?"

Karl smiled. "Almost right. A combination feint, decoy, ambush, and double bluff." He turned to Tennetty. "You willing to take a few chances?"

She nodded. "As many as you are, Karl Cullinane."

Good, he thought, *here's where you can die to settle your score for Chak. You deserve—*

He caught himself. No, that wasn't right. There was enough evil in the world, more than enough. There was no need to add to it by betraying one of his own people.

"Tennetty," he said, "ride back and tell Aveneer to set out guards with crossbows, then bed everybody down until dusk. I'll want him to bring his people forward then. Dig up eight volunteers who don't mind trying something a bit risky, and bring them back with you at dusk—oh, and bring Erek, too."

"Make that seven volunteers, Tennetty," Slovotsky said. "I haven't volunteered for a long time; I want to make sure I remember how."

"No." Karl shook his head. "Before this is over, you're going to remember why it's been so long. Besides, I've got something else for you. Get moving, Tennetty. Remember, it's eight volunteers, with their horses."

Slovotsky stared into his face. "What are you up to, Karl? Am I supposed to sneak through the Holts' camp while the fight is going on, or is it something even more idiotic?"

"How did you guess?" He jerked his thumb over his shoulder. "Go back into the woods and get some sleep. You're going to need it."

A cool night breeze whispered through the branches, caressed his face.

The night was clear and almost cloudless. Which was just as well, for once; rain would make it anywhere from difficult to impossible for Karl's people to reload.

He patted at Stick's neck, then reached across to check the short horn bow lashed to his saddle horn, and the quiver, crammed full of short arrows, that was stuck tightly in his rifle boot. There would be no guns, not for the first rush. Guns would announce who they were, and that had to be avoided.

He swore, uncomfortable in the cold steel breastplate and helmet, but there wasn't a remedy for that, not this time. This was one time that putting up with his armor's weight was going to be a necessity, even if the damn breastplate and its underlying padding did seem to weigh half a ton. It would deflect anything but an unlucky point-blank shot, and it was more than likely that he'd need that luck and that breastplate before too long.

He looked over at Tennetty. "Think we've given Slovotsky enough time?" It would take Walter a while to work his way close enough to the keep to take advantage of the diversion.

She nodded.

"Then let's do it." He hoisted himself to the saddle, then leaned forward and reached down to hitch at his greaves. The damn armor kept slipping.

He made sure that his sword was firmly seated in its scabbard, although he hoped that he wouldn't actually have to use it on this run. If Karl ended up in sword range of any of the Holts, that would mean that everything had fallen apart. Still, he'd rather have it and not use it than the other way around.

At his right, Tennetty and the eight others were already mounted, their horses snorting and pawing the ground in impatience. No guns for them, either; they carried only crossbows and bolts, except for Bonard, who had a horn bow like Karl's.

Aveneer signaled for Erek and Frandred to raise their lamps; the two mounted them on the trees on either side of the path, the baffles barely letting traces of light peep through.

"Let's go," Karl whispered, digging in his heels and ducking his head as Stick stepped over the stone fence and into the fallow field, the others following.

He spurred the horse into a canter, and then a trot.

There were things about This Side that still amazed Karl, even after all this time. The number of soldiers around the keep, for one. Back at school, there had been dorms with more people than the thousand or so laying siege to Furnael's keep.

It seemed strange that something as impressive-sounding as a siege was capable of being carried out by only a thousand or so soldiers. Maybe it really shouldn't have; hell, Richard Lion-heart's Crusade expedition hadn't numbered more than eight thousand, and that was a force that had been raised throughout all of England. Maybe it was reasonable that the whole Holtun-Bieme war was being fought by just a few tens of thousands of soldiers on both sides.

But it still looked funny.

The Holtish commander had divided his force of a thousand men into four groups, each one camped just out of bowshot of one of the four walls of the keep.

They hadn't been divided equally, of course. That would have been foolish. The largest group, slightly more than a third of the Holtish force, was camped opposite the keep's main gate. Another two hundred and fifty were planted across from the minor gate, the two remaining groups of about a hundred and fifty each camped opposite the remaining two walls.

It was an intelligent arrangement, one that prevented the keep's defenders from safely attempting any sort of horseback smash-and-retreat sortie; in the time that it would have taken Furnael's forces to raise even the small portcullis, both of the smaller Holtish forces could have joined the attackers at the rear gate and used the opportunity to force an entry.

Furnael and his people were sealed in, tight.

Karl rode slowly across the fallow field toward the main force of the Holts, the others strung out to his left.

Off in the distance, he could barely see the main gate of the keep, its iron portcullis visible against the flickering flames of a watchfire inside the keep. Karl had ridden through that gate years before; now, he hoped that Slovotsky had worked close enough to it to alert those inside when the time was right.

He transferred the reins to his teeth and unlashed his bow, nocking an arrow.

The Holts clearly weren't ready for an attack from outside; Karl had closed to within two hundred yards of the guards' fire when a soldier leaped to his feet and shouted a warning into the night.

"Do it," Karl said, drawing back the arrow to its steel head, then sending it whistling off into the night. Karl was an indifferent shot with a shortbow or longbow; no sense in trying for an accuracy that he didn't have, not from Stick's pitching back.

He drew another arrow and fired it at a forty-five-degree angle, aiming as best he could for the center of the encampment.

Tennetty steadied her crossbow and pulled the trigger. A Holtish soldier screamed and grabbed at the bolt in his thigh, then fell forward.

"Aim higher, dammit!" Karl yelled. "This isn't the time to play sharpshooter." A low shot would just plow into the ground; a high one might find flesh deeper in the camp.

"No closer, anyone," he said. The nearest of the Holts were at just about maximum effective range for the slaver rifles.

He let another shaft fly, noting with surprise and pleasure that as the arrow fell it caught a Holtish soldier in the throat.

Screams and shouts echoed through the camp. Karl unstrapped his lantern from his saddle and dashed it to the ground. Stick danced away from the flaring fire that marked his position, just in case any of the Holts had missed the point.

As gunshots sounded from the camp, Karl quelled an urge to dive from the saddle. At this range, the enemy's guns were next to useless. They would have to mount up and give chase. Which was just fine.

"Ready another volley." He nocked an arrow and waited for the crossbowmen to load their weapons. "Aim high, now, and . . . fire!"

Nine bows went off in a volley, immediately rewarded by more cries and screams from the Holts.

It had been only a few moments since the fight had started, but already a troop of a hundred, perhaps a hundred and twenty, soldiers were mounting up, preparing to repel the attack. Good. Both the size and the speed of the troop spoke well for the abilities of the Holtish commander, and Karl was counting on him to be good at his job.

"Secure weapons and prepare to run," he called out, already tying down his own bow.

One of Karl's horsemen started to bring his horse around.

"Hold your position!" Karl snapped. "Run before I tell you to and I'll shoot you down myself."

It was going to be tricky. They would have to draw the Holtish along with them, not letting them get close enough to do any damage, not outdistancing them altogether. *About ten seconds,* he thought. Nine. Eight. Seven.

To hell with it. "Run for it!" He wheeled Stick about and galloped for the trees, the others following him.

Their baffles now fully aside, the lanterns at the tree line beckoned to him; the path broke through the forest exactly halfway between the two. Stick galloped for the path, hooves throwing soft earth into the air as the stallion leaped over the low stone wall.

It was fortunate that the path back into the forest was straight: Stick's hooves had trouble finding it; branches and brambles beat against Karl's helmet and face until he had to close his eyes tightly for fear of losing them. Behind him, the others crashed through into the forest.

A signal rocket screamed into the sky; Karl opened his eyes to see it explode high above the trees in a shower of white-and-blue fire.

Aveneer's basso cut through the night: "Fire!"

Seventy rifles went off in a volley, their almost simultaneous *whip-cracks* sounding more like a sudden flurry of popcorn popping than anything else.

Horses and men screamed.

The path widened. Karl pulled Stick to a stop and dismounted from the horse's back, while Tennetty and the others galloped beyond him.

"Second section," Aveneer's basso boomed, somewhere off in the distance, *"fire!"*

Again, the crack of seventy rifles firing in a volley sounded; Karl dashed back down the path.

Aveneer's first section, the one that had fired the initial volley, advanced over the dark and bloody ground, their rifles now slung, using their swords and knives to administer the *coup de grace* to wounded animals and humans alike. Of the hundred cavalrymen who had pursued Karl and his nine warriors, barely a dozen had survived unscathed, and those few were riding hell-for-leather back toward the main Holtish camp.

Karl began stripping off his armor as Erek ran up with Karl's rifle, pistols, and a large leather pouch; he accepted Karl's breastplate, helmet, and greaves in return.

"Message to Aveneer—deliver, wait for a response," Karl said. "Begins: No casualties on my team; Tennetty and others moving into position. Orders: Advance by section, volley fire and leapfrog. Send another runner back with Erek. Query: Any casualties? Ends. Go."

The boy ran off.

Karl primed his rifle's pan. *Now we'll see if the third part works.* The first part of his plan had worked like a charm: A hundred Holts lay dead on the ground, and the Holtish were buzzing like bees. The second part had either succeeded or failed by now; either Slovotsky had or hadn't been able to take advantage of the distraction to get within throwing and shouting range of one of Furnael's warriors manning the ramparts of the keep.

But the third part depended on just how good the Holtish commander was. When what had appeared to be a small Biemish raiding party had approached, his first response had been the conservative one of sending out an apparently overlarge troop of cavalry.

But then, when the guns had gone off, his whole picture of what was going on would have, and should have, changed. As far as the commander had known, his side was the only one in this war that had guns—the only other force in the world with guns and powder was Karl Cullinane and his warriors—so he would identify Karl as his opponent. Or, perhaps, he would consider the possibility that his slaver allies had turned on him.

Either way, it would be a whole new development. And what would a good commander do when confronted with an attacking force of indeterminate size?

In another tactical situation the right response would be different, but here the commander knew he was already up against the keep's defenders, and had arrayed his forces for a siege; the conservative response, the safe reaction, would be to withdraw his entire force along the Prince's Road toward Holtun and barony Adahan, probably sending a cavalry detachment through to make sure that the way was clear.

His command should be more important to him than his mission. If he was good enough.

Karl stepped out through the trees and into the starlight. While the cavalrymen mounted up, a large contingent of Holtish soldiers were setting up a quick line defense, bringing guns and bows around to face Aveneer's slowly advancing sections.

"First section, fire!" Aveneer called out.

Karl crossed his fingers. It didn't look good; the Holts were setting up for defense, not withdrawal.

"You've got guts," he whispered to his unseen adversary. "Too damn much guts." Hadn't the bastard decided that he was outnumbered? Was he about to try a last run, himself?

Erek ran up, one of Aveneer's younger warriors beside him.

"He says," Erek said, panting, " 'Understood; firing by your order. Casualties low: seven wounded, none dead.' " Erek shook his head. "I don't think he's seen everything, Karl. Some of those horsemen broke through the line."

Easily a mile away, two more signal rockets momentarily brightened the night, as if to say, *We're on our way.*

Karl let himself ignore the report on casualties for the time being. *I'll worry about it later, when I know how many lives my being clever cost this time.* "It looks like Tennetty and the rest of the horseborne squad got to their signal rockets," he said. "And made it into position."

"Yes, Karl." The boy smiled. "Will the Holts run?"

"Count on it," he said.

I hope so, his thought echoed. *Okay, General Patton. How about now?*

"Second section, *fire!*"

That started a rout. The small detachment camped opposite the gateless northern wall broke and ran, some soldiers fighting each other for possession of a horse, others dropping their weapons and running down the road.

Karl couldn't see the other small detachment, but he was willing to bet that they'd be the next to break.

The group camped opposite the keep's rear gate began to move out, but in an orderly fashion: foot soldiers double-timing toward the road, cavalrymen with crossbows riding ahead to clear the way. Apparently their commander had decided that discretion was the better part of valor.

Good. But the main force wasn't moving, and with the one remaining small force, those almost three hundred men were enough to hold off Karl's people indefinitely, unless Karl was willing to shed a lot of Aveneer's men's blood.

"Erek—message to Valeran, return. Begins: Do it. Ends."

Again, the boy dashed off, this time in a different direction.

This was the last trick Karl had up his sleeve. If it didn't work, things were going to get very messy. If the hundred men now under Valeran's command weren't enough to persuade the Holtish commander that there was a huge force opposing him, Karl would have to count on Slovotsky's being able to get more than his note through to Furnael, on Furnael's believing him, *and* on Furnael's being able to take effective action.

All of which wasn't too likely, not in combination.

Well off on the right flank, Valeran's group stepped out of the forest, firing in volley.

But the Holts held, firing and reloading their guns and bows.

And then it happened: The main gate to the keep began to creak open, accompanied by battle cries from within the keep's walls.

The Holts had had enough; their line broke.

Karl beckoned at Aveneer's runner. "To Aveneer, and return. Begins: Belay volley fire. All reload, advance. Targets only by eye and ear. Ends. Go." The runner ran off.

At a brightening on the horizon, Karl's head jerked around. A gout of flame scoured the eastern sky.

Flame? What the hell was going on?

What . . . think . . . on?

"Ellegon!"

He could barely hear the mental voice as the dragon roared across the sky, well above the range of the most powerful crossbows as he vented fire and steam, hastening the Holts in their headlong flight.

The air cavalry is here. I see I'm a bit late. Hope I didn't inconvenience you too much.

No, not at all. It gave me the chance to figure out how about two hundred and fifty could send four times that number running, Karl thought, letting his mental voice drip with sarcasm. *Thanks for the experience, Ellegon.*

No problem.

Karl felt the dragon probe more deeply.

I'm sorry about Chak. We'll have to talk about him.

Later. Business first. "Erek, get over here—*move* it, boy. Message for Aveneer, return. Begins: Belay attack. Nobody takes a step forward of your first section until further orders."

With the Holts on the run, and with Ellegon in the skies to make sure they kept running, there was no reason to take any chance on getting someone killed by friendly fire. Furnael's people had been under siege for a while; it was likely that they were more than a little trigger-happy. "Healing draughts to be dispensed as needed," he went on. "Ends. Message for Valeran. Begins: Acquire three prisoners for interrogation. Keep your distance from Biemish until further orders. Ends. Go."

His neck muscles were already starting to unkink. It was as though a huge weight had been lifted from his shoulders; Ellegon's presence in his mind buoyed him like a lifejacket.

Lightning crackled from the dragon's back, the white ribbons descending into the midst of the fleeing Holts, now more mob than army.

Lightning? *Ellegon must have picked up Henrad and*—no, not lightning. Henrad wasn't up to anything that difficult.

Ellegon, tell me Andrea isn't with you.

There was no answer.

Please.

It was her idea, Karl, not mine. The same for Ahira. I told them you wouldn't like it, he said petulantly.

Ahira? What the hell is going on at Home? Are the children—

The children are fine. Kirah and all of them are staying with the Engineers for the time being. Ellegon banked, wheeling across the sky. *Let me bring her to you—*

"No!" *Stay the hell up in the sky until everything settles down.*

He would have to talk to Furnael, and—

No, better—tell Aveneer to move one of his companies back to the campsite, and then you can land there. First things first. He had intended to go down and talk to the baron, but this had to take priority. *Can you reach Slovotsky?*

Yes.

Tell him I'll be a while. Then get your scaly self over to the LZ, on the double.

Yes, Karl. It's good to see you again, too.

Despite everything, he smiled. "Right. . . . Hey, you—yes, *you.* Get me my horse."

CHAPTER TWENTY

Several Acquaintances
Renewed

Only the brave know how to forgive. . . .

—Laurence Sterne

Karl pulled the stallion to a halt, then swung his leg over and lowered himself slowly to the ground. He reached up and tied Stick's reins around a branch of a tree; unlike Carrot, Stick wouldn't stay ground-hitched, although the stallion usually respected a light hitching.

Are you sure enough of that that if your horse tries to run, I can eat it?

Ellegon sprawled on the grass, his massive saurian head cradled on his crossed forelegs.

No. And why is it that you always want to snack on my *horses?*

Everyone always says that when it comes to horseflesh, you've got great taste.

Apparently, the dragon had included Andy-Andy in on the conversation. She groaned as she stooped to pick up a fist-sized stone and bounced it off his thick hide, before turning back to her work.

Ahira and Thomen Furnael sat on the grass, resting against one of the dragon's treetrunk forelegs, while Andy-Andy and Ranella directed ten of Aveneer's warriors in the unpacking of the dragon's harnesses and the huge wicker basket.

"Leave that keg alone," Ranella said, indicating a small one that was tied tightly into a padded nook of the basket. "Do not try to move it, do not drop anything on it, do not even look cross-eyed at it."

"Okay, what the hell's going on?" Karl said, glaring at Ahira and Andy-Andy. "I sent for—"

"Shh." Andy-Andy smiled as she threw her arms around his neck and gave him a quick kiss. "Mendicants can't be choosicants. Hey, *you*—easy with that box." She pushed away from him and walked over to where Ranella was directing the unloading.

"Help is what you sent for, and you got it," the dwarf snapped. "As I remember it, nobody elected you God, Karl."

"Just what are you doing here, Mr. Mayor?"

"Call me Ahira." The dwarf shrugged. "I'm not mayor anymore. I lost a vote of confidence four tendays ago. Which is why I'm here—"

It hit Karl like a slap. "You *what?*"

"I lost. Chton called another vote of confidence, and a lot of the farmers who would have voted the way you wanted them to didn't vote for me." He shrugged again.

"You left Home with Chton as mayor? You—"

"Do I look stupid? I didn't have enough votes to hold on to the job, but the Joiners couldn't get enough support to win a clear majority, either."

"So who—"

"Riccetti, of course."

"Now, wait a minute. How did you get him past Chton's faction?"

Ahira turned to look at Andy-Andy. "Should I tell him? Or did you really want to try that experiment?"

"Experiment?"

She ignored him for a moment, talking quietly to Ranella. "You can handle the rest of it, yes?"

"Yes, Andrea."

Andy-Andy turned and walked over to Karl. "The experiment is to see if someone can actually die of curiosity."

Enough. How safe are we?

Not an unfriendly thought as far as my mind can reach. Why?— oh. The dragon snorted, parboiling a stretch of grass.

"Ahira, I don't want anybody going down toward Furnael Keep until the mopping-up is done. When that happens, you can take Thomen to his father, but not until then."

The boy spoke up. "But, Karl Cullinane, this is my home. I know—"

"You may know every rock, tree, and bramble, boy, but we're on the fringes of a war. I'm *not* going to have to tell your father that I got his other son killed, understood?" He turned back to Ahira and switched to English. "Slovotsky is down there; coordinate things through him. Keep the kid alive, kapish?"

"Yes, Karl." The dwarf hefted his battleaxe. "It's good to be back in business."

Karl snorted. "A hell of a lot you remember." He walked over to the carrying basket and pulled out three blankets, throwing them over his shoulder. Without a word, he scooped up Andy-Andy in his arms.

If I remember right, there's a tiny clearing about a quarter mile this way. Tune us out, and make sure we're left alone.

Yes, Karl. Have fun.

"Karl!" She struggled against his grip. "What do you think you're doing—"

"It's pretty damn obvious what I'm doing, Andrea. The question is, do you intend to stop me?"

"And if I do?"

He shrugged. "Then you will."

"That's fine, then." She leaned her head against his chest. "Just so I have a choice. I missed you too, you know."

"Don't tell me, show me."

Andy-Andy peered over his shoulder. "We're out of sight, Karl. You can put me down now," she said. Her voice was flat, business-like.

He lowered her legs to the ground, then released her. "You didn't buy the act?"

She shook her head. "I know you too well. That pseudomacho act probably fooled everyone except maybe Ahira. I still don't know why you bother with it, though."

"Got to keep up the image, beautiful." He sighed. Getting the job done depended on whether others would follow him, and that depended in large part on his image. There was another side to it, too: Sending his friends out to die was bad enough; public breastbeating wouldn't make it one whit better. But this wasn't public.

He swallowed. "Let me give it to you straight: Chak was killed outside of Enkiar."

A brief intake of breath, and then: "How?"

He shook his head. "He . . . decided that stopping the slaver powder from getting through was more important than his own life." He pounded his fist against a tree, sending chips of bark flying away. "The little *bastard* . . ."

He dropped to his knees. As she crouched beside him and wrapped her arms around his neck, he closed his eyes, buried his face against her breasts, and finally let the tears flow.

After a while, she reached into her robes and rummaged through an inside pocket for a cloth, then handed it to him. "Better wipe your nose, and give your eyes a chance to clear up, hero," she said, her voice infinitely gentle, despite her words. "You'll blow your image to hell otherwise."

"Thanks." He forced a calm tone. "Now, tell me: What the hell is going on back Home? Did Ahira blow the vote, or was Chton too good for him?"

She shook her head. "I think he blew it, maybe even deliberately. Gwellin's finally decided to go back to Endell—" She raised an eyebrow. "That isn't a surprise to you?"

"No," Karl said. "He mentioned it a while back."

"In any case, he invited Ahira to go along with him. Ahira said no, but . . . after that, it seemed like he was . . . deliberately going out of his way to annoy people. You remember the dispute between Lou and Keremin?"

"Something about some farmland?"

"Right. Keremin was in the wrong, but it's an honest disagreement. When Ahira manhandled him—in front of a dozen farmers, Karl—and told him to stop trying to steal the fields . . ." She shook her head. "He earned himself another enemy. And then he insisted on working out with Daven. Ahira beat him badly in front of his own men."

Was it conscious or not? Had the dwarf deliberately been trying to get himself thrown out of office, or had it been an unconscious unwillingness to hold on to the responsibility?

He didn't ask. If anyone would know, Ellegon would—best to save it for later.

"I tried to smooth it over," she went on, "but I didn't get far. When the town meeting came up, Ahira just didn't have the votes, not without you there to back him up."

"So how did you get enough of the Joiners to agree to Riccetti as mayor? Magic?"

"Better than that." She grinned. "Sneakiness. I had Riccetti explain to one of Chton's Joiners that the Engineers weren't interested in *any* trade with Therranj, not if Chton became mayor. Apparently, Chton figured out that Khoral wouldn't take that at all well, so he decided to outsmart us: Chton *nominated* Riccetti. Clever move, really: It satisfies Khoral by letting him try to negotiate with Riccetti directly, and lets Chton drive a wedge between us and Lou."

"But Chton ought to know that won't work. Lou's loyalty isn't in question." *Is it?*

"Well, it wasn't." She breathed on her fingernails and buffed them against her chest. "Uhh . . . it seems that Riccetti has long had a *horrible* crush on me, and that he made some moves on me in your absence. And when I was overheard telling him to keep his filthy hands off me . . ."

Cute. A phony division for Chton to try to exploit. But just a bit *too* tricky. "I think you've been hanging around Walter Slovotsky for too long."

"Oh?"

"That's his style, not yours."

"And where is it written that I can't learn?"

He didn't answer that. Obviously she could learn the sneaky side of Home politics. *Matter of fact, there's a lot she could teach me. My natural inclination would have been to stick my thumb in Chton's eye.* "Last question: Why did Ahira come along with you?"

She didn't answer for a moment. "I don't know; he just volunteered. Gwellin agreed to hold off going back to Endell until he returns. Tell me, if you had to guess what one thing he'd miss most about Home, what would it be?"

"Close call—it'd be either Janie or Walter." Karl sucked air in through his teeth. "He's going to ask Walter to come along with him, and bring Kirah and Janie."

She nodded. "That's my guess."

Damn. Well, there wasn't anything that could be done about it now. But maybe, later on, either Ahira could be talked out of asking, or Slovotsky could be talked out of saying yes. "Do me a favor. Keep your head down and your eyes open, okay?"

"Okay." She smiled thinly up at him. "But tell me: What would you say if I told you to do the same thing?"

"I'd say that I already do." He helped her to her feet. "C'mon, let's join the others."

A smile creeping over her face, she shook her head. "No. I've got a better idea." Extending a tanned forefinger, she ran a fingernail up his arm. "Since we're trying to maintain an image and all . . ."

Fingercombing the dirt and leaves from his hair, Karl led the way back to the clearing.

Ranella had most of the gear unpacked, and spread out on tarpaulins on the ground. There seemed to be about two hundred guns, plus several kegs that undoubtedly contained powder and shot, as well as some lead ingots, no doubt for bullets. He nodded silent approval; running bullets was easy enough, and ingots took up less space than premade rounds.

"Karl Cullinane," Ranella said, nodding. "It is good to see you, Karl."

He raised an eyebrow, and opened his mouth to ask why an apprentice Engineer didn't treat a journeyman with a bit more formality, but caught himself. Riccetti must have promoted her during Karl's absence.

"Journeyman Ranella," he said, returning her nod. "It's good to see you, as well."

Her face fell. She had expected him to snap at her, and had been looking forward to flaunting her new status at him.

"What have we here?" he asked.

"Quite a lot, Karl. Fifty-two pistols, one hundred and sixty shotguns, thirty-three rifles—"

"Where did you get all these?"

"You said to bring every weapon we could, so we . . . requisitioned Daven's team's old rifles and most of your squads' weapons. Nehera is working full-time on barrels until they are replaced. Apprentices are taking care of the stocks, locks, rifling, and boring."

That still would be one hell of a lot of work for the dwarf. Turning a flat bar of iron into a rifle barrel took hundreds of welding heats, and even though Nehera could work on several barrels in rotation, he would have to sleep sometime.

Well, Karl would send word to Riccetti not to work Nehera too hard.

Don't be silly. Ellegon snorted, sending Aveneers' men reaching reflexively for their swordhilts. *Lou Riccetti is not as old and wise as some people, but he is no fool, either. He will see to Nehera's health.*

Karl nodded. *Good point.* "What else do we have?"

"Three thousand rounds in that sack, Karl—lead ingots, a bullet-running kit. Those two barrels contain gunpowder—and the Engineer sent along a surprise."

"Yes?" Karl raised an eyebrow.

"Do you see those two small kegs, Karl?"

"Yes."

"One of them contains a gross of the Engineer's new grenades. They're loaded with . . . guncotton." She raised a palm. "The Engineer said to inform you that he has not solved the instability problem—but we have kept it cold." She shrugged. "He won't swear how long it'll go without self-detonating, but he said he would be surprised if any of them go before another six tendays. Now, Karl, the other hogshead contains very carefully packaged detonators—"

"Detonators?"

"Fulminate of mercury, Karl. Silver fulminate goes off if you blink at it. This is stable. Relatively."

He repressed a shudder. Fulminate of mercury was touchy stuff. Almost anything could set it off—heat, friction, a sudden blow. "Any special instructions for the detonators?"

"No, Karl." She shook her head. "Other than not to insert the detonators into the grenades—or keep them near the grenades—until you're ready to strike them."

"Strike them?"

She smiled. "He said that would impress you. He's rigged a sulfur-tipped fuse. You rub the fuse tip against a rough surface until it catches fire, and then throw." She held up a cautionary finger. "There is no guarantee that it won't explode on impact, though."

Surprise, surprise. Still, that sounded good. "Assuming that things go well down there, I'll requisition some space in Furnael Keep for a magazine—mmm, make that several magazines." It would be best to keep the grenades spread out; if one self-detonated, it would send the others sky-high. "You'll take charge of that—talk to Frandred and Aveneer about guards."

"Understood, Karl."

Ranella had been giving his first name a thorough workout. He let a chuckle escape, then dismissed her questioning look with a shake of his head. "Very well. Later, I'd like to—"

The pounding of a horse's hooves sounded from down the path.

Erek rode up, then descended from the saddle of his mottled pony in what was more of a barely controlled fall than a voluntary dismount. "Aveneer . . . reports," he said, gasping for breath.

"Trouble?"

Erek shook his head. "No. He says . . ." He paused, panting, then tried to start again.

Karl held up a hand. "Ta havath, Erek," he said. *Sometimes,* he thought, *it feels like I spend half my life telling people to take it easy.* "If there's no problem, then take a moment and catch your breath."

Erek nodded, then waited while his breathing settled down. "Aveneer reports . . . that all is clear. Walter . . . Slovotsky reports that the baron will . . . see you."

"Andy? Could you get Erek some water?" He clapped a hand to the boy's shoulder. "I want you to rest, Erek. I won't need a runner for a while."

"Yes . . . Karl."

Karl beckoned to Thomen. "Let's get you to your father, boy."

Baron Zherr Furnael was waiting for them just inside Furnael Keep's main gate, fifty of his warriors keeping him company while the rest manned the ramparts.

Karl almost didn't recognize the baron; the years hadn't treated Zherr Furnael well. Before, he had been a solidly built man, sporting a slight potbelly; now, his leather tunic hung on him loosely, as though it had been made for a larger man, a younger one, less skeletal.

Deep lines matted the baron's face; the whites of his eyes had developed a definite yellow tinge. Worse, Furnael had developed a nervous twitch around his left eye; he constantly seemed to be winking.

But there was still an echo of his old inner strength. He threw an arm around Thomen's shoulders for only a moment, then stood with his shoulders back, his spine ramrod-straight, his face somber as he faced Karl.

"Greetings, Karl Cullinane. It has been a long time." Furnael's voice was more fragile than it had been, but a trace of its old power was still there.

Karl dismounted, handing the reins to one of Furnael's men. He wasn't sure how Furnael would feel about him. Would the baron blame Karl for Rahff?

Right now, he needed Furnael's cooperation as much as the baron had needed Karl's help in breaking the siege; it took a great deal of effort not to break into an idiot smile when Furnael extended a hand.

The baron's grip was astonishingly weak. Karl tried to keep an acknowledgment of that from his face, then regretted his success when he saw the implied pity mirrored in Furnael's eyes.

Releasing Karl's hand, Furnael turned to one of his men and called for his horse. "We have much to discuss, Karl Cullinane. Will you ride with me?"

"Of course, Baron. I am at your service."

An echo of a smile pierced through the gloom that hung over Furnael like a shroud. "That, Karl Cullinane, remains to be seen."

Six years before, on the night that Furnael had indentured Rahff to Karl, the two of them had ridden down the road from Furnael Keep to the row of clean shacks that served as Furnael's agricultural slaves' quarters.

Although the question of whether or not that night was going to end with spilled blood had hovered over them like a crimson specter, it had been a pleasant ride: lush fields of corn and wheat had whispered gently in the night wind; they had talked idly, while Furnael had dismounted from Pirate's back to remove a stray stone from the smooth dirt road.

There had been changes. Now, ruined fields sprawled on either side of the deeply rutted road, the cornstalks trampled by booted feet and shod hooves. The Holts hadn't wanted head-high cornstalks obscuring their view, possibly hiding an enemy; what they hadn't harvested for their own use they had trampled or burned, like a jackal covering the remnants of a too-large meal with its own vomit.

Furnael pulled on the reins of the brown gelding, then dismounted, beckoning at Karl to do likewise.

"Not quite like last time, eh, Karl Cullinane?" The baron stared at him unblinkingly. "You look older."

"I feel older. About a million years, if not one whit wiser."

"Yes." Furnael sighed. "Yes, that's a feeling I can sympathize with. Remember when you offered to take on the Aershtyn raiders if I would free all the slaves in my barony?"

Karl nodded. "Maybe I should have tried harder to persuade you. I've often wondered about that."

"No." Furnael shook his head. "I wasn't . . . equipped to believe that you were serious. Not then. Not until word of you and your Home raiders trickled back. Many good men have died because I didn't believe you. Rahff, for one. . . ." The baron stood silently for a moment. "Did you know that I had my best friend killed half a year ago?"

"No, I didn't." Karl shook his head. "Baron . . . Adahan of Holtun?"

"Yes. Vertum was one of Uldren's better strategists; it was necessary to order him assassinated." Furnael clenched his fists momentarily. "I am grateful that Bren is up north; perhaps at least Vertum's son will survive."

Karl breathed a sigh of relief. With Bren up north, at least he wouldn't have to kill Rahff's best friend.

Furnael chuckled hollowly, as though reading Karl's mind. "And what if someone else kills Bren? Will that make him any less dead?" He clapped a hand to Karl's shoulder. "We think alike, Karl Cullinane. Tell me: How did my son die?" the baron asked, his voice infinitely weary.

"I sent a letter with a trader, years ago," Karl said, toying with Stick's reins.

"Your letter only said that he died honorably, protecting another. *How* did he die, Karl Cullinane? You must tell me. I . . . need to know."

"Understood." Karl sucked air through his teeth. "Do you remember Aeia, Baron?"

Again, Furnael's face momentarily became an echo instead of a ghost of what it had been. "Call me Zherr, Karl. And yes, I remember her. The Mel child that you were returning to Melawei."

"She didn't stay in Melawei; she's my adopted daughter, now. A slaver was trying to kill her. Rahff stopped him. I don't know . . . maybe I hadn't trained him well enough; perhaps he just wasn't fast enough. Before I could intervene, the slaver . . . ran him through."

"He died quickly?"

"It must have been almost painless," Karl lied reflexively. Didn't Furnael have the right to know that his son had died in agony, his belly slit open by a slaver's sword?

Probably. *But I'm not going to be the one to tell him.*

"The man who killed him . . ." Furnael's eyes burned with an inner fire. "Did you . . . ?"

"I broke the bastard's neck." Karl spread his hands. "With these hands, Zherr."

"Good. Now . . . it seems that what is left of my barony is in your debt. How can we repay it?"

"For one thing, all my people need food and rest. Aveneer's soldiers have been on a forced march for more days than they care to count. I'd like your people to see that they're fed, and given a chance to rest."

"Done. Your plan is to move on the Holts' slaver allies, I take it."

"Yes." *And then to—somehow—shut this war down, deny the buzzards and the slavers their profits.* "Have you heard of a burn-scarred slaver working with the Holts?"

"That I have." Furnael nodded. "Name of Ahrmin?"

"Right. He led the slaving raid in Melawei when we were there, and he's backing the Holts, providing them with their slaver gunpowder." Karl reached up and stroked Stick's muzzle. "I'll have one of my people interrogate the prisoners, and we'll see if we can find out exactly where on Mount Aershtyn the raiders are camped, precisely what resources they have there. I'm willing to bet that somewhere on Aershtyn is the guild's headquarters in the Middle Lands."

"But even so . . ." Furnael shrugged. "What good will that do? No matter where they're camped, there's no way you could approach them without being spotted at least a day in advance. With a chance to prepare for an attack—"

"You're forgetting Ellegon. While the main force is working its way up and hanging on to their attention, I'll have the dragon drop me and a few others in from behind." Karl hitched at his sword, forcing a smile. "If we can do it, if we can break the back of the Holt-slaver alliance, maybe the Holts will sue for peace."

That was the best shot, if it all could be done quickly. It would require Prince Pirondael and his barons to accept an unsatisfactory truce, in place of a war they were losing, while Holtish Prince Uldren and his barons would end the war knowing that the tide of battle was about to turn against them.

Winning a cease-fire instead of losing a war would make both sides feel very clever . . . for a while; within ten years, both sides would probably claim that they would have won if the peace hadn't been forced on them.

Karl repressed a sigh. He could spot at least three major weaknesses in his plan, but at least it had a chance.

Furnael held out a hand. "It is good to see you, my friend."

Karl accepted the baron's hand, and was pleased to find that the grip was stronger now. "Zherr . . ." He closed his eyes and forced himself to say it. "I'm sorry about Rahff. If only . . ."

"No." The baron shook his head. "We both have to go on." He

easily pulled himself to his horse's back. "There's a war to be won."
He slapped himself on the leg and laughed as he spurred his horse.
"Damn me, but there's a war to be won!"

Karl smiled. Furnael had been given just the barest taste of possible victory, of possible life for his barony and his people; and the baron had shed about twenty years.

So Karl kept quiet as he spurred Stick, all the while thinking: *No, Zherr. There isn't. There's a war to be stopped.*

CHAPTER TWENTY-ONE

Ahrmin

Whom they fear they hate.

—Quintus Ennius

"Master Ahrmin?" Fenrius' basso boomed from outside his tent. "It is time to go."

Painfully, slowly, Ahrmin got to his feet and limped out of his tent, squinting in the early-morning sunlight. His carriage was waiting for him; he let Fenrius help him through the door and onto the padded seat.

The slaver camp at the base of Aershtyn was different from its cousin halfway up the slopes. Up there were the pens and corrals holding the well-chained cream of the captured Biemish population, guarded only by the few guildsmen necessary to keep them safely confined.

But this camp was a military operation, a place where Pandathaway-made powder was stored, guns made and repaired. Until today —now, the camp was breaking up, as Ahrmin's guildsmen prepared to move out.

It would be difficult to move three hundred men silently, and when they joined up with Prince Uldren's Holtish troops it would be impossible. Fortunately, the element of surprise wasn't always necessary.

The problem with you, Karl Cullinane, isn't that you challenge me.

Were that all, I would still have you killed, but you wouldn't haunt my dreams so. If you were only the murderer of my father, I would have you killed slowly.

But I was wrong about you: You are not only my enemy; you challenge the fabric of what is. I can't allow myself the luxury of killing you slowly; it is vastly more important that I kill you surely.

"You're sure of the assassins?" he asked Fenrius.

"Nothing is certain," the big man said, choosing his words carefully, "but they are said to be competent. I am . . . confident that he will be dead, or at least out of action, by the time we get there."

"Good." No, surprise wasn't necessary. Not when your enemy was trapped like a bug in a well-corked bottle. Then, all that was necessary was to heat the bottle. . . . "Very good. Make sure the barrels are tied down." Ahrmin leaned out the window, his good left hand pointing to the wagon that contained the huge barrels of powder; the massive, well-oiled oaken barrels were sealed so tightly that neither air nor water could have penetrated their sides.

"Yes, Master Ahrmin." Fenrius snapped his fingers and pointed toward the wagon; a dozen journeyman slavers ran to it, giving tie ropes another examination.

"You have had word from the Holts?"

"Nothing new." Fenrius shrugged. "Prince Uldren has pulled out most of his army from the battle in Arondael, as promised—although I'm not sure he believed the message—"

"*I* believed the message. And that is more than sufficient. As Uldren knows." If Uldren hadn't been willing to cooperate fully, well, the Biemish would have made adequate allies. Perhaps better ones— it was unlikely that Pirondael would stupidly fail to press home a tactical advantage, the way Uldren had in the north. It was clear to Ahrmin that Prince Pirondael was determined to benefit from every possible advantage.

Still, switching alliances hadn't been necessary; Uldren knew that his own survival depended on slaver powder and slaver guns.

"There should be more than enough for the task—once we join them." Fenrius gestured toward the tarpaulin-covered cylinder, twice the length of a tall man, that was mounted on the largest of the flatbed wagons.

Ahrmin nodded. "True. Have you seen the latest shipment from Hivael?"

"Yes." Fenrius nodded happily. "A hundred slaves came through this morning."

"I take it they aren't like that last batch?"

"No, not at all. Baron Drahan seems to have understood your message."

Ahrmin smiled. "A simple matter of withholding powder until their commitments were met. And with the shipment to Keranahan destroyed, the shortage was acute."

"Perhaps, Master Ahrmin, but it was effective." Fenrius smiled his approval. "I held back a dozen women. Definitely not culls." He smiled thinly. "Prime stock, although perhaps a bit spiritless."

"Fine. Send two of the best to me as a diversion for the trip."

"Yes, Master Ahrmin. At once."

That was a pleasant prospect. The trip was likely to be agonizingly long; best to have a distraction. "When they are delivered to me, move us out."

"Yes, Master Ahrmin."

Ahrmin leaned back against his cushions. Soon. It would be soon.

You and I have a score to settle, Karl Cullinane. It is only proper that a . . . version of one of your own devices will kill you.

CHAPTER TWENTY-TWO

Betrayal

If you pick up a starving dog and make him prosperous, he will not bite you. This is the principal difference between a dog and a man.

—Mark Twain

The aftermath of the siege and the battle was, in more ways than one, a bloody mess.

Karl happily left the beginnings of reconstruction to Furnael and his people. War could ruin in weeks what had been built up over many years; it would be a long time before the barony was back to anything near its former prosperity. The lack of people to work the fields was compensated for only by the lack of mouths for the keep's siege stores to feed.

Furnael now had an excess of land in what would have been a buyer's market—if there had been any buyers. Of course, there were none: The populations of the neighboring baronies had been decimated, slaves and freefarmers alike clapped into chains and shipped off to be sold along the Cirric coast, to work in the mines of Port Orduin and Sciforth, plow fields in Lundescarne, or serve in fine houses in Pandathaway and Aeryk.

There was a chance that some could be freed, up on the slopes of Aershtyn, where a few escapees reported that the slavers had their camp, a staging ground for what the captured Holtish prisoners said was to be a vast human cattle drive to Pandathaway.

Maybe they could be freed. But there were preparations to be made. The most important ones were the ones that Karl found most pleasant: resting and eating. Aveneer's team was road-weary almost to the point of exhaustion; Valeran's people and the mercenaries who had signed on in Biemestren weren't in much better shape. Even Karl had to admit that regular meals and regular sleeping hours had their attractions.

Well, the regular sleeping hours *would* have been nice. There was just too much work to do. The foremost priority was maintenance on the firearms. There were flints to be cut, frizzens to be rewelded, bent triggers to be straightened, barrels to be freshed out, split stocks to be glued or replaced. That had to be left to Ranella and Slovotsky, who spent their days closeted in the keep's smithy, the doors always heavily guarded.

The gunsmithing, though, interfered with another high priority—reshoeing of the horses. Most of the animals were long overdue, and the necessity that they be reshod created a logistics problem: All gunsmithing procedures were secret, and had to be conducted in the privacy of Furnael Keep's sole smithy, but shoeing required some of the same facilities.

The solution was more work for Karl. While he wasn't enough of a smith to turn bar stock into horseshoes, he could take shoes that Ranella made in the smithy and then fit them to the horses.

Of course, the shoes did have to be adjusted, and that required an anvil—and a forge. Or a reasonable facsimile.

Stop that, Ellegon—you're scaring the—would you please *try to broadcast calm?* Karl thought as he ducked aside, trying to avoid the brown mare's kick.

He was almost successful: The hoof just barely caught him on the right thigh, knocking his leg out from underneath him. It felt as if he had been hit by a hammer; he fell to the ground and rolled to safety.

Rubbing at his thigh, he glared at Theren and Migdal while they struggled with the horse. "I thought you were supposed to be helping me shoe this fleabag," he said, keeping his voice calm and friendly for the mare's benefit, not theirs.

"Sorry, Karl," Migdal said, pulling down on the reins.

Erek ran over and helped him to his feet. He stood on his good leg for a moment, debating whether or not to just pack it in for the day and let this idiot mare go only three-quarters reshod. It was always the last horse that could break a bone, just as it was that one last run down the ski slope that had once broken his leg.

Distant fingers touched his mind.

That's true. But remember: There was a very simple reason that it was the last run in which you broke your leg.

Oh? What was it?

After you broke your leg, you weren't interested in skiing anymore.

Always got to keep me honest, eh?

It's a tough job, but somebody's got to do it. Ellegon closed both eyes.

"Okay, people, let's give it another try. Just one more shoe and we finish this one off—then I'm calling it quits for the day." And a rather productive day at that, he thought, eyeing the late-afternoon sun with satisfaction.

There wasn't a whole lot of thrill in this stint as a farrier, but there was a certain something to it. Karl had always found a certain magic in metalworking, and while shoeing was something that a real smith would have found almost agonizingly routine, Karl liked it. Working with horses and working with metal, both at the same time—what could be better?

"Retirement," he muttered to himself. He set his nippers down next to the anvil and reached for the right rear hoof, turning around and pinning the hoof between his thighs.

Now, keep the animal calm, okay?

Ellegon gave out a mental sniff as he lay on the ground on the other side of the low brick wall that had a one-foot-square hole in it. *Go to sleep,* he began to sing, his mental voice low, but intense, *go to sleep, little horsie . . .*

Karl felt his own eyelids start to sag shut. "Stop that!" *All right, you made your point. Now cut that out. Just don't scare the horse, okay?*

The dragon didn't answer; Karl decided to take that for an assent.

He picked up his nippers and began to loosen the old nails. Sometimes the hardest part was getting the old shoe off, particularly if the foot had had time to overgrow it too much.

As this one had. He grunted as he pulled out the last nail, then pried the shoe off, throwing it on the all-too-large pile of used shoes. Accepting the wood-handled trimming knife from Erek, Karl quickly trimmed the sole, the frog, and the hoof wall, then tossed the knife back to Erek, who handed him the rasp in exchange.

Rasp gripped tightly, Karl gave the bottom of the hoof wall two dozen quick strokes, then eyed the hoof.

Not quite right, but almost. He tried an additional half-dozen quick passes with the rasp, then looked again. Better, nice and level. The toe length looked about right, too. He rasped away the splinters around the old nail holes, then held out his hand for a shoe.

Damn. "Anything less round? These feet are about as pointed as I've seen today."

Erek handed him another. Close, but not quite.

That is what I'm here for, isn't it?

Straightening, Karl let the foot drop and walked over to the brick wall.

Well, it really wasn't much of a wall, just a six-foot-long, four-foot-high stack of bricks with a hole in the middle, right next to where the small anvil stood on its stump. Karl gripped the shoe with a yard-long pair of pincers and stuck it through the hole in the wall.

Ellegon breathed fire, the backwash of heat almost sending Karl stumbling away. Instead, he closed his eyes and forced himself to hold on.

That should do it.

Karl pulled the red-hot shoe back through the hole and brought it over to the anvil. A few quick taps with the hammer, then he dipped it into a pail of water, ducking his head aside to avoid the hissing steam. He brought the shoe over to the mare and picked up the horse's foot, comparing.

Not a bad fit, not bad at all, he decided as he brought the shoe back for Ellegon to heat. It took only a few seconds before he was able to bring the hot shoe back to the horse, lift the hoof, and set the shoe against it, watching the hoof smoke as the shoe burned itself into place.

Quickly, he nailed the shoe in, bent the excess length of nails down, clipped them off, and clinched the nails.

His thigh was still throbbing where the horse had kicked him.

Enough. He let the foot drop. "I'll let you rasp off the edges," he said to Migdal. "I'm done for the day."

He eyed the setting sun, then waved up at one of Furnael's guards on the ramparts. No need to ask if the watchman had spotted anything unusual; that would have resulted in an immediate alarm.

Where's Andy? he thought, as he exchanged his tools and apron for his sword, pistols, and pouch.

Up in your rooms, Ellegon answered. *Doing some work with Henrad.*

Anything you can interrupt?

A pause. *Nothing dangerous.*

Good. Relay: I'm done for the day—any chance we can get some time to ourselves?

She says: "Give me about an hour—Henrad's almost got this cantrip down, and I don't want to break quite yet."

Fine. It'll give me a chance to take a bath.

Thank goodness for small favors, the dragon said, sniffing in distaste.

Karl laughed. "Come heat the water for me," he said, rubbing at his thigh as he limped across the broken-ground courtyard toward the bathhouse, the dragon lumbering along beside him like a four-legged bus.

Over by the east wall, Valeran was teaching a class in Lundish swordsmanship, both of his blades flashing in the light of the sun that hung just over the wall of the keep. Karl didn't dare interrupt him; what if, up on the slopes of Aershtyn, one of the warriors Valeran was teaching missed a parry?

Not everything that goes wrong is your fault, Karl.

Maybe not. But why does it always feel that way?

Egotism.

Thanks.

You're welcome.

Karl passed by the low stone smithy. Wisps of smoke floated up from its brick chimney, only to be shattered in the breeze. Two guards stood with their backs to the door, while the clattering of metal on metal came from inside.

Karl nodded to them as he walked by and into the low bathhouse next door.

The room was dark and dank. Karl set his weapons and his amulet on a dry spot on the rude shelf before stripping off his clothes and pumping water into the huge oaken tub. Ellegon snaked his head inside and dipped his mouth into the tub. Almost immediately the water started hissing and bubbling.

Touch—carefully, now.

Karl dipped a hand into the water. It was nicely warm.

Then I'll be on my way.

"What's up?"

Ahira wants some help with the timbers he's clearing out of the Holts' tunnels, and I have to get my patrol out of the way if I'm going to help him.

"Fine."

About his leaving . . . do you want me to—

"No. I don't want you peeping my fam—my friends for me."

Without another word, the dragon ducked his head back through the door. Momentarily, wind whipped dust in through the open door . . .

. . . and then silence.

After rinsing the dirt from his body with the icy water from the pump, Karl went to the tub and lowered himself slowly, gingerly, into the steaming water. As always, what had been comfortably warm to his hand felt as if it would parboil his calves and thighs, as well as more delicate parts of his anatomy.

But he forced himself to sit back against the oak sides of the tub and relax in the heat. Gradually, the tension in his neck and shoulders eased. He rubbed his hands against his face, then shook his head to clear the water from his eyes before leaning back.

Aershtyn was going to be bad, there was no doubt about it. If the slavers had as large a collection of slaves there as Karl suspected, they would guard them well.

And that probably meant guns. Karl didn't like the idea of sending his people up against guns. That was how Chak—

No. His hands clenched into fists. No, he couldn't keep thinking about Chak. That was the way of it: Good people had died, were going to die before this was all over.

There wasn't any cheap way out. There never was.

A round cake of scented soap lay on the rough table next to the tub. Karl picked it up and began to work up a violet-smelling lather. *Smell like a goddamn flower, I will.*

His face washed and rinsed, he lay back and tried to relax. But the water cooled all too quickly. He could either get out now, lie in a tepid bath—

Or do something else. "Guard," he called out, careful to make his voice both loud and calm.

Almost immediately, Restius stuck his grizzled face through the door. "You called, Karl?"

"Yes. Knock on the smithy door and see if Slovotsky would be willing to join me for a moment. Wait," he said as Restius started to leave. "Not so quick. Ask him to bring a red-hot bit of bar stock," he said, splashing the water. "A large bit."

Restius smiled. "I see." He disappeared, returning in a few minutes with Walter Slovotsky.

Walter held a large iron bar in his massive pincers. Even in the light coming through the open door, it glowed redly, although it was only a dull red.

"My, but we're getting fancy," Slovotsky said as he dipped one end in the tub, the water quickly burbling, boiling. "How's this?"

"Better," Karl said, working his hands underwater and kicking his feet to spread the hot water around. "Much better. I owe you one. If you want the next bath, I'll heat it for you. Deal?"

"Deal." Slovotsky made no motion to leave. He lowered the pincers to the ground and threw a hip over the edge of the tub. "Got something to talk to you about." He pursed his lips, opened his mouth, closed it.

"Well? You getting shy in your old age?"

"Me? No, it's just that . . . How long do you think it'll be before we finish up here?"

Karl shrugged. "Well, I figure we'll move on Aershtyn in about three weeks. That should be over quickly. It's shutting down the damn war after that that bothers me—that could take anywhere from a few tendays to . . ." He let his voice trail off.

"To however long you'll put into it before you give up." Slovotsky nodded. "Which is probably the way it's going to be. Listen to Furnael's people, Karl, *listen* to them. They don't just want peace, they want revenge." He shrugged. "Can't say as I blame them, but that's not the point."

"And is how long this war is going to go on. Is it?"

Slovotsky didn't meet his eyes.

Karl reached out and gripped his hand. "Walter, be a bit bolder. Remember how it used to be? You weren't ashamed to look me in the eye after the time you made it with my wife—"

"Hey!" Slovotsky's head jerked up. "Andy wasn't your wife, not then."

"True enough."

"But I wasn't all that eager to discuss it with you, even then."

"True again. But that wasn't because you were ashamed, was it?"

"No." Walter chuckled. "That was because I didn't want my head bashed in."

"I won't bash your head in. Not even if you take Kirah and Janie and go to Endell with Ahira."

Slovotsky's jaw dropped. "You knew?"

"Andy worked it out."

They sat in silence for a moment until Karl snorted and tossed the soap away. Somehow, even warm, the bath wasn't comfortable, not anymore.

"Hand me that towel, will you?" he asked as he pushed himself to his feet and stepped out of the tub.

He dried himself quickly, then slipped his amulet over his head and began to dress. "What do you want from me, Walter? My permission? You don't need that." He buckled his swordbelt around his waist, his hand going to its hilt for a moment.

Slovotsky looked him straight in the eye. "Maybe . . . maybe sometimes it feels as if I do, Karl. It's just that all of this . . ." His awkward gesture seemed to include the entire universe. "It's starting to get to me. I can remember a time when the most violent thing I'd ever done was sacking a quarterback, Karl. It's . . . I don't know how to say it."

He started to turn away. Karl caught his arm.

"Listen to me," Karl said. "You don't need my permission, but if you want my blessing, you've got it. We've . . . been through a lot together, Walter, and I love you like a brother. If you really need to spend a few years away from the action, then you do it. That's an order—understood?"

"Understood." Slovotsky smiled weakly. "Besides, it may not come to that. Who knows? I could get myself killed on this Aershtyn thing."

"Always looking at the bright side, eh?"

"Always."

They emerged into a golden, dusky light.

Slovotsky held out a hand. "Thanks, Karl. I appreciate it." He seemed to be about to say something else.

Karl took his hand. "Walter—"

Alert! Danger! Warning! came the distant voice.

Karl's head jerked around. Nobody else was reacting.

"What is it, Karl?"

"Ellegon—can't you hear him?"

Slovotsky shook his head.

Ellegon, what is it?

He felt that Ellegon was trying to answer, but he couldn't hear him. The dragon must have been at his extreme range, and only Karl's mindlink was tight enough to pick up Ellegon's broadcast, and that only irregularly, unpredictably.

"There's trouble." Karl cupped his hands around his mouth and called up to the watchman. "Sound the alert!"

The warrior began beating rhythmically on the alarm gong.

"Walter," Karl snapped, "get your squad armed and up on the ramparts. Take charge there. Erek! Where the hell's that—" He stopped himself as the boy ran up. "Message to Piell, Chak—" He clenched his fists. "Belay that last. Add Aveneer. Begins: Ellegon has sounded an alert. Nature unknown. I'll be at the main gate. Arm your people, report via message runner to me there. Ends. Message to Valeran. Mount up and bring your men and my horse to main gate. Ends. Message to Baron Furnael: Begins: Trouble. Am at main gate. If it pleases you, meet me there with your chief man-at-arms. Ends. Go."

Karl? The distant voice was clearer, firmer. *Can you hear me?*

Yes, dammit. I've sounded the alert. What's going on?

The dragon swooped over the ramparts and dropped into the courtyard, sending up puffs of dust as he landed heavily on the sunbaked dirt. *I'm not sure. Did we want a troop of about five hundred Holtish cavalry to be about half a day's ride east of us on the Prince's Road?*

"No—did you say *east?*" That didn't make any sense. Biemestren lay in that direction. How had the Holtish worked their way that deeply into Bieme, and why? It didn't make any tactical sense, not after the way that Karl had broken the siege.

They could have been sent before the breaking of the siege, but any force sent to reinforce the Holtish siegers would surely have been sent in via the west, through Holtun.

It just didn't make any sense, none at all, unless—

"Ellegon, check the west road. Now."

The west road?

"Yes, the west road, dammit." It was the only explanation. A cavalry force of that size wouldn't be sent to reinforce a siege. It had to be intended to block an escape.

An escape from what? From whatever was moving in on them from the west. "Get airborne, do a nice, high recon until you see something interesting, and then get back here. Move it, dammit."

You're welcome. His leathery wings a blur, the dragon leaped into the air and flew over the ramparts. *I will keep you in—* Ellegon screamed; his mind opened.

Pain tore through Karl's chest as three oily-headed crossbow bolts sank into his massive chest, passing through his thick hide as though it weren't there. He tried to flap his wings, struggled to pull upward with his inner strength, but he crashed to the ground and—

"Karl!" Furnael slapped his face again.

He shook his head as he lurched to his feet. "No! Ellegon—"

On the ramparts, a dozen guns fired in volley. Slovotsky turned to call down to Karl. "The dragon is *down*. We've fired on four crossbowmen, driving them back into the woods."

Hooves clattered as Valeran, leading Stick, arrived with his twenty mounted men.

"Four bowmen—watch for them." Karl leaped to the horse's back and spurred him through the gate, Valeran and his men galloping along behind.

Ellegon lay writhing on the ground by the side of the road, half in, half out of the ditch, his grunts and screams strangely animalistic, his flailing treetrunk legs sending huge volleys of dirt into the air.

Three crossbow bolts projected from his chest, their fletchings barely visible.

Karl dismounted from Stick's back. "Go," he shouted to Valeran. "Find them. I want them dead."

There was nothing to do as the huge dragon lay there, dying. Dragonbane was a poison to Ellegon, and every second it was working its way deeper into the dragon's body.

No. I won't give up. Ellegon had been able to survive his only other contact with the stuff, more than three centuries before. There was a chance that he could survive this. The poison would have to be gotten out—but how? Karl couldn't even break through the wall of pain around the dragon's mind.

I have to. Ellegon, he thought, *can you hear me?*

Yes. But the word was accompanied by nauseating waves of pain. Clutching at his chest, Karl crumpled to the ground.

No, *don't,* he thought, as the mindlink faded. *Don't answer. Just hear me. I have to get those bolts out of you. Try not to move.*

He worked his way in between the writhing forelegs, only to be batted aside by a fluttering wingtip that knocked him off his feet.

"No, Ellegon. Don't move." The three bolts were spread out across the dragon's chest, all but one above Karl's reach.

He quickly pulled that one out and tossed it away, then tried to climb up the dragon's side to get at another.

But his toes couldn't find purchase among Ellegon's hard scales. There was just no way to reach them.

"Karl!" A hand slammed down on his shoulder. "Lift me!" Andy screamed at him, a long-bladed knife in her hands.

Karl stooped, clamped his hands around her ankles, and lifted her up, holding her tightly as high as he could.

The dragon screamed again—

Don't move, Ellegon. Please don't move. If you knock us away, you'll die.

Karl . . . The mental voice was distant. *My friend . . . I'm afraid that this is goodbye—*

"No, dammit, don't you *dare* die on me, you scaly bastard. Not you, Ellegon. Andy—"

"Shut up," she hissed. "I've almost gotten the second one."

The dragon's mental presence was fading quickly, and his struggles were slowing, not from control, but from weakness.

"*Got* it," she exclaimed. "Take five big steps to your right so I can get at the last one."

While it felt like hours, Karl knew that it was only a few seconds later that she cried out, "Got it. Let me down."

He lowered her, shaking the tears from his eyes. "No, that's not enough. We've got to do something about the poison in the wounds."

Think, dammit, think. He looked up the dragon's side to the red holes in Ellegon's gray hide, and at the slow ooze of thick blood dripping down Ellegon's scales. The trouble was that dragonbane was poison, a chemical poison that dragons, virtually immune to most forms of physical attack, were subject to.

Andy-Andy buried her head against his chest, the bloody bolts falling from her hands. "He's not going to make it, Karl." The dragon's breathing was almost imperceptible.

"Shut up. Let me think." There had to be something to do, some way to clear the poison out of—

Got it!

He opened his pouch and pulled out his powder horn. "We'll burn it away," he shouted. "With gunpowder." Drawing his beltknife, he snatched at the hem of her robes and cut a swatch off, then used the rag to dry the most accessible of Ellegon's wounds as best he could.

He handed her the knife. "Give me another swatch," he said. He packed the wound with the fresh cloth, then opened his powder horn and tipped a third of the powder into the cloth. "Valeran!" he shouted, "get me a torch, some fire—now!"

Her face brightened. "Lift me."

He braced his back against the dragon's chest, caught her by the waist, and lifted her. As she planted her feet on his shoulders, he passed up the horn. "Do the same thing I did. Then get as much powder as you can into the swatches."

In moments the remaining wounds were packed with gunpowder. Lowering Andy-Andy to the ground, Karl accepted the torch from Valeran and touched it to the nearest of the wounds.

It puffed into flame and acrid smoke. He touched the torch to the other two rents in Ellegon's hide, and again they burned.

Andy gripped his arm. "Do you think—?"

The dragon was still breathing, but that was all. *Ellegon? Can you hear me? Dammit,* say *something.*

He shook his head. "I don't know. And I don't know what the hell else to do. We'll just have to wait." He bent over and kissed Andy-Andy gently on the forehead. "Make that 'I'll just have to wait.' This area isn't secure, yet." He turned to Valeran. "Put a guard around him—borrow men from Aveneer. I want a full circle, twice as wide as a bowshot, well lit with watchfires. There may be other assassins around. They're not to get within crossbow range—*nobody* is to get within crossbow range—understood?"

"Understood." Valeran nodded. "But—"

Karl turned. *"Erek!* Gather all team leaders and seconds for a full staff meeting, main dining hall; ask the baron's permission. Invite him and Thomen to join us—particularly Thomen. Go."

The boy nodded and ran off.

Valeran looked as though he was about to ask why, then shrugged. "Yes, Karl. But I was trying to tell you that we captured one." He led Karl around to the other side of the dragon and pointed to a greasy little man who lay on the ground, tightly bound, next to Norfan's horse. "Do you want me to hand him over to Tennetty?"

"Yeah." He nodded.

"Instructions?"

"She's to make him talk, and then she's to make him die."

Karl stood at the head of the long table, gathering his thoughts, trying to forget about Ellegon for the moment. There was nothing that could be done about the dragon now, but this meeting was critical.

Gathered around the table, the others sat quietly, waiting for the storm to break.

Sitting together at the far end of the table, Valeran, Frandred, and Aveneer talked calmly, in soft tones, as though nothing at all bothered them.

Karl had never truly understood that mentality. He understood the necessity of generating the image, of course, but the calm resolution that one was going to die in battle, and that this coming battle might easily be *the* battle, well, that was something Karl could simulate, but never quite understand. That was something he had given up when he had deliberately subsumed his Barak persona.

Sitting next to him, Andy-Andy reached over and squeezed his hand momentarily, then dropped it. *Relay, please*—he caught himself. *Damn.* "I'm glad you're here," he whispered, smiling back at her.

"Hate sleeping alone that much, do you?" She smiled back.

"Right."

Next to her, Tennetty and Ahira sat quietly, their faces more impassive than calm. But the dwarf's brow was furrowed. His stubby fingers steepled in front of his aquiline nose, he occasionally glanced over at Karl, then resumed his own thoughts.

Karl let a chuckle escape his lips. Ahira was trying to anticipate him. There had been a time when the dwarf was a better military tactician than Karl, but practice and study had honed Karl's skills. Still, Ahira's ability to think well under pressure was something to reckon with . . . or to rely on, depending.

On the dwarf's right, Piell sat back on his high-backed chair, feigning calm, while opposite Ahira, Walter Slovotsky waited patiently, his all-is-well-with-any-universe-clever-enough-to-contain-Walter-Slovotsky smile intact, as always.

Next to Slovotsky, Zherr Furnael sat stiffly, looking like a compromise between the way he had been six years before and the way Karl had found him. Well, a compromise it would have to be. Furnael was the key to everything, and if the baron could just hold himself together for a few more years, maybe . . .

Thomen sat quietly next to his father, his eyes watching everyone, missing nothing. Thomen was different from his brother: Rahff had been much more of a talker, less of a watcher.

"It's going to be tough, people," Karl said. "The first item of business is getting Ellegon in through the gates. Andy, can you levitate him?"

"I've been expecting that. And I . . . think so." She nodded, biting her lip uncertainly. "I may be able to lift him, but that doesn't mean I can float him in here—and with his mass . . ."

"That's easily solved. We tie some ropes to his legs and everyone helps pull him in through the main gate." He looked over at Furnael. "If he does survive, he's going to need to eat a *lot* of food. You can start with your scrawniest animals—he won't care."

"It will be done." The baron nodded. "We have some smoked beef in the cellars that has turned. If that wouldn't do Ellegon harm—"

"Turned?" Slovotsky raised an eyebrow. "Why haven't you disposed of it?"

Furnael answered slowly. "Because, Walter Slovotsky, when you are under siege you would rather your people have moldy beef to eat than see them starve in front of your eyes. That is . . ." He pinched the bridge of his nose between thumb and forefinger. "My apologies. I was asking—would the meat be bad for the dragon?"

"Not at all," Karl said. "He doesn't poison easily."

Aveneer raised his head. "I don't understand all this hurry. It can't be because of five hundred cavalrymen a day's ride away to the east, so I—"

"Wait," Ahira interrupted. "How do you know it's not?"

Aveneer threw his head back and laughed. "You may have observed that Karl Cullinane does not panic easily. Five hundred cavalrymen would not panic him, not when we've that many effectives here, most armed with guns."

"No, it's not the horsemen." Karl shook his head. "They're only there to cut off our remaining avenue of escape. The reason that I'm worried is that I'm all but certain there are at least two thousand heavily armed soldiers only a few days to the west. I've been sold out, people, and Ahrmin is about to arrive and try to collect."

"Surely," Valeran said, studying the fingernails he was cleaning with the point of a dagger that he hadn't been holding moments before, "you aren't accusing anyone here? I realize that I am new to your service, but I've never been fond of being the target of a false accusation."

Tennetty pushed back her chair and rose slowly, her hand on the hilt of her sword. "If it is you—"

"*No,* Tennetty," Karl snapped. "It's not Valeran. Think it through.

"Holtish cavalry moving in from the east on the Prince's Road is an obvious suggestion that there's more trouble brewing in from the west. They can't be here to reinforce the siege—they wouldn't chance swinging in through Bieme if that were the case. Doesn't look like a normal military procedure, does it?

"The attack on Ellegon cinched it." He looked at Tennetty. "You interrogated the surviving assassin. Who were they after?"

"Ellegon. At least, that's what he said."

"Right. Think about it. Assassins armed with dragonbane, sent to kill Ellegon. That has to mean that whoever is behind this is after me —and who has known that I'm here long enough to prepare and send out assassins?"

The words hung in the air for a moment.

"Not the Holts," Furnael said, tenting his fingers in front of his chin. "If they had known about you and your people, they would have been prepared for your lifting of the siege, and reinforced their positions, not sacrificed the horsemen who chased after you, then retreated. You're saying that your betrayer is Biemish, some traitor in Biemestren?"

Karl nodded. "In a sense. Assume that I'm right, assume that a large part of the Holtish army is headed this way—who would benefit?"

Furnael shrugged. "The Holts, of course, if they can take the keep."

"Nonsense. The Holts already had the keep under control; they could have cracked it like an egg anytime they wanted to divert the manpower from the north. But they didn't do that, did they?"

Furnael wrinkled his brow. "No, but . . ."

"But who else stood to benefit? Who had already written off barony Furnael as a lost cause? Who would love to divert a few thousand Holts and their slaver allies south—"

"Wait—"

"—and who would gain by weakening the Holtish advance in the north, possibly taking advantage of the situation to order a counterattack? Tell me, Baron, *who?*"

"Son of a *bitch!*" Slovotsky nodded. "Pirondael." He threw up his hands. "Look at it from his point of view. It'd be a gorgeous bit of betrayal. It was common knowledge in Enkiar that Ahrmin's as irrational on the subject of you as you are on the subject of him—why wouldn't Pirondael know? He's counting on the little bastard's taking off after you with every gun and soldier he can muster."

He pushed his chair back from the table and began pacing up and down. "Shit, Karl, that changes *everything.* We don't have any line of retreat at all. Even if we could somehow punch through the Holtish cavalry at our back door, we can't sneak hundreds of warriors through Bieme."

Furnael sat up straight. "Bieme is not your enemy, not even if—"

"Nonsense, Baron," Andy-Andy snapped. "If your prince has betrayed Karl, he'll know it, and he'll be deathly afraid of my husband. As he has a right to be." She looked up at Karl. "Assuming that I don't get to him first."

Furnael shook his head. "I find this difficult to believe. My prince would not dishonor his crown this way."

"You're confusing the myth with the reality, Zherr. Wearing a crown doesn't make a man honorable." Karl turned to Slovotsky. "Walter, how many men do you think you could sneak past the Holts?"

"Depends. You thinking about sending me back to Biemestren?"

Karl nodded.

"Damn." Slovotsky shrugged. "Then you'd better tell me what you want me to do."

"I want you to find out if I'm right or not about Pirondael's betraying us. If I'm wrong, you've got it easy: Talk him into sending some reinforcements."

"If you think that's easy, would you please tell me what you consider hard?"

"If I'm right, then I think it's time we put a new prince under that crown of Pirondael's, and make sure that the new prince sends out reinforce—"

"Who?" Furnael snarled. "Both of my prince's sons have died in this cursed war; Evalyn is long past child-bearing. The succession is in doubt. The best claim is probably Baron Tyrnael—"

"Not if we seat the crown firmly on *your* head, Zherr." Karl looked the baron straight in the eye. "Not if we . . . persuade Pirondael to abdicate in your favor."

Furnael looked him straight in the eye. "You are asking me to commit treason, Karl Cullinane."

"But what if I'm right? What if he's betrayed you, your barony, and your son?" Karl pointed toward Thomen. "He'll die here, as surely as the rest of us."

Furnael sat back in his chair. "It does come to that, doesn't it?" For a long moment he sat motionless, his eyes fixed on Karl's.

Then he shook his head. "No. There's no way it can be done. I can't be in two places at once. How can I defend my barony and decide whether or not Pirondael is guilty?"

"You can't, Baron. You're going to have to go along with Slovotsky, and decide for yourself." Slowly, Karl drew his sword and balanced the flat of the blade on the palms of his hands. "We'll button up here; I can't go anywhere until Ellegon's well enough to travel, anyway. I'll do my best to safeguard Furnael Keep for you. You have the word of Karl Cullinane on that."

Furnael hesitated. Karl wanted to take that for assent, but he sensed that if he pushed the baron at this moment, it would only push him away from what had to be done.

Finally, Furnael nodded. "We shall do it."

"Fine." Karl slipped the sword back into its sheath. "Walter, I want you out of here before sunup. How many do you want to take with you? Twenty, thirty?"

Slovotsky spat. "Don't be silly. That'd be suicide. It's got to be a tiny group, to have any chance of getting through, and into the castle." He leaned back in his chair and closed his eyes, sitting silently for so long that Karl was beginning to wonder if there was something wrong.

Slovotsky's eyes snapped open; he shrugged. "Okay. The group is me, the baron, either Henrad or Andrea—"

"Not Andy. I need her here."

"Make it Henrad, then—I'm going to need some magic. And I'll need someone to handle the horses—Restius should do for that—and one other. Ahira?"

The dwarf nodded. "I was hoping you'd ask." He pushed his chair back away from the table. "We'd better decide on equipment and get packed." Ahira looked up at Karl. "Are you sure you can hold out here until we can relieve you?"

Karl shrugged. "No. But I'd better. You see another way?"

"No. I'm worrying about the dragon. Do you think he's going to be okay?"

"I don't know. We'll just have to wait and see."

Not . . . terribly long. The voice was distant, and it was weak.

But it was there.

Karl didn't know whether to laugh or cry.

He settled for slapping his hands together. "Okay, people, let's get to work."

CHAPTER TWENTY-THREE

Biemestren Revisited

It is a bad plan that admits of no modification.

—Publilius Syrus

Walter Slovotsky moved quietly through the dark night, slipping in and out of the shadows of Biemestren Castle like a wraith.

Two hundred yards to the west, a dozen peasant shacks huddled up against the outer wall like moss against a tree. Four hundred yards to the east was the outer wall's main gate. But this stretch of wall was empty, the grasses growing almost chest-high.

"Just a short way, Baron," he whispered to Furnael. The baron's breathing was heavy; he considered offering Furnael a hand, but decided that the old man's pride would be wounded.

This wasn't a job for an old man. On the other hand, complaining about Furnael didn't make sense; the baron, after all, was a manifestly necessary component of any plan to put the baron on the throne.

So? Who says I have to be logical all the time? I'm Walter Slovotsky, dammit, not Leonard Nimoy.

To his left, Henrad stumbled. Ahira's hand whipped out, caught and lifted him, setting Henrad back on his feet before the boy could fall.

Slovotsky shook his head. Henrad might be coming along well in his magical studies, but he'd be about as useful on a quiet recon as a belled cow. He kept looking behind him, as though he could see where Restius waited with the horses, or possibly what was going on a week's ride away at Furnael Keep.

Walter shook his head. That was going to be a bitch if the Holts and slavers were attacking with any kind of seriousness.

Karl me boy, I sure hope that you're every bit as good as everybody else thinks you are.

Granted, the defense had the edge in this kind of warfare, but it wasn't an insuperable one. Everything really depended on how many of the Holts were moving on Furnael Keep. Or *had* moved on Furnael Keep; it could actually all be over by now. Come to think of it—

Whoa. Methinks you'd better get your mind back on what you're supposed to be doing, Walter me boy. You're doing with your mind what Henrad is doing with his eyes.

Despite the silent complaining, he was pleased with how things were going, so far. Though it was obviously bad for morale for someone in authority to gripe openly, a constant stream of silent complaints helped Walter keep himself sane. Relatively sane, at least.

Besides, being impressed with his own abilities was something he still hadn't gotten over. In the old days, he was large and reasonably well coordinated, but it would have been difficult to think of himself as terribly graceful.

Spiderman, watch my smoke, he thought. Then: *Walter, Walter, remember Slovotsky's Law Number Seven: Thou shalt always cover thy ass.*

The castle guard wasn't set up badly, but whoever had set out the guards had been more capable at maintaining order than security: two-man watchfires were scattered evenly on the outer ramparts, touring sentries only on the inner curtain wall.

It didn't take a military genius to deduce a manpower shortage; the main gate on the outer wall was only lightly manned, and the northern bastion wasn't manned at all.

Still, that wasn't surprising, Walter decided. The bastion was supposed to be a strongpoint for an active defense of the castle, not a lookout tower. Pirondael—or the commander of the House Guard, more likely—expected to know in advance about any attack in force, and would man the bastion when appropriate.

Slovotsky nodded his approval. The commander of the House Guard was right; any large force would have been spotted long since.

On the other hand, the ramparts overhead were silent and empty, which pleased Slovotsky as the four of them crouched in the dark at the base of the wall. Overhead, the massive stone merlons at the top of the wall stood invitingly.

Ahira beckoned to him. "Ready? Or do you need a rest?"

Slovotsky shook his head. "We human flies don't need rest."

"Eh?"

"Do it, Ahira, do it."

While Walter slipped into his suede climbing gloves, the dwarf reached over his shoulder and unfastened a long braided-leather rope from his rucksack. Ahira measured the merlon by eye, adjusting the size of his loop.

He swung the rope several times around his head and threw.

The loop settled raggedly around the stone merlon; Ahira twitched at the rope to settle it into place, then pulled it tight.

"You're on," the dwarf said, taking a strain on the rope.

The trick to climbing up a rope was to let the feet and the leg muscles do as much of the work as possible; only the foolish relied on the weaker shoulder muscles any more than absolutely necessary.

Walter Slovotsky swarmed up the rope like a squirrel up a tree. At the top of the wall, he lowered himself to the stone walkway and listened. That was one of the tricks of the trade: At night, the ears were every bit as important as the eyes. The whisk of a leather sole on stone could carry hundreds of yards through the dark.

Halfway around the jagged curve of the outer wall was the main gate, and there a fire blazed orange against the night. Walter closed his eyes, held his breath, and listened.

Perhaps the wind brought him faint murmurings of the distant guards' voices. Perhaps not. In any case, there was nothing closer, nothing except for the night sounds of insects, and the distant sound of voices from the village shacks.

He reached over the merlon and tugged on the rope three times, waited a moment, then tugged twice again. In a few moments, Ahira was at his side. After pulling up the rope, and rigging a sling on one end, they lowered it and pulled Henrad up, then Furnael.

"What next?" Ahira said, as he coiled the rope and lashed it to his belt.

"Stay here for a moment," Walter whispered as he slipped away from the other three. It was still well before midnight, and there were hours of darkness left; best to use that darkness liberally, safely.

He found a stone staircase only a few hundred feet away, then went back for the others and led them to it, down the stairs, and into the tall grasses of the outer ward.

The slope was steep as they climbed quietly through the night toward the inner wall, slipping into the shadows.

Walter decided that Karl had been right: This would be a difficult slope to fight up. The defenders wouldn't even have to kill you to stop you; all they would have to do would be to get you to lose your balance and you'd roll down the grassy slope to the bottom. Certainly it would be nearly impossible to set up siege towers or ladders at the top of the motte.

Walter beckoned to Henrad. "Are you getting anything yet?"

The boy shook his head. "Nothing. I don't think there's a wizard in the area. Except for me."

Ahira snorted. "Don't put on airs, Henrad."

The absence of Pirondael's wizard surprised Walter for a moment, but only a moment.

Actually, it made sense; Furnael's wizard had deserted at the start of the war. Most wizards seemed to be abject cowards when it came to physical danger, although they often weren't. It was just that in any kind of combat situation, the other side's having an active wizard was such a huge disadvantage that any successful strategy necessitated killing the wizard.

That tended to discourage all but the more powerful wizards from getting involved in combat situations, and usually the more powerful wizards were far more interested in augmenting their own abilities than in using them.

"Henrad," Walter whispered to the boy. "Be sure you're ready to zap the hell out of any group of guards before they can raise a cry."

"Zap?"

I just plain gotta remember to persuade Andy to teach these people more colloquial English. "Be ready to put them to sleep, then. Understood?"

"Yes, Walter Slovotsky."

The inner wall was a different sort of problem than the outer wall had been. Not only was its circumference studded with manned guard towers, but Walter could hear the slap of sandals as a guard walked his tour above.

This was one of the times that Walter almost wished Karl Cullinane were running this one instead of him.

He sighed. No, it was best this way; keeping Furnael Keep intact wasn't something that Walter would have wanted to try. Besides,

Karl wouldn't have done this right—he would have tended toward silencing a guard or two, hoping to make it down the wall and into the fortress itself by speed alone, expecting to power his way through any opposition.

That would have been suicide here. This wasn't like a typical slaver camp, where the guards would usually sit in one place, waiting for eventual relief. That sort of thing was easy: All you had to do was hit an outer guard station just after it had been relieved, and you would have scads of time to get set up and move in.

This was different. It was like planning on jumping through the blades of a whirring fan without being cut into bloody little slices.

Not getting cut into bloody little slices is, after all, the key to a sound plan, he thought, suppressing a chuckle.

He told the others to wait at the foot of the wall, then slipped off into the night. Maybe the inner gate was up; perhaps they could slip in that way.

No good. The portcullis hadn't been lowered, but the whole area around the gateway was lit by dozens of smoking, flickering torches —too well lit. He could probably slip in, but that was too much to expect of the others.

Damn.

Ahira, Furnael, and Henrad were waiting where he had left them. Above, he could hear the slap of the sandals of an approaching guard, walking his tour on the ramparts.

Walter put his mouth to Ahira's ear. "Can't use the gate," he whispered. "So we've got to do it the hard way. The timing's going to be critical here. Get out the rope."

Unless he missed his guess, a guard walked by this part of the wall at least every fifteen minutes, which left barely enough time. Assuming, of course, that there weren't extra sentries posted, or that a soldier on duty in the nearest tower didn't happen to step out into the night to clear his head and spot them. If that happened, Henrad's Sleep spell wouldn't do them any good, not after one quick shout.

As the guard's footsteps vanished in the distance, Walter nodded to the dwarf. "Do it."

Again, the dwarf unfastened the long braided-leather rope and adjusted the size of his loop. He whipped the rope several times around his head and threw.

It missed. Slovotsky raised an eyebrow. Missing when it counted wasn't what he was used to from the dwarf.

"Better do better, Jimmy me boy," he said.

Ahira glared at him and threw again. This time the loop settled down around the jutting merlon as though God Himself had slipped it on. One quick tug and it was tight.

Slovotsky swarmed up the rope and slipped to his belly on the rampart. Nothing.

Again, he tugged on the rope, rising to help Ahira up, then the two of them pulled the other two up. He led the others down a staircase and into the shadow of the wall of the inner courtyard.

Well, that's the easy part.

"Henrad," he whispered. "Locate her—and be quiet about it, boy."

"Yes, Walter Slovotsky." The apprentice wizard nodded. "Consider it done," he said, a trifle too smugly. Still, a short-distance Location spell wasn't supposed to be terribly difficult, not when the object of the search was already well known to the wizard.

As the boy quietly murmured the harsh words that could only be heard and forgotten, Walter glanced down at his amulet, which was hardly flashing at all.

Still, it was flashing, and there was no need to ask for trouble; he unlooped it from his neck and tucked it into an inner pocket of his blousy black pantaloons.

"She is . . . in a suite on the second story of the keep, directly opposite a guardroom. Beralyn is . . . awake, and irritated at the noise the guards are making across the hall. . . . There is a female servant in her outer chamber, although she believes that the woman is sleeping on duty."

Walter turned to Furnael. "Do you know where this suite is?"

Furnael nodded, his face grim. "Yes. What are you going to do about the guards? Even if Karl Cullinane's accusations against Prince Pirondael are true, they're not to blame. It would be—"

"I'm not after their blood." *Did you say "Prince Pirondael," Baron? You're not calling him "my prince" anymore, eh? Good.* It looked, more and more, as if Furnael was accepting Karl's accusations against Pirondael. "Besides, they're essential to the plan—I *can't* kill them. Have some faith." He nodded to Ahira and Henrad. "Let's go."

After all the difficulties getting over the walls, getting into the residence tower itself was almost an anticlimax.

They waited in the shadows until nobody was in sight, then simply walked in through the arched front door and made their way quietly up the dark stone staircase.

Walter kept one of his throwing knives ready in his hand. Though he wasn't after any innocent's blood, if they were spotted, blood would be shed in any event.

And if somebody's going to bleed, I'd just as soon it not be little ol' me. It was only fair, after all: The rest of the universe consisted of millions and millions of people who collectively had millions and millions of gallons of blood; Walter Slovotsky had only his meager few quarts, all of which he continually put to good use.

The tower was quiet. That was the advantage of doing this in the middle of the night, after all: As long as they avoided anyone who could sound the alarm and wake the soldiers in the adjacent barracks, all they had to worry about was those few guardsmen on duty.

They reached the second-floor landing and crept into the hall. The door to Beralyn's suite stood open, the entrance room lit by a single oil lamp. The room across the hall was well lit. Walter could make out several voices talking quietly; there were at least four soldiers talking in the room, perhaps as many as eight.

He nodded to Henrad. "Once more, Henrad," he whispered, then turned to the dwarf. "Watch your timing, Ahira."

The dwarf raised an eyebrow. "Nervous, are we?"

"No, I'm not nervous," he whispered back. "What the hell do I have to be nervous about? I'm really calm about sneaking around inside a castle that's next to a barracks, both of which are inside two separate walls, all of which means that if anybody—*anybody*—raises an alarm I'll be dead within minutes, if I'm lucky. So what the hell do I have to be nervous about?"

"Damned if I know."

Henrad knelt on the floor, murmuring the words that could only be heard and forgotten, the rough syllables that vanished on the ear like a sugar crystal on the tongue, leaving behind only a vague memory.

As Henrad completed the spell, Ahira, his speed belying the shortness of his dwarf's legs, dashed around the corner and into the room.

Walter shuddered, waiting for the clamor of steel on steel or steel on stone that would alert someone, somewhere, that something untoward was going on, but . . .

Nothing.

He walked around the corner. Ahira had already relieved the seven sleeping soldiers of their swords and quietly stacked the weapons in the corner of the room. As the dwarf spotted him, he flashed Walter a quick smile.

Whew! Walter leaned back against the wall. That was out of the way. Next . . .

He beckoned to Henrad. "Help the dwarf tie them up, and bring them into position. Now it's Furnael's and my turn."

The dark archway into Beralyn's suite beckoned to them. Walter slipped inside, opening his pouch and removing several strips of cloth from it.

This was almost too easy. The serving girl was sleeping over by the window, starlight streaming in and splashing over where she sat back in the chair, fast asleep, her mouth open. He wadded a fistful of cloth into a gag, then beckoned to Furnael, pointing at the door beyond.

Furnael crept through the doorway and vanished from Walter's sight into Beralyn's sleeping room.

Walter rubbed his fingers together as he crumpled the cloth tight, then carefully pushed it into the serving girl's open mouth. Her eyes flew open; she gathered in a quick breath for a scream. He punched her in the solar plexus; she folded over like a blanket.

Within five seconds, she was fully gagged and tied.

John Norman, eat your heart out, he thought, then instantly regretted it. The poor girl was scared stiff; if this hadn't been necessary, it would have been an inexcusable thing to do to her. As it was, he wasn't terribly proud of himself.

Furnael pushed his way out through the curtains of the other room, carrying a lamp. "Beralyn is dressing; she will be along directly."

Dressing? *Damn* all women. This was something that could be done in pajamas, or whatever the hell Beralyn wore to bed. "Wonderful. She can come on up with Ahira." He hefted the bound form of the serving girl to his shoulder and walked out through the door.

The stairs up to the third floor waited for him. Walter hesitated for a moment, gathering his nerve.

Ahira tapped him on the shoulder. "If you need help—"

"Then we're already dead meat." He shrugged. "I don't have the slightest idea what you ought to do if you hear fighting sounds from upstairs, but make it good."

He crept up the stairway toward Pirondael's sleeping chambers, Furnael following along behind him. He peered out of the shadows. Two fully armored soldiers stood in front of the door, each with a spear in hand. They stood at full attention, although their eyes were glazed over, their shoulders stooped just a trifle.

Damn. Walter ducked back and hefted a throwing knife.

"No," Furnael whispered quietly, laying a hand on his shoulder. There wasn't time to argue. Walter pushed him back and stood.

Pain sparked through his head like an explosion; the world went gray as he felt strong fingers prying the knife out of his hand.

No, he thought, *I can't—*

Through force of will alone, he kept himself from slipping away into the darkness.

He could hear Furnael rise and walk down the hall.

"I am Baron Zherr Furnael," Furnael said in a firm voice. "You will awaken Prince Pirondael and tell him I am here to see him."

"How—"

"Now, fellow."

Walter pushed himself to his feet and peered around the corner. One of the guards had vanished into the sleeping chambers, but the other, not looking at all sleepy anymore, stood between Furnael and the doorway.

Damn you, Furnael. Walter lifted a throwing knife, moved out into the hall, and threw, all in one smooth motion.

Later, he couldn't decide whether or not he had done it on purpose, but the hilt of the knife caught the guard directly between the eyes with a solid *thwock;* he collapsed like a marionette with its strings cut.

Walter caught his spear before it could clatter against the wall and lowered it to the ground, then quickly tied and gagged the guard before he paused to glare at Furnael.

The baron looked back at him impassively. *If this can't be done honorably,* his look seemed to say, *then it shall not be done at all.*

Up yours, Walter thought, resolving—assuming they got out of this alive—to spend some time with the baron and a baseball bat, before his own self-honesty made him admit that in the relief of getting out of this alive he'd surely be more glad than anything else.

Besides, where would I get a baseball bat?

Footsteps sounded from inside the room. "The prince will see you shortly," the other guard said, as he stuck his head out through the curtains.

His eyes grew wide; his mouth opened—

Walter caught him in the throat with a backhanded slap, then clapped both hands on the soldier's naked ears. Leaving the collapsing soldier to Furnael, he dashed through the curtains, already drawing another throwing knife, praying he wouldn't have to use it.

The prince, dressed only in a nightshirt, was fumbling in the dark, trying to load a crossbow, when Walter rushed in.

Walter tackled him; and they rolled around on the thick carpet for a difficult few moments before Walter could get a proper hold on the larger man.

But finally he had one of the prince's arms twisted up into a hammerlock and the point of a knife barely pricking the skin over Pirondael's jugular.

"I think this counts as a gotcha, fatso," he said in English, then switched to Erendra. "I advise caution, your majesty—and silence."

He raised his voice fractionally. "All set in here, Baron." Walter frog-marched the prince over to the bed and pushed him face-down as Furnael entered the sleeping chamber and began lighting the several lamps scattered about the walls. "Search the bed for weapons, while I keep an eye on your prince."

The baron quickly pawed through the bedding, sweeping a dress dagger from the nightstand and onto the floor. "Nothing else, Walter Slovotsky."

"Good. Load the crossbow, please, then give it here."

Furnael slipped the bolt into the slot, nocked it, and handed it to Walter.

"Take a seat, Baron," Walter said. "The show starts in just a couple of minutes." He curled his fingers around the trigger as he let go of the prince. "You can turn over now, your majesty," he said merrily. He pulled a stool over next to the nearest wall, rapped on it to assure himself of its solidity, then sat down. "Now, I'm renowned for being one of the best shots with a crossbow that ever there was," he lied. "Matter of fact, back where I come from, an officious official once forced me to knock an apple off my son's head from a good hundred paces away . . . so, I wouldn't think that there's going to be any difficulty about putting this bolt through your throat if you cry for help, is there?"

The prince shook his head.

"I can't hear you."

"No," Pirondael whispered.

"No, no," Walter said. "Don't whisper. There's nothing that attracts attention like a whispering voice." He had to repress a smile when the prince looked at him as though he were insane. "Just talk in normal tones. Now: Karl Cullinane sends his greetings. Karl's a bit irritated with you for betraying us, and he sent the baron, Ellegon, and me to see about bringing back an explanation."

The prince's feigned look of surprise and shock came just a heartbeat too late.

"Then it's true." Furnael sucked air in through his teeth. "All along, I'd wished that there was another explanation."

"That counts as gin, shithead," Walter said to the prince, then switched back to Erendra. "Why, Pirondael?"

Pirondael spread his hands. "I do not know what you are talking about, Walter Slovotsky. I've . . . betrayed no one."

"Then how do you explain that the Holts knew enough to send assassins with dragonbane ahead? Other than our own people, there were only four who knew that we were expecting him: you, two of your soldiers, and Beralyn. None of the other three had any reason to betray us. You did. It didn't work, but," he said, eyeing the window, "Ellegon's irritated. He'll be along before morning to explain that in person." Walter leaned back against the wall. "So, we've got a bit of a wait."

"What did you say about the dragon?" Pirondael said, raising his voice just a trifle.

Walter ignored him as he turned to address Furnael. "You know why people don't like dragons, Baron?"

"No, Walter Slovotsky. I don't."

"It's not just that they're large and carnivorous, although that helps. But there are a lot of things in the world that are large and carnivorous, and—*I wouldn't move too far, Pirondael*—people don't fear them the way they do dragons.

"The real reason," he went on, as Pirondael folded his hands back in his lap, "is that dragons can read minds. They know what you're thinking, and if that's not enough, they can probe for everything you've ever done. Every dirty little secret, every private disgrace that you've tried to forget—every betrayal, Pirondael."

"I've betrayed no one, Walter Slovotsky."

Slovotsky shrugged. "Tell that to Ellegon. He'll eat you, if you've betrayed us. Too bad; the baron here would just banish you, load you up with gold, and let you and a small band hit the road."

"Banish *me?*"

"That's the other part of the deal that lets you get out of facing the dragon. You'd have to abdicate in Furnael's favor."

Pirondael laughed. "So. Now we know what this is all about." His face grew somber. "And I'd thought better of you, Zherr. I wouldn't have thought you a traitor."

"*Traitor?*" Furnael snarled. "You call me a traitor? I haven't breathed an unfaithful breath, Pirondael, not until I was persuaded you sold out my barony, my people, and my friends."

"Hah. Sold out *indeed.* Barony Furnael was already lost, Baron. I'd been forced to write it off to the Holts. It was dead. If the corpse could serve Bieme, then—"

"I *held!*" Furnael slammed his fist against the wall. "And would have held out forever, if need be. But you, you treated us like gamepieces on a board—"

"Save me your noble pretensions, Baron. Put yourself in my place —what would you have done?"

Furnael paused for a moment. "I don't know," he said softly. "But I would have kept faith with my people, Pirondael. As I always have."

"Honorable of you," Pirondael sneered. "Very honorable. I did what I thought best for Bieme, and I'm not ashamed of it."

"You wouldn't be." Furnael strode to the curtain over the doorway and jerked it from its hooks. "But you ought to be."

The bound forms of ten soldiers of the House Guard stood silently there, Ahira, Henrad, and Beralyn collectively brandishing more than enough sharpened steel to assure their silence.

Furnael spun the nearest of the guards about and slashed the rope binding his hands. "What do you say to this, Guard Captain?"

It's nutcutting time, Walter thought. This was what it all depended on. If the kind of soldier who would remain proudly on station on the losing side of a war didn't care about what kind of man he had pledged his life to defend, then everything was shortly going to go to hell.

But if Pirondael's guards *did* care, if it *was* important to them that their prince be a man of honor, and not the kind of sniggling opportunist that the prince had proved himself to be . . .

The captain stood and faced Pirondael, tears streaming freely down his grizzled cheeks. "I would have served you to the last, *your majesty,*" he said, pronouncing the title like a curse. "I would have died protecting your body, pig." Wiping the tears away, he turned to Walter Slovotsky. "You mean to put Baron Furnael on the throne?" he asked quietly.

"If not, I've come a long way for damn little." Walter nodded.

"He's got as good a claim as anyone. And he doesn't betray his people or his friends."

"And what would you do with this?" He jerked a thumb toward the prince.

"If he abdicates in Furnael's favor, it would be up to Prince Furnael, no?"

"Banishment," Furnael said. "If he abdicates."

"Generous." The captain nodded. He held out a hand to the dwarf. "Give me a sword."

Ahira raised an eyebrow. *Well?* his expression asked.

Furnael didn't wait. He jerked his sword out of his scabbard and threw it hilt-first to the captain, who caught it, then balanced it on the flat of his palms.

"I swear my loyalty to you, Zherr Furnael," the captain said, "for as long as you are worthy of it." He offered Furnael the sword.

"Keep it," the baron said. "And these others?"

The captain nodded. "They are my men, majesty. I wouldn't have them in my company if they weren't worth having."

"Then please unbind their hands, friend Ahira."

"Excuse me." Walter raised a hand. "If you two will stop playing kiss-my-ring for a minute, we've still got an abdication to arrange."

The sword whistled through the air until the point rested just beneath Pirondael's chin, the hilt held firmly in the captain's hand. "I do not think there will be any problem," he said. "Will there, Pirondael?"

"N-no. I abdicate in favor of Tyr—" The prince went into a spasm of choking as the flat of the captain's sword slapped him across the throat.

"No. The choice is ours, not yours," the captain snarled. "Do you agree to that? Nod your head more briskly, Pirondael. Good. Taren, procure paper and a pen, and fetch the Warder of the Seal. No explanations—just bring him."

Walter looked at Furnael.

The baron laughed. "If you don't want to trust Captain—what *is* your name?"

"Garavar, majesty."

"Not majesty yet. As I was saying, Walter Slovotsky, if you do not wish to trust Garavar, who will be chief captain of my personal guard, I'll be more than happy to listen to alternatives."

Walter laughed. "Then be on your way," he said, gesturing with the crossbow.

That was a mistake. He never knew where Pirondael got the knife. It could have been hidden in the bedding and missed by Furnael in his search; it could have been concealed somewhere on Pirondael's ample person.

Six inches of steel flickered through the air until stopped by Furnael's throat.

Walter centered the crossbow on Pirondael's chest and jerked the trigger. The bolt caught the prince's shoulder. Walter whipped one of his throwing knives through the air, relishing in the meaty thunk as it sunk into Pirondael's chest, directly over the heart. A last knife caught Pirondael's twitching outflung palm, pinning it to the headboard.

He dropped his crossbow and rushed to Furnael's side. No good. There was no time to send for healing draughts.

Furnael was dead.

He crouched there for a long moment, until Garavar's shaking of his shoulder brought him back to the here-and-now.

Beralyn cradled the body in her lap, weeping silently, her husband's dead face hidden in her hair. Before, she had been able to face her husband's death almost casually, but not here, not now.

He glanced over at the bed. Pirondael's blind eyes stared glassily back at him.

Garavar shook his shoulder again. "What do we do now, Walter Slovotsky? Have you any good ideas?"

Walter stood, and forced himself to nod. *Shit. I'd better think fast. Technically, the heir is probably somebody like Tyrnael—or Thomen, maybe, if we assume that Pirondael actually abdicated in Furnael's favor. I guess we can wrap his hand around the seal long enough to stamp anything we want.*

But that won't do it. Tyrnael would probably have all our heads just on general principles, and Bieme doesn't need either a sixteen-year-old prince or some sort of regency.

"Yes," he said. "I have a suggestion. Pirondael abdicated in favor of whoever we choose, didn't he?" He took a deep breath.

Forgive me, my friend. "Now . . ."

CHAPTER TWENTY-FOUR

The Defense of Furnael Keep

In war more than anywhere else in the world things happen differently from what we had expected. . . .

—Karl von Clausewitz

Karl Cullinane walked the ramparts, looking off to where the Holts waited. His eyes teared, partly from the glare of the setting sun, partly from the acrid smoke that the light breeze wafted his way.

"Belay firing," he called out, his words picked up and echoed down the line of two hundred riflemen. Slowly, the ragged volley died out. "Clean and reload; oil patches, only," he said. "Aveneer, take over. Fire only at reasonable targets."

He turned and climbed down the ladder to the courtyard below, then walked over to where Ellegon lay sprawled on the dirt. The dragon's eyes were almost impossibly bleary, but they still glowed with life.

What is going on, Karl? Ellegon's mental voice was still weak, but growing firmer as every day brought the dragon more strength. Just today, he had been able to lift his head from the ground for the first time.

"Damned if I know," he said, reaching out and rubbing his fingers against the hard scales of the dragon's jaw. "They're redeploying a bit, but nothing much." Just the sort of idle shuffling of positions that would keep the defenders worried, but it didn't look as if the Holts were really getting ready for an assault, not yet.

It just didn't make any sense. After Tennetty's last recon, she had reported that the Holts were doing absolutely nothing, other than holding position. No building at all—no ladders, no siege engines, no beams being cut for shoring the walls of tunnels—nothing. Somewhere between thirty-two hundred and four thousand Holtish troops were sitting there, the nearest just out of rifleshot, all of them waiting.

Now I know how a candle on a birthday cake feels. But even so, even if Ahrmin is on his way, why the wait?

Why would the top Holtish commander be willing to let line troops stand idle, when they could undoubtedly be put to good use in the north after polishing off Furnael Keep?

What could they be waiting for?

I don't know. Maybe Tennetty would have some ideas?

Speaking of Tennetty . . . where is she?

On the northern . . . rampart. I've sent for her; she's on her way.

"Shh," Karl whispered. "Save your strength. Sleep, if you can."

Young dragons don't need much sleep.

"You don't look all that young right now."

Good point. The plate-sized eyes sagged shut.

Tennetty's slim form appeared atop the rampart; she bounded down the rungs to the bottom.

"You sent for me?" she asked, her index finger working its way under her eyepatch as if of its own volition.

"I was considering it—but Ellegon decided for me," he said, as he beckoned her over to the well in the center of the courtyard. He worked the crank and raised the bucket, scooping out a dipperful for Tennetty first, and then for himself.

The water was cool and wonderful as he tilted his head back, pouring it in his mouth, relishing the way the icy overflow ran down his beard and onto his chest.

That was the nice thing about now: Every sense was sharp, every sensation special, even the slightly metallic taste of Furnael Keep well water. Karl nodded softly to himself. It was easy to forgive your friends, at the end of it all.

"Move it, you," a merry basso sounded from the ramparts, as Aveneer brought the two hundred riflemen down from their full alert, passing out watch assignments for the night.

Karl nodded in approval. The Holts almost certainly weren't going to try for some sort of tricky night assault, but there was no sense in taking chances.

He turned to Tennetty. "You think we're going to get any visitors tonight?"

She shook her head. "No. And I don't understand it. I haven't seen any evidence of their building siege towers or engines—or even ladders."

He nodded. "Me neither. It's like we're all waiting for someone, or something. But I don't understand why."

"Ahrmin, of course . . . I can see that he'd want to be in on the end." She fingered the amulet around her neck. "But why would the Holts want to wait for him?"

"I don't know."

Tennetty cocked her head to one side. "Want me to find out, Karl?"

"What say *we* find out?"

She shook her head. "I don't think you can sneak well enough. Maybe Piell and me?"

"I've got a better idea; let's go talk to Andy." He walked toward the nearest door into the keep proper and headed for the suite that he and Andy-Andy were using.

She was seated in front of a flickering lamp that stood on a wide wooden table; a huge leather book was open in front of her as she carefully studied the words that Karl couldn't even see.

He knew better than to interfere while she was studying, so he waited until she lifted her head before he cleared his throat.

"Karl." She smiled as she turned in the chair and rose to her feet, stretching catlike in her gray robes. "Are they still out of range?"

"Yeah. Funniest damn siege I've ever seen. How's your invisibility spell these days?"

"Good enough," she said, then paused for a moment as she sucked air in through her teeth. "You're planning on taking a walk tonight?"

"Tennetty and I are, if you can manage it."

Tennetty raised her eyebrow. "Be still, my heart."

The tension between the two of them had evaporated in the past days. A small part of it was that he needed somebody around who he was used to working with; with Chak dead, Piell occupied with his longbow squad, and Walter and Ahira gone, Tennetty was about the only one remaining from his original team he was really used to.

The big reason, of course, was simpler.

I'm not going to make it alive out of this one, he thought. There was no sense in taking hard feelings to the grave, not when the object of the anger was really a friend. Tennetty had had a horrible breach of judgment back in Enkiar, true, but she was a friend.

And death was a time to forgive one's friends, a time for gentle goodbyes.

"When are the two of you planning on leaving?" Andy-Andy asked.

He reached out and rubbed his thumb gently against her jaw. "About midnight, I thought. Give us some time to ourselves, before."

"Good." She smiled up at him. "I guess I didn't wear you out last night."

"Apparently not."

The conviction that his own end was near had brought a fierce passion to their lovemaking, and he didn't feel like stinting himself. Not when the end approached so quickly.

Maybe, if Walter and Furnael were successful in Biemestren, relief would be on its way, eventually. Hell, if they had actually gotten to Biemestren, and in the unlikely event that (a) they could put Furnael on the throne quickly, and (b) Furnael had ordered the House Guard to ride immediately, and (c) the House Guard had obeyed, and with alacrity, and (d) if they came in enough force to break through the Holtish roadblock on the west road, then relief could arrive in another week or so.

But that wasn't about to happen.

It probably wouldn't make a difference, or not enough of one. Since the Holts weren't building catapults and onagers, it was likely that already-built ones were on their way down the road.

Maybe that was it. But certainly Karl and the defenders didn't have forever. The Holts either knew or had to assume that the dragon was recovering within the walls; they and the slavers among them would have no desire to stall the assault until the dragon was recovered enough to fight.

He shook his head. Hell, they could take the keep by rushing it with siege ladders, if they didn't have a more elegant, a less costly way.

But maybe, just perhaps, the Holts would hold off until Ellegon got well enough to flee, if not to fight.

And then, beautiful, we can get you out of here. You, Thomen

Furnael, perhaps Erek and Ranella. I'll give the orders, and see that it's done.

And then, he thought, lifting her from the chair, gathering her in his arms, *we'll give Ahrmin and the rest of those bastards a last run that'll make them wake up screaming for the rest of their lives.*

Tennetty cleared her throat. "You want me to put together a couple of kits? Crossbows, I suppose—can't use guns. . . . Andrea? Can you include the bows and everything in the spell?"

"Yes, but . . ." Andy-Andy pushed away from him. "I . . . can't keep you invisible for much time at all." She wrinkled her brow as she looked up at Karl. "Just a few minutes, if it's going to be both of you. Enough time to get out—"

"But not enough to get back in, eh?" He smiled. "Shouldn't be a problem. We'll leave just after dark, and coordinate our return with Aveneer. Tennetty, include a signal rocket in our kit, and two grenades each, plus fuses." He smiled at Andy-Andy as he jerked his thumb toward their sleeping quarters. "I'll be with you in a minute."

Andy-Andy smiled gently back at him and walked away, her spell book tucked carefully under her arm.

He turned to Tennetty. "There's something I've been meaning to talk to you about—"

"I know; consider it said." She eyed him levelly. "I'd better get us packed up for tonight." She started to walk away, then turned back. "It's all been worth it . . . hasn't it, Karl?"

You know, Tennetty, I've never heard you sound unsure of yourself before. I'm not sure I like it.

He forced a smile. "Count on it. Now get lost for a while."

Aveneer was waiting for them near the front gate. His eyes sparkled in the light of the torches as he shook his massive head. "It's not been my experience that generals do their own scouting, Karl," he said, "and I don't like the idea."

Frandred nodded, then shook his head. "Bad idea, Karl, bad."

Karl had never liked the way that Aveneer's second-in-command always had to say something twice. It reminded him of a retarded boy who had been his neighbor, long ago. Long, long ago . . .

"You think that man of yours is a better scout than I am?"

Aveneer nodded. "Possibly."

"He is, of course he is."

Karl nodded a false agreement. "Then fine, bring him up. One thing, though: Would he be able to tell a mobile gunshop from a mobile smithy?"

"No, but that's not relevant." Aveneer shook his head. "It wouldn't be his responsibility to decide, but to report."

"Right." He crooked a finger and beckoned Aveneer close. "And it isn't your responsibility," he whispered, "to tell me what my job is; it's your responsibility to carry out my orders. Understood?"

Aveneer pulled back and snorted. "True. But I'd be a bit careful, were I you. Eh?" He clapped his hand to Karl's shoulder. "You wouldn't want to get killed prematurely." He clasped Karl's hand in his. "Just in case you don't return, any advice?"

"Nothing much." Karl shrugged. "Except the obvious. Hold off using the grenades until the very last. You've got to get them bunched in order to get the right payoff. When they rush, I'd try for volley fire, instead of fire-at-will—you might be able to break the rush." He walked to the portcullis and looked out.

Perhaps five hundred yards down the road leading from the keep, the nearest of the Holtish encampments waited, campfires blazing away into the night. He slipped the heavy bolts on the man-high door that formed part of the base of the portcullis and then walked back to where Andy-Andy and Tennetty stood waiting.

He quickly stripped off his jerkin and leggings, then pulled a loose pair of shorts on over his shoes, belting the shorts tightly around his waist. That was a trick that Walter Slovotsky had taught him, long ago: On a recon, it was best to keep as little as possible between your skin and the air. It was almost as though he grew extra nerves; it was certain that he felt more vulnerable when creeping almost naked through the night.

Tennetty smeared the greasepaint over his skin, then strapped a crossbow across his back and handed him a drawstring-topped leather quiver, which he tied to his right thigh.

He looked at his swordbelt, debating whether or not it was right to take it. No, he decided; the crossbow and quiver were already going to be enough trouble to handle, and if this recon came down to swordplay, he was already in too deep.

He nodded to himself. Best to go as lightly armed as possible. He selected a Nehera-made bowie and belted its scabbard around his waist, thonging the knife into the scabbard. Logical; he wouldn't need the saber, but a knife could be handy.

To hell with logic. He belted on the saber.

Tennetty had already armed herself and stood ready, her fists clenching and unclenching.

Karl turned to his wife. "Do it," he said.

Andy-Andy began to murmur the words of the spell, the harsh, flat sounds that could only be forgotten, never saved in the mind.

The world slowly went gray around him, until it settled into a total black. That was the trouble with a simple invisibility spell: It made its subject totally transparent to light, and that included his retinas. Transparent retinas couldn't react to light.

But this wasn't a simple invisibility spell; Andy wasn't done. Her hand reached out and touched his forehead, the fingertips sliding down until she touched his eyelids.

The pressure of her fingers increased as the words of the spell finished.

She released his lids; he opened his eyes. Two feet away and a foot below his eye level, he could see the dark discontinuity that marked where Tennetty's eye was.

Karl looked down. He could see right through himself, all the way down to the outline of his bootprints in the dirt.

He reached out and took Tennetty's hand.

"Let's go," he whispered. They would have to touch each other; in the darkness outside the keep, he wouldn't be able to see her any more than the Holts could see him.

They stepped out through the door and into the night. Down the road, eager-eyed sentries had perhaps already noted the open door, and were probably waiting to see if this time it meant that somebody was leaving the keep, trying to slip away.

But they had been keeping watch for five nights now, and every night Karl had ordered the small door opened, then closed several times, both when Tennetty was trying to sneak away for a quiet recon and not. By now, the watchers were probably persuaded that this was simply intended to spook them.

Karl and Tennetty walked swiftly down the road.

By the time they had faded back into visibility, they were far down the road, well concealed in the trees.

The main Holtish camp spread out in front of them. Despite the greater size of his force, the leader of this expedition had followed the same general plan as the leader of the last one. He had split off three cavalry units to camp separately opposite the keep's other walls, and even put his main camp on the same ground his predecessor had chosen.

But that was where the similarity ended. This Holtish general was much more security-conscious. There were twelve watchfires spread around the camp's perimeter, each manned by at least twenty guards. And even within the camp there was added security: The inner portion of his main camp was a corral-like compound, perhaps forty yards across, containing what Karl was sure was the powder magazine, as well as several boxy travel wagons—one of them a wizard's wagon, no doubt.

There was something else in that corral as well, something that scouts hadn't reported seeing. But it was almost hidden between the wagons and covered by a tarpaulin, and all he could tell was that it was longer than it was wide, which didn't do a damn bit of good.

"That . . . thing in the compound wasn't there last night." Tennetty looked at him. "Do you think we could get in there?" she whispered, her words barely carrying the few inches to his ear.

"Not and get out, that's for sure."

"I wasn't talking about getting out. If we could blow up their magazine, scatter the powder, the morning dew would finish the job for us."

A nice idea in principle, but it just wouldn't work. The interior of the camp was clearly too well guarded—he wouldn't even be able to get within throwing range. Besides, unless it was very well thrown, a grenade probably wouldn't break open the barrels containing the Holts' reserve supply of slaver powder.

He shook his head. "I don't think even Walter could get in there." Damn. He lifted his amulet. It was flashing red, though; clearly, the Holts had added a wizard in the past few days, as well as whatever that thing under the tarp was.

He looked up at the overhanging branches of the dying oak. It might be possible to get about twenty, maybe twenty-five feet up, and that might give a decent view of whatever was going on in the camp. "How's your tree-climbing?"

"Better than yours. And quieter. Give me a hand up." She quickly stripped off her weapons and boots. Karl cocked and loaded both crossbows, then set them carefully on the ground before boosting Tennetty up to an overhanging branch.

Silently, she climbed, while Karl kept watch. She would be almost invisible to anyone looking, but only almost. Off in the distance, Karl could hear something moving through the field. He hoped that Tennetty could hear it, too, but loosed his sword in its scabbard in case she couldn't.

The sound grew closer; a whisk of leather on grass.

Great. Patrolling Holts weren't what he needed right now, but it looked as if he was going to get them anyway. If he was lucky, as they passed by his position they'd be discussing whatever strategy the Holtish general was planning for the morning.

He wasn't lucky. Two Holtish soldiers, each armed with a slaver rifle, walked by, only yards from where Karl huddled in the shadow of the old oak's projecting roots. It seemed for a moment as though one of them looked directly at him before the Holt's gaze swung by, but perhaps he was mistaken.

In a few minutes, they were gone.

Tennetty dropped lightly from an overhanging branch. "Unless they've got another cripple with them, he's *there*. I saw him coming out of the magazine with a wizard."

"Ahrmin?"

"Who else? He was showing the wizard that ram."

"Ram?"

"The . . . thing near the powder magazine. Ahrmin had the covering off for a moment. It's a ram, a damn large one."

That was strange. A ram attack, intended to breach the keep's walls, ought to be accompanied by some other sort of attack elsewhere; by itself, the ram and its crew would be too vulnerable to concentrated fire from the defenders. So where were the onagers and catapults or the siege ladders?

A chill washed across him. "Describe this ram."

"Strange-looking thing. Like a long metal sausage, about twice as long as you're tall. It's mounted on a cart. I guess they're going to have some sort of rigging for horses to propel the thing, but the wagon it's on is rigged for pulling, not pushing." She shrugged. "And why it has a hole in one end . . ."

A hole?

Omigod. "That's not a ram. It's a cannon." Which explained what the Holts had been waiting for. A cannon could shatter the walls, or, firing chainshot or grapeshot, quickly reduce the defenders on the walls to bloody hunks of flesh. The Holts had been holding up the attack, waiting for this to arrive.

His heart thudding in his chest, he forced himself to breathe slowly. He would have to see that Andy-Andy was smuggled out, and not tomorrow, but tonight. The cannon that they had waited for had arrived; the Holts would attack in the morning.

But would she go? And who could he trust to smuggle her out of here? *Damn* Walter Slovotsky for taking Ahira.

Tennetty. It would have to be Tennetty.

"What is a cannon?" Tennetty whispered.

"Like a big rifle. Except that it can knock down walls."

"Knock down—I see." She nodded sagely. "How do you counter a cannon?"

"You spike it—" He caught himself. Maybe? No. There were ample guards around, and a wizard within the compound, likely there either to assist in the attack or to keep the slaver powder from picking up water from the air and self-detonating. "Or you do what Chak did, except on a large scale. Without enough powder, a cannon is useless."

She nodded wisely. "Then we'd better get to it, no?"

Ridiculous. Absolutely ridiculous. There wasn't a chance in a billion that the two of them could get through the Holts and into the magazine, and there wasn't a chance in a million that a large group could.

But a group didn't have to. Only one had to, if that one knew what to do. If in the noise and confusion, one man could break through to the magazine or have just enough time to spike the cannon, that might buy some time for Slovotsky to put Furnael on the throne and bring relief to the keep.

At the very least, it would force the Holts to switch strategies, and spend some time building ladders or siege engines.

"Karl, we may never get another chance at him. We've got to—"

"Don't tell me what we have to do. Ahrmin is secondary, dammit. The cannon's the first priority. Listen," he said. "Get back to the keep—"

"No. You can't do it yourself."

"Damn right, Tennetty. Bring back as many people as you're sure you can smuggle out without being seen. No guns; we're not going to have time to reload, and even if we pull this off, they're going to need them in the keep. But load up with grenades. And all of the smith's hammers and a dozen spikes."

"And if we can do that . . . ?"

"The magazine and the cannon first. Then we kill the little bastard."

"Fine." She smiled, and turned to leave.

He caught her arm. "One more thing: Bring my clothes. I don't want to die half-naked."

It felt as if it took forever for Tennetty to get back. By the time she arrived, seven others in tow, Karl had made and rejected a thousand different, useless plans for getting in and out of the Holts' camp all by himself.

Seven others. That was all she had brought back. Karl didn't admonish her; she knew better than he did how many she could sneak out of the castle.

But she could easily have picked a worse seven: Piell, Firkh, Hervean, Rahnidge, Thermen, Erek . . . and Aveneer.

"I thought I left you in command," Karl said to the red-bearded Nyph, as he handed Aveneer his share of the grenades. It worked out to nine each, with two extras, both of which Karl appropriated for himself.

"You did. And *I* left Valeran in command." Aveneer shrugged. "I've spent far too much of my life away from the center of things. Figured that this one time I'd make absolutely sure I don't die of old age."

Karl shrugged. There was nothing that could be done about that now, even if he didn't want Aveneer and his battleaxe around.

Which he very much did. "Fine," Karl said. "First thing, we've got to be sure that we take out the wizard." He lifted his amulet. "This won't provide much protection, but it's all that we've got—"

"No." Tennetty looked over at him soberly. "Andrea sends a message: The wizard is hers. When she hears the sound of the first grenade going off, she will—how did she put it—'brighten her fire.' The Holts' wizard will see that as a challenge."

Ellegon, relay—He caught himself. He was out of range, and there wasn't a damn thing that he could do. Except—"My orders stand. If you see the wizard, take him out. Understood?"

Tennetty looked him square in the face. "Even if that means missing the magazine? Or the cannon?"

He grabbed her by the tunic. "You challenging my orders, Tennetty?"

She raised her palms. "No. I'm asking what they are. Think about it."

Andy . . . He forced himself to keep his harsh whisper under control. "Get the magazine and the cannon. No matter what."

Accepting his tunic from Tennetty, Karl drew it on and belted it tightly around his hips with a length of rope. After inserting the fuses in the detonators and the detonators in the grenades, he carefully tucked them into his tunic, their iron sides cold against his belly, then buckled on his swordbelt, with the pouch tied tightly to its right side.

"Keep an even spacing," he said. "Not too close—if a shot hits you in the wrong place, you're going up, complete with grenades."

Tennetty smiled. "Right, right. Do we get to it or not?"

There had been a time, long, long ago, when a younger Karl Cullinane wouldn't have been able to face the idea of walking into the lion's mouth.

But that was long, long ago. He looked from face to face, trying to come up with the right words.

He couldn't find any.

"Follow me," he said.

On hands and knees, they crept through the waist-high grasses in the dark, Tennetty and Piell armed with crossbows in addition to their grenades. With a bit of luck, perhaps all nine of them could get to the Holts' outer perimeter before they were spotted.

Their luck was not in; when they were still a good fifty yards from the outer edge of the cleared area that marked the Holtish camp, a harsh voice called out a warning; a shot rang out, a bullet hissed overhead.

Piell rose, his crossbow discharging. The bolt caught the watchman in the chest; he screamed hideously. Hervean rose to his feet, a sizzling grenade in his hand.

But the Holtish guards reacted quickly; Piell and Hervean were cut down by a flurry of gunfire, Hervean's grenade exploding while still in his hands, miraculously not triggering any of his or Piell's remaining grenades.

Already on his feet and on the run, Karl struck the tip of a fuse on his swordbelt buckle and sent a grenade hissing toward the Holts. It landed in between three of them and exploded, sending bodies and pieces of bodies flying into the night.

An explosion on his right shook him from his feet. As he rose, he pulled out another grenade, struck it, threw it, then another.

Three Holtish swordsmen came at him. Karl drew his saber and parried the first's lunge, letting the rush carry the man past, while he speared the next one through the throat.

The third one smiled as he lunged for Karl.

The smile vanished as he went down, a crossbow bolt transfixing his neck. Tennetty laughed as she sent another grenade hissing off into the Holts. Karl drew one from his tunic and threw it into the watchfire, not bothering to strike it. It blew almost immediately, turning the fire into a shower of sparks and flinders.

Karl couldn't see what had happened to most of the others; all except Tennetty and Aveneer had been carried away from him.

"This way," he shouted, as the three of them worked their way farther into the camp, Aveneer using his axe like a scythe to clear the way, Karl and Tennetty lighting and throwing grenades one-handed, their swords weaving like snakes.

The flat of his sword parallel to the ground, Karl speared a Holt through the chest, then kicked the body off his wet blade before turning to cut down one on Tennetty's back.

Less than a hundred yards in front of him, the Holts' wizard stood within the inner camp, halfway between the magazine shed and the cannon.

Lightning issued from the wizard's fingertips, crackling off into the night.

Andy—"No!" He fought his way toward the wizard, but a heavy blow hit him on the right side, just above the waist, knocking him down before he heard the rifle's crack. As he tried to get to his feet, a booted foot caught him in the chest, knocking him back, half out of breath.

Instinct brought his sword up, slipping the saber's tip up the other's thigh and into his groin, Karl lurched away, giving his saber a savage twist before he leaped to his feet. Another Holt was bringing a rifle to bear on Tennetty; Karl booted the weapon out of the man's hands, then caught him by the hair, the Holt's body spasming twice as he absorbed two shots meant for Karl.

He drew his saber across the Holt's throat before sending him on his way, then decided that it had been too long since he'd set off a grenade, and quickly lit off two.

Thunder echoed the grenades' explosion.

Now I'll get the wiz—

Where *was* the Holts' wizard? Where he had stood but moments before, there was nothing, nothing but a small crater.

He felt Tennetty pulling at his arm. Momentarily, the screaming and the shooting rushed around them like a stream around an out-thrust rock.

"I took out the wizard," she shouted. "Hope you don't mind."

There wasn't time to thank her. "I'm going for the cannon. Cover me."

She fended off two attackers as he dashed toward the cannon, dropping his sword and drawing the spike and hammer from his pouch.

A heavy weight landed on his back; he thrust back an elbow, then swung the smith's hammer around, feeling the Holt's skull cave in like an eggshell.

Spiking the cannon took only a second, but as he dropped his hammer and stooped to retrieve his sword, a sharp blow to his back knocked him down to the ground. He clawed inside his tunic for another grenade, but they had all bounced away in the dark, and the weakness in his side and back was spreading.

There was another explosion somewhere off to the rear, but that wouldn't do any good. The magazine was ahead, not behind.

He started to crawl toward it as thunder shattered the sky into rain.

A dark mass crashed into him from the side; blindly, his hand clawed at the other's face, only to encounter an eyepatch. "Tennetty!"

She smiled weakly at him, her mouth working, but no sound issuing from between her bloody lips as her eyes sagged shut.

I'm sorry, Tennetty, Rahff, Fialt, Erek, Aveneer, Chak—all of you—

But *rain?* It wasn't rainy season—

Andy. It was a goodbye from Andy, her way of telling him that she had survived. The Holts' wizard wouldn't have started a rainstorm, even if he could have; you couldn't reload in the rain, because the powder would get wet. And the Holts were under attack; they would want to reload. Now, they couldn't—

No, they couldn't, could they? Real gunpowder would become wet and useless in the rain.

But slaver gunpowder had to stay safely under cover, or it would turn back into superheated steam.

The powder would get wet. His fumbling fingers tore at Tennetty's tunic until he found a grenade. He struck the fuse against his thumbnail and flicked it toward the magazine shack.

The powder would get wet. The explosion tore off one wall of the shack, sending the barrels inside clattering.

He gathered Tennetty against his chest as he heard the crack of splitting wood . . .

. . . and the largest explosion of all, that shattered the world into white-hot sparks of pain that quickly went black.

CHAPTER TWENTY-FIVE

Arta Myrdhyn

What though the field be lost?
All is not lost; th' unconquerable will,
And study of revenge, immortal hate,
And courage never to submit or yield.

—John Milton

For a long time, there was nothing. Nobody was there . . . and no body was there.

And then there was a spark, and the spark thought: *So this is what being dead feels like.*

"I doubt that you have nearly enough information to decide that yet, Karl," an airy tenor voice out of his past said. "Although if you ever do find out for certain, I would be most grateful if you would let me know. If you *can* let me know, that is. It's something I have wondered about for . . . for a long time." Deighton chuckled thinly, a hollow sound.

There was no question; the voice was Deighton's. Professor Arthur Simpson Deighton, Ph.D. Lecturer in, though not practitioner of, ethics; gamemaster, wizard.

The bastard who sent us all across.

"My parentage is not at issue here. And I won't accept the blame for the second time, Karl. As I recall, you had a knife to my throat." A thin chuckle echoed through the empty universe. "Although I would gladly have done it simply for the asking . . . as you may have surmised by now."

Where are you, Deighton? Hell, where am I, for that matter?

"Matter, Karl, has rather little to do with it. Would you settle for illusion? It will be quite persuasive, I can promise you that."

What the—

"I'll take that as an assent."

There were no loud sounds or bright lights. The universe simply came back, until Karl Cullinane was sitting in a wooden chair at the battered mahogany table in Room 109 of the Student Union.

The room was as they'd left it on that long-ago night: books and coats piled against the wall and on the extra chairs; pens, pencils, paper, and dice scattered around the battered surface of the old mahogany table. He looked up at the overhead lights. Strange, so strange to see fluorescent lights again. No flicker, just a steady light.

Slowly, gingerly, he got to his feet, waiting for his wounds to start hurting.

But they didn't. He felt fine, except that he wasn't himself, not the self he should have been, not here. While he was wearing jeans and a slightly tight plaid shirt—just as he had way back then—he was still himself from the Other Side, not the skinny Karl Cullinane of This Side.

He flexed his right biceps in the sleeve; the fabric split along the seam.

"And yes, if you prick yourself, you will bleed," the directionless voice said. "But it is all illusion. Have an illusionary cup of coffee, and perhaps a phantom cigarette. You may feel better."

He looked down at the table. A white porcelain mug of coffee sat steaming next to a battered half-empty pack of Camel Filters.

"Drink up, Karl."

He shrugged and picked up the coffee cup, then took a cautious sip.

Good Colombian beans, gently roasted, well laced with rich cream and sugar. Karl had once thought coffee an acquired addiction, but one that could be broken with a bit of abstinence. He now knew he was wrong: This was absolutely delicious. He picked up the cellophane-wrapped pack of cigarettes and extracted one, snickering at the Surgeon General's warning.

I don't suppose us dead folks have to worry about whether something is hazardous to our health. He stuck the filter between his lips. "Light?"

"As I told you, you are not dead. Still, an illusory cigarette is harmless. Enjoy." The end of the cigarette flared into flame.

Karl inhaled the rich smoke . . .

. . . and doubled over in a spasm of coughing. He threw the cigarette away.

"I said it was harmless, not unirritating."

"Fine." He wiped his mouth with the back of his hand. "Deighton —or should I call you Arta Myrdhyn?"

"Either will serve."

"Why don't you show yourself?"

"If you'd like." Across the table from him, the air shimmered momentarily, and there he sat, just as Karl had seen him on a night more than seven years before. A thin, stoop-shouldered man in a tan wool suit, puffing on the bulldog briar pipe that was responsible for the burns that marked the pockets and arms of the suit.

Deighton removed the pipe from his mouth and touched it to his lined forehead in a brief, mocking salute.

"How have you been, Karl?" He puffed a cloud of smoke into the air.

Karl considered lunging across the table for Deighton, but decided against it. This was either some sort of very real dream or it was Deighton's turf. Either way, jumping Deighton was unlikely to get any results.

"I've had friends die because of you, Arta Myrdhyn," he said.

"True." Deighton nodded slowly, gravely. "True enough. And I assure you that I'm as aware of that as you are. Including Jason Parker, by the way. It was rather nice of Andrea to name your son after him." His face grew pensive for a moment. "I . . . truly didn't mean any of you any harm. And I truly would tell you everything, Karl, if there weren't sufficient reasons not to."

"What do you want?"

"We had an agreement, Karl Cullinane." The pleasant demeanor vanished, as Deighton's eyes turned icy. "You agreed to keep my sword for your son, hold it for him until he was ready to use it. In return for that promise, you were allowed to use it against that young fool Thyren. But you didn't keep your promise, Karl."

Karl pushed himself to his feet. "Not my son, bastard. You keep your filthy hands off of him."

"Sit down."

Karl gathered himself for a leap—

—but found himself sitting in the chair.

"Illusion, remember? My illusion, not yours." Deighton puffed at the pipe for several seconds. "I'll offer you another deal: Fetch the sword for Jason, hold it for him until he's ready for it, and I'll send you back."

Karl dialed for a calm voice. "I thought you said this was an illusion," he said, pleased to find that he could talk calmly. "How can you send me back?"

"Right . . . now, I guess you would call it?—right now, Karl, your body is lying on the battlefield, a knife's edge from death. Normally, I couldn't communicate with you across the barrier between This Side and the Other Side, but this is . . . a special circumstance. While you're not on This Side at all, you're not fully on the Other Side. Does that make sense to you?"

Deighton cocked his head to one side as he steepled his fingers in front of his chin. "I couldn't bring you back from the dead, and I wouldn't push you over the precipice, but I will . . . use my best efforts to hold you on the side of life, for the time being. If, that is, we have an agreement."

"No deals." Karl shook his head. "No deals, Art. You're not going to play around with my son's life the way you have with mine," he said, instantly resolute. He was surprised at himself. There had been a time when he had had difficulty with commitment, even when it was only a matter of committing himself to a course of study.

But that had been long, long ago.

"Yes," Deighton said, studying him closely, "there have been some changes. It is clear nothing I would be willing to do would make you change your mind." He rose to his feet. "Well, I suppose that is that," he said matter-of-factly, tossing his pipe aside. It vanished.

The room started to melt away, the colors running together. Karl braced himself for the final darkness. *Goodbye, Andy . . .*

"Oh, don't be so melodramatic." The room solidified again. "You may dispense with the heroics for now. Save them for when they're appropriate. As they will be. I still have to send you back," Deighton said, shaking a finger at him, "although you really ought to be more careful. It's unlikely I'll be able to do even this little for you next time we meet."

"Next time?"

Deighton nodded. "Once more, Karl Cullinane. Once more."

Suddenly, Deighton stood at his side. The old man stuck out a hand. "Be well, Karl Cullinane. Take good care of that son of yours. He's awfully important, as you've suspected."

Karl didn't take the hand. "I will take care of my son, Deighton, whether you want me to or not."

"I'd expect no less."

"Just tell me one thing, please—why?"

"I can't tell you. Not now."

"Will you ever?"

"No." Deighton caught his lip between his teeth. "I'm sorry, Karl. I can't explain it to you right now, and I doubt I'll have the opportunity the next time we meet." He clapped his hand to Karl's shoulder. "Be well, my friend."

"You're no friend of mine!"

Deighton looked surprised. "Of course not. But you are one of mine. It is my fond hope that you will do me a great favor, the next time we meet. Until then, be well."

"Wait—"

"One more thing: Ahrmin isn't dead. He got away again. While I can't blame you for this one, you really ought to have been more thorough in Melawei, Karl."

Deighton smiled genially. "Be well."

The room melted away.

CHAPTER TWENTY-SIX

The Silver Crown

Uneasy lies the head that wears a crown.

—William Shakespeare

"Karl," Andy-Andy's voice called to him, sweeter in his ears than anything he had ever heard. It occurred to him that she had been calling his name over and over again—for minutes, or was it hours?

She sounds worried. His eyelids weren't heavier than twin Volkswagens, so he opened them. It didn't make much of a difference: The room was dark, and it was far too much effort to focus. He was stretched out on a down mattress, the heavy blankets piled on his chest threatening to interfere with his breathing.

"Karl," she said urgently, "can you hear me?"

"Of course I can hear you," he tried to say, but the words came out as *glmph.*

He can hear you perfectly well. Ellegon's mental voice was firm. *Karl, don't talk. Just use your mind—assuming you have one. I'll relay.*

Fine. Got to tell her about Deighton—

Save that for later.

But—

But nothing; you've been dreaming about nothing else since they brought you within range. I know it all.

Ellegon—

Shut up and listen. You're the luckiest human that ever there was. As far as blood goes, Andrea thinks you're down more than a quart, so you have to take it easy. We pulled five bullets out of your hide; none of them hit anything vital. And not only did you fall into the cannon's blast shadow—that's what saved your life—but Andrea got to you with the healing draughts quickly enough to save everything except most of three fingers on your left hand. You've been hovering on the edge for eleven days now, and we've all been worrying about whether or not you were ever coming out. Happy?

His eyelids had increased in mass until they were much heavier than Buicks, so he let them sag shut.

Tennetty, Aveneer, Erek—did they—

Tennetty's fine, Karl. She cracked some ribs, that's all. Although once we figured out that you were going to be okay, she did have some words about you pawing around inside her tunic. Says if you want to do that again you should ask really prettily.

Ellegon, you're not telling me about the others. Did any of them—

No. None of them made it.

His fists started to clench, but he didn't even have the strength to do that. *The Holts and the slavers—*

Chased all to hell and gone. After the explosion, Valeran led a rifle company out after them. The Holts couldn't use their own guns, not with Andrea keeping up a light drizzle; Valeran captured about two hundred, killed more than three times that number, and sent the rest running. Now go back to sleep.

The next time he woke, light was streaming in through the mottled glass window, splashing warmly, brightly on the bed.

Andy-Andy was next to him, sitting on a low stool, her face only a couple of feet from his. She smiled at him as she reached out and took his hand.

"Hello there," she said, her calm, level voice belying the exhaustion written in her face. The dark shadows under her red-rimmed eyes showed that she clearly needed a night's sleep.

"Hi." Lifting and dropping his hand to pat the mattress next to him wasn't quite impossible. "Get . . . in."

"Really?" She brightened. "You're getting better quickly, but not that quickly."

"No. Sleep."

"Maybe later. Would you like some broth?"

I've already sent down to the kitchen for the food. Andrea, I've got to tell him.

"It can *wait!*" she hissed.

That is a matter of opinion. Mine differs from yours. Karl, Walter wants you to know that Pirondael did abdicate, just as you wanted, but Furnael didn't survive through Biemestren.

Furnael was dead. That meant that Thomen was now the prince? A bit young, but Beralyn might be a decent regent.

Guess again. Thomen is Baron Furnael; his mother will be regent, but only of barony Furnael.

Wait. If Pirondael abdicated in Zherr Furnael's favor, then—

*But he *didn't.* What Prince Pirondael agreed to do was to abdicate in favor of Captain Garavar's selection. As far as Garavar and the rest of the House Guard are concerned, that pretty much settles it: Garavar picks the next prince, and if the rest of the barons don't like it, they can try to revolt.*

Who's this Garavar person?

Officially, he's a guard captain in the House Guard. Unofficially, he's the Biemish commander-in-chief, although that'll have to be ratified by the new prince.

Great. So who is the prince? Some—

You.

Very funny.

I thought so, too. But Captain Garavar of the House Guard is here along with all of the House Guard except for a skeleton force that's waiting at Biemestren castle, and Garavar and the two thousand House Guardsmen don't think it funny at all. Matter of fact, he's pretty damn impressed with the firepower your majesty is bringing to the throne, including one spiked slaver cannon, a few hundred real gunpowder guns, a dozen hand grenades, and—ahem!—one slightly damaged dragon. Dowager Baroness Beralyn has dispatched messengers to the remaining barons, pledging barony Furnael's loyalty to your majesty, and explaining that you and five hundred men just scattered two regiments of Holts and slavers all to hell—which ought to impress them.

This is all crazy, you know.

That is entirely a matter of opinion. If I were you, I'd try to get used to it. Now go back to sleep.

But—

That wasn't a suggestion.

None of it made any sense to him.
Sleep, on the other hand, did.

Sleep, food, and rest gradually brought back some of his strength. Within three days, Andrea decided that he could have visitors, as long as they didn't tire him.

Walter Slovotsky was the first. "Hey, Prince, how you doing?" he asked, manifestly pleased with himself. As usual.

Karl pushed away the bowl of soup that Andy-Andy was trying to force on him. "No more beef stock. I want a beef*steak*. Thick one. Pan-fried. With butter, lots of it. And corn—on the cob. And maybe some deep-fried chotte—"

"Whoa, hero." She laughed, kissing him lightly on the forehead. "Take it slow." She gave him another sisterly peck.

Karl quietly resolved to even the score for that, and shortly.

Sex. All this one thinks about is—

Shh.

Andy-Andy rose to leave the room, stopping for a moment to whisper to Walter that she wanted him to make the visit short.

"Well," Slovotsky said, shaking his head, "I'll keep it as short as possible; there's a lot to catch up on."

"Think about it." Her face stern, she held a hand in front of Walter's face and murmured a few harsh syllables. Sparks arced from her thumb to her forefinger. "Just a few minutes, I said."

"Right. Just a couple of minutes. One minute. Thirty seconds—whatever you say." Slovotsky waited until the door shut behind her. "Whew!" He shook his head. "I'll be happy to get back to Kirah. *My* wife isn't deadly." He threw a hip over the edge of the bed. "How long you figure you'll be laid up?"

Karl sat up all the way, his head spinning only slowly. "Another couple of days and I'll be on my feet. Probably be quite a while before I'm back to par, but . . ." He eyed the fresh bandages covering the still-painful stumps of the three missing outer fingers on his left hand. "It could be worse."

"Good. I'm going to send Garavar in here in a couple of minutes." Slovotsky snorted. "I'll tell you, there was a time when I regretted getting him and the House Guard to go along with Pirondael's abdication—I'd planned on showing him an upright Karl Cullinane, not a comatose one."

"What is this nonsense about my being a prince?"

"Not nonsense. Bieme's all yours—unless *you* abdicate. Which I wouldn't suggest. There've been enough changes—"

"But why *me?*" *Dammit, Walter, this isn't my sort of thing, and you*—

"Garavar went along with it because there had to be somebody, and your name was the one on the table." Slovotsky shrugged. "I pushed for you because the only way I can think of for this war to be ended is for the Holts to sue for peace quickly. And that wouldn't happen with some revenge-minded baron on the Biemish throne.

"Which is where you come in. After word percolates through Holtun of your defeat of two regiments of combined Holtish and slaver troops, you're going to be the most feared man in the Middle Lands. If the Holtish don't come to the peace table, my guess is that with Andy making sure that the Holts can't use their guns, Valeran's improvised brigade can go through them like shit through a goose."

"But I'd intended on ending the war—"

"In your own way." Walter spread his hands. "Which might or might not work. This will. Whatsamatter, don't you want the crown?"

Karl clenched his fists. "Don't give me that—"

"Then fine. Give it to Thomen, and let Beralyn rule as regent. That'll be a fine gift to Furnael's son."

"Now, wait—"

"Or let the barons fight over which one gets it. They *might* settle it quickly enough so that Bieme doesn't necessarily lose the war. Bieme might even win, Karl—and instead of Bieme's being chopped up and sold to Pandathaway on the installment plan, it'll be Holtun that gets the axe."

"Not while I'm alive, it won't."

Slovotsky nodded. "And not while you're prince, either. Here's one hell of a chance for you to make some changes, Karl. Go ahead and use it." He turned to the door and raised his voice. "Garavar! He'll see you now."

Garavar was a large, grizzled man of about fifty. His features were regular, and his hands of normal size, but he had something of Aveneer's expression around the eyes, the same look of eagles.

"Your majesty?" he said, as he walked slowly into the room, an aged wooden box in his hands.

Karl sighed. Walter was right. He was stuck with it, for now. But not forever.

Of course not forever. You're not even going to live forever.

Good point.

Thank you.

"I am Karl Cullinane," he said carefully.

"I am Garavar, of the House Guard. With the others, I have been . . . managing as best I can, waiting for you to be able to take over your duties."

"Fine." Karl swung his feet over the edge of the bed. "Give me a hand, both of you. Walter, get me some clothes. There's work to be done."

"Andy-Andy said—"

"If I'm prince, then I outrank her, no? Move. Captain," he said, forcing himself not to waver as he pushed himself to his feet, "I'll want a staff meeting tonight. Frandred, Valeran, Beralyn, my wife, Tennetty, plus you and anyone from the House Guard you think needs inviting. In the meantime . . . Ellegon, are you flying yet?"

Just short distances. I . . . still have a ways to go. And the same goes for you—

"Shut up. Captain, tell Valeran I want a recon of the slaver camp on Aershtyn, and I want it yesterday."

The warrior nodded gravely. "Yes, your majesty. You intend to send a detachment up Aershtyn?"

Karl snorted as Walter helped him on with his breechclout and leggings, then slipped a clean tunic over his head. "I plan on *leading* a detachment up Aershtyn, Captain."

"With all due respect, princes don't—"

Kneeling to slip Karl's boots on, Walter threw back his head and laughed. "With all due respect, Captain, this prince is going to do whatever the hell he damn well pleases. Get used to it." He belted Karl's saber around his waist. "Better give him what's in the box."

Garavar opened it. Inside lay a circlet of silver, studded with diamonds, rubies, and emeralds. "You could wear a simple cap of maintenance, if you'd prefer, but—"

"This will do for now." Karl took the crown and set it on his own head. It didn't feel steady there; he had to hold himself up straight to make sure it didn't slip off.

Probably I can improvise some sort of bobby pin, but . . . first things first. "Captain Garavar, as of now, nobody owns people in Bieme. Anybody who thinks he owns anybody else—"

"Ta havath, Karl." Slovotsky chuckled. "Garavar's already had that explained to him, complete with ruffles and flourishes. No point in bothering with any proclamations right now; no matter how you yell and scream, there aren't going to be any changes, not until the war settles down. Hmm . . . what *are* you going to do about the former slaves?"

"Sharecropping is a step up, no? *No*, not sharecropping," he decided, remembering little Petros' fierce devotion to his scraggly field. "Better: We'll give the former slaves some of the barons' land, and allow the barons reasonable taxation privileges."

I'll soon be known as Karl the Tyrant by the barons, but that's their problem. Government needn't worry about the strong and wealthy; they could always take care of themselves. "Give me your arm," he said. "I've got work to do."

CHAPTER TWENTY-SEVEN

Goodbyes

Why is it, Maecenas, that no man living is content with the lot that either his choice has given him or that chance has thrown to him, but each has praise for those who follow other paths?

—Horace

Andy-Andy and Tennetty standing at his side, Karl said goodbye to Walter and Ahira at the keep's gates.

Their mounts and their packhorses were champing at their bits, possibly because of the way that Ellegon was eyeing them interestedly.

"You sure you don't want an escort?" Karl asked. "If you'll just wait a couple of weeks, I can send Ranella with you—and I could send a company with you as far as Biemestren right now."

Karl, since when does putting something off make it not happen?

I don't know. But how can I say goodbye to either of these two?

Briefly and matter-of-factly, if you don't want to nauseate a recovering dragon.

Sitting uncomfortably in his pony's saddle, Ahira shook his head. " 'Tis best done quickly, eh?"

Adjusting a rifle in its saddle boot, Slovotsky shrugged. "Seems that way to me, too. Hey, who knows? Endell might turn out to be a real drag; I may get so bored in a year or so that I'll need to get back into harness. Hell, we might even still be Home when you and Ellegon show up to pick up the kids."

"I'd like that."

"Karl." The dwarf looked down at him. "I have to say this again: If you ever need either of us . . . you'll know where to find us, Karl. Come if you can; send word if you can't. This isn't goodbye—just so long."

I need you two now, he thought. But he couldn't say that. Not in front of everyone.

Damn. He reached up and shook hands first with Ahira, then with Walter. "I'll miss you, both of you."

Slovotsky snorted. *"Tell* me about it." He clasped hands briefly with Tennetty, then vaulted from the saddle to kiss Andy-Andy thoroughly, whispering softly in her ear as he held her close.

You're supposed to be jealous.

Shut up, Karl explained.

Walter's all-is-well-with-a-universe-whose-center-holds-Walter-Slovotsky smile seemed a bit forced as he climbed back up to the fore-and-aft-peaked saddle, making sure that the packhorse's leads were still tightly bound to it.

Andy-Andy walked over to Ahira, threw her arm around his waist, and buried her face against his thigh, not saying anything, while the dwarf ran gentle fingers through her hair. She turned away, her face wet.

"Watch your butt, Karl. Or Andy's; it's much prettier," Walter Slovotsky said as he and the dwarf turned their horses around and rode them slowly through the open gate, the three packhorses trailing behind. "And remember Slovotsky's Law Number Twenty-nine: 'It ain't over 'til it's over, and maybe not then, either.' "

Karl watched them for a long time, until they had vanished around the bend.

Finally, he turned to Tennetty. "Once we hit the slavers on Aershtyn, you want to hitch a ride Home with Ellegon and take over our raider team?"

"No." Idly, she fumbled in her pouch, pulling out her glass eye, holding it up with thumb and forefinger, considering it in the daylight. "We're going to have to rush this Aershtyn raid, so that you and Ellegon can take off soon enough to get back to the valley before Gwellin leaves."

"Oh? Why is that?"

"You're going to see if you can persuade Daherrin to take over the team, instead of going back to Endell. Gwellin wouldn't go for it, but I think Daherrin might."

"So, you want Aveneer's team instead?"

"Frandred's team, now," she said firmly. "Granted, he'll give every order twice, but that won't hurt anything."

"So what are you going to do?"

She tossed the glass eye high into the air, then let it *thunk* into the palm of her hand. Tucking it back in her pouch, she adjusted her eyepatch and smiled up at him. "I'm going to watch your back. Somebody's got to make sure it doesn't sprout knives."

How about me—

"You?" Tennetty spat. "You who can't even dodge a quartet of clumsy crossbowmen? You're going to watch out for Karl? Who's going to watch out for you?"

Ellegon didn't answer; he just lowered his massive head to his crossed forelegs and closed his eyes.

Andy-Andy smiled her approval.

Karl turned away from all of them for a moment, forcing his shoulders not to sag, though even his cap of maintenance seemed heavy.

But it wasn't really the cloth cap or this absurd title that weighed on him. Karl had long ago taken on a task vastly more important, far more difficult, than governing a two-bit principality, and neither a manipulating wizard nor a crippled slaver was going to stand in his way. There were going to be some changes made, no matter what.

Karl. All the playfulness was now gone from Ellegon's mental voice; it was gentle but serious. *Do you think that Walter and Ahira don't know that? Do you think that they aren't committed to it? Taking a vacation isn't the abandonment of a vocation, Karl.*

I know that.

And so do Walter, Ahira, Lou, Andrea, Tennetty, and all the rest. They're every bit as committed as you and I are, my friend. Gentle fingers stroked his mind. *The phrase is: "and we mutually pledge to each other our lives, our fortunes, and our sacred honor." And we shall keep the flame burning.* Ellegon sent a gout of fire roaring into the sky. *In more ways than one.*

"Fine by me." Karl Cullinane straightened his shoulders, then wiped his eyes before he turned back to the others. "We've got a lot to do. Let's get started."

EPILOGUE

Ahrmin

Fortune is like glass—the brighter the glitter, the more easily broken.

> —Publilius Syrus

Ahrmin looked around the Aershtyn camp, shaking his head ruefully. The slave drive to Pandathaway had to start within a matter of days, or it surely would never leave. It was a certainty that Karl Cullinane would be sending a force up the slopes of Aershtyn to steal the slaves; Ahrmin had no intention of being around when that happened. Under other circumstances, he would have wanted to try to ambush Cullinane, but not this time. This was Cullinane's moment; best to let him win. There would be another day.

Just one more time, Karl Cullinane. . . .

It was even possible that Cullinane and that damned dragon of his would somehow manage to ambush the drive en route to Pandathaway. Ahrmin had no intention of being around for that, either. Let Fenrius take the caravan to Pandathaway; Ahrmin would travel more quickly by himself.

He shook his head. The assault on Cullinane at Furnael Keep had been a disaster, but Ahrmin had survived disasters before. The trick wasn't simply to survive, but to turn the setback into an advance.

Things didn't work out as well as you must think, Karl Cullinane, he thought. Until now, Cullinane had been able to move freely about, magically protected from being Located; the only place in the Eren region in which he ever could surely be found was that blasted valley of his. And that had been too well defended.

But now it was different. Cullinane was pinned down in Bieme; that would make him more vulnerable, not less so. Let him wear a crown for a year or two; a crown could be separated from a head as easily as the head could be separated from its shoulders.

We aren't done with each other, Karl Cullinane, Ahrmin thought. *You have won two battles, that is all.*

The third battle and the war will be mine.

"Fenrius," he said, "saddle my horse. I want an escort of twelve men ready to leave before nightfall. You will bring the chain to Pandathaway; I will meet you there."

"Yes, Master Ahrmin."

The next time we meet, Karl Cullinane, you die, he thought, completely certain that it would come to pass.

Ahrmin smiled.

ABOUT THE AUTHOR

Joel Rosenberg was born in Winnipeg, Manitoba, Canada, in 1954, and raised in eastern North Dakota and northern Connecticut. He attended the University of Connecticut, where he met and married Felicia Herman.

Joel's occupations, before settling down to writing full-time, have run the usual gamut, including driving a truck, caring for the institutionalized retarded, bookkeeping, gambling, motel desk-clerking, and a two-week stint of passing himself off as a head chef.

Joel's first sale, an op-ed piece favoring nuclear power, was published in *The New York Times*. His stories have appeared in *Isaac Asimov's Science Fiction Magazine, Perpetual Light, Amazing Science Fiction Stories,* and TSR's *The Dragon.*

Joel's hobbies include backgammon, poker, bridge, and several other sorts of gaming, as well as cooking; his broiled butterfly leg of lamb has to be tasted to be believed.

He now lives in New Haven, Connecticut, with his wife and the traditional two cats.

Ties of Blood and Silver, Joel's science fiction novel, is available in a Signet edition.